# BloodFeuds

A Novel of

# WARWORLD

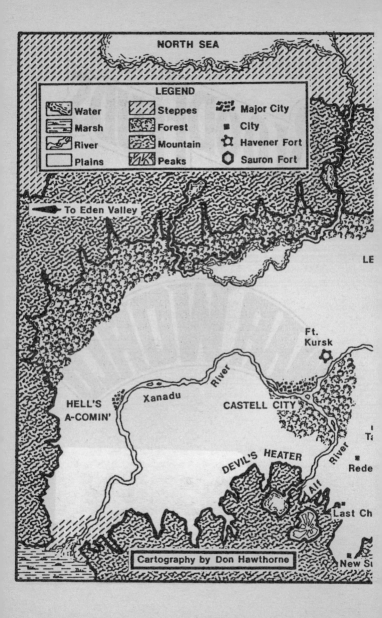

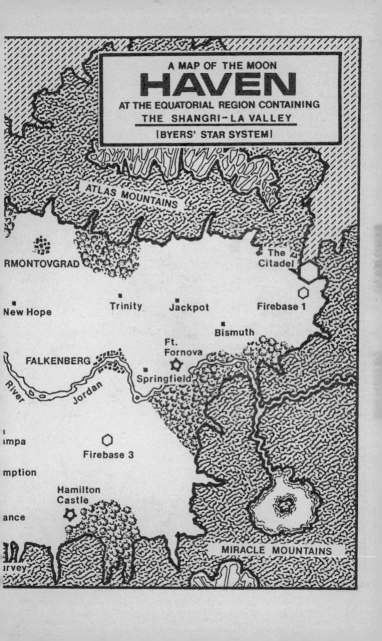

DAS MOUNTAINS

PROMONTORIUM

New Hope

The
Cliquot

Trinity, Starport          Firebase 1

Bismuth

Ft.
Geneva

Springfield

FALKENBERG
RIVER

101 km

Firebase 3

Hamilton
Castle

THE OLD MOUNTAINS

# BLOOD FEUD . . .

Troop Leader Ufthak yawned and poured himself a cup of not-quite-coffee from the insulated flask that hung on his belt. The mild stimulant was welcome, the warmth even more so. Sentry-go was tedious duty, nowhere more so than at the northern edge of Tallinn Valley where it widened out onto the steppe, at no time more than now — second-cycle night, truenight, was extra dark and extra cold.

The sky seemed naked without either Byers' Sun or Cat's Eye to light it, Ufthak thought. Then he laughed at himself — pretty fancy language for a noncom. What would happen next? He'd probably start writing poetry.

"At which point they pension me off," he said aloud. Then he laughed harder. There was no such thing as a pensioned-off Soldier on Haven.

As if to relieve his boredom, a band of nomads came cantering by, closer to his post than they usually dared approach. Some of them drew within a couple of hundred meters, their heat-signatures clear to his eyes. Ufthak frowned and glanced over to the far side of the valley. Sure enough, plainsmen were also making a display in front of the other sentry post. Ufthak glowered. What in the name of bad genes were they up to?

The Troop Leader clicked the change lever of his assault rifle from safety to semi-automatic. If the nomads thought they could lull him out of alertness, they were welcome to try. A lot of them would end up dead before they realized they were wrong.

All of Ufthak's enhanced senses focused on the riders ahead. The tiny noises behind him were too faint even for enhanced senses, until someone jumped down into the firing pit in back of him. He started to whirl, too late. Iron-hard fingers jerked his head back. A knife's fiery kiss licked across his throat.

The last thing he felt before he went into the dark was embarrassment at letting cattle trick him so.

*. . . AND NO MERCY!*

# PROLOGUE

In the beginning there was the CoDominium, an alliance of nations that hated each other, banded together to keep an uneasy peace. Under that peace many worlds were found and colonized: Sparta, Covenant, Friedland, Meiji, Frystaat, Sauron, Dayan. Then the CoDominium's explorers found Haven, moon of a gas giant planet circling Byers' Sun, a full year's travel from Earth by Alderson Drive. There the CoDominium sent Earth's human refuse: religious fanatics, the rebellious folk of inconvenient nationalities, the obstinate practitioners of outmoded customs, those who were in the way. Most died, for Haven was a harsh world of drought and thin air and endless cold. When the CoDominium fell — and Earth with it — three in every four on Haven died with the machines that supported them.

The kings of Sparta rebuilt civilization under the First Empire of Man. They found Haven of marginal usefulness, recruiting soldiers from its fierce and hardy peoples, sending them the Empire's exiles and criminals in return. For four hundred years the Empire's peace lay on Haven — usually very lightly, beyond the few cities — and there was as much prosperity as a grudging planet could support.

The Empire of Man fell in the Secession Wars; the folk of the planet Sauron, genetically engineered as the ultimate soldiers, led the rebellion. When it ended, civilization was nearly dead among the stars — and Sauron was wholly dead, blasted from space until the continents cracked down to the molten core. One shipload of the Soldiers escaped the destruction of their homeworld, fleeing in search of refuge. The refuge they found was Haven, and to make it secure they destroyed every remaining vestige of high technology on a world already poor and backward. Once more there was a great death, and in the midst of that dying the long war against the Saurons began.

Three hundred years later the struggle continued, with intervals of uneasy equipoise. . . .

# Book I
## *THE SEED*

# ● CHAPTER ONE

The fluorescent panels in the delivery room flickered and almost died. There was nothing anyone could do about it. The fortress of Angband at the mouth of the Tallinn Valley was half a continent away from the Citadel, center of Sauron power. The last supply shipment had reached the Base six Haven years — forty-six Terran-years — before. The last shipment of men had been considerably more recent, but none of them had been engineers; the Citadel guarded those like precious gems. Soldiers in Angband and the other Bases were Soldiers only. When the panels finally quit for good, they would do without. It was three hundred T-years since most high technology on Haven had died in a burst of nuclear fire, as the *Dol Guldur*'s crew made the planet safe for the last fleeing remnants of the Race. The Sauron refugees' descent into barbarism was taking much longer, but it was just as sure.

This time, though, the silvery light came back. The woman—girl, really; she could not have had more than fourteen T-years —writhing in the stirrups noticed neither dimming nor return. Eyes screwed shut, she pushed with all her might.

Her partner, a Chief Assault Leader named Dagor, touched her cheek. "Soon now, Badri," he murmured. "Soon it will be done."

Angband Base's Breedmaster stood between Badri's legs, ready to receive the baby when it came. "Don't worry. This is what the cattle women are for," he told Dagor. "And if she dies giving birth to a Soldier, well, fair exchange."

The scar under Dagor's left eye went pale. Almost, he grabbed for the Breedmaster's throat. "Shut up, Grima," he growled.

He made himself subside. They were far from friends,

but he needed Grima's skill to bring Badri through safe. On Haven, no birth was ever easy. And despite his harsh words, the Breedmaster knew his obstetrics. He would not let a successful breeder die if he could prevent it. Especially one like Badri, who was probably between a quarter and a half of Soldier blood herself; it was not only among the tribute maidens taken to the Base that the Soldiers of Angband sowed the genes of the Race.

Badri shrieked. Dagor squeezed her hand, willing himself not to use his enhanced strength to crush it. She was very strong, more evidence of Soldier ancestry — but he was full-blood, and immensely stronger.

Grima grunted in satisfaction. "Here we are." His hands reached where, Dagor thought, only he himself had any business touching. But the Breedmaster knew what he was doing. He guided the baby out, sponged mucus from its mouth. It began to cry.

"A girl," Grima said, with a faint sneer Dagor's way.

The Chief Assault Leader's iron shoulders sagged. Soldiers always wanted — Soldiers always needed — to breed more Soldiers. Dagor knew the chromosome that decided the baby's sex came from him. He could not help frowning at Badri even so. *Well, the girl will be useful for the crossback breeding program,* he consoled himself. One female to every three males was the Soldier norm; that, and the lethal recessives, were the reason they levied breeding-stock from their subjects.

Grima delivered the raw-liver horror of the afterbirth. Dagor expected his woman's travail to end then, but her belly still rippled with contractions. Grima palpated it, stared, palpated again. "There's another baby in there," he exclaimed, startled out of his usual air of omniscience.

Badri's struggle to give birth began again. She was close to exhaustion now; Dagor was learning firsthand why the process was called labor. "You should have known she was carrying twins," he snarled at Grima.

Above a linen mask, the Breedmaster's eyes were harassed. "More than half the time, the first indication of twins is birth," he said. "If this were the Citadel, with the technology they still have there, maybe. As is, keep quiet and let me — and your woman — work. Just be thankful I hadn't started sewing up the episiotomy yet." Dagor scowled, but nodded.

Not too much later, as the Chief Assault Leader reckoned time — an age went by for Badri — another baby let out its first indignant cry. "A boy this time," Grima said, with a faint air of satisfaction. "Now I sew."

"Well done," Dagor told Badri. He doubted she heard. Her head lolled, her eyes were half-closed, her breath came slow and deep. She was, the Chief Assault Leader thought, falling asleep. He did not blame her a bit.

First one newborn, then the other squalled as Grima stabbed tiny heels to draw blood. "Don't let your woman get too attached to them yet," he warned. "The genetics have to check out."

"Get on with it, then," Dagor snarled, though the Breedmaster outranked him. Scowling, Grima stalked out of the delivery room. Dagor shouted for a servant to see to the twins.

Back in the laboratory where only he was allowed to go, Grima frowned as he ran his checks. The babies' blood clotted Soldier-fast, that was certain. The rest of his test had to be more indirect. Some — too many — reagents were not changing color as they should when they found Soldier genes.

But almost all his reagents were old. For some, his predecessors had found equivalents brewed from Haven's plant life. For most, there were none. And so he made do with tiny driblets of the chemicals the last shipment from the Citadel had brought, hoping the driblets were enough to react to genes whose presence they were supposed to mark, hoping also that the complex chemicals had not decayed too much over the decades.

His frown deepened. If the reagents told the truth — *if* — these twins were marginal Soldiers at best. He suspected some of the chemicals were too far gone to be useful any more, but what were his suspicions against the hard evidence of the test tubes? It was not *likely* that a pair as

genetically compatible as Dagor and Badri had produced
offspring who were simply deficient in Soldier genes —
more probable that they would hand on a lethal overdose
of augmented traits. Dagor was Citadel-born, sent out as
part of the breeding program himself. Nearly pure-strain,
of high quality.

It was *possible* that the recombination had selected only
cattle traits, however; breeding was a lottery.

"Marginal, marginal, marginal," he said under his breath.
That meant the decision lay in his hands. He enjoyed the
strength accruing to him from this power of life and death,
but with power went risks. Chief Assault Leader Dagor, for
instance, was up and coming, and would not take kindly to
having two of his children ordered set out for stobor. Never
mind that he had several more by unassigned breeders; his
primary bond was with Badri.

On the other hand, Brigade Leader Azog, Battlemaster of
Angband Base, had been looking askance at the rising young
Chief Assault Leader lately. Subordinates with too much am-
bition could be dangerous; every senior officer knew that.

Grima pondered, rubbing his chin. Breedmasters, by
the nature of things, had to be conservative; conserving
genes was their job. Given the choice between displeasing
Dagor and displeasing Brigade Leader Azog, Grima
hesitated only a moment.

"There is no choice," he told the Chief Assault Leader a few
minutes later. There was a choice, he knew, but he had already made it. He spoke only to salve Dagor's anger. "These
newborns do not meet our standards. They must be culled."

Badri wept helplessly. Dagor soothed her as best he
could, which was none too well: "They have only cattle
genes in them. They could never serve the Base, serve the
Race, as they must."

"*They are my children!*" Badri screamed. She clawed at his
face. He seized her wrist with the thoughtless, automatic
speed his enhanced reflexes gave him. She wept louder,
turned her nails against her own cheeks.

Dagor offered the only promise he could: "Maybe some
woman of the cattle will take them in."

Badri stared, hope wild in her eyes. Better than she, Dagor knew how forlorn it was. Stobor, cliff lions, and cold claimed exposed babies, not cattle women. But every Base's exposure ground was unpatrolled, to give each mother the chance to think her infant might be the lucky one, rescued by people instead of death. Nobody counted the small bones, for the same reason.

Dagor had once thought that weakness: simple euthanasia of unacceptable infants would have been quicker and cleaner. Now he saw for himself the wisdom of the scheme. Even Soldiers had to be able to live at peace with their women.

## • CHAPTER TWO

They had not been married long, the Judge Lapidoth bar Shmuel and Dvora bat Lizabet, when they rode up the Bashan Pass and out of Eden Valley. They were still in the Pale — Fort Kidmi and the northern border were three weeks away, if you had good horses and pushed hard — but the steppe was not the valley. Here on the windswept upland, packs of stobor, tamerlane prides, and solitary land gators were still a menace; worse were bandits, sometimes nomad raiding parties slipping past the patrols. Worst of all, the Saurons' Angband Base loomed beyond the frontier at the entrance to Tallinn Valley. The People — haBandari, in their own tongue — had been at war with the Saurons since the first of the accursed breed set foot on Haven.

Dvora waved up at the steep tumbles of rock on either side of the pass; low blocky fortresses armored them like a cliff lion's scaly mane. Someone blew a ram's-horn trumpet back. The pass was crowded with traders' caravans from half the world, haBandari herders taking their horse-herds down to the lowlands for birthing, or women making the same journey for the same reason. Many of those women were from outside the Pale, paying rent here rather than tribute to the Saurons for use of Tallinn Valley. The Bandari asked only goods. The Saurons demanded women as well.

Traffic thinned as they turned north, until by the second week there was only the odd herdsman's tented camp or a ranchhouse to mark this as inhabited land, that and the graded crushed-rock surface of the road. By Earth standards they travelled through an Arctic wilderness of lichen, scrub, and adapted Terran grass, but humans had lived on Haven for a thousand T-years. To Havenite eyes, this was rich land; as rich as anything outside a lowland valley, or the great continent-spanning equatorial depression of the

Shangri-La. It was cold enough to crinkle the hair in their nostrils in the thirty-six hour darkness of truenight, but trueday and dimday were warm with summer, and they had hospitality for most stopovers. If not, the double sleeping bag that had been a wedding gift was warm enough, with two.

Now and then they stopped to hear a dispute over grazing of herds or an inheritance. Dvora was as cheerful as if she had won her first case. Her husband grinned; she had, by talking him into taking her along as assistant and recorder — the alternative was death by precedent and brief. The Law allowed that a man who was newly wed might stay home to cheer his wife, but in these days of Diaspora on Haven the Law frequently yielded to necessity.

"So you come along to cheer me instead," he said, as they rode side by side. Their stirrup-irons made an occasional musical *ting*; the pack-muskylopes behind blew out a blubbery cry through their hair-filled nostrils.

Dvora smiled at him around a stick of biltong she was chewing on. "Keep the *sklems* up here from skinning you, you mean," she said indistinctly, her strong white teeth busy with the hard dried meat. Lapidoth was tall for one of the Bandari, his long braid of hair a rufous brown; his wife was more typical, of medium height, olive-skinned, dark of hair and eye.

The ruby on her left hand glinted in the pallid light of Byers' Sun; it had been his mother's and her mother's before that until he came along, the eldest of four brothers and no sisters at all. God only knew how many generations of women had treasured it, a surprising vanity for people like themselves. Dvora prized it not just for its beauty, but for the words with which he had accompanied the gift. "Who can find a virtuous woman? For her worth is far above rubies."

Not part of the ceremony, yet Dvora had not hesitated to improvise as well. Her hand had trembled once, convulsively, in his, but then she had spoken without faltering: "I will do you good and not evil all the days of my life." Apparently, she thought that breaking precedent to ride out with him fell into that category. ("It does!" she had insisted. "The Proverbs say we're supposed to bring food from afar, not fear the snow, consider a field and buy it, and you can't do that locked up.")

"Who's next?" he said as they halted at a crossroads well.

Nothing moved across the rolling land but the shadow of an ice-eagle circling against the great reddish disk of Cat's Eye, falling huge and faint on a distant herd of sheep. Lapidoth chuckled as he hauled up the skin bucket of water and splashed it into the trough by the well, watching the shepherdess' dogs chivvy the bleating herd into a tight clump; she would be waiting with her bow in hand.

"Botha, *pleksman*," the Judge's wife said. Yeoman ranch-holder. "Tax evasion, claim for exemption due to hardship," she recited, then: "Hee-yee, back there!" The riding crop in her hand snapped at the nose of one of the muskylopes, as it tried to shoulder her pony aside at the trough and the horse shied at the sweep of a curled horn. The clumsy, shaggy beasts were native to Haven's steppes and hence needed less water than the Terran horses. Not that that prevented them from trying to take more than their share.

*Rather like Botha*, Lapidoth thought; then he put all prejudgment aside with a practiced effort of will.

They turned aside onto the plaintiff's land; it was nearly a quarter-cycle's journey to the *wowenwerf*, the homestead of Bothasplek. Nothing much showed aboveground but kraals, the skeletal frame of a windmill-pump, a few fields of irrigated fodder and greens . . . and the felt-and-leather tents of Botha's neighbors, who had come to the trial as law, custom and desire for a break in the routine of rural life demanded. Smoke blew from the chimneys in the turf roofs, bringing to Lapidoth and Dvora the taste of ash and the promise of warmth.

"Botha bar Hans fan Tellerman, stand forth!" Lapidoth said, in his best ceremonial voice.

The central room of Botha's ranch house was the usual type, three-quarters sunken into the ground, fieldstone below and whitewashed rammed earth above. Bedrooms for him and his wife and his children, his younger brother and *his* family, his widowed sister and *her* children, and the half-dozen young clansfolk who worked for him on shares gave off the main room; farther down a corridor were storerooms, kitchens, loom-shed, smithy, and ice-lined pantry. There were good, colored rugs in the central room, around a ceramic *chagal* stove; tools and weapons were racked on the walls. Bothasplek was household and business and military unit all in one, as was common in the Pale's portion of the steppe, and universal near the northern border.

Right now the circular room was crowded with neighbors and kinsmen and even the second assistant of the chief of *Kumpanie Tellerman*, Clan Tellerman, who happened to be up near the border too. He held the status of *aluf* — commander's power over his kinsmen. Muskylope-oil lanterns lent steady amber light and buttery scent to the air.

"What have you to say?" Lapidoth asked.

The written and oral depositions were over, and the accused had a right to reply in summation.

Botha blinked, his big hands working. He was a square-built, square-faced man with a deep chest, a typical high-steppe Bandari in his worn leathers. His hands and face bore scars; this was the frontier, after all. The lack of respect in his voice was not typical at all.

"I deny that the assessment itself is just," he said. "I've lost stock to *hotnot* raiders twice this last Haven year" — almost eight T-years; most people still used both systems, as was convenient — "and what did Fort Kidmi do for me, that I should waste labor and working-stock helping them?"

"And you were caught smuggling twice last year," one of the neighbors broke in, "and fined for it, bar Hans. More sheep than you lost to the raiders — more sheep than you *say* were lost to the *hotnots*, and you're too friendly by half with them for my taste."

There were two words for *foreigner* in Bandarit; *gayam* meant anyone not of the People and was a mild insult. *Hotnot* meant high-plains nomad, savage, and was a serious slur.

"Order," Lapidoth said, as the accused cursed and shook his fist, and arm-waving discussions erupted. The offenses were all there in the records, anyway. "Botha bar Hans, of *Kumpanie Tellerman*, do you dispute the facts of this case as stated?"

"I dispute your right to tell me what to do on my own land, you Eden Valley pimp of a fan Reenan!" he barked, his wind-burned olive skin flushing darker. There was a shocked murmur, and the chief's assistant spoke sharply:

"A little more respect for the blood of the Founder, you!" he said, half-rising. Fan Reenan was Piet van Reenan's clan; all the clans descended from unit-commanders in the original band of refugees Piet had led. "And this land isn't yours, it's the clan's land, given you in trust as it was to Hans bar Yitzhak before you—and your father never shorted his dues."

"Thank you, *aluf* fan Tellerman," Lapidoth said, "but no more interjections, please." He consulted with the lawspeakers on either side, local folk with no direct interest and of known integrity.

"Botha bar Hans, in the name of *kapetein* and of the People, by the Law we keep, hear the sentence of the Judge of the People.

"You withheld your road dues, and paying them will not cause you to suffer hardship. The dues are assessed on all, for the defense of all; so says the Law. You will pay to the commander at Fort Kidmi the labor of three fit adults for seven cycles; this you owe. For the offense of late payment, as much again or its value in silver or other goods; your *aluf* or your clan chief to make the assessment. No others of your clan are to aid you in this payment."

A gratified murmur; Botha was not popular with his local kinfolk.

Botha stood silent, glaring. Lapidoth went on: "And you will remit the illegal charges for water, grass and campground you have imposed on those who came to this law-speaking."

At that the accused did speak, or howled: "There are too many! Their beasts are eating my home-pasture bare!"

"Then you're overgrazing it," Lapidoth said, looking to

the Tellerman *aluf*. A man's clan chief allocated land, and saw that the holder did not abuse it. The *aluf* nodded. It would be looked into.

Botha ground his teeth audibly. Lapidoth said: "Here are thirty neighbors and landsmen of the accused, folk of the same district. Do any dispute this verdict? Let them speak here, or hold to the peace of the Law."

Silence. "Judgment is given."

As Dvora's pony paused to investigate a knotted patch of ground cover, Lapidoth turned to her.

"I want to be off Botha's land before first-cycle night so we don't have to accept any more of his hospitality!"

Both of them had grown heartily tired of watching him watch them at mealtimes, or hearing him apologize for the necessity of serving *tref* food, which he had probably ordered up on purpose — unlike the farmers back in Eden, most haBandari kept the basic dietary laws whether they were *Ivrit*, Christian or sacrificed to the *anima* of the Founders. The People as a whole were about one-third of each, varying from clan to clan.

Even the local fan Tellerman clansmen didn't like Botha bar Hans.

"I feel sorry for his sister," Dvora said.

"Why?" Lapidoth asked.

"She's pregnant. One of the ranch hands, I think."

Her husband nodded. Embarrassing at the least, by Bandari morals — they were not a prudish folk, but they respected marriage; and she would have to leave soon for the fan Tellerman hospice in the Eden Valley, where higher air pressure made it safe to bear children. Safer, at least. Coming from a household fined for lawbreaking would heighten the embarrassment to a real ordeal. He smiled as she pressed her hand to her own stomach; another four T-months to their own first.

"She should give her brother better advice," Lapidoth said.

"She said he hasn't been listening lately — she needed a shoulder to cry on. Evidently Botha had a run of bad luck a few years ago, and it embittered him. He's a hater by nature — didn't you see his eyes? Wouldn't put it past him to ambush us." *Just because you're paranoid doesn't mean they're not out to get you,* she always said. Paranoia was a survival trait on Haven. Lapidoth tugged at the strap of his rifle; he was authorized to carry one of the expensive weapons. Not that Botha would *really* be that stupid; still . . .

"Come on, slowpoke!" he cried, his voice carrying too loudly in the thin steppe air.

Dvora's pony, a trade from Botha's kraals and about as cantankerous as the man himself, jerked the reins through her fingers and started to browse on a tangle of brownish ground scrub. Dvora first tugged, then sawed on the reins, to no effect. Trust a horse of Botha's to have an iron mouth as well as an iron constitution! The crossbreed was a poor match for her own gentle Eden Valley mare, but she was stone-lamed back at Bothasplek. Finally Dvora got its head up and tightened her grip on the reins, only to be thrown forward as it grabbed another mouthful.

*"Ai-ya!"*

A shriek of bloodthirsty glee cut through the air, and a dropping shaft struck Dvora's mount in the rump just behind the blanket-roll at the cantle of her saddle. If she had not been sprawled on the pony's neck, the arrow would have struck her. The pony bolted, bucking and twisting. Dvora wrapped her arms about its neck and clung, but she was too far off balance to begin with. Her grip broke: she tumbled end over end, and lay still.

Lapidoth swore horribly as the bandits boiled up out of the hollow; Bandarit was an excellent language for profanity, having inherited richly from both *Ivrit* and Afrikaans in that respect. He clamped legs to signal the horse to stillness and brought the rifle up. *Crack*, and a long billow of dirty-white smoke; the archer leading the gang pitched backward out of the saddle with a hole in his leather breastplate. Lapidoth's hands worked rapidly; bite a cartridge open, drop a pinch into the pan, work the lever to open the breech and push the charge and bullet in with a thumb. Lever back to lock the breech, pull back the hammer. Sight low on the charging figure, horribly near;

*squeeze* the trigger, *ting* the flint comes down on the frizzen in a shower of sparks and *crack* again. This time the bullet struck the horse rather than the man, but he went out of the saddle in a fall that landed him on his head.

The third man was riding at him, no time to reload again. *Sh'ma, Yisroel,* Lapidoth had time to think, raising the empty gun to protect himself; no time to draw his saber. The bandit was snarling, sweeping back a meter-long yataghan for an overarm cut. Then his face dissolved in a shower of bone and blood as a pistol shot exploded from behind Lapidoth.

Limbs and bladder threatened to give way as he slid from the saddle, but he controlled himself enough to stumble to his wife's side. Somehow, Dvora had managed to fall as softly as she could — *I'll never say that ground scrub has no purpose for existence except to break a muskylope's leg again,* he vowed. God, what a woman! Half dazed as she must have been, she had managed to reach her pistol, aim and fire in time to save his neck.

She still held the heavy double-barreled flintlock. It shook in her hand, and she brought up her wrist to steady herself. Still, the barrel drooped; just as well, Lapidoth thought, seeing his wife's eyes glazed with horror and what he hoped wasn't concussion. Her braids tumbled free of her knitted cap; one dangled in the mud and blood that smeared her face.

"Dvora?" he called, making his voice gentle. As far as he knew, she had never killed, never seen violent death before. Every Bandari trained for war, but training was not the same.

"I got him," she announced, her voice faltering. "He would have killed you."

"Killed *us*," Lapidoth said, and knelt beside her. "Many daughters have done virtuously, but thou excellest them all," he whispered in *Ivrit* and smoothed back her hair. She let her head sag and allowed him to straighten her, feeling over her limbs for breaks.

"Nothing . . . I think . . . get the muskies. . . ." she whispered. "Their horses too. Don't worry . . . about me."

No one could let a chance to catch and claim horses or muskylopes go by. And the bandits' saddlebags might hold extra food, some evidence of whether they were outlaws from Dede Korkut's strictly ruled yurts or honored members of a particularly feral tribe. Or Botha's men in disguise; they were nondescript, dressed in nomad felt, but that could be subterfuge. There were Caucasoid genes among many steppe tribes, and Turkic blood cropped out among haBandari now and then. Although the stink was strong evidence; the People were a cleanly folk.

"Go *on!*" Dvora pushed at his leg. "I'll build a fire. . . ."

Rather than upset her further, he mounted and collected the beasts, who hadn't strayed far. A quick search of their baggage yielded five daggers, a skin of mare's milk, some herbal-smelling smears that he discarded when Dvora grimaced at them, and a *firman*, a letter to Botha. He read the Turkic script well enough, even this semi-literate scrawl; it was from Mustafa, a Rolling Plains outlaw who called himself a chief and led a varying number of sheep-stealers, backstabbers and horse thieves in the country northeast of the Pale, up Rungpe way.

Ambush, was it? By Yeweh, Botha could run for Tallinn Valley and live under the Saurons' banner of the Lidless Eye after this. Stoning would be all he could expect from his own people or the *kapetein's* justice — killing by stealth, bringing in outsiders to attack a fellow Bandari and offering violence to a pregnant woman.

"Mustafa," he murmured to Dvora. "And Botha. They were in this together. This proves it."

"A wonder they can read," she said, her voice acid though shaky. Then her eyes went wide, and she coiled in on herself, her lips pale and moving in silent protest, oath or prayer.

"Can you ride?" he asked. Even shaken as she was, she might be better off riding through the night to Tallinn Town than camping here. He tucked the *firman* into her saddlebags and pulled out a blanket to wrap around her as she rode.

But Dvora was shaking her head. Fear clenched in his belly as she tugged at the leather breeches she wore, lowering them in a gesture incongruous this far from the peace of their bedroom. They were stained with blood.

"I'm going to lose it," she whispered, amazed.

"The fall?" Lapidoth was personally going to kill that damned pony if it had made her miscarry.

"The fall, maybe. And the altitude. I was told, if I were spotting, not to worry too much, just lie down and keep warm. It started yesterday, but we had to get out of there. . . ."

*Lie down and keep warm.* On the steppe, a quarter of it permafrost and liable to freezing temperatures even eight Terran months into the two-year-long summer. Wonderful. Their first child. Easy to say that it might never have survived; Lapidoth wanted to howl. Instead, he patted Dvora's hand. He still had a life to worry about. His wife's.

"I'll build a fire, heat water . . ." Damn, he wished she hadn't ridden out with him.

Dvora's hand was lax, pallid, but the pulse in her wrist, though weak, was steady. Now, Lapidoth thought, if only she didn't hemorrhage, they had every chance of getting her to safety. *Rest till Byers' Star rises*, he thought. At dawn, they would set out.

"But we have to move," she whispered. "They could come back, see what happened to their friends."

"You can't ride," he told her. "At least sleep till morning." It was late dimday; she should stay sleeping while it was relatively warm. When they had to move it would be early truenight, and the motion would help keep her from freezing.

"No!" She started to rise, and he restrained her. "Tie me to the saddle. . . . I'll make it. . . ." Then, with a flicker of her usual wit, "You don't want me to get all upset, do you?"

Caught between the cliff lion and the tamerlane, Lapidoth thought. He took what seemed like an age to lift her to the pony's back, settle her in warmly, and tie her to the saddle.

"Horses," she murmured. "I'll lead them; you guide." Slowly they started off, a tiny, feeble party under the unwinking gaze of the Cat's Eye. It provided enough light for Lapidoth to scout out their way. They were nearing Angband's territory now, where the Sauron fortress loomed over the Tallinn Valley. Lapidoth hoped against hope to see riders on the steppe: they might be nomads of Dede Korkut's tribe, friendly to the Pale — but they could be bandits, just as likely.

He turned back toward Dvora, who had drifted into uneasy, muttering sleep. Her forehead was only slightly warm; he tucked the blankets more firmly about her, thankful that childbed fever had not claimed her out here with no *mediko* or salves. Carefully, not to disturb her, he detached the reins of the spare horses from her saddle. If worse came to worst, they would provide a diversion.

For an instant, the shots and screams of Dvora's nightmare blended into reality. She waked, screamed, a huge hand clamped against her mouth. She tried to bring her teeth to bear.

"Quiet!" Lapidoth hissed at her. "We just got unlucky."

He stood at her stirrup, adjusting saddlegirth and the ties that bound her. "I'll try to distract them; you get through. Take the *firman* back to the Pale . . . there's proof. Throw a big rock at Botha's execution."

"No!" she cried, despite his muffling fingers. "Don't throw yourself away . . ."

"I'm not a hero, remember? I'll be as careful as I can," he told her. Then he mounted, slapped her pony on its rump, sweaty despite the cold, and rode in the opposite direction, leading the captured horses until, with a shout, he could set them galloping in a panic.

*I'll be as careful as I can.* As the gelding broke into a stumbling run, Dvora realized he had promised her nothing at all. And, as the shouting and shooting rose, then subsided, she realized he would never tell her anything again.

With nothing else to do, she rode on, tears freezing on her face. Her skin was growing hotter, more taut, even as she wept. Possibly, she had a fever. If she were fortunate, she would die of it. If she were very fortunate, she might even deliver the evidence, and then die. Dizziness wrapped her in an embrace rougher than Lapidoth had ever dared, and she rode on through the night.

\* \* \*

The pony's gait slowed to a trot, then to a dispirited stumble. Once or twice it stopped to graze, and she lay dozing, waking when it moved. The last time that happened, she found herself covered with sweat. Her forehead was cooler and she was shivering, but with honest cold, not fever.

"Sentenced to life," she muttered to herself, grasping the reins in hands disgustingly weak.

Life without Lapidoth — and she had had him for such a short time! She pulled off her glove, wiped her face, then clenched her thighs, numb after the countless hours of riding through the day and early into first-cycle night. The packing between them . . . she should change it, but it lacked the heat and wetness of too-heavy bleeding. *Stronger than I thought. Damn.*

She must be near the town now, unless the pony had wandered in circles for most of the night. If she was going to live — which, barring bandits, looked likely — she would have something to show for it: her vengeance on the people who had robbed her of husband and child-to-be. *I will have justice.* Never forget; never forgive.

Only one thing would stop her. If the Saurons found her, she had every intention of blowing out her brains with her pistol. The People did not surrender to that enemy, ever — still less a woman to be forced into their accursed breeding program. Lapidoth's ring winked on her finger. "Strength and honor are her clothing, and she will rejoice in times to come." Yeah, sure.

Then she heard the wailing, a thin, plaintive noise that forced a shiver up her spine. She glanced around her and saw in the far distance the looming, windowless bulk of Angband through the truenight blackness. Sick and dazed, she had ridden far too close to it. And now she rode across the culling ground that was so much a part of the Saurons' bloody history, on the homeworld and here: the blasted land where children who did not meet the standards of . . . *the Master Race* — her mind spat out the epithet from hatred that was old before mankind ever soared from Terra — were set out to die. . . .

Or to be taken up. By nomads, by haBandari travellers
— it had been done for centuries; it was a mitzvah, a
righteous deed. Some children were too frail to live, the
powerful Sauron legacy overstressing tiny bodies, striking
them dead just as surely as a plague. But others . . . no
reason others might not be claimed, grow up healthy.

Grow up hers.

The cries came more and more faintly. Whatever child
wailed out there, hungry and abandoned, would not survive until morning; the cold or stobor, drawn to the sound
and the smell of a lonely infant, would see to that.

*A child to replace the babe I lost.* The thought became obsession, then armor for her weakened body. She reached
down and slipped loose the ties that bound her to the saddle. *Lapidoth's knots,* she thought, undoing the familiar
tangles. Then she blinked away the tears. She would ride in
quickly, quietly, seize the child, and be gone.

A hundred meters from where she thought the child lay,
she dismounted and tethered her pony, then advanced
with all the trailcraft she had. Ahead of her she heard stumbling, and her hand went to her pistol. Did Saurons
stumble? Not with their night sight; and what would it be to
them if others took up their discards . . . her baby! Already,
she thought of the child lying in her path as hers; that the
Saurons could toss it out to die filled her with rage as hot as
what she felt for Lapidoth's killers.

Now she could hear how the cries changed. There were
two voices; two infants! Children which, if they thrived,
would have the Sauron genes, and would grow and raise
more children, strengthening the breed. Such children, if
they survived exposure, usually thrived. If her own breasts
could not produce milk, she would need a very strong wet
nurse indeed, she thought. She quickened her pace. *Just a
little longer*, she thought at the babies ahead. *Your mother's
coming!*

Second-cycle night at Angband Base: black and freezing,
with neither Byers' Sun nor Cat's Eye in the sky for light
and warmth. Two tiny voices cried in the frigid darkness.

Both were weaker than they had been an hour before. Soon both would be still forever, unless . . .

Kisirja came stumbling, drawn by the sound, but not drawn enough to dare show a torch. Aye, Saurons were not known to shoot at skulkers on the exposure ground, but no one on Haven ever felt easy putting Saurons and mercy in the same thought.

Kisirja stooped by the abandoned infants, scooped one up in firewalker-fur gloves, pressed it against her. Warmth and softness made the baby quiet. "Mine now," Kisirja crooned. "Mine." She held it inside her sheepskin coat.

"Mine now," Dvora heard another woman croon. "Mine." A rustle told her that the interloper had placed one of the infinitely precious children inside her heavy coat. Dvora drew closer, saw the woman stoop, her gloved hand touching the second child. . . .

*Not both! One is for me!* Dvora cried to herself, strode forward, and snatched up the child. How good its tiny body felt in her arms! She could almost believe this was the child she had carried in herself, not whatever it was that Lapidoth had buried (*"Don't look, Dvora; you don't want to see"*) beneath scrub and a few flat rocks. Her child . . . and his.

She had to give the other woman credit for speed; she jumped back, ready to fight. Though she tried to keep even her breathing quiet, the infant she held betrayed her location with a squall that already sounded stronger for the warmth it took from her body.

"Who are you?" the woman whispered in Turkic. "What do you want?"

*What do you think?* Dvora chuckled faintly, appalled that she could laugh. She summoned her own knowledge of the speech of the tribe.

"The same as you, child of the steppe. The Bandari hate the Saurons no less than you, but we need their genes if we ever hope to meet them on equal terms. And there are two babies here, so we need not even fight. Go in peace."

It was a bluff. Dvora felt the bleeding start between her legs again. She barely had strength to stand, much less fight a woman of the steppes, hardened by life among the yurts and sheep flocks. Usually, the nomads respected haBandari, left them alone. Perhaps this one... *please God*...

She heard a faint choke of breath that she identified as a sigh of relief.

"Allah and the spirits grant you the same peace, ha-Bandari," the tribeswoman said and hurried away. Dvora could see her releasing her muskylope from the Finnegan's fig to which it had been tethered. Dvora waited, gathering her strength for the long stagger back to her own beast. Curiously, she seemed to draw strength from the tiny bundle that squirmed inside her garments, seeking nourishment from breasts that might never fill.

It took one infinity of struggle to stumble back to the gelding and another to mount it, to tie herself to the saddle and finally to urge it into unwilling movement toward Tallinn Town.

Before she fell into an uneasy sleep, the child resting against her heart, she rehearsed the story she would tell in Tallinn Town. She hadn't miscarried on the steppe, but given birth; despite all odds, the babe had survived, and so had she. That much of the story she would invent. Lapidoth's sacrifice and death — she would die before she altered the truth of that by so much as a breath. She would have the satisfaction of Botha's condemnation and death.

And the truth of the child's birth would remain for her own people. *Chaya*, she thought. Her grandmother's name. *My daughter, Chaya.*

"Allah and the spirits grant you the same peace, haBandari," Kisirja said. She knew nothing but relief that they could share. The Bandari lived southward; the ones who came north were traders, but they were also warriors whom few dared to rob. She hadn't heard this one approach, while she'd made enough noise on the exposure ground to wake a gorged tamerlane.

The other baby quieted as the Bandari woman picked it up. Somewhere not far away, a stobor started yowling, then another and another, until a whole pack was at cry with a sound like the laughter of demons. Kisirja hurried toward her muskylope, which was tethered to a Finnegan's fig out of sight of Angband Base.

If the Bandari woman had a mount, it was nowhere near Kisirja's. She untied her muskylope and climbed onto its broad, flat back. She tugged on its ears to send it back toward the clan's yurts. She wanted to gallop, but not during second-cycle night.

Not much later, the stobor pack trotted through the exposure ground. The nasty little predators soon left, hungry still.

# ● CHAPTER THREE

The baby nursed and nursed, as if there were no tomorrow. "Hungrier than mine, he is," said the woman who
held him at one breast and her own, much bigger,
daughter at the other. She did not sound angry, but rather
indulgent, motherly, almost proud.

"He has every reason to be," Kisirja answered. Under her,
the yurt swayed and rolled, as if at sea. Horses snorted, muskylopes grunted. Kisirja was only glad Nilufer had given
birth three T-months before, and so had milk to spare.
Otherwise they would have lost the child she'd rescued.

"What will you call him?" Nilufer asked.

Kisirja had thought about that all through the long, cold
journey home. "His name will be Juchi."

" 'The Guest.' " Nilufer smiled. "Yes, that is very good.
Juchi he shall be."

When at last he'd drunk his fill, Juchi burped lustily against
his wet nurse's shoulder. His head stayed steady and upright
on his shoulders, instead of wobbling like most newborns'.
The nomad tribes near Angband had fostered enough babes
over the centuries that such was not uncommon, though.

He had some Sauron genes in him, then, Kisirja
thought. But the Saurons did not cull just babies in whom
their strain was too weak. If it was too strong, an infant
could die of a heart attack like an old man or spasm to
death when overenhanced reflexes sent it into convulsions
at the slightest sound. Whether Juchi was a permanent
guest remained to be seen.

"May Allah and the spirits make it so," Kisirja murmured. Nilufer nodded, understanding her perfectly.

Juchi burped again, sighed in contentment. The wet
nurse handed him to Kisirja. He looked up at her. Even
baby-round, his face was longer than those of most

children born in the yurts, and his eyes had no folds of skin to narrow them. Kisirja did not care. He was hers now, for however long she had him.

Brigade Leader Azog thumbed on the Threat Analysis Computer. As the screen lit, he smiled at the machine. It was one of the last pieces of high-tech gear the Base had that still worked. The computer console contrasted strangely with the massive stones of the walls and the steelwood of the ceiling. The core of the Base had been a native hill fort before the Saurons came, and they had thriftily incorporated what went before. There had been little steel or concrete or synthetic available here anyway, even in the days when the *Dol Guldur*'s wreckage still smoldered. The armored fiber-optic and power cables overhead were slung between massive forged-iron brackets screwed into the ceiling beams.

Azog punched in the first of his usual questions: THREATS TO ANGBAND BASE — RANK ORDER. His typing was one-fingered but rapid, a curious blend of lack of practice and Sauron speed. Once the TAC had been able to speak aloud — it could still listen, and give commands through the screens. Commands for data, mostly; data of every kind, important and seemingly inconsequential. It would demand that they interrogate a prisoner again and again, sometimes; even if the answers were always identical save for phrasing. And the pickups were everywhere in the Base, perhaps elsewhere as well.

It was well worth the trouble.

The TAC muttered to itself. Words appeared on the screen: THREATS TO ANGBAND BASE:

1. THE CITADEL
2. THE BANDARI
3. STEPPE NOMADS, CLAN OF DEDE KORKUT
4. TOWN OF TALLINN
5. STEPPE BANDITS, MUSTAFA'S BAND

OTHERS TOO LOW A PROBABILITY TO BE EVALUATED.

Azog eyed the screen, frowning a little. The Citadel and the Bandari were always one and two on the TAC's list; the Citadel because it might wish to bring the outlying Bases under tighter control, and the Bandari . . . well, that feud had started the day the first stone of Angband was laid. Piet van Reenan himself, the Bandari Founder, had died in single combat against a Sauron from Angband Base . . . haBandari legend said he'd *killed* a Sauron and crippled another, possibly a Cyborg, before dying.

The last time Azog had checked the TAC, ten or twelve cycles before, the nomads had been fifth on the list. The time before that, no clan had even been named. He wondered what this Dede Korkut was up to. Maybe one of his shamans had tried cooking up smokeless powder and not blown himself sky high in the attempt. The TAC could evaluate and link clues too small for even the most perceptive human observer, although it volunteered nothing.

Frowning still, the Brigade Leader cleared the screen. He typed his second ritual question: THREATS TO CO, ANGBAND BASE, RANK ORDER. Again the TAC went into its own private ritual of thought. The answer took so long to come out that Azog wondered if it was working as it should.

Just as he began to worry in earnest, he got his answer: THREATS TO CO, ANGBAND BASE:

1. SENIOR ASSAULT GROUP LEADER DAGOR
2. STEPPE NOMADS, CLAN OF DEDE KORKUT
3. BREEDMASTER GRIMA

OTHERS TOO LOW A PROBABILITY TO BE EVALUATED.

Now Azog was frankly scowling. END, he typed, and the screen went dark. His own thoughts cleared more slowly. He'd commanded Angband Base for close to twenty T-years, far longer than any other CO since the *Dol Guldur* landed on Haven and the Citadel sent out an expedition to found Angband in the far southwest. In all that time, he'd never seen anything but one of his fellow Soldiers listed as a threat to him personally. Dagor was no surprise; a pure-bred Soldier of the Citadel's strain, likeable as his race counted such things. Charismatic, that was the word.

*I wish they'd sent us machinery instead of men,* he thought once more; but the Citadel had more men to spare. As the equipment from the *Dol Guldur* wore out, most of it was never replaced, and each Base hoarded what it had.

He had anticipated that Dagor might become a problem. What were those cursed nomads up to?

The Brigade Leader's eyes lit. Had he been a man who laughed, he would have chortled. Instead, he nodded in slow satisfaction. This was what the battle manuals called an elegant solution.

"Why you?" Badri demanded.

Dagor shrugged. "Because I am ordered." He went on checking his combat kit, methodical as a good Soldier ought to be. He was especially careful examining his ammunition; most of the pistol cartridges were reloads. He set aside a couple that did not satisfy him.

He was leaving his assault rifle behind, heading out as a man who could be anyone rather than a Soldier. Since many Haveners tried to kill Soldiers on sight, that might prove useful. It made him feel very vulnerable, but, he told himself, a lone raider ought to feel that way. And he was his own best weapon, always.

"You are too senior for a seek-and-destroy mission," Badri insisted. The two Haven years — fifteen T-years — that had passed since her first breeding had refined young-girl prettiness to a dangerous beauty. Black eyes sparked above a proud scimitar of a nose; her cheekbones seemed high and unconquerable as the cliffs that walled off Tallinn Valley.

The years had refined her wits, too, making her in all ways a fit companion for the Soldier who, folk whispered, would next wear Brigade Leader's leaves. Quietly, quietly, she fed those whispers.

Dagor shrugged again. "I know. But I am not senior enough to refuse." To rebel, he meant, and they both knew it. In that as in all things, timing was critical. If he moved against Azog now, he would fail; and Angband Base would continue its long decay into a mere feudal outpost with legends about its ancestry. "Once I return, though, with the added prestige of having ended a threat to the Base . . ."

". . . when Azog has not gone into the field in a Haven year or more," Badri finished for him. It was not cowardice that kept the Brigade Leader at his desk, only good sense

— combat stress killed more middle-aged Soldiers than any foe. And for a Soldier, Azog was downright elderly. Troopers noticed, though, and also noticed that Dagor was still of an age to lead from the front.

"Aye," he said. "Once I return, I think the time will have come at last to settle accounts with him."

"And with Grima." Badri's voice was flat, determined. Since the twins the Breedmaster had forced her to expose, she'd given Dagor two more sons, neither of whom Grima had dared condemn. Neither still lived. One had died in hand-to-hand combat training, the other from a fall.

The Breedmaster had had no part in their deaths. She blamed him for them anyway, for ruining her children's luck. And even were that nonsense, without him she would have had two children who lived.

Dagor had his own reasons for wanting Grima dead. "Aye, he's Azog's toady, sure enough. When I come back, I'll set the Base to rights. The risk to me, I'm certain, is less than Azog hopes."

"It had better be." Badri clasped him with almost Soldier's strength, kissed him fiercely. Reluctantly, he pulled away. "Duty," he said, reminding himself as much as her. Her genes were not as enhanced, he thought, but she was almost all Soldier just the same. The thought ran against indoctrination. He believed it even so.

Still, once he was out on the steppe, trotting north fast and tireless as a muskylope, he found himself eager to meet these nomads who had the presumption to menace Angband Base. Time to remind the barbarous cattle, it seemed, just what the cost of facing Soldiers was. He smiled, an expression that had as much to do with good humor as a tamerlane's reptilian grin. He would enjoy administering the lesson.

Juchi rode along, every now and then shouting from muskylope-back to keep the sheep going in the direction they were supposed to. He wondered which were stupider, sheep or muskylopes. It was one of the endless arguments that kept the clan amused through the long, cold second-cycle nights.

'licker of motion, far off the steppe. Without his willing it, Juchi's eyes leaped the intervening distance. The flicker expanded into a man: a man wearing a shaggy sheepskin cape much like his own. Whoever the stranger was, though, he did not move like a nomad — he was far too self-assured on foot.

Juchi tilted up his fur hat so he could scratch his head. He glanced at the sheep. They were, for a wonder, going in the right direction. If they did start fouling up, Salur on the other side of the flock could deal with them for a while. Anyone alone and afoot on the steppe needed checking out.

Sometimes Juchi's extraordinary vision made him underestimate how far away things were. The muskylope's steady amble also helped deceive him. Not until he looked back at the flock did he realize he had ridden close to three kilometers.

He grew uneasily aware that he had only a knife at his belt; he could not afford a good saber, and there was no point in carrying a bow on muskylope-back, since you rode lying flat on your belly. He slowed his mount, thought about heading back to Salur, who could afford a horse and *was* carrying a bow. Pride forbade it. In any case, there was but one traveller, not carrying a bowcase or quiver; without a mount, he probably had no gun. Juchi rode on.

Dagor waited for the nomad to approach. His feet ached inside his boots. Just because he could run like a muskylope did not mean he enjoyed it. And here came a muskylope for him to ride. That the beast belonged to the young man lying on it never entered his mind.

The youth asked formally, "Who comes seeking the yurts of Dede Korkut?"

Dagor grinned: the very clan he'd been looking for! And here was a lovely way to start making life miserable for them. He produced his pistol, watched the cattle lad's eyes get round. "I require your muskylope. Kindly climb down."

"No," the youth said, as if not believing his ears.

Dagor gestured with the pistol. "Mind your tongue, boy, and I may decide to let you live. Now climb down!" He put some crack in his voice, as if dressing down one of his troopers.

As the youth descended, his hand went halfway to the hilt of his knife. Then he thought better of it and stood very stiff. "Thief," he whispered.

"Robber," Dagon corrected genially. He gestured with the pistol again, more sharply this time. "Now move away from that muskylope."

The nomad went red; he had, Dagor thought, more Caucasoid genes than most steppe-rovers. But he did not stand aside. "He's mine," he protested with the innocence of the young. "You can't just come and take him away from me."

"Can't I?" The Senior Assault Group Leader did all he could do not to burst out laughing. "How do you propose to stop me?"

The plainsboy surprised him by blurting, "I'll fight you for him."

"Why shouldn't I just shoot you and save myself the trouble?" As Dagor spoke, though, he lowered the pistol. Man to man, hand to hand — that was what Soldiers were bred for. Let this upstart cattle boy learn — briefly — who and what he faced. "Knives, or just hands?"

"Hands." The young man took the knife from his belt and tossed it in back of him. He fell into a crouch that said he knew something of what he was about.

Dagor shrugged off his cape, then his pack. He threw his pistol twenty meters behind him. If the nomad wanted it, he would have to go through Dagor to get it. The Soldier took off his own knife and, as he did, his foe jumped him.

He'd expected that. Indeed, he'd been ostentatiously slow disarming himself, to lure the nomad in. His foot lashed out to break the youth's knee. After that, he thought with grim enjoyment, he would finish him at leisure.

But the nomad's knee was not there. Dagor was almost too slow to skip aside from his rush, and still took a buffet that made his ear ring. He shook his head to clear it, stared in amazement at the plainsboy. "You're quick," he said with grudging respect. "Very quick."

"So are you," said the nomad, who sounded as disconcerted as Dagor.

They circled, each of them more wary now. Another flurry of arms and legs, a brief thrashing on the ground, and they broke free from each other once more. Dagor felt a dagger when he breathed—one of his foe's flailing feet must have cracked a rib. Blood ran from the steppe nomad's nose; a couple of fingers on his right hand stuck out at an unnatural angle, broken or dislocated.

Dagor willed his pain to unimportance. He had to be getting old, he thought, to let a puppy—and a puppy from the cattle, at that—lay a finger on him, let alone hurt him. Old? He had to be getting senile! All right, the fellow was fast and strong for an unaugmented man, but that was all he was, all he could be. Perhaps a few genes from a great-grandmother who entertained a passing Soldier, or a culled reject. It did not suffice.

*No more play now*, Dagor thought, and waded back into the fight.

Even when he lay on the ground with the nomad's arm like a steel bar at the back of his neck, he could not believe what had happened to him. "I will spare you if you yield," his opponent panted.

Instead, as any Soldier would, Dagor tried once more to twist free. That steel bar came down. He felt—he heard—his vertebrae crack apart, then felt nothing at all. "Badri," he whispered, and died.

"More kvass, my son?" Before Juchi could answer, Kisirja handed him the leather flask. He drank, belched with nomad politeness, drank again. The fermented mares' milk mounted to his head, helped blur the hurts he had taken in the fight with the outlaw. Not too much: Juchi already had a name for a hard head in his cups.

He belched again, touched the pistol on his belt. After endless searching, he'd found it and the ammunition the outlaw had carried for it. Better than either had been the awe on Salur's face when he brought his prizes back to the flock.

"Who was the bandit?" Kisirja asked, for about the tenth time. "Who could he have been?"

Juchi shrugged, as he had each time she'd asked. "By his gear, he could have been anyone. He was very fast and strong, stronger than anybody I've wrestled in the clan."

"Could he have been" — Kisirja felt a sudden spasm of fear, remembering what she had drilled herself never to think of: how Juchi had come to her, come to the clan — "a Sauron?"

He stared at her. "How could I hope to best a Sauron, my mother?" The tribes all had a little Sauron blood; how not, after three hundred years? In some it cropped out more than others, difficult to tell among normal variation. But an unaugmented man was still cattle to a full-bred Sauron warrior.

"It is a Sauron weapon — see, it has brass cartridges such as the Bases make — but those have been known to fall into human hands. No, I think he must have been a bandit of some sort, perhaps exiled from the Bandari. They have Frystaat blood, many of them, which makes them fast and tough, but as I say, I can't be sure. I'll never be sure, just glad that I'm here."

"As am I, my son." A haBandari outlaw, Kisirja mused. That was possible, maybe even probable. For the first time in years, she wondered what had become of the exposed Sauron babe the Bandari woman had taken when she found Juchi.

And, for the first time in even more years, she found herself feeling odd to hear Juchi call her "mother." No one in the clan had ever told him he was not theirs by birth. The nomads stole babes from Bases' exposure grounds now and again, aye, but they feared the Saurons too much to let those babes learn their heritage. The genes were valuable, and indeed cropped up naturally from time to time. Everything that went with them . . . Kisirja shivered.

Juchi hugged her, tight enough to make her bones creak. "Don't worry, my mother. There was but the one of him, and he is not coming back to rob honest men any more."

"Good." Kisirja smiled and did all the things she needed to do to reassure him. Even his embrace, though, somehow only made her own worries worse. That effortless, casual strength —she felt like a filebeak that had hatched a land gator's egg.

The land gator named Juchi was, for the moment, quite nicely tame. "I have to go now, my mother. The clan chief himself invited me to his yurt, to see the pistol and hear my story." He puffed out his chest and did his best to strut in the cramped confines of the yurt, then kissed Kisirja and hurried off to guest with Dede Korkut.

Kisirja should have been proud. She was proud, and all her forebodings, she told herself, were merely the fright of any mother at her son's brush with danger. After a while, she made herself believe it.

"He is not coming back," the Breedmaster said.

"How can you be sure?" Badri wanted to scream it at him. Ice rode her words instead. Ice was better for dealing with the likes of Grima. "He's only been gone twenty cycles." It was the truth: Dagor was too fine a soldier, and too much a Soldier, for her to imagine any mere human vanquishing him.

"I fear I can." The Breedmaster did not sound as though he feared it; he sounded glad. "And not only do I believe it, so does Brigade Leader Azog. He has ordered me to put your name on the reassignment list. You are not as young as you once were, but you have at least a Haven year's worth of fertility left to give to the Race, maybe close to two. You may yet bear many children, many Soldiers."

Badri fought panic, felt herself losing. She had seen this happen to other women at Angband Base, but had never thought it could be her fate. Dagor, dying in combat against cattle? As well imagine Byers' Sun going out. Without thinking, she looked up to see if the star still shone. It did, of course. But Dagor was gone.

"Children." She forced the word out through the lips that did not want to shape it. "Children by whom?"

Grima smiled. Badri wished he hadn't; the expression stretched his face in directions it was not meant to go. "By me," he said. "Our genetic compatibility index is very high." His eyes slowly travelled the length of her body, stripping her naked — no, worse, spread and exposed — under her gray tunic and trousers.

"No," she whispered.

"Why not?" That smile returned; suddenly Badri preferred it to the hungry expression it replaced. "I am Breedmaster, no mere trooper to despise. One day, who can say, I may rank higher yet. As my consort, you will be a person of consequence. If you refuse me, do you think another would risk my anger by choosing you?"

Numbly, Badri shook her head. The Breedmaster could do too much harm to a Soldier who opposed him. She thought again of her twins, more than half a lifetime gone now. How could she lie with the man who had ordered them set out for stobor? But even Dagor had accepted that, reluctantly, for the good of the Race. Now, though, Grima was as much as saying that he might twist birth analyses for his own purposes.

Through her confusion, his voice pursued her, tying off her future as inexorably as the noose of a hangman bush: "Shall I visit you after mainmeal, then?"

She felt the noose's spikes sink into her neck as she muttered, "Yes."

Much, much later, after Grima finally left the cubicle she had shared so long with Dagor, she lay alone on the bed, huddled and shivering. The Breedmaster had been worse even than she'd imagined, cruel, selfish, caring nothing about her save as a receptacle—several receptacles — for his lust, and, almost worst of all, with his Soldier's strength utterly tireless. Had he not had work to do, he might have been here with her yet.

He'd enjoyed himself, too, she thought furiously, no matter how still and unresponsive she lay. "We'll do this many more times," he'd promised as he was dressing.

"I'll kill him," she said into her pillow. But how? How could she, of mere human stock, kill an enhanced Soldier? Grima never relaxed, not even in the moments just after he spent. And if she tried and failed, he would only relish punishing her. The thought of giving him pleasure in any way made her want to retch.

Instead she washed herself, again and again and again, as if soap and hot water could scrub away the feel of his mouth chewing at her breast, his hands rough on her most secret places. "I'll kill him," she vowed. "One day, somehow, I will."

Doubtless he did not even remember leaving her twins out for the stobor. Badri did. She would never forget, even though she did not know if they had lived or died.

"Shulamit," Miriam bat Lizbet said, exhaustion and sadness in her voice. "Her name would have been Shulamit."

"It will be," her sister Dvora the Judge said, resting a hand on her shoulder and looking down at the tear-streaked face. "The *medikos* say you can try again in a couple of T-years. The name will keep. You're very young for this, anyway."

They were all sitting in a curtained alcove in Strang's small, scrubbed infirmary. Miriam and her Yohann — he was in soldier's leathers, in from a patrol sweep to the north. He had the classic haBandari build, square and muscular-stocky, with a thick braid of black hair; only his eyes were unusual, bright blue. They were misted too, as he sat holding her hand. This had been their first try for a child. Stillbirth was nothing unusual — not anywhere on Haven — but the pain was none the less for that.

"Yes," Miriam said, eyes drooping with sleep as she looked up at her elder sister; perhaps that explained her words. "You should marry again, Dvora," she whispered. "Have more of your own."

Dvora stiffened slightly. "Chaya is trouble enough," she said, forcing a smile into her voice. "Speaking of which, I should collect her. You sleep."

She bent down to kiss the younger woman's forehead, exchanged a quick hug with her brother-in-law. Then, as she was Judge, she had to stop briefly at the other bedsides, to congratulate and dandle. Each birth was a victory for the People, a victory as important as a battle won. Labor, even in the protection and relatively high air pressure of the valley, was long and exhausting. Even given the febrifuges and antibiotics that three T-centuries of ingenious Bandari kitchen chemists had devised from herbs and molds, childbirth on Haven was still a risky business. Usually it was a pleasant duty — happiness was contagious — but this time ...

Emerging from Strang's infirmary into the cold of the first-cycle night, she tensed. Her hand, on which Lapidoth's ruby gleamed like a gout of blood, dropped to her beltknife. The streets hereabouts were narrow between blank adobe walls, built when the Eden Valley's capital had been called Strong-in-the-Lord rather than Strang; before van Reenan's band first came, in the days of the Wasting, just after the arrival of the *Dol Guldur.* Sound echoed far.

Children shouting; that was all. If her daughter Chaya were here, doubtless Chaya would put name to every voice and tell her exactly how each child was feeling. Dvora frowned. The Pale's children were not brought up to shout like *wildechaverim*, like wild little animals, or to run heedlessly through crowded streets. And ... *there.* A knot of young figures, dodging among a string of dromedaries loaded high with rugs, past a cart piled with sacks of rye, around a rabbi and his cluster of students —

Just as well that she saw them, rather than one of the Eden farmers with his stern ways and even sterner belt. *I almost died,* Dvora thought, as she did every time she visited the newborn. When she miscarried on the steppe, only her native toughness and pure Litvak stubbornness (a phrase her father had often used to describe her mother) had pulled her through.

*Dizziness ... heat pouring down her thighs ... her body cooling even as she bucked and spasmed to expel what had already died ... Lapidoth holding her hand, weeping over it as he drew her back from a too-easy death ... her hand shook, pulsing, the bloodlight in the ruby dancing ... so cold by the small fire that was all they dared kindle ... the torturous ride tied to a muskylope, as her strength returned ... and then the thin wails of cold and hunger ... weakening even as she neared them. ...*

She had spent months in Tallinn Town, recovering and hiding from the woman-hungry Saurons, until she healed enough to join a merchant train back to the valley where *medikos* of her own kind — not the tribal midwives whose skill and cleanliness she profoundly distrusted — observed her, tested her and warned her a second pregnancy would bring risk.

She was almost relieved: if she dared not conceive, she need not remarry, need not risk loss such as Lapidoth's death had caused her. By then, too, she had had her work: the laborious and successful preparation of the case against Botha, followed by the Judgeship that had been her husband's.

Dvora shuddered, remembering Botha's eyes, and the weight of the rock in her hand. He had been a strong man, and an unpopular one — the circle of neighbors had carefully avoided throwing at his head, and he had stayed alive and conscious until he was almost covered in stones.

Then the Pale and Dede Korkut's men had ridden out against the bandit Mustafa, the first time that the two communities had worked together. Lapidoth would have been proud to see that. Now she rode circuit as Judge, well-guarded. That was going well . . . and the young *kapetein*, Mordekai bar Pretorius, called on her for advice more and more often. Sometimes he even took it, too. It was by Dvora's suggestion that a team of *Sayerets* — the Scouts — now waited in various disguises, as merchants, pilgrims, even travelling holy men, by the culling grounds of the Sauron Bases within reach of the Pale. What had been done occasionally by merchant caravans passing a Base was now done by system, on a much larger scale — secretly, of course.

The running feet pounded closer and then into sight. She recognized some of her daughter's classmates.

"Is it the swordsmith?" she asked, stepping forward into their path. Young Heber bar Non was back in the Pale, looking for a wife, it was rumored, although he was young for that. He had wandered over half of Haven — as far as the Shangri-La — and then succeeded his father in running the forge in Tallinn Town, northwest of Eden. Well enough, Dvora had thought at the time. A match between the swordsmith and a girl of Eden Valley might be good for trade, unless it drew the Lidless Eye of Angband Base down upon him.

"Or perhaps you *sklems* are running around yelling to announce a Sauron raid?"

At the sight of their valley's Judge, the children jolted to a whispering halt.

"Here she comes! Here comes the Judge!"

She had sat in judgment over too many of these children's parents not to know what the guilty huddle, the downcast eyes and thinned mouths meant.

"Sauron . . . Sauron . . . how'd she *know*?" came the whispers, as she stood there, ostentatiously tapping her foot.

"*Laila tov*, Judge," came the voice of her friend Barak's son.

"Using *Ivrit* to get round me, are you, Avi?" she asked. Her breath wreathed about her like a pale cloud in the night air. "How are you going to get round your teachers if you come in late and have time enough just to do your chores, not your schoolwork?" That finished Avi. What about the others? "Well, are you going to explain so we can all go home, or do we stand in the cold all night?" she demanded, waiting with her arms crossed. "And speaking of home, where's my daughter?"

A few of the children — youngsters in their teens, really —looked like Edenites. They *were* adults by the standards of their people, who seldom kept children in school long; the thronging chores of fields, barns and dairy were more important, among the farmer folk.

*Gayamske koff*, she muttered inwardly in Bandarit: *heads like savages*. Even after three hundred T-years of coexistence, haBandari and the original settlers of Eden still had their differences; and, wouldn't you just know it, child-rearing — the most vital and precarious thing on this whole iceball! — was chief among them.

Muttering and hissing rose from the boys and girls who faced her. Most were near or a little past Eden Valley adulthood of two Haven years, bar or bat mitzvah age. Her own daughter had gone through the *mikveh*, the ritual bath that only the very strictest of haBandari knew how to conduct, besides the usual coming-of-age ceremony. There had been need, need to establish clearly that Chaya was hers, Bandari and *Ivrit*, but . . . she shook that thought from her mind. Thirteen or fourteen was the age at which young men and women could own land, sign contracts, bear arms and marry. And yet they were children to her, and they looked younger each year.

"Well? Do you want to tell me why you're all making more noise than a cliff lion battling for his mate?"

Avi, who sported a fine black eye, looked resigned, opened his mouth, then shut it, clearly reluctant to betray a classmate.

Dvora shivered and sighed. "Someone tell me what's going on before I call your parents!" she snapped. The huddle tightened, then divided, leaving two of the strangers standing before her. Their heavy clothes were wrinkled and torn, and dried blood still crusted the mouth and nose of the boy who stood between her and the girl, clearly his sister. He tried to stick out chest and jaw, and quailed as Dvora glared at him.

"I'm Joseph-Beloved-of-God," he said, "and this is my sister, Hagar. We came in for the day. And my father says . . ."

"Tell her!" cried another girl. "Tell the Judge that you tried to boss her daughter, and when Chaya ignored you, you called her a 'breed' and said she should have been thrown out at birth like a Sauron cull!"

The boy paled beneath the grime and blood, and Hagar's eyes widened, her mouth opening in dismay.

*Her daughter.* Dvora shut her eyes in pain that racked her heart as badly as the pains of her miscarriage, so many years ago. Adults still called her Lapidoth's child . . . but no hiding the Sauron blood, not when it ran so strong. Chaya had it in overflowing measure. She was also the Judge's daughter, under every eye. And hence . . .

*The shoemaker's child goes barefoot,* thought Dvora, *the baker's child has no bread, and the Judge's daughter has the story of her birth thrown at her by strangers.*

"That's prejudice." Dvora made herself shake her head. *Highly dangerous prejudice*, she thought. Especially now that part-Saurons were becoming numerous, with the new policy.

Useless to punish the children, who doubtless repeated what they heard at home. "Chaya is my daughter and your neighbor." She drew on her memories of Bible quizzes throughout the years of her schooling. "*For ye were strangers in the land of Egypt —* " she intoned impressively. "Who of us isn't a stranger here?" she demanded. "Who of us can avoid working together if we are not all to starve, freeze or fall to bandits or Saurons?

"Think about it!" Her voice took on the resonant, lecturing tones that, she had learned, gave her verdicts the greatest weight. "For this, Ruth bat Boaz hung from the cross and was lifted down by Piet van Reenan? For this, a gentle girl had turned general and rebel? So two young fools on their first visit to town could overturn three hundred T-years of work?"

*What did you expect? One lifetime isn't enough — even if it's yours. Or your husband's.* Memories of Lapidoth, thoughts of how angry this would make him, made her frown even more deeply.

As often as not, the Edenites still used Bible names — when they weren't burdening children with something like Sword-of-the-Lord or Fly-from-Fornication. The Bandari shared the old scriptures with them. Apart from that, very little — including the ways of men and women, and whether children should follow unquestioning in their father's or mother's steps, to plow and spade or loom and kitchen. Joined by force, they were not one people, not wholly — any more than the nomad women forced to wed with the Saurons were one with their appalling mates.

She waited, holding this Joseph's eyes, outglaring the Cat's Eye with her own anger, her own fear, until his eyes fell.

"And you, Hagar, do you know the story of your own name? I'd suggest you go home and read about it. And both of you, keep silent, if you cannot speak decently. Whether the girl you insulted was my own child or not, your childishness weakens the valley just as surely as if you sowed a field with salt. Now, get out of here, all of you! I shall talk to you and your father later."

And she would, too. If that kind of bigotry was springing up in the outlying settlements, she would have to. *The black eye and bloody nose that I saw will be nothing. They'll use guns and knives next, and we'll have riots, pogroms, civil war. And if we don't finish each other off, the bandits will.*

Hagar and Joseph fled, Hagar's sobs loud in the night air. Let them worry for a bit about offending the Judge; punishment enough, when she rode out to their farm. After she found out where it was. Among the million or so other things that she would have to do. First, though, to find her daughter. The other children dispersed more slowly.

"I think Chaya hid in the bunker." Avi's words floated behind him like a message from the *p'rknz*, the spirits.

The stablehand looked a little startled when Dvora slid a bow into the case on her saddle and rode out into truenight, bundled to the ears. He said nothing, nor did the officer at the gate in Strang's city wall; if the Judge chose to ride out, that was her business. It was five or six hours' journey up into the Bashan Pass, rising all the time. The soft yellow lights of the city fell away behind her, hidden by the folds of the foothills below the Shield range; the scattering of farmhouse lanterns thinned away as well. She passed a pair of riders on patrol; one dipped his lance as he recognized her. Then she was alone with her thoughts and the hollow *tock* of hooves on the gravelled road.

The bunker had been built when the Elder of Strong-in-the-Lord still ruled Eden Valley. Three hundred T-years ago the exiles from Frystaat and the New Vilnius refugees who had made up the proto-Bandari took this valley, and the bunker had been captured without the loss of a single man on either side. The site of a victory that neither group wanted to talk about, it had fallen into ruins. The modern forts were better sited, kilometers farther up.

A cliff lioness could have made her lair here, birthed cubs for all Dvora knew. Or some outcast, more clever and more desperate than most, could have risked the Bandari guards to hole up there, waiting his chance to steal women, drugs or weapons. It wasn't safe for a child or a young woman to wander about distressed, unaccompanied, and unarmed, though Dvora knew that whatever else her daughter was, she was never without protection. Dvora loose-tied her horse to a snag of rock — it would be able to pull away if stobor or cliff lions came — and took the faint ancient pathway.

The climb to the old bunker left Dvora panting, sweating under her sheepskins despite the cold of the night. She set her feet carefully, testing her footing. A pebble landed in her path.

"You might have warned me what some of the outbackers would say." Chaya's voice floated over her head, accusing and too collected for a girl's.

"Told you what?" Dvora said, guilt sharpening her voice. "That there's always a serpent in Eden? In *this* Eden, it's fools and bigots. That's life, daughter, and you'd better face it. And face me, too, while you're at it."

Most would have made a noisy, scrabbling production of climbing down from the fragment of roof that jutted out above Dvora. Chaya managed it in a quick, smooth dismount, her sheepskin jacket flaring open about her. As always, Dvora noted how well suited her daughter was to the stark Haven environment. Sturdy and strong, she carried no extra weight beyond what would keep her warm. She breathed easily in the thin air, but did not display the barrel-chested, hyperdeveloped rib cage of high-altitude dwellers. As the Cat's Eye flashed, she glanced aside. Moisture flickered briefly in her eyes, then dried; her high cheekbones bore no traces of tears.

*Conservation of body fluids*, Dvora thought, and wondered once again why the Saurons had chosen to discard her daughter. On a planet full of enemies, Saurons were *the* enemy; but like the People, they needed what girl children they might have. Why discard a girl? Saurons culled for undesirable traits; yet Chaya seemed healthy in every way.

"You didn't fight," Dvora stated, rather than asked.

"They're still walking, aren't they? I wish you'd let me join the *Sayerets*," Chaya said. She patted a beltknife in a tooled leather sheath. Both looked new, yet familiar. "I'm quiet, fast, strong; no one would see me. Doesn't matter, does it, if a half-breed monster keeps you safe so long as you don't have to look at her?"

So that was why she had fought the idea of training to be a Judge! She feared that defendant and plaintiff alike had already condemned her as an outsider. *Judge then, Judge. The case of Chaya bat Dvora versus Eden Valley. Dare I make such a case, even for my own child?*

"And Barak says . . ." Chaya went on, beginning to quote the commander of the *Sayerets*.

"Barak talks too much!" Dvora snapped. "All right, so you'd make a fine *Sayeret*. But I had to make that rule, and I can't make an exception of it. Stop trying to make me feel guilty." Women were to be barred from the *Sayerets* until they had children — in which case, they would probably not want to enlist in a unit under arms most of the time, unlike their clan reserve regiments. She reached out to her daughter, but the girl stepped back.

"Tell me again," said Chaya. "I know, I grew up knowing that I'm at least half Sauron. But tell me again."

"This is no place for it," Dvora replied. "Anything could come, a tamerlane, a bandit." *A Sauron*, she had almost said, but stopped in time. "Or someone with a complaint. I don't know which would be worse, right now!" That forced a shaky laugh from Chaya.

"Let's go. We'll go back to the house; I'll make a cup of tea; you'll have something to eat; then we'll talk. All right?"

Sauron Chaya might be, but she was also a child, glad to have someone to comfort her. *For as long as I can, daughter. And I don't have to be a prophet to know that that won't be much longer.* She remembered where she had seen toolwork like that on Chaya's beltknife: Heber's work. She had dreamed of training up her daughter to be Judge after her, but the heart had its own logic.

The eggbush tea was strong and sweet in the large, crude mugs that Chaya had made years ago in school. The firelight was dimming, and the lamps had burned down almost to extinction. Chaya liked the dimness; she could see well enough in trueday light, but a fraction of that was most comfortable for her. No need to say why.

Perhaps the nomads had the right of it; Lapidoth had once told Dvora they never revealed the ancestry of a child from the culling ground for fear of Sauron vengeance. Bandari were used to free speech, and to using their eyes and minds, as well. At least most people didn't *mention* it, in public.

Was this marriage with Heber her daughter's way of punishing for her refusal to admit women to the *Sayerets*? *You could be anything else*, she had cried once. *Only don't leave me!* And was that fair? Was that just?

*Here is another case for you, Dvora.* She could hear Lapidoth's voice, quizzing her as he had in the days when he was the Judge and she a student. *Two people come before you, a parent and child. The child is offered a chance to make a new, rich life; the parent has attempted to restrain the child.*

What will you decide?

Put that way, there was no case at all, except between her desires and her conscience. She had spent a lifetime making conscience the victor; and she would not give up now.

*The girl doesn't know how to tell you. She needs your help.*

Faced with that familiar, beloved need, Dvora suddenly knew how to begin.

Chaya moved slightly, the dusky light gleaming off the bone and metal hilt of that fine new knife.

"Nice beltknife," Dvora said. "What did you pay for it?"

"Heber gave it to me," Chaya replied, her olive coloring suddenly more vivid. "He said he'd come by tonight." Her pupils grew enormous, despite what was, for her, the relative brightness of the house.

To be wife to a swordsmith in Tallinn Town? To scuttle from the menfolk who came to guest, and to efface herself? That was no life for her Chaya. And besides, was Heber even *Ivrit* anymore, even Bandari?

"To ask for you? I assume you want me to give my consent." A girl was formally marriageable after her bat mitzvah, although a parent's consent was needed until the eighteenth T-year. "What else do you want me to say?"

"It's not what you think," Chaya muttered. "I'll travel with him, learn to forge swords myself . . . wear a mask against the glare. And I'll be . . ."

*Free of this place.* Not for the first time, Dvora could cheerfully have cursed Barak and the other *Sayerets*, that young maniac Hammer-of-God he'd picked up — the one who not only killed raiders but sneaked into their yurts and left the heads for sleeping kinfolk to find — all the tough warriors whose honor was expressed in edged steel. There were other ways, other honors, as Chaya must learn in Tallinn, if she did not learn it here in the Pale. *And it could be worse. If she ran away and joined up as a caravan guard, she could end up a continent away, not three weeks' ride.*

"Look at me, girl," Dvora said in her Judge-voice. "You asked for the story of your birth."

That had been a while ago, when she noticed that she was stronger than the other children, including the boys. She had thought it was Frystaat blood — the inheritance of the Founder's people, who were high-G adapted. That was the common assumption when a child showed abilities far beyond the norm, although after all these centuries the genes for such abilities came as much from fostered Sauron culls as the Founder.

With Chaya, no such pretense was possible. The memory of her face when she learned her strength was instead the legacy of the People's worst enemies was a bitter one.

"Do you want to hear it again with him, or do you want to tell him?"

Whatever else her daughter was, she was no coward. That was not surprising. Neither were her parents, whichever set. Chaya raised her head, her eyes flaring like the Cat's Eye that had long sunk into second-cycle night. "I'll do it. Tell me again, so I can make it live for him."

# ● CHAPTER FOUR

Brigade Leader Azog typed in his first question:
THREATS TO ANGBAND BASE — RANK ORDER.

The TAC performed its electronic equivalent of thought, then replied, THREATS TO ANGBAND BASE:

1. THE CITADEL
2. STEPPE NOMADS, CLAN OF DEDE KORKUT
3. THE BANDARI

OTHERS TOO LOW A PROBABILITY TO BE EVALUATED.

The Brigade Leader scowled. He understood why the rankings had changed, but could not remember a time when nomads represented a greater danger to the Base than the Bandari. How had they taken out Dagor? That was a good man gone, even if a rival; had Azog known the Senior Assault Group Leader would perish without accomplishing anything at all, he might not have sent him out alone.

Azog put his second question to the TAC: THREATS TO CO, ANGBAND BASE, RANK ORDER.

This time the machine's reply was prompt: THREATS TO CO, ANGBAND BASE:

1. BREEDMASTER GRIMA

OTHERS TOO LOW A PROBABILITY TO BE EVALUATED.

The Brigade Leader stared. Only one threat? The others that dogged his tracks had not disappeared. That meant one of two things: either the TAC had malfunctioned at last, or Grima's threat was so overwhelming that it made all others pale beside it.

Azog could not afford, did not intend, to take a chance. Just as his finger stabbed for the button to summon the Breedmaster, the intercom buzzed. "Who is it?" the Brigade Leader snarled.

"Breedmaster Grima, Brigade Leader," came the reply. Azog's grin was all teeth, like that of a cliff lion about to spring. "Come in, Breedmaster. I was thinking of you." He made sure his sidearm was loose in his holster. "Well, Grima," he said as the other Soldier sat across the desk from him, "what can I do for you?"

Grima steepled his fingers. "I came" — he glanced at his wrist chrono — "to say good-bye, Brigade Leader."

"Odd," Azog said, "for I was just about to summon you to give you the same message."

The Breedmaster nodded, unsurprised. "I thought that might be so. Were you less suspicious, you might have been allowed to last another couple of cycles. As is — " He spread his hands in regret.

Azog laughed, or tried to. For some reason, his throat did not work as it should. Full of sudden alarm, he reached for his pistol. At least he *thought* he reached for it, but his hand did not move. And when he tried to suck in a deep, furious breath, he found his lungs frozen as well.

The Breedmaster checked his chrono again. "Distillate of oxbane has an *extremely* precise latent period before it manifests itself," he remarked, as if expounding on the poison to one of his assistants. "As I said, I do apologize for having to up the dose to a lethal level so soon, but you left me little choice."

Azog could not even blink now. He felt his heart stutter, beat, stutter again, stop. He watched the office go dark, first the corners where spiderwebs linked beam and stone, then the desk under the fluorescents. He knew the lights were not failing. Not this time. Not, for him, ever again.

*"At them!"* Bugles blared, some of brass, more carved from horns of herdbeasts. Horses, muskylopes, and men rushed forward. "Dede Korkut!" the men screamed.

Another line, about as ragtag as the attackers, stood in defense on a low ridge. "Suleiman!" they screamed back.

"Suleiman the sheep stealer! Suleiman the sheep bugger!" Dede Korkut's warriors yelled. The men armed with muskets and bows began to shoot; those who carried pistols or scimitars or lances waited for the fight to come to close quarters.

Suleiman's warriors returned fire. Here and there a man or a beast fell, to lie still or, more often, writhing and shrieking. Had they had more firearms or more discipline, they could have chewed the attackers to bloody rags. As it was, Dede Korkut's clansmen took casualties, but came on.

At their fore ran Juchi, afoot. Not breathing hard, he stayed even with the mounted men to either side of him. Arrows and bullets sang by. The leading warriors on horses and muskylopes began pulling up at last, waiting for their comrades to reach them and add to their firepower.

Juchi ran on. Suleiman's men shouted and turned more of their weapons on him. But he was no easy target, not running as he did, fast as a horse but with a man's agility. Most arrows or bullets flew behind him; his speed made the nomads mistake their aim.

Then, suddenly, he was into the line of defenders. Suleiman's men stopped shooting at him, for fear of hitting their comrades instead. They converged with knives, swords, clubbed muskets, ready to make an end of this lone madman in their midst. They moved on him in no special order — what need for that, against one?

They quickly learned. A gray-faced warrior reeled away, clutching the spouting stump of his wrist after Juchi's blade stole hand from arm. Another was down and motionless, half his face sheared away. An instant later another fell, his cheekbone crushed by a left-handed buffet after he thought to rush in on Juchi's unweaponed side.

Worse was that none of their blades would bite on him. Faster than thought, he slipped away again and again, to stun, to maim, to kill. "Demon!" one of Suleiman's men shrieked as he flopped, hamstrung, somewhere near the middle of Juchi's path of slaughter.

Juchi took no notice. This, to him, was easy as weapons drill; easier, for his own clansmen had learned to respect, if not always to believe, his speed, and so fought him almost always on the defensive. Suleiman's warriors paid dearly for thinking him no different from one of themselves.

They paid, in fact, with the battle, though Juchi realized that only when he found no more targets to strike. Then

Dede Korkut's men were all around him, pounding his back, lifting him off his feet so he could see the last of Suleiman's folk fleeing for their lives.

"We rolled 'em up!" someone bawled in his ear. "Cut 'em in half and rolled 'em up! You threw fifty meters' worth of 'em into confusion, and we poured through and smashed 'em. They won't come sniffing after our sheep again for the next ten Haven years."

Juchi found himself standing before Dede Korkut. The clan chief's hair, he noticed with surprise, was almost entirely white — how had it escaped him till now that Dede Korkut was an old man? To a youth, ever growing and changing, he had seemed eternal as the steppe.

"Bravely, splendidly done!" Dede Korkut told him. As Juchi bowed to acknowledge the praise, the chief raised his voice: "Hail Juchi, new warleader of the clan!"

The clansmen shouted approval. "Juchi!" "Juchi warleader!" "Hail Juchi!" "Hurrah!" They crowded round the new hero to clasp his hand, pound him on the back, and, finally, raise him to their shoulders.

Such praise from his own people — from men, most of them far older than he — did what the exertion of combat had quite failed to do. Juchi's heart pounded till he thought he would burst with pride.

Another wave of pain washed over Badri. It would have doubled her up on herself had she not been held immobile by the obstetrical table's stirrups. Blood flowed from between her legs, blood and all but formless clumps of tissue.

"Pity," Grima murmured. "It would have been a Soldier." He reached inside Badri with his curette, scraping away the remains of what might have become a life. When at last he was satisfied, he packed her womb with gauze, saying, "I'll monitor your blood pressure round the clock for the next cycle, but I think the risk of hemorrhage is small. Very clean, as miscarriages go."

Badri heard his words as if from very far away. She was tired, so tired — worse, she thought, than after any of her births, even the lost twins so long ago. She was even too tired to resent Grima's brisk, competent care. But then, she thought, he would have done the same for any of Angband Base's domestic animals.

No sooner had that thought entered her mind than his words confirmed it: "You'll be ready for breeding again as soon as your courses resume."

"As you say," she whispered. She did not argue with him, not any more. But she knew that if she conceived again, she would also miscarry once more. She still had a supply of the herb one of the other women had brought her from Tallinn Town. Grima would get no sons on her.

And yet — the man she hated, the man she slept with, was no one's fool. One miscarriage might befall anyone. Two, especially from a woman who had always birthed well before, would surely raise his ever-ready suspicions. That made aborting again much more than a physical risk.

He'd been talking, she wasn't sure for how long. Finally some of his words penetrated her exhaustion: " — have to meet with the Weaponsmaster again, over the threat of this cursed nomad tribe. The TAC makes it out as more dangerous to us than even the Citadel, which strikes me as insane — but then, the TAC often says things like that, and turns out to be right in the end. It must have to do with the way it swallows data like a land gator scavenging. . . . You rest now. I'll be back presently."

"As you say," Badri repeated. Grima tramped away. For a moment, she was simply glad he had gone. Then she started to think again. Like the Breedmaster-turned-Brigade Leader, she had no idea how a steppe tribe could threaten the might of Angband Base. Unlike him, she had oracular faith in the Threat Analysis Computer. The machine's job was to know everything. If it said Dede Korkut's plainsmen were dangerous, then dangerous they were. How much more dangerous would they be, she wondered suddenly, if they had an ally inside the Base? When at last she fell asleep, she was smiling.

"Fine work," the Sauron's woman said.

She was tall, as tall as Chaya, with a beauty the Bandari woman could not match, and she had ordered her escort of Sauron Soldiers out of the swordsmith's shop with peremptory authority. They had gone willingly enough; edged weapons were not much used by the Soldiers. Rifles, or hand to hand, were their style.

"That is mine," Chaya said. She had become no mean smith herself, in the T-year or so since her marriage to Heber. "I —"

There was a cry from one of the other women, a young girl hugely pregnant with what was surely her first child. She tottered, reaching out blindly toward a rack of knives. Chaya moved before she could think, catching the limp weight with one hand and the toppling rack with the other; the edged metal rattled, but she had stopped the motion before the weapons could fall free.

The tall woman was beside her almost as swiftly, and they lowered the girl to the floor. "Ah, Dokuz," she murmured. "Unlucky the name, unlucky the day." She turned her head as the Soldiers burst through the doorway, looking ready to guard, kill and interrogate all in one.

"Dokuz is ill," she said. "Fetch a stretcher, and one of you alert the Breedmaster." Her nostrils flared at that, and Chaya's hearing — if nobody else's — could detect the cold hatred in the last word.

The Soldiers looked at each other, and obeyed.

"You are brave, to run toward falling knives," the woman said to Chaya. "Your name?"

"Brave?" Chaya said. "No, I merely do what must be done." She paused. "I am Chaya bat Dvora, wife to Heber the swordsmith."

The Sauron's woman nodded, respect in her eyes. Chaya judged she had been human once — *had lived in a human community,* she corrected herself — for she had not quite the chiseled look of a full-blood, and those came rarely into Tallinn Town.

"And your name?" she went on, suddenly wanting to speak more with this woman who bore herself with such pride.

"Badri," she said. Chaya's eyes widened slightly. The

Brigade Leader's principal woman — and his bitter enemy, if rumor did not lie. Soldiers came into Tallinn town, often enough; to trade, to drink and to whore in the taverns. Put enough clownfruit brandy into him, and even a Soldier would babble.

Badri cast a glance over her shoulder. The Soldiers had returned, with two conscripted Tallinn Town civilians and an arrangement of poles and blankets. They bore the half-conscious Dokuz away.

"I hope her delivery is easy," Chaya said.

"I, too," Badri said, her voice carefully neutral.

*What keeps her?* Chaya thought. There were horses outside; what prevented her from commandeering one and riding far and fast? The position she held, consort to the Sauron leader? Somehow Chaya doubted that.

Badri followed her glance. "No, we are *trusted*" — the word brought a bitter twist to her lips — "to shop in town. For those who were born here, our kin are hostage; for the others, how could they find the yurts of their clans? And they would only seize more women, if we fled." She gave Chaya a long, considering look. "I had heard that Heber went to the Pale for a wife. You help him, you say?"

For answer, Chaya held out her hands. The callus was hard and even on her fingers and palms. She did not speak; the Saurons permitted links between the Pale and Tallinn Town, but they did not love them.

"Good," Badri said. "He needs a strong wife." She leaned forward. "We can all use strong friends," she said after a moment. "We should speak — the three of us."

Chaya felt a jolt of fear. *Has Heber been talking?* she asked herself. Here in Tallinn, the ancient hate between Sauron and haBandari ran hotter even than it did in the Pale, and seeing their rule made her understand how Heber felt. But it also made her understand their strength and cunning . . . now, with Tallinn at peace, the Saurons of Angband seemingly content, and her mother Judge in the Pale, was no time to emulate the Zealots of ancient Jerusalem.

But *if*, if only — she used every enhancement of her senses to judge Badri's voice, tone, the set of her eyes. "Perhaps we should," she said, in as casual a tone as she could muster. "I'll mention it to Heber."

Even wearing the smoked glass, Chaya squinted in the firelight as she added measured amounts of charcoal. The small steel crucible must be watched, she knew, with especial care. In it, Heber sought to recreate the *wootz* that, thousands of years ago, the ancestors of people like Badri and the chieftain Dede Korkut had wrought into swords and used to conquer half a world.

Filtered by the glass, the light in the forge was blood red. The metal would be even bloodier, the cherry red that meant that the *wootz* was ready to pour. The hot acrid smell of molten metal and burning charcoal filled her nostrils.

It would be forged, folded, heated and quenched, over and over. In the old days, it would have been quenched in the body of a slave. Heber, God protect them all for fools, meant to quench these blades and hundreds like them in the bodies of their masters, the Saurons of Angband Base.

She half-wished she had never mentioned Badri's name.

Footsteps sounded outside. Chaya's keen hearing told her that they approached the forge. She whirled, one hand reaching for the knife hidden in a storage bin. A pistol would have been more sure, but who had ever heard of a swordsmith relying on firearms? Besides, a bullet astray near a crucible . . . Chaya didn't want to think of that either.

"Ho, the forge!" It was Heber's voice. The doors were doubled: one let him into the building; the second protected the forge against gusts of wind or squalls that the outer door might admit.

Even through the filtered glass, Chaya found pleasure in watching him. Heber was not especially tall, either for the Bandari or the townsfolk, but he seemed bigger, perhaps because his trade had added muscle to his shoulders. He needed that strength to hammer out the blades; but it was good, very good for other things as well. As always, she smiled at the man, and then smiled more secretly to herself.

He shook his head slightly at her, not needing Sauron sight to know what she was thinking.

"How did your trip go?" she said.

His smile grew broader. "The *khan* was pleased," he said.

Love and fear fought in her as she saw the laughter dancing in his eyes. "Tell me," she said.

The swordsmith who based himself at Tallinn Town put aside his scimitars and daggers in their velvet trays. "Thank you for your kindly guesting of me, excellent *khan*," he said, bowing as he sat cross-legged in Dede Korkut's yurt.

The nomad chief bowed in return. "You are always welcome here — the quality of your edges guarantees it." The prominent clansmen with him, many of whom had just bought new blades from the smith, nodded their agreement.

The swordsmith bowed again. "I thank you once more, excellent *khan*." He hesitated, went on. "Excellent *khan*, could I but have your ear alone for a brief spell of time, I could perhaps set a weapon in your hands sharper than any scimitar."

Dede Korkut's eyebrows rose. "What would you tell me that my nobles may not hear?" he demanded. The swordsmith sat quietly and did not reply. Dede Korkut frowned, rubbed the few thin white hairs on his chin that he was pleased to call a beard. At last he said, "Very well." He gestured for the rest of the plainsmen to leave the yurt. They filed out, more or less resentfully. "Juchi, you stay," Dede Korkut commanded.

It was Heber's turn to frown. "I would sooner speak to but one pair of ears."

"He is the clan's warleader, and my heir," Dede Korkut said flatly.

The swordsmith still did not yield. "He is young."

"As the ancient *shaikh* Ishaq Asinaf once observed, it is a fault of which everyone is guilty at one time or another," Dede Korkut said. "He does not speak out of turn. If you doubt it, then leave, and take your precious business with you."

For a moment, Juchi thought the swordsmith would do exactly that.

In the end, though, Heber fixed Dede Korkut's warleader with a hard stare, warning, "Lives ride on this, my own not least."

"I hear," Juchi said. "I understand." He visibly composed himself to listen, resolving to show no reaction to whatever wild scheme the smith was about to unfold.

*That* resolve was at once tested to the utmost, for the fellow asked Dede Korkut, "How would your clan like to seize Tallinn Valley?"

Behind his impassive mask, Juchi had all he could do to keep from shouting. Every band on the plains dreamed of taking a valley for its very own, to make sure all its women's births would be safe. Like the rest of the steppe-rovers, Dede Korkut's clan paid tribute for the privilege of sending its pregnant women to a land of decent air pressure: either to the Saurons for Tallinn Valley or to the Bandari for Eden Valley to the southeast of it. There were others, but they were hostile, or too far away. The Shangri-La was best of all, but the Sauron Citadel squatted at the entrance — which was a full T-year's travel, in any case.

By the spark that leaped in Dede Korkut's eye, Juchi was sure the clan chief was dreaming along with him. Dede Korkut's response, though, was dry: "I presume you have this arranged with the Saurons."

"No," the swordsmith said, and Juchi got ready to throw him bodily out of the yurt. Then the man from Tallinn Town went on, "But with one of their women, aye."

"What good will that do?" Dede Korkut said. "Their women are not the folk we have to fight."

"Hold a moment, mighty *khan*," Juchi said, his mind leaping forward with the agility of youth. "Saurons, from all I've heard, are great fighters, true enough. But there are not many of them, and much of their strength, especially the strength of their fortress, lies in the excellence of its magic."

"Technology," Heber corrected him.

"Whatever it may be," Juchi said impatiently. "If the

woman corrupts it so they do not realize we are upon them until the moment, we may accomplish much. If." He let the word hang in the air, stared a challenge at the smith.

The man studied him in return, then slowly nodded. "Your chief was right, young warleader, in bidding you stay. You see through to the essence of the scheme. At an hour you choose, the Sauron fort's systems can be made to fail. And when they do, if you strike quick and hard enough — "

"You speak always of our striking," Dede Korkut said. "How will the folk of Tallinn Town respond when battle is joined? If they are with us, they will aid us greatly. If they stand with the Saurons, the attack is not worth making."

"Tallinn Town has no love for Angband Base," Heber said after some small pause for thought. "The taxes the Saurons extort far outweigh the protection they give — not to mention the women taken against their will. For now, the town knows nothing of what I discuss with you. Were it otherwise, you may be sure this secret would not stay secret long. But most folk in the town, most in Tallinn Valley, will be for you, come the day."

Dede Korkut rocked back and forth. *"Aiii,* Shaitan could put no greater temptation before me than you dangle now. Victory would make the clan great. But if we fail — " He shuddered. "If we fail, the clan dies."

"How say you, then?" The swordsmith kept his voice steady, even sat relaxed, but Juchi smelled his sharp sweat. "I can offer information, the crippling of Angband's defenses . . . and perhaps weapons more potent than these swords. My wife's mother," he went on with delicate emphasis, "is Judge of the Pale."

The clan chief did not directly answer, turning rather to the warleader he had chosen. "Can this thing be done?"

Juchi had been turning that very question over in his mind. "Perhaps it can," he said. "Perhaps it can."

The swordsmith let out the breath he had been holding. "I shall pass this word back to the one who gave me the message. We go forward, then." He rose, bowed — now to Juchi as well as to Dede Korkut — and left the chief's yurt.

The two nomads were briefly silent. Dede Korkut leaned backward against his pillows, slightly blue around the lips; Juchi put a hand on his shoulder.

"It is nothing," the *khan* said. "Old age is a disease from which none recover . . . but I hope I will live to see the sons of Iblis in Angband overthrown."

Juchi nodded. "We will have to examine this further before we do in fact go forward. It could be a trick of the Saurons, to lure us to destruction."

"That thought I had also," Dede Korkut said. "This Heber bar Non may live in Tallinn Town, but he is of the Bandari. They have their own purposes . . . and any two of them could cheat Shaitan at dice."

"True. But they have dealt fairly with us — hard bargainers, but just. More, their hate for the Saurons is old and black."

"And if the swordsmith speaks truly . . . oh, if he does!" Dede Korkut clapped Juchi on the shoulder. "If he does, you will lead our warriors."

"Good," Juchi said. "I begin to have some ideas that may help us, come the day. We will be fighting Angband Base as much as the Saurons inside, I think. And the Base cannot run away. . . ." All at once, he began to laugh.

"Where is the joke?" Dede Korkut asked.

Juchi told him. After a moment's startlement, the clan chief laughed too.

"Wife," Heber said, and the formality of his voice warned her that he was not alone, "prepare food for our guests. I go to welcome them."

*Wife.*

Chaya stiffened. As often as she and her husband had had to play the game, she never liked being relegated to the position of tribal servant. But there were, God knew, worse roles in life; and she had met women who played them. Deliberately, she waited until Heber had ushered in his guests, then made much of dropping her head and scurrying modestly into the kitchens. But she had seen what she wished to see: one of Heber's guests was Dede

Korkut the chieftain — that silver hair was unmistakable despite the hat he had jerked down over as much of it as he could. The other was a younger man, taller than Heber.

The chieftain's son? Chaya hadn't known that Dede Korkut had one. His heir, she concluded as she poured batter on heated metal to make flatbread and scooped stew into bowls. He did not look like a nomad, apart from his dress; too tall, and brown-haired, with a rather beaky, sculpted face.

When the trays were loaded, she called her servant to bring them to the principal guesting room, then dismissed the girl to her home. The guesting room was located, somewhat unconventionally, in the living quarters, and Heber had had her furnish it with rugs and cushions and leather hangings, so it resembled the yurt of a prosperous tribesman. Here, he showed his most favored customers his most expensive swords — there was little market for weapons in Tallinn Valley itself, where the Sauron "peace" hung heavy. And here they met to discuss what Chaya simultaneously feared and longed for: the downfall of Angband Base.

Chaya glanced at her husband: stay or leave?

"*Khan*," Heber spoke before the older man could protest, "you brought your heir Juchi into our . . . discussions. My wife, Chaya, must stay."

"A woman?" asked the younger tribesman.

"I greet the guest," Chaya said, low-voiced and polite, in Turkic. The *khan* chuckled at her words, which were a pun, as she very well knew.

"*Khatun* Chaya is Bandari, the daughter of the Judge of Eden Valley."

"The lady may be a princess among her kind," said Juchi, "but she is no warrior."

"With respect," Heber said, "it is a woman among the Saurons who can unlock the secrets of their minefields to us. A woman," he went on, "who as women will, meets her friend — her friend Chaya — to gossip of women's doings, such as no Soldier will take notice of."

The two nomads grinned acknowledgment of the stratagem. *Which is part truth*, Chaya thought. She and

Badri *were* friends; the Brigade Leader's woman was even more lonely than she.

Dede Korkut nodded. "And if one woman can fight the Saurons, why not another?" He paused for a moment, touching a hand to his chest, and struggling for breath. At their looks of concern, he waved the hand in irritated dismissal. "It is nothing. *Khatun?*"

"It is not as a warrior that I can serve." Chaya decided that the time had come to speak for herself. "But as a pledge of support from the Pale. Speak the word, and the Bandari will flock to your standard."

The warleader Juchi smiled. "Perhaps . . . and perhaps they would stay flocked, once Tallinn Valley is rid of the Saurons," he said drily.

He went on directly to Chaya: "You claim, *khatun*, that your word will bring us aid. We do not expect the warriors of the Pale to abandon their own and march so far, but Angband may summon aid from Quilland Base; that is a long journey, and the two Bases have not been overfriendly, but it may be that all Saurons will unite against 'cattle.' " He spat the Sauron word. "To reach us, such a force must cross near the northeastern border of the Pale. Bandari fighters might guard our rear while we attack — but how shall you command them from Tallinn Town?"

From her left hand, Chaya stripped her ruby ring and let it clatter onto the low brass table. "Some among your men ride as they will. Let them ride to Eden Valley to give my mother *this*, and our warriors will ride out."

"More women?" Juchi seemed to scoff, but a chuckle underlay the deep, almost familiar rumble of his voice. For a warleader, he was easy to talk to, Chaya thought; their thought processes were curiously alike, even when he felt he had to jeer at her.

"My mother, the Judge Dvora, is no warleader. She decides on matters of law, and the *kapetein* rules the Pale. Rather will the warrior Barak bar Sandor lead the warriors of the Pale to the steppes. If by some chance Quilland Base sends to these Saurons' aid, Barak's warriors will hold them," Chaya said.

Heber smiled. "I believe you know the man Barak," he remarked. "And the *Sayerets*, the fighters he leads."

The *khan* shook his head, shuddered slightly. "Barak I know," he said. "If he sends his men, let him come himself and not let that young madman they call the Hammer-of-God command — but against the Saurons, even the Hammer would be welcome."

Twice and three times, Chaya retreated to the kitchen to fetch more food and drink. The last time she emerged, she carried a skin of mares' milk, traded for with the tribes against just such a necessity. She stood in what would have been darkness for anyone who lacked her night sight watching the faces of the other conspirators, who had fought and refought in words and maps their way across the battle plain before Angband, but who were, once again, brought up short before the fortress' mighty walls.

"We could encircle Angband with warriors for ten years and never get in!" lamented the old man Dede Korkut. Though the night was young — second-cycle had not even begun — his eyes were red, and he peered as if he had difficulty focusing.

"It is too dim for you, *khan*," Heber said. "Let me . . ." He threw fuel on the fire, and light flared up.

Chaya, who had chosen that moment to approach holding the skin of mares' milk, stumbled. She regained her balance quickly, managing neither to drop the skin nor to swear.

"When the fire flares up, my sight is no better than a drillbit's," she complained. "Wait — drillbits!"

Juchi and the *khan* laughed together; after a moment, Chaya joined in. Heber looked from one to the other.

Drillbits were known for their adamantine teeth and for their greed. Notoriously difficult to control, drillbits could literally chew through walls — assuming you could get them to start.

"I laugh that the *khatun* and I think so much alike," Juchi said. "I too had the notion of using drillbits against Angband's walls. But" — he shrugged — "how to do so without the Saurons' noticing? Bait, perhaps, but they would *see* us planting bait. Still, the idea teases at my mind."

Chaya reached into a turquoise bowl that held a garish array of tennis fruit, Finnegan's figs, and red-and-white splotched clownfruit. She caught one up, balanced it in one hand, then tossed it into the air.

"Let me speak as a woman," she said. "It has always been hard to restrain the children from insulting the Saurons. How if we do not even try?" She mimed throwing the clownfruit at her husband.

"Coat the walls with fruit pulp, and the drillbits will gnaw through them for us. They're so stupid they'll burrow a meter or more to find the rest — and Angband's are about a meter thick at the base. Built of soft tufa, too."

"And the Saurons? Would they not try to harm our sons? Would they not wonder at the waste of food?" On Haven little was wasted, even in a prosperous corner like the Tallinn Valley.

"Overripe clownfruit," Chaya said. More nods. Clownfruit were native Haven flora, although humans could eat them, until they went overripe; then they generated a toxic alkaloid that not even distilling would remove. The drillbits wouldn't mind — they liked them that way.

"The Saurons too live with women, who would not see other women's children hurt for so little." *Please God, let that be so!* "And the Saurons are men and warriors, who like being laughed at as little as any other men. What would they have said? That in their pride, they grudge little children a messy game?"

After a moment, all three men began to laugh uproariously. The skin of mares' milk was passed, this time to her first. She was laughing so hard that the white fluid nearly came out her nose, and she neglected to belch politely.

The men of Dede Korkut's tribe gashed their cheeks in grief. They rode about the grave-mound in a wide circle, with the blood drying on their faces, hammering the hilts of their sabers on their shields and howling like tamerlanes; behind them the women keened and wailed, a clump of dark felt against the dun-brown of the steppe. Within the great pile of rock Dede Korkut lay as his fathers before him, with his bow and sword by his side, dressed in fine cloth, a cup of gold filled with kvass to hand. Around the mound his dead horses stood erect, impaled on stakes, to accompany their master to Paradise. Cat's Eye loomed behind the grave in the west, as if weeping; all about stood the tumbled bones and stones of previous burials, for this had been the resting place of the tribe's *khans* and nobles for centuries.

Heber bar Non and Chaya bat Dvora stood at a little distance; they had brought gifts to the grave-feast, but this was a matter for close kin. When only the women of the *khan*'s own family continued their keening, and the followers from other encampments had withdrawn to their yurts, they sought Juchi.

"Excellent *khan*," Heber said, bowing.

Chaya copied the gesture: travelling outside Tallinn, she had returned to Bandari dress. It attracted little attention, here near the borders of the Pale, but the weight of the saber on her belt felt a little strange.

"Not yet," Juchi said. His hard sculpted face was drawn with genuine grief; the cuts on his cheeks had already clotted, looking like old scars except for the line of dried blood. He stroked his beard. "Come."

They ducked into the warleader's yurt; a servant brought kvass, and Juchi sprinkled the ceremonial drops on the little stuffed idol over the entrance.

"This first pouring I give to the spirit of the yurt," he murmured. Then, turning to his guests: "Not yet am I *khan* of the tribe, but soon. Dede Korkut named me his successor. I must journey to all the encampments, but that is custom, no more. He had no living sons, and his nephew Tarik is not yet a man of moment."

Heber leaned forward. "And our plan, O *khan*?"

Juchi raised his head for a moment, as if listening to make sure they were not overheard. "Yes to that also, swordsmith. The warriors have gathered for the funeral — that will arouse no suspicion in Angband, although they would hear of an ordinary muster. We strike. If," he went on, "the boys are ready."

"They are, *khan*," Chaya said firmly. "It was more difficult than getting the maps of the minefields, but it is done. There is a price, though." Juchi's eyebrows rose. "Many of the mothers have daughters who were taken to the Base. If they are widowed, their children orphaned . . ."

Juchi stroked his beard again. "Hmmm. *If* we take the Base, there will be plunder aplenty. Let some of it go to dowries for the widows — some of the weapons, even. Will that serve?"

Chaya nodded. "As for the orphans, those whom their kin in Tallinn won't take, the People will. Bandari do not hold a child's parents against it" — *most of us don't, much* — "and we will be glad to take them in. Our Law commands that we do, when there is an opportunity."

The nomad chief nodded. "Good. Best they leave Tallinn Valley; a father's blood calls for blood, and I would not wish them growing up to vengeance around me. Yet slaying the helpless is an ill thing, if it can be arranged otherwise." The skin passed again. "Forgive my discourtesy, but you should leave quickly. We begin at once, and the Saurons have many spies."

"This is a filthy sport the boys of the town have," Grima snarled. "Filthy! We should shoot a few, to teach the rest a lesson."

"It does no harm," Badri said, doing her best to soothe the Brigade Leader. He gave her a curious look; usually she cared not a jot for his feelings. She went on, "And shooting children will surely forfeit whatever goodwill that has managed to grow up over the years between Angband Base and Tallinn Town."

"I have no goodwill toward these rascals." Grima rose, and seized Badri's wrist in an unbreakable grip. "Come, see for yourself the mischief they make." He gave Badri no choice, but dragged her along with him as he stamped through the outer court and ascended to the top of the wall. He scowled down at the boys outside. "Look!"

Badri looked. Boys and a few girls frisked about. One reached into the sheepskin bag he carried, and drew out an overripe clownfruit. He hurled it at a friend. The other boy

ducked. The clownfruit splattered against the gray stone of
Angband Base's outwall. It slowly slid to the ground, leaving behind a yellow splash of juice. The distinctive
bitter-oily smell of the fruit in its overripe state rose; useless
even for compost, since it would kill the introduced Terran
bacteria and earthworms that tried to eat it.

As if that first throw had been a signal — *an opening shot*,
Badri thought — all the children started flinging fruit at
one another. Since they could dodge and the wall could
not, it got much messier than they did. Pulp and juice
brought stone to bright, even gaudy, life, as if it was the canvas of some ancient abstract expressionist.

Grima was a Soldier; he had never heard of abstract
expressionism. Turning to Badri, he growled, "The little idiots have been at it since first-cycle sunrise, close to
one hundred and twenty hours now. The whole wall is
smeared with this filth."

"I'm sure they'll give it up soon," she answered mildly,
glancing at the small but brilliant point of light that was
Byers' Sun. It hung low in the west, slowly sinking toward
the jagged horizon. "With both the sun and Cat's Eye gone
from the sky, it will be too cold for the boys to play such
games—and too dark for them to admire their handiwork."

"Admire!" Grima turned such a dusky shade of purple
that Badri wondered if he was about to have a stroke:
apoplexy often felled Saurons no longer young. But the
Brigade Leader mastered himself, and his woman her disappointment. He ground out, "If it weren't for the waste of
ammunition, I *would* order them shot."

That was not *quite* true. The Soldiers ruled by terror, but
like most weapons terror was more effective as a threat
than a reality. An occasional gruesome execution served
well enough to keep the fear alive. Killing a valley child for
a prank was likely to spark more rebellion and sabotage
than it was worth. Still . . .

"They're only children," Badri said. "They're harm-
less." She bit down on a giggle as she imagined young
Soldiers behaving so. Then the laugh choked itself off.
Even young Soldiers were anything but harmless.

Grima shook his fist at the town boys. "Get out of here!" he yelled.

Soldiers' uniforms, from any distance, looked alike regardless of rank. It was easy for the children to assume the Brigade Leader was just another grouchy trooper. One of them threw a big red-and-white fruit at him. Luckily for everyone, it missed.

"I'll fine their fathers, that's what I'll do," Grima snarled. "Enough to make them hurt — you, get their names! Then *they'll* beat the little bad-genes brats black and blue."

Grima stormed down off the wall. He was as angry as Badri had ever seen him. Considering how the two of them got along, that was saying something. She followed, her face the expressionless mask to which she schooled herself. Behind the shield she held up against the Brigade Leader, she exulted.

Troop Leader Ufthak yawned and poured himself a cup of not-quite-coffee from the insulated flask that hung on his belt. The mild stimulant was welcome, the warmth even more so. Sentry-go was tedious duty, nowhere more so than at the northern edge of Tallinn Valley where it widened out onto the steppe, at no time more than now — second-cycle night, truenight, was extra dark and extra cold.

The sky seemed naked without either Byers' Sun or Cat's Eye to light it, Ufthak thought. Then he laughed at himself — pretty fancy language for a noncom. What would happen next? He'd probably start writing poetry.

"At which point they pension me off," he said aloud. Then he laughed harder. There was no such thing as a pensioned-off Soldier on Haven.

As if to relieve his boredom, a band of nomads came cantering by, closer to his post than they usually dared approach. Some of them drew within a couple of hundred meters, their heat-signatures clear to his eyes. Ufthak frowned and glanced over to the far side of the valley. Sure enough, plainsmen were also making a display in front of the other sentry post. Ufthak glowered. What in the name of bad genes were they up to?

The Troop Leader clicked the change lever of his assault rifle from safety to semi-automatic. If the nomads thought they could lull him out of alertness, they were welcome to try. A lot of them would end up dead before they realized they were wrong.

All of Ufthak's enhanced senses focused on the riders ahead. The tiny noises behind him were too faint even for enhanced senses, until someone jumped down into the firing pit in back of him. He started to whirl, too late. Iron-hard fingers jerked his head back. A knife's fiery kiss licked across his throat.

The last thing he felt before he went into the dark was embarrassment at letting cattle trick him so.

Juchi climbed out of the Sauron sentry post, waved his dagger and the dead sentinel's assault rifle to show he had succeeded. His keen ears caught the sound of a struggle in the pit on the opposite side of the valley. He dashed that way, only to see two nomads scrambling out, one supporting the other.

He pursed his lips, silently blew through them. Four men had gone after that other sentry. He just thanked Allah and the spirits that neither Sauron had managed to get off a shot.

The fortress was a couple of kilometers back into the valley. The warriors there might not have heard, or might have assumed the sentries had things under control. But Saurons had enhanced ears and lively suspicions. The last thing Juchi wanted to do was rouse them.

As the plainsmen in the bands that had distracted the sentries realized the way south was open, one of their number galloped away from the mouth of the valley. He soon returned, leading all the fighting men of Dede Korkut's clan, with Heber bar Non and a band of grim-faced volunteers from Tallinn Valley as well. With him came the grenades, Pale-made, and extra charges of gunpowder and shot for the tribe's muskets.

"Now comes the tricky part," Juchi said softly, when everyone had settled their gear.

"Aye." One of the nomads nodded. "We'd've had a go at

the Saurons in their fort long years ago, were it not for the minefields here."

"Now we know where the mines are, though, with the knowing stolen from Angband Base's own computer," Juchi said. His men murmured in awe; to them as to him, *computer* was but a word to conjure with, as vague and splendid as *demon*.

Juchi studied the map the swordsmith had brought to the clan. "Follow me," he ordered. "Single file, each man walking as best he can in the footsteps of the man ahead. Anyone who steps on a mine, I will punish without mercy." The warriors stared, then chuckled softly.

They made it through without losing a man. Juchi knew nothing but relief, not least for himself. The map was not an actual printout, but the swordsmith's reconstruction of data smuggled out of the base. Even to do so much — Juchi marveled at the courage of the woman who sent the smith what she'd picked from the mechanical brain.

If all went as he hoped, he thought suddenly, he would meet her soon. Now, though, for the one role in the mission he could not play. "Boys forward," he whispered. A couple of dozen lads, all of them between nine and fifteen T-years, came up to him. "You know what to do," he told them. They nodded, slipped off toward Angband Base.

Up on the wall, Senior Trooper Gorbag came to alertness at the sound of running feet approaching. Then he heard children laugh, heard an overripe clownfruit splatter off the stone below him.

"Get out of here, you gene-poor cattle bastards!" he shouted. The children took no notice of him. He went back to walking his beat; the Brigade Leader tolerated this nonsense for the moment, even if he did not love it. The cattle in Tallinn Town would be the ones grinding their teeth when the fines were announced.

He heard a couple of other sentries shout challenges, then realize they were just spotting more miserable boys. "For a bottle of beer, I'd blow them all away," he said when he came up to the Soldier on the next stretch of wall.

The other Soldier laughed. "For half a bottle," he said.

Not all the boys were armed with fruit this time. Most carried drillbits instead, carried them most carefully by the ropes that bound the burrowers' front and hind legs together. They made sure the animals' heads could not reach anything but air, made especially sure those irresistible teeth came nowhere near their own precious flesh.

Ihsan's drillbit had a particularly evil temper. It kept twisting its meter-long ratlike body, kept trying to jerk its head around so it could bite his hand. As plainly as it could without words, it told him it was angry and hungry and wanted its freedom right now, if not sooner.

"Yes, yes," Ihsan muttered, lugging it toward the wall. He set it down in front of a fruit-besplashed place and cut its bonds with his beltknife.

The drillbit's teeth sank into the spot where it smelled fruit. Those diamond-like incisors cared nothing about stone; the best armor-piercing arrowheads were ground from drillbit teeth. As Ihsan watched, the beast started to burrow into the wall. The youth did not watch long, but turned and ran.

Gorbag yawned as he came down from his turn at sentry-go. Sleep would be welcome, sleep and then his woman. Or maybe, he thought hopefully, the other way around.

He was at the base of the wall when he heard a sound that did not belong. It reminded him — he frowned at the image his mind called up — it reminded him of a man chewing on a mouthful of ball bearings.

He scratched his head. "What the — ?" To his amazement, a chunk of wall about the size of his fist suddenly crumbled to dust. The hole grew larger. A streamlined head poked through, and peered nearsightedly up at him.

Gorbag's precious discipline went south. He was too horrified to shoot. He screamed instead, as if he were some rich, pampered Tallinn Town woman watching a mouse scuttle across her polished floor.

"Drillbit!" he shouted again and again. "*Drillbit!*" Moments later, the same cry rose from another part of the wall.

* * *

Grima cursed his enhanced hearing. He had been about to mount Badri when the shouting started. He thought about going ahead regardless — she seemed even more furious about submitting than usual, which always turned him on.

Then he realized what the troopers were yelling. He cursed again, this time out loud and foully. Wearing only an erection, he dashed for the wall.

His ardor wilted in the chill of second-cycle truenight. The rest of his body ignored the cold. The Soldiers in the courtyard had the good sense not to notice how he was dressed.

Someone had finally decided to kill one of the drillbits. Another one waddled, obscenely fat, close by the wall. The Brigade Leader's bare foot lashed out, slammed the animal into the stone. It twitched and died.

Even as it did, though, a new outcry arose twenty meters away. Another brown bullet head, ridiculous nose twitching, started to emerge from what should have been solid rock.

Grima dapped a hand to his forehead. "The whole frigging wall might be honeycombed with 'em!" he shouted — screamed might be a better word, if screams came in deep, rasping baritone.

"What do we do, sir?" a Soldier asked nervously. The Brigade Leader snatched the rifle out of the man's hands, fired at the newest drillbit. The unaimed round spanged off stone thirty centimeters from its head. The drillbit squeaked and pulled back into its hole.

Grima suppressed an impulse to yell back toward the barracks. "You — Trooper Mim — go set off the general alert." It would be undignified for the Brigade Leader to run around shouting naked people out of bed over quasi-rodents.

As soon as Grima dashed away, Badri scrambled out of bed. She grudged the time she needed to throw on a robe, but took it nonetheless. Unlike her lord and master — lips skinned back from teeth in a carnivore grin at that thought — she would draw questions, running through the corridors naked. As it happened, no one saw her before she got to Angband Base Command Central; the commander's quarters were close by, for emergencies. She barred the door behind her — Command Central, she'd learned from the TAC, was intended to be a last redoubt against enemy assault no matter what happened to the rest of the base. Hence this single door. For once Sauron military paranoia would be turned against the Soldiers, she thought.

Too bad for the Saurons. Badri began pulling switches.

"I told Mim to set off the general alert!" Grima cried once more, furious not just at the drillbits but now also at his own men. Was everyone asleep in the second-cycle darkness? Red lights should have been flashing, sirens wailing, and Soldiers piling out of the barracks, ready for anything. A minute more and he'd say to hell with dignity and begin yelling and kicking butts himself.

Only the Soldiers on the wall rushed toward the Brigade Leader's voice. Then all the lights in the courtyard went out.

Beyond the side of the wall opposite the one where the drillbits had been released, Juchi and his men stood waiting. When Angband Base plunged into blackness, the nomad warleader thumped the plainsman next to him on the shoulder. The whole band dashed forward, scaling ladders and knotted ropes at the ready.

The first inkling Grima had of something seriously wrong — as opposed to a monumental fuckup — came when Mim ran out of the main barracks, shouting, "Sir, sir, Command Central is locked from inside, and whoever's in there won't acknowledge orders!"

While the Brigade Leader was still trying to digest that, the courtyard lights came back on. They showed men on the walls, armed men not in Soldier field-gray. The nomads started shooting down at the troopers by Grima. Grenades arched down, exploding in sulfur-smelling puffs and sending potsherd shrapnel whining off the inner walls of Angband.

The Soldiers returned fire. Stunned, outnumbered, and

pinned down as they were, they nonetheless tumbled invaders from their perches. But the plainsmen's bows — they even had a couple of assault rifles, Grima saw with dismay — hissed death through the Brigade Leader's companions. Muskets loaded with buckshot roared, filling the courtyard with lead and dirty smoke. The grenades flew again and again; a dud came to rest by his foot, and he recognized the make. Bandari, although the men on the walls were nomads, screaming *Allahu Akbar* and Turkic warcries.

One lone voice cried *HaBandar!* instead. His weapon had the sharper *crack* of a rifled musket; two paces from Grima, a Soldier jackknifed backwards. The hole in his stomach was small, but the exit-wound in his back was the size of a small dinner plate: a 12mm-rifle slug of soft lead creates massive tissue damage, much worse than a round ball of the same caliber. Grima did not need to give orders about that. Two streams of bullets from assault rifles battered the Bandari, whoever he was, down off the wall to crumpled death.

Gunfire did what the dead alarm had failed to do — it brought Soldiers bouncing out of bed, weapons at the ready. And when the first of them charged out through the doorways, the foes on the wall cut them down before even Soldier's reactions could save them.

"Dede Korkut!" the nomads yelled. "Dede Korkut!"

Grima's heart, already thuttering near panic, almost stopped altogether when he heard that cry. Here was the danger against which the TAC had warned him, the danger that had caught him all too literally naked. He had thought the danger past when the report of the old chief's death came in, a T-year before.

The plainsmen were descending into the courtyard now, and more and more of them were on the walls. This had to be the whole tribe, Grima thought, appalled, and all its firepower. Somehow they'd made it through the minefield. Men from Tallinn Town as well — hundreds, there must be thousands of cattle swarming over the wall.

Connecting that improbability with the failure of the general alarm and the Assault Leader's dreadful news, the

Brigade Leader groaned, "Treason!" And devastatingly effective treason, too—Grima was almost the only Soldier in the courtyard still standing. Against the guns the nomads had massed, against the surprise and disadvantageous position, genetically enhanced fighting ability did not count enough.

Bullets singing around him, Grima ran for the barracks. Somehow he tumbled through the doorway still unwounded. The Soldiers inside were not trying to come out any more. That, they'd learned, was deadly. Instead they were shooting from loophole windows and, from the screams outside, doing no little damage.

"That's the way!" the Brigade Leader shouted. "They haven't taken us yet!" With the rations stored in its underground cellars, the hall could stand a longer siege than any nomad tribe could afford to undertake. And when the nomads had to withdraw . . . Grima snarled, thinking of the revenge the Soldiers would take.

Then fire-fighting foam gushed from forgotten ceiling fixtures unused since Angband Base was built. The stuff was choking to breathe; worse, when it got in a trooper's eyes, it burned like fire and left him blind for . . . Grima did not know for how long. Long enough. As the shooting from the barracks slackened, the plainsmen, still yelling like their imaginary demons, swarmed into the hall.

What happened next was butchery. It was not all one-sided; even blind, Soldiers could dispatch whatever foes came within their reach. But few of the nomads were so unwise. They spent ammunition with such prodigality that Grima wondered whether they would have enough left to hold Angband Base if they took it.

That, however, was not his problem. Getting the traitor out of Command Central was. He could still see out of one eye, after a fashion — and, somewhere back in his quarters, he had a key to a secret entrance to the Base's ultimate strongpoint.

Badri was wrong. In military paranoia if nowhere else, the Soldiers let imagination run free. He might yet turn the battle against the invaders.

Grima ran through the corridors, dodging blinded Soldiers and shouting his name over and over so they would not shoot at what they could not see.

Women's screams mingled with warriors'. Some fought side by side with the Soldiers. Others struck at their one-time partners with anything they had. Grima saw one stab a trooper in the back with a pair of scissors. The Brigade Leader broke her neck and ran on.

Badri was not in his cubicle. He did not know whether to be glad — he might have had to kill her, too. After frantic rummaging through desk drawers, he snatched the key he needed, then ran for all he was worth toward Command Central.

Silent as a stalking cliff lion, Juchi chased the naked Sauron through the chaos of Angband Base's death throes. He could have shot him more than once, but the officer — he'd heard and seen the fellow giving orders — looked to have some definite purpose in mind. That, Juchi thought, might be worth learning.

So he waited until the Sauron bent to turn a key and swing open a tiny hidden door before he fired a burst from around a corner. He heard the meaty *chunnk* of bullets smacking flesh, peered cautiously to see what he had done.

The Sauron was down but not quite out; he snapped a shot that *craacked* past Juchi closer than he ever wanted to think about. Juchi returned fire, emptying the assault rifle's magazine. Not even Sauron flesh withstood that second burst. When Juchi looked again, he saw the naked Soldier sprawled in death.

Pausing only to stick in a fresh clip (his last, he noted, and reminded himself to make sure someone salvaged the good brass cartridges he'd used), he stepped through the door the Sauron had opened. At the end of a narrow, winding corridor was another door. He opened it.

When Badri saw a piece of the wall of her little fortress within a fortress begin to open inward, she knew she was dead. *So unfair*, she lamented, *so unfair*. But then, maybe not. She had had her vengeance on Angband Base; perhaps it was only right that the Base have vengeance on her.

She stood, straightened, awaited her fate with a strange calm. Here inside Command Central, she had no weapon. For that matter, how much good was a weapon likely to do against a battle-ready Soldier? She was sure only a Sauron could have sniffed out the hidden way, about which not even she had known. Thus she gasped when the door revealed instead a nomad warrior, shaggy in fur cap, sheepskin jacket and boots, heavy wool trousers, and a young man's brown beard sprouting from cheeks and chin.

He swung his rifle toward her, abruptly checked the motion. She realized her robe had fallen open. She made no move to pull it shut. Let the plainsman see all he wanted, if that kept her alive.

He said something in his own language. She shook her head; she had no more than a few words of the plains speech. He tried again, this time in stumbling Russki:

"Who — you?"

That she could follow; most of the folk of Tallinn Town and Valley had Russki for their native tongue. She gave her name, waved around. "This is Command Central. This is where I fight for you."

His grin was enormous, and looked even more so with his teeth so white against his unshaven face. "Badri?" he shouted. "You Badri? I Juchi, warleader Dede Korkut's clan. We have Angband Base, Badri. We win. Between you, fighters of clan, we win!" He threw his arms wide.

She sprang forward. Even the prod of the assault rifle in the small of her back as Juchi's embrace enfolded her was only a brief annoyance. He smelled of stale sweat and smokeless powder. Badri did not care, not now, not in the savage rush, stronger than vodka, of a victory she had never expected to win.

He tilted her chin up. His face felt strange against hers; she had never kissed a bearded man before. Triumph burned as hot in her as in him. The kiss went on and on. She felt her loins turn liquid. Afterwards, she was never sure which of them drew the other down to the floor.

* * *

This far from Base, not even Chaya could hear the screams and the shooting.

*Waiting. That's the hardest part.* She wanted to pace, to shout, even to scream frustration at the men who claimed the work of fighting and left her and their wives to wait and to fear. The women of Tallinn were quiet, schooled to waiting while their fates were decided. Even the youngest bride sat calmly, restraining a toddler while its mother nursed a baby.

They were all calm, all quiet. The screaming and lamentations would come later, if they were needed. In the half-light of the shelter Chaya could see the women's eyes. Shadowed and liquid, their glances shot to the door every time someone thought she heard a sound. Waiting made your ears play tricks on you. She exchanged glances with some of the other women. Each had been selected for strength and composure; each bore a pistol.

If their menfolk lost, they would not die unavenged. And, if all went well, the women would follow them into death, not to be slaves to Saurons. Chaya wondered how many of them could hold to that resolve.

She stretched and shifted in her place, trying not to become stiff with waiting as the night dragged on.

"Quiet!" she hissed to silence a whispered conversation. Moving with as much care as if she sought to avoid ambush, she edged toward the door.

"Footsteps," she mouthed at the older women and saw them draw their pistols from their layered clothing. Then she sagged with relief as a series of taps sounded on the door. "It's the signal!" she said, speaking aloud for the first time that night.

Tears rolled down the women's faces; and she would have wept too . . . but her tears dried so very quickly.

Juchi had sent youths to reassure the women and command them not, the youths repeated, not to venture into the Base to care for the wounded menfolk. The injured would be brought out. Repeat: they would be brought out. Chaya grinned at the very young men, who bore messily bandaged wounds and their female relatives' shrill attention with obvious forbearance and more than a little pride. This might well be their first time in authority over their mothers and aunts; it was too much to expect that they would take no satisfaction in the role of returning, victorious warriors. Hurriedly, they recounted the battle: so many Saurons slain, so many vanished.

Vanished? Some might try to cross the steppe, make for Quilland Base; and Barak's warriors would be waiting for them. Then they saw her, and their jubilation faded. "Chaya *Khatun* . . ." one spoke hesitantly.

"We knew there would be dead." Her voice sounded cold and strange. "Who else?"

An odd way to phrase it. But, just from the way they looked at her, she knew. Heber was dead. Somewhere in that thrice-damned fort, her husband lay dead, hacked or torn to pieces, a bullet in his brain . . . it did not matter. The man who had loved her when all around her called her a freak lay dead.

The women raised the wail of tribal lamentation until Chaya's too-keen hearing could not bear it. She moved forward, her whole body cold, despite the press of bodies.

"I beg you," she said, still in that lifeless voice. "My work here is done for now. I must go out."

"Where, *khatun*?" One of the youths made as if to stand between her and the door. He might never have backed down from the Saurons, but fell back at her glance.

"The Saurons stole a life from me. They owe me a life in return."

She went out into the night. Briefly she stopped at the forge to pick up weapons, supplies and tools. She harnessed a muskylope and rode out of Tallinn Town.

When the muskylope staggered and all but pitched forward onto its knees, Chaya slid from its broad back and made camp. She kindled a tiny fire, sheltering it from the winds that tore across the steppe. She herself might have spotted it from afar, however; and that was good.

She drew her heavy sheepskin coat about her and huddled by the small flames. She did not expect it to warm her; nothing could warm her since the announcement of

Heber's death. They would wonder, those townsfolk, why she did not wail with the other wives, why she would not be present to claim and wash her husband's body. She did not want to see it.

Saurons would be wandering the steppe tonight, Saurons and, very probably, her own kinsfolk from the Pale. Either way, she would claim a life to replace the life that had been reft from her . . . only she was so weary: not a weariness of the flesh, but a draining of the spirit.

Which would come first, she wondered, Saurons or Bandari? And which did she want to see?

At the outermost limits of her hearing sounded a chuckle, surprised and satisfied. Chaya's lips peeled back from her teeth. So. She tensed, listening for footsteps. Only one man, then. No, a man, a Sauron. She had to hope he would be battle-stunned enough that he would not wonder why one of the "cattle" wandered alone on the steppe during second-cycle night, but would take advantage of whatever he found: shelter, fire, food, a woman if he was still capable.

She drew out her pistol, looked at it, set it aside. That was too quick, too dignified. Moving quickly, but as quietly as she could, she drew out the tools she had taken from the forge and hid them beneath the blankets and furs of her bedroll. The footsteps grew louder, more assured. No trooper, not even one from a beaten Sauron post, could believe himself to be overmatched by cattle.

What would he say if he knew this "cattle" was a Sauron cull? Probably the same thing. Best not threaten him at all, at least at first.

When the Sauron entered the tiny circle cast by Chaya's fire, he found her sitting cross-legged, stirring a fragrant pot of stew. Again, she heard him chuckle, and turned her shudder of revulsion into what she hoped he would think was a shiver of pure terror. So easy, so very easy to reassure himself, faced only with a woman of the "cattle," wasn't it?

"Don't be timid, girl." The Sauron's voice was hoarse. He used Americ; then, at her carefully blank stare, changed to Turkic. "You're as lost as I am, aren't you? Well, don't worry. We'll join forces. I can use a woman. . . ."

She bet he could. She made herself cower back as he hunkered down by the fire, so near to her that her resolve almost failed her.

"Give me some of that," he ordered.

She filled one bowl, then another. Then she emptied the pot and, in a great frenzy of anxiousness to please, brought out a flask of almost-coffee. He drank deeply, then belched, a sound that had nothing to do with the courtesies of the tribes. She tried, nonetheless, to look pleased.

"Well-trained, are you?" he said as he wiped his greasy mouth on his sleeve. "Whose are you . . . never mind that; you're mine now. What's your name?"

Disdaining a lie, she told him. "And yours?"

"Gorbag. Trooper Gorbag, at your service. As you are at mine," he announced, and lunged at her.

She gasped and held her breath, glad that she had not eaten, lest she vomit all over the man who pushed her onto the sheepskins she had spread out. Because the wind was cold, he undid the minimum possible of his garments and hers. She clenched her fingers into the curls of the fleece on which she lay, and wished he would spend himself quickly. Her body, the body of a woman half-Sauron, adapted to survive in a world that prized fertility, moved to accommodate him. Her mind ranged far away, even as her fingers clutched the shoulders of the instrument of her vengeance.

*Make hate to me, Sauron, and then I will make hate to you.* If it took that Gorbag . . . *Greasebag*, she thought, or *Scumbag* would have been better names . . . forever, she would still lie beneath his thrusting, grunting hulk. But at last he climaxed, pulled free, and fell asleep, exhausted past self-protection by defeat, the cold of night on the steppe, and sex. Chaya forced herself to lie still, his head on her breasts, until the snoring started. She had not known that Saurons snored like cattle. Then she reached for what lay beneath the sheepskins: hammer and spike from Heber's forge. Reached for them, raised them — and froze.

*No. Not even if I die for it. I cannot, cannot bear to kill him as he lies on top of me. I have to move.*

The unnatural calm that had enthralled her since she heard of her husband's death broke as a hammer smashes brittle iron, and she recoiled, shoving Gorbag onto the sheepskins. He grunted, rolled, and woke. With an intake of breath that was almost a shriek, Chaya leapt on him, straddling him with her own Sauron strength. Gorbag's eyes glowed into awareness. He had a moment of knowledge and fear before she thrust the spike against his temple and hammered it home. He spasmed like some immensely powerful insect, kicked, voided and died.

Knife in hand, Chaya raised herself from where he'd tossed her as he died. He lay face down, and she was glad of that. A single stroke of Heber's keen steel severed head from neck; Saurons, she saw, bled like cattle and died just as easily. She pulled her clothing about herself, grimacing at the moisture on her thighs. That too was part of her vengeance. She had always known when she was ripe to conceive, and she had had hopes that, after the battle to destroy Angband, she and Heber . . .

*Don't think of that,* she told herself. The dry heaves and the cramps snatched her up, anyway. At last she was empty; at least, most of her. She was sure she had conceived of this . . . *Already, I forget his name* . . . She would take his son, as she had taken his life; and she would bring the boy up as her own husband's son.

She harnessed the muskylope, kicked earth over the dying fire, muffled the Sauron's head in the defiled sheepskin, and tied it to the saddle. She left the tent and the headless corpse behind her as she rode toward Eden Valley.

"Hold! We have you in our sights!"

The sky was paling; the sun would rise at her back, giving her a brief advantage. Then she recognized the voice.

*"Avi?"* she called, shocked at how plaintive her voice sounded. Mutters from the force ahead of her told her she had guessed right. "It's Chaya bat Dvora, who married Heber . . ." Her voice was breaking.

A horse — a big one — walked forward. Barak bar Sandor always chose the biggest horses. A big man, for all that he was little more than a boy in years. "Chaya? What are you doing alone out here?"

"I wasn't," she said. "The battle; it's over and we won. I was coming to tell you. . . ."

"And Heber . . ."

"Gone. But there is this."

She untied and held up the Sauron's clotted head.

"The Lord gives, and the Lord takes; blessed be the name of the Lord." An Edenite accent, a tall gangling youth with mad pale eyes. Hammer-of-God Jackson. Chaya looked into the fixed, exalted stare and nodded. *I'm mad too, for this night,* she thought.

She heard murmurs of pity and sympathy, and Barak rode closer. She forced herself not to recoil when he enveloped her in what he meant to be a comforting hug.

And then, never mind that her tears dried too fast, she wept until she was sick.

# ● CHAPTER FIVE

Sitting up in the bed that had once been Grima's, Badri said, not for the first time, "I am too old for you. Soon you will see some maiden you fancy, and tire of me." She kept her tone light, as always when she spoke of such things, but the fear was there, underneath.

Juchi reached out to caress her breast. "You are you, and I am happy," he said, also not for the first time. Then, smiling wickedly, he went on, "And what with Sauron technology and Sauron plunder, you lived better than we did out on the plains. I would never have guessed the age you claim, not within ten T-years."

"You flatter me outrageously." Badri pressed his hand to her. "Don't stop." Half a T-year before, she never could have been so fluent in Russki. Love was a strong incentive.

He grinned at her. "I hadn't planned to." He stretched luxuriously; he was not used to sleeping (or rather, at the moment, resting) so soft. But his wits were still alert. "We are a good pair for a whole flock of reasons. This for one — " He squeezed gently; she shivered a little. "And for another, a different sort, what better match to link the clan and Tallinn Valley?"

"None better," she nodded. "But matches made for that sort of reason are more often endured than enjoyed." She leaned toward him. His left hand came up to join his right; he held her breasts as if they were the two balanced pans of a scale.

She might have picked the odd image from his mind, for he said, "I think they're heavier than they were. Are you pregnant?"

She considered that. "We'll have a pretty good idea somewhere around the end of first cycle." Then she threw herself on him. "I hope I am!" She'd never said anything like that before, not even with Dagor. And with Grima, the idea of children had been a nightmare.

"I'm not sure I do," he said. She frowned at him, surprised and hurt, till he went on. "It would mean I'd have to stay away from you for a while, and I don't want to do that."

He rolled her over, pinned her with his greater weight. He was, she thought as he slid into her, rutty as any Sauron she'd ever heard of. Of course, he was also very young. For her part, she knew only joy that their first joining had been followed by so many more.

She knew only joy. . . . Her arms went round his neck, pulling him even closer to her.

This once, Badri wished the Saurons still held Angband Base. She was used to the attentions of a Breedmaster or his aide, not a nomad midwife dressed in furs and muttering charms. The midwife, though, said, "*Eee*, from the speed of your labor, you've done *this* a time or three. Have trouble with any of your others?"

"The — " Badri stopped as a contraction washed over her. "The first time was twins. The others, no."

"You probably won't this time either, then. All I'll need do is catch the baby as it falls out, I expect." With the small part of her mind not engaged in birthing her child, Badri hoped the plainswoman was right.

So it proved. After what seemed forever but was less than six hours, the midwife said in satisfied tones, "A fine girl — four kilos, I'd guess. Here, you hold her and I'll go tell Juchi."

Badri took the baby and set it on her breast. "He's not in the fortress. His mother still stays in her yurt, and she's very ill. Otherwise he'd be here with me."

"Of course he would." The midwife shook her head, annoyed at herself. "Yes. Kisirja. How could I have forgotten?" She shook her head again, not in the same way. "Very ill, aye. May Allah and the spirits be merciful to her, in this world and the next."

Fever wasted Kisirja's face. It had only grown worse through the three days that made up two cycles — two orbits of Haven round Cat's Eye. A hundred thirty hours of fever were plenty to ravage anyone. Juchi held her hand, sponged her brow, did all the other things that made Kisirja more comfortable but did no other good, no real good.

"Juchi," she whispered.

"I'm here, my mother," he said.

She smiled. "Good." She still knew him, then. For the past little while, he had not been sure. But now her hands tightened on his, with more strength than she'd shown in most of a day. "You're a good boy, a fine man, Juchi."

"Thank you, my mother."

"A good boy," Kisirja repeated. "As fine as if I'd borne you myself. A fine man." Her wits were wandering after all, Juchi thought. He took the folded cloth from her forehead, dipped it once more into the bowl of cool water beside her. As the fever grew, he'd had to do that ever more often.

Some time not much later, Kisirja drew in a long, deep breath, as if she were about to say something. Her eyes opened wide, held Juchi's. He watched awareness fade in them. When it was gone, he reached down and eased them shut.

He drew his dagger, slashed each cheek in nomad mourning. The cuts stopped bleeding almost at once. The grief took longer.

In the five T-years since the fall of Angband Base, a good deal had changed in the lands it ruled. A wall of mud-brick surrounded Tallinn Town now, and the folk had learned much. Self-defense was one of those things; Juchi *Khan* kept his promise, and ruled the settled folk as part of his own people, not conquered subjects. That meant that they must bear their part in defending the combined territories of tribe and valley; which meant learning to fight, something new to them except for the merchants whose buisness took them travelling. These past many years, the Saurons had defended Tallinn Valley, scorning any help from cattle. Now the Saurons were gone from this part of Haven, and the clan that had been Dede Korkut's and was now Juchi's needed their bows and swords and sinews.

"Cover drill," Juchi shouted. The townsmen dove into

foxholes, and emerged aiming crossbows, muskets and the
odd Sauron rifle. Juchi shook his head. "Too slow, too slow.
Half of you would have been shot, the rest ridden over, by a
charge of mounted archers. Get out and try it again."

His pupils groaned. The *khan* grinned without sympathy. "Suleiman's men won't have pity on you. Don't
expect me to, either."

"Suleiman's men won't know the way through the
minefield," one of the bolder men said.

"Mines are like sentries," Juchi told him. "They warn,
they slow. They don't stop. We have to have warriors for
that. Fear kept people out of this valley, fear of the Saurons.
Now that the clan and town hold it instead, folk will test us
to see if we are strong enough to keep it. I'm surprised the
challenge has taken this long to come."

"But — " The townsman was still not cowed, not quite.
Juchi grinned at him.

"Enough words." He tossed aside his weapons belt. "If
you want to argue, come do it with hands and feet."

The man from Tallinn Town gulped and shook his head.
His folk had not taken long to learn what the nomads
already knew: no one bested Juchi in single combat.

"All right, then. You've wasted enough time complaining to catch your breath. So — cover drill!" The raw
recruits sprang for their holes again.

Juchi worked them a while longer before he let them go.
He walked back to the fortress his warriors now occupied.
Badri and their daughter Aisha stood not far outside the bul-
let-scarred barracks hall. Aisha squealed and sprinted
toward her father. He picked her up, flung her high in the
air, caught her, flung her again, spun round and round like a
top. When he set the little girl down, she took a couple of lurching steps and fell on her bottom, gurgling with laughter.

Badri came up more slowly: she was far along with their
second child. He leaned forward over her protruding belly
to kiss her. "How does it look?" she asked him.

He shrugged. "About as before. The latest scout in says
Suleiman's warriors, and maybe another clan's with his, are
gathered a few hours' ride north of the mouth of the valley.

They have no herds with them; they can't be there for any reason but fighting."

Before the clan took Tallinn, that would have meant immediate combat; now he could move the flocks and noncombatants into the safety of the valley, and keep them there longer than Suleiman could wait. The enemy would have to come to him, and fight him on his own terms near his secure base.

"No, they mean to take all we have." She took his arm. "Come with me. I have something to show you, something of the fortress you have not seen yet."

"Can I come too?" Aisha asked. She was able to stand again.

"No, you play out here for a while," Badri said. Aisha stamped her foot. Badri swatted her on the bottom, just hard enough to let the little girl know she meant what she said. Aisha started throwing pebbles at the wall.

"What is this thing you have to show me?" Juchi asked. He heard the nervousness in his own voice. He sometimes was forced to remember that Badri had lived most of her life at Angband Base, that she took for granted the technology which — where it survived — he still found unnerving.

She did not answer him until they were inside the chamber next to the one they shared. Dust lay thick here; it was not a bedroom, and perhaps had not been entered since the Base fell. The fluorescent ceiling panels came on, though, when Badri flicked a switch; their unwavering light cast patterns of shade on the rough-finished stone of the walls, the crinkled edges of the papers abandoned on desks and shelves. The dangling loops of cable threw shadows across Badri's face as she walked to the keyboard and the dark screen. Juchi stared with superstitious awe at the machine on the dusty desk. "A — computer?" he whispered.

"A computer," Badri said briskly. She felt around behind it, clicked another switch. The screen lit. She went on, "Grima used it, and all the Brigade Leaders before him. He let me watch sometimes, never thinking I would see how to make it work myself. Most of what I sent to your clan, most of what I did on the night you attacked, I learned here."

Juchi imagined vengeful Saurons somehow stored inside. "You mean — it can work for us?"

But Badri said, "Why not? We hold the Base now. Grima spent a lot of time feeding it information, but he said it could extrapolate, too — and that it watched and listened even when the terminal was off. Watch." She typed the first command she had seen Grima use so often:

THREATS TO ANGBAND BASE: RANK ORDER.

Juchi stared as the Americ letters appeared one by one on the screen. He stared again, and had to hold himself in place by force of will, when more letters appeared without anyone having typed them: THREATS TO ANGBAND BASE:

1. CLANS OF SULEIMAN AND AYDIN
2. CLAN LEADER, CLAN OF JUCHI
3. MOTHER OF CLAN LEADER, CLAN OF JUCHI
4. THE CITADEL

OTHERS TOO LOW A PROBABILITY TO BE EVALUATED.

When Badri read the words, Juchi laughed, as anyone will when magic is clearly seen to be fraud. "No wonder Grima lost, if he put his faith in this thing. My mother has been dead as long as Aisha's been alive." He touched the faded scar on each cheek.

But Badri stared at the screen in some perplexity. "It was always right before. I had to order it not to put me on any of its lists, or Grima would have caught on to me." She tapped a fingernail against her teeth. "Let me try something else."

She typed again: THREATS TO CO, ANGBAND BASE, RANK ORDER. "I hope it thinks that's you," she said.

He gestured harshly. "Hush!" The answer showed below the question.

THREATS TO CO, ANGBAND BASE, the TAC wrote:

1. CLAN LEADER, CLAN OF JUCHI
2. MOTHER OF CLAN LEADER, CLAN OF JUCHI

OTHERS TOO LOW A PROBABILITY TO BE EVALUATED.

"Just read that to me," Juchi said.

Badri did, then typed END in disgust. "I'm sorry," she said, touching Juchi's hand. "I thought it would help. But then, Grima always worried about how long the machine would keep working. I suppose it's finally dead."

"Senile, anyhow." Juchi laughed again. "If the steppe clans had known this was what Angband Base used for brains, they would have attacked a hundred T-years ago."

"It really did come up with right answers," Badri insisted. But even she had to admit: "It isn't coming up with them now."

"It certainly isn't." Juchi gave her another cantilevered kiss. "I thank you for showing it to me. Were it what it once was"—*What you say it once was*, he thought—"it could have been valuable."

Badri shrugged, still puzzled. "If we need wisdom beyond our own," she said, "we can always go visit the Pale and ask Judge Dvora."

"Off to bed with you," Chaya said.

Her son pouted for a second, then sighed at the tone of command in his mother's voice. She lifted him for a hug, feeling the strength that was already in his arms — strength like hers, from the same source.

"Good sleep, Grandmother," he said politely, when Chaya set him down. He leaned over the coverlet to kiss the older woman's cheek.

The room seemed larger without his active presence. The muskylope-oil lamps showed plastered, painted walls and a wool hanging woven to show the Three — Piet, Ruth and Ilona, the Founders. A small tile stove kept the room warm and boiled a pot of herbs. The medicinal smell mingled with the sachet's scent of musky-sweet wildflowers; under that was a faint odor of age and sickness. Dvora's hands plucked at the coverlet, gnarled and wasted thin. So was her face, fallen in on the strong bones, but her eyes held calm intelligence beneath a feverish glitter.

"A good boy," she said, looking after him. "A strong boy; as he'll need to be."

Chaya nodded. The boy's birth, a little more than two Haven years ago, had been hard; but the babe had been bigger than most, stronger, almost preternaturally aware. *The Sauron admixture.* She could not remember what his father looked like. *His father was Heber,* she insisted to herself,

and knew it for a lie. There had been no hiding what Chaya
was, but Barak . . . people would accept that Heber had been
his father, and put his abilities down to his mother's blood.
At least most would, and those who knew better would keep
silent. It was a little less conspicuous now, with all the
orphans from Angband growing up Bandari.

"So." Dvora smiled. "A Judge you will be, after all. Our
lives run in circles, bringing us back where we'd never
thought to be, *nu?*"

"It's a living," Chaya said, looking away from the affec-
tionate irony. "Apart from making swords and killing
Saurons, about the only thing I've shown any talent for."

It was lucky much of the Pale's Law was tradition, inherited
not just from the long-destroyed settlements at Degania and
New Vilnius, but from the other strains as well. Balt and Litvak, exiled Israeli kibbutznik and mutant hell-planet Boer
had long since melded into the People . . . and then there were
the farming folk of Eden, Americ by race, Christians of a forbidding dourness by faith, still not wholly reconciled to
inclusion in the Pale of Settlement after all these generations.

With Barak and his protégé at her side, Chaya had made
very sure that no Saurons lingered near the ruins of Angband,
disguised as tribal folk or bandits until they could warn their
fellows. Increasingly, she'd taken over her mother's duties as
Judge; and the folk of Tallinn had asked her to come there, as
well. Juchi had not begrudged it; the families were close, and
he felt in her debt, for Heber. She thought she'd repaid Dvora
for her earlier unhappiness. And she thought she was ful-
filling her father's and her husband's dream of joining Pale
and Tallinn valleys into one people. Just as, three hundred
T-years before, Boer and sabra, Balt and neo-Hassid had been
joined to make the Bandari; and as Bandari and Edenite had
been . . . more or less . . . joined.

There was plenty of work, and you could find forgetfulness in work. Five hundred Sauron children from Angband,
and as many again of their women — some tribute maidens,
some Sauron-born; all to be integrated into the clans, with
incomprehension and prejudice in plenty on both sides.
That had been her special charge, and a success.

"Oh, power is a strong lover," Dvora said. "But you'll find he's a cold, demanding one as well, and fickle."

Chaya shook her head, half in negation, half in rueful acknowledgement. "Besides," she said, "I'm not *the* Judge. Yet. Considering my heritage . . ."

"Which can't be officially acknowledged." Dvora chuckled at the legalism, then wheezed; her daughter held her head up and helped her drink the extract of *timurgaunt* — Tamerlane's Gauntlet — that strengthened the heart. It helped, but not as much as it had. Fluid was building up, pressing on the heart and on the lungs. Heart failure was a great killer on Haven, for those lucky enough to live past middle age: constant cold and air thinner than humans had been bred to bear. "You *are* my daughter."

"Miriam's your sister; she'd be a better choice."

"Miriam is busy smithing, when she isn't making babies," Dvora said. "You're it, my girl; Judge after me."

The office was not officially hereditary, but if the child was qualified, the parent counted for a good deal; the People were careful of such things. "Hush, rest a while," Chaya said.

"This came to me the night of the battle," Dvora said when her breathing had eased a little. She slipped from her withered hand the ruby that Chaya had once used as a signal. "It is time to give it back to you."

She closed her eyes and lay quietly until her daughter thought that she was sleeping; Chaya smoothed the coverlet and brown linen sheets, preparing to leave.

But Dvora rose. Her voice was wild, and her eyes seemed to look beyond the room — beyond Strang, or the waking world. "Awake, awake, Dvora!" she cried, more shaman than Judge in that moment. "Did you think that I did not know?"

"Know what?"

"As I did with you, giving a dead man the name of father to a Sauron child. Lightning was never Heber's child." The old, filmy eyes flashed with their former cunning.

"A life for a life," Chaya said, stony calm.

Dvora nodded. "I do not fault you, though I shudder, perhaps, at what you did. But the time when I needed to pass judgment on anything is long gone. Now, I merely *know;* and you must know too. Do you recall, daughter, the night before Heber asked for you, I told you how I found you on the steppe?" Chaya nodded.

"We've never spoken of that since, yet, seeing Lightning, I have thought about it often." Her ringless hands reached out to clasp her adopted daughter's.

"There were two babies left to die, you recall. You, and a boy. A brother." Dvora fell back, exhausted by her words. "Good . . . bye," she said.

Chaya stared for a moment, then sprang to the door. *"Mediko, mediko!"* she shouted, her voice raw with fear.

The man rushed in, blinking with sleep, then paused by the bedside, folding the twisted hands on the sheet. Chaya stopped him with a gesture, then closed her mother's eyes herself.

"The Lord gives, and the Lord takes — " she began, but her voice choked.

" — blessed be the name of the Lord," the *mediko* finished for her.

Numbness descended; she was hardly aware of friendly hands urging her out of the room.

Dvora bat Lizabet was buried by the side of her husband, who had also been a Judge among the People, on a hillside outside Strang. An ancient rusted cross in the shape of an X stood on the hill, where Boaz the Prophet had hung his daughter Ruth for rebellion. That had been in the time when van Reenan's band came to the Eden Valley, refugees from the Wasting the *Dol Guldur* brought to Haven. Captain Piet van Reenan had taken Ruth down from the cross of iron, and together they had overthrown Boaz; from him and Ilona ben Zvi and Ruth Boazdaughter flowed the blood that still ruled as *kapeteins* of the People . . . as often as Judges, too. The ruler's conscience, living proof that Power must be subject to Law.

Ruth lay here beneath a marble slab carved with the last power tool in Eden Valley. All her successors lay here too — ragged piles of stone from the terrible years of the People's beginnings, then others carved with increasing skill, until the latest bore chisel-work as fine as the pre-Wasting machines could have made. Lapidoth's carried his name, and a single sentence: *Greater love than this has no man*. Ruth's stone held her dying words. As Dvora's child, Chaya must now recite that ancient farewell to the crowd that covered the hill slope and the fields beyond, nearly to the high stone walls of Strang:

" . . . *Let your grief be light*," she went on, "*it's only when a parent buries a child that grief is heavy; this is the way of nature. But remember me, remember all of us. Remember that you can see farther if you stand on our shoulders. . . . From my sister Ilona's heritage, remember that we are nothing without the Law that binds us one to another. From mine, remember that the Law was made for us, not we for the Law; love is the final commandment. From Piet: be strong, for without strength and courage there can be no Law, nor love, nor peace. Together we are the People.*"

More and more voices joined hers, a thousandfold whisper across the plain, through the ruddy darkness of dimday. Any of the People could recite it; this was spoken every year at the Ruth's Day service, and at most funerals. All of them joined her on the final:

"*Good-bye.*"

Tears flowed down her face, drying quickly; beside her Barak wept — and his tears too, glistened only for a second beneath Cat's Eye. Many of the crowd were in tears. All Judges were respected, but Dvora had been loved. Dvora's sister Miriam stood by the graveside, with her infant daughter in her arms; the baby cried thinly as her mother's tears dripped on her face.

Juchi and his family were present as well; he had cut his face in his own people's gesture of mourning, used only for a great leader or the closest of kin.

"Your grief is mine, Chaya *Khatun*," he said quietly, in good Bandarit. "Judge Dvora was a strong ally and a good friend." Beside him, Badri had covered her face with her shawl, head bowed in sadness; Aisha buried her face in her mother's skirts, against the swollen belly of her pregnancy.

A few cycles later, Suleiman and his allies attacked — although not so many allies as there might have been, if the Pale had not thrown the weight of its diplomacy behind its friends. Juchi's clan and the men of Tallinn Town threw them back. Among the prisoners they took was a fair-sized contingent from the clan of Aydin.

Juchi wondered about that, a little. He tried to remember whether the scouts had known just who Suleiman's main partner was. He didn't think so. Even clan shamans made lucky guesses every so often.

And when the triumphant warriors came back to the fortress, he found that Badri had presented him with a son. That drove all thoughts of the ancient computer from his head.

She wanted to call the boy Dagor. It was a likely enough sounding name. He didn't argue with her.

The clan, Juchi thought, was fat. For some of his men, that was literally true: he watched a couple of middle-aged warriors walking into Tallinn Town to buy something or other, and their bellies hung over their belts. In the old days, out on the steppe, a fat nomad, save maybe a shaman, would have been hard to imagine. Life was too harsh. Juchi shrugged; the younger men were with the flocks, and training hard.

The old days ... Juchi laughed a little, and shook his head. Hard to believe more than a dozen T-years had slipped by since Angband Base fell. His own body belied them. It was as firm, hard, and tireless now as then. Just the other day, though, Badri had plucked a white hair from his beard. He shook his head again. Nothing, he thought, lasted forever.

Even that little philosophizing, far from profound, was unlike him. He left off as a horseman rode up. The messenger dismounted and bowed. "*Khan*, I brought your words to Suleiman. He agrees that they hold wisdom."

"Good," Juchi said. "He will meet with me, then?"

"Aye, *khan*, in two cycles' time. He asks if you would meet with him here or out on the steppe."

"On the steppe," Juchi said at once. "He and his men would only spy if we invited them into the valley—into *our* valley."

"Aye," the messenger said again.

"You need not tell him I said that, though. Tell him ... hmm ... tell him that, as we are plainsmen too, the plains are the fitting place to discuss our differences and to settle once and for all the boundaries of our clans' grazing lands."

The messenger nodded, mumbling to himself as he memorized the words. Then he grinned. "Shall I also tell him that we'll run his men into the Northern Sea if he doesn't keep within the bounds we set him?"

Juchi grinned back. "*He* knows that already. If he didn't, he'd still be fighting instead of talking. He's stubborn as a stone."

"He's jealous, is what he is," the messenger said.

"I suppose so. Every nomad *khan* dreams of taking a valley for himself."

"But you didn't dream — you did it. We did it. And every time Suleiman comes sniffing around, we send him away with a bloody nose."

"I told you — that's why he's finally willing to talk."

"No doubt you're right, *khan*." The messenger sketched a salute, climbed back on his horse, and headed north at a trot.

Juchi walked into the courtyard of the fortress, and almost got trampled by a mob of boys playing football. That was what his clan called the game, anyhow. To the children from Tallinn Town, it was soccer. He'd never met the odd-sounding word till his people conquered Angband Base; he wondered idly if the locals had borrowed it from Saurons.

His own son was at the head of the yelling pack, running and dodging as fast and lithe as the rest of the boys, though they were anywhere from two to four T-years older. Juchi remembered his own childhood. He'd been more than a match for children his age, too.

As he watched, Dagor booted the ball past the other team's goalie and into the makeshift net. "Good shot, Dagor, lad!" he called, waving to his son. Soon the boy would be old enough for warrior's sports, tent-pegging with a lance and *buzkashi*.

Dagor's grin, already enormous, grew even wider as he waved back. The boy's comrades swarmed over him, lifted him onto their shoulders. Again Juchi thought of his own youth, of the day he'd been named warleader. Seeing

Dagor get such acclaim so young made him want to burst with pride.

When he found Badri, he spoke of the football game before he mentioned the talks Suleiman had agreed to. "Why meet him on the steppe?" Badri asked.

As he had for the messenger, he explained his reasons. Badri nodded when he was done. "That makes sense," she agreed. "But remember — and never let Suleiman forget — that you are not *just* of the plains. You hold Tallinn Valley, too. Go out to the steppe, then, but go with all the trappings, all the ceremonial, that shows you to be a lord as well as a *khan*, if you know what I'm saying."

"Yes, I do." He kissed her. "Your advice is always good. That's one reason I've never looked — well, never more than looked — at anyone else." By law he was entitled to four wives, and by custom and wealth a chief could have many women. He kissed her again. "But it's only one reason. There are others."

"Let me shut the door first," she said.

When the time came for Juchi to ride out to meet Suleiman, he remembered what Badri had suggested. He put on a linen tunic instead of the wool and leather he usually wore, to remind the other *khan* he ruled farmers as well as plainsmen.

And he decided to be lavish when he armed himself. He did not just sling his assault rifle on his back and have done. He put on crisscrossing belts of shiny brass cartridges, too, one over each shoulder — let Suleiman see that Angband Base's machine shop could still turn out cartridge cases.

A sword and a knife hung from the left side of his belt. He started to put another knife on the right, then had a better idea. He rummaged through a leather sack he did not remember opening since he came to the fortress. Sure enough, the pistol he had taken from that arrogant robber on the steppe was inside.

He buckled it on. Since he got his rifle, he'd had no need for the lesser firearm. He was not even sure the rounds would still fire. Today, though, he did not care. He only needed it as one more thing with which to overawe Suleiman.

Feeling quite the fearsome warrior, he swaggered out to Badri. "How do I look?" he asked.

Her lips quirked. " 'Overwhelming' is the word that comes to mind."

He smiled too, but answered, "Good. That's the word I want to come to mind."

Then Badri noticed the pistol. "You've never worn that before."

"Why bother, when I have the assault rifle?" He reached over his shoulder and patted the Kalashnikov's barrel.

"No reason at all," Badri said. "I just didn't know you had it, that's all. May I see it?"

"Of course." Juchi saw nothing odd in the request. Before she was a plainsman's woman, Badri had been a Sauron's woman. He would have been more surprised were she not interested in weapons. He took the pistol from its holster and showed it to her.

*"Where did you get this?"*

Juchi blinked. The words tumbled out in a harsh whisper, unlike anything he'd ever heard Badri use before. She was staring from him to the pistol and back again. She had gone pale. That alarmed him. In all the time he'd known her, he'd never seen her show fear.

"I took it from a bandit I killed, out on the steppe a couple of T-years before we won Tallinn Valley. He was going to steal my muskylope, but he took me up when I said I'd fight him for it. I broke his neck."

The pride the memory put into his voice faltered as he looked at her face. "What's wrong? Tell me, Badri, please."

"This pistol belonged to a Soldier once. A couple of T-years before Angband Base fell, he went out to the plains to scout a clan that the computer — the computer you don't believe in — said was growing dangerous. It was the clan of Dede Korkut. He never came back."

Badri spoke mechanically, as if by keeping all emotion from her words she could keep it from her heart as well. Then, at last, her voice broke. She looked down at the floor as she went on, "His — his name was Dagor."

"The name you gave our son." Now Juchi's voice too was empty and cold.

"The name I gave my son. Dagor and I had three sons, three sons and a daughter. None of them lived. The girl and one boy were twins, Sauron culls, set out for stobor. I was just a girl myself, then. The other two, later, had accidents. It happens. He was far from a bad man, Juchi — I've known a bad man. His name, at least, deserved — deserves — to go on."

"As you say." After a moment, Juchi found he could bear to have a son named for Badri's onetime consort. After all, the man — the Sauron — was fifteen T-years dead and gone, while he and Badri were very much together. He found he could not even blame her for not saying where young Dagor's name came from. The quiet had kept the peace, and with any luck both quiet and peace might have lasted forever.

"You — broke his neck, you said?" Badri asked. Juchi nodded. "How could that be? Dagor was a Soldier, a Sauron."

Juchi understood what she meant. No one, not even a man with Frystaat blood, could match reflexes with a Sauron in unarmed combat. He said slowly, "Maybe I took the pistol from a bandit, one of a band, say, that had ambushed Dagor."

"That must be it!" Badri brightened a little. She had long since known, long since accepted, that Dagor was dead. Thinking the man she loved now was the one who had slain him was something else again. "What did he look like, this bandit you killed?"

"I'll never forget him," Juchi said. "He gave me maybe the toughest fight I ever had. He was a few centimeters taller than I am. He had more reach, too, and knew what to do with it. He was Caucasoid, more or less — dark eyes, but fair skin and light brown hair, a little lighter than mine. He had a short white scar, just below one eye — the left one, I think."

"You have painted me Dagor's image in words." Badri shook her head, over and over. "How could that be?" she repeated. Then, fierce as a tamerlane, she burst out, "Who — what — was your mother, Juchi? Why did the computer call her such a threat to the Base? Why did the computer call you such a threat to the Base?"

"Because it's daft," Juchi growled. "Because it's old and mad. I wish someone had put a bullet through it when we took Angband Base. Then it wouldn't be here to worry you."

To his relief, Badri changed the subject. "How old are you, Juchi? Exactly how old, I mean."

He needed to think. "As near as I can reckon it, a bit over four Haven years — say, about thirty-one T-years." He had no idea why she wanted to know, nor did he care. Talking of anything but Dagor — Dagor the elder, he amended — suited him fine. "I hope that satisfies you. Whether or not, though, I have to leave. Suleiman is waiting."

He walked to the door. Behind him, very softly, Badri whispered, "Who was your mother, Juchi? Oh, who?" He did not turn back.

"It is agreed, then." Suleiman's wrinkles arranged themselves into a smile. "We shall not graze our herds southwest of a line drawn straight north from the fifth ridge to the west of your valley, nor shall your herds graze north or east of that same line."

"It is agreed, aye." Juchi's voice was hollow. He knew he should have been able to claim grazing lands stretching two or three ridges farther northeast, but his heart was not in the dickering, not today.

He still had no truck with the flashing words Badri had read him from the computer screen. They were too far outside his experience for him to take them seriously. But what his mother had said while she was dying came back now to trouble his thoughts. What if her wits had not been caught in fever's grip? What then?

*What indeed?* he thought. How could he hope to find out? Kisirja was dead. Whom else could he hope to ask? He pounded a fist into his thigh. Who better than his wet nurse? He'd had little to do with Nilufer since the clan came to Tallinn Valley; her family grazed their herds on the far limits of the tribe's territories and visited seldom. Now with her sons' sons married, she had come to live in the softer climate near the town.

As fast as politeness allowed, or maybe a little faster, he took leave of Suleiman. The old *khan* did not seem offended. Compared to grazing land, manners were a trifle.

On the ride back to the valley, Juchi wondered if he shouldn't let the whole thing drop. But no, he couldn't, not now, not with Badri so upset. And his own curiosity was roused. He'd always been sure of who he was. Now, suddenly, he doubted. Allah and the spirits willing, Nilufer would set his mind at ease.

Nilufer was a widow these days. She lived in a small yurt close by the larger one that belonged to her eldest son. She poked her head through the door-curtain in surprise when Juchi called from the outside, asking leave to enter.

"Honor to the *khan*! Of course you are welcome!" She held the curtain wide. "Come, come! Will you take tea?"

"Thank you. You are gracious." The rituals of hospitality let Juchi adapt to the gloom inside the black-felt yurt. He sat cross-legged on a threadbare rug, sipped Nilufer's tea, nibbled a strip of jerked mutton.

After the polite and pointless small talk that accompanied meat and drink, Nilufer asked, "How may I serve the *khan*?" Her eyes twinkled. "I fear my breasts are too old to please him now."

Juchi laughed. After so much strain, that felt strange and good. He said, "As a matter of fact, your breasts are the very reason I came." That made Nilufer giggle, but Juchi went on, "No, no, I speak the truth. I want you to tell me why I needed a wet nurse when I was a baby."

"Why does any baby need a wet nurse?" Nilufer said. "Your mother had no milk to give you." But the sparkle was gone from her face and voice. Something else replaced it — caution, Juchi judged. She was not telling all she knew.

"That I gathered," he said. "Why was it so?"

"I couldn't rightly tell you, *khan*, not for certain," Nilufer said. She could not meet his eyes, either.

"Why not?" he persisted. "My mother must have given you some reason. Was I perhaps an unusually difficult birth?"

He watched her seize the pretext. "Yes, that's it, that's just what she said, poor thing," she said eagerly.

"You're lying." His voice was a whiplash. Nilufer flinched away from it. "What is it you don't want to tell me? How can it matter, after so long?"

"You won't be angry with me?" she quavered.

"No, not for the truth, by Allah and the spirits. I swear it." He realized he had got up on one knee, had moved toward her as if in threat. No, not as if. He eased himself back to the rug. "I will not be angry at you."

"All right. All right." A little spirit returned to her voice. "As you say, it was long ago, and the Saurons are gone from Angband Base now — all of them but you."

"What? Me? You're mad, old woman." Juchi laughed harshly. "Do you say my mother slipped away from the tents to sleep with a Sauron Soldier?"

"She slipped away from the tents, aye, but not to sleep with the Saurons — rather, to rob them. They cast out infants that did not suit them. Most the beasts took, or the cold, but not all. You were one of the lucky few."

"I don't believe you." *I don't want to believe you,* he thought. He found a question that had to make a liar of her: "If what you say is true, why has no one ever told me this fable before?"

"At first, *khan*, it was for fear that if you knew you were of Sauron blood, you might flee the clan and go back to Angband Base. After a while, I suppose, folk had got into the habit of silence. But now that the Saurons are long gone, I don't see what difference it makes whether you know. And if you doubt me, Juchi *Khan*, think on the meaning of your name."

"Guest," Juchi whispered. His world tottered round him. "Juchi."

"The same word," Nilufer nodded. "You've been a cherished guest, an honored guest, and now a great and mighty guest. But always, as I told you, you were a lucky guest. Both babes the Saurons set out that night were lucky."

"*Both* babes?" Juchi stared at her. "What new tale is this?"

"One not everyone knows. But your mother — Kisirja, I mean, Allah and the spirits give her peace — your mother told me that two babies, both newborn, lay exposed by

Angband Base then. Just as she picked up the one that was you, a Bandari woman took the other."

His world had tottered. Now it crashed down. "That would have been a girl," he said in a dead voice.

"I really couldn't tell you one way or the other. Your mother never said."

"Yes, she did. Just a few hours ago. My mother."

Nilufer scratched her head. "What's that?"

Juchi did not answer. Instead he turned and leaped out through the door-curtain. Nilufer stared after him. He sped toward the fortress, swift and straight as an arrow from a compound bow.

"Allah," Nilufer exclaimed. He'd left his horse behind. "I wonder what the poor fellow's trouble is. I hope it's not something I said."

Juchi ran.

His father, dead under his hands. His wife, his mother; his daughter, his sister; his son, his brother.

"What have I done?" he cried. "Allah, what have we done?"

The fortress where he lived — the fortress where he'd been born — was a couple of kilometers away. He ran through fields of ripening barley. As he ran, he thought only of his own field, his field of double sowing, the field in which he'd grown and where he'd sown his children. He groaned, and ran on.

Men were working in the fields. They shouted as he trampled the grain. When he did not swerve, they chased him. He outran them. That had always been easy. Now he knew why.

The fortress drew nearer, nearer. He ran through the gates. Men waved, called out to ask how the parley with Suleiman had gone or simply to greet him. He answered none of them, but sped to the barracks hall.

There at last his way was blocked. The clan's shaman stood in the doorway. Tireshyas had been plump on the steppe. Now he was so fat that any doorway he stood in, he filled. When he saw Juchi, he went white. "Lord *khan*, your wife—"

"My wife," Juchi's voice, his eyes, were so terrible that Tireshyas fell back a pace. "My wife! You are one of those who knew I sprang not from the clan but from a Sauron's woman, not so?"

Already agitated and now frightened and confused, the shaman stuttered, "Well, well, yes, lord *khan*, yes, but—"

"And you knew I took a Sauron's woman to wife." Juchi stepped forward, filling the space from which Tireshyas had retreated. "And you never thought to wonder if the two might be the same. My mother. My wife. Badri."

Horror filled Tireshyas' face. "Lord *khan*, she is — " Again Juchi interrupted, this time with a kick that sank deep into the soft flab of Tireshyas' belly. The shaman flew backward and crashed to the floor.

Juchi sprang over him. "Badri! Where are you? I'm coming for you!" In his own ears, the words sounded more like stobor's howl than speech.

He heard people behind him. Behind did not matter. They could never catch him. Then someone came out into the hall, right in front of him. He did not know if the man would try to stop him. He did not care. He hammered him down and ran on.

The door to the chamber where he and Badri slept, the door to the chamber where their children had begun, the door to the chamber where, for all he knew, he had begun — that door was open. Juchi went in. "Badri!"

No reply. She was not there. He unslung his assault rifle. He'd find her soon, and then . . . half a burst for her and the rest, as much as he could fire before finger slipped from trigger, for him. And even that was not enough. How could one quick instant of pain make amends for — for the twisted thing their lives had proved to be?

"Badri." Cradling the rifle, he went out to the hall again. The doorway next to his was also ajar, unlocked, as it had not been in a Haven year and more. Through it he saw the dusty glow of the computer screen. He growled, deep in his throat. The cursed computer had been his doom. He would drag it down to hell with him.

He wanted to shoot it in the belly at close range as if it

were a human enemy, and watch it die. He darted into its — *its lair,* he thought.

He did not fire. The light from the screen let him see a tiny motion, off to one side. He whirled toward it. "Badri," he whispered. He had found her.

She was dead. Hanging by a rope fastened to one of the wrought-iron hooks that held the cables, her face dark and distorted. She wore a wool cape, held in place by a heavy golden brooch, steppe work that he had given her. A chair lay overturned behind her.

Juchi let the rifle fail. "Ah, Badri," he cried, half in anguish, half in envy. "You found the truth before me!"

He drew his knife and cut her down. How long he held her, lost and alone in his worse than grief, he never knew. When he looked up, the doorway was full of staring, silent faces.

"Let me by," someone said, her voice small but insistent. "Let me by. I must see."

"No!" Juchi groaned wildly to the unheeding faces. "Not her! Not my — " He choked, could not go on. What word ought he to use? Daughter? Sister?

Aisha pushed through the crowd. Juchi watched the color drain from her cheeks. Her eyes, black and enormous and staring, were Badri's eyes. And his own. "Father?" she whispered. "Mother?"

Seeing her, the sweet child-woman who never should have been, Juchi knew he could never face her, not now, not ever again.

He undid Badri's brooch, weighed it long in his hand. With a great shout of pain and fury, he plunged the pin first into one eye, then the other, again and again and again. The last sound he heard before he fainted was Aisha's scream.

Screams came from the ruined fortress. Chaya's son stiffened. He did not think of it as a place of danger; they had been coming here on visits all his life, and he had called the *khatun* Badri "aunt" from almost the day he learned the word. With the rapid movements that had made the people of the Pale and Tallinn Valley nickname him Lightning, he was up and running toward the gate.

Her son came running back. "It's *Tantie* Badri, Mother!" he cried. "She is dead, hanged, and *Khan* Juchi has blinded himself. They are calling for you."

His face was pale around the eyes and mouth, and his throat worked. She rose more slowly from her seat beside the camel, sorrow dulling her. Now the truth was revealed, it hurt even worse than she had feared that it might. Juchi. In all ways but one, her match. And in that one way . . . he belonged to Badri.

Belonged in two ways, God help them all. Was this God's curse upon them? What had they done? What had any of them done?

Of all the secrets that she had heard as a Judge, this was the hardest to bear; even harder than the secret of her own son's birth. And she kept it, for the good of the folk she served.

They were waiting for her outside her home, the people of town and tribe. "My son has told me," she said, waving aside their explanations and exclamations of horror. "Bring me to them."

"Aisha found her own mother, hanging . . ."

"The poor girl, brought up a princess, and who will wed her now?"

"Son and daughter, accursed, accursed . . ."

"Who will guard us now?"

*I must protect my . . . my niece. And my nephew too, if we are to salvage anything from this disaster.*

"Quiet!" Chaya snapped. "The girl is guiltless. And it will be a wonder if she is not scared witless." *But she will not be. She comes of good stock.*

Just as Chaya quickened her pace, two of the elder men came up to her. "Judge," they said, "surely incest is a crime."

"And will you try the dead and blind for what they did not know?"

"You have always said ignorance is no escape from the Law."

Chaya slipped past the drillbit-gnawed fragments of retaining wall. Hearing the shrill mourning of the women and Juchi's pleas for death, she shivered and quickened her pace.

"Who is it now?" cried Juchi. "Who has come to look upon the monster?"

His head was wrapped in bloody bandages, but it snapped toward her with the keen hearing they shared. "The Judge? Chaya *Khatun*? You have courage beyond the lot of most women . . . all but one, Allah grant her pity! I beg you, kill me."

It would be a mercy. It would be the kindest thing that Chaya could do for her brother. It would be fratricide, the oldest crime. She dared not. And, if she were to save anything at all from this tragedy, she must not even explain why.

"I have told him," the tribe's shaman Tireshyas said, "that, accursed as he is, anyone who slays him will take on an immense burden of ill luck. Do you agree with me that he must leave this place?"

To wander lost? Better he had died the night he had been set out. Then Angband Base would still stand; Chaya's child would never have been born; and another generation would have grown up in slavery. She could not wish his life — and hers — undone. They had wrought too long and too well together, even though their lives had been built upon a lie.

Now, because of that lie and the concealments that went with it, their work might easily lie in ruins by tonight. If they had only known — and spoken — the truth! She was at fault there too, having known (or at least suspected) and kept silent all these years.

Yet Juchi was her brother, her ally, too, for more than half her life. She could not condemn him to death wandering the steppe.

"In all I did, I sought for good," he mourned.

Tireshyas turned to him. "And in all you did, you were confounded." He picked up a stick and handed it to him. "If still you strive for good, you will do as I have asked, and leave us."

Juchi bowed his mutilated head. "I will. Maybe among strangers I can find the end I seek."

"Father, oh, Father!" That was Aisha's voice, and it broke the former *khan*, who sobbed dryly, without eyes or tears.

"Care for my children," he said. "Their part in this was innocent."

Did Chaya imagine that his sightless eyes turned toward her? "I promise," she said, even as the shaman gravely agreed. He looked at her over Juchi's head and nodded. Perhaps away from the tribe, they would have a chance at some kind of decent life.

"Would you let them see you one last time?" the shaman asked Juchi. "Aisha begs for nothing else."

*No!* Chaya did not know how she kept from screaming.

"If you have any pity," Juchi begged, "spare me that!"

Tireshyas opened a door and admitted a young man whom Chaya had seen before: Juchi's escort past the valley's minefields. It was a hard mercy, not to waste even a mine on an outcast, but Chaya understood. Who knew how Juchi's death might curse the tribe?

Juchi shuffled out the door leaning on a stick, one hand on the young man's shoulder. Behind him, Tireshyas made a sign against evil.

A scream went up among the women. Chaya ran forward. Aisha had broken free of the women who held her and was running toward her father and her guide.

"No!" Juchi cried, but she flung herself at his feet, the scarf falling from her dark, disheveled braids. Tears sparkled on her high cheekbones, so like her parents' — or Chaya's own; and she sobbed, forgetting calm, forgetting dignity, forgetting the modesty of an unwed girl and all else but that her father (and brother) was vanishing from her life.

Again he shook his head, and gestured at his guide. The young man bent to raise her. Aisha jerked away, and rose on her own. She wiped hands across her face and drew herself up, abruptly cold and dignified.

"Can you deny you love me? Will you add that to what you have cost me?" she asked. Her eyes were wild with guilt as Juchi flinched under her words, weakening as he had not weakened when she had wept and flung herself at his feet.

"I can see through the minefields as well as you," she told the young man who might, had life been gentler, have offered Juchi riches for the right to wed her. "You may go back now."

Juchi embraced his daughter, hiding his ruined face against her slender shoulder. Head up, she glared at the watchers as she comforted her father. Then she led him away. Their path turned twice, and they were out of sight.

Chaya's eyes filmed with tears, then cleared.

"If this is anyone's fault," she said, "it lies on the heads of the Saurons and their accursed breeding program."

*Cursing your own, are you, girl?* she asked wryly. Nevertheless, that brought mutters of agreement. You could always blame a misfortune on the Evil Eye or the Saurons, anywhere on Haven — and as far as the Saurons were concerned, she thought, it was no less than the truth.

"I say we must have the truth," she declared to the shaman. "The truth, the whole truth, and nothing but the truth, so help me God. And," she took a deep breath, "I shall begin."

She pulled off her glove and worked her ruby ring free.

Beckoning to her son, she handed him the ring.

"Take this . . ." She drew a deep breath. "Take it and give it to your cousin."

She turned to face the town and tribe she had judged for all these years. It was time that they judge her as they had already judged her family. More than the fate of a few people hung on their decision. They could separate; they could even swear a blood feud. Or they could all spend their lives trying to repair what had been done.

"But for you!" she cried out, turning eastward. Toward the Citadel, toward the Saurons. "For you, monsters, destroyers, accursed of God — for the Saurons there will never be forgiveness. *Eye for eye, tooth for a tooth; limb for limb, stripe for stripe — and for a life, a life!*"

# Book II
## *THE SOWING*

# ● CHAPTER SIX

Breedmaster Titus nodded, satisfied. "Another strong Soldier for the Citadel," he said.

The Soldier's mother smiled. "Of course," she said. "He's mine." Her smile took on an edge. "I could have wished him a Cyborg. Perhaps, the next?"

"Perhaps," said the Breedmaster. But he committed himself to nothing. A Cyborg, unlike a common Soldier, was as much made as born. The biomechanicals had to be cultured in nutrient vats from cells brought from Old Sauron, and implanted *in utero*, with no certainty that the fetus would prove viable; much of the Citadel's remaining biotechnology was devoted to them, and the trace elements required for the process were scoured from half the planet. There were six mature Cyborgs in the Citadel, and only another fourteen out in the Bases. One young adult besides, and one child, in the Citadel. The Citadel's resources would stretch to no more.

Titus would have given them up altogether. The process was grossly inefficient, and anything but cost effective. But the mythos demanded Cyborgs: Cyborgs, therefore, he had to have.

Sieglinde seemed oblivious to the pause, which in any case had consumed but a fraction of a second. He gave her the rest of her due, as was his duty. "That is four sons you have given to the Race. You are to be commended."

She inclined her head. She understood necessity as well as he. The Race had long since used up its heritage from the homeworld, the thousands of fertilized ova to be brought to term in the wombs of captive women. Now there were none left; and Soldiers were reduced to merely human expedients: breeding like cattle, and with cattle, in a process only a little more effective than a lottery.

Sieglinde was a rarity even by the standards of Old Sauron, a woman of pure Soldier stock who was both viable and fertile. Her three older sons were all healthy, no evidence yet of lethal recessives. So too was this one. Yes, thought Titus. She had done well. Well enough, perhaps, to grant her what she asked for.

He would not say so, of course. That would have been premature. It was enough that she knew that he was pleased. More than that, a Soldier did not need.

Sieglinde sighed a little. She was Soldier bred and born, and birth was her battlefield. Now that her child was accepted into the Race, she could let herself yield a little to her body's need for rest.

The Breedmaster took her son from her arms. He was lively even for a Soldier, flailing against the hands that held him. His reflexes, the Breedmaster had said, were near the upper edge of the optimum range. He would be lethally quick, but not so quick that he startled himself into a convulsion. His nightsight would be excellent, but he would not be dayblind. His hearing was keen enough to set him twisting and staring at the rustle of paper in the Breedmaster's pocket. He was full Sauron of impeccable line. He would grow into a commander of Soldiers.

"The next one," she said from the edge of sleep, "*will* be a Cyborg."

Cyborg Rank Bonn extricated himself carefully from the rubble of the practice-room wall. Someone rather too clever for his own good had set a drillbit to excavating it, to see if the story that drillbits had brought down the walls of Angband Base was true. The boy had been sent to a Base even more distant and forsaken than that one, and set to work testing his ingenuity on the remnants of machinery there.

Bonn thought the wall had been repaired adequately. It had not been strong enough to resist the full weight of a Cyborg Rank, thrown all but effortlessly by the young Soldier who stood with hands at sides, waiting. Bonn flexed a shoulder. His bones were as flexible, and as strong, as good steel. They were not as young as they had been, or as impervious to an encounter with plaster over mortared stone.

He brushed plaster from his gi and frowned. "There is such a thing," he said, "as excessive force."

"There is such a thing also as the teaching of a lesson," said his adversary coolly. "One should never underestimate one's opponent."

Bonn bent his head a degree. "One should also judge one's response. You will be held responsible for the restoration of the wall."

His pupil's head bent a half-degree. "Sir."

"Soldier." He bowed stiffly. The other bowed with considerably more grace. "Dismissed."

He watched the young one go. Young, he thought, and reckless. But gifted in the arts of combat. As was only fitting in one born Cyborg, of the best blood in the Citadel.

It was a pity that women in these days were not admitted to the rank of the death's head. She was the only Cyborg of her generation, thanks to a succession of overly conservative Breedmasters, followed by Titus, who, though Cyborg himself, was both conservative in regard to making Cyborgs, and inclined to experiment with them when he made them. She was needed above all to breed sons who could, the Breedmaster willing, be made Cyborgs. She had a daughter already, Cyborg as she was, and showing a remarkable degree of promise for one so young.

*And need the Breedmaster be willing?* Bonn thought. Sigrid was the Breedmaster's heir. She was trained in the techniques — she had taken part in her daughter's making.

Suppose, thought the Cyborg Rank. Suppose that the Breedmaster could be circumvented, new Cyborgs made, a line of super-Soldiers begun upon Haven. Suppose that this could be done. Then the world would change. Indeed, it would.

For now, however, he must focus on the immediate goal. Sigrid was ready to conceive. Cyborg Rank Bonn was prepared to oblige her.

He nodded to himself. He would ask her soon, when she had had time to ponder the lesson. She was close to the peak of her fertility. His nose had caught it in the match; and he'd been, truth to tell, distracted. He had paid amply for that distraction.

He paused. Had she known it? And exploited it?

Well for her if she had. A Soldier used every weapon in his — or her — arsenal.

He was almost smiling as he went to the next of his duties.

Sigrid stepped out of the bath. Lakshmi offered her a warmed towel. It was a decadence, but the servant could be as stubborn as her mistress when it came to providing what was proper.

Her skin loved the feel of warmth and softness and skilled hands, rubbing away the aches of training. She arched and purred.

Lakshmi giggled. "Just like a cat," she said in her sing-song accent. "So strong, too. Like steel and silk."

Sigrid shook her off. The tribute maiden followed, gently persistent. Sigrid shrugged and stood still. Her breasts were tender, and not only with bruises. She was ready to conceive again.

She looked down at Lakshmi as the girl bent to dry her feet. She was close to whelping, herself. It would be time soon to send her to the breeding pens. She had asked Sigrid to birth her child: sentimental, and typical of cattle, but efficient enough. Sigrid was a capable technician. Even the Breedmaster had been heard to admit it.

Sigrid's sister, Sieglinde, had quarters in the officers' wing, with access to the crèche as befit the mother of four sons. She had two of her sons with her, young Galen whom Sigrid had entered in the database just that morning, and Harad escaping his nurse to fling himself headlong at Sigrid. She scooped him out of the air. He did not screech as cattle children did, even those who were part Soldier. She nodded approval. "But you should never trust anyone to catch you if you jump," she said.

"You did," he said.

"I might have chosen not to."

"Not you," said Harad.

She dropped him. He curled into a ball and rolled, and bounced to his feet, grinning at her. She allowed herself the ghost of a smile.

"You are so good with the children," said Sieglinde. "When are you going to have another?"

"Soon," said Sigrid. She walked past her sister to the window, which looked down on the boys' court. It was empty now in half-night, with the sun just set but Cat's Eye already dominating the sky. Its light was kinder to Cyborg eyes than full day.

"Make it sooner," Sieglinde said. "Signy is what? Two T-years? Three? It's past time you gave her a brother."

Sigrid shrugged.

The children's nurses took them away, Harad protesting volubly, if softly, that he wanted to stay with Sigrid. Sigrid found her jaw was clenched. Her whole body was tight, tight enough to make her bruises throb. Bonn had given a good account of himself before she used his own mass to launch him into the wall.

His mass, and her anger. She could admit it here, in the cool Eyelight, with Sieglinde watching her in silence.

"You don't want another baby, do you?"

Sigrid's shoulders stiffened. She relaxed them muscle by muscle. "Why do you think that?"

"You'd have one if you wanted one," Sieglinde said. "Cyborg Rank Bonn fancies you, you know. He might have to duel Cyborg Rank Metz. Or Assault Leader Udun. Or — "

Sigrid repressed the impulse to whip about. Sieglinde was baiting her. Sieglinde often did. "Do you know," said Sigrid with perfect calm, "how tired I am of being run after like a bitch in heat?"

"Of course I do," said Sieglinde. "I take them when you turn them away."

Sigrid did turn then, but slowly. Sieglinde's face was placid. "You're jealous," Sigrid said.

"Not really," Sieglinde said. "I want a Cyborg son. You could have one for the asking. I mind that. But I like bedding and birthing. You hate them both."

"I like bedding," Sigrid said. "Birthing is battle like any other. But not if it's the only battle I'll ever see."

"What better battle can a woman fight?"

There was no proper answer to that. Sigrid gave it the one she had. "I would have it all. The woman's battle. The man's. Everything that makes life worth living."

Sieglinde regarded her without comprehension. The perfect Soldier's woman, was Sieglinde. She obeyed without question, bore sons without complaint. She never fretted that she must not pass the walls of the Citadel, nor risk her precious genes and her precious womb in any field but that to which she was born.

There was something missing in her. Some spark; some edge. Her sons had it and to spare. She was but a vessel. A womb.

What Sieglinde lacked, Sigrid had in full measure. Too full. A child born with too much of the heritage died far more quickly than a child born with too little. The latter, after all, was only cattle. The former was more than nature could bear.

Sigrid looked back and down. Her fingers, clenching behind her on the window ledge, had crumbled the stone.

Her voice was raw, grating in her throat. "I should have been left for the stobor."

"You almost were." Sieglinde blinked gravely in Sigrid's silence. "You're dangerous, you know. Lady Moria told me that. She said the Breedmaster was going to expose you. Then he decided to keep you, to see what you would be. He's curious, Breedmaster is. Lady Moria says that's a vice, except in a scientist."

Sigrid laughed. "Of course he never intended to expose you."

"No," said Sieglinde. "I'm exactly what he wanted."

Sigrid opened her mouth. Shut it. Blinked once.

Sigrid was, genetically and by training, a Cyborg. That was more than a simple super-Soldier, a supremely efficient killing machine. It was also an enhanced intelligence, and a greatly enhanced ability to process data.

That ability was housed in what was, after all, a human

system. A young one, and fully female. Its gonads did its thinking for it rather more often than she liked to admit. That was a failing even of Cyborgs.

"He wanted me," said Sieglinde. "Not you as you turned out to be. Cyborgs are difficult. Cyborg women worst of all, because they can't be risked, and yet they live to risk themselves. He wanted a woman who would be what he needed her to be. Strong, to breed strong sons. Calm, to bear what a woman must bear."

"I am the best that he has bred," Sigrid said.

"And the worst," said Sieglinde. "I am the future as he sees it. Our women are too few. Too valuable. They can't be permitted to be rash. Without a core of purebred women, the genes of the Race will dilute into the pool of the cattle like the air of a small planet into space."

"He'd breed the wits right out of you," said Sigrid, no more than a whisper. "Out of us."

"It's for the good of the Race," Sieglinde said. Perfect, placid Sieglinde, who was content to be as she was. "See, you're all in knots. Wouldn't you rather be happy?"

"Happy." Sigrid laughed like a bullet cracking through bone. "I was never bred to be happy. And now I see . . ."

"Now you see what you never wanted to see. I'm the best of what will be. You are an aberration."

There was not even malice in it. Sieglinde knew it for truth.

"Our father," said Sigrid, and she did not often call him that; it was not what he was, who was Breedmaster of the Citadel before all other bonds of blood or breeding, "our father is a master of his art. Even Caius never dreamed as he dreams."

"Breedmaster Caius never thought of it. He came from Old Sauron. He didn't see everything that this world would make us."

"Our father sees it," said Sigrid, "but does he know what it is he sees? Women like cattle, true cattle, witless and content, breeding daughters like themselves, and sons like the best of our Soldiers. What would the Lady Althene have said to that, who was Second Rank on the *Fomoria*? What would she call this thing?"

"Efficiency," said Sieglinde.

"She would call it degeneracy. The Race is more than its sons. It is its daughters, too. Take away their part and you lessen us all."

"Is that why you won't give the race a son?"

Sigrid stared at her sister. Sieglinde was as placid as ever, unafraid of the danger that was in Sigrid, because she could not imagine that anyone — even Sigrid, even maddened — could wish to harm her.

"There," said Sigrid, spitting out the words. "There. He's bred out rebellion, and he's bred out sense. The best of a woman of the Race is that she too can fight, she too can defend herself and her blood. He would have her defenseless; protected, never protector. He'd weaken us by half, to serve his own convenience."

Sieglinde did not understand. She was not even annoyed. Her glance was pitying. "You're always so angry," she said. "Aren't you afraid you'll take a fit and die like Sigurd?"

"Sigurd was flawed. Breedmaster knew it too late. I have no such flaw."

"Maybe not," said Sieglinde. She yawned. "He only lived fifteen T-years. You've lived twenty. It's a pity. It wouldn't have mattered if he wanted to go out and fight. That's what Cyborgs do."

"Yes," said Sigrid, cold and still. "That's what Cyborgs do."

"Cyborgs fight," said the Breedmaster, "and train the young. Women breed, and bear the young."

"What of a Cyborg who is a woman?"

Breedmaster Titus turned from the terminal to look at Sigrid. His eyes were as cold as hers should have been. But the anger was too great. It had festered too long. It made her say what she knew better than to say, with passion as ill restrained as in her sparring with Cyborg Rank Bonn.

"Let me go," she said. "Give me what you give any young Soldier fresh from the crèche: his freedom, his proving, his manhood. Let me do a deed that benefits the Race."

"You have done it," said the Breedmaster. "You gave it a

daughter who is Cyborg. It is time you gave it another: a son this time, to fight for us and to train our young."

"I shall give the Race a son," said Sigrid. "Many sons. But what of me? What of what I am? You had me trained as a Soldier is trained. You taught me as you teach your assistants—"

"So that you may be Breedmaster when I am gone."

The interruption was completely unlike the Breedmaster. It was not a surprise. Sigrid had known since she began who would be Breedmaster after Titus. If she lived so long.

"You waste me," she said, "keeping me like cattle."

"I keep you because you are too valuable to waste. Should I risk your knowledge and your heritage as I risk a Soldier, simply because you ask for it? A Soldier is valuable, yes, but he exists to prove himself. If he is fit, he survives. If he is not fit, he dies before he can pass on his genes. You," said the Breedmaster, "are unquestionably fit. You lack wisdom, but that will come. You lack control, but that can be remedied. Your duty is here. Here you will stay."

There was no moving him. He did not see what for her was necessity. A Cyborg was the ultimate Soldier. What a Soldier would do simply because he was ordered to do it, a Cyborg was bred and trained to consider, at lightspeed, and to make his own decisions. Soldiers did not rebel. Cyborgs could, and did. Not en masse since the Revolt that saw the destruction of too many of their number and the end of too many bloodlines. But a lone Cyborg could conclude from the available data that his orders were inefficient or harmful to the Race, and choose to disobey them.

These orders were efficient. For the Breedmaster. These orders were beneficial. To the Breedmaster. Sigrid was indeed too valuable to risk.

She was also too dangerous to keep penned. She was by nature a fighting animal. Controlled combat in the practice rooms was not enough. Controlled exercise on the lands of the Citadel was insufficient. She could feel the bonds of reason fraying — the fits of anger, the sudden, unbridled surges of strength.

Pregnancy was a cure, of sorts. Her body would subside into the calm of gestation. Her mind would fray further, but her mind was not what the Breedmaster wanted. Her genes and her womb were all he cared for.

Something was wrong with that reasoning. She could not for the moment see what. She was gone from the Breedmaster's office, with no memory of dismissal. If that disturbed him, then well enough.

Something moved, out on the steppe. The Sauron sentry came to watchful alertness, discarding like an unwanted cloak the boredom that is a sentry's normal lot in time of peace. His fingers caressed the trigger of the Gatling gun that covered part of the approach to Shangri-La Valley. This was a busy pass, but also a very large one, and it had been some little while since he had seen any travellers.

Even with his enhanced vision, the moving speck was only that, a speck. He brought binoculars to bear. The speck resolved itself into a pair of human figures, afoot. The sentry frowned, actively suspicious now. Haven's nomads were universally mounted, on horses or camels if they had them, on native muskylopes if they did not. *Dismounted nomad* was a contradiction in terms.

The two people slowly approached the entrance to the valley. One appeared to be leading the other. The sentry forgot them for the moment. By themselves, they had to be harmless. But if they were intended to distract him so that raiders could attack the mouth of the deft that led into the valley, they would fail. The Soldiers laughed at sneakier ploys than that.

At last, reluctantly, the sentry decided there were only the two of them. One was a woman, still of childbearing years but no longer young. She was not visibly pregnant, either, so there went the most obvious reason for her coming to the valley. The other, the man she was leading, had gray hair and a white, wispy beard that blew in the cold breeze. He walked awkwardly; the sentry needed a moment more to realize he was blind. Not only did his eyes stay closed, the lids seemed sunken into their sockets, as if no eyeballs lay beneath them.

For all his genetic modifications, the sentry felt ice walk up his spine. The tale was from half a continent away, but it was not the sort that shrank in the telling; over a generation's time it had come to Shangri-La Valley. Unlike most folk on Haven, Sauron Soldiers were not supposed to be superstitious. All the same, the sentry jerked his hand away from the Gatling as if it had suddenly become red-hot. That blind man had known worse than bullets. Shivering and doing his best to blame it on the weather, the sentry let the woman lead the man into the pass.

Dirt and clumpy grass lay underfoot, by their irregular pressure against the soles of his boots and by the sound they made as he scuffed through them. More sounds came from either side: echoes from the nearby canyon walls. "Careful here," his daughter said; her hand on his arm was his sole link to a world wider than what he could feel and hear. "The slope gets ever steeper. Don't stumble."

"I shan't, Aisha, unless I trip," Juchi said. He heard the futile pride in his voice; his senses, those he still had, were swift and keen. Automatically, he cocked his head for a better look at the terrain over which he'd pass. Futile again. . . . "Where are we now?" he asked.

"Halfway through the cleft," Aisha answered. "The Citadel sits above us on the rocks, armed and armored like a tamerlane, and folk from half the world pass by on their way to Nûrnen. The rubble of the great Wall reaches to the hills on the south."

The Great Quake had brought down the Wall, a century before; it had stretched from the mountains on the north to those on the south, and had been a century and a half a-building. Legends of it were sung around fires from one end of the continent to the other. It must have been a wonder to see, although the Citadel was wonder enough, rising in concentric tiers around a central spike set flush against the mountain's wall. Only the mountain itself, which towered two thousand meters above the keep, reduced the inhuman scale of those great works. Even the lowest and outermost of the walls was higher than a bow-shot was long.

Juchi sighed, long and slow. "I never dreamed I

would see it." He laughed harshly at himself. Like the head-cocking gesture, the word remained, half a lifetime after his eyes were gone. He sighed again. "I've wandered farther than ever I dreamed I would, back in the days when I rode with Dede Korkut's clan. And what did it gain me in the end?"

"Great glory," his daughter answered stoutly. "Who but you ever drove the Saurons from one of their lairs, made a whole valley free of them?"

"A greater curse," Juchi said. "Who but I slew my father, lay afterward with my mother; who but I bred children who were also my sibs? How can I atone for such sin, make myself free of it? Blinding did no good; my mind sees still."

Aisha said, "You have borne it, where a lesser man would have fled into death."

Juchi's laugh held nothing of humor. "That is your fault more than mine. Had you obeyed and left me, death would have found me soon enough. Many times, oh, how many times, I've wished it had."

"No." Aisha had been a stubborn child; that had changed not at all since she grew to womanhood. She went on, "Allah and the spirits must have had reason for twisting your life as they did. Before its end, they will grant that you know that reason."

"Then they'd best hurry," Juchi said. "I cannot see my beard, but I know it is the color of snow. I need not see to know how my bones ache, how my heart pounds, how my lungs burn with every step I take. Soon I will die whether you let me or no, daughter of mine."

"That is why we have come at last to Shangri-La Valley. Here sit the Saurons in their power, the Saurons but for whom your curse would never have arisen. By the god, by the spirits, I will see that you have justice from them before the end. If they do not give it to you, I will take it from them myself." Aisha spat on the trail to show her contempt for the overlords of Haven.

"What do they know of justice?" Juchi said. *My daughter hates the Saurons far more than I,* he thought. "They know only force. And why not? It has served them well over the years. And their blood is ours as well, in me through the father I slew; in you, poor child, through me."

*And perhaps I come to the Shangri-La seeking death, not justice.* He had longed for death, but shrunk from suicide. The Saurons might well oblige him with what he had lost the right to hope for long ago — a warrior's end in battle.

"I wish only that you would leave me to my fate, child," he said.

"I am no child," Aisha said wearily; how many times had they argued this round and round? "And I do not willingly claim their blood, while you, Father, you struck a great blow against it."

"You may not claim the blood, but the blood will claim you," Juchi said.

Aisha did not answer, not in words. The pressure of her hand on his arm changed; she was moving forward again. Juchi followed. From the breeze that blew into his face, he tried to scent out what lay ahead in the valley.

With every step he took, the air seemed to grow thicker. That, he knew, was his imagination, but the Shangri-La Valley was far and away the greatest lowland Haven boasted, millions of square kilometers in extent and ringed with mountains. Women came from thousands of kilometers around to bear their babies here; the steppe tribes paid the Saurons a steep price for the privilege, in goods and in women. So did the merchants who thronged through the pass to trade.

The breeze brought the fresh, green scents of growing crops. By Haven's standards, the climate of the Shangri-La Valley was tropical; a man from the Terra now long lost in legend would have judged it no worse than austere. It was mild enough to let wheat survive. In the Tallinn Valley, oats and rye were the staple crops. Of course, the Tallinn Valley could have been dropped unnoticed anywhere here.

The breeze also carried the odors characteristic of man, and man in large numbers: smoke and sweat (the amount of labor required to wrest a living from even the most salubrious parts of Haven was plenty to raise sweat even in the moon's icy climate) and ordure. Falkenberg and Castell

City and Hell's A'-Comin' had been cities once, before the Saurons smote them from the sky. Towns still stood not far from where the bombs had landed. Other towns had grown by the Sauron Bases, large ones here in the valley, smaller ones on the steppe.

Another, newer city lay close to the inner mouth of the valley. Nûrnen had grown up to serve the Citadel, the Saurons' greatest center on Haven. After more than three hundred T-years as masters of the moon, the Saurons were not averse to such luxuries as it could provide them. Further, the more work the humans they contemptuously called cattle did for them, the less they had to do for themselves and the more they could remain fighting machines. That suited them. Thus Nûrnen throve.

"Take me into Nûrnen," Juchi said suddenly.

Aisha stopped. "Why do you want to go there? Of all the towns on Haven, Nûrnen loves the Saurons best."

"Just so," Juchi said. "Through all the long years since they came, simply hating them has not availed. They are too strong, and their strength repels hatred as armor will turn a sword stroke. Those who love them may know where they are truly weak."

The noise Aisha made, deep down in her throat, did not betoken agreement. But she led Juchi into Nûrnen all the same. She had guided him for more than twenty T-years now. When he gave her a destination, she got him there. Whatever she thought of the life she led, she never complained.

"I've given you a long, empty time, my daughter," Juchi said.

"You did not give it to me; I chose it for myself," Aisha answered. "And how could I have found a better one? Who would have taken me into house or yurt, bearing the burden of ill luck I carry?"

"Through me, all through me. You could have left me behind, left your name and birth behind, gone off and lived among folk who knew nothing of your misfortune."

"You tried that, Father. Yet your name and birth returned to work your fate. Why do you think it would have been different for me?"

To that, Juchi had no good answer. Allah and the spirits accomplished a man's fate as they would, not so as to delight him. The best he could hope to do was bear it with courage.

Soon after the pass opened out into Shangri-La Valley, Aisha stopped to pick a couple of clownfruit from a tree. She gave one to Juchi. As he bit into it, the mixture of sweet and tart brought to mind a perfect mental picture of the red-and-white fruit. Even after so long without eyes, he knew what things looked like. Yet it was a sign of Sauron power that food grew thus, unguarded.

She guided their steps onto the shoulder of the paved road that wound through the ruins of the Wall and down into the lower plateau where the city stood.

"Here are the Saurons' gallows," Aisha said tightly.

"Aye," Juchi said. "I can smell them."

Men — and a few women — hung from the long row of gibbets; some by their necks, or by their feet, or in iron cages. Most were dead. They bore placards listing their crimes: BANDIT OLEG and the caravans he had attacked, or RIVER PIRATE BARTON with a tally of ships. Some were much simpler: INSOLENCE or RESISTANCE TO A SOLDIER.

Before long they entered Nûrnen. First, outlying villas and farms for wealthy merchants, and truck-gardens rented by peasants. Then smithies, forges, machine-shops; the Saurons permitted more technology here than in most places, as a useful supplement to the manufactories in the Citadel itself. The clamor of busy streets surrounded Juchi: men and women afoot and on horseback, wagons with squealing wheels, the rhythmic footfalls of litter-bearers. Cobbles or blocks of volcanic tufa made a strange footing beneath his boots, more used to the clumpy grass of the steppes.

"Turn here," Aisha said, directing his footsteps south.

The plateau that held Nûrnen fell in a series of gigantic steps. Highest and nearest to the Citadel was Saurontown, in which dwelt Soldiers who had reason to live outside the bleak, looming fortress above. The streets were a regular grid, the buildings stark and plain, handsome in an austere fashion. Most of the people wore plain gray, or livery of the Citadel; only the odd entertainer or harlot made a splash of color, although some of the gardens shone in bright contrast to the buildings.

A broad stretch of cleared land and steep switchback streets separated Saurontown from Nûrnen proper. The only other paved roads Aisha had ever seen were in the Pale, and those were mere tracks compared to these. Below was a vast sprawl of buildings; she looked up from guiding her father/brother's steps and stopped to gape.

"Is it very great?" Juchi said, a trifle wistfully. "Greater than Strang?"

"Beyond belief," Aisha said. Almost to the edge of sight, buildings sprawled about a twisting maze of streets; tumbledown hovels and lofty churches, the mansions of great merchants with trees showing over their courtyard walls, covered bazaars stretching for hectares, huge public squares with precious water shooting from fountains. "Strang could be lost a dozen times here."

Juchi shook his head; he had been awed on his visits to the Pale. "I can hear a great roaring," he said. "Like nothing else I have ever heard. They say a hundred and fifty thousands of people live in Nûrnen — before this, I did not believe it."

"Neither did I," Aisha said. Then, staunchly: "But each one of them walks on two legs or rides on four, as we do."

They walked. They were used to that, but never to a place where one could walk and walk and still be among buildings and people.

"This is a street of silversmiths, Father. A caravanserai where merchants may rent space for their beasts. Here is a market for slaves . . . and here is a tavern."

The blast of heat from the door, the noise inside, and the smell of beer and tennis-fruit brandy had already told Juchi as much. The noise faded a little while the drinkers sized up the pair. A moment later, it picked up again: they were judged harmless, at least at first glance. Juchi almost smiled at that. He'd worked more harm than any tavern tough could dream of.

"Here is a stool," Aisha said. Juchi felt for it with his hand, sat down. Someone approached the table — a barmaid, by the rustle of skirts.

"What'll it be, sir, lady?" she asked, her voice losing some of its professional good cheer as she got a look at Juchi's face. She spoke Russki, but with a different accent from that of Tallinn Valley, an accent that grew stronger as she lost some of her calm.

"Kvass," Juchi said.

"Beer for me." Aisha had farmer's tastes in some things. "And a roast chicken for the two of us to share."

"I'll bring your drinks right away. The chicken will take just a little while — we're cooking three of them now, and they should be done soon." The barmaid hesitated, then said, "Maybe you'd better show me your money first, since by the look of you, you're new in town."

Aisha fumbled in the pouch she wore at her belt. A moment later, silver rang sweetly on the tabletop. "Will that do?" she asked.

"Oh, yes, ma'am." The barmaid retreated in a hurry. She came back very quickly, set a mug of beer in front of Aisha and a skin of kvass before Juchi. He tasted it, and made a sour face. Town taverns had a habit of serving a thin, weak brew, and this one was no exception. Someone new came up to the table; a man, and no lightweight, either, not from his stride. He reeked of fear.

"The taverner," Aisha whispered to Juchi. She raised her voice to speak to the man: "How may we help you, good sir?"

"I'd talk to your companion, if I could," the fellow said. Hearing Aisha use Russki, he answered in the same language, though his voice had a shrill Americ accent: the Saurons spoke Americ among themselves, and Juchi had heard it more than any other tongue on the streets of Nûrnen. Americ made him nervous. It was the language Badri had known best. He pulled his mind back to the here and now, back from the image of Badri that hung always before his eyes.

"I will speak with you, good sir. Ask what you would." That openness made the taverner hem and haw, and Juchi had never heard of a bashful taverner. He knew what was coming:

"Forgive me if I offend, graybeard, but there are tales

that cling to an old blind man who travels with a woman younger than he is."

"I am the man of whom those tales tell," Juchi answered calmly, as he had many times before. The tavern went deathly still. Juchi's shoulders moved up and down in a silent sigh. That had happened many times, too.

The taverner gulped, loud enough for Juchi to have heard even without his genetically augmented ears. Legends, by their very nature, dealt with the long ago and far away. To have one sitting at a table had to disconcert the taverner. He needed close to half a minute to gather himself after that gulp. At last he said, "I don't want your trade here. I ask you politely to leave in quiet and peace."

"Our silver is as good as anyone else's," Aisha said hotly. She took slights harder than Juchi, who felt he deserved them. The legs of her stool bumped on the rough planks of the floor as she started to get up so she could argue with the taverner face to face.

Juchi set a hand on her arm to stop her. "Wait, daughter." He turned his empty eyes toward the taverner. The man gulped again. Juchi kept his voice mild: "Tell me, sir, if you would, why you want me — want us — to leave."

"Because — because — " The taverner stopped, took a deep breath, tried once more: "Because you are who you are, curse it, and because you did what you did. And because Nûrnen is a town that depends on the Soldiers and their goodwill. They'd not think kindly of me if I let you stay."

"Those are fair reasons," Juchi said. "We will go." Aisha started to protest further. He shook his head at her. "Come, lead me away. I would not stay where I am not welcome. Is it any wonder, then, that I have wandered through all these many years?"

"Everywhere you travel," Aisha said, "folk treat you unjustly."

"No, only with horror, and horror I have earned. Now let us go."

As Aisha led Juchi toward the door, a man at a table he passed said, "And good riddance to you, too, mother-fucker." He laughed at his own wit.

Juchi reached out and effortlessly lifted the man with one hand. The fellow squawked and kicked at him. Juchi felt the muscle shift, heard the whisper of cloth against moving flesh. His body twisted to one side before the booted foot could find its target.

"Motherfucker!" the man yelled again. His hand slapped against the hilt of his knife. At effectively the same instant, Juchi's hand closed on his wrist. Juchi squeezed and twisted. Bones crunched. The man screamed. Juchi threw him away. He smashed against something hard. Juchi stood in a warrior's crouch, waiting to hear if he got up. He did not.

"Horror I have earned. I grant this," Juchi said. "The contempt of such a dog I have not earned. Come, Aisha; lead me away from this place where I am not welcome."

He reached out his hand for hers. She took it, and guided him toward the doorway. Behind him, someone said softly, "More Soldier blood in him than in most Soldiers, by the saints. Look to Strong Sven, somebody — see if he'll ever get up again."

"Let him lie there," someone else replied. "He picked on a blind man; he deserves what he got. Maybe he'll keep his stupid mouth shut next time."

Slightly warmed by that, Juchi followed Aisha down the street. He listened and tried to learn. Nûrnen was indeed a town on good terms with the Saurons. The best indicator of that was how seldom he heard the term. Like the taverner and the other man in his establishment, most people called them Soldiers, their own name for themselves. Juchi did not care one way or the other. Just as he was what he was, they were what they were, and names did not matter.

"Most names," he amended out loud. Aisha made a questioning noise. "Never mind," he told her. He could still feel the quick, precise motions his muscles had made as he chastised the foulmouthed fool. The memory would stay with him. That was his trouble, he thought. He was blind, but the memories stayed with him.

Soldiers lined up for a meal in one of the Citadel's

refectories. It was first come, first served, regardless of rank. If a simple Section Leader took his place in line before a Chief Assault Group Leader, he was served before him, too. The Soldiers did not make distinctions among themselves where distinctions were unnecessary.

Glorund the Cyborg was no simple Section Leader. Nor was he merely a Chief Assault Group Leader. Nevertheless, the Battlemaster took his tray and waited his turn with everyone else. Once a young officer, an Assault Group Leader with, everyone said, a promising future ahead, had stood aside for him. The fellow was a blank-collar-tab Soldier within half a cycle, and bound for duty on the most barren part of the steppe Glorund could find. After that, no one curried favor with him in the refectory line.

In these days, family groups often ate together in their private quarters, particularly among the lower-ranked Soldiers. Glorund disapproved; he would have preferred the old ways, when Soldiers all slept in barracks and ate together. It was not practical to go back — water flowed uphill more easily than a privilege could be retracted once granted — but he intended to see there was no further degeneration.

The refectory workers who slapped food onto the tray were all from Nûrnen. Soldiers did not need to cook; therefore, they did not cook. The food was nourishing but unexciting — stewed heartfruit, a meatloaf made from ground mutton and muskylope, a chunk of rye bread, a mug of beer. Glorund, like lower-ranking Soldiers, was no gourmet. No geneticist had ever found a good enough reason to bother amplifying the sense of taste. Still less for Soldiers, who could eat anything a scavenging land gator could, and did at need.

Glorund's ears, however, were not only genetically modified but also boasted the bioengineered implants that accompanied the Cyborg death's heads on his collar tabs. He heard, and listened to, every conversation in the refectory. Differential signal processing let him pay attention to each of them in turn. That was useful; even people who knew intellectually what he could do sometimes made interesting slips if the refectory was crowded. He was particularly interested in mentions of the name of Carcharoth, his Chief of Staff and so his main rival for supreme power. The younger Cyborg had been showing slight but dangerous signs of impatience along with his ambition.

What he got from his scanning was something entirely different. "The blind man's come into the valley," he heard a Soldier say who'd been on sentry-go. His modifications did not literally let his ears prick up, but he willed into being the mental analog of that primitive physical process. If he heard the word *blind* again, he would key on it, correlate it with this first mention.

To Glorund, to all the high-ranking Soldiers of the Citadel, there was only one blind man, the one responsible for the loss of Angband Base and Tallinn Valley. Not for the first time, he thought the Citadel should have mounted a real punitive expedition, no matter that Angband Base lay far, far to the west. Cattle should never be allowed to get the notion that they could beat Soldiers. So often in combat, what men believed counted for as much as what was true. Granted, Quilland Base, the nearest outpost, was semi-independent and prickly about it (Angband had been virtually a domain of its own for a century before its fall), but the thing could have been managed.

But more cautious heads had prevailed back then: Soldiers who had argued that an attack on Tallinn Valley would draw in the Bandari. And in the end Juchi had destroyed himself more thoroughly than any mere outsiders could have done. The most difficult lesson for Soldiers to learn was that abrupt, straightforward aggression was not always the best solution to a problem. Though to be sure, what was left of Tallinn was a Bandari protectorate these days.

" — blind man smashed him against a table, broke three of his ribs."

Glorund hadn't been consciously following that conversational track; the gossip of other ranks seldom held much of value. Now he replayed it, and learned of the bar fight in Nûrnen. Haven was a tough, unforgiving place; few handicapped folk could survive here. Fewer still could hope to win a fight against a sighted foe. Even for Juchi, that did not seem likely, not so many years after his fall. For anyone else, though, it seemed impossible. Glorund kept eating. His metabolism was augmented, too, to power his implants. He needed twice the calories of an ordinary Soldier, or three times those of an unmodified man. No matter what he decided to do, he had to fuel up first, as if he were a pirate's steamboat taking on wood before it sailed. When he was done, he rose from his bench, stacked his tray, and left the refectory. He did not even pause to draw weapons: what need for them, against the old blind man he sought? He did stop a moment at the Citadel's outer gate, to record a message that he was going into Nûrnen for a while. He needed no one's authorization to proceed; Soldiers, and especially Cyborgs, were supposed to use their initiative.

Nûrnen was a dozen kilometers from the Citadel, down the pass and out its throat: a couple of hours' walk for an unmodified man, half an hour's run for the finest unmodified athlete. Glorund got there in less than twenty minutes, and was not breathing hard when he arrived. The paved road was crowded — it always was. The tonnage of supplies needed to keep ten thousand Soldiers and their women, children and servants fed was considerable. The Cyborg took the cleared grass strip beyond the roadside ditch. He paused to button his greatcoat just outside of town, to hide his collar tabs. That a Cyborg was in Nûrnen would have raced through the place as quickly as word of Juchi's presence had reached the Citadel. Sooner or later it would get around anyhow, but better later than sooner.

He needed to ask fewer questions than an ordinary man would have. He simply strolled through the streets as if window shopping and let his enhanced ears do his work for him. He kept keying on *blind*. By the time he'd heard it three times, he knew in which tavern Juchi had had his fight — the Sozzled Stobor, down by Silver Street. He paused on the way to buy a couple of barbecued lamb ribs. When he was done with them, he tossed the gnawed bones into the street. There they lay; he hadn't left enough meat on them to interest scavengers.

The taverner bowed low as he came in; any Soldier automatically expected that much deference in Nûrnen, and was likely to turn a place inside out if he didn't get it. "Clownfruit brandy," Glorund said.

A barmaid fetched it for him. She was pretty. He watched her appreciatively. He had a wife back in the Citadel and a dozen or so children from unpartnered tribute maidens, but any Soldier was supposed to disseminate his genes as widely as he could, doubly so for Cyborgs — it improved the quality of the tribute stock. Soldier genes were common everywhere within a thousand kilometers of the Citadel, and for lesser distances around the other Bases.

*Maybe another time,* Glorund thought with mild regret. He'd come into Nûrnen for a purpose more important if less enjoyable than spreading a barmaid's legs.

He had another shot of brandy, then ordered bread and cheese to go with it. "You eat like a land gator," the barmaid said as she watched him methodically demolish the meal. She meant it as a compliment; on Haven, being able to put away large amounts of food in a hurry was a survival characteristic.

Glorund smiled back at her, thinking that perhaps he would bed her after all. That, too, was a genetic imperative. But no. First things first. He stretched and yawned, giving a good impression of a man who felt lazy and loose. "Hear you had a strange sort of brawl in here not so long ago," he remarked casually. "Raisa," he added. A Cyborg's infallible memory had many uses. Cattle attached great value to those in power remembering their names.

That was all the prompting she needed; if she was as eager to screw as she was to talk, he thought, she might well wear him out, Cyborg Soldier though he was. "We sure did," she said. "Blind man — Ivan over there" — she pointed to the taverner — "says he's Juchi the Accursed, whaled the stuffing out of Strong Sven. Everybody in town knows Strong Sven, and nobody wants to quarrel with him. He has a good bit of Soldier blood in him, or so they say."

"Half the people of Nûrnen have some Soldier blood in them," Glorund said. An understatement; half had enough to notice. All the same, the identity of Juchi's opponent had startled him. A T-year before, Strong Sven had fought a Soldier to a standstill. The Soldier was no prize, genetically speaking, but he hadn't been left out for stobor, either. So Strong Sven unquestionably was of mixed blood. And what did that say about Juchi?

Ivan the taverner spoke up: "I wouldn't let Juchi stay here, not after he admitted who he was. I like the Soldiers, I do, and I want naught to do with anyone who fought and hurt your folk." He puffed out his chest in righteous — and possibly even sincere — indignation. As he deflated, his right hand moved in a sign the people of Shangri-La Valley had learned from the steppe nomads. He added, "Besides, I didn't want his ill luck rubbing off on my place."

"Where would he have gone, then?" Glorund asked. As long as the cattle were so forthcoming, he would pump them for all they were worth.

Just for an instant, his thoughts went back to the barmaid. She was the one who answered: "When they went out the door, they turned left, going south through town. Maybe they were trying to get a place to rest, but who would give them one, knowing what they were?"

It was a good question. Glorund knew that not all of Nûrnen was as pleased with the Soldiers and their constant presence as Ivan professed to be. Still, Nûrnen depended on the Citadel for its livelihood. Few townsfolk would risk their overlords' wrath for the sake of a couple of wanderers. The Battlemaster threw down a silver coin with the shark shape of the *Dol Guldur* stamped on one side and the old Americ motto KILL 'EM ALL AND LET GOD SORT 'EM OUT on the other. Coppers jingled as Ivan started to make change. "Keep it," Glorund said. "You've helped me."

As he went out into the street, he glanced up at the sky. Byers' Sun stood almost at the zenith; Cat's Eye was low in the east: second cycle, third day noon, more or less. Another thirty-five hours of daylight, at any rate. Sleeping patterns on Haven tended to the peculiar. Some people catnapped when they felt like it, regardless of where — or whether — Byers' Sun and Cat's Eye were in the sky. Some tried to keep a rhythm of long stretches of awareness and long sleeps. Soldiers, for their part, usually went without sleep as long as they could, then slept hard for ten hours or so. Glorund had to think of Juchi as a Soldier. Likely he and the woman would not have settled down to rest, not here in a city where so many people had reason to despise them, but they would have pushed on into the valley. If they did stop to sleep, it would be away from people.

Working through the logic took but a moment. As soon as he saw the end of the chain, Glorund went into a Soldier's trot. Like a broken-field runner, he dodged round the people and carts crowding Nûrnen streets. Some Soldiers got into trouble when they tried moving quickly in town: they forgot that people would seek to dodge out of their way, and sometimes zigged into them when they should have zagged away.

Glorund was a Cyborg. He made no such simple mistakes. He saw a kilometer and a half of street as a single unit, plotted his course through it with accuracy and finesse. His processing equipment and reaction time let him treat the journey as a series of freeze-frames, with the men, women, horses and muskylopes essentially motionless as he moved past them.

Soon he was past the southern limits of the town. The road was paved in the center with stone blocks like an old Roman road on Terra, and intended for much the same purpose: moving armies of Soldiers into and out of the valley. It was convenient for heavy haulers, carts drawn by oxen and muskylopes, as well as the sprung carriages of the wealthy, and saddle horses reined down to a walk or a trot. Faster mounted traffic loped or galloped by on the wide graded shoulders. Pedestrians, unless they wanted to chance being trampled, usually opted for the softer ground just off the road.

He slowed and examined the road's edges with care. He knew the shoes a man from Nûrnen or another valley town was likely to wear, knew also the boot styles of the local nomads and, of course, of his fellow Soldiers. All those, save to some degree the nomads, he mentally eliminated; his eyes literally took no notice of them. That disposed of more than eighty percent of his possibles; the rest he studied more closely. He did not need long to settle on two pairs of prints as most likely to belong to Juchi and his guide.

One of those sets of prints was a good deal smaller than the other. Since Juchi's guide was known to be a woman, that alone made those two pairs a decent bet to be the ones he sought. Legend said she was his daughter, his sister or both at once, but Glorund, with resolute Cyborg rationality, discounted legend. Data counted for more, and data he had: the smaller set of feet — the ones he'd tentatively identified as belonging to Juchi's companion — took firm if short strides. The other set of prints, the ones from the larger feet, was scuffed and dragged along through the dirt, very much as if the person who made those tracks could not see where he was going.

Glorund grinned a carnivore grin and resumed his effortless Soldier's trot. Now to see to revenge for Angband Base. It would be late revenge, and minimal, but not to be discarded on account of that. Word of how Juchi met his end would also become legend, legend that would grow and make fear of the Soldiers grow with it. Glorund's grin stretched wider. Not entirely incidentally, the news of the Battlemaster's dealing personally with a problem which had dogged the Citadel for a generation would solidify his support . . . and weaken that of a certain overly ambitious Chief of Staff.

Unlike an unaugmented tracker, the Battlemaster did not have to slow to keep track of his quarry's trail. Now he simply screened from his vision centers all footprints in the road save the two pairs he sought. Sometimes Cyborgs made mistakes by programming themselves to ignore data that later proved important. Glorund did not think he was making a mistake, not here.

As he ran on, the trail grew fresher. He was not taken by surprise when Juchi and the woman with him left the road to turn down a narrow country lane, then headed for the shelter of an apple orchard not far away. He mentally checked his weaponry. He had a knife, and he had himself. That was plenty. Juchi, after all, was unlikely to be toting an assault rifle. As for the woman with him, well, she was a woman, and largely (altogether, if the legend was a lie, as legends mostly were) of cattle stock. He screened her from his consideration as thoroughly as he had the irrelevant footprints.

He added two things to his inventory of weapons. He had privacy here, and he had plenty of time. Grinning still, he trotted toward the orchard.

Aisha looked up from the small fire she was building. Her nostrils flared, testing the wind, and she tilted her head to listen. "A man is coming."

"Yes, I hear him." Juchi turned his head toward the sound. Even after so long, he sometimes expected to see what he was hearing. Whoever the approaching stranger was, he had a gait like a muskylope's, tireless and easy. Juchi heard his quick footfalls but only calm, steady breathing, as if the fellow were just ambling along.

Suddenly Juchi did see, in his mind's eye that no brooch could pierce. He saw himself as a young man out on the steppe, saw another man approaching him at a trot. It had been just such a trot as this. The man had been his Sauron father Dagor. Just before Juchi killed him.

The fellow now was in among the trees, weaving between them faster than a man had any business doing. Aisha said, "He has a gray greatcoat." Hatred was bitter in her voice.

"He is a Sauron," Juchi said. "Well, if he wants me, he has me. I shall not run from him, nor would it do me any good to try."

They waited; Aisha was painfully conscious that the rapid pounding of her heart would be audible to the Sauron . . . and that Juchi's was as calm as that of a man asleep.

Less than a minute later, the Sauron came into the clearing.

"Greetings, guest," Juchi said. "Will you share salt and bread with us?"

"Yes," the Sauron answered, "but afterwards I will kill you all the same."

Aisha drew in a sharp breath and started forward a little, her hand moving toward her knife. Juchi set a hand on her arm and shook his head. He turned back to the Sauron. "You are honest, at any rate. Shall we talk awhile first, that I may learn who so boldly seeks my death?"

"As you wish. I just now thought to myself that I have all the time I need to do as I will with you," the Sauron said. "Think not to escape, either, for I am no mere Soldier. I am Glorund, Battlemaster of the Citadel. I know you cannot see them, but I wear the death's heads on my collar tabs."

Cloth rustled. He was loosening his greatcoat, then.

"He speaks the truth," Aisha said, her voice quavering. "He is a Cyborg."

"I did not think he came here to boast and lie," Juchi said. He was calm. He'd passed beyond fear for his life in the moment he'd plunged his wife/mother's brooch into his eyes. He nodded to Glorund. "Well, Battlemaster, so you will take your revenge for Angband Base, will you?"

"Exactly so," Glorund answered. "Our reach is shorter than it was in the long-ago days; we have not maintained as much technology as we might wish. But we still know what examples are worth. Now that I have you, the cattle will quiver in fear and horror whenever they speak of your death. That serves the Citadel."

Juchi shrugged. "Men quiver in fear and horror when they speak of me now," he said. "Allah and the spirits know I have deserved death. But no one yet has dared call me coward. I shall not flee you. Indeed, I warn you that I will strike back if I may. I began fighting Saurons long ago; the habit is hard to break."

"Strike if you wish," Glorund said. "It will not avail you." Juchi had not dealt with Saurons for many years, but he remembered the arrogance they could put in their voices, the certainty that things would be as they said and only as they said. Glorund had it in full measure.

"You condemn me for taking Angband Base," Juchi said. "Why should I not condemn you and all your kind for what you have done to Haven?"

"Because you have not the power," Glorund answered at

once. "Haven is ours because we are strong enough to hold it, to shape it as we will." Yes, he was arrogant, arrogant as a cliff lion stretching in front of a herd of muskylopes.

Juchi had thought that way once, till his own downfall led him to a different view. He said, "Your kind, Sauron, did not have the power to hold Angband Base. Thus by your own argument you ought to leave me in such little peace as may be mine."

"Had you stayed in that faraway valley, you would be right. But you are here now, in the Shangri-La Valley, the stronghold of the Soldiers, and here, I gather, by your own free choice. That makes you a fool, and for fools the death penalty is certain. I am but the instrument the universe chooses to carry out the sentence."

"Why not say you are a god and have done?" Aisha spat.

"There are no gods," Glorund answered. "I am a Soldier and a Cyborg. Here and now, that is all I need to be. I am a lord among the Soldiers, and the Soldiers are lords among the human cattle of this world."

"Do you take pride in that?" Juchi asked.

"Why should I not?" Unmistakably, Glorund was preening. "Year by year, we breed more Soldiers, shape this world in our image."

"And year by year, your reach grows shorter. You said as much yourself. When your kind came to Haven, you came in a starship. Where is your starship now, Sauron? You had fliers, they say. Where are your fliers now? You call your folk great conquerors? Were you not then fleeing defeat, like a beaten nomad tribe driven from good pasture country to badlands where grass hardly grows? Boast of your might, and hear your boasts ring hollow in your ears."

Aisha clapped her hands in delight at her father's defiance. Juchi hoped to hear some sign of anger from Glorund, the sharpness of an indrawn breath or the small mineral noise of teeth grinding together. From an ordinary man, even from an ordinary Sauron, he knew he would have won them. Yet Glorund still sat as relaxed as if they were talking about the best way to trim muskylope hooves. The biomechanical implants that made him a Cyborg gave him inhuman calm.

*Inhuman is good word for it,* Juchi thought. Many doubted whether Cyborgs truly were human beings any more, or only war machines fueled on bread and meat instead of coal. Juchi was glad no Cyborg had led at Angband Base. That fight had been hard enough as it was. But had he died in it, he would not have gone on to sin as he had. Maybe better, then, if a Cyborg had been there. He'd chased round such thoughts countless times in his years of wandering, never to any profit. That did not keep him from getting caught up in them, from wishing his life somehow could have been different.

He realized he'd missed something Glorund said. "I'm sorry," he said. "I was woolgathering."

"A fit trade for a nomad," the Sauron said, the first trace of wit Juchi had heard from him. "Let me try again: aye, we were defeated. The herds of cattle trampled down our forefathers by weight of numbers. Is that warfare? Half a dozen drillbits may gnaw flesh from a man's bones. Does that make them mightier than men?"

"The fellow they gnawed will never worry about the question again," Aisha put in. "He lost, and so did you. So will you all, until no bearer of the Lidless Eye walks alive on Haven."

"And what have you Saurons done with Haven since you came here?" Juchi demanded. "Have you made it better? Stronger? Or have you simply gone about the planet destroying anything that might get in the way of your quest for power?"

"Those who rule brook no rivals," Glorund answered. "So has it always been, on every world; so shall it always be. Accept a rival to your power and one day you will find you have a master."

"But your power is not based only on the fighting magic you Saurons carry in your bodies," Juchi said.

"By the Lidless Eye, what else is there, you bad-genes wretch?" The Battlemaster's words still came out in that perfectly controlled tone, but they betrayed anger all the same.

Juchi nodded to himself. Flick a Sauron on his fighting ability and he bled. Juchi did not intend to let him clot. He pressed on: "You won Haven with machine magic, and slew everyone else's machines when you came. You had to — machines can kill from farther away than any Sauron's arm can reach. But now that that magic is gone for everyone else, it is dying for you as well. And fight as boldly as you will, how can you ever hope to leave Haven again without the machine magic you've spent all these years killing?"

"When we have fully mastered the world, we will restore technology — under our control," Glorund answered. "It can be done; Cyborgs can outthink men of the cattle as well as outfight them."

Juchi snorted rudely. "I've wandered widely across Haven this last half of my life. Though I do not see, I hear and I know. Aye, you hold Shangri-La Valley tight, here with your Citadel. Here you still retain some of your magic, enough to conjure Cyborgs — for now. But for how much longer, even here? In the other and lesser valleys where Sauron fortresses still dominate, they have lost the art. And, Battlemaster Glorund, think on this — is a Citadel a place from which to fare forth to conquer all the world, or is it a place to huddle, warded against a world that hates you?"

Glorund sat some time silent. In that silence, Juchi was reminded of the electronic ruminations of the Threat Analysis Computer at Angband Base. He wondered how Glorund was analyzing the data he had presented, how the Cyborg went about weighing those data against the ones he already possessed. No matter how Juchi had scoffed at it, the Threat Analysis Computer had proved abominably right. Could Glorund's augmented flesh and blood match the machine?

Juchi never learned the answer to that question, for Glorund said, "I can tell you what the Citadel and its valley are. They are the fitting place for you to die."

"Aye, Sauron, that is so, but not for the reason you think." Unobtrusively Juchi shifted his weight, readying himself for the attack that, he knew, would come at any moment. While Glorund hesitated still, he took the chance to get in the last word: "What better spot for me to lie than in the center of Sauron wickedness? Perhaps your land will gain some atonement from me, as I have already rid one part of Haven of your foul breed."

*     *     *

What would have been killing rage in an unmodified man ripped through Glorund. The Cyborg Battlemaster felt it only as an augmented urge to be rid of Juchi once and for all. He had no need for the rush of adrenaline that sped the hearts and reflexes of cattle, even of Soldiers. All his bodily systems functioned at peak efficiency at all times. Without gathering himself, without changing expression, he leapt at the blind man whose very existence mocked the Soldiers, who would not be silent, and who somehow kept piercing, deflecting, the cool, perfect stream of Glorund's own logic.

A man of the cattle would have died before he ever realized Glorund had moved. The Battlemaster learned in that instant that part of Juchi's legend, at least, was true. He reacted to Glorund's attack with speed many of the Soldiers at the Citadel might have envied, knocked aside the first blow intended to snap his spine, struck out with the dagger that had appeared in his right hand.

Glorund chopped at his wrist. That should have sent the knife spinning away. Juchi held on, grappling with Glorund. His every kick, every hand-blow was cleverly aimed, Soldier-fast and Soldier-strong. The knife scored a fiery line across Glorund's ribs before the Battlemaster finally managed to knock it out of Juchi's hand.

"The Breedmaster who left you out for stobor was an idiot," Glorund said.

Juchi's only answer was to butt him under the chin. Even Glorund saw stars for a moment. Juchi's blindness mattered little in the hand-to-hand struggle in which they were engaged. Both men fought more by ear and by feel than by eye — and Juchi, however he had learned them, knew all the tricks in the warrior's bag. But however skilled, however swift, however strong he was, he was no Cyborg. He hurt Glorund once or twice. Even so much surprised the Battlemaster. But Glorund made Juchi first groan and then scream.

"There," he snarled, snapping Juchi's right arm against his own shin. "And there." He rammed his knee into his enemy's midsection. "And there!" A final savage twist broke

Juchi's neck. It was not the slow, lingering kill Glorund had looked for, but it would serve.

Juchi's will to live was stubborn as any Soldier's. His lips shaped one last word: "Badri," he whispered with all the breath left in him. Then at last he died. Glorund started to scramble free.

With a wordless scream, Aisha leaped on the Battlemaster's back. Glorund had looked for that, looked for it with anticipation. He would, he thought, have her two or three times and then either kill her or take her back to the Citadel for breaking. He swept out an arm to roll her off him. It was a casual sweep, not one he would have made against an opponent he took seriously. But he still thought of Juchi's legend as legend and no more; he did not believe Aisha was truly Juchi's daughter and sister both, did not believe she too could hold Soldier genes. Cyborg logic was very seldom wrong. When it was, the surprise was all the more shocking.

Aisha's fist smashing down on his arm brought home to him he that had made a mistake; she not only had Soldier genes, she had a goodly proportion of them. *Her father had a three-quarter sire and one-half dam*, the passionless computer part of his brain calculated. *She had a five-eighths sire and one-half dam. Fairly pure strain, of excellent quality. Reflexes in the upper seven percent of Soldier range.*

He twisted desperately now, in full earnest. He was as fast as a leaping cliff lion. He was not fast enough to keep her from drawing her knife across his throat.

Blood spurted, hideously crimson. Soldiers clotted far faster than ordinary mortals; Cyborgs held their circulatory systems under conscious control. Glorund could will away bleeding in an arm, in a leg, in his belly. But in his neck — ! Whether his brain lost oxygen from bleeding or from his own willfully imposed internal tourniquet, the result would be the same, and as bad.

Pieces of the world went gray in front of him. The color even of his own gushing blood faded. He kicked out at Aisha. If he was to die, he wanted to take her down with him, lest her genes be passed on to those who hated Soldiers.

He thought he felt his booted foot strike home, thought

he heard her cry out in pain. But all his senses were fading now, not just his vision. When he fell to the ground, he hardly knew he lay against it.

Was his bleeding slowing? He forced a hand to claw its way up his side to the wound that opened his neck. Yes, the fountain had dwindled to a trickle. If he stayed very still, he might yet live.

Something dark appeared over him. He concentrated. Aisha. She still had that dagger. He tried to raise a hand to protect himself. Too slow. He knew he was too slow. The point, sharp and cold, pierced his left eye and drove deep. All he felt at the end was enormous embarrassment.

Slowly, ever so slowly, Aisha got to her feet. She bit her lips against a shriek as the broken ends of ribs grated against each other. Even dying, Glorund had been faster and stronger and deadlier than anything she had imagined. Now she understood how and why the Saurons ruled so much of Haven. How they had ever been stopped, why they did not rule the human part of the galaxy, was something else again. She wanted desperately to pant, to suck in great gulps of air to fight her exhaustion. Her ribs would not permit it. She sipped instead, and trembled all over. "Father," she whispered. "I have given you justice."

A noise, not far away — Her head whipped around. Her fist clenched on the hilt of her dagger. The blade was still red with Glorund's blood. Even as she made the gesture, she felt its futility. If that was a Sauron coming through the apple trees, she was dead. Only wildest luck and surprise had let her slay the Battlemaster. She would not enjoy surprise here, not standing over Glorund's butchered corpse. And as for luck, surely she had used it all in killing him. Her shoulders sagged in resignation; she waited for her end.

But she still did have some luck left, she realized when the newcomer walked into the clearing. He was no Sauron, only a peasant dressed in sheepskin jacket and baggy trousers of undyed wool. He carried nothing more lethal than a mattock.

His eyes widened as they went from her face to the dagger

to the two bodies sprawled close by, back to her face, back to the bodies. They almost popped from his head when he noticed that one of those bodies wore a greatcoat of Sauron field-gray. He shifted the mattock to his left hand so he could move the other over his heart. Aisha had seen that violent crisscross gesture in some of the valleys she'd visited. It belonged to a faith many farmers still followed.

"You killed them both?" the peasant whispered in Russki. He gripped the mattock in both hands and fell back into a clumsy posture of defense.

Aisha shook her head. The motion hurt. Every motion hurt. "No," she answered wearily. "The Sauron killed my father. I killed the Sauron."

"You are a woman," the peasant said, as if it were accusation rather than simple statement of fact. "How could you slay a Sauron Soldier?"

"I am called Aisha. My father is Juchi." She pointed to the corpse that was not Glorund's. Juchi's death had not hit her yet, save to make her numb — she noticed that she still spoke of him in the present tense.

This time the peasant dropped the mattock to crisscross himself. "The accursed one," he whispered.

"So people have named him," Aisha agreed, more wearily still. "He taught me to fight — before misfortune cast him down, he was a great warrior. And I — I share his blood." The third repetition of the peasant's ritual crisscrossing began to bore her. She said, "If you're going to run screaming to your Sauron masters, do it. I won't flee. I'm sick to death of wandering."

"Don't talk like a fool," the peasant said, crisscrossing himself yet again. "We bury these bodies, we maybe have time to run away, Bog willing." He picked up the mattock and set to work. Dirt flew.

"Why do you need to run away?" Aisha asked.

"This happens on the land I work for the Saurons, so they will blame me." He paused to wipe sweat from his forehead. "Drag the bodies over here while I work."

Aisha obeyed. She did not relish the idea of her father sharing a grave with a Sauron but, as Juchi himself had said, perhaps that was only just. Glorund's greatcoat came open as she hauled him by his boots to the edge of the growing hole.

The peasant kept digging for another couple of minutes. Then he happened to look over at Glorund's collar tabs, and saw the death's heads embroidered there. As if drawn by a lodestone, his gaze swung back to Aisha. "You slew — a Cyborg?"

Now, at last, he did not bother crisscrossing himself. He did not bother digging any more, either. He whirled and threw his mattock as far as he could. It clattered off a tree trunk. He lumbered away, back toward the road.

"Where are you going?" Aisha called after him.

"What does it matter?" he yelled over his shoulder. "Wherever I run, it will not be far enough. But I must try." The thump of his heavy strides faded as he dodged through the apple trees. Aisha felt a sudden, almost overwhelming surge of pity for him — she was grimly certain that he was right, that he would be hunted down and killed. His crisscross Bog would not save him when the Saurons learned their ruler was dead.

And what of herself? Only minutes before, when she'd thought the peasant a Sauron, she'd been ready to give up and die. Now she found that was no longer so. She looked down at her father. Yielding tamely to the Saurons would spit in the face of everything for which he'd lived. She could not fight them all, not here in Shangri-La Valley. That she had killed Glorund the Battlemaster was a greater victory than she had any right to expect. She must escape, to strike a harder blow later.

Which left getting away. The foolish peasant had fled at random, and probably would not go more than a few kilometers from this land he'd been working all his life. He could no more conceive of taking refuge on the steppe than of building a shuttle and escaping into space.

But the plains and their clans were Aisha's second home. Aye, the Saurons might seek her there, but seeking and finding were not the same. Before she consciously came to a decision, she was jogging toward the steppe. It was a slow jog, with knives in it, but she kept on.

She skirted the town of Nûrnen, staying off the main road in favor of the farmers' tracks that snaked their way through the fields. At the inner margin of the pass she turned south into a district of rough hills and canyons that lay between the road and the southern mountains; shepherd's pathways there led out onto the steppe.

She jogged on, ignoring her hurt, ignoring how tired she was. All her life she'd been able to do that at need. She seldom thought about why it was so. Now she did, acknowledging the Sauron blood that ran in her veins through Juchi. She felt that she was putting it to its proper use, as he had before her — using it against those who had brought it, all unwanted, to Haven.

Had the Saurons in the Citadel or in their sentry posts at the outer mouth of the cleft wanted her, they could have taken her. She knew that. They had assault rifles and Gatlings and no doubt deadlier weapons as well, leftovers from the starship that had carried them here. But now, without Juchi at her side, no one took any special notice of her. She seemed just another woman who had finished her business in Shangri-La Valley and was on her way back to her clan.

She kept jogging for several kilometers after she left the pass. Only when the tall grass behind her had swallowed up the way back to the lowlands did she stop to wonder what to do, where to go next. For long minutes her mind remained perilously blank. All her adult life she had led her father/brother about, served as his eyes and as the staff in his hand. She'd wanted nothing more. Now he was gone. She still knew no grief, only vast emptiness. Without Juchi, what point to her own life? What could she do? What could she be?

"I am Aisha," she said. The wind still blew the words away. She said them again. The wind still blew. What did her name mean? Her voice firmed as she declared: "It will mean what I make it mean."

She still had no idea what that would be. She turned northwest, toward distant Tallinn Valley where she had been born, and began to find out.

# ● CHAPTER SEVEN

As Cat's Eye left the zenith and began its descent over the far horizon of the valley, Sigrid passed the guard on the Citadel's gate. He glimpsed her face and did not presume to challenge her. She was allowed at least to step beyond the walls of the Citadel. For the present.

The Citadel was in turmoil with the death of Battlemaster Glorund. There was no question as to who would be Battlemaster after him: Carcharoth had made that clear the moment the news came in. So far no one had seen fit to challenge him. Sigrid doubted that anyone would. The Cyborgs were in shock. One of their own, and a Battlemaster besides, killed by cattle.

Breedmaster Titus would support whoever held the position; he was content with his own office, which he — and Sigrid — believed to be more powerful by far. The Battlemaster dealt with the defense of the Citadel. The Breedmaster ruled its heart. It was the Breedmaster who culled the newborn, made the Cyborgs, decided whose bloodline would live and whose would die.

As she walked out of the Citadel, making no secret of her going and so concealing it more effectively than if she had tried to make a hidden escape, she heard the bell that called the First Council to discuss the debacle. Their function was purely ceremonial. The real decisions would be made in the Battlemaster's office, in the Breedmaster's laboratory, in the Cyborgs' quarters.

Had she been a male, she would have been needed in the councils, at least among the Cyborgs; they were too few to ignore any of their number, however junior his status. As a female she was an anomaly, her status neither junior nor senior, simply *other*. She could have attended the conference, even been listened to, but in her current state of high fertility, she would have been a potentially disastrous distraction.

Her womb, they needed. The rest of her, no. Rather the contrary, at the moment.

She was as free as she would ever be. Free to go where she would, to make what decisions she pleased. It was a peculiar sensation for a Soldier, not unusual for a Cyborg. In her current state of restless irritability, it was a blessing of sorts. She could not process data rationally while she remained in the Citadel. Nûrnen might distract her, might even yield data that would prove useful to the Race.

That her departure at this juncture could be construed as desertion and dereliction of duty, she well knew. She was prepared to justify it. If those justifications amounted to rationalization, then so be it. She could always point out that her playing truant in Nûrnen was preferable to hurling Cyborg Ranks through dojo walls.

The center of Nûrnen was twelve kilometers from the Citadel, down the pass and out the throat into the red Eyelight of the valley. Sigrid took the road at Cyborg pace, as fast as a horse could gallop, pushing herself a little to work off her temper. Even so, she was barely breathing hard as she came from farmlands to suburbs to the crowded buildings of the city proper; to Saurontown, that was built on the slope that looked toward the Citadel. In certain lights, to certain minds, the shadow of the stronghold seemed to lay long and black across the dwellings of those Soldiers and Soldier stock who would not or could not live within the guarded walls.

Sigrid did not pause in Saurontown. The computer in her brain recorded the crowding of faces, the positions of bodies in her path, the ruler-straight avenues and the right-angled turns defined by buildings as square-cut and unadorned as the uniform she wore. She was not hailed or stopped. A Soldier in Citadel gray, moving as fast as a Cyborg could move, was no obstacle to trifle with.

Beyond Saurontown, in what some of the younger Soldiers were pleased to call Cattletown — which Sigrid, severely, called Nûrnen proper — the city changed. The streets began to meander. Houses and public buildings lost their uniformity, sometimes wildly: on one corner a pediment of severe and classical simplicity, on the next extravagant, painted and gilded rococo, on the one after that a simple whitewashed cube with a high arched gate and a scent within of exotic perfumes, and beside it a structure like a nomad's yurt writ huge in stone.

The streets were thronged with people. Lean, rangy, plain-coated Nûrnenites, at times indistinguishable from the dwellers in Saurontown. Plump valley merchants puffing in what to them was thin air; stolid toil-worn valley farmers. Lean, cord-muscled, turbaned Ashkabad camel drivers. Big fair-haired fur-hatted Kossacki looking incomplete without their horses. Little bandy-legged Mongols looking furious without theirs. Even a black-haired, braided, stobor-hide-clad savage who could only be a Dinneh, half a world away from his homeland, and in his impassive face eyes as wide and wondering as a child's. Other types and faces and modes of dress that Sigrid had never troubled to study, all thronging together in streets that could barely contain them, spreading out in the plazas and the market squares but clumping thick where the bazaars themselves were; and everywhere a stink and a clamor and a seethe of unregenerate, unengineered humanity.

Cattle.

But cattle who could think.

There was no room for temper here. There was barely room for a lean whip of a Cyborg woman. Some who noticed her field gray and knew it for what it was took care to move out of her way. Many did not. Most of those could not: the press was too great. Even she was slowed to walking pace, and then to a crawl.

She could have pushed through. She chose not to. She chose a current of people and followed it. Her directional sense assured that she would not be lost, even where the streets were most convoluted.

She sidestepped a nomad whose head came precisely to her shoulder. He was wrapped in furs; he reeked of unwashed man and unwashed whore. His breath was a melange of unspeakable odors, the most recent a tavern sampler of cheap fruit wine, bad beer and ill-brewed kvass. He staggered against her. Almost she failed to stop the reflex that would have snapped his neck. It caught him instead with force enough to jar his bones, and set him upright. His head rolled back. His grin revealed appalling teeth.

Suddenly she was supporting his whole weight. She would have dropped him, but there was nowhere to do so without his being trampled. Little care as she had for the life of so inferior a specimen, she cared less to cause an incident. And an incident there would be, if a nomad died in the center of Nûrnen with the Citadel's only Cyborg woman as a witness. Then she would be confined to the Citadel, and even this small freedom denied her. Soldiers were authorized to take terminal action — kill — at the least sign of resistance, or on their own initiative. That did not mean they could slaughter at whim; that was bad tactics, liable to produce resource-wasting resistance.

She shouldered the limp, redolent weight, and looked about.

There was a tavern within a few strides — the one, no doubt, from which he had emerged. She could drop him there and then go her ways. Such as those were.

"Hoi! What you doing?"

Another of them. She had not noticed him except peripherally, as one notices a buzzing insect. Now he forced himself on her attention. He was slightly more sober than the other had been, or slightly less sozzled. He was also, she observed, slightly more presentable. Taller, to begin with: fully as high as her chin. Marginally cleaner. Noticeably younger. His kind grew little beard in any case, but cultivated what moustache they could; his, though not as sparse as some, was soft, a boy's.

"What you doing?" he repeated. "Where you go with Ogadai?"

He was speaking the language of the Citadel, and capably enough at that. She answered in plains Turkic. "Is he yours?"

The nomad blinked and shifted languages; his version of the lingua franca of the steppe was accented with something barking and guttural. "He's my cousin." He scowled. His hand dropped to the hilt of his saber. "Where are you taking him? You take him up there" — his head jerked toward the east and the, from here, invisible Citadel — "I'll kill you."

"Killing there would be, cattle boy," said Sigrid, beginning to be amused. "But I would be the one who did it. Do you want this sack of kvass? Take him. I have no use for him."

The nomad half-drew his saber. His fury was a pheromone reek, so sharp that Sigrid twitched. "What do you call him? What do you call my cousin, the *khan*'s son, the pride of the clan?"

"Drunk," said Sigrid, "and stinking. Are you going to draw your saber? If you do, be reminded. It's a felony to draw on a Soldier in Nûrnen."

For a moment she expected — hoped — that he would draw. But the saber slammed back in its sheath. The nomad spat, just missing her foot. "Give me back my cousin."

Not a coward, she decided. More prudent than most of his kind knew how to be. And young — eighteen T-years, twenty at most. "If you were a woman," she informed him, "you would make a fair mother of Soldiers."

She stepped past him. She was ready if need be to use the drunken nomad for a shield against a dagger in the back. But none came. When she stepped into the near-darkness of the tavern — a blink, a pause, and her eyes had focused, in their element now and seeing everything with sharp-edged clarity — she was aware of him behind her. He was still angry.

She stood in spreading silence. There was, she noticed, a respectable crowd. Nomads, Nûrnenites, a squire from the central Shangri-La, a lone Cossack. No Soldiers.

She walked through the stillness. A corner vacated itself. She dumped her burden in it.

She'd intended to leave as she had arrived. But she had not eaten since her session with Bonn, and the haunch that turned on the spit looked edible, even savory. She left the snoring nomad where he lay and claimed another corner, barely lit but more than bright enough for her comfort. A barmaid crept up, half shaking, half defiant. "Beer," said Sigrid, "and meat. Bread if you have it. Double portions."

"I know," the girl said in Russki-accented Americ. Valley Russki; Sigrid could place the dialect, about a hundred and fifty kilometers west of the Citadel. The girl was greenish at her own temerity; but she left with dignity, not running, even swinging her hips a little.

Sigrid raised a brow at that. No Soldier would have taken her for a man, but Soldiers were capable of observation. She was tall — Cyborgs were. Field-gray covered what scant curves she had. She wore her hair cut short for practicality. Her face was fine-boned for a Cyborg's, strong for a woman's: Soldier norm, near enough. No beauty, Sieglinde would say. Her beauty was in her genes.

Which was nothing that cattle could see, let alone understand. The young nomad stood in front of her table, blocking what light there was. He had seen his cousin carried to another room. That, it seemed, was solicitude enough for the man's person. His honor was a frailer thing.

"You said foul things of my cousin," the boy said.

"They were true," said Sigrid.

"They were not honorable."

"Was he?"

That almost brought the saber out again, but prudence conquered once more. Sigrid found herself almost admiring the child. He was not for her. She was for full Soldiers, and for Cyborgs; women's reproductive potential was more limited than men's, and must be conserved. But he was attractive in his way. Intelligent. Compact, even graceful, in his movements. Well-muscled under the furs. *Pity*, she thought. She might have enjoyed the diversion.

"Sit down," she said.

He was startled enough to obey. And to take the mug when the barmaid brought it, but not to drink what was in it. Sigrid tasted the beer. Not bad. It was hardly true, what people said of Cyborgs: that they could not taste anything. They would eat anything, yes, to keep their bodies functioning. But they preferred quality if they could get it. She drained the mug and signaled for another.

The nomad gulped down his own.

"Do you have a name?" Sigrid asked him.

"Temujin," he answered. He jerked, once the word was out, and made a sign with his fingers. "Take your spell off me!"

"No spell," she said. Except, possibly, pheromones. She had never sat close to a cattle male before when she was fully fertile. He still seemed unaware that she was female: her voice was deep enough to seem sexless. "A very . . . noble name," she said. One of the ancient role-models the Soldiers had taken, back on Old Sauron, the homeworld. Temujin, later called Genghis Khan, Universal Emperor. This one did not look likely to emulate his predecessor.

He flushed. "What is *your* name?" he asked roughly. Defiant as the barmaid was, but rather less afraid. He would have deduced that, if the Soldier had his name, the Soldier would not take his life — an invalid extrapolation from nomad custom.

He evidently did not know Soldiers well.

Sigrid pondered his question. Then she answered it. "Sigurd," she said. Slurring it, possibly. Sigurd, Sigrid: let him hear what he wished to hear.

"Sigurd," he said. There was a fresh mug of beer in front of him. He drank it in a long swallow. "You could have killed my cousin."

"I almost did." She pondered her third mug of beer. It would not intoxicate her. Her body was processing its alcohol, its sugar and what little further nutrition it contained.

"Why didn't you?"

He was a little owl-eyed. Cattle could not drink; she wondered why they tried. "It would have been . . . inconvenient. Mildly."

"In — con — venient." He nodded. "Messy. Blood feuds."

"In a manner of speaking," Sigrid said. A male Cyborg might have killed in any event; like all males, they tended to irrationality.

The barmaid brought meat, bread, stewed acorn squash. There was more than a double portion. Triple, in fact.

"You eat like a starving tamerlane," said Temujin. He was putting away a fair amount himself, for an unaltered human. High metabolism, or nomad thrift. One stuffed oneself when one could, for when one had nothing.

As much as he ate, he drank easily twice that. Sigrid was ready to leave him to it once her stomach was full, but something in his now disjointed babblings brought her up short.

" — foaled on the high steppe, and lived to do it again; and the foals lived too, daughters as hardy as their mother."

"What?"

Her voice was sharp enough to give him pause. He blinked at her. "Mare," he said with elaborate patience. "Foaled on the steppe. No valley. Foaled right up there, where the air was thin enough to make a Sherpa dizzy."

"Nonsense," said Sigrid. "Nothing Terran breeds safely on the heights."

"She does," said Temujin. "The mare. I saw her, days from any valley, with a day-old foal. And not her first, either. Her — herdsmen swore to that."

Sigrid heard the catch in his voice, the flicker of a pause. "Who are these herdsmen?"

His eyes narrowed to vanishing. He was trying, no doubt, to look shrewd. "Herdsmen," he said. "Nomads."

"Mongols? Turks?"

He hesitated again, again for the briefest instant. "No," he said. Truth: his scent lacked the sharpness of a lie. "Not either. Another tribe. 'Way upcountry."

"And they have a mare who foals outside of valleys." Sigrid curled her lip. "Are you sure you saw her? Or was it your cousin? Or your cousin's friend? Or a friend of that friend, who heard the story from a traveller?"

Temujin snapped erect. It was not as dramatic as he might have hoped: he wobbled and nearly fell over. He caught himself and thumped his chest. "I saw it. I, Temujin of the Black Horse clan of the White Horde. With my own eyes I saw it."

"And there was a valley inside of a day's journey, just

deep enough to foal in, but they never told you of that," said Sigrid.

His fist crashed down on the table. The tavern was filling up, but even in that uproar the sound was as sharp as a shot. Sigrid took note of who flinched, who stared and who took care not to notice. None of the latter two was close enough to hear with unaugmented ears.

Temujin did not shout at her, which was interesting. He spat the words through clenched teeth. "There is a valley. Oh, yes. But not close enough for that mare to have foaled in it."

"So? Then it is one of the tribes that pays tribute to the Citadel or the outlying Bases? Or are they beholden to Tallinn, or" — her nostrils thinned — "Eden?"

"None of them. Not one!" He grinned a wolf's grin, all armament and no mirth. "They're a free tribe. They pay tribute to no one. They don't need your valleys — they have their own."

He was much too far gone in beer and kvass to know what he was saying. So far gone that he seemed almost sober.

His grin widened, one would have thought, impossibly. "But do you know what they do need?"

She encouraged him with silence.

"Men."

She raised a brow.

"They have none," he said. "They don't keep their sons, or raise them past babyhood. They're all women. Women who" — he paused to savor the Soldier's incredulity — "fight."

Sigrid had no incredulity to give him. "Women can fight. No matter how their men may deny it."

He was much too sozzled to notice her bitterness. He leaned across the table. The end of one of his braids trailed in gravy. He never noticed. "They'd like you," he said. "They like your kind, if they can get it. Which isn't often. They have to kill it after, you see — after they've got what they need. They foster out the sons to tribes who'll take Sauron get. The daughters they keep, and train for war."

"How do you know this? Have you seen it?"

"I saw a baby who looked like you. Ice and ash. And a

woman who picked up a man and the pony he was on, and dumped them into the fire." He squinted. "Looked like you, too. She did. But they run odd, that kind. 'S not true what Och — Ozh — Ogadai said. Don't cut off a breast to shoot better. Mine had both. Beautiful handfuls. Beautiful, she was."

"Why did you leave her?"

He sniffed loudly. "She left me. Got what she wanted. Skinny little girl-baby. Popped her out, took a look, said 'Thank you, good-bye, be good boy-toy and go back home where you belong.'"

"We have never," said Sigrid, "heard a word of this."

By now he was listing visibly. He squinted at her. " 'Course not. Secret. Swear oaths. Promise — not — " He hiccuped. And choked.

She heaved him up. No one, she noticed, stared. She hauled him out the back, past people who goggled and scurried and fled. In the black, urine-reeking alley, she dropped him. He caught himself against the wall: fortunate for him. Otherwise he might have drowned in his own vomit.

"Tell me," said Sigrid, "where you found this tribe."

He was on his knees, shaking and gagging. Realizing at last, maybe, what he had said, and to whom.

She set a precise toe in his side, and as he doubled, upended him. He fell sprawling. "Tell me where," she said.

It took time. He was defiant. He was strong: he did not scream. But she was stronger. He told her what she wanted to know. Who, and where, and how to come there. There were ways to disorganize a personality, alternating pain and other, subtler types of stimuli; and he was very vulnerable to her pheromones. Almost comically so, compared to a male of her own race.

When he was done, he was no longer drunk and was in no more pain than he should be. He would walk back to his sot of a cousin. He would ride well enough, come waketime. He would have no women for a while, but that would reverse itself. Sigrid was nothing if not thrifty, and he was good stock, for cattle. A male Soldier, she reflected, might well have damaged him permanently. But that was inefficient, and wasteful of resources.

He, of course, knew none of that. His eyes on her were black and burning. "You will die for this," he said.

She regarded him in honest surprise. "Why?"

"My honor —"

A bark of laughter escaped her. It made him jump, and gasp for what it did to his hurts. "There is no honor. Only strength. And I am stronger."

"Not always."

"Always," said Sigrid. "Send us your daughters when they are grown. They'll win much honor in the Citadel."

He spat. He aimed, no doubt, for her face. It went wide.

"I do regret," she said, "that you are not for me."

He surged up. She was ready for him. But not before he had grasped what even a drunken Mongol could not mistake. She laughed — twice in a day: she was growing frivolous. "Yes, I am a woman."

"There are no Sauron women."

"Oh," she said, "but there are." She had him in her arms, almost like a lover. He was not, unfortunately, up to a sharing of his genes. She patted him as if he had been Harad, then lowered him to as clean a patch of pavement as there was in that vile place. "See, I leave you your pride. When you are ready, you may walk. I've harmed nothing that will not heal."

Nothing but his honor. His eyes were smoldering with it. She nodded, a salute of sorts, and left him.

Bloody light from the Cat's Eye glared over the steppe. The wind lashed the high, coarse grasses into waves like the seas of lost Earth. Aisha had heard stories of them, but the only tides she could sense pulsed in her temples. The only salt she tasted came to her lips after she coughed, and she had been coughing too often as she ran, slowed to a trot, then to a walk, one hand pressed cautiously against her aching side.

She ran her tongue over dry lips. The last thing she had drunk was the thin, sour beer they had served in that Soldier-loving tavern in Nûrnen, that slut of a town. And she, even she, with her Sauron blood, was cold now and sleepy enough to scare her. She and Juchi had come far during this day cycle; now it was getting toward Haven's long night. All her life, she had rested in the dark when she could. . . .

And now her father would rest forever. Tears filmed her eyes briefly, then dried. He had died hard, but at the end, he had had her mother's — and his — name on his lips. And she had avenged him. Aisha's own lips snarled. *I could not offer him a proper funeral.* The last duty of a child. *I cannot die before I kill more Saurons!* she screamed to herself. *I must avenge him!*

She knew — and mourned — what became of her father. But what would become of her? She coughed again and spat, a dark glob. Control, she warned herself. Enough blood in her lungs and even she could drown.

Would the tribe take her back? She feared not. Once, the tribe had been "we." Now, it was "they"; and, touched by her father and mother's curse, she was an outsider. She would be lucky if she was not killed on sight. *Haven*, she remembered, once had meant harbor. There was no haven, no harbor for her anywhere, unless she made one for herself.

Tallinn . . . she had counted it home long, long ago: a vanished haven of intricate red rugs and supple leather walls and care. She shut her eyes until red lights went off beneath her lids. So much red — blood from her father's ruined eyes, blood gouting from his mouth as he died, then from the Cyborg's eye, the glare of the Cat's Eye, the pain, like a coal held to her lungs, of ribs grinding against each other. Even the sullen luster of what she had worn into exile: the great ruby that the Judge of the Bandari had sent her by her son's hand.

A thousand times in the past twenty years, she had thought of selling it. Juchi needed medicines; she needed a sharp knife; they both needed better boots and winterwear. Once, she had even approached a Bandari trade caravan and held out the ring. The ruby — for what she and her father must have. Even the greedy, sly Bandari recoiled from it, excusing themselves to whispering with heads together, the occasional glance flicked back at her. They had forgotten her hearing, augmented by her mother's crime.

" . . . *Give* them what they need. It's a mitzvah anyhow."

She had wanted to hurl his charity in his big-beaked face. For her father's sake, she could not. So she accepted the gifts. She'd even managed to thank the man. And she had never told her father that she had traded pride for warmth. His shoulders had shuddered that night when he thought she slept; he had no tears, but she knew he mourned what he feared she'd traded. As she might have done, she realized. She just might.

They had never spoken of it.

Aisha shivered at the memory. Odd: she was no longer cold. Heat spread out from that burning coal at her side. Like the heat of a fire within a yurt after a long day's ride, it was heat that sapped her strength and made her yearn only for sleep.

Her father slept forever. Surely, no one would begrudge her just one little hour of rest in the Cat's light. Even the coarse waving grass of the steppe looked inviting as new-washed fleece. Her knees were loosening, her pace slowing. . . .

If she slept now, she would never rise. She met the Cat's Eye with a feral snarl and forced herself into a jog. The impact of her feet on the hard earth and the stabbing in her chest made her gasp. The cold air, rushing into her open mouth, nearly stopped her breath altogether with its impact.

She coughed, and it felt as if she had swallowed clown-fruit brandy that some fool had set on fire. She spat it out; blood followed — more blood than she had will to stop.

*Father, I avenged you!* She took that comfort, at least, down with her into red-tinged darkness. It was not enough — Saurons still lived — but it was something.

The steppe glowed. Heat-light tendrils drifted from the ground, up through the long grass into the cooling air. Here and there a small life starred the rustling stems with its body warmth, like a wavering, moving fire sliding through silvery dapples. A huge-winged ice-eagle trailed its presence through the wavering currents of the air; those swirled like liquids mixing in a clear glass. Westward the snowpeaks of the Atlas reared against stars — stars and glaciers bright with visible light, drinking heat-light from the mottled slopes below, with billowing cloud shapes flowing up the pass from Nûrnen and Shangri-La. The air carried the scents of human, horse, muskylope, drillbit, rabbit, sheep; a kilometer or so upwind, the acrid half-reptile smell of a tamerlane pride, a big male and three females, cubs. . . .

Barak bar Heber — some called him bar Chaya, his mother being Judge and his father dead before his birth — shook his head and sighed. There were no words for what he saw with IR-sensitive eyes, not in Bandarit or Turkic or Americ or Russki. His mother knew what he meant, some others — orphans from Angband, children from the culling-grounds. But there were no words. . . .

*What would a poet with the right language make of it?* he wondered.

Hooves thudded nearer. He looked back. The caravan was making speed: thirty-two Bandari merchant wains, huge wagons with man-high wheels rimmed in tires of woven drillbit gut, their padded pelts stretched tight over the hoops. Thirty pair of draught-muskylopes pulled each, and a sprawling, brawling mass of men, women and animals surged around them. It was less disorderly than it looked — he and the merchant chief Josepha bat Golda had been in command for a T-year now, all the long way from the Pale — but dangerous, this close to the Citadel. And nearly illegal, under the codes of haBandari and Sauron alike. Goods from the Pale and the continent-spanning Bandari trade routes for the wealth of Nûrnen; thousand-knot rugs for ingots of raw copper, iridescent glass for dried Terran fruits that grew nowhere but in the Shangri-La, Dinneh-trapped pelts and spices from Sna Babra on the western ocean for orthosilk and perfume and platinum.

Most of the return load was good minted silver, something that would draw steppe-rovers like flies to a weeping honeytree all the way back to the Pale. There were also twenty-eight children from the culling-fields of the Citadel and Nûrnen's Saurontown, collected by the Pale's agents. Most precious of all were the reports in his own head, from those agents and the network of spies they ran, a spiderweb reaching into the Citadel itself — human-norm workers, mostly, although not *every* Sauron was as incorruptible as their myths would have it.

The two riders pulling up behind him were quarrelling as they came. Barak grinned; Josepha and the *mediko* Karl bar Edgar fan Haller had been at that since he was a pup. *Oom* Karl — any Bandari of the older generation was an uncle, more or less — had been far too quiet since his wife died last year. It was more than normal mourning. Perhaps because she died while he was away, and of a bad birthing, he blamed himself for not being there.

"Guards all deployed, everything *recht*," Barak said, preempting Josepha's open mouth.

She scowled: a woman of middle years, full-figured — what the People called *zuftig* — streaks of white in her braids along with the jewelry that showed her status as master merchant. Her long caftan-coat was embroidered and her saddle tooled and studded with silver, but the weapons had seen use. Nobody spent half a lifetime carrying prize loot across Haven without fighting hard and often. He valued her experience, but not quite as much as she thought he should.

"You're young yet," she said. "Not even six." Haven reckoning, but there were times he was convinced she'd transposed that to T-years.

"That's why you got me cheap," he pointed out. Karl fan Haller snickered and took up his own conversation:

"You should have got that cart for the milch-goats. They go dry, you're going to have twenty-eight unhappy babies on your hands."

"*I'm not providing a sit-down ride for bliddy nanny goats for six bliddy thousand bliddy kilometers!*" she said. "Don't you tell the mother of six about babies, you —"

They went stone-still as Barak flung up his hand. He whistled sharply, swung the arm around his head, held up three fingers and then made a fist and pumped it twice.

Three of the caravan guards rode up at a sharp canter. "Over there," he said, jerking his head west and north. Directly toward the Citadel; the Bandari had camped thirty klicks out, doing their trading second-hand, mostly. Far enough that everyone could pretend they weren't there. "Not sure. One man, I think, from the sound."

Odd breathing, too liquid. He cocked his head . . . no, the wind covered it, and the direction was wrong for scent. "Let's go."

A stirring in the long grass, moving against the wind. The reddish brightness of heat, in the shape of a man sprawled flat. Iron-copper scent of blood, too much, sound of phlegm rattling in the lungs. One injured traveller, alone on the steppe. The trail was visible for a little way in crushed grass and residual heat, leading straight back to the Shangri-La. *Too hot. Fever.* And a mealy undertone to the scent, less salt than a human norm sweated — like his own. Together with the mere fact of being alone on the steppe, that spelled one thing. *Sauron.* Finishing off a wounded enemy was mercy. Finishing off a Sauron was positively a mitzvah; Barak's teeth skinned back from his lips.

"Cover me," he said. "There, see?"

"Ya." His *rasal* — sergeant — pulled the rifle from its scabbard and dismounted. His horse lay down, and the man dropped behind it, laying the rifle across the saddle and thumbing back the hammer. "Got it."

The other two nocked arrows to their bows. "Let me go see, Barak," one said; a young woman, tall, with blond braids coiled around her head.

"Sannie," Barak said without looking around. "It's bad enough when Josepha tries to mother me."

He heard her grunt, and ignored it. Sannie was a good sort, dogged and skilled; he liked her — perhaps loved, he wasn't sure — but she kept *pushing* at him.

No matter. He reached behind him and pulled the three-meter lance from its tubular scabbard, nudged to put the horse to a canter. One hard thrust, and another enemy of the People would be gone. Hadn't they thrown his mother and his uncle Juchi out to die? Dvora had rescued Chaya like Moses from the bulrushes (he thought of those as some sort of steppe grass), but Yeweh knew what evil had come of Juchi's abandonment, and would come — a good man condemned to horror. The hooves drummed. The long whetted steel of the lancehead dipped.

The Sauron's face showed above the grass, stark white. "*No!*" Barak shouted, hauling the horse aside and throwing himself from the saddle, weapon tossed into the grass. "Cousin Aisha!"

Fevered, delirious. Her flailing blows would have cracked a normal man's bones even now; he held her immobile, ignoring the blood and fluid that sprayed into his face from her wide-stretched mouth. "Hurry," he panted over his shoulder.

Karl fan Haller's hands were steady as he soaked a pad in ether. "Not too much," he muttered. "Hold — "

*Give your cousin this*, Barak remembered, as the thrashing form sank into quiet. The ruby ring he'd carried to her; Juchi standing with the bandage around his ruined eyes, Aisha beside him . . . It rested between her breasts on a thong, now. And she looked a decade older than he, not the same thirty T-years. She looked as if she was dying, and her body was burning up. Not just the higher temperature normal to the supercharged Sauron body, but a killing fever.

"I'll get a horse-litter," Karl fan Haller said; it was three klicks back to the caravan and the infirmary-wagon.

Barak shook his head, standing, cradling Aisha with infinite gentleness. He turned and began to trot with gliding smoothness, as fast as the riders who followed him.

It was not Juchi who was accursed, Aisha moaned, but herself. She lay on soft blankets, but confined in a tiny yurt that reeked of herbs and sickness. Worse yet, it never ceased to sway and jolt as if some giant's hand shook it. And worst of all, Shaitan had sent a thousand djinnis to torment her. She shivered, then sweated in the next instant; and always a raspy-voiced djinni hovered over her with an arsenal of stinks, steams, needles and foul tastes. . . . "Damn fool runs with a shattered rib . . . a wonder she didn't die of a punctured lung . . . or freeze . . ." The muttering trailed away into long words that Aisha was certain were incantations. All in a language she had not spoken since girlhood, and imperfectly then: Bandarit.

It was a ritual the djinni did, and it would call for blood. She knew it, she just knew that in a moment the djinni would stick her with yet another knife, and she had to get away.

"Barak! Come hold this madwoman!" shouted the djinni, and the armed man who had seen her in shameful illness and watched as she fell thrust into the dark, tiny space and held her down while, sure enough, the djinni stuck her with yet another knife, needle, thorn . . . it didn't matter . . . she was slipping out into a warm tide of sleep.

Hard to believe, as she fought out of the riptide, only to sink again, that a djinni tended her with a father's care.

Something remained to be said, before she could drift happily away. "Not . . . not right . . ." she muttered, " . . . shouldn't be here . . ."

"What's that about?" muttered the man who, shamefully, watched her once again.

"She was born in the tribes," the djinni explained. Odd that his voice no longer rasped so harshly on her ears. The tide was so warm, so pleasant. In a little while, she would forget. . . . "And she's delirious, or close to it. So she's returned to the ways she knew as a child. She's unmarried; by all the customs she ever followed, it's highly improper for either of us to be here."

She muttered and tried to nod. "Easy there . . . easy . . ." muttered the djinni. "I'm Karl. I'm a doctor. *Mediko. Hakim.*" He patted her hand as if she were still an innocent who had not forfeited the protection of her tribe. She wanted to cling to that hand; her weakness shamed her.

"Barak! Company coming!" A low urgent voice called, and a series of whistled notes followed.

"Saurons," muttered the doctor. "Steady there, lady. Easy . . . we won't let them get you."

She was too weak to move. They would find her and they would take her. Take her like that thrice-accursed Glorund, who had thought to have her on the ground beside her father's body, and whose own body now moldered in the pit that was too good for it.

"*Shaysse!*" Barak whirled toward the opening of the tiny yurt. "*Oom* Karl, get your supplies together. If they get to you . . ."

"I know the drill," the doctor nodded. "But you won't let them reach me. Give the Saurons hell, will you?"

Barak's teeth flashed in the lamplight. "My pleasure. And, by the way, tell her it's all family, will you?"

Aisha tossed her head, her too-sensitive hearing bringing her the few low-voiced words she needed to know that Barak and his guards were readying what they hoped need only be a show of force. Muffled hammerings and the click of metal told her the caravan would be defended with everything from stakes to grenades. Odd to sense oncoming battle, know herself as one of its causes, yet be protected. It was a luxury she did not think she should indulge in. She tried to lever herself up, but fell back, dizzy.

Another click sounded beside her. Her eyes fluttered open; the healer held a tight-stoppered pot with a long fuse. Near him, but not too near his weapon, was the lamp.

"You . . ." she moaned.

"I won't let them take us. Or my medicines. Now, *sha*, be still. Or I put you out again."

Now Aisha could hear the regular trot . . . trot . . . trot of Saurons patrolling the steppe.

A whistle came from outside.

"Stop right there." Barak's voice, not the caravan master's. Knowing the Saurons' hearing — how not? it was no keener than his own — he didn't even bother raising his voice.

The Saurons stopped. They were not even breathing hard.

"Who commands here?" a voice said in Americ.

"Josepha bat Golda is master merchant; I'm Barak bar Heber. I run the guard corps," Barak's voice replied in the same language, the Eden Valley dialect of it. "Who're you, chief of the Citadel shithouse detail?"

"If this is the shithouse, I've got the detail," the Sauron said. "Halt for inspection."

*Oom* Karl shrugged. "They've got guts even for Saurons, taking on a fully equipped caravan." He pressed an eye to one of the lacing holes in the wagon's canvas tilt, and stared out.

Aisha snarled. She would have liked to wind their guts around a Finnegan's fig tree.

"We're looking for a woman," Chief Assault Leader Sharku said. He and the half-dozen Soldiers behind him carried assault rifles, and ignored the glowering hostility of the caravan crew that so grossly outnumbered them.

"When aren't you?" the guard corps chief — Barak, his name was — retorted.

In his mottled leather armor and horsehair-crested helmet he loomed taller than Sharku, bulked larger. That might have intimidated a plainsman. Sharku ignored it, too. He had his assault rifle, he had the Citadel behind him, and he had utter confidence that without either he could have broken the Bandari in half.

The caravan master, standing fully armed beside Barak, chuckled and leaned on the long steel war-hammer she carried. "Sorry. We don't trade our kinswomen."

"This one's no kin of . . ." Sharku broke off. New pieces fit together in his mind. He'd been used to thinking of the tale of Juchi as nine parts nomad manure to one of truth, till it rose up and kicked the Citadel in the balls. "A woman, not too young, though not as old as this hard-mouthed jade." He gestured dismissively at Josepha, savored her glare.

Barak just stared back at him. If the Bandari was used to intimidating plainsmen, Sharku was used to intimidating cattle generally. Neither had any luck now.

"She's probably injured," Sharku amplified, pushing ahead regardless.

"What makes you think a woman, not too young, injured, could survive alone on the steppe?" Barak asked.

Silence stretched between them. Sharku kept his face impassive, though inside he scowled. But there was no help for the admission, not when legend was becoming sober fact. "She's got Soldier blood," he ground out.

\* \* \*

The healer drew a careful breath. His eyes glittered warning at Aisha as he turned to lay a finger over his lips.

"What's she to you, Saurons?" Barak's voice was full of lordly disdain. "Aside from the obvious."

Aisha bared her teeth. Not fearing them as he probably should, *Oom* Karl laid his hand over her mouth. She would have wagered her hope of Paradise that the Saurons wouldn't admit that a woman had killed their precious Cyborg Battlemaster.

She could almost see the Sauron shrugging. "No matter. Just remember, your kind's not welcome in the valley. We've tacked up Juchi and his worthless accomplice to warn cattle what rebellion costs. All they're good for now. Take my warning now instead of theirs — stay clear." His Americ was flat, uncompromising; Aisha hated him at once.

All that poor man's mutters of Bog and his crisscrossing hadn't spared him a death as painful as her father's; and not even her father's honor and her own spared him this last exposure and her family such shame. Tears ran out of the corners of her eyes, then dried. Allah Himself would mourn; she had failed in a child's obligation to provide her father with a worthy burial.

Well, he would have more Saurons for company, she thought, all but growling. Starting with these. Drawing a deep breath, she tried to tap the reserves of wild strength she had always had.

"Lie *back*! I may be no match for your strength, but if I have to, I'll knock you a good one on the back of the head. Let's see you fight me with a concussion." Delirious Aisha might be; she wasn't stupid. She lay back, waiting and listening for the Sauron's next question. The physician's lips thinned and he checked his weapon.

Sharku sniffed, probing the air with his enhanced sense of smell. He pointed with the muzzle of his assault rifle toward a wagon. "There's a woman in there."

"That's my aunt," Barak told him. Sharku normally had no trouble telling when a man of the cattle was lying; body language and odor gave him away. Now . . . he wasn't sure. The guard captain went on, "She just had a miscarriage. Again. So you wouldn't be interested."

"If she's your aunt, she'd be old for us anyhow," Sharku answered. Now he got a scowl from Barak.

Behind him, one of the Soldiers added, "We get no sport from these Bandari bitches. She'd probably knife us in our beds."

Watching Barak swell with pride, Sharku wanted to kick the stupid clot. Instead of insulting the Bandari, he'd given him face. Too many Soldiers had no notion of how to deal with the lesser folk of Haven.

The same big-mouthed idiot went on to the fellow beside him, "I don't care whether she's fertile or not. I wouldn't mind some fun."

He had, to give him what minimal credit he deserved, spoken quietly. Barak shouldn't have heard him. But the guard captain had; Sharku's eyes narrowed.

"Don't even think about it," the Bandari said, softly enough that an unaugmented man standing beside him wouldn't have caught it, under the sound of wind and the noise of the caravan settling itself for battle.

*Touch of Soldier blood there himself, maybe,* Sharku thought. That was getting disconcertingly common. Why wasn't anything ever simple? Now they wouldn't accomplish thing one without a fight.

He scanned the line of wagons without moving his eyes. Something like twenty men who looked like full-time fighters. Four rifles — the Bandari made excellent flintlock breechloaders. Sixteen or so bows. Another thirty or forty ostlers and traders and whatnot crowding up behind; it was hard to tell with the restless movement of the muskylope teams. They had pikes, hammers, billhooks, axes, crossbows . . . and from the way they sorted themselves out, some experience of drill.

Not good.

Aisha had had no miscarriage, no child. *I never will,* she

thought. It struck her as unutterably sad. But Barak her kinsman was facing Saurons out there. He should not do so alone, she resolved.

Karl's lips moved soundlessly: "Don't even think it."

She chuckled, which plainly puzzled him.

She wondered if her first impression — that he was djinni, not man — had been right after all. In the darkness, his eyes seemed to glow. She imagined her own did too, reflecting in the tiny lamp: lambent and feral, like those of a creature wounded unto death, but with one last battle in her.

"He is of my blood," she whispered back. "But not accursed. I cannot —"

"You cannot interfere. By God, woman, letting the Saurons know we've got you would be the worst thing you could do."

"The Battlemaster will pin our hides to the stake next to the motherfucker's," a Sauron hissed outside, "if we don't bring her or her body back to tack up instead."

Aisha felt a surge of fierce pride. She had *killed* the Battlemaster; this must be a new one.

"We're going to have to search that wagon," Sharku said. He didn't like it; he knew he might have been wrong, and he hadn't come out here to embarrass himself in front of cattle. *Everyone back at the Citadel is running around like a brain-shot land gator*, he thought. Having the Battlemaster found with his throat cut was *not* your everyday occurrence. The First Council was meeting in round-the-clock sessions, for what that was worth.

"You and what *h'gana*?" Barak asked him. "Smart Soldier like you, you should think of better ideas."

"What do you have in mind?" Sharku asked softly. One on one, he knew he could take the Bandari, even if the fellow did have Soldier blood. But if Barak knew that, too, he gave no sign. Whatever else they were, the Bandari weren't weaklings.

And it wasn't going to be one on one. More caravan guards had appeared and quietly surrounded the squad of

Soldiers. Sharku heard rifle hammers snick, bows creak as they were drawn. His men shifted their feet, gritty soil *scrutching* under their boots. The odds had just swung violently. Any Soldier could calculate the chances with three or four weapons aimed at every man in the patrol.

The Soldiers would win . . . but there might not be more than one or two left standing when it was over.

"What do I have in mind?" Barak retorted. "You shagging ass out of here, if you want to see the women you *do* have again. As for us, we're headed back to the Pale for Ruth's Day. And expecting to join up with another caravan pretty soon. So you'd better get moving."

Bluff? Sharku weighed it. He thought his men could beat the guards even if they were outnumbered five to one. He wasn't quite sure, though, not against Bandari — and he was sure he'd take casualties trying. And if he did that and the woman wasn't in the wagon after all . . . he'd be lucky if he got himself posted anywhere as close as Quilland Base. The Soldiers hadn't made themselves masters of so much of Haven by wasting scarce manpower in futile last stands. They didn't tolerate failure in commanders, either.

"Anything else you wanted?" Barak prompted.

*Arrogant bastard,* Sharku thought. "You'd better stay out of Nûrnen, Bandari, or you're liable to end up in pieces on pikes yourself."

"I promise, I won't be back unless I plan on moving in," Barak said.

"That stay could prove unpleasantly permanent."

"Not when I've got you circled."

Almost, Sharku gave the order to attack then, just to prove to the Bandari that he wasn't as smart as he thought he was. But the Chief Assault Leader held back. *A Soldier has discipline,* he reminded himself. Let the cattle posture if they would. He did say, "I look forward to our next meeting."

"I've had enough of your pretty blue eyes to last me a lifetime," Barak said, "but any time you like. Now we're going to get moving — like I said, we have to make it back to the Pale. Open it up, *chaverim,* let's go. As for you, Sauron — " He jerked his chin back toward the Citadel.

Sharku ostentatiously turned his back. He hoped the Bandari would try something, so he got the excuse he needed to turn his men loose on them. But they didn't. He walked away.

The thud of retreating footsteps vibrated in the wood of the wagon. Aisha let out a breath she had forgotten she was holding. Fire licked against her ribs, and she flinched.

*Oom* Karl sighed gustily, too. "Got off easy, for now," he said. "Now, I'm going to make sure you sleep. . . ."

"My father," she muttered. "He was dead, and they defile his body. I must turn back to Nûrnen and avenge him." She began to climb from her blankets.

He had a sharp-pointed glass knife in his hand. Before Aisha could catch his wrist, he scratched her arm.

She raised a hand to punish him for the scratch, but her head swam. The shadows in the tiny wagon closed in and engulfed her.

# ● CHAPTER EIGHT

The *kapetein*'s house in Strang was not particularly magnificent, although it had grown over the years. It was old; the main walls had been built under the Empire of Man, four and a half centuries ago, of adobe stabilized with a plastic that still kept the bricks fresh and crisp after so many savage Haven winters. The foundations had been built on an earlier house, one reared by the first settlers of the Eden Valley — a heretical offshoot sect of the Church of New Harmony, back in the dying days of the CoDominium. Men had lived here, women had borne children here, for almost all the stretch of human exploration beyond Terra.

Boaz, last Prophet of Eden, had been taken prisoner in the bedroom above — by his daughter Ruth, when she freed Strong-in-the-Lord from him, with the aid of Piet van Reenan and his band. From here, Piet had gone forth to kill and die in single combat against the champion of new-founded Angband Base; he had killed a Soldier with his hands, and fought a Cyborg to a standstill, to win a favorable treaty. And now the twenty-first *kapetein* to succeed him lay in a reclining chair, his face pale and lips blue with the disease that would kill him. He would not be the first ruler of the People to die old and in bed, but he would be in a distinct minority. The hands that plucked at the heavy wool blankets trembled, but the fierce black eyes were steady.

The room was long, ten meters by five, with a stove and table; around it sat his advisors and co-rulers. Chaya bat Dvora fan Zvi, the Judge. Barak bar Sandor fan Reenan, *kommandant h'gana*, supreme commander of the armies of the People; sixty T-years, more white than gray in his beard, but tough as a gnarled old root.

And Hammer-of-God Jackson, commander of the *Sayerets*, the Scouts, grizzled and middle-aged, scarred by every weapon used on Haven. First Edenite farmboy to climb that high in many years, tall and lanky, his leg still encased in a cast from his latest mission.

"You don't look well, *aluf*," he said with concern, looking closely at his ruler.

"Dying men usually don't," *Kapetein* Mordekai bar Pretorius said. "The Lord gives, the Lord takes — "

" — blessed be the name of the Lord," all four concluded — Jackson the Christian, Mordekai and Chaya the *Ivriot* and Barak, who sacrificed to the spirits of the Founders.

"I'll last till spring, maybe," Mordekai said. "I doubt I'll see another Ruth's Day." A Haven winter was three T-years long, and it was just beginning to loosen its grip in the Pale, in the season of awesome storms. Cat's Eye was swinging inward on its elliptical orbit.

He looked up to the portrait of Piet van Reenan at the other end of the room; life-size, and tradition held it had been done by his wife Ruth bat Boaz soon after the Bandari came to Eden. A man in his thirties — getting on into middle age for a Frystaater; the high-G adaptation shortened their lives — and built like a brick. Dressed in the khaki uniform and soft body-armor of *Jarnsveldt's Jaegers*, the Imperial special-forces unit recruited on his homeworld, and carrying an assault rifle in his hands. The rifle itself hung on the wall above the picture. Useless now; nobody on Haven, not even the Saurons, could duplicate the stressed-composite synthetics of the structure, or make the stabilized matrix-carbon caseless shells. Much less the computer system that was as much a part of it as the trigger. . . .

That odd combination of teak-colored skin and bright blond hair still showed up in the People occasionally; Piet had had many children, and he was not the only Frystaater in the original band. The eyes . . . Mordekai had seen that picture most days of a long life. The eyes of a man who'd been as kind as he could be, and when necessary, as ruthless as a tamerlane. What were the last words? Ah, yes: "*We are the Kings who die for the People.*"

He must have murmured that aloud: the others were looking at him in concern. "No, not senile yet — and for the good of the People, I have to keep this aching carcass moving a while longer. Hammer. Your report."

The Edenite nodded and opened a thick folder. The crinkling rustle of linen-rag paper sounded as he set it out: page after page of neatly written notes in the blocky Bandarit print, and foldout maps.

"The road," he began, "is proceeding pretty much as planned — slowly." Even after so many years as a professional soldier, his Bandarit carried a slight Americ twang. Mordekai thought it an affectation, to remind everyone of his origins. *As if anyone forgets.* "It's a different world, down there in the Shangri-La . . . and the way there is through Hellmouth — "

Fort Gilead had marked the southern border of the Pale for two hundred years. North was the giant cul-de-sac of high steppe between the Iron Limper mountains and the Afritsberg that ringed the Shangri-La, with Eden Valley on the eastern fringe. South was seven hundred kilometers of escarpment, all the way to the seacoast near where the Xanadu River broke through the mountains and drained the Shangri-La to the ocean.

Hammer-of-God Jackson watched with impassive face as the operation went on in the fort's infirmary. The patient was unconscious — haBandari *medikos* had rediscovered ether three generations ago — and the commander was profoundly grateful. It was slow work, removing a snapper worm. The long thin threadlike body glistened in the lantern light as the surgeon wound it on the spool, gently, millimeter by millimeter, keeping just enough tension on the length that ran down to the exit wound on the patient's abdomen. Too much and it would snap, and all would be to do again. You had to get the head, or the worm would grow back — and eventually spawn. What happened after *that* didn't bear thinking about. It was rare, and like all Haven life, a snapper worm couldn't live indefinitely off Terran tissue, but sometimes there were enough Haven elements in the content of the gut to sustain it. Too little tension, and the worm wouldn't withdraw.

"Still enthusiastic about your trip, *aluf*?" the *Sayeret* officer said, as they walked out to their waiting muskylopes. Snapper worms were rare elsewhere, but swarmed in the wet country farther south. "I can tell you, the Xanadu road isn't like chasing *hotnots* up on the northern border."

Hammer-of-God Jackson turned to look at him; he'd commanded the Scouts for a long time, but the units down here in the south were almost a different outfit altogether. The younger man met the cold pale gaze for a few moments, then looked away. "Boy," Hammer said, "the Lord God of Hosts — through Barak bar Sandor, *kommandant h'gana* — has set me a task; I will not turn my hand from it. Nor will you."

They mounted their beasts and lay along the broad backs; horses were less useful here, not enough Terran grass in the grazing and too many predators. Their way stretched south, past the wind-powered sawmills that creaked and groaned on the hills — most of the Pale's timber came from these fringes — and onto a plain eight-meter stretch of road surfaced in crushed rock.

"Let's go. *Trek*."

"What's he saying?" Hammer-of-God asked, tossing his head slightly. The broad-brimmed hat he wore shed droplets of rain in a minor shower, lost in the drizzle that fell steadily about them.

The savage jabbered again, gesturing; his scrawny form glistened in the dimday light. He was clothed in tight leather — nobody sane left his skin bare in the escarpment wilderness — and the leather was cunningly stained and mottled, with patches of vegetation sewn to it to break up his outlines. The spear in his hand was tipped with a leaf-shaped blade of beautifully worked obsidian, the axe at his belt of the same material, except for the haft. That was a human thighbone. The knife next to it was of steel, Pale-made. The man's stink was all his own, and indescribable.

"He's saying," the Bandari interpreter said, "that we must pay more for his tribe's labor. More spearheads and knives, more cloth and beads and brandy."

"Why?"

Hammer-of-God would have bet these forest-runners would do *anything* for the trade goods the Bandari brought. He looked over to the road-camp; it was built of squared logs, an eerie sight on most of Haven, dry and cold and almost bare of trees, where every scrap of wood was precious. The camp was fortified as well and separated from the native camp by a ditch stuck with sharpened stakes. The sentries who paced about wore Pale armor of metal-edged leather backed with drillbit gut; their cloaks were mottled like the savage's clothing and worn carefully to keep their bowstrings or the priming-pans of their rifles dry. Behind the camp was the latest piece of engineering Sapper's people had made: an iron-chain suspension bridge just wide enough for a light cart, over a steep gully nearly three hundred meters deep. Beyond that the trail switchbacked north up the face of a forested mountain: not a large mountain by Haven standards; the top wasn't even covered in ice, and the air was breathable. Thick, in fact. The ground dropped steadily as it went south, but it was steep, rain-soaked, and consisted of a crumbly volcanic tufa that collapsed regularly.

There was hardly a level spot in the whole hundred thousand square kilometers of wilderness, except for gully-beds that turned into raging whitewater deathtraps every time a cloud came in from the distant sea and hit the rising, cooling ground of the hills. Which, this time of year, was about every second Haven day; the lower you went, the earlier spring came. Hammer-of-God had been born in the Eden Valley, where crops grew only if watered by man; he had spent most of his adult life on the high steppe, an Arctic desert where tribes fought wars over trickles of springs.

*I never thought you could have* too much *water,* he thought with a slight shudder. The smell of it was all around him, musty and dank and chill, colder than a winter storm on the steppe, because you were never *dry.* The branches of the trees clicked together — bulbous, distorted shapes, all native Haven flora but of types he'd never seen before. The horizon was no farther away than the edge of the clearing, utterly alien to the huge spaces and empty landscapes of upland Haven.

Ahead of the work-camp was a stretch that would have to be tunneled. Off in the dimday darkness, something squalled. A cliff lion, by the sound, but hoarser than the mountain breed he was used to. Bolder, as well; in the Pale, they had mostly learned to avoid men. Here, the natives avoided *them*. Likewise the tamerlane prides, the swarming woods-stobor, the giant drillbits that undermined any human construction. Ruddy firelight showed through the window-slits of the blockhouse; the engineers and surveyors and soldiers would be sitting about the flames, trying to dry out, trying to keep their equipment from rotting, treating their fungus infections with alcohol and salves. Full winter was better; at least then all it did was freeze and snow into drifts roof-high. Impossible to work then, of course.

"He says," the interpreter replied to Hammer's half-forgotten question, after a fresh spell of jabbering, "that the tribes to the south are offering the same goods, better and cheaper."

The barbarian chief smiled nastily; his front teeth were filed to points, and they showed yellow and sharp. He rummaged in a bag at his waist and brought out something that glinted. Hammer-of-God took it and turned it over. A glass bottle, blue-green and rather crudely blown. He sniffed at the neck. Something alcoholic, a fruit brandy — clownfruit, he thought.

*From the lowlands.* Traded overland among the sparse barbarian tribes of the escarpment, hand to hand, slowly. The hair on his spine tried to bristle under the sodden leather. Another two hundred kilometers to the sea. To the great delta of the Xanadu River and the Saurons' Khanut Base. *Outpost of Antichrist,* he thought with swelling eagerness. *Like Israel with the Amelekites of old, Lord, we will smite them!* He nearly fell to his knees in thankfulness . . . but no, he must deal with this savage first.

*Preserve me from sinful pride, Lord,* he prayed. *Give me a humble and contrite heart. If we are victorious, to Thee are all praise and glory owed, for nothing is done save by Thy will.*

He forced his mind back to worldly things. The savage

chief's face was almost unreadable, under scars that were ritual and scars made by the stone-headed weapons of his kin, under grease and dirt and weeping sores. But Hammer-of-God had a lifetime's experience with primitives; mind you, this one made a nomad *khan's* council look like a meeting of rabbis, but the principles were the same.

"Ask him," he said sardonically to the interpreter, "how many weapons his tribe's enemies are willing to sell him."

The beady black eyes shifted, and a gabble broke forth — accompanied by breath that stank of rotten meat and bad digestion. There was not enough Terran growth here to provide all the nutrients a human needed, and the natives showed it. That might be one reason they were so few, and all cannibals, too. . . .

"He says we must give him many, many knives and thunder-sticks — that's rifles, *aluf* — and our bows, and help him against his enemies, who are sons of . . . don't know that word . . . and eat their own mothers raw." The interpreter smiled thinly. "Which, *aluf*, is probably true, that last bit."

The road would be turning east here, into the high country. It would not do at all to have the Saurons get wind of it, although from what the Bandari could tell they did little intelligence work among the escarpment tribes — complacency and arrogance, but then that was natural enough, when nobody dared openly challenge you for centuries on end. The Bandari would pay the natives more, a trickle of Pale-made goods would drift down to the seacoast, but not enough to excite suspicion. Softly, gently, when you were stalking Saurons. Either by strategy or in person.

Hammer-of-God settled down to bargain. That was another skill an Edenite who rose high among the Bandari clans must learn perforce.

"Good piece of work, that, the way you beat them down," *Kapetein* Mordekai said. "Yeweh knows, I have enough trouble getting this project paid for out of the 'black' funds. The timber and pelt sales help, but not enough."

"We had him by the throat, *myn kapetein*," Hammer-of-God said, looking up from his papers. "The completed

section of the road ended there. It took us twenty days" —
better than twenty-six hundred mortal hours — "to get
over the surveyor's trails to the edge of the escarpment,
even with native guides. From there, not so bad. Much like
the rest of the Atlas, although the wildlife was like nothing
I've seen, probably because the peaks were lower and it
rains more. The scholars've got some speculations about
it." Selected wisemen from the schools of Ilona'sstaadt had
accompanied him, recording and cataloging. "Then
through the cleft, into the Shangri-La —"

Spit filled Hammer-of-God's mouth at the smell of
roasting lamb ribs. After eating only Haven produce for
too long, the body developed cravings near to madness for
Terran-descended foods.

"How much?" he said.

The vendor's eyes opened wide at the sight of the silver
coin he offered. It was Sauron and stamped with KILL 'EM
ALL AND LET GOD SORT 'EM OUT on the other. Hammer-of-
God had always felt a certain grim amusement at that —
such sound piety from the godless abominations of the
Citadel. He presumed they had souls; they would be very
surprised when God did sort them out — into the flame that
burned forever, into the embrace of the Worm that died not.
After his trip down the Xanadu road, he felt he had a small
sampling of what that would be like. If there was a corner of
Hell that was wet and cold, rather than hot and dry.

The surprise was not for the coin; they circulated all
though the Shangri-La Valley, even here at the western
end. The peasant was shocked that hard currency
should be offered to *him*; Hammer-of-God cursed his
own forgetfulness, but the error was made.

"*These Sons spend money like water*," the man muttered to
himself in Russki; Hammer-of-God could understand it,
for the speech of Tallinn Valley was similar. The man mis-
took him for a visitor from the neighboring people, the
Sons of Liberty.

"Here — here, excellence, take all you wish!" he said
much louder, in Americ.

Again, the dialect was not impossibly different from the one the soldier from the Pale had grown up speaking. With his height and sandy hair he could have been any of that breed, from a dozen different parts of Haven.

The man handed him a woven straw platter of the succulent meat, doused in a red sauce, with a hunk of dark rye bread and some pickled cabbage on the side. A double handful of the carved wooden tokens the locals used for change came with it, each marked with a crossed hammer and sickle.

"The Saurons must oppress these people with Satanic malice," Hammer murmured to the operative beside him as he ate, swiftly and with pleasure.

The terraced fields outside had been fantastically rich by the standards of the Pale, of anywhere but the Shangri-La, with orchards of Terran fruit as well as Finnegan's fig and clownfruit. Potatoes were well along, even this early in the year — the climate in the lowlands was mild, only a hundred meters above sea level at this end of the valley, and blessed with rain from the clouds that came through the Xanadu gap. Great fields of rye and barley and oats, even wheat, were grown without irrigation. There were lush pastures and fat herds; nobody here would have to worry about drought or about taking the beasts to a valley for birthing. This whole vast land — from the Afritsberg heights glacier glinting in the west to the Citadel four thousand kilometers to the east — *was* a single valley.

Yet the village — a substantial town for these parts with a population of a thousand or more — was dirty and straggling, at least in this section. Dusty dirt roads, wells and privies scattered about, low crumbling rammed-earth huts with peeling whitewash. Children, naked or in linen shifts, ran and screamed among chickens and pi-dogs and pigs; women went by about their tasks, dressed in long bleached-tow dresses and colorful headscarves. Men wore baggy breeches, long shirt-tunics belted at the waist, and boots or wooden shoes, and were vastly bearded, vastly dirty and ragged as well. The only well-made buildings were a tavern with a scattering of drunks lying outside it and the small onion-domed church. The town looked as if it had decayed even before it was built; after the bustle of the Pale's urban settlements, it was shocking. So was the smell, not honest farmyard manure but filth bred of apathy.

The operative had been here longer. He laughed sourly. "Oh, the Saurons squeeze them hard enough," he said in a whisper, moving away from the vendor. The man at the little stall did not seem surprised that two men talking in the street took such precautions about being overheard. "But you only have to look up the hill to see why it's like this here."

The heights above the village were crowned with a fort. Its solid earthworks rose five meters high, inside a deep ditch with stone walls above that, muzzles of brass cannon showing through. The gate was an imposing structure of massive timbers — Terran trees grew well here in the eastern foothills of the Afritsberg — with towers on either side. From a high flagpole flapped a proud red banner.

"That's where the governor of this area lives?" Hammer said.

"The chairman of the *kolkhoz*, yes," the operative said, using the local Russki dialect's terms for *overlord* and *feudal estate*. "There's one like that around every manor-house in this country — and it's a *big* country. The whole corner of the valley northwest of Hell's-A'-Comin'."

"Not bad." Hammer-of-God evaluated the fortress with a practiced eye. "Even with explosives, that would take a while to pry open, if it's well supplied."

"Believe me, Chairman Yegor Vladimirovitch keeps every grain of barley in the district locked up in his very own warehouses, as Pharaoh did," the spy-emissary said. He looked up at the thud of hooves. "Speak of the devil. Time for our little charade — just like the *Parim* festival back home."

A party of soldiers was riding into the village straight ahead, with peasants scattering and bowing low before them, each brushing the earth with one hand as he did so. First came a standard-bearer, with the same red flag that flew above the fort, a hammer and sickle in its corner — the standard of the New Soviet Men. Next came another banner, quartered with blazons that must represent the local lord's family. Behind them a hundred or so cavalry.

*Well-equipped*, Hammer-of-God judged. They all had flintlock pistols and sabers and bowl-shaped iron helmets, and wore green-gray wool uniforms. About half had lances, and all either a short carbine or a nomad-style compound bow and quiver. The infantry behind them were similarly dressed and carried flintlocks or crossbows over their shoulders, short machetelike swords at their belts.

*And not badly trained*, he decided. They marched in good order and silently; they looked tough, too. Proud men, arrogant — and a few arrogant women in the ranks of the horse-soldiers, which was very rare among anyone of the peoples that Hammer-of-God knew but the Bandari.

"Halt!" A figure in a steel breastplate beside the standard-bearer threw up a hand — *her* hand, Hammer-of-God saw, as she removed her helmet and long blonde hair fell free around a cold white face.

"You, dogs — what do you do here?" she demanded.

Hammer bowed; the operative took his cap in his hands and answered: "We are honest traders, noble *sudarinia*" — "lady" in Russki — " come to make a few kopeks."

He pointed to their pack-muskylopes, each with a pair of canvas-wrapped wooden crates in a frame across its back.

"Swine!" The woman struck him across the back and shoulders with her riding whip. She would have been quite pretty without the sneer. "Do you *Ami* dogs think we are savages here on the *kolkhoz* of Yegor Vladimirovitch, that traders can come to exploit our poor peasants without leave or permits or payment of tax? Seize them, and their inferior foreign trash too! My father will give them People's Justice!"

The peasants listening recoiled and moaned in horror at the dreaded words, crossing themselves and gabbling prayers.

Hammer-of-God Jackson felt considerably better about his mission after he'd been shown into the fortress. That was partly because of the gallows at the entrance where men hung after being knouted or having their feet crushed in the *butuks*, but mostly because of the clean, well-kept look of the gaily colored and fancifully carved buildings and the sleek, well-dressed, well-fed people amid the swept, cobbled lanes. *Accursed are they who hear not the groans of the poor,* he thought. Once again, God was using him to strike hammer blows upon the sinful. The Saurons with the New Soviet Men, and vice versa.

The infantry marched away to their barracks; the Chairman's daughter stood while servants relieved her of her armor and then followed her straight to a council chamber along with the officers of the cavalry troop. The soldier of the Pale noted that all of those wore red stars on their helmets and on shoulder-flashes. Yegor Vladimirovitch himself awaited; he was a thick-bodied man, bearded to the navel, dressed in a tunic of shimmering green material and trousers of the same; his broad waist was confined with a silver belt, and his boots were tooled with colored figures. As the officers entered the room they ground their heels in the mosaic portrait of a man's face — an ordinary-looking man, with a high forehead and a blood-colored birthmark on it. Then they bowed to two iconlike figures hung on the wall below the crossed banners of the New Soviet Men and Yegor Vladimirovitch. One was balding and wore a short neat beard; the other was clean-shaven with a bushy moustache.

"Good. Sit, eat my bread and salt; we will speak," Yegor said. His little blue eyes were cold and flat above his bushy whiskers, but they lighted at the sight of the long crates being carried into the room. "I hope a true envoy is here, not some *zhid* dog."

The operative — his name was Shmuel bar Pinkas fan Zvi — ground his teeth but kept silent. Hammer-of-God inclined his head and introduced himself.

Yegor did likewise; there were several other New Soviet nobles there plus another group of the same Caucasoid physical type, although sharper-faced on average. These were dressed very differently: broad-brimmed high-crowned hats of felt, or fur caps with tails at the back, checked shirts, leather vests, fringed leggings over their tight blue canvas trousers with polished copper studs. All of them carried multiple pistols and heavy clip-pointed fighting knives, and they spoke Americ with a nasal twang that made it hard for Hammer-of-God to follow.

*Ah*, he thought, *the Sons of Liberty*. Their leader had a flintlock revolver — probably not altogether practical; the Pale's gunsmiths had experimented and found them not worth the trouble.

"Rancher Delgado of Bwena Wista," the man said, jerking a thumb at his chest. He and his countrymen wore sweeping moustaches but clean-shaven chins. "These're my top hands, Smith, Billy-Bob."

Hammer-of-God blinked, groping for translations. According to the briefing, the Sons of Liberty barely had a government; what there was seemed to consist mainly of standing in circles and arguing furiously. Very much like haBandari, except that the People eventually came to conclusions and acted. In an emergency, very quickly indeed.

"I won't make speeches," Hammer-of-God said, speaking slowly in Russki, the common language of the meeting. "I gather you gentlemen are ready to rise against the Saurons."

"*Da!*" Yegor roared, one hand tugging at his beard. "By St. Vladimir and St. Yozef, we can tolerate them no longer! They exploit us with their tribute until we starve —"

Hammer-of-God carefully kept his eyes off Yegor's ample belly. The peasants outside had looked gaunt enough.

" — and every season their tribute rises. They walk among us like overlords. Me, Yegor Vladimirovitch, a Party man who is the son and grandson and great-grandson of Party members, aye, of noble birth for generations uncounted — me they treat as if I were nothing but some filthy *dvornik*, a porter to be kicked aside. They demand more and more women, too. Not just peasant wenches such as any man might tumble for amusement if he can stand the stink, but free women, *nomenklaturniks*, even those of the Chairman class. It is not to be borne!"

He tossed back a glass of vodka and waited for the others to do likewise. Seemingly inured to the ritual, the Sons of Liberty drank. Hammer-of-God let his sit before him; if he tried to match this wild bull muskylope, he'd end the session under the table.

Yegor went on: "And they have taken our *kolkhozes* along the Xanadu River, *and divided them among the peasants in individual holdings.*" He spoke as if the words fouled his mouth. "These the poor peasants must sharecrop for the Sauron exploiters. The ignorant peasants, they have no idea of true ideology — many have run away from their rightful Chairmen to the river lands. We cannot endure it. At whatever risk, we must force them to reduce their demands — to return to the level of my grandfather's time at least. If we show them it is too expensive, they may compromise."

*I doubt it*, Hammer-of-God thought silently. The Citadel did not compromise so easily.

Rancher Delgado had been watching Yegor with a skeptical eye. When the New Soviet Man finished, he thumped the table with his fist: "We don't much care what happens to these slave-driving bastards," he said frankly, ignoring the bristle from the New Soviet nobles at the table, "but we're being squeezed too; gals, money, you name it, they take it. The Saurons, they give the river-town merchants more 'n' more monopolies — it's hurtin' our trade, and we trade a lot."

Shmuel leaned close and whispered in Hammer-of-God's ear: "They've got some manufacturing capacity, too." Since it was in Bandarit, nobody else there could follow.

"And," Delgado went on, "they're taking more of our land — whenever they want more, they just tell us to get off. We're free men, not serfs! We figure, a lot of us, they'll go on takin' more until it's all gone. Their numbers is growin'. Better to fight 'em now, while we have some chance, even if it's slim."

Hammer-of-God narrowed his eyes in respect; the Son chieftain seemed to have a more realistic idea of what was involved than Yegor. Another whisper in his ear: "The New Soviet Men have a much bigger standing army, but the

Sons' militia is fearsome. They've been fighting each other on and off for generations."

That was standard procedure for areas the Saurons didn't govern closely. They approved of the eugenic culling effect of war, and it was good divide-and-conquer tactics as well.

"Let me show you what we have to offer," Hammer-of-God said.

When the crates were opened, even these practiced bargainers could not control the gleam in their eyes, the instinctive crooking of fingers that longed to stroke and hold. Weapons were the best currency almost anywhere on Haven, and these men were all fighting chiefs.

He took up one of the breechloaders, demonstrated the action, passed it to Yegor's daughter. "For the *sudarinia* Vala Yegorova," he said.

"*Horrosho!*" she exclaimed, swinging it up and dry-firing out the window. Flint tinged on steel in a shower of sparks. "Most fine! A thousand meters' range, you say?" She worked the action, peering down the barrel from the breech.

"If you're a good shot," he answered. "Six rounds a minute, and it can be loaded lying down."

More whistles and oaths at that. "So," Yegor said, handling one of the grenades, picking up a pair of binoculars. "Yet the accursed Saurons' assault rifles can fire hundreds of rounds as far."

"You were ready to face them with crossbows and muskets," Hammer-of-God pointed out. "Wouldn't you rather have these?"

Yegor nodded, eyes narrow. *Time to bargain.* "We can't," Hammer-of-God went on, "supply enough of these to equip all your troops — we can't even equip all our *own* troops with them. They're too expensive, not just money but skilled labor and materials. The same for the ammunition. We can supply quite a few, though. Perhaps we can help you set up clandestine manufacturing of more of your own. Certainly the ammunition, that isn't nearly as difficult."

Rancher Delgado stroked a moustache. His eyes were dreamy as he rested them on the rifle. " 'Mout be," he said judiciously. "Better be careful the Saurons don't get wind of it."

Everyone nodded fervently. "This will take time," Hammer-of-God said. "Time, and a great deal of care. Now," he added, "you haven't fought the Saurons very much, have you?"

Reluctant "no's" around the table. "We haBandari" — no point in complicating things unduly by mentioning relations between clan and Edenite — "have fought them often for three hundred T-years and we've never paid one girl to the Saurons in tribute, or one sheep."

They were impressed. That much knowledge of the People had drifted even here; and apart from the secret of the Xanadu road, the only way to reach the Pale from this area was to go all the way east to the Citadel, then around the Atlas mountains back west on the high steppe — half a Haven year's journey, if you were lucky.

"We also hold Tallinn Valley, where Angband Base once stood." By treaty of alliance with the folk there, but that was another complication he need not mention. "If we're to aid you, it's going to be on our terms."

*Kapetein* Mordekai coughed. Chaya went to his side and uncorked a thick glass bottle, poured out a spoonful.

"That stuff tastes like stale muskylope piss," he grunted.

"I'm glad you've got such a wide range of culinary experience, Mordekai," she said, "but take your medicine anyway."

"Gahh." The ruler swallowed water to wash it away and turned to Hammer. "You think these *gayam*'ll go along with it?"

"If the Lord softens their hearts," Hammer-of-God said.

"Or their heads," Barak mused, looking down at the map and tracing lines. "Because whatever we do, the Sauron *mamzrim* will kick their *totchkis* so hard their teeth will march out on review. What sort of force can they muster for a revolt?"

"The New Soviet Men, maybe seventy thousand troops," the Edenite soldier said.

His voice took on something of Yegor Vladimirovitch's bear growl: "*All picked fighters*, nomenklaturnikis *of the warrior class*." Then in his own his own voice: "The Sons of Liberty, more than that — those are militiamen, mostly, but fierce. Their one-minute men — odd name, isn't it? — their first-line militia, are about sixty thousand strong and in the same class as the New Soviet regulars. Better equipped, less disciplined. Say a hundred forty to a hundred eighty thousand effectives altogether, plus the rest of the Sons' militia. The New Soviets' peasant levies as much again in raw numbers, though I've got doubts about their reliability."

Barak whistled silently. "Impressive." The whole Pale held only three quarters of a million people, from the babes in arms to *Kapetein* Mordekai himself. Of the clans of the People, half a million.

"*Aluf*, the population densities down in the Shangri-La *are* impressive. But there are fifty thousand adult Saurons in the valley too. Counting only fighting men in their prime years." He paused. "So far, we've only talked with a few powerful magnates from each people, not the central governments — no secrets once *they* know. The plan is for the conspirators to rise in revolt, which means their peers will have to join them because the retaliation will fall on all of them anyway. Given what our clandestine-ops people estimate of the sentiment against the Saurons there, that'll probably happen. Particularly after a T-year or so more of increased Sauron squeezing and some propaganda by us; they don't know much about the persuasive arts, so they'll be vulnerable. A lot will depend on what arms we can give them."

Mordekai smiled. "Show him, Barak," he said.

Barak grinned like a tamerlane and brought a box of metal parts from under the table. He dumped them out, stirred them around, and began clicking them together, tightening a screw occasionally with a small tool. In less than a minute, a complete firelock for a rifle took shape.

"Just and righteous altogether are the judgments of the Lord — Blessed be His Name!" Hammer-of-God proclaimed. "Interchangeable parts!"

"Amen," Mordekai said. "Still a lot of hand labor involved, fitting and filing to match the jigs — but we've got the measurement problem licked at last. The ancients used light somehow, to measure things. We know that. We can't, Yeweh knows we tried long enough — but the fan Gimbutases finally figured out how to do the same thing with a machine made of screws shaped on watchmaker's equipment. Rifles still won't be *cheap*, but we'll have more. Which means we can send more over the mountains."

Hammer-of-God nodded. "That'll be important. This weapon we're forging down there — it's a one-shot wonder. It'll hurt the enemy, when we use it, but we can only do it once. And if we wait too long, it'll go off of its own accord."

Mordekai nodded. "Still, hurting the Saurons however we can is definitely a mitzvah."

"From your mouth to His ears," Chaya said, and shrugged. "As long as *they* can't hurt *us*. Our shield has always been the year's travel between here and the Citadel. With the new road — and they'll know about it, once our weapons and staff advisors start showing up in a valley rebellion — that'll be cut down considerably. The Saurons could move forces west along the Jordan and Xanadu rivers, and have a strong supply base within a month's journey of Fort Gilead."

Hammer-of-God bowed acknowledgement of the Judge's acumen. Barak snorted. "I don't think we've got much to worry about," he said. "Hammer?"

"*Aluf*, Judge," Hammer-of-God said. "I've been up and down that track. Iskander of the Silver Hand couldn't fight his way up the Escarpment from the Xanadu mouth. Not without ancient weapons, nukes. It's *hell* in there."

"And if they had nukes left — or delivery systems — they would have used them on us already," Mordekai said.

"True, *myn kapetein*," Hammer-of-God said. "And even if they could fight an offensive through that wilderness, they couldn't *get* troops through it, not without a road. If we did a fighting retreat, they'd have to advance right into our guns in fortified positions — and we could destroy the tunnels and bridges as we pulled back. We couldn't have built that road with any opposition, and the Saurons couldn't rebuild it. Although they could have built one if they'd done it secretly, the way we did."

"So," Mordekai said. "With a little luck, the rising will be enough to distract them while we attack Khanut Base, at the mouth of the Xanadu. With our little surprises." They all smiled grimly; Clan Gimbutas, the great smiths and engineers of the People, had been preparing some other nasty shocks for the Pale's enemies. "Khanut's isolated from the valley by a hundred kilometers of mountain canyons; the only link's the old Imperial tunnel system."

A railway ran through it. With immense labor, the Saurons had repaired it and kept the way open; but to build it anew would take technology that no longer existed anywhere — save perhaps Sparta, if the Imperial capital planet had indeed survived the Seccession Wars that destroyed Old Sauron. Nobody knew.

"If we blow that, they'd have to canoe down the rapids to reach Khanut."

A chuckle; those rapids included a hundred-foot plunge, and the sides were sheer most of the way. The People destroyed Sauron or Ancient works whenever they could. What the Bandari used, they knew how to build more of. The Saurons mostly lived off their ancestors' leavings.

Mordekai went on: "We take Khanut Base, *we* control the mouth of the Xanadu and access to the sea — and we can take that whole stretch of coastal lowland. A dozen times bigger than Eden Valley, richer . . . and no way for the god-rotted Sauron *mamzrim* to get at it in force!"

Chaya nodded; her lips thinned to a grim line. "And we *definitely* owe the Saurons all the grief we can deliver," she said. Her slab-and-angle face showed an implacable determination, very Sauron itself. "My husband Heber . . . and all the others over all the years."

"For Piet," Barak said.

Chaya inclined her head. "Exactly . . . and for the Wasting. The People *pay* their debts — to the last jot and tittle." And with a grin as predatory as Barak's: "No profit without risk," she said, quoting an old Bandarit saying.

Mordekai nodded. Then he flipped to the last pages of his copy of the report. "You're pretty short with this last bit," he said. "*It was necessary to demonstrate our abilities to the conspirators.*"

Hammer-of-God looked down into his cup of eggbush tea. "There was a skirmish; I was injured," he growled, thumping his elbow on the cast. "Damned stupid. *Gayamske naktness.*" Barbarian folly.

"The *medikos* won't let me have so much as a glass of brandy," the *kapetein* said. "Pleasures are scant in my life. Humor an old man. Tell me."

It was not something Hammer-of-God had seen before, but it was familiar enough from tales. A Sauron patrol, coming in with its tribute of women. They needed many; fetuses high in Sauron genes miscarried more often than not, and that was bad for the mothers' health. Many women died, and many newborns were culled as insufficiently pure — exposed, or sometimes turned over to subject-communities, these days. These girls were from the Sons' territories, most dressed in tight blue trousers and checked shirts, huddled in a clump of misery. All except the dozen or so the Saurons were amusing themselves with by the fire; those were naked. Occasionally a scream cut through the dull roar of the rapids behind the camp.

*Flaunt your wickedness, agents of Antichrist,* he thought. The taste of anger was cold, colder than the steppe blizzards, colder than his soul had been when his son died. Died in his first engagement, a skirmish against the outposts of Quilland Base, two thousand kilometers northwest of this spot. Died slowly of gangrene. *The mills of God grind slow, but they grind exceeding fine, and your Dark Lord will not save you from His justice.*

The rapids were one reason for picking this spot. Their fog of noise reduced the terrible range of Sauron hearing. For scent, the breeze blew in from the Xanadu River, behind them; you had to be careful about that, with Saurons. Their noses were not as keen as a dog's or a stobor's, but easily equal to that of a horse. To hide the heat their bodies gave off, all of them were dressed in felt cloaks soaked in water. The evaporation kept their heat-signatures more or less to the ambient, on a mild fresh spring day here in the lowlands. The river bank was overgrown with huge copper beeches; the light of the campfire flickered on their undersides. Boats were drawn up along the shoreline, enough to transport the whole party downstream to the railhead, where the train would take them through the mountains and down to Khanut Base.

*No. They shall be delivered; make me your instrument, O Lord.* Twenty of his own *Sayerets*, reconnaissance commandos and scouts. Six of them had scope-sighted rifles. Nearly a hundred of the elite household troops of the New Soviet nobles, the Chairmen: what they called *speznaz*. All of them were equipped with Bandari rifles, and Hammer-of-God had tested their training himself. They were really not bad at all; in every other respect the New Soviet Men had the most misgoverned, corrupt and sheerly incompetent state Hammer-of-God Jackson had ever had the misfortune to visit, but they didn't neglect war. Nobody had moved a muscle while the Saurons came down the tributary and made their camp.

He raised the binoculars. Yes, all of the servants of darkness were occupied on the women, except for two standing guard with their assault rifles cradled in their arms. Purely a formality; was this not the Xanadu River, artery of Sauron dominion in the heart of their power, the Shangri-La?

"Now," he said.

*Crack.* The sniper beside him fired. One of the standing Saurons folded backwards as a spot appeared on his chest; thirty grams of soft lead exploded out of his back, carrying a chunk of his spine and pieces of heart and lung along with it.

As if that had been the signal — and it had — a hundred and twenty rifles crashed. The other Sauron was hit four times before he struck the ground. Even so he was returning fire, and a New Soviet Man fell screaming from a tree that had been his shooting-blind. Hammer-of-God felt his stomach clench. If only one of the Saurons escaped, all was for nothing — but he must prove himself to the suspicious New Soviet nobles, or the plan was wasted effort. He watched as another Sauron leaped up from the woman he was taking and started a dive for his rifle; she grappled him around the ankles. Only for the second it took him to break her neck, but a Pale-made rifle slug clipped the top of his head like an egg while he did it. Muzzle-flashes strobed from the assault rifles. Bandari and New Soviet Men died.

The Sauron commander shouted orders; Hammer-of-God recognized the clipped syllables of the Battle Tongue. Two Saurons leaped up and sprinted for the beach, while the survivors gave cover. That was just long enough for a reload; thirty rounds or so tore up the ground around them, and struck both. They kept moving. Once they were in the water it would be impossible to be sure if they were dead. The sniper beside Hammer-of-God finished his slow reload and raised his weapon, working a screw below the long brass telescope that topped it.

"Mmmm-*hmmm*," he muttered, let out a soft breath, and fired.

The Sauron he had been aiming at ran two more paces and fell facedown. The other fell, rose again, staggered under a half-dozen hits, fell, crawled. More and more hidden riflemen fired at him; at the last, only his fingers moved, clawing the mud as they tried to drag his body along in obedience to the last order.

"Heads up!" a voice called in Bandarit.

Hammer-of-God and the sniper looked around in alarm. A Sauron rocketed up out of the hollow beyond the camp, faster than a horse, dodging and weaving like a dancer. Wounded, naked, covered in blood, but still beautiful and deadly as a cliff lion. The sniper's movements speeded up; he snapped back the hammer of his rifle and fired.

"Missed. *Shaysse!*"

They were his last words; the Sauron was upon them, gray eyes glinting out of a blood-mask, teeth laid bare where a bullet had shattered his jaw. That made the fixed calm of his face more terrible than any berserker's grimace. His first backhand smashed in the side of the sniper's skull. Hammer-of-God twisted and fired his own rifle; he missed, and something *hit* him. There was a whirling impact, and he was half a dozen meters away, smashed up against the roots of a tree, fumbling at his waist for his pistol. He was numb in a way all too familiar which meant that something very bad had happened to his body. Events moved slowly; the double-barreled pistol slid up, like something in a dream. Everything was very slow except the Sauron, and he was moving at normal speed, then looming over Hammer-of-God like the Angel of Death. Bladed hand raised to kill, eyes calm above the ruin of his lower face, where the ripped tongue showed through torn lips and shattered bone. Then his eyes bulged. Bulged and popped, and the rest of the staring face shattered with the bullet that had taken him in the back of the head. His body toppled like a tree across Hammer-of-God's legs and lay twitching like a pithed kermitoid.

*Then* the pain started.

"*Mercy of Christ, get him off!*" the soldier of the Pale shouted — even then, shouted rather than screamed, still in control. Two of the *Sayerets* flung the corpse away. One knelt to slice the mangled leather of Hammer's trouser leg, and swore softly at what he'd revealed.

"Get the *mediko*," he said. Bone fragments stuck out of the leg, above the knee. He pulled a flask from his belt, emptied it over the wound, then applied pressure above it to control the bleeding.

Vala Yegorova walked up, her new Bandari rifle cradled in her arms. She watched with detached sympathy as the *mediko* began his work. "He will lose that leg, at the least," she said.

"Shut up, *gayam*," the woman tending him said. "We're physicians in my clan, not your witch doctors." She clicked her tongue when he refused the ether-soaked pad that would have brought unconsciousness. "No? Here then, *aluf*, bite down on this."

Hammer took the leather strap between his teeth — not for the first time in his career — and locked his fingers on the smooth-barked tree beneath him.

"Ready?" the *mediko* said. "All right, you two — straighten it, but *gently*. Firm, but gentle. *Now*."

Light vanished in gray shot with black and red. When he could see again, he spat out the mouthpiece and panted, "All?"

The New Soviet Woman nodded. "Each one accounted for. We will carry them to a lime kiln and burn them to ash; it is not far. The rifles we will hide with yours."

Hammer nodded, conscious of the sweat rolling down his face in huge greasy drops. He fumbled for the strap again. The *mediko* was spreading out a sheet and swabbing down her hands while her assistant unfolded the leather instrument case.

"Now?" he said to her.

"Yes, now," she replied with the certainty of her trade. "Getting the damaged tissue and dirt out of there is the first priority. For this, I *will* put you under — and you need a saline drip, as well."

"A moment," he said, nodding curtly, and turning back to Shmuel and the *gayam* woman. A cruel respect showed in her face. "Keep secret," he ground out. "Mission priority . . . and Shmuel, *move*."

The *mediko*'s hand clamped a pad of gauze over his face. A whirling, then blackness.

"There's more, isn't there?" Mordekai asked.

Hammer-of-God smiled wryly. "Yes, I could never hide anything from you, could I, *myn kapetein*? This *polkonik* Vala Yegorova took me pretty literally."

Chaya's head came up. "The girls?"

"Lime kiln," he said briefly. *How did I fail You, Lord?* he asked himself yet again. "Nothing Shmuel could do, with only twenty of the People — and my orders, and me unconscious and strapped to a litter."

Mordekai looked at his face, then made a small sign to the others. *Don't push him.*

"Well, that's the nature of savages," he said. "The plan is working, and that was what we ordered you to do." He paused. "The election, that's the next thing on our agenda."

He held up a hand. "Oh, please, no mealy-mouthing. I am dying. We need a good candidate. I've held this office for seven Haven years, it's a record. Barak would make a good successor —"

"*Not if Piet came down from that picture and begged me!*" Barak shouted, suddenly on the edge of his chair.

Mordekai's laugh turned into a cough again, but he waved aside Chaya's offer of more medicine. "It would make me sleep. Barak, I commend your attitude — they had to drag *me* screaming and kicking into this job. Your grandmother among others, Chaya bat Dvora. Of course, *you* wouldn't want it, *nu*?"

"I'm not eligible," she said tightly. "The Law says —

" — a descendant of Piet van Reenan, by either of his wives." The Founder had married twice, to Ruth bat Boaz, first Judge, and Ilona ben Zvi, first *kommandant h'gana*. To unite the peoples . . .

"Dvora bat Lizabet —" Barak began hopefully.

" — was not my mother-in-blood. In spirit, yes. My blood-mother was Badri."

"Not officially," Mordekai said. When Chaya turned on him, shocked, he smiled with bland wickedness; it made his face look like an ancient wrinkled child's. "Chaya, *myn tochter*, there are plenty who have an equally fictitious 'right' through their *fathers*. That's why we *Ivrit* always said the mother made the difference. Maternity is a matter of fact —"

" — paternity is a matter of opinion," she finished for him. "And too many people know the facts of mine, you old scoundrel."

"There's your son, young Barak. Barak bar Heber — and Heber was of the blood, nobody would dispute that."

Chaya fell silent, her lips thinning. "Eh, you don't want him bound to this job like I've been, *nu*?" Mordekai said. "Bound to it like Ruth's cross of iron. You're thinking like a mother. Be Judge instead."

She shook her head. Barak nodded, slowly. "Young Barak's a good choice. Not *too* young. Five and a half, thirty-five T-years. Good officer. Strong like an ox — being *kapetein* drains a man, unless he's a golem like Mordekai here. Strong mind and will, too — something we'll need in these times. It's been quiet these last thirty years; nothing worse than the Aydin War. Now things are moving. Us, the Saurons, the tribes . . . I can feel it in my bones. Now we need a strong leader." He inclined his head to the portrait. "May the Founder's spirit send us one."

The *kapetein* spoke musingly. "Odd . . . I hadn't thought much of it, but the strongest contender for my shoes is part-Sauron." He looked at Barak. "How many of your officers are children we took in after Angband Base fell?"

"Quite a few, now you mention it," Barak said, cup halfway to his lips. "Quite a few."

"And a lot of the others are doing very well, too," Chaya said. "As merchant-apprentices, scholars . . . they're sought after as sons and daughters-in-law. Not like I was. Times change, sometimes for the better, thank Yeweh." A worried frown: "You think it'll cause problems?"

"I don't think so," Barak put in. "It's been . . . what, fifty T-years now we've had teams watching the culling fields? A lot of *them* have done well, too. Raful bar Teger, the one who got that working" — he nodded at the firelock assembled from standardized parts — "he was one. My Chief of Staff, he's another. That's off the top of my head; there aren't any public records."

"Dvora's idea, Yeweh bless her rest," Mordekai said. He seemed to be amused. "And a good one. No, no great problem. Sauron rearing, Sauron training and belief, that's most of what makes a Sauron. Ours are just folk of the People . . . like you, Judge Chaya bat Dvora fan Reenan. With a little something extra, eh?"

For a few minutes Mordekai was silent, his eyelids drooping, until they thought he slept. Then he looked up. "Young Hammer here would be a good *kapetein*."

The Edenite leaped as if jabbed with a drillbit tooth, then grimaced at the pain in his leg. "*No*, by the Lord!" Then he barked laughter; the *kapetein* had always known how to shake him out of himself. "I'm pure Edenite peasant since back before the Founder's time — thank the Lord for His mercy."

"Barak's away," Chaya pointed out. "Josepha's caravan."

"I'll try to hold on until he gets back," Mordekai said, smiling when she flushed. "Chaya, there are nearly fifteen hundred who are eligible. How many would be good at sitting at the head of this table?" He shrugged expressively in the People's manner, palms up. "I should know? But there are exactly six I'd be *happy* to see take it — two are in this room, and a third is your son."

He shrugged again. "What do the *medikos* say about your leg, young Hammer?"

"Half a T-year until I walk again," he said. "I'll limp, but I should be able to ride, aye, get about, do enough of a man's work to earn my bread."

Barak grunted. "You're not so young that I need your trigger finger and your sword arm more than your brain, Hammer," he said.

Hammer shook his head. "I'll work my farm, that's where I'm going." His blue eyes met the dark glare of the general's. "Don't talk duty to me, Barak. I'm sick of killing. Thirty-five years I've been running your errands. I want to put my hands in the dirt again. See my daughters and their children more than once a T-year." He touched his leg. "God sent me to you, to fight the good fight for Christ. Now God is telling me to go home."

Barak's face darkened. "*He who lives by the sword —* " he began, ignoring the white lines around Hammer-of-God's mouth.

" — shall go home and sit by a warm fire," Mordekai said. His voice was soft, but it stilled the *kommandant*'s incipient bull-roar. The old man reached for the silver-headed stick that leaned against his chair and rapped it sharply on the ground. The door opened. "*Aluf* Hammer-of-God needs help to his bedroom," he said.

And then the door closed behind Hammer-of-God's rigid back: "Sixty T-years, and still can't control your temper, Barak?" The general growled wordlessly. "If you ever *do* wear my shoes, you'll have to learn when to bellow . . . and when to wait."

"I want him to wear *my* shoes, when I'm gone," Barak said.

"Possible, if Yeweh wills — or there may be something else waiting for him. Right now he needs time at home, to forgive himself. And that's a stubborn man; hector him and he'll pull the other way, like a willful muskylope breaking your cart."

He sighed. "Yes, yes," he said to their looks of concern. "I'll sleep now." Then, bright-eyed for a moment: "I *hope* I last until young Barak comes home. Some people . . . Fate follows them, things happen around them. You're one, Chaya bat Dvora; your son is another; so are your kinfolk . . . born of your mother and brother. For good or ill, Fate follows you all. That's all I regret, that I won't be here to see it."

beside the bowl.

"Eat," she said. . . . . . . . . . . . . . . . . . . . . . . . . . . . . . . . . . .

. . . . . . . . . . . . . . . . . . . . . . . . . . . . . . . . . . . . . . . . . . . . .
to eat herself full. . . . . . . . . . . . . . . . . . . . . . . . . . . . . . . . . . .

. . . . . . . . . . . . . . . . . . . . . . . . . . . . . . . . . . . . . . . . . . . . .
. . . . . . . . . . . . . . your . . . . . . . he said, and . . . . . . . . . .

You Bandari have the Saurons . . . . . . . . . . . . . . . . . . . . . . . .

. . . . . . . . . . . . . . . . . . . . . . . . . . . . . . . . . . . . . . . . . . . . . . .
shrugged — mostly she said the rest should . . . . . . . . . .

# ● CHAPTER NINE

"I can walk," Aisha said fretfully. She was tired of the
narrow cot of the infirmary wagon, tired of long lurching
days with nothing to see but the swaying strings of herbs
strung to the hoops overhead.

"Not yet," her nephew Barak said firmly. "But you can
come out for supper. Come on, *tanta*, the fresh air will do
you good."

She had been sponge-bathed, dressed in a new robe, and
wrapped in a tanned muskylope hide. Barak lifted her, as
easily as he might a child.

"Too thin," he said, ducking through the opened rear
tilt of the wagon and dropping to the ground. "But we'll
cure that, *nu*?"

The wagons had been drawn up in a circle, as they were
every camp-time. Bandari travel-wains had no wooden
tongue at the front, only a long trek-chain, with the muskylopes yoked on either side. When the big vehicles were
pulled into the wagon-burg, the circular fort, the chains
lashed them together. Outside, the herds were grazing
under mounted guards, barely visible in the last slivers of
dimday light declining into truenight. Inside was a small
town. Leather roofs unrolled like curtains from rests along
the wagon hoops, strung to poles; walls were let down and
lashed into place. The inner doors were kept laced open
for now, and the wagon Barak carried her to was an
Aladdin's cave of rugs and blankets. Fires had been lit
before most of the wagons, and the smell of cooking filled
the air.

"Eat," *Oom* Karl said, tucking her in. He had a
healer's neat hands and eye for detail. With a smile she
did not understand he said again, "Eat, *myn libkin*, eat."

Aisha looked down at the bowl of muskylope stew. "I

think you must be trying to fatten me for the slaughter, djinni," she said, with a scowl that was half a laugh.

Sannie came with a stack of hot thin wheatcakes, made from batter poured on an iron plate. She peeled off half a dozen and dropped them on the boiled-leather plate beside the bowl.

"Eat," she said.

Aisha took the bowl in her left hand, rolled up one of the flatbreads with her right, and scooped up the food. Karl sprinkled some coarse gray salt on it for her. It was so *good* to eat herself full.

"You need more food than ordinary folk," the *mediko* said.

Aisha stiffened slightly. Karl shook his head. "You're not responsible for your ancestry," he said sharply. "And none of it's bad in itself."

She looked at him round-eyed. "But — " she exclaimed. "You Bandari hate the Saurons worse than any others!"

He nodded. "We hate their bloody deeds, *Khatun* Aisha, their tyrannies and murders. Bandari don't — " he paused, shrugged " — mostly don't and the rest shouldn't, hate people for their ancestry alone. Yeweh and the Founders know all the ancestors of the People saw what comes of *that*. You're stronger and faster and you see farther; so does Barak, and Chaya — whom we made our Judge, remember. Where's the evil in that? It's what you *do* with yourself that matters."

Wordlessly, Aisha held out the emptied bowl. He went to the fire to fill it for her again, and brought back a rolled straw sack of *latkke*, powdered-potato pancakes fried in hot muskylope oil. The edges were crisp, the centers rich with onions and cheese.

"It's all so *good*," she said, savoring the rich tastes.

"You expect bad eating in a caravan of spice merchants?" Josepha bat Golda strolled over and squatted down on her heels. "Back among the living, I see."

Aisha nodded. Out among the fires, someone was tuning a fiddle, scraping the bow across the strings. To the west, the last sliver of Cat's Eye sank; two of the sister moons floated ghostly above it, translucent silver crescents. There was just light enough to touch the great peaks of the

Atlas to the south, a last gleam on the savage glaciers that crowned the peaks. Sparks from the fires swirled upward into the night, lost among the frosted arch of stars.

"Spices and condiments," another merchant said from the tilt of his wagon next to theirs. "Fine brandies, candied fruits."

"And glass and mirrors, paper and ink," still another called.

"Fine steel, tooled harness, rich furs — "

Barak returned from a circuit of the camp and sprawled on the cushions.

" *'Have we not Indian carpets, dark as wine?'* " he quoted. Aisha recognized the tone of a bard reciting poetry, if not the lines. Karl did, and took them up:

" *'For we have rose-candy, we have spikenard — '* " Josepha bat Golda caught the rhythm:

" *'Mastic and terebinth and oil and spice — '* " More voices joined them:

" *'And such sweet jams, meticulously jarred,*
*As God's own Prophet eats, in Paradise.'* "

There was laughter, but Barak's strong baritone continued alone:

" *'And we have manuscripts in peacock styles,*
*By Ali of Damascus; we have swords,*
*Engraved with apes and storks and crocodiles,*
*And heavy beaten necklaces, for Lords.*
*Yet we travel not for trafficking alone;*
*By hotter winds our fiery hearts are fanned.*
*For lust of knowing what should not be known,*
*We take the Golden Road to Samarkand.'* "

Barak gestured grandly at the night. Off in the distance a herdsman called, a Bactrian gave its burbling complaint. Farther still something squalled hungrily, and the animals shifted in the darkness.

"That's why I travel with the caravans," he said. "Not for your miser's pay, *Tanta* Josepha. The Pale's a grand place, but it can get confining. *Ama* Chaya will get me to settle down soon enough. What would the People be without their traders? Dull as dust."

"Not to mention poor." Josepha's voice was dry. "Watch

the eloquence, Barak my lad, or you'll talk yourself into the *kapetein's* shoes."

He shuddered theatrically and flicked his fingers in a gesture against ill luck learned from the tribes. The master merchant went on: "That's like saying, what would we be without our ranchers?"

"Hungry," someone replied. "No scholars?"

"Ignorant. No warriors?"

"Dead, very dead."

More laughter. Sannie came by again, slapped down a tray of sweet pastries, and flopped after it to lie with her head in Barak's lap. "You have any *idea* what it's like making those on a camp oven?" she said. "Ai, leave one for me!"

Barak winked around a mouthful of baklava. "I should marry you just for your cooking," he said. She reached back to thump him in the ribs.

"I marry you, I expect you to hire a cook," she said. "I deserve it."

They went off hand in hand; the fiddler was warmed up, and some of the younger folk were dancing. Aisha leaned back in the nest of cushions and let her mind drift. Later she was conscious of strong arms lifting her back to the wagon. And a voice:

*"Sweet to ride forth at evening from the wells,*
*When shadows pass, gigantic, on the sand —*
*And softly through the silence beat the bells,*
*Along the Golden Road to Samarkand."*


"I don't think they're friendly," Barak said. "One hundred twenty . . . three of them." His eyes narrowed; Aisha recognized the particular way they did it. Sauron vision, focused like a telescope or a hawk's eyes.

She did the same, shifting a little in the saddle; it was a long while since she'd had a good horse — Juchi had rarely been able to afford even a muskylope, while they wandered. The riders sprang out to view, across a kilometer. They were all of fighting age, heavily armed, with long twisted strings of black wool hanging from their caps and preceded by a standard of nine dark horsetails.

"Those aren't White Sheep Turks," Josepha said. She was using a brass telescope, and Karl fan Haller had his binoculars out. "Omin Hotal had better look to his sheep and camels."

"And his head," Barak went on grimly. "Those are the *Kara Asva*, the Black Horse Horde. A bad-natured tribe, and this bunch are a war-party on *razziah*, or I'm the Grand Lama Maitreya. From the number of horsetails, there are more of them about. That's an *Aga Bey*'s standard."

"And none of them averse to paddling their paws in our goods, if we give them a chance." The chief merchant spat in the dirt. "Friendlies don't follow you for a day, without trying to parley."

"Trying to make us nervous," Barak said.

"Succeeding," Karl fan Haller replied. Aisha had been a little surprised to see him included among the leaders' deliberations, but among Bandari a *mediko* was highly respected. "They've got us outnumbered. Shall we circle the wagons?"

"Not much else we *can* do, except pay ransom, and I'll see them hung by their testicles first," Josepha said grimly. "Hate to stop. We're low on water, and I've got my doubts about the next well — it's chancy."

"*Nu?*" Barak sat in thought, drumming his fingers on the peak of his saddle. Then he showed his teeth; Aisha had learned a Bandarit term for that expression. It was a *shit-kicking* grin. He pulled his bow from the case at his saddlebow and dismounted.

"*Oive*, Barak, getting delusions of demigodhood, are we?" Josepha said sarcastically. The raiding party had ridden closer when the caravan stopped, but they were still nearly nine hundred meters away.

Barak was silent, still grinning. He selected an arrow from the quiver, a long slim one fletched with ice-eagle feathers and tipped with a narrow chisel-shaped point of polished drillbit tooth. Thoughtfully, he rolled it over his thumbnail to test the straightness, then tossed a pinch of dirt into the air, studied the way the grass tufts blew between him and the *Kara Asva* chieftain. Aisha watched with awe; not even the fabled *bogatyri* of legend could make such a shot. Bandari bows always looked a little odd to her — they had a rigid central section and flat limbs pinned to it, about the thickness of a man's thumb, and the string looped over small bronze wheels at the ends. The arms on Barak's bow were twice the usual thickness, and besides wood and sinew and horn, they were backed with strips of forged *wootz* steel.

He drew, not seeming to aim consciously, the point of the shaft coming up to a forty-five-degree angle. There was no sound but the creak of the bow, the hum of the string. Off in the distance, the Black Horse warriors were pointing and laughing . . . and he loosed.

The arrow disappeared, literally too fast to see. Aisha focused on the chieftain beneath the standard of the horse-tails; he was a broad-shouldered man, his body and legs sheathed in armor of overlapping steel splints laced together. He braced both hands on the front of his saddle and stood in the stirrups to look ahead, expecting to see the arrow quivering in the steppe as a gesture of defiance.

The noise must have warned him. He looked up, and it took him squarely in the face; the point came out below the rear brim of his helmet. The body slid from the saddle and hit the ground with a thump, twitched a few times, and died.

Aisha understood why the *Kara Avsa* tribesmen looked silently down, then slung their chief across his saddle and turned away, heeling their horses into the distance-eating canter of nomads in a hurry. A kill by rifle bullet might have brought a charge on the caravan, would certainly have made the dead chief's kinsmen and *noyok*, sworn vassals, hungry for blood revenge. So would an arrow at normal range. In either case, they would have hung on the caravan's trail like stobor behind a muskylope herd. That shaft slicing down impossibly out of the sky was something human men could not counter; it was something only a hero—or a demon—could do.

"Barak!" one of the caravan guards shouted. They rushed forward to lift him to their shoulders. "*Barak! Barak! Barak!*"

Aisha felt a blush starting from somewhere around the level of her belly. "Bathe?" she said. "In *plain sight*?"

"Yes, it's all true." The healer laughed at her, reading her thoughts once more. She kept her eyes averted from him, looking at Sannie instead — who was not wearing anything either. "We bathe, whether we need to or not. And you could use the sun on that skin of yours. We all could; that's why the nomads get rickets so often, not enough sun on their hides, not to mention ringworm and scabies. So, out with you. Doctor's orders."

She stepped down from the wagon, hugging the rough wool of the blanket about herself, and stalked into the patch of volcanic sand.

"I promise, no one's going to look at you," Karl bar Edgar said kindly. "Anything you've got, we've already seen. And right now, we've seen it in better shape."

He must have seen her bare while she was sick, but he ostentatiously turned his back and walked over to where Barak sat. She flushed like a fool for relief — and aggravation. Thank Allah and the spirits, it was mostly women here, like a *hammam* . . . but the men were not far away, and they wore *nothing*. Gritting her teeth, she let fall the blanket and crouched. It was a warm day for a Haven spring on the high steppe. Most of the others looked comfortable enough. They rubbed themselves down with the pumice-like dust; there was barely enough water for humans and horses, and the last well had been dry. Sheep had died of thirst, and people grew rank if they let the grease stay on their skins too long.

She was still — despite her age — a maiden. That too was a matter for shame, not to do her duty to her family and bear children to carry on the name in honor. But in all her life, the only man before whom she had ever undressed was her father/brother.

Everyone, she noticed, kept weapons close at hand, despite the sentries. The Bandari women sunned themselves and braided one another's hair, gossiping with the brutal frankness she knew from the women's baths in a dozen towns, except that here they called comments over to the men from time to time, amid laughter and giggles from the younger girls.

"Like this," Sannie said, scrubbing at her flanks with the

sand. She was stocky, muscular for a woman, with a little more spare flesh than Aisha had even after six cycles of being urged by everyone around to stuff herself.

"I know how to wash," Aisha snapped. *Do they think I'm a total savage?* she thought resentfully. Anyone who lived on the high steppe knew how to dust-bathe; water was often scarce. Those tribes who washed at all, that is; some just sewed themselves into a new layer of felt clothing as the old one rotted off. Her clan had always been more punctilious than most about the religious obligations — good Muslims washed before prayer — and Badri had taught Juchi and her children something of a Sauron's neatness.

"Here." Sannie returned with her own clothes and a package for Aisha.

"What is it?"

"Clothes. Your old ones were *schmutzig*, filthy. We had to throw them away."

"I cannot . . ."

"If it's the money, count them as a bounty. Didn't you kill the last Battlemaster of the Citadel? Look at it this way, we give value for value. We're in *your* debt."

"No," Aisha snapped.

Sannie sighed, then called over to the men's side: "Ai, Barak!"

Aisha lowered her eyes as her . . . cousin/nephew . . . came to them, but he was already partly dressed, bare feet but trousered legs. The *mediko* stood beside him.

"*Tanta*," Barak said, patience in his tone, "am I not the son of your mother's daughter?"

*Is he going to claim authority over me?* she thought rebelliously. He *was* the eldest male close kin present. . . .

"Yes," she said.

"And isn't it the custom among the tribes of the black tents just as much as the People, that kinfolk aid each other? Among the Bandari, it's the Law."

Aisha opened her mouth, then closed it again. More than half her life she had wandered with Juchi. Sometimes they had found work, for a little while, in places that did not know their name. More often they must starve or take charity from people who shoved food or silver at them and begged them to move on lest their curse bring ill luck to the land. Every mouthful given, in aversion or still worse in pity, had burned her gullet.

*He claims me as kin for all to hear*, she thought. And he said a place was hers by right. She fought down quick tears, and fought down hope too. "I will dress," she said.

"Good."

She unfolded the package; the clothes were clean and well made, but slightly worn with use. They smelled of the dried steppe wildflowers the Bandari put between layers in their clothes-chests. Sannie showed her the unfamiliar ties and buckles.

"What are these?" she asked, holding them up; ribbons, with silver threads woven in them.

"For the braids," Sannie said. "Here, Ilona, help me."

Aisha felt another set of fingers braid back her long black hair, tying it off with the ribbons. Her eyes went hot again, and she mumbled thanks.

"By Allah and the spirits, am I related to *everyone* in the Pale?" Aisha demanded.

She and Karl bar Edgar rode side by side, a little off from the caravan and its dust cloud. He had been explaining the complex network of marriage and adoption that tied her into the clans of the People through Chaya and Barak.

"Not everyone," the healer said, smiling. He did that more often, these last few months, and some of the deep sadness was gone from his eyes. Now you could see the lines beside them came more from laughter than frowns. "Not to me, for example. Nor to Chief Elder Goforward Meeker, if it comes to that. Or Hammer-of-God Jackson."

Even in Juchi's tribe, tied to the Pale by treaty and alliance, that had been a name to frighten children with. She shuddered. "Praise the Merciful, the Lovingkind for that."

Barak rode up. The guards were still full-armed and alert, and the man beside him was sweating under the armor and padding; it was a warm high-summer day, halfway through the Haven season. It would be a bold bandit gang that dared attack a caravan this close to the border of the Pale — but Haven bred plenty of *those*.

"Slandering poor *Oom* Hammer?" he said. "It's all a *mishpocha*, one big family, anyway. . . . We're nearly to the caravanserai," he added, pointing.

Aisha focused on the still-distant building. It was the standard sort of stopping-place on the better-travelled steppe routes, built in the Bandari style. A big square courtyard walled in stone, heaps of cut hay for animals, sleeping cubicles, and a tall water-cistern with a windmill pump. She frowned, then looked off toward the horizon. Yes, that snag of worn-down volcanic hill was familiar. The caravanserai, new-built of unweathered ashlar blocks, was not, and the road beside it was also new. It was wide enough for two wagons, neatly cambered and ditched on either side and covered in pounded crushed rock.

"Isn't this the pasture of — who leads my tribe now —"

"Tarik Shukkur *Khan*," Karl said.

"Tarik the Hunter? Still?" Aisha said, slightly surprised. "He must be ancient." He was a nephew of Dede Korkut. "Why this road, then?"

"It leads to Tallinn Valley and town," Karl said. "We, ah — " he coughed.

Barak came to his rescue: "We have a treaty of protection with them now," he said, "and a garrison to hold the valley mouth — we built a new fort, *not* on Angband's ruins, and a town wall."

Aisha glowered at her kinsman. Juchi had made the tribe great by making them overlords and protectors of Tallinn — and popular overlords, mild and just as well as strong and rightly feared. Tarik was no Juchi for ability, but he was a good man, as she remembered. Now it seemed the Pale had swallowed his inheritance.

Karl bar Edgar looked embarrassed. Barak shrugged in his armor. "After Juchi . . . left . . . the encampments of your tribe were thrown into confusion. . . ."

*Believing the spirits had stolen their luck*, Aisha thought. A demoralized tribe was easy prey for enemies. Guilt stabbed her.

"Then Quilland Base sent an expedition to Angband," Barak said.

"To rebuild it?" Aisha's voice was sharp with surprise. She would have heard of that, surely.

"So we thought. But they left again — and raided the Pale. Tried for the northernmost pass into Eden Valley, though it's high and rough. We sent them back bewailing their dead — if Saurons can mourn — sent them home sorry and sore, at least, and harried them north past the border. Then we stood on the defensive; it was a hard fight. But the Sauron *mamzrim*" — he spat to one side — "had left a cache of weapons in the ruins of Angband. It was," he added grudgingly, "clever."

He used the Bandarit term: *slym*. That could mean intelligence, but carried overtones of sneaky cunning. A man who had *slymgetheid* could outwit you and leave you all unknowing. Josepha bat Golda, for example, was universally acknowledged to be *slym*.

"Every tribe within half a year's travelling time came running." They would, for a chance at Sauron weapons. "But the weapons were booby-trapped. Then the tribes started fighting over them, and in the intervals, plundering the Tallinn Valley and the encampments of your folk. They sent to us for help — they were being destroyed. We call it the Aydin War. Afterwards they were both still weak, so they needed continued aid."

"And Tarik Shukkur *Khan* has a . . . treaty of protection with you now, too?"

"A treaty of perpetual friendship," Karl said gently.

*I'd like to stuff you back into your bottle, djinni,* Aisha thought. *And I would, too, if the cork weren't already stuck.* . . . . A treaty of perpetual friendship that allowed for garrisons and roads from the Pale. She spurred her horse a little ahead and rode alone for the rest of the day.

"A bath!" Karl bar Edgar said with deep feeling. "A bath in *water*. A *hot* bath."

Aisha smiled back at him; he was a difficult man to remain angry with, although she was still a little distant with Barak. The trail had been very dry, the last little while, as Haven summer drew to its peak. They all wore masks of dust, cut through with sweat-runnels in the heat of trueday — although truenight was still chilly; this was the high steppe, after all.

*Burg Kidmi* — Fort Front, the northern anchor of the Pale's defenses — bulked ahead of them, along roads increasingly crowded. It stood on a height, partly built of squared stone and massive earthworks, partly chiseled out of the basalt rock itself, all in the form of a six-pointed star. Symbolic, and highly practical; it had the foursquare solidity Aisha was coming to associate with the works of the People, just as you could tell something of Sauron make by its angular austerity. Along the battlements and bunkers were brass cannon and long swivel-guns, catapults for hurling barrels of gunpowder, conduits for pouring the moat and sloping glacis full of burning coal-oil and musky-lope lard.

It wasn't large, to one who had seen the Citadel, but impressive enough; the small town at its foot swarmed with trade, and so did the larger settlement of merchants' tents. Karl nodded proudly at her glance.

"It's only fallen once," he said. "One hundred and seventy-six T-years ago, to a combined expedition from Angband and Quilland Bases. The last of the defenders blew up the magazine when the Saurons came over the wall. Their losses were so great they pulled back. We rebuilt it stronger than ever."

From the tallest gate-tower flew the flag of the People; a six-pointed white star superimposed on a leaping antelope, flanked by flaming swords.

Karl's eyes narrowed suddenly. "Is that a black ribbon below the flag?"

Aisha focused her eyes. "Yes," she said. "A long pennant."

"Lord have mercy," the healer whispered. Aisha looked a question. "Someone of very high rank is ill; we put up the ribbon to ask for prayers — when the *medikos* say they can't do any more, and it's in God's hands. It's probably the *kapetein*. He's old, he hasn't been well. Christ have mercy."

The enhanced ears of Juchi's daughter caught the

silence that spread through the caravan. Even Josepha bat Golda stopped her conversation with a fellow merchant; and that had been going on for hours, a blow-by-blow description of a barter deal with a Hayq trader — Pale merino wool for coarser carpet makings, via an exchange of promissory notes in Ashkabad. An accomplishment to boast of, getting the better of an Armenian. . . .

"Yeweh spare him," Barak said, riding up. His face was stricken, but behind him Sannie's eyes seemed to glow with hero worship. "Mordekai's been *kapetein* since before I was born — he was elected the year before my grandmother Dvora brought Chaya back to the Pale."

"From your mouth to His ear," Karl said. "And Christ's mercy on him, Barak — but he's an old, old man."

"A great man," Barak said. "The greatest of our *kapeteins* since Piet himself, maybe."

*Juchi should have died like this!* Aisha cried within herself. She tried to force herself to share her kinfolk's grief, but could not. *Old and loved, sons and grandsons at his side, his people mourning him, his name held in honor forever!*

"In a coma since last truenight," Yohan bar Non fan Daugvalipilis said. "The *medikos* say it's in God's hands."

The Bandari officer was a tall man with an ice-eagle's face and eyes paler than ice; his braid was ash-blond. If it were not for his Bandari dress and language and way of moving, Aisha would have instantly judged him Sauron — he had turned toward her when they were brought into the fortress of *Burg Kidmi*, and his nostrils flared to take her scent.

"It's like Cat's Eye disappearing," Barak said, shaking his head. "I can hardly believe it."

"You'd better. I love him like a father myself — but for him my mother would have been cast out on the steppe after Angband, and we'd have starved or worse. Thanks to him, him and Chaya and old Barak, I have a nation and a family and a high rank. But all men die, my friend, and he wouldn't want us standing around grieving when there's work to be done. I've got orders from your namesake — as soon as you get back, on to Strang you go, by relays of fast horses. Things are shifting like permafrost in spring. It's the bad side of having a man like Mordekai for so long; all the other factions have gotten hungry."

"I don't want it," Barak said softly. "I really don't."

"Does that matter?" Yohann dropped below human-norm audibility: "What matters is who wants *you*. A lot do. A lot don't, including those who aren't happy with Mordekai's policies toward us Orphans. Which are Chaya's policies, too."

"No factions based on blood!" Barak said sharply.

Yohann nodded. "Not from this side, surely," he said, speaking normally again. "You see why it's important to get you back, though. Incidentally, *I'm* under orders to stay here and keep an eye on Tarik's people; some of them have been meddling where they shouldn't." A brief smile. "Saves me having to forgive my mother-in-law for Ruth's Day — a small mercy. Her cooking is awful and she spoils my children rotten when we're on speaking terms with her."

Aisha broke in: "I go also. I have an interest in this. My aunt . . . my half-sister . . . Chaya would wish me to be there."

The commander's office was a plain whitewashed cube, high in the keep of Fort Kidmi. Through an open window came the *heep . . . heep . . . heep* of someone drilling troops; across from it was a stove, empty and swept in summer. There were filing cabinets, maps, a stone abacus with fanciful carving; the only decoration on the walls was a charcoal sketch of a smiling round-faced woman with a baby in her arms and two children standing by her. Yohann's eyes on hers were cold and measuring.

Barak broke in. "It's a family matter — *mishpocha*," he said.

The man with the Soldier's face made a purely haBandari shrug. "It was a blank *kitb*," he said; an open-ended requisition order. Good for mounts at any of the road-stations . . . or simply from anyone passing by, in extremity. "Judge Chaya will need her family there. So, I put Aisha bat Badri's name on the *kitb*."

"And mine," Karl bar Edgar said. "Since she's my patient."

"That'll be hard travel," Barak warned. Aisha was of Sauron blood, but for all that she was no expert rider, by nomad or Bandari standards. Barak had blood and skill both, and was a warrior in his prime. Karl was unaugmented human and no longer young.

"You're taking my patient, you're taking me," Karl told him. He glanced at Aisha and smiled crookedly. "Can't get away from your *mediko* that easy, *khatun*."

Yohann bar Non nodded and wrote their names on the order.

"May the *anima* of the Founders ride with you," he said, shaking Barak's hand. "Do what you must. *Am Bandari hai!*"

"The People live," Barak said, echoing the other man's words. "Shalom."

Strang was hushed, but crowded to bursting. The throngs in the streets pressed aside to let them past, murmuring Barak's name. Aisha watched them through a blur of exhaustion; the horses were fresh, changed at the Bashan Pass station, but the humans were reeling. Sannie sat slumped, cracked lips bleeding, and Karl bar Edgar was nearly unconscious. They cantered into the irregular square before the *kapetein*'s house, to find it packed so densely that they had to dismount. Aisha helped Karl down from his horse and supported him for a moment. They went forward slowly, toward the line of soldiers that kept the crowd from the verandah — Edenite infantry with muskets, although they kept them slung and linked arms to thrust back the watchers.

When they were halfway to the steps a figure appeared on the second-story balcony. Aisha's vision snapped close; her sister/aunt Chaya, in Bandari formal clothes, her face drawn. She looked much older than Aisha's last memory of her, but that was vivid — the day when Juchi left Tallinn was not something she would ever forget. Then another man came out; Barak bar Sandor. He seemed much the same, except that his braid and short beard were mostly white now, rather than gray-streaked. More people crowded out, a mullah — they called such a man "rabbi" here, a tall funereal-looking Edenite in black, some younger figures who Aisha supposed must be the *kapetein*'s grandchildren or even great-grandchildren.

Chaya raised her hands. "*Kapetein* Mordekai bar Pretorius fan Reenan has been gathered to his fathers," she said, and bowed her head.

Something between a sigh and a moan swept over the crowd. Aisha felt Karl bar Edgar stagger against her. He knelt, and the crowd rippled as they did likewise. Karl was sobbing; Barak's shoulders moved jerkily too. He reached down and brought up a palmful of dirt, smearing it across his face and cheeks. Then he grabbed the collar of his jacket and ripped it half across with effortless strength.

"The Lord gives, the Lord takes — " Chaya intoned, a catch in her voice.

" — Blessed be the name of the Lord," swept across the square and the city in a voice like a strong wind.

"*Yisgadal v'yiskadash . . .*" Barak said, in a voice thick with tears. Bandari prayers? Aisha knew enough now to recognize *Ivrit*, their holy tongue, but not to understand it.

*The will of Allah*, Aisha thought, touching her face with dirt and tearing her new clothes for courtesy's sake. This Bandari *kha-khan* had died full of years and honor. He would be buried among his fathers. Guilt was more sour than oxbane, envy sharper than the teeth of drillbits. Juchi's body fed maggots on the Saurons' pikes, seven thousand kilometers away.

Most of those she saw were weeping. Most of those who did not, looked lost and frightened. It was natural enough, she supposed. *Kapetein* Mordekai had ruled from their grandfathers' day. Under him the People had grown in numbers and knowledge and wealth; they had pushed back the threat of Angband which had lain over every generation since Piet's day, and made Tallinn theirs. Mordekai had extended their borders, left the Pale second only to the Citadel among the kingdoms of Haven in power, and infinitely happier and more just. She heard the question that ran from one to the next: *Who will be father to the land now?*

Some were without sorrow or fear; Aisha saw well-hidden pleasure in a few. Sannie's gaze fairly blazed with hope; her lover would rule the Pale, and she at his side.

*Juchi, Juchi*, Aisha keened within her soul, as she had not keened aloud when he died. She did not listen as Chaya spoke ritual words: established the period of mourning, explained how the Judge and *kommandant h'gana* would rule together until the election of a new *kapetein*. Her tears flowed now, brief Sauron tears, but it was for her own father and his stolen life, for what might have been. Let the Bandari think she mourned their ruler.

Chaya was concluding: " . . . and when we asked him, his last word was 'Barak.' " The weeping died to a low mutter, and Chaya's son stiffened. So did the grizzled old soldier on the balcony beside her. "Then he died. Barak bar Sandor has said he does not wish his name placed in nomination — but that is a matter for you, the People; it is by your will the *kapetein* rules, not his own. For ten cycles we will mourn; then we will choose. This is the eve of Ruth's Day, when we remind ourselves that strength and law joined love to make us one People. Go; renew the bond."

"There's a saying we have," said Karl bar Edgar. *"May you live in interesting times*. It's a curse." His voice cracked with tiredness, and he staggered occasionally as they were escorted through the crowd. It was breaking up anyway, quieter than usual for Bandari. Even the grim-faced Edenite soldiers around them seemed subdued; a few of them were crying too. The tears looked odd on their expressionless shaven faces.

"The Judge will be down soon," their officer said, once they reached a quieter spot by the side of the house.

"I know the saying," Aisha told Karl. "You stole it from the tribes." She forced herself not to bow her head or wring her hands — she was a suppliant here, but she had her pride — and stood upright. A little pair of worn silver scrolls hung over the door; she wondered what they signified.

The physician muttered under his breath. "This isn't the time I'd . . . you couldn't be coming here at a worse time. The old story about Judge Chaya being part Sauron." He shook his head. "No question about Barak's father, though. Even if Heber did choose to work in Tallinn."

"He's still of *Oom* Piet's line," Sannie pointed out.

Aisha shrugged. For one who was accursed, all times were bad. She was outcast. What was it to her if the Bandari fought over their laws? And what bloodline was as corrupt as hers? *What if Chaya recoils from me?* Her memories of that day in Tallinn might be false, the lies of hope, or Chaya might have changed. *Where shall I go?* Wandering the world seemed natural while she did it. Now she'd had spell of something else, and the prospect of going back sickened her soul.

"Look," said *Oom* Karl. "I'm a healer. If I say it's normal to worry, you shouldn't blame yourself."

"Fine words for *coward*!" Aisha flared at him. "All right, then. I *am* afraid. Now you can despise me for that *and* for my family's curse. Watch the barbarian. Make sure she bathes. Show her how decent folk do it, just in case. And then you can watch how she walks. Watch how she talks. Watch to see if she eats differently, and comment on her manners. And watch out, for the time will come when she does something dreadful that will bring everyone she . . ." her voice wobbled. Furious, she went on, ". . . cares about to ruin. I've spent a lifetime doing that."

"Too long," murmured the physician. To Aisha's astonishment, he patted her hand. She jerked it away as if the touch had been a hot coal. "I meant what I said. You come to us in sad times. But Judge Chaya will do her best for you."

The door opened. Chaya came through, still in her long embroidered coat, but with her graying hair freed from its braids. She went straight to Aisha, holding out her arms. "My niece," she said. "Welcome home."

To her horror, Aisha was shaking. She felt Judge Chaya's shoulders shake too, then steady; and she embraced the older woman, her aunt and sister.

"Let's get her out of here," Chaya muttered. "If she breaks she'll hate herself." The Judge paused as if considering. "Worse than she already does."

Aisha felt herself steered into a building, thrust into a leather-framed chair, and held, always held, by those strong hands. Other footsteps followed; for once Aisha couldn't count them.

"No, Karl, I don't think she needs a sedative. Did she cry

once while you were nursing her back to health? Not even once? Then she has got to cry it all out. *Tell* me about it, little one, little sister."

Little one? The last person who called her that had been her father — when he still had his sight. It was the compassion in Chaya's words and voice that broke her where exile and even the caravan's care of her had not. Aisha tried to break free of the Judge's grip. When she could not escape, she turned her face into the chair's high back and wept, sinking down until she was curled up on its broad seat like an injured child.

This time her tears poured down without drying. That too was a survival reflex; here, in this moist place, her body could afford the release.

"They didn't even bury him," she sobbed. "The Cyborg . . . he broke my father's arm — I heard him scream. He told my father, 'The Breedmaster who threw you out was an idiot.' He *looked* at me, and I had to fight him or he would have . . ." She shuddered, fighting for control, and she drew deep breaths of the valley air. "I killed him, but they have slain my father's honor."

Chaya rocked her as if she were a child. What a luxury, to be weak, to be little. She didn't think she ought to allow it. She didn't think she could stop it.

"I didn't hear this," Chaya remarked over Aisha's tumbled braids. "What have the *mamzrim*, the Sauron bastards, done this time?"

"Ran into a Sauron patrol on our way back from Nûrnen or thereabouts. Apparently" — Barak lowered his voice — "they dug old Juchi up, quartered him, and put him on stakes by the road for everyone to see. She overheard, of course."

Mother and son sat beside her and held her with a strength equal to her own. She wanted to stand, to scream, to strike out and *smash* the Sauron faces, to *kill* —

"Karl, you had reports . . . ?" Chaya prompted.

"I haven't released my patient," Karl announced, and collapsed.

● **CHAPTER TEN**

"It's a mess," Chaya said frankly, over their breakfast.

The house of the Judge was familiar to Aisha, but dimly, as if in an old dream. Juchi had brought her here once or twice on visits, when he was *khan* in Tallinn Town. Dreams: a little dark-haired girl running through rooms with high ceilings, rooms that smelled of wax and polish and herbs; a kind old lady who gave her sweets and smiled. She hadn't been able to say "Dvora" properly, and the Judge had smiled at her accent. Chaya had been a tall, gawky young woman with no time for her.

Barak and Aisha had recovered well enough after ten hours of sleep. Sannie and Karl fan Haller still looked as if they had been riding with the Wild Hunt, but they did justice to the eggs and potato pancakes.

"Mordekai not even buried yet, and the factions are out in force," Chaya continued. "Why the Law says we have to take so long for the election is a mystery to me."

"Because we enjoy arguing and dickering and intriguing so much," Barak said through a mouthful of pancakes. He reached for the loaf and hacked off a slice. "Yeweh, how sick I got of flatbread. And because, *ama*, as you told me back when, in the old days it took cycles and cycles to get the news to all the outback folk and give them time to talk it over."

He sipped eggbush tea with goat's milk. "You haven't said it yet, *ama*," he added. His eyes were blue-green, a darker color than his mother's.

"And I'm not going to," she said with the hint of a snap. "I'm Judge. I'm impartial."

"And fibbing," he said. "You do and you don't. I know why you do, but why don't you? You always told me not to dither about things."

"*You* don't want the job; why shouldn't I feel the same way?"

He grinned; it was a charming expression. Aisha could tell he knew it. Chaya knew he knew and he knew that, too. It was a game they played with each other, as they must have done since he was a small boy. Nostalgia had a taste like wild honeytree sap, she found — sweet, but bitter underneath.

"I do want it, and I don't," he said.

"Who's dithering now, then?"

Sannie blinked eyes still red with the exhaustion of their ride from Fort Kidmi. "Barak will be the greatest *kapetein* since Piet," she declared.

Barak turned the smile on her; even sodden and aching with tiredness, she blossomed into near-prettiness. "Oh, I don't know," he said, teasing.

*No man dislikes seeing worship in a woman's eyes*, Aisha thought sardonically.

"Maybe *ama* here would make the greatest *kapetein* since Mordekai, instead. Then I could have all the fun while she does the work."

"Just like childhood over again, *nu*?" Chaya shook her head. Then, more seriously: "I'm not eligible."

"Barak is," Sannie persisted. "Heber bar Non was of the blood on both sides — from Ilona and Ruth."

Chaya's face stiffened slightly; Aisha thought only she and Barak would have caught it.

"It's early days yet," Barak pointed out. "Sannie, you know what I'd really like? A good, long steam and soak in the Chukur Square baths — I've been dreaming about it since we hit the steppe. If you'll reserve us a place, I'll join you in a bit."

After Sannie left, Chaya reached over and tweaked his braid. "You should marry that girl. Three years together and nobody else for either — it'll be a scandal if you don't. *And* it's unfair; she'll want children."

"That's debatable, with me," Barak said.

"No, it's not. Do you love her, or not?"

"She also wants to be the *kapetein's* wife."

"That's not an answer. She wants to be *your* wife first and foremost. Do you love her?"

"I do and I don't," he said.

Chaya sighed. "A long trip, but you don't look much different," she said.

Barak chuckled and filled his cup again. "Neither do you."

"Liar. I creak; I get up in the night more often. A decade or so either way of your age, you don't seem to change. Don't believe it, son; it doesn't last, any more than youth does."

"How would you know?" Barak asked. "Being young and beautiful forever and all."

"Go!" Chaya slapped him on the shoulder. "If you won't mind your mother, go play with Sannie in the tub, and practice some of the lies you'll be telling your friends in the taverns. Don't think I didn't hear — drawing the bow of Oddheykos, indeed. Go on with you, leave an old woman in peace."

Laughing, they embraced; he dropped a kiss on Aisha's cheek, and nodded to the healer. "What a gossip you could be, if you hadn't taken the *mediko*'s oath, eh, *Oom* Karl?"

Aisha waited until Barak was out of earshot; that took some time, even with the thick door between. "Why doesn't he want children?" she asked. "I heard it in his voice when you spoke about Sannie wanting them."

The others looked at her sharply. "Told you she was no fool," Karl said to Chaya, raising his eyebrows. At her nod, he continued: "Barak was married."

"She died?" Aisha said. Karl shook his head. "He put her aside?"

"She divorced him," the fan Haller said. Aisha stared at him in shock. *Bandari law*, she thought. *Very strange*.

Chaya sighed and stirred her tea. "She was an Orphan — our word for the children we took from Angband. I think at first Barak wanted her because he could embrace her without fear; our strength isn't always a blessing. But he loved her very much, and she him. They had twin daughters — beautiful children. Then the girls caught the summer-milk fever; one died, the other was left blind and lame."

"We don't know what causes it," Karl said, his fists clenching in a physician's frustration. "Someday . . ."

"The next time . . . you know the Sauron mating problem?"

Aisha nodded. Even after three hundred years of selection, Sauron-Sauron matings were risky; the purer the blood, the greater the risk of miscarriage and deformity as the recessives matched. Back on Old Sauron, the Soldier and other high castes had used an extensive technology for reproduction. Here they nursed the few children born to purebloods, outcrossed the males on as many Havener women as possible, then inbred the offspring to reconcentrate the Soldier genes, culling ruthlessly throughout. Horsebreeders used the same technique, and it was working — but very slowly. In the first generation on Haven the Saurons' population had exploded, fed by the forty thousand fertilized ova they brought and implanted in captive women. Once they were thrown back on nature's methods, it had taken all three centuries to get the population back up to the first generation's level.

"Two more pregnancies, both miscarried — the last one nearly killed her."

"I was there," Karl said somberly; his fingers made pellets of bread, odd in a man usually free from nervous habits. "We know so little, compared to the Ancients! I've read the first Allon's notes — Piet's own *mediko*, during the Wasting, they've been translated, the language has changed — and he complains again and again that without the machines he was used to, only his courses in medical history were of any use." He sighed. "All we could tell her was that if she had any more children by Barak, she'd likely die. Then she asked if she could have them by another man, one with no Sauron blood." A shrug. "It's our oath, we had to answer with the truth. Probably yes."

"She wanted children more than she wanted Barak," Chaya said. "It nearly killed him — he even tried to refuse to sign the *get*. It was a scandal. Sannie's the first woman he's taken up with for more than a day or two since. She ran away from home to be with him; I wasn't joking, if he doesn't marry her, it *will* be a scandal, and a bad one. But marriage means children, and he's nervous of childbearing."

"It's always a risk," Karl agreed. Old grief touched his face; Aisha remembered his wife had died in childbed. "I'd better be going — old Itzhak will want my reports on those children we rescued from the god-rotted Saurons in Nûrnen." He hesitated, then turned to Chaya. "Your Honor, may I call on your niece?"

"Why of course, old friend," she said with equal politeness. "If she's agreeable." When he was gone, she laughed. "Still a fan Haller," she said. To Aisha's questioning look: "They're very formal and conservative in that clan."

"I don't understand," Aisha said.

"You don't? Well, niece, you're a conqueror like Juchi — the heart of at least one loyal subject, at least. He was asking permission to court you."

The blush that spread up from her navel was even worse than the one she'd felt when she went to bathe in the dust.

Ruth's Day, Aisha recalled, was supposed to be a day of reconciliation. *This will take more than one day,* Aisha thought.

The funeral came first; out on a high place near the city, on the same ridge to the west that held the Judges' graveyard, but a little separate from it. Piet van Reenan's grave was the highest, an inclined slab of basalt, as if he lay looking out over the land he had won. A later generation had inscribed his last words on it in letters of gold:

*We are the kings who die for the People.*

The twenty-first grave was ready, dug down into the broken tufa of the subsoil. With endless labor, the Bandari had made this a garden, shaded by poplar trees and laced about with hardy flowers. The paths were dark with people, flowing out over the plain and down across the cultivated land to the walls of Strang.

Despite her envy, the bitterness of Juchi's fate, Aisha found herself moved. They really seemed to be mourning him as they might their own fathers.

Suddenly the shrill familiar sound of tribal keening cut through the air, through the chant of the rabbi in his white-and-blue shawl. Startled, she looked up from her thoughts.

More than a few of her own people were here, she realized.

Not just Turkic nomads, from her own tribe—many from her own clan and sept. Men and women both, common herders and nobles. Numbers of them had cut their cheeks, as they would for a great *khan* of their own folk, including Tarik Shukkur *Khan*, who came as one of the pallbearers. That was a great honor, she knew — by Bandari thinking. Blood glistened on Tarik's cheeks. That might be policy, but why would the others do so? She looked again. Nobles and commons alike looked prosperous, the ordinary herders well-fed and their clothes sound; Tarik's coat fairly glowed with embossed gilt felt.

*Perhaps this treaty of friendship is not so bad*, she thought grudgingly. If her tribe were vassals, they were well-treated ones. She waited through the ceremony, with fear and longing.

When their turn came, the chiefs of the tribe approached Chaya. When they saw Juchi's daughter — when they recognized her, under the Bandari clothes — they checked for a moment in astonishment, their narrow slanted eyes going wide. Then they came on once more, bowing with hand to brow, lips, and heart.

"And I present your kinswoman and mine, returned after long journeying, as you may have heard," Chaya said at last, after the ritual courtesies.

She spoke the tribe's language with easy fluency. *Better than I after all these years among outlanders*, Aisha thought. *How strange*. Turkic was the common tongue of the steppes, even among those who had other languages, but the folk who had been Dede Korkut's had their own dialect of it, salted with Russki loanwords from their long association with Tallinn Valley, with the odd Americ phrase picked up from the Saurons of Angband, even a little Bandarit.

"Indeed," Tarik said smoothly, "we have heard. Praise to the Merciful, the Lovingkind, that he guides her steps once more toward home." He was a broad-shouldered man, a notable archer and a great hunter in his youth. The question in his tone was very subtle. "We welcome her who returns in honor, victorious as a *ghazi* over the servants of Shaitan. She would be welcome among us."

*I begin to see why he is still* khan, Aisha thought; she had learned much of ruling, from watching Juchi and listening to him speak. Some of the others showed naked fear, but the *khan*'s face was blandly friendly. His power did not rest on Bandari lancepoints alone.

"My niece will be staying with me, as I am her nearest kin; I am sure she thanks the *khan* for his graciousness." A verbal nudge; Aisha started and nodded. "Until she has a household of her own, perhaps."

That made the nomads' eyes even rounder. *Who would marry the offspring of the Accursed One?* Aisha blushed; so did Karl fan Haller. With the peculiar delicacy of the tribes, they went on to talk of other matters, touching on business.

The nomads listened to the Judge: they *listened*, Aisha marveled, they actually *listened* to a woman who raised her voice and spoke with authority in public. It was one thing among Bandari: such was their custom. It was quite another to see hardened warriors of her own people nodding respectfully as she spoke.

"I'll see you at the ceremony, niece," Chaya said. The opening of Ruth's Day, in an hour or so. She turned briskly and walked away. Karl fan Haller left a little more reluctantly.

Aisha swallowed, fighting the urge to put her hand over her face. Her tribe did not veil — few steppe nomads did, as opposed to Muslim farmers or townsmen — but she felt naked under their stares. Soon only the *khan* was left, and two younger men; she recognized one as Kemal the Archer, a grand-nephew of Dede Korkut and nephew of Tarik. A handsome man, as he had been a comely youth; amber-skinned, and his slanted eyes were an unusual dark green rimmed with darker blue.

"Kemal, my son-in-law and nephew," Tarik said, confirming her memory and adding to it. "Ihsan, his *adana*." A blood-brother and close companion, then; both men were hard-eyed and quiet. Ihsan was missing the little finger of his right hand and a part of the next. They were a few years older than she, Aisha realized suddenly. *When I thought of them at all, it was as gangling youths.* They had not aged in her mind, while she and Juchi wandered the world.

"I hope all goes well for the people of our tents, excellent *khan*," Aisha said awkwardly.

"Well enough now, Aisha *Khatun*," he replied. Several nomads within earshot glanced at each other as they heard the title. "Although for many cycles after you . . . left . . . our *kismet* was greviously bad."

"We were fools and suffered the price of folly," Kemal said flatly. "Excellent *khan*. We pay it still."

Tarik smiled crookedly and ran a hand down his beard. "Civil war," he explained to Aisha. "War between brothers — I and Kaidan, Kemal's father. Though I swear by Allah and the spirits it was no wish of mine."

"Some think it the curse of Juchi," Kemal said, looking at her boldly. "Others that we earned it by casting out him and his children."

"Dagor?" Aisha said suddenly. Her belly, well-filled though it was, chilled. She had known he would never hold their father's power, but she had thought him at least safe among kindred.

"Kaidan sent him for fostering to the Kutrigurs of Jayul's clan," Tarik said gently. Aisha ground her teeth. *Fosterling* was another word for *hostage*. The *khan* went on: "It was one cause among many of the break between Kaidan and me. He also made alliance with the clans of Suleiman and Aydin, who rode like lords among our people and harried our subjects in Tallinn Valley."

"That was unwise," Kemal conceded.

"He felt the Bandari had gathered too much power among us."

"That was *not* unwise," Kemal said; his uncle and father-in-law shrugged.

"*Inshallah*," Tarik said. "Then the Saurons came and left their blighted weapons in the ruins of Angband. The clans of Suleiman and Aydin fell out and fought over them — after sending in our men to trip the boobytraps. So died my youngest brother Scaroglu."

Kemal spat on the pathway and swore with vicious inventiveness, grinding the spittle in with his heel. "The Saurons set us against each other," he said. "Accursed of God, sons of Iblis, they torment us as a boy might throw stones at a kermitoid by the waterhole, for sport."

"As the ancient *kaphar* sage said," Tarik observed dryly, "the boys throw stones in sport, but the kermitoids die in earnest. By the time I called in the Bandari — I and the men of Tallinn, what was left of them — half our people were dead, and many more of our fighting men."

Aisha looked at him, appalled. *Half!* she thought. Blood drained from her face. *Juchi's seed is accursed indeed!* She looked around, half expecting to see the ground tremble and crack beneath her feet.

Now it was Kemal's turn to shrug. "We were caught between the stobor and the tamerlanes. Better to have merciful conquerors than cruel ones."

"We are left our own laws and religion," Tarik observed judiciously. "We govern ourselves by our own custom on our own land."

"Except for our new *relatives*," Kemal said; Ihsan nodded abruptly. Aisha sensed that the discussion was an old one, one of those arguments that chased its own tail, like a stobor pack chasing a muskylope around a hill.

Kemal turned to her. "There were many widows and young maidens without suitors," he said. Aisha nodded — not without a sudden blush: *I have a suitor*. Although the law of Islam said a man could take four wives, few could afford it, especially after a costly war. "For some reason the Bandari seem to have more men than women; Allah and the spirits know, their women seem much like men to me. There were marriages, after the war."

"Should the women die childless, starve, or turn harlot?" Tarik asked.

"No," Kemal spat out. "But they live amongst us still, under Bandari law, not ours." To Aisha he added: "With so many sonless families, they inherited grazing and water rights, you see."

"A woman follows her husband's clan," the *khan* said.

"Well enough, if they follow him far away! Living among us, the husbands teach their daughters shameless habits, and ours visit them — visit their aunts and sisters — and grow envious. Also the commoners grow insolent to their chiefs, seeking to speak in council. And we may not make war or *razziah* without the Pale's permission. That lies hard upon our honor."

"But when war does come, the Pale rides at our side," Tarik said. "We have free use of Tallinn and Eden for our pregnant women and our flocks, and much trade. We grow fat."

"So do cattle," Kemal snapped. Tarik's manner grew less mild; he glared, and after a moment Kemal dropped his eyes.

"You are my heir and father of my grandson," Tarik said. And unspoken: *But I am not dead yet, and heirs may be unmade.* When he was satisfied that dominance had been restored, he commanded, "Escort your kinswoman."

They were dismissed; Kemal turned at once, a bit stiff, but obedient. Aisha found herself following him. They walked down toward Strang.

"It is a long time, Aisha," Kemal said.

She nodded. She did not understand why he seemed so apprehensive of this meeting. Tarik's son-in-law, possibly the next chief, married at least once to sleek women with no hint of a family curse about them. It was she who stood defeated, a beggar at her sister/aunt's ample table.

"You must have many sons," she ventured.

"Three. The eldest is a man himself, with a wife and yurts of his own. And — all dishonored by the dishonor the Sauron sons of pigs put on Juchi. We are kin, all of us, in the tribe. It shames us for one of our own to lie rotting under the Cat's Eye. Under Juchi, we had honor and respect."

*You cast him out!* Anger and a kind of astonished gratitude warred in Aisha and kept her silent.

"And it shames our warriors that a woman slew the Battlemaster of the Citadel — a demon-Cyborg — while we sit on our swords and watch our sheep."

*That I believe*, she thought. With nothing recent but a disgraceful war of brothers, the warriors of the black tents would be itching for something to restore their honor.

"Niece," Chaya said affectionately to Aisha, then turned back to a group of others: "*No* petitions on Ruth's Day. *Oive*, don't I get any time with my family at all?" They moved off, grumbling slightly.

"Hectic," Barak said.

"How should it be?" Chaya said. She did not inquire what had gone on between Aisha and her tribal kinfolk, turning again to her son. "The Edenites are raising Cain again. A lot of the fan Hallers egg them on."

Barak smiled down at her; he was a tall man. "You're the one who always says the Edenites have to be made part of the People," he teased. "The fan Hallers are friendly with them."

"Yes, but" — Chaya lowered her voice, until no one without enhanced ears could have caught what she said — "it's supposed to be *us* influencing *them*. Some of those fan Hallers might as well be farmers themselves." She sighed. "The *plaatsmen* are complaining about being under-represented in the voting again."

Barak shrugged. "They don't let their women vote for their council of Church Elders," he said with the resignation of someone rehashing an old argument, "so that cuts their weight in half in elections for the *kapetein* or Judge. Let 'em enfranchise their women, if they want more say — the clans do." To him it seemed reasonable and fair, and not the least manipulative or coercive.

"I thought they might, or at least some of the more enlightened congregations," Chaya said. "They were talking about it, but . . . Then Kosti bar Agridas fan Gimbutas, you know, Agridas of Eisenstaadt's third son, his family own those smelting furnaces — "

Barak groaned and slapped his forehead; the horse he was leading stuck its nose in his ear. "Don't tell me. A girl, right? *That* one . . . don't know how he manages to walk. Or why his family isn't ruined with paternity settlements." Bandari law was strict on the matter.

"Not just a girl. Daughter of Chief Elder Praisegod Jenkins, promised in marriage to Elder Goforward Meeker."

Barak thought for a moment. "Wait. That old goat could be her father, and he's had *two* wives — "

" — both worn into early graves, yes. I don't *blame* the girl, and it's entirely legal, and Kosti's going to marry her" — Chaya's eyes went grim with an unspoken *he'd better* — "which means she'll be safely in Clan Gimbutas. But the timing is rotten; every Elder in the Valley is raving about seduction and whoredom and whatnot."

"You'd think the younger Edenites would realize," Barak said dryly, "that those bloodsucking old vultures are getting their money *and* their potential brides."

"The Elders have God working for them, or so they claim. And then, old *Kapetein* Mordekai, rest his soul . . . he sure picked his moment. The Elders respected him; they like a man in authority, and one with some white in his beard. Mordekai knew how to talk to them." She shook her head. "I'm glad to see you home, son."

"They're not going to like *me*, much," Barak pointed out. "They'd like *Oom* Barak more. Though I'm popular enough with the clans."

"Yes, and a lot of Tarik's tribe *do* like you," she said. "Barak *bahadur*," she added, using the tribal term for *hero*.

He shrugged off her teasing. "They don't have the vote either."

"No, but they've got a legitimate interest in how the election comes out," Chaya said. "If they — and the Tallinn folk — are to be under our authority, and I don't see any alternative, then they've got to have a say in the decisions. We are not Saurons; we don't rule serfs or slaves."

Aisha broke in. "*Tanta*," she said — it was much more comfortable than thinking of the older woman as her sister — "why are there more men than women among the Bandari? That's part of it, isn't it?"

Karl bar Edgar coughed. Aisha looked up in time to see the Judge transfix the physician with a glance.

Chaya sighed. "Some secrets can't be kept forever. But this must go no further?"

At Aisha's nod, the *mediko* said: "What Dvora did for Chaya . . . since then, we've had spies and soldiers in disguise doing it. All over Haven."

Aisha's feet checked; she almost tripped. "You dare to, after Juchi?" she whispered.

He shook his head vehemently. "That was ignorance — ignorance born of fear of the Saurons. We keep careful records to prevent inbreeding and for genetic compatibility.

There was a woman who worked in the Breedmaster's lab in Angband, she stayed here afterward — married one of my teachers — and she showed us how."

"But," Chaya said.

"But," Karl echoed. "Three boys to every girl from the culling fields. That seems to be a dominant trait, too, so many of the ones we've adopted are having mostly sons; it's fifty years now, thousands of families."

"Speaking of reports, Karl . . ."

" . . . I'd better get in the ones for the children we brought back from Nûrnen," he said, then added shyly: "There's an amateur theatrical at the Forum tomorrow, Aisha. Would you care to join me?"

Aisha stammered, then nodded. Chaya smiled.

"Now, get going before your cousin Clan Chief Hans bar Rhodevik fan Haller thinks we're trying to bribe you. Besides, young Kemal is probably prowling back and forth, dying to interrogate someone. He'd like to renegotiate the treaty, I think, with a new *kapetein* who doesn't have the support Mordekai had. I don't like it when any of the warriors from the tribes get that impatient. People have a way of dying."

"Of conspicuous knife wounds," the *mediko* agreed. "Bad for your patients."

"Apart from the damage to my patients, they cause feuds. And this near Ruth's Day, and with the election . . ."

"Definitely counterproductive." Karl and Chaya grinned at each other, allies for the moment.

Karl nodded, his face thoughtful. "Allies, they call us. Honored brothers. Right. Like Cain and Abel. I can drive that, at least, through my cousins' thick heads."

His hand went out, almost irresolute, and Chaya's grasp on Aisha's shoulder tightened.

"Aisha is *my* kin, remember? I'll take care of her for you."

He was out the door before Aisha could thank him.

"I think," Chaya said deliberately, "he likes you. And he's a fine man. I think we might help you build a very acceptable future. His wife has been dead long enough, and I have worried for him. He's mourned too long."

Aisha jerked away. "I have to go back. I have to avenge my father."

"He — my brother is dead," Chaya said flatly. "I left my husband Heber for others to bury and came back here where I was needed. And that was my life, and that was my honor."

"With a young son . . ."

"Barak wasn't born yet," Chaya said.

"They didn't bury my father. They dug him up! It stinks to heaven, and Allah weeps."

"God," Barak muttered, "don't let Hans fan Haller hear you say that."

"Quiet!" Chaya snapped. "Aisha, you are our blood kin. We'll do what we can. Judge's honor. *My* honor."

All over the Pale, books were being balanced before Ruth's Day. People who had not spoken for a Haven year, clans that had snapped at neighbors or snapped up conveniently straying livestock were talking again, hesitantly. It was not easy — whether you were Bandari or Edenite — to admit error, and no easier to accept forgiveness than to offer it. And a few people would be skimping all year after paying back their debts.

Aisha, dressed in yet another fine new set of clothes, wool and linen this time, followed Judge Chaya and Barak toward the city's meeting place. The streets of Strang were as crowded as Nûrnen, on a smaller scale, and nearly as intimidating to someone who had spent most of her life in the empty lands. She leaped as a cage on wheels rocked by with a tamerlane inside. It was an adult male, longer than a man and about as heavy, with a ruff of scales armoring its face and neck and shoulders, and long teeth that overlapped its jaws. The beast recoiled at her movement, snarling and lowering its head.

"We have some of Judge Ruth's belongings. Would you care to see them?" Chaya asked.

"Watch it," muttered Barak.

"Oh?" Chaya raised a surprisingly elegant brow. "Kemal. He's coming our way."

Aisha braced herself as Judge Chaya greeted him in the language of the tribes and smiled as he flicked fingers at heart, brow, and lips. "*Khatun* . . . Judge, I must speak with you," he began, though he faced Barak.

"We are on our way to show our kinsman Judge Ruth's belongings. Come with us?" asked Chaya. She turned to lead the way.

The hall was new, taller and more airy than the older buildings of Strang; the arched doorways and windows were covered with whimsical carvings in stone, bug-eyed dwarves, clothed rabbits, an armored man carrying a huge clock. Folk stood aside respectfully as Chaya and her party came to the door, with murmurs of "shalom" and "*laila tov.*"

The Judge's hands worked deftly, unfastening a lock. "I say," she began, "that this is Ruth's Day when debts are acknowledged, quarrels are resolved, and all books are balanced. I honor you as a good guest."

She switched into the language of the tribes, in which the name *Juchi* meant *guest.*

"The man you speak of was cast out by his tribe, but acknowledged by his blood kin, who stand here. We shall not let him suffer dishonor, nor share in it. But you must decide, guest of the Pale. Is it to your honor to join in avenging a man whom all believe to be accursed?"

Blood rose to Kemal's face. "The Saurons shame us," he said.

"Only if we let them. My kinswoman killed a Cyborg; do you think she will let her father's disgrace live?"

The nomad's eyes widened. He nodded to the Judge, then bowed to Aisha as if she were still a princess in the yurts, and strode off.

Smiling thinly, the Judge led the way into the meeting hall. The noises of the crowd died, and they stood alone in a huge room. Aisha stared about her, fascinated, for the hall had windows — not just skins stretched across openings cut into the walls, but windows wrought of precious, colored glass. All her life, she had heard stories of the wealth of the Bandari; she had eaten their food, worn their clothes, and profited from their medicines. But the luxury of those windows, with their stars and stags, their hammers, their swords, and all the other sigils of the Pale, startled her.

A table had been set up and covered with an embroidered cloth. On it rested treasure that none of the Bandari would covet, fond as they were of riches. Its value lay only in that once it had belonged to Ruth bat Boaz: the innocent vanity of frayed ribbons in pale colors, perhaps given her by Piet van Reenan; a book, encased in some shiny stuff, with letters that Aisha could not read and a picture of a frail, blonde girl in a blue robe on its cover; some simple first-aid supplies; the gleaming, well-kept menace of a handgun that had not fired in three hundred T-years.

Beside the relics of the first Judge lay a heavy chain from which hung a large enameled medallion — a springbok superimposed on a six-pointed white star and framed by flaming swords on a field of blue. It would go to the next *kapetein*, Aisha thought. Chaya had told her that while the office was vacant the Judge ruled and kept the insignia of office, signifying that Power was the servant of Law. Barak avoided even looking at it. So did his elder namesake, when he clumped in through the door with a horseman's rolling stride.

" 'Duty is heavier than a mountain,' " he quoted: one of the Founder's sayings. " 'So a man should have a strong back before he takes up leadership.' "

Chaya nodded. "But Piet did it," she said, and turned to Aisha: "Her father hung her on a cross for defying him when Ruth was the age you were, Aisha, when you led your father into exile. Do you understand what I am saying? If she could recover from her own father's attempt to kill her, and rise to be Judge over the Pale and the mother of healthy children, you too . . ."

*I see you nod,* tanta, *sister, when the djinni you call Karl bar Edgar comes to my side. What future do you plan for me? Sufferance in a clan that does not want me?* "There goes our kinsman and his barbarian woman?" *Watched, corrected and not reminded of everyone's generosity and patience more than thrice a day? Sooner would I flee to the steppe and make my way alone to Nûrnen.*

She turned to Chaya, and the reproaches died on her lips. The Judge wore Badri's face, and her mother — *their* mother — had always wanted the best for her daughter. That evil, not good, had come of Badri's care was not her fault. Light glinted off the book in which another woman cursed by her blood kin had found delight. Ruth bat Boaz's father was not her fault. Her care, perhaps, and a sorrow that would abide unto death: but she bore no blame.

"On Ruth's Day, we forgive," Chaya murmured. "It is no bad thing to start by forgiving yourself."

They sat in the Judge's bench, near the front. The silence of the great room gave way to a low murmur as the crowd filed in.

Tears welled in Aisha's eyes. *How had Chaya known?* Again, Aisha did not begrudge them. Nor was she the only one, in the crowd of clansfolk who pressed into that room and sat on the narrow benches, to weep that day. She pressed her hands over her eyes as old Barak, who still commanded the armies of the Pale, spoke of the *kapetein*, who had been friend and brother to him. When young Barak laid an arm across her shoulders, she did not jerk away from its comfort.

She blinked away sorrow and glanced around. Quick reassurance glinted at her from Karl's eyes. How different he was from his stolid kin! Sitting well behind him was *meid* Sannie, who glared at Aisha as if resenting her place near Barak.

The Bandari kept good order during the Memorial, if good order included the whispers of children, the footsteps of elders whose bladders would not let them sit still for the long speeches, the hasty, apologetic *pad, pad, pad* of mothers removing children who whimpered at the breast. The adults were quiet during the speeches; Aisha, schooled to the watchfulness of an untold number of camps in which she was the only guard, shivered with the tension in the air.

A General Council had been called. Members of *kumpanies* — Bandarit for clans — and Church Elders not already present were travelling from outlying areas. The election of a new *kapetein* was too important to be left to proxies; and this vote, Aisha knew, was trouble.

*Who will wear the chain of office?* the tension seemed to demand. One by one it focused on the leaders who sat near Aisha, at the front of the hall. *You are too frail*, it told some, such as the dead *kapetein*'s brother. *You? Unlikely*, to another. *It won't be you*, to the sour-faced Haller chief who sat, master of his kin, glaring at clans he could not master. *It might be you*. As if aware of the scrutiny, Barak shivered.

"What an election!" he said. "The two leading candidates running *against* themselves, and the third watching everyone else running *away* from him."

"Oh, Hans bar Rhodevik?" Sannie said dismissively. "He hasn't a prayer. Why, they might as well elect Praisegod Jenkins and have done with it."

"Praisegod controls a quarter of the vote," Chaya pointed out. "In a three-way race, don't discount it, Sannie." She sighed. "Maybe we should have elections more frequently, for practice — we seem to have lost the knack."

Sannie watched Barak intently, as if trying to make out which part of him was Sauron and which, Bandari. She would be a difficult kinswoman, Aisha thought.

Byers' Star was westering when the service ended. A cold wind drove the clouds from the pale sky. Then the sun seemed to brighten; warmth even seemed to come from the baleful Cat's Eye: Ruth's Day came at the time of year when there was no darkness; after the first harvest of the year, before the labor of planting the next.

Barak groaned and stretched. "I can't sit for that long," he complained. "And with all those eyes on me."

"They'll be watching you at the feast, too," Chaya warned.

"I'll be too hungry to mind. Let's go!" He laughed and flung one arm about his mother, the other about Aisha, making a great show of hurrying his womenfolk along.

For all Barak's hurry, they were not the first to the feast. What seemed like hundreds of hungry Bandari and Edenites clustered about trestle tables where roast lambs lay, surrounded by kebabs, stews, roasts and more usual fare such as cheeses, flat breads and salads. On another table, guarded by women and under heavy assault by the children of every clan, rested sweets: baklava and other pastries, dried fruits and decorated eggs. Other tables were set up in the streets and squares for groups of friends and family. Distant kin circulated, babies were admired, gossip exchanged.

Already, a few red-faced men — Edenite farmers from the look of them — leaned against yet another table on which rested a veritable army of bottles — *vadaka*, whisky, mead, ice-wine and the treacherous liqueurs Aisha had never seen, much less sipped. Behind it stood barrels of ale.

Tarik and his nobles made their appearance, treated with careful courtesy. Nobody used the word *hotnot* in their presence, although some seemed to be thinking it. Kemal and his followers stayed longer, drank and ate and belched politely — and very few of them were overly scrupulous about the Koranic injunction against alcohol — but their eyes never ceased the watchful flick . . . flick . . . flick of a beast wondering whether to challenge the pack leader. One of the nomads began to sway back and forth where he sat. Kemal snapped out an order, and one of his fellows led him away.

"Nipping at the whisky, I bet," muttered Barak. "I hope he's a quiet drunk. What about you, Aisha?"

*I don't drink much. I don't eat much. Usually haven't had the chance.* The feast would be ordeal, not celebration, for her. *Watch the barbarian eat. See her do it all wrong.*

"You'd drink kvass, wouldn't you?" Barak asked her.

"I prefer ale."

"We can do that. Mother, your usual?" He disappeared into the crowd.

"I take it you don't eat pork." Chaya led Aisha toward the tables. Without seeming to guide or observe her, she helped her fill a plate with more food than she had seen at once since she was a child. Barak returned with the ale. The talk and the food relaxed Aisha, and she found herself laughing, even when *Oom* Karl wandered by and offered, with a grin, to pay his admission to their table with a round of drinks. Not bothering to pull up a chair, he leaned an arm over hers as if he had a perfect right.

Chaya caught her eye and winked. Kemal, passing by with Josepha bat Golda and some other merchants, nodded gravely at the way her new clan seemed to accept her. Her relief at his approval didn't even annoy her as she thought it should. And when *meid* Sannie glared, she was able to smile and beckon her over. If Barak were to become *kapetein*, he would need a wife, and Sannie was smart and strong.

Sannie scowled. *Ya Allah! Does she think my cousin would even* look *at me? There's been enough of that in this family!* And turned her back.

Barak chuckled. "She gets like that. She'll be back."

Two men wearing the sigil of Gimbutas came up, one holding an extra beer, which he handed Sannie.

"She's probably trying to make Barak jealous. Hasn't worked," Karl said. "He's going to marry her — he just isn't ready to settle down yet. It's all a matter of time, time to heal. You'll see."

Two of Sannie's cousins came up beside her and wrapped arms about her, shouting that another caravan had just come in, and Sannie must come see.

Two caravan guards, a very young man and woman, strode toward Aisha's table, arms linked. The man had a long rope of blond hair, conspicuous against his dark skin and green eyes; Frystaat looks. The woman's blue eyes flashed, and her personality, though she was little more than a girl, blazed more fiercely than anyone's but Judge Chaya's. Following her, almost trotting to keep up, was a younger girl enough like her to be her sister.

"*Cousin!*" the elder girl said, and then at Aisha's inquiring look, "No, really — I'm Shulamit bat Miriam fan Gimbutas — Miriam bat Lizbet, Judge Dvora's younger sister. A lot younger!" She grinned irrepressibly. "So we're relatives."

A little awkwardly, Aisha exchanged the embrace and kiss on the cheek of kin. "But . . . Judge Chaya is fan Reenan?" she said.

"*Ya.* My mother married to a fan Gimbutas — my father, Yohann bar Rimza fan Gimbutas — so she took his clan." A brief scowl. "The Saurons killed him, lousy *mamzrim.* Anyway," she went on, "this big lump of gorgeous stupidity here" — she thumped the young man beside her on the shoulder; it sounded like a fist hitting hard wood — "is Karl bar Yigal fan Reenan, and the little imp of wickedness with the pimples—"

"I do *not* have pimples!" the younger girl burst out, then blushed.

"Yes you do—is named Erika bat Miriam fan Gimbutas. My half-sister," she added with mock distaste.

Karl bar Edgar groaned when the youngsters left. "They're back! I don't know what's worst. Having another Karl about who gets into fights, having him fight with Shulamit there or having them on good terms with each other."

"Thing is, you just don't like being called Little Karl," someone threw at the healer, and he whimpered theatrically. "Not when Big Karl is young enough to be your son."

Aisha felt the healer twitch under her hand.

"You want Shulamit and Big Karl to stay on good terms with each other," Barak said. "When they fight, they throw things. But you can't break a bedroll when you pound it."

Aisha surprised herself by flushing like a young maid, then laughing. She felt engulfed by clan, by friends, by kinfolk who did not reject her.

*Let it be real. Praise Allah, let it be real.*

Aisha sat on temporary bleachers under the stars, and watched the entertainment. Most of the skits were obscure to her; they were satirical, based on local gossip and relationships she didn't know. One or two did strike home. There was a tall brown-haired warrior of amazing strength, who chased away bandits and land gators (that was four men under a startlingly lifelike model of boiled leather and papier-mâché and paint), but then fainted in terror when a blonde girl pinched his buttocks. She dragged him off by an ankle, waving a club triumphantly in the air.

Aisha glanced at Barak; he was laughing almost hard enough to fall off his cushion with one arm around Sannie's waist. The next troupe showed an old warrior and a young warrior loaded with slave-shackles, flogged and dragged protesting toward an altar with a chain of office on it. When they got there, each kept trying to hand the chain to the other, while a figure in a gray, tufted chin-beard—

evidently Karl bar Edgar's kinsman Hans — danced around snatching at it. Every once in a while the two men dodging the chain would turn and boot his backside.

The skits ended in a roar of laughter, loudest of all from the ones who'd taken the brunt of the jokes. Everyone trooped down off the bleachers. Barak and Sannie were arm in arm: he was reciting a particularly scurrilous set of lines, and she was giggling and poking him in the ribs.

When they stopped at the Judge's house, everyone but Aisha and Karl withdrew to a slight distance. As if it were the most natural thing in the world, Karl bar Edgar kissed her lightly on the lips. She was still tingling as she walked up to her room.

The grief of the funeral, the excitement of Ruth's Day — a festival at which you *had* to forgive anyone who came with the proper words could be wearing — vanished in the excitement of the election. Barak and Barak took to giving speeches together; each praised the other and listed his own shortcomings. The Bandari audiences, ordinary clansmen and chiefs and proxies who held the delegated votes of those unable or unwilling to come to the valley, were entertained, but they listened closely to the speeches and asked questions. When the candidates had gone — only three were seriously considered — they spoke among themselves, in uproarious arm-waving confusion that still served to settle points and build consensus.

Summer warmed, and storms stalked huge across the horizons. The dams in the foothills to the east filled as warmth came at last to the high Afritsberg that separated Eden from Shangri-La and the glaciers gave up their moisture. Herds had been driven down to the lowlands to fatten on the stubble-fields and reaped hay meadows of first-harvest and enrich them with manure. Soon they would have to return to the high steppe, where the rested grazing and patches of warming permafrost would carry them until secondharvest. The Valley would plow and plant, more lavishly since there was more water this time than for firstharvest; thirdharvest was most abundant of all, most years. Already produce was being salted, smoked and frozen down for the long Haven winter, three T-years of it.

The Bandari made politics and in the intervals between, held feasts and games. Aisha saw with some pleasure that her tribesfolk did not do too badly at riding and shooting contests, though they seldom won at *karat* or footracing. She had learned enough Bandarit to begin to appreciate the music and poetry; her head whirled when Karl took her among the scholars and showed her the fruits of their work. She almost thought him a djinni again when he showed her the drawings from the great new telescope: Cat's Eye, the sister moons, orbital debris from stations blasted to fragments by the *Dol Guldur*. Even more impressive, she came to realize that much of what she saw was *new* knowledge, not reconstructed from scraps of the Ancients but worked out from the beginnings.

"We found we couldn't *use* so much of what they knew," Karl explained to her; he always did that, treating her as someone who could follow his thought. "They were like grown men who knew how to run. A baby can't; he has to learn step by step, and all we have is fragments of instructions on the most advanced techniques. We've decided we have to go back to those beginnings and redo it. At least we know something of what's possible—that's a huge advantage."

She met his children by his first wife; grown men and women, mostly; the youngest had two Haven years. That was ordeal, not pleasure, but she took some pride in carrying it off. He winked at her afterwards, and she blushed as she always did, with as much pleasure as embarrassment.

"*HhhhhhhhnnnggggaaaHHHH!*" Barak groaned.

He and young Karl bar Yigal sat across from each other, hands locked, mouths wide as they gulped for air. The muscles stood out on their arms like bands of iron, and more writhed on their bare torsos. Power enough to snap steel or uproot young trees strained against itself. Karl was only about eighteen T-years, but already thicker-built than Chaya's son; it was bull against cliff lion. *Sauron against Frystaat*, Aisha thought. Still the massive dark arm bent backward, slowly, slowly. Then it slammed into the wood, hard enough to make the cups and dishes bounce.

"Ai!" Barak said, shaking his hand. "You've got a grip like a tamerlane's mouth. Have some mercy on an old man, *youngk*!"

Young Karl worked his own fingers. "You should talk?"

Spectators were cheering and paying up bets; Shulamit and Sannie handed their lovers towels to wipe down their sweat-slick bodies, then handed them their shirts. The two women smiled at each other in perfect accord.

It was the last of the public feasts before the election, and the air fairly crackled with tension. There had been a few fights, and one criminal case—one of Kemal's men, who kept fondling a woman after she told him to leave off. The punishment for that was booting, running down a double line of citizens and being slapped and kicked. The man had been crawling and moaning by the time he reached the end.

*Serves him right*, Aisha thought, shaking off the memory. No reason not to be happy, now. No reason but her father; and that matter was stored away, down in the depths of her mind. Not forgotten. Never that.

"I'll try again when you've been *kapetein* for a while," young Karl said, grinning; his smile looked very white against his dark face. "Sitting on a cushion, eating *latkkes* and worrying about paying for an irrigation canal in Tallinn — your muscles will turn to muskylope lard. Shulamit and I'll be out with the caravans, living hard. It'll be a pushover."

Barak made a sign against ill luck and reached for his stein. "You'll have to be more respectful then, you young *sklem*," he said.

"Maybe," Karl said. "But Shulamit won't."

The girl stuck out her tongue at both of them. "Come on, Sannie," she said. "Let's go look at the cloth merchants' stalls again."

Karl fan Haller looked up from peeling a clownfruit; he had been popping segments into Aisha's mouth. "It's an even split," he said. "A third for you, a third for Barak, about a quarter for my stiff-necked cousin, the rest undecided."

"How do you know?" Chaya asked, watching the two

young women saunter off arm-in-arm. Her sister, Miriam, farther down the table, was looking too, shaking her head, with an expression almost identical to that of young Karl's mother's beside her. *None of us is going to get the ideal child-in-law*, she thought. *But what mother does?*

"*Medikos* hear things," Karl bar Edgar said. "Also, we gossip." He frowned. "The worst thing I've heard is a rumor about Barak — that he's some sort of front for a plot by the Orphans and the cull-children to take over and make this a second Citadel, if you please." He shrugged, not noticing that Chaya had stiffened. "Nobody's buying that, of course — except some Edenites and a few paranoiacs. Everyone knows about Heber; and besides, most of the Orphans are for *Oom* Barak."

One or two tribesmen wove by — Kemal couldn't keep a watch on all of them, apparently. They eyed her owlishly as she sat holding Karl's hand. Aisha started to look down, then met their eyes with what was not boldness for a woman of the Bandari. *This* was her clan now.

The long, long feast went on. Later in it, an old man with light eyes strode toward the table.

"Ho, *aluf*!" called Karl. He released Aisha's hand, almost surprised to find himself holding it.

"What's wrong with him?" Aisha asked. For all the kvass she had drunk, she was instantly sober, instantly alert. The man was Avi bar Shimon fan Allon, the oldest healer in the Valley, so much respected that he never accompanied warriors or caravans, but worked with the women's doctors, helping to birth the next generation. Chief of *Kumpanie Allon*, Karl bar Edgar's teacher.

"Dammit, I'm not on call," muttered Karl. "All we need . . ."

The newcomer's face was sweaty. His hands shook visibly, not with age, but with anger. Seeing him, Karl Haller rose so fast he almost overset his chair.

"*Oom* Avi," he said. "What's happened? Has there been an accident?"

"There certainly has been," said the old *mediko*. Aisha rose and tried to give him her chair.

"Thank you," he said to her with absent courtesy. "I

haven't seen you before. First time in the valley? First child?"

*He doesn't know me. He thinks I'm someone's wife. I could pass for normal here. I could. I could.*

"My niece," Chaya told him firmly. "Aisha."

Now was the time for him to recoil at the outcast. Instead he looked at her with close interest for a second, then shook his head, dismissing the subject. "Hold on, Karl. I said there was an accident."

"I'll have to get my kit unless . . ." But the elder healer's hands were empty.

"No one's hurt. But some pork-eater broke into the archives next to the Strang infirmary, the genetics section. No, no drugs or knives are missing. And you don't know how relieved I am about that."

"We can station guards," Barak suggested. "But what *was* taken?"

The fire began to cool in Avi's eyes. When Barak slid a drink across the table, he picked it up in hands that no longer shook with rage. "Medical records. All my files have been rifled, Brigit's work, the personal files. Pawed through by some *mamzrim* in a hurry."

Avi bar Shimon had married a woman from Angband Base, one whom he met while poring over what medical technology had survived the nomad sack. Being Soldier-born herself, she had worked in the infirmary there in a menial capacity, helping the Breedmaster's assistant. Afterwards she had helped Avi set up a simpler system for the Pale, guarding against excessive inbreeding in the Sauron children.

The Judge had to have been standing ten meters away in a crowd that made about as much noise as a tamerlane balked of its dinner. But she heard. Almost at once she was at her son's side, listening, her eyes flicking across the tables of feasters, trying to pick out who was and who was not there. Naturally, Kemal stood at her side: the watcher at the feast. It was as important for him to ferret out signs of trouble as it was for him to see a show of Bandari strength. Alliances could rise and fall for less.

"Who would be interested in medical records?" Barak asked.

"Should I know?" Allon snapped, giving the distinctive haBandari shrug; hands flipped palm up and shoulders hunched. "You maybe. Your mother. Your own doctor. Your records were one of the set that's gone missing."

Barak looked at the old healer, puzzled. Then he threw back his head and laughed.

"For what?" he asked. "The arm I broke when I tried to shoot *Kapetein* Mordekai's rifle when I was eight? Every scratch I took in training? Obviously, someone's pouring from a bad barrel of beer! Why don't we get a new one and forget all this?"

"I need those records, bar Heber!" snapped Allon. "There's other things in them than broken arms!"

"*Shaysse!*" hissed Karl bar Edgar . . . fan Haller. "The old man just lost it. Yes, my esteemed cousin Hans. Watch out, here he comes."

Hans bar Rhodevik fan Haller stalked in. He was angry; rumor had it he had been furious with *Kapetein* Mordekai for two decades at the old man's stubborn refusal to die at a reasonable age. Not a popular man, Hans bar Rhodevik, even with his own fan Hallers — although most of them would vote for him out of clan loyalty, and they were numerous.

"You're not going to be a candidate, of course," he announced to Barak. He had never been noted for good manners, but that was impolite in the extreme.

Barak was still chuckling from his exchange with Avi. "I haven't decided yet, *aluf*," he said politely; the man was a clan chief, after all. "You can be sure I'll tell you when I do."

Hans had clipped his beard to a chin-tuft, a style more common among Edenites than Bandari. It jutted forward as his face tightened with anger, and someone at another table went *baaaaa* in imitation of a billygoat.

Maybe it was the kvass and ale. Aisha blinked at him and smothered a giggle. Barak laughed, and even Judge Chaya grinned.

"I'm waiting to see if you die in a fit, *Sauron!*" shouted Hans fan Haller. "Sauron blood and cull blood — maybe they didn't throw your worthless mamma on the scrap heap for nothing!"

"You fucking bastard!" Barak leaped for the older man's throat. Three men hurled themselves forward to stop the fight. Barak tossed them aside like rag dolls, then stopped himself, drew himself up and spat at Hans' feet.

"Out of respect for your years, I'll ignore that — once," he grated. The words fell into a pool of tense silence. "Speak like that about my mother — and the Judge — again, and you can meet me north of *Burg Kidmi*." Outside the Pale, whose law forbade dueling. He turned on his heel and stalked away.

Judge Chaya stood, as frozen as Aisha herself, watching Karl. They must know what was in those records — another curse? Please Allah it would not bring ruin down upon this last of her kin: Chaya blind, Chaya cast out to wander . . . hardened as Aisha thought herself to be, she cringed until the screams alerted her once more.

Aisha had heard tribesmen scream in rage. She had heard outraged Bandari before. But she had never imagined the sheer volume of outrage and curses that she heard now.

"I don't give a damn, fan Haller," the old healer spat. "Confidential be damned. Sealed files be damned. Those are medical records, and we need them. Make up your mind, man. Are you a *mediko* or a politician?"

"I'm trying to keep the damn Pale from splintering!" the younger man shouted. "I suggest you do the same."

She reached for her beltknife. They all had beltknives, even Kemal and his men, who backed toward each other. Their eyes flicked around the infuriated Bandari. Abruptly, Aisha's own blood cooled. Time, as she thought of it, slowed, and her thoughts clicked past like beads on an abacus, adding into a sum she didn't like.

Something about those looks. They meant more than concern that the brawl turn into a riot and from there deteriorate to a feud in which not even honored guests were safe. They were more than apprehension; call it satisfaction, perhaps? Aisha didn't like the look of them.

She took Chaya aside as the disturbance was quelled; old Hans fan Haller stalked away, muttering loudly about

Sauron instability and assault. Men and women looked at each other dubiously; violence before the elections was a bad omen.

"*Tanta*, I must know," she said. "How did Kemal's father die?"

"In the war," Chaya said, seeming surprised.

"No, *exactly* how?"

The Judge dropped her voice with apparent reluctance. "We don't speak of it much. He wouldn't break with the Aydin, even after all the rest did — even Kemal, he didn't come over but he took his sworn men and pulled up into the hills, wouldn't fight with his father against the tribe."

"*Who killed him?*"

"Hammer-of-God Jackson," Chaya whispered. "Killed him and the Aydin *Khan* both, and threw their heads into a meeting of the Aydin chiefs." Then more sharply: "Why now?"

"Because I sense something," Aisha said. A peripheral flick of her own memory, and she recalled that *meid* Sannie had left with cousins.

Cousins? Cousins who called themselves Gimbutas — and she a fan Haller, of an almost Edenite *kumpanie*? Fan Haller were tricksy . . . like nomads. Cousins from an outlying territory, perhaps cousins who lived outside the Pale altogether.

The murmurs were turning to shouts again in the street.

"SHUT IT DOWN!" bellowed Judge Chaya with all the power in her Sauron-bred body.

Aisha smelled blood in the air, the result of some lucky punches. Its hot-copper scent made her adrenaline spike up, to be subsumed in that readiness that was the mark of the Sauron-born.

Kemal and his men froze, hands falling away from their beltknives. Carefully, as if setting up an ambush, they began to back out of the crowd. Aisha followed them with her eyes, aware that the Judge was administering a tongue-lashing such as she hoped never to deserve: something about "reasonable concern for future health" turned into a blistering attack on lack of respect for Bandari customs: "disgrace before important guests" and "indecent breach of mourning for our *kapetein*." The Sauron part of Aisha's memory would "store" that lecture for when she had time to retrieve it from memory. Maybe in a hundred years.

For now, however, she concentrated on being inconspicuous, on passing unnoticed in a storm of reproaches and accusing glares. Like Kemal, she backed away from the center of the fight into the shadows, where she could hide and think and plan. She had never been good at thinking and planning more than a day ahead. No practice at it. One thing, though, she knew.

This was not a time to warn Judge Chaya that the Pale was filled with spies. Perhaps, if she could bring proof, none of those stares would touch her. She would have brought honor to the Bandari — and perhaps they could help her restore her own.

Gradually the shouting subsided — into sullenness on the part of some of the Edenites, mutters broken by Karl bar Edgar's earnest, persuasive voice; and into loud, even drunken self-blame on the part of the Bandari, who began to stage a reconciliation that would have made a wedding festival staid.

Aisha prowled, her senses alert to catch the *warmth* of the spies that she always sensed but no one else save but her father (and the Judge or another Sauron) could, her nostrils flaring to catch the scent of the men she suspected. Her boots squeaked with newness, so she shed them and walked about the town in felt slippers, then barefoot out past the walls into the sprawling tent-city of those in for festival and election. She wanted silence for her thoughts and her own concealment.

Could she be certain Kemal had set spies? How could she find out? And even if she did, how could she bring proof against them, exile that she was? This was a problem Judge Chaya *might* have been able to handle with all the resources of the Pale behind her. And why? What revenge? Ah. Hans bar Rhodevik would make a rotten *kapetein*. And he was a strong man physically, middle-aged, likely to live another four or five Haven years. If the Pale was torn with internal dissension, the tribe of Tarik — of Kemal, by then —would stand some chance of restoring its independence and driving out the new-found and unwelcome kinsfolk. Even of retaking Tallinn, although she had heard that many Bandari were settled there on the devastated lands.

The Cat's Eye jeered down at her. *You had a girl's training and then a refugee's. What do you think you can do?*

Not trip over the child who wandered into her path, surely. "*Meid? Tanta*," the girl corrected herself. Her eyes held an unchildlike curiosity that reminded Aisha of Karl bar Edgar, but without the sorrow at the back of the eyes. She wished she could bring this problem to him. That was the problem when a wild thing was tamed; it looked to the tamer for protection and aid. "Why aren't you at the feast?"

Aisha put out a hand to tip up the girl's chin. Like all children in the Pale, she was respectful but utterly at ease with adults: in the Pale, all adults were protectors of children, or else painfully dead.

"I had eaten and drunk enough," she answered with the first words that came to mind. "And you? Why aren't you there, little cousin?"

"I followed my sister Shulamit and her friend Karl . . ." Her eyes creased into merriment, and Aisha revised upward her estimate of the child's age. "No, not like that. They said they went on a new hunt. Not for stobor or even tamerlanes, but for men. I heard them say it. For spies."

Aisha stared at the girl. *Allah, do you send a child to aid me?* She would have sworn those two youngsters had eyes only for each other. *Everyone is the hero in her own story*, she reminded herself, *though she may be but a servant in yours.*

"I like you," Erika confided. "You don't laugh at me for what I said. Shulamit said people would laugh if I told them."

"You are Bandari," Aisha said. "Even young as you are, you would not say . . ."

"They go to find proof now, Shulamit and Karl do. But they make noise when they hunt!" Outrage quivered in the girl's soft voice. "You don't make noise when you walk." She pointed at Aisha's bare feet.

"Why do you tell me?"

"Because you are kin to us, and to Barak and the Judge. You know . . ." She glanced around before mouthing the name of the nomad chieftain, not daring even a breath of sound. "I watched you."

Had Aisha been all that much older than this Erika when she left Tallinn? That seemed as long ago now as the time when Haven turned cold.

Aisha squatted down beside the girl. "What makes you think . . .?" she whispered.

"Shulamit travels much. She says she never saw the cousins who call themselves Gimbutas before, and when she greeted them, they watched her as if she were a *nafkeh*, a whore," she translated. "Our clan would not do so. Some fan Hallers might, or *plaatsmen*."

Aisha cocked her head at the girl. *Where?* Wide-eyed, Erika pointed. *That way.* Aisha glanced down at her feet and grinned in appreciation: not having Sauron blood, the girl couldn't risk losing toes or worse by going barefoot. But she had worn soft slippers rather than boots. A clever child. Allah send she have a better fate than Aisha.

Silently they prowled, past yurt, wagon and house. Lamps, torches and fires confused the senses Aisha had learned to rely on in her years of wandering the steppes; the nightsounds of a town, sinking to rest after the emotions of a feast, a binge and a near-riot, blocked her hearing.

"This isn't going to work," she whispered to Erika. "Go find your sister and go home."

"They said it would be someplace private." Her eyes danced with sudden, wholly unmalicious humor. "They know a lot of places to go. That's why they thought they could find the spies."

A boy and a girl, scarcely adult, more intent on each other than on caution; Aisha wanted to groan.

"Do you know of such places?" she asked the girl.

Erika promptly raised a hand and began to tick off a list

on her fingers; there seemed to be a lot of them, all well-known. Nobody would want to chance a *really* unknown spot — too dangerous if something went wrong.

*Privacy*, Aisha thought. It was scarcer than the ruby that glittered on her hand, either in the tribes or among the Bandari. And yet, if reports had been stolen and were to be passed to the men who wanted them, it must be done in private. Assuming the spies were Kemal's men, she didn't think an exchange could be made in Kemal's yurts — too closely watched, among haBandari herdsfolk with even more distrust of outsiders than the valley dwellers. Assuming — which she didn't — that the spies were Gimbutas, she couldn't imagine any privacy at all in that clan; and, again, if they masqueraded as Gimbutas, they wouldn't risk exposure.

The Bandari of Eden . . . memories clicked and flashed into place: the bunker where Ruth had been held, where Judge Chaya had hidden as a child. Honored now, but little used, and far enough away that no one might watch it. It was a wild guess, but it was better than the nothing she had turned up in a long night of searching.

*You know*, Aisha told herself, *you could be making all this up, you and a little, left-out meid who wants attention. Can't you see it now?* "Oh, that's our crazy cousin." *Really a great political asset, just when you mean to help.*

She recognized that voice; it was the inner killer you heard when the winds lashed you, you hadn't eaten for days, you had a fever, and all you thought you wanted was to lie down and sleep forever. She had practice in ignoring it, and she hadn't lived this long by distrusting her hunches.

First, get the child away.

"Erika, do you know where Judge Chaya lives?" A quick nod. *She is this child's aunt, of course she knows*, Juchi's daughter reminded herself. "I want you to get her, please. And tell her that her niece, Aisha bat Juchi — can you remember that? — thinks she's found some answers." Even now she could not feel easy with the Bandari custom of girls' taking their mothers' rather than their fathers' names; it seemed disrespectful. "You can say you helped; you did. Ask her if she can come to the bunker" — Erika's eyes widened — "as soon as she can. Armed. Then, *you go home*, do you hear me? And if you meet your sister and Big Karl, tell them to go home, too."

"*Ja, tanta.*" Erika nodded and padded off so fast that Aisha would have taken hot iron in her hand and sworn that the girl would obey all her instructions. Except, perhaps the last one.

The Judge was half Sauron. And Barak wouldn't let her go alone. Three half-breeds ought to be enough to take out a nest of spies. At a Sauron's best pace the journey to the bunker was barely an hour, in the thick, oxygen-rich air of Eden.

Aisha ran.

# ● CHAPTER ELEVEN

The Cyborg Aisha had slain knew by training as well as instinct *how* to use the senses she fumbled even now to control. No point regretting it. She ghosted up the final set of switchbacks toward the Bashan Pass, counting on truenight darkness and her earth-colored clothes to keep non-Sauron eyes from seeing her. There were a few travellers, even this late. They were plain to her view, fuzzy outline shapes of body heat against the stone-cold earth. Once a patrol heading west on horseback, leading pack-muskylopes. She hid behind a tall tilted slab of rock, motionless as the soldiers halted. One stood in his stirrups.

"Anything?" his commander called.

"Movement. Shall I take a look?"

"No, it's a rock-dassie or drillbit," the officer said after a moment. "We've a long way to Fort Gilead. *Trek.*"

They cantered off. The next was a train of Bactrian camels burbling complaint as tired drovers whacked them on toward the valley to the east. They looked at her incuriously as she trotted past, dodging the bales of wool strapped to the camels' pack-saddles. Then she was at the saddle of the pass, higher even than the steppe; she could feel her heart and lungs adjust smoothly, breathing deeper and pumping harder.

She climbed from the broader modern road to the old disused track higher up the slope. There was no warmth there, not even reflected UV, with Cat's Eye down. Her nightvision picked out just enough to keep her feet from stumbling as she worked her way up to the old bunker — but there was a slight glow from the narrow slit windows and the buckled splinters of the door.

Stealthily Aisha crept toward the bunker. The approaches and the half-ruined stonework offered sturdy places for hands and feet: she didn't want to leave a blood trail on the rocks for men or beasts, nor to take the pathway. She took a deep breath and waited, utterly motionless, surveying the place with all her senses. From within a cracked wall came the sense of warmth. Well enough, but it could be a beast, or beasts. She flared her nostrils. Human scent, unmistakable, but without the spoor of rut. Not youngsters crept off together, then. She sank to the ground and crept closer, peering from the top of a boulder through the door. Four people: she counted the invisible sources of heat.

Aisha edged closer . . . no, that handhold looked as if it would crumble . . . three points anchored . . . lever the leg *over* now, quietly, you fat musky!

The pulse in her temples distracted her, so she ignored it, focusing on the heat, the voices up ahead. By instinct, she crept up the rocks, picking a vantage-point, where she could listen and watch and, if the time came, when the time came, intervene. One long leap away from the old trap-door that gaped in the flat roof.

"What do they say?" The voice bore the accent of her tribe, but weighted with heavy sarcasm. "Bring the *hakim* along, you said; one *hakim* can understand the words of another." A hooded lantern flared, the reflected glow blinding to her night-adapted eyes for a second.

Aisha heard whispered curses and a scrabbling through pages. "They're in Bandarit, even to the letters. Allah wither them! No, keep the lantern covered, fatherless one!"

"Then we get someone to read them," came a third voice. *Kemal.* "The fool slut who helped us gain them. Fetch her. She can refuse us nothing now."

"I'll go, lord," said a voice she recognized at once. Ihsan, Kemal's *adana.*

Aisha shifted into shadow as one of the nomads slipped from the bunker. She would know his scent again, if anyone would believe her.

Who was the woman? Sannie? Somehow, that made sense. She wanted Barak, and she wanted him to be *kapetein.* Seize the records before someone else did, and hide them. If nothing in them hurt Barak, betray Kemal

and let them be "found." Or find them yourself and reap
the harvest of gratitude that might follow and be wife to the
*kapetein* — and healer of the rift between Edenite and Bandari, if Sannie cared for that.

But if the medical records held . . . oh, Aisha did not
know what, taints in the blood, the threat of disease, the
nomads had what they could not read and would probably
destroy. And the files would hold no dangers for Barak.

It was all dishonor, greater than her own in leaving her
father's corpse unburied.

Grimly, Aisha shook her head. If they planned hunts as
badly as they planned this, they would have starved to
death. The wind blew and she sheltered against the rock as
the night passed. How long, dammit, how long would the
Judge take to come or Sannie to betray herself? She had
wintered on the steppe, and the Eden Valley's weather was
gentle in comparison; but she didn't think she could wait
that long before she *must* attack.

"Douse that flame! Someone's coming!"

Darkness.

Aisha didn't think Barak or the Judge would make the
noise she heard, a confident *crunch, crunch, crunch* of boots
on rock. The breathing was of a middle-aged man who
found the going rough. Obviously, someone did not fear
disclosure. Other bootsteps followed, several men. She
rose, squinting to reduce the risk of her reflective Sauron
eyes showing in the darkness. Now she knew she must see
or die, of curiosity if nothing worse.

A new light flashed into the darkness, deliberately glinting on the long double barrel of a Bandari pistol. "You've
got the medical records? Hand them over."

The light flared up as the cover was withdrawn from the
lantern, and Aisha flattened herself. She was above the
mens' heads, unlikely to be seen if she did not move or
speak. The man who spoke had a tuft of chin-beard shot
with gray.

Hans fan Haller? Had *he* set the spies?

"What do you know of this, Bandari?" Kemal spat.

Hans bar Rhodevick fan Haller laughed. "More than

you, *hotnot*." Hands clapped to sword-hilts at the insult, then paused uncertainly. The men behind the fan Haller chief carried bows, except for two with wide-muzzled flintlock shotguns. Those pointed into the bunker, and it took little imagination to see what their buckshot would do in that enclosed space.

"D'you think I haven't tried to get a look at those records?" Hans bar Rhodevick said. "To know who among us are Sauron spawn, to what degree — and what the *real* parentage of our would-be *kapetein* Barak is. He's too strong and fast, curse him — too strong and fast to have only his dam's Sauron strain. Karl bar Edgar wouldn't go along, curse *him*.

"So I had Sannie watched; she could get in there, say she was thinking of a marriage and needed access to the files, make an impression of the key. Her father's a locksmith. Should have known she'd do something stupid like bring them to you. These women . . . what we get for letting them think they run things . . . even our esteemed Judge."

Incongruously, Kemal laughed. "You'd shoot a guest?"

"I'd say you outwore your welcome when you turned spy. So I'll take these, and you can just leave quietly. Or you can have a fight and be known as the men who turned on their hosts. The *dead* men who turned on their hosts."

How many people had come up here? Aisha wondered. The more who knew of this, the less chance for decent concealment.

"The new *kapetein* would hardly approve of this."

Haller gestured at the records. "*I'll* be the new *kapetein*. His vote will collapse, and enough will come to me. *Those* prove he's no more fit to be *kapetein* — "

A woman's voice pierced the night. "Than who? Than you, Hans bar Rhodevik fan Haller? Someone who'd be in the Elders' pockets — as if the clans would stand for that, even most of fan Haller? Someone who'd set Bandari against Bandari for the sins of their fathers? Or had you planned to hold whatever *might* be in those records over Barak's head? Blackmail is as much a crime, you know, as theft. Or spying."

So quietly that Aisha never heard it, Judge Chaya and her son had come up the rocks and into position. Two clicks sounded. The nomads crowded in the doorway of the bunker looked about frantically, and so did the fan Haller clansmen, but all were blinded by the night and the unshielded lantern.

"I would like to know," the Judge's voice was assured, even a little amused, "who is whose catspaw in this. Sannie? A willing tool. She might not even guess who put her up to it. Or did someone, one of her own clan, egg her on? *Steal* the records since your attempt to force Karl to disclose their contents failed miserably. Never mind what harm it might do our medical care. Steal them, discredit Kemal for spying, throw me out of office? That's another way to look at it. Or, let's look at it from Kemal's point of view. Cast the Bandari into ferment, maybe into civil war, and then break away, if you can. A pretty mess."

"You're a fine one to talk about messes," the fan Haller snarled at the unseen Judge. "Righteous, aren't you? You don't want your son to be *kapetein*? You want it so bad you can taste it. But he's just not qualified, is he? Not of old Piet's line, is he? We know that, just as we know why that woman you brought in wears the ring you used to have. She's bad seed, isn't she? You all are. We never saw you with your husband. How do we know . . ."

The broadhead arrow that punched through Hans fan Haller came from behind Aisha. It slapped through his chest and out his back to quiver in the hard dirt of the trail. He looked astonished, then agonized and then like nothing at all. As the other fan Haller clansmen whirled, trying to find the source of the shot, the tribesmen jumped. The shotguns roared into the night, stabbing orange flame, but they had already been wrestled upwards. Aisha saw knives glint and then streams of blood, rapidly cooling in the night.

Barak dropped to his feet and walked toward the bunker, another shaft on the string. Even without his mother out in the darkness, hand-to-hand he outnumbered the four nomads all by himself. "Everyone don't move. Fan Haller just went too far. And you heard it. One move and you'll go farther."

Kemal chuckled. "What about you?"

Barak shrugged. To Aisha's senses, his breath and pulse were normal — Soldier normal — and he wasn't sweating at all. Half-blood that he was, he should have shown more stress than that. "A man's mother, she's sacred, or should be."

They all knew why Chaya's son was called Lightning; they might as well have been disarmed, in the same room with him. "All right, Kemal. This has all gone too far. Hand over the records."

Kemal prodded at Hans with his toe. "I never liked him," he said. "This was well done, all but the blood feud it will bring." He shrugged and made a sign to his followers. They wiped and sheathed their blades. "Let there be peace between us for this night. I have eaten the salt of your house and am your guest, at least." He handed over a thick file of papers.

"We don't have feuds," said Barak. "We have Laws. I'll have to stand trial."

Kemal grinned sardonically. "So you say. Say it again if you live that long. But hear what I say, man of Law: if the Pale casts you out for this night's work, I'll make a place for you in the tribe."

Aisha understood him. Kemal hated his people's subjection to the Pale, and he had despised Hans bar Rhodevik. Barak he respected as a warrior and honest enemy. Evidently Barak bar Heber felt the same way, from his answering smile.

Absently, Barak flipped through the crumpled leaves of the medical record file. "Sure. After all, I'm of your blood. Just like Aisha. Come on in, why don't you, cousin? You too, mother. Let's make it a *mishpocha*."

Kemal shook his head as if admiring what? Enemy? Ally? Aisha sought for a word and found it: *accomplice*.

Judge Chaya slipped in between two boulders. "Cover the light," she commanded. The hood closed around it, all but a narrow bull's-eye. "We ought to burn those," she muttered.

Barak laughed, a sound Aisha distrusted. "Kemal, you were right about Law, weren't you? God, that I should live to see the day. The Judge urging her son to break the Law? Why?"

He bent over the records. "I could understand concern over my . . . our Sauron blood. But I'd have thought it was diluted. You're only half-blood, so I'm a quarter Sauron. Shouldn't make for any trouble. Unless." He froze. "Unless . . ."

Aisha stood, and slid down to the ground. Light glinted off the ruby on her hand and caught Chaya's attention. Abruptly, she seemed to shrink in on herself; for the first time, she looked old. She stared at Aisha, who knew in that moment that both faced the same nightmare every day of their lives.

"Blood," Judge Chaya murmured. "So much blood. Always calling for more." She looked down at the bodies lying in the darkness that spread out from beneath them. "The God-bloody Saurons." Her eyes darkened as if she stared into hell. "They took him from me. Took Heber, before we could make the child we wanted together, we were waiting until . . . And I never even saw his body, I had nothing of him."

"*Ama* . . ." Barak's voice was gentle.

"She's got to let it out." Aisha's voice was so ruthless she could barely recognize it. "All these years, the wound has festered. What did you do, kinswoman? The Saurons stole a life from you, so you . . . stole one back?"

Chaya nodded. "You aren't the only woman who kills Saurons, girl. Left him dead on the plain with a spike through his head. My son's *mine*. The Sauron was just the means to get him."

"So I'm not of Piet's line on either side," Barak said. He didn't sound as if it had hit him, yet. But it would, very soon, it would. "You didn't want to admit what you'd done. Instead, you discouraged thoughts of me becoming *kapetein*. But what if I had? What would have become of your Law if I had?"

"It was all in the blood!" Chaya snarled, then seized control of herself. "The Law would have been broken. But no one would have known. Just me. I would have taken the blame on my soul. The Pale would have had a strong leader. *And would that have been so bad?*"

"It can't happen now," Barak said.

Chaya nodded her head and dared to look at her son. "You don't hate me?"

"I just wish you'd told me earlier. I could have done something to take myself out of the running. I knew I could *do* the job; I just didn't *want* it much. Well." He stared down at Hans' body. "At least now I've taken care of that."

"What about us?" asked Kemal.

He and his men knew too much now to live. He stank of fear to Aisha, and he had to know that the three who faced him could smell it; but she was proud of his courage in that moment.

"Dishonored," said the Judge. "Spying. Conspiring with *him*. I wouldn't stoop to kill you. Tell about this night's work, and I'll see no one believes you. Ever. Get out of here. Come back with your warriors and we'll give you a fight. Come back with more spies — " She spat.

"Some more are coming," Barak observed, almost as if he counted heads at a feast. "They're not making very good time."

*But then, they don't have Sauron blood.*

"A tribesman," Aisha said. "Kemal sent him to bring in Sannie." Her lips quivered. "He wanted her to translate the medical records for him. Want me to tell her that her services aren't required?"

Barak shook his head. "She has to see. Too much has been hidden." He sighed. "It's my fault as much as hers. I made her wait too long. I took counsel of my fears; always a stupid thing to do."

"It would not have been treason if my plan had worked," Kemal said.

"*Why is it that treason never prospers?*" Chaya said. She laid a coat over Hans bar Rhodevik's staring eyes. "Why, if it prospers, none dare call it treason."

Color flushed Kemal's high cheekbones. "And my blood is still dishonored." He gestured at Aisha.

"I'm not about to kill myself to cleanse it," she told him.

He shook his head. "Not what I meant, girl. Your father, not you. We cast him out. You *chose* to go with him, a loyal daughter, worthy of honor. It's not your fault."

She shed years in that moment, years and defenses. Tears rose briefly, then subsided. Karl the *hakim* had said the same thing. Forgiveness. Mercy. Those were . . . what? Miracles? Avenging one's blood, though, was a Law.

"But it is my blood," Aisha said softly. "And my father's cries up to heaven for vengeance." *Saurons, see your evil turned on yourselves.* Nobody could hate with the grim persistence of a Sauron, except one of their kind raised on the steppe.

"You go." Kemal gestured to his men. "I'll see this through."

"But, *khan* . . ." one of them began.

"I said, go! I am no *khan*, who am a dishonored man. You will say nothing of what passed this night. Or do I slay you for your disobedience? Tell Tarik, I shall return when I have cleansed my name; that only. If I can. *Go!*"

The nomads left quickly, pushing past their comrade on the way. He was walking with his hands tied behind his back and Sannie's saber-point resting lightly on his sheepskin coat, directly over the liver.

"If you *hotnots* think — " she began, then stopped. The Bandari and her captive gaped identical "O's" of shock at the bodies and at Barak and his mother.

"Come on in, Sannie," said Barak.

The young woman's eyes widened with dismay, whether at the sight of Barak or the bodies on the bunker's floor, Aisha couldn't say. But only for a moment. In the next, she controlled herself as well as any half-Sauron woman might.

"What did you hope to gain?" Chaya asked gently. "You couldn't have known what was in those records."

"He, *Oom* Hans, he wanted to know, thought there might be *something* when Karl wouldn't talk. I knew *Oom* Hans musn't get them, and somebody had to before he did. I thought . . . I thought . . . best to get rid of them, the *hotnots* would do it and then they'd be blamed and nobody would believe — and you would have been *kapetein*, Barak. And the Pale would have been strong. *All* of us, Eden and clansfolk, just as Karl's dinned into my ears since before I could ride. *And would that have been so bad?*"

Even Kemal burst out laughing. Sannie flushed with shame.

Chaya shook her head. "For the first time, Sannie, I think I could approve of you as a daughter-in-law. My thoughts exactly. But it's too late now. And the Law is the Law, no matter how much good we think we might have done by breaking it."

"Well, it's virtually bliddy unanimous," *Oom* Barak said, "thanks to you!"

The chalkboard with the tally was up behind his head. Eight in ten of the legal electors and their registered proxies had chosen Barak bar Sandor fan Reenan as the twenty-second *kapetein* in lawful succession to Piet.

The conspirators stood in front of the *kapetein*'s table, even Chaya who had just decked him with the chain of office. The celebration was still going on outside, along with a wild flood of rumors. Old Barak was alone at the head of the table — *you will have to get used to that, being alone,* Chaya thought — but Tarik Shukkur *Khan* stood respectfully to one side.

"You needn't act as if we'd had you sentenced to death," Chaya said.

Barak grunted. "What'm I to do with you, then?"

Young Barak grinned. "You could have me sentenced to stoning for murder," he said cheerfully.

"And me for conspiracy, treason and spying," Kemal added.

Barak and Kemal looked at each other and nodded; they were nearly of an age. Both looked younger this morning, as if the failure of all their plans had somehow made them boys again. Practically speaking, the risk of such a sentence was nil, but *Kapetein* Barak would have to find some conduit for the outrage *Kumpanie* Haller and its allies felt, at the least. A pure pardon would bring rioting. That was the *kapetein*'s problem, and the younger men were both profoundly relieved at that.

"You should send me forth," Aisha said with an old bitterness. "The curse of my blood has brought ruin enough."

The *kapetein* grunted again. "Bliddy likely," he said. "It's *tsouris* we brought on ourselves with greed and stupidity. You saved us. I should exile you? Just what we need now, more causes for hatred among ourselves, more blood, more feuds."

Suddenly Chaya spoke. "What's the saying? If anything goes wrong, blame it on the Evil Eye — "

" — the Evil Eye or the Saurons," the new *kapetein* finished for her. "Well?"

"Who's responsible for all this?" Chaya asked, her voice rising.

Aisha's eyes kindled for the first time since the bunker, and she spoke: "Yes! The bloody Saurons — their meddling, their casting Juchi and Chaya out to die, their accursed breeding program, their tyranny — *that* is the cause of all this!"

Tarik stroked his beard and smiled his enigmatic smile. "Oh, most excellent," he said. "I could not tolerate the execution of my heir, however guilty. Not and hold the loyalty I need to rule, but . . ."

" . . . but if I choose exile, all is settled?" Kemal said. There was whole-hearted respect in the glance he turned on the older man. "Exile, and the honorable path of vengeance as a *ghazi* fighting the holy war against an enemy whom all men hate and fear. Did you plan this, excellent *khan*?"

Tarik shrugged. "No. But one must always be ready for the knocking hooves of opportunity."

*Kapetein* Barak snorted laughter. "So you, young Barak, and this prince of his people, and your cousin Aisha, will announce that Yeweh and the *anima* of the Founders command you to tear down the Citadel with your bare hands?"

"Allah and the spirits," Kemal corrected.

"And I as well," Chaya said.

*Oom* Barak shook his head. "The Judge can't leave the Pale."

"The Judge can't be accessory to a murder!" Chaya said.

"The fan Haller was in conspiracy against the Pale!"

"That didn't give either me or Barak the right to execute him on the spot! I resign!"

*Kapetein* Barak throttled back his temper with a visible effort. "I don't accept it."

"What are you going to do, have me Judge from behind bars?"

"I'll appoint a deputy, by the *anima* of Piet, and you can step back in when you return," he grumbled. *Which will be never*, they all knew.

"So." *Oom* Barak sighed. "Yes, that will do. Everyone will agree to ignore details and blame it all on the Saurons; you four will hare off into the wilderness . . ."

" . . . five," said Ihsan. "Your father's ghost would haunt me otherwise, Kemal; and you are my *adana*. And the tribe is full of eager swords who will ride as your *noyok*, your sworn men, on a *jihad* such as this. Is not Aisha at our head?"

"Are you mad?" Kemal demanded of him. "Who will care for my son?"

"I," Tarik answered. "He will make a fine heir, and one who is also my grandson, and so cannot . . ."

Kemal's nod held bitter admiration. "So you will be rid of me, have an heir who is linked to you by blood as well as by marriage, and rid the encampments of the wildest of the young men," he said. "*Shabash*, Tarik Shukkur *Khan*!"

Chaya nodded to herself. *Best for the People as well.* So old Mordekai's plan would come to fruition — and in the end, generations hence, Tarik's folk would be Bandari themselves. The *khan* probably knew; but it would be long after his lifespan, and his family would still have power — as chiefs of *Kumpanie Tarik*.

"Six of us," Sannie said, looking at young Barak. "Please?"

He nodded. She slumped with relief.

"Now," the *kapetein* said. "Let's figure out how we're going to explain this to *them*." He jerked a thumb over his shoulder at the noise of the crowd.

Aisha found she was not sorry to be leaving. Always, if she had made the Pale her home, she would have had the sense that she was betraying her blood for the life it had denied her. The decision left her feeling light, as if she had recovered from another fever, but relieved.

*I would have been a curse to him*, she thought. The pain was distant, lost amid so many others. *A home, children — these are not for me. Better thus.*

*Kapetein* Barak had been generous even in his anger. They rode out on good horses, leading strings of remounts; there were silver and goods on their pack-muskylopes. To Chaya's surprise, a trickle of men and women came to join them even before they left the Pale, youngsters mostly, friends and admirers of her son. They stubbornly ignored orders to leave, as stubbornly ignored Barak's blasphemous refusal to command them.

At the last, a few people turned out to see them off from *Burg Kidmi* itself. One of them was young *meid* Erika. Her mother Miriam stood talking with Chaya, but the girl ran up to Aisha and held out her fist. In it was a gold chain, with a medallion enameled in blue: the Eye that wards off evil.

"It's old," the girl said. "To keep off the Lidless Eye."

Aisha leaned down and kissed her. "Keep it for yourself. And may Allah grant you a happier fate than mine." The girl retreated, a little crestfallen but keeping her head up proudly.

Young Karl and his Shulamit were there as well. Naked longing was in their eyes as they watched the six make ready.

"My father forbade," young Karl said to Barak and Chaya.

"My mother *and* my foster-father forbade," Shulamit echoed.

"Good," Barak and Chaya said, without a heartbeat's difference. Then they laughed.

"Go home, *youngk*," Barak said, fisting him on the shoulder. "The Pale needs you. *Am Bandari Hai!*"

"They need you worse!" Karl cast over his shoulder, as he rode off toward his father's caravan. "Bring me the Battlemaster's head, and I'll let you beat me at arm-wrestling again!"

Aisha smiled to see them go. *Was I ever that young?* she wondered. "I just regret . . ." Her voice trailed off. She glanced over and met her sister/aunt's eyes.

*You* haven't *had much of a life, have you, Aisha?* she read the thought there.

Chaya had promised her a life, a place, even a home and

husband of her own. Instead, she had joined Aisha in exile and a quest for vengeance. Aisha shrugged, wordless. At least, when her sister and aunt's life fell apart, she had a new purpose she could turn to. It was more than their mother Badri had, dead by her own hand in the ruins of her life. They would not die for nothing, if it came to that.

She ordered herself not to glance around. Karl bar Edgar fan Haller must be sick of the thought of her, much less the sight. And he had his clan, stunned by the death of their leader, to comfort. If anyone would listen to him.

A word Aisha had heard in the Pale crept into her thoughts. *Dayenu.* Enough. It would have been enough to slay the Sauron Battlemaster. It would have been enough to die cleanly on the steppe, to find kinsfolk, honor, even, and aid for this private *jihad* of hers. Not much of a life? It was hers. And it was enough.

They rode in silence, without banners.

At the border of the Pale, a silent rider waited for them. His leathers were worn and comfortable, his armor somewhat less so, as if he seldom wore it. But he carried his weapons easily, and the thick roll behind his saddle was marked with the twisted serpents of his art. And the sorrow too many people had marked seemed gone.

"And what do you think *you're* doing?" Aisha yelled at him, abruptly, gloriously furious.

"The way you're acting, I wouldn't let the lot of you cross a cow pasture alone," Karl retorted. "Someone's got to look after you. Also a lot of my clansmen aren't exactly happy with me. You're not the only ones who've made the Pale too hot to hold you."

Aisha's fury melted into something strange. Something like — happiness?

*Now we are seven*, she thought.

Enough? It was more than enough.

# ● CHAPTER TWELVE

Sigrid rode openly over the crest of the hill, and stopped
just below it. Long kilometers lay behind her, long days of
Haven, and a longer, bleaker night, when she had made
choices, Cyborg-choices, choices that would be interpreted
as betrayal. Even if she returned with the mare that foaled
on the high steppe, and with an account of a tribe that
escaped every record, and every tale but one that came to
Nûrnen or the Citadel. That there was such a tribe, she was
certain. She had seen its outriders. The mare she rode was
one of its own. It was not the one she came for. That one
would not be wandering near a cliff lion's kill, with bit and
saddle still on her and the foamed sweat of terror dried on
her neck.

The lion was dead, as dead as the woman it had killed.
Its hide was Sigrid's cloak, its hollowed head her helmet.
She would tan it properly when she came to the tribe. She
did not entertain the possibility that they would reject her.
She was what they dreamed of: Soldier, and woman, and
rebel.

The challenge came, it seemed, out of the rocks under
her horse's feet. The mare shied. Sigrid turned the shy into
a sidle, mare's head turned aside, shoulder pointed toward
the voice.

"Who walks on Katlin's land?"

"One who would see the heart of it," Sigrid answered,
raising her voice above the wind, but not too far. She saw
the glow of body warmth behind the tallest of a tumble of
stones, heard the rustle and creak of leather, scented the
sharpness of smoke and sweat and unwashed skin.

"That mare is one of ours," the sentry said.

"So was her rider," said Sigrid. "She is dead. I avenged
her death."

Sigrid heard the hiss of breath sucked in. "Vilny? Vilny's dead?" The voice stopped, then began again, louder than before, and harsh. "Who are you? Where do you come from?"

"I am one who would ride with Katlin's daughters, if Katlin's eldest daughter will have me."

The sentry came from behind the stones, a tall woman, spare and weathered, with graying hair in a braid over her shoulder. She wore a short sword and a knife, and carried a loaded crossbow, which she leveled on Sigrid's heart. Her eyes were hard: narrow Mongol eyes in a high-cheeked face, but her hair was fair brown among the silver. Sigrid met her stare calmly, sitting astride the now quiet mare.

She took her time in examining Sigrid. Sigrid waited with a hunter's patience. Yes, this one had Soldier genes, but much diluted: most of her breeding would be nomad, and whatever oddity had begun this oddest of tribes. Americ, she deduced, and Northeuropean — Terran in any case. The tales she had pried out of nomads and travellers on her journey north had made her sure of one thing: this was an old tribe, though no Soldier had ever admitted to hearing of it.

Soldiers had not known to ask, nor maybe would they have cared if they had known. Katlinsfolk kept to themselves. They did not wage wars of conquest. They did not allow themselves to be conquered; but since they were few and remote and offered no threat, they would have been suffered until it became expedient to bring them under Sauron dominion.

Now they had something of value — vast value if true. A mutation. A Terran animal that could breed and bear young on the high steppes of Haven.

The Breedmaster's heir of the Citadel could have asked for no greater gift, and no better proving. Had she been a Soldier, she could have returned with the cliff lion's hide and been reckoned man enough. But she was Cyborg, and she was, on this journey, a renegade. She would come back with everything that she had gone for, or she would not come back at all.

At last the sentry spoke. "You are a Sauron." She sounded surprised. But not, Sigrid noticed, afraid.

Sigrid nodded once.

The woman lowered the crossbow a fraction. "I will take Vilny's horse. You will walk to the next cairn. The one there will take you where you wish to go."

"How will she know," asked Sigrid, "that I have your leave?"

"She will know." The woman held out her hands.

Sigrid set the reins in them. The mare went quietly enough. Sigrid turned her back on the sentry and walked where she was directed. She heard the woman draw breath as if to speak, heard the creak and jingle as she shrugged. There was no soft, deadly snap of the crossbow's trigger, though Sigrid was braced for it, to leap and roll and vanish into a fold of the earth. *Clear that crossbow has not shot — too fast anyway.*

The guard at the next cairn was younger, little more than a child. She did not speak to Sigrid, only took her in with wide fascinated eyes and spun, flicking her hand in a command: *Follow.* Sigrid followed.

Every step she took, she took under surveillance. There were crossbows trained on her, and as she drew closer to the clanfire, pistols, even an assault rifle. A Soldier had died for that one, she was sure. The woman who carried it stood out in the open, and the light of Byers' Star turned her hair as bright as brass. Sigrid acknowledged her with a lift of the chin.

The Soldier's daughter was the last line of defense. The rise on which she stood dropped away to a relative level and an encampment like any other on the steppe: a huddle of yurts round a central, slightly higher structure, a scattering of goats and sheep and horses amid the shaggy bulk of muskylopes, grazing under the watchful eyes of herders mounted and afoot. Dogs ran at heel or stirrup or moved among the animals, nipping a straggler here, facing down a runaway there. The animals came in both sexes. The herders were all women; likewise the dwellers in the camp and the children underfoot. There were no bearded faces.

No men; no boys, unless there were a few among the fur-wrapped, big-eyed youngest.

Sigrid's guide led her to the central and highest dome of felt upon its wagon. In front of it, instead of the horsetail standard which would have marked a nomad's clan, stood a spear, and on the spear a skull. Years and weather had polished it until it gleamed. The wind whistled through its empty eye sockets.

"An enemy?" Sigrid inquired of her guide.

The girl shook her head. "Clan-founder," she said. "Margit."

As if the name had been a signal, the flap of the yurt swung open. A woman stepped out. She was old, and she walked stiffly, but it was clear that she had been a fighter in her day. Another came behind her, and that one was young, and startling to look at. All the faces that Sigrid had seen had been like those of the first, outermost sentry: nomad crossed on Americ and Northeuropean stock, with a suggestion of Frystaat or Edenite or Bandari, and of course the rare, unmistakable Soldier. This was a type rarer still — Sigrid would have said impossible, unless the woman had been bred with care from a near-pure line. Similar stock had gone into a number of the Soldier blood-lines, but never so close to its original.

This was Maasai. The name was preserved in the Citadel's database, with the rest of the legends and the lost races. Native Terran warrior stock, badly depleted around the time of the CoDominion's founding, but restored and recreated in the first experiments in what would become the Soldiers. Here was a living relic of the old line.

A woman as tall as Sigrid and even leaner, even in leather and furs. A face molded out of bronze, with high wide cheekbones, wide-flaring nostrils, full-lipped mouth. Tight-kinked hair wound in plaits, pulled back together and knotted in a broad leather band. Body that moved as a predator moves, with smooth unconscious power.

Sigrid's vitals twisted with pure lust. Not for the woman — that was not one of Sigrid's aberrations — but for what she was; for the genes she carried, and would pass to her children.

It required discipline to turn from her, to hear what the elder of the women was saying. "I am Margit," she said in the language of the Citadel, or one very like it; changed, but not so much as to be incomprehensible. "I welcome you to the clan of Margit of the Katlinsfolk."

"Sigrid," said Sigrid. "Of the Citadel."

No one seemed astonished or even afraid. The eyes on her were curious, no more; and if wary, only as wary as anyone needed to be in front of a stranger. Margit — it seemed to be her title as well as her name — inclined her head and beckoned. "Come to my hearth," she said.

That was in fact the clanfire, the fire laid in a bed of stones in front of the chieftain's yurt. The Maasai woman tended it, feeding it with cakes of dried muskylope dung, while the chieftain and her guest settled on rugs and cushions brought by young women. None was shy or meek as women would have been in a nomad camp. They made it clear that this was service freely given, and bearing honor with it.

"You have no men here," Sigrid said after a round or three of amenities. There was the inevitable kvass, and bread warm from the hearth, and roasted meat — muskylope, mutton, goat — and goat cheese. Sigrid's appetite was a matter for much amusement. "She eats like a man," someone had said, sparking Sigrid's observation.

"No," said Margit. "We have no men. Do you think that we need them?"

Mockery glinted in the old woman's eyes. Sigrid acknowledged it with the twitch of a smile. "For protection, no. For breeding, certainly. Unless you have technologies which even we of the Citadel have lost?"

Margit laughed. "We breed our daughters in the old way. The best way, most would tell you."

"Without men?"

"There are men in plenty in the world. When the season comes, when the clans gather, our allies send their young men; or the young men come themselves, out of curiosity. With them we breed our daughters."

"And sons."

"The sons go back to their fathers. Or," said Margit, "if the fathers will not have them, we give them to the earth."

"To the stobor."

"To the earth," Margit repeated. "You do the same, they tell us."

"We cull," said Sigrid. "We make no distinction of gender. Only of viability."

Margit nodded. It might have been an old woman's palsy, but her eyes were shrewd under the wrinkled lids. "Your kind have come here. They breed strong children. Too many, unfortunately, are sons."

"Three in four," Sigrid said. "Their fathers claimed them, then?"

"Their fathers died."

Sigrid sat unmoving. "So I was told. And you are free of the yoke."

"Have you come to take vengeance?"

"No," said Sigrid. "Any Soldier who died at your hands would not have been fit to carry on the Race."

"Even if he died by treachery?"

"That is a failure of intelligence."

"How cold you are," said a new voice, "and how hard."

Sigrid did not turn to face the Maasai woman. She had no need to see what her other senses so perfectly encompassed. "I am a Soldier."

"You are more than a Soldier."

Sigrid turned then. The Maasai was smiling.

"I am the Eyes of the clan," the woman said. "You are not what the Soldiers were who came to us."

"I am a woman," said Sigrid.

The Maasai laughed. "So you are! You would never have passed the first guard if you had not been. No, Soldier woman: there is more to you than you would like us to see. What goddess set the steel in your bones?"

"Genetics," said Sigrid. She was growing — not afraid. No. But wary. "You too have Soldier blood."

"Not as you know it," the Maasai said. "I am the Eyes of the clan. So was my mother before me, and her mother, and hers, down the long years of this world."

Sigrid's eyes narrowed. Data clicked together. "Parthenogenesis," she said. "We are told — I was taught — that those experiments failed."

"So you are told," said the Maasai. "I had not known there were Cyborg women."

"They are rare," Sigrid said.

"How they must have loathed to see you go!"

"If they saw me, I failed every test of my skill."

"I doubt you failed," said the Maasai. "I dreamed you, Cyborg woman. I saw a great savior, and a great danger. You will be our salvation, or our destruction."

"That," said Sigrid, "is superstitious nonsense."

"Of course," said the Maasai. "It is no less true for that."

Sigrid sat perfectly erect on the rug, propped by no cushion, as she had sat since she came to the clanfire. Her face, she knew, wore no expression at all. Her breathing was steady. Her heart beat at precisely its normal rate. Her body was hers to control, within and without.

Her mind was not so easily mastered. This high-steppe shaman with her beautiful genes, this daughter of no father, was completely alien and profoundly disturbing. The Breedmaster's heir itched to take her apart, to see what she was made of. The Soldier yearned for the same, but in another sense altogether. The Cyborg, collating data, found her impossible; but there was no denying the evidence of augmented senses when it sat within arm's reach, clearly aware of the danger and just as clearly unperturbed by it.

Sigrid had come to steal a mare. She had found a treasure at least as valuable. "Are there more like you," Sigrid asked of the Maasai, "or are you alone in this generation?"

"Stay with us," said the Maasai, "and see."

They trusted her. That was the strangest of many strange things among these people: they knew what she was, and they kept no secrets. They saw no need. They had always disposed of the Soldiers who came to them. And Sigrid was a woman.

They were not innocents, or weaklings. They had preserved their tribe's integrity against every enemy who came against it, since the early days on Haven.

*     *     *

"Katlin was a convict," Margit said by the clanfire, two cycles after Sigrid's coming. This was a lesson they all knew, from the way they listened, youngest closest, lips moving as if to recite the words with their chieftain. "She had been a terrorist, a warrior for women, when women were like cattle, and men were their masters."

"As they are among the nomads," the girlchildren murmured together, as in a ritual.

"So she was sent away," Margit said, "in BuReloc's ship, in the belly of the hellbeast, roaring from star to star. Others died on that journey. Still more died on Haven, under the yoke. But she grew stronger. And — much stranger — she lost her hate. She learned to pity the men who held her prisoner. She swore an oath."

"A great oath," the children said.

"A very great oath," said Margit. "The greatest oath of all. To be no man's chattel. To take her fellows as she could, and go away, and raise her daughters to be free."

"And they were free," the children said.

"So they were," said Margit. "But it was a long fight, and a hard one. They were few at first, the Katlinsfolk. There were only Katlin, and Margit —"

"Margit!" the children chorused.

Margit smiled. "And Margit, and Kyoko, and Djuna, and Marisa, and Lais, and France who died birthing the first daughter of the tribe; and that was France, too, for her mother's remembrance."

"And there was the other one," the children said, "the one whose name is hidden."

"The other," said Margit, "came later, walking across the steppe, alone and unarmed and carrying her mother on her back. She had found a place, she said, to bear the child that swelled her belly. She would lead Katlin's folk to it, because her dreams had told her she must. Katlin's folk laughed," Margit said, "just as you laughed, Soldier woman, and called her dreaming nonsense. But they followed her, because others of them were bearing, and they would die if they went back to the valley they had left, but they would die if they remained on the high steppe. They followed the stranger, and her mother whose face was exactly like her own. And they found the valley she had spoken of."

"Katlinsvale," the children said.

"Katlinsvale," said Margit. "The deep place, the hidden place, the place where no man goes. There the stranger bore her daughter, and the daughter had her mother's face. There the others bore their children, and all were daughters but one, and that one was a gift to the earth."

"To the stobor," Sigrid said.

"To the earth," said Margit, as if that too were ritual. "So are we free, and our valley is free, and we take men only as we choose."

"As we choose," the children said. Grinning and tumbling over one another if they were youngest, or departing with dignity if they were old enough to be in training for war.

Impressive, judged Sigrid, watching the women at mounted exercises. They had settled on a very practical mode of fighting for their gender and their resources: mounted archery in the main, with recurved bows such as the Mongols had, and the small crossbow, and the lance, with the saber for close-in fighting. More advanced weapons were rare. Those who had them seemed to regard them more as heirlooms than as usable tools of war — sensible enough in the circumstances. Ammunition would be hard to come by, this far out on the steppe.

They were good at what they did. They had discipline, unusual for nomads. They fought in units, with duty rosters, and every woman of age or in condition to fight was expected to serve; even if she was pregnant, until she went to the valley. As units they lived, ate and slept. They hunted as units, herded as units, saw to the camp in relays according to the roster.

Sigrid, as a guest, did as she pleased. If she stayed she would be expected to live as the others lived, under their laws. Laws which, she conceded, were not ill-conceived.

They maintained order without repression; they enforced discipline without compulsion.

She liked these people, this way of living. She came to that knowledge with reluctance, almost with dismay. Liking was a weakness — in a Soldier undesirable, in a Cyborg unconscionable.

"You forget," said the Maasai, "that you are human as well as Soldier."

Sigrid had grown to expect that the Maasai should read her, however well she masked herself. That the woman's ancestor had been augmented was beyond question; those augments gave her, at times, almost a Cyborg's perception.

"You never laugh," the Maasai said. "You almost never smile. Yet you have it in you to be as any woman is. What fools your Soldiers were, to train you as they did."

"I was trained as a Soldier."

"As a man," said the Maasai. "You are not a man. You are yourself."

"Cold," said Sigrid. "Hard. I was bred so."

"So you think," said the Maasai. And walked away as she was given to doing, having said all that she intended to say. Done all the damage that, for the moment, she intended to do.

The dogs that watched the herds were a breed new to Sigrid, who in her studies had learned the breeds of hawk and hound and horse as well as human. Big dogs but wiry, thick-coated for Haven's cold, blindingly fast and impressively strong and quite remarkably intelligent.

One of them had taken to accompanying her when she walked in the camp. It was a he, and it had a sister, smaller and more flighty, who would not let Sigrid touch her as the other did, but hovered at a distance, watching warily, and followed where its brother went.

The male moved as she stood in the silence of the Maasai's leaving, to thrust a cold nose into her palm. She looked down and thought of wringing its neck. It looked up, plumed tail wagging slightly. Not subservient. Not doglike in its devotion. But determined, clearly, to remind her that it had conceived a preference for her.

Its sister crouched beyond, at five meters precisely. The

brother's eyes were brown. The sister's were eerily silver: blind, it seemed, but keen enough in the testing, narrowed now and fixed on Sigrid.

She laughed, startling herself. "Do I need herding, then?" she asked the bitch.

The bitch crouched lower. Leaped, circled, crouched again. Waiting. Guarding her herd of one, her odd sheep.

The mare was not kept under any particular guard. That might have been taken for foolishness, but Sigrid was inclined to call it prudence: hiding the beast in plain sight. She was nothing unusual to look at. A bay like most of the horses this clan bred, no distinctive markings, no particular turn of speed or intelligence. Her foals were slightly better — she had been bred to good stallions. None of them would have caught Sigrid's eye had they not been pointed out to her, and that before she even asked. Foolishness again. Or a deeper reading of herself and her purposes than she might have believed cattle capable of.

Paranoia was a form of wisdom. Margit had said that. She denied she had learned it from a Soldier. It was a maxim of Katlin's, handed down from the beginning.

Soldiers tended to underestimate cattle. The word itself was a trap; use of it and, worse than that, belief in it, had killed Soldiers more than once. Katlinsfolk were not only cattle but female.

But Sigrid was female, and she had been trained rigorously to know the enemy for what they were. Less than she, yes, one on one; but so were Soldiers. She did not let herself rest secure that she was among barbarians, and innocents at that, so sure of her sympathy with their gender and their cause that they could imagine no threat from her. If they trusted her, then they believed they had defenses against her.

The dogs that watched the horses watched her as she walked through the herd. The horses ignored her for the most part or raised heads from their grazing, curious but calm. The foals aped their dams or pretended massive, snorting, wheeling terror, but with ears up and tails high, no more capable of true deception than they were of standing still.

The mare's youngest foal was one of the spirited ones, bay like its dam, but with a promise of greater height and fineness. It moved well, high and light. More than steppe pony was in that bloodline. Someone, somewhere, had brought in Terran desert stock, testing it maybe, to see if it would take to the highlands, and this foal had thrown back to it. The deep girth and broad nostrils adapted well to the thin air. The high tail could be a difficulty in a climate that needed to preserve heat more than to shed it, but the coat looked more than adequate, shorter than the other foals', but thick and well insulated.

Its dam was a little slimmer in the leg than the run of the herd, a little finer in the head, but still a thickset, blocky, shaggy-coated steppe pony. She allowed Sigrid to approach her, kept on grazing calmly while Sigrid's hands ran over her. It had been impossible to pack in proper examination equipment; a whole laboratory would just have been enough, and a shuttle to carry it in, and while she was at it, a ship's sickbay full of instruments from Old Sauron. As it was, she had her hands and her senses and some little training in horse-doctoring. They told her nothing but that this was a mare of some dozen T-years, who had had several foals, who was sound and evidently sensible, and already pregnant with a new foal. Its sire prowled the herd's edge, a big clay-colored brute with a hammer head and a mean eye. No doubt they had bred him for size. He appeared to have little else to commend him.

The filly slipped in under Sigrid's arm and attacked the mare's udder. Sigrid stepped back. She did not expect that anyone who watched might be deceived, but for appearance's sake she examined another mare or two. None would have done for the Citadel. Too small for the run of Soldiers. Sturdy enough to carry weight, certainly, but the weight would not be exceptionally comfortable with its feet dragging on the ground.

Sigrid took a long circuit back to the center of the camp. She would take the mare and the two older fillies. The yearling she would leave. The suckling was a problem; she would have to consider it. Most efficient to leave the creature behind, but it looked to be the best of the mare's foals. She could carry it if need be: it was small enough.

There was the matter of the guards, of the dogs and of the distance from this camp to the Citadel, long kilometers of steppe populated by nomads for whom horse stealing was a high art and Soldier killing a feat every young hellion dreamed of. Sigrid was under no illusion that her task would be easy. Or that she would be welcomed back without penalty.

The Maasai was waiting for her by the clanfire. "You are summoned," the woman said, "to the Mother Clan." She was calm about it, as if she had expected it. The inevitable hangers-on and listeners-in were not. This, it was apparent, was a great honor.

Sigrid was as calm as the Maasai, but it was a very different calm: the stillness of the hunter. Here, maybe, was a part of the trap. To separate her from what she came for. To take her deeper into the tribe's territory; to surround her with a ring of watchful clans.

She could refuse. No rope or chain could hold her. And when the clan took its sleeptime — in truenight, this point in the cycle — she would take the horses and go.

But there was the Maasai, who was as valuable a finding as the mare. And there was her own curiosity. She wanted to see this Mother Clan. She wanted to look on this valley that was in no records of the Citadel. It was data that would be useful when the Citadel brought this tribe under its control. There were priceless genetic treasures here, in humans and in horses. She wanted them; needed them; as an unaugmented human needs the gold he hoards in his strongboxes; for the beauty as well as the utility.

If he saw her — What would he do if he saw her?

*Court her?* Temujin wondered. *Kill her?* The nomad's laugh was bitter. The Sauron bitch would laugh till her cold pale eyes dissolved in tears of mirth if he offered bride price for her. And to whom could he offer it? The Citadel? That would but set all the filthy Saurons howling with laughter.

Kill her, then? He laughed again, no less ruefully. As well face a stobor pack, armed only with a pile of over-ripe tennis-ball fruit.

But he could not get her out of his mind. She'd robbed him of honor, robbed him of pride, squeezed knowledge from him like a man wringing a damp rag dry. All the *tngri* of sky, earth and water — and all the demons — knew he'd tried to forget her.

No use. For somehow, Sauron arrogance was in her transmuted to the sort of spirit a nomad dreams to find in the finest of horses, a spirit that would never yield to any greater force, that never acknowledged any greater force than itself. But if one bearing such a spirit could be per-suaded to cooperate . . . oh, if . . .

When he thought about it rationally, he knew he was ob-sessed. But he had fewer than three Haven years on him — say, twenty T-years, more or less. The young yield easily to obsession, and often call it love. And so here he was, riding back to Nûrnen to seek her out. Searching for her in Kat-linsvale would be worse than useless; having betrayed the secret of the women's tribe, he could await only painful death there.

She could have returned by now, with the mares he'd told her of. Nûrnen was his best chance. One way or another, he would have his reckoning there.

The town loomed ahead, less than a klick off now. He could see it, hear it. The wind blew behind him, from the pass the Citadel warded down into Shangri-La Valley. Otherwise, he would have smelled Nûrnen, too. Even with the wind at his back, he imagined the smell, the half-foul, half-rich reek of a city that existed to serve the Citadel.

Ahead, something was mounted on pikes jabbed into the ground to either side of the road: several somethings, as a matter of fact. Temujin reined in for a longer look. His stomach did a slow flipflop. Sick spit poured into his mouth. Once — quite a while ago, given their present wind-cured state — these had been the constituent parts of . . . two men, Temujin judged. The two heads were closest to the roadway.

Placards hung beneath them. In several languages —
the Sauron's own Americ, the Russki that was widely
spoken through Haven's valleys, Turkic written in Latin
and Arabic letters, the sinuous Uighur script Temujin read
most readily, even in the blocky, angular Bandarit alphabet
— they announced the victims' names, stations and crimes.

One placard was very much to the point. All it said was
THE PEASANT YEGOR — ACCOMPLICE. Temujin snorted.
Whatever the peasant Yegor had been accomplice to, it had
brought him a nasty end.

Temujin's gaze swung to the placard under the other
head. This one had more text. It read: JUCHI THE BANDIT,
BROUGHT HERE TO JUSTICE FOR HIS VICIOUS CRIMES.
THUS PERISH ALL WHO CHALLENGE THE DOMINION OF
THE SOLDIERS.

Juchi . . . Temujin's lips shaped a soundless whistle. Tales
of Juchi had accreted round whatever core of truth there
was like layers of nacre round a sandgrain, forming at last a
shimmering hotsprings oyster pearl of legend. Temujin
did not know how much of the story of incest and murder
and suicide and mutilation to believe; that tale had been
growing since before he was born. He did know Juchi'd
had something to do with the fall of the Saurons' Angband
Base, northwest of the Pale and far to the south of his own
people's grazing lands.

He also knew, or thought he knew, that blind accursed
Juchi was accompanied in his wanderings by his daughter
(or sister? or both?) Aisha. Where was Aisha's quartered
body, then? Who was this poor Yegor whom the Saurons
had mutilated in her place?

He read Juchi's placard again, and spat on the ground in
scorn. *Soldiers*, indeed! They were Saurons, nothing better.
They could call themselves muskylopes if they cared to; it
would not change their nature by jot or tittle.

And he had gone and become besotted of one of them.
He knew it was stupid; he knew it was worse than stupid.
Had she somehow ensorcelled him, other than by being
herself? He didn't think so, but would he know it if he *were*
ensorcelled?

"Eternal Blue Sky," he muttered under his breath, realizing that if by some miracle — or would it be disaster? — he gained Sigrid (about as likely as the return of the lost Imperial 77th, the Land Gators, in full battle regalia), he might be wiser to speak of her and her kind as Soldiers. One day, surely, his tongue would slip, and she would tear him in half.

He'd had practice in laughing at himself, had Temujin. Every time he did it, it came easier, so that by now it was almost second nature. Laughter kept the wound in his soul from stinging as it would have otherwise. So did kvass and the tipples the farmer folk brewed from fruits and grains: beer, stout, stronger drinks like vodka and tennis-fruit brandy.

He dug heels into his pony's sides. The beast obediently stretched into a trot toward the city. He knew he should go back to the lands of his people and take up the threads of his life. He knew Sigrid was probably not in Nûrnen; it was just the next-most-likely place, after Katlinsvale — and he dared not go *there*. Even if the Katlinsfolk had taken Sigrid in, they'd roast him over a slow fire for blabbing. No man he'd talked to mentioned her being there, but that meant little. Yes, he should turn around, right now.

"Sigrid," Temujin whispered, and kept his face toward Nûrnen.

A tiny flicker of motion, out on the dun steppe near the horizon. Without his consciously willing it, Chief Assault Leader Sharku's eyes went into telescopic mode. The Soldier's sight leapt across kilometers. The tiny flicker resolved itself: men on horseback, advance guards for a group of yurts behind. One of the guards carried the clan's standard, a white sheepskin tied to the top of a tall pole.

Sharku held up his left hand. The Soldiers reined in. "Nomads ahead," he said. "Either they're the Ak-Koyunlu Turks, or someone's setting an ambush."

The second ranker of the four-man party, Chief Assault Leader Mumak, grunted out a minimum ration of laughter. "Be a sorry looking ambush after it closes on us." He stroked the magazine of his assault rifle as if it were a tribute maiden's bare breast.

The junior Soldier, a newly fledged Assault Leader named Ufthak, asked Sharku, "Shall we dismount?" His long, thin face betrayed hot eagerness to close with the plainsmen, regardless of whether they were in fact hostile. Very Soldierly was the motto stamped on the coins minted at the Citadel: KILL 'EM ALL AND LET GOD SORT 'EM OUT.

Sharku considered, shook his head. "No, we'll stay on our horses. Horses are swank to the nomads. If those are the Ak-Koyunlu up ahead, they're friendlies — haven't missed a tribute payment in twenty T-years. And if they aren't the White Sheep Turks, we can afford to let 'em make the first move before we get off our beasts."

Prestige was important to a Tribute Party, out collecting goods and women from the Citadel's subject tribes. That was why the troop behind him consisted solely of officers — impressive for the cattle, a pain in the ass for the man sent to lead. Two types of officers got assigned this duty: promising young commanders in training to rule and administer — which implied ability to deal with the cattle in some manner other than shooting them — and those best kept out of the way. There had been a time when the Soldiers spoke little to the cattle except "obey or die." They had long since learned that it saved ammunition and effort to command cattle in their own symbolic language. The Soldiers were nothing if not efficient.

Had good horseflesh not impressed the nomads, Sharku would have preferred to approach them on foot. He could run as fast as a horse could gallop, lope as fast as a horse could trot, and hold his gait long after even a steppe pony broke down. Afoot, he was also more maneuverable than any horse could hope to be, and a much smaller target to boot.

"They'd better be who they claim they are," Mumak said. "Me, I've gone too long without any. Fighting's fine, but I'd sooner fuck."

That was good for an argument any time Soldiers gathered; about half preferred one, half the other. The arguments never settled anything, and only led to more fights. Sharku didn't feel like dealing with a fight right now — although the old argument was better than chewing over the weird and disturbing fate of Battlemaster Glorund. He held up his hand again to forestall discussion. "We'll just have to see what comes, that's all."

From a Soldier, that passed for wit. "What comes, eh?" said Snaga, a Chief Assault Leader junior to Mumak, though a couple of T-years older. Sharku was one of the ones everyone preferred to have out of the way, except when he led a small unit into combat. Envy tinged his voice as he went on: "You don't even care whether you get your dick wet or not, do you, not with Chichek waiting for you back at the Citadel."

"The day I don't care if I get my dick wet or not, Snaga, you can leave my carcass out for drillbits to chew, because I won't need it any more," Sharku retorted.

Snaga, who'd likely never be promoted again if he lived another hundred T-years, prudently shut up. Despite automatic defense of his own machismo, though, Sharku's face wrinkled into an unfamiliar smile. Chichek was indeed a woman in ten thousand.

Her name meant *flower* in the Turkic dialect of the steppes. Like most tribute maidens, she'd come to the Citadel nervous and afraid. She had more reason for nerves and fear than most: her father Gasim headed the Rolling Plains tribe, which made her outright hostage as well as payment for her people's birthing privileges in the Shangri-La Valley. She'd come in unassigned, and fallen to Sharku purely by lot.

And then — well, the Soldiers knew the unexpected happened sometimes. Instead of shrinking from Sharku's touch, Chichek the flower had flowered under it. Enthusiasm will flatter any man; Sharku did his best to keep on pleasing the girl (who really was flower-pretty, in the moon-faced, slant-eyed nomad way). He watched with more than a little self-satisfaction as her quickly kindled passion deepened into love.

He still wondered just when he'd begun to love her, too, as opposed to finding her a delightfully pleasant convenience. He supposed it was the day, five T-years gone now, when she'd handed him their firstborn son. Gimilzor

(whom Chichek sometimes called Gulsheri, the name of
Gasim's dead father) was a lad to reckon with; his proud
father hoped he'd rise high, someday. Breedmaster Titus
thought he might, if he lived up to his genes. Perhaps as
high as Battlemaster. He wasn't a Cyborg, true, but
Cyborgs were rare and getting rarer; the time was coming
when a good plain Soldier might aspire to any rank he
chose. The first ruler of the Citadel — the legendery Diettinger himself — had not been a Cyborg, after all. Neither
had his successors, although the Battlemasters were the
real rulers now. Gimilzor could rise higher than his father.

Sharku shook his big fair head, faintly puzzled. Somewhere down deep, he knew he'd have fallen in love with
Chichek no matter how the child turned out. The
birthstruggle was what had united them, not its outcome. A
Soldier had but to recall the fate of Old Sauron the
homeworld to know that not all struggles, however noble,
are crowned with success.

Faint across distance and through cool, thin highland air,
a valveless trumpet sounded, snapping Sharku back to the
here and now. The notes were as they should have been, a
call to parley. Sharku wondered whether he and his men had
been seen or if the trumpeter simply began the parley call as
soon as he was close to where he expected to meet the Soldiers. The latter, most likely; the Chief Assault Leader
doubted anyone with unaugmented eyes could have picked
out his party from background clutter at this distance.

Of course, the Bandari sold telescopes or binoculars
sometimes for a fabulous price, or more often gave them as
presents of vast worth to tribes they wished to influence.
Sharku scowled; the White Sheep had better not been
intriguing in *that* direction.

"Forward," he said, and urged his pony into a trot. Feeling the wind in his face as the animal carried him along,
feeling its muscles surge beneath him, drew from him a
scowl rather than contentment. How could the plainsmen
make such a fuss over their horses? He was a better
traveller than this stupid beast any day. The Soldier's
Americ dialect had a curious name for a person who'd

rather sit around on his backside than actually do anything. Aboard a horse, Sharku felt like a couch potato.

When Soldiers and nomads had drawn a couple of klicks closer to each other, the Turks' scouts suddenly recoiled, like stobor drawing back from a carcass when cliff lions approached. The trumpeter began to play louder and faster. Chuckling, Sharku said: "Now they know we're here."

He made sure he had a round in the chamber of his assault rifle, but kept the change lever in the safe position. As junior most Soldier, Ufthak unfurled the standard that answered to the Turks' white sheepskin. Blazing crimson on space-black, the Lidless Eye fluttered free.

The nomad scouts halted. Only the man who bore the tribal emblem rode forward, he and one other. Again Sharku's vision overleaped intervening distance. The second Turk was a middle-aged man with graying hair, wearing a jacket edged with cliff lion fur and a pair of gold bracelets on his right arm. His pony's trappings also glittered with gold.

"That's Omin Hotal all right — their chief," the Chief Assault Leader said. "I recognize him; I've taken tribute from the White Sheep Turks before. Doesn't look like they're going to get gay with us this time around, either. They're good cattle."

"Too bad," Snaga said, his *voce* not quite *sotto* enough. He was of the sooner-fight-than-fuck school.

On approaching within a hundred meters, Omin Hotal's standard bearer dipped the white sheepskin in salute to the Lidless Eye. Ufthak did not return the compliment; Soldiers never saluted cattle.

"Peace be upon you, envoys of the Citadel," Omin Hotal called. "May Allah and the spirits grant you broad flocks and many sons."

"Upon you peace as well, bold chieftain," Sharku replied. He knew his Turkic bore a whistling Americ accent, but he was fluent enough; talking with Chichek helped keep him so. He also knew both he and Omin Hotal lied when they wished aloud for peace — both preferred conquest. Ritual was ritual, though, so on with it: "May Allah and the spirits grant the generous wish to him who made it."

"I welcome you as a guest to my yurts," Omin Hotal intoned. Sharku shot him a look full of sharp suspicion. The word he'd used for guest, *juchi*, was also a name bitter as oxbane in Soldiers' ears. If the chief aimed at mockery, he played a dangerous game. Sharku decided to let it pass —once.

The Chief Assault Leader said: "I am honored to partake of your bread and salt." *What a liar this duty makes of me,* he thought. He wished he could tell the unwashed, fanatical barbarian just what he truly thought of him. Soldiers were not supposed to have such counterproductive emotions. If they did, they did not display them.

If Omin Hotal had similar thoughts about the party of Soldiers—and he likely did—he concealed them behind a smiling mask. He said, "Come. We shall eat; we shall drink; we shall talk. Afterward, as it pleases you, you may take such other pleasures as are men's."

The butter-bland mask did not slip. Sharku respected him for that, to the limited degree he respected any cattle. Of course, the chief was stuck here between drillbits before and tamerlanes behind. Nomad custom set great store on the virtue of women, but clan survival demanded that they surrender tribute maidens to the Soldiers. Though survival counted for more, yielding meant humiliation. Omin Hotal handled it better than most clan leaders.

The chief said, "Come with me, then, Chief Assault Leader Sharku of the Citadel, and your fellows with you." He wheeled his pony and rode back toward the main body of the clan. His standard bearer followed: among plainsmen, the chief *was* the clan, the standard only symbol.

The Soldiers' usage was different. Ufthak rode first with the Lidless Eye, proclaiming the Citadel greater than its representatives here. Sharku followed, then Mumak and Snaga. They went past Omin Hotal's scouts without so much as a sideways glance. Sharku had already sized them up from afar. They were tough enough men, by cattle standards; Omin Hotal would gather the best of the younger warriors from all the encampments of the White Sheep Turks for his personal guard. A couple carried black-powder carbines. Like the Soldiers' horses, those were more for show than for use. Horn- and sinew-reinforced bows were the plainsmen's real weapons of choice, with *shamshirs* for close-in work. Leather cuirasses dipped in boiling wax reflected the light of Byers' Star with an almost metallic glitter.

The scouts came back behind the Soldiers. Sharku would not lose face by turning his head, but used every speck of enhanced hearing to listen for the click of a carbine lock, the rattle of an arrow against its mates in a quiver as it was drawn. If the cattle were foolish enough to try something, they'd regret it. *Each man his own army* was the Soldiers' way.

Nothing untoward befell. Omin Hotal dismounted and stood waiting for Sharku to arrive. The Chief Assault Leader reined in his mount a couple of meters in front of the plainsman. Omin Hotal stepped forward, held the head of Sharku's horse while the Soldier descended from it. The nomad bowed low. "Enter my yurt, Soldier of the Citadel; use it as you would your own."

"You do me too much honor, chief of the White Sheep Turks," Sharku said, though he would have been outraged had Omin Hotal done him any less. He could easily have sprung from the ground up to the doorway of the wheeled cart, but a two-step stool took away the need.

Given the nomads' primitive technology, the yurt was a fine piece of engineering. Its framework of woven sticks arched up into an igloo shape, almost as if its rude builders had heard of the geodesic dome. The thick layers of felted wool and muskylope fur covered the framework, one over it and the other inside. The dead air trapped between them added to the insulation.

The outer layer of felt was whitened with lime. The inner felt wall, as Sharku saw when he slipped between the cloth lips of the entrance, was covered with felt vines and trees, animals and birds. Their bright colors shouted at him. He wondered how they looked to the cattle; his eyes needed less light to respond to color than theirs. But he supposed the nomad women would not have made them if all their beauty went to waste.

Organa, Omin Hotal's principal wife, sat crosslegged to the left — the woman's side — of the doorway. She bent forward until her forehead touched the felt of the flooring. "Allah and the spirits grant you peace, Soldier," she murmured.

"And to you and yours, Organa *Khatun*," Sharku answered. He seated himself to the right of the yurt's entrance. So, one by one, did his three companions. Omin Hotal waited outside a few minutes, calling out instructions of one sort or another to his men. Even that pause showed deference: he allowed the Soldiers to be alone with his woman. That she was too old and dried up to be worth having mattered not at all; as with ironic wishes for peace, symbolism worked here.

The chief came in, knocked his forehead on the floor, then sat at Sharku's left hand. "Give the guests kvass, woman!" he shouted angrily. "Have the spirits stolen your manners?"

"I am sorry, my husband," Organa said — yet another ritual. The skin lay right behind her. She poured the cloudy liquid into ram's-horn cups, gave one to each Soldier and the last to Omin Hotal. Her turn would come later.

The nomad chief dipped a forefinger into the fermented mare's milk, sprinkled a couple of drops over a little stuffed felt idol hung above the entrance. He muttered in Turkic: "In Allah's name these drops I do not drink, but give them to the spirit of the yurt, that he may watch over us and keep us safe."

Sharku, as was his right, raised the first cup to his lips. He drank with loud slurping noises, as any polite nomad would have. The other Soldiers drained their cups in turn, and used the conscious control they had over their diaphragms to belch titanically. Omin Hotal beamed with pride at the compliment and drank last.

Dried muskylope dung burned on an iron pan in the center of the yurt. Its pungent smoke rose through the round opening at the center of the dome above. Today's fire was for warmth only, not for cooking as it normally would have been. Omin Hotal said, "Our tribute maidens will fetch the meal they have prepared to honor you, Soldiers of the Citadel."

The chief's timing was good. A pretty girl bowed her way into the yurt and set before the Soldiers a tray full of strips of horsemeat dried and preserved by sun and cold. Little wicker bowls round the edge of the tray held sauces for dipping, some sweet, others fiery. Under flowery perfume, Sharku smelled the girl's sharp fear. He smelled that scent every time he went out to collect tribute maidens.

The horsemeat was hard as leather. Sharku demolished strip after strip with jaws stronger than an unaugmented man's. The girl stared in amazement at how fast the Soldiers emptied the tray. The fear-stink eased; on the steppe, gluttony was something to admire. She was almost smiling as she retreated.

Organa poured more kvass, this time for herself as well as the men. It bit Sharku's tongue like vinegar, but left a pleasing aftertaste of almonds. He drank cup after cup. He metabolized ethanol too fast to get drunk on anything that wasn't distilled. Omin Hotal, as host, had to try to keep up with him. The nomad chief's face grew very red.

Another tribute maiden brought in wheaten griddlecakes with clarified butter and sweet syrup. The flour for the cakes had to have come from a lowlands valley; on the plains they were a luxury. The Soldiers wolfed them down. Omin Hotal giggled. "Would that Allah had given me your bellies," he said. Organa poured again.

After two courses, Sharku could with propriety inquire, "How has your clan fared since last we met, chief of the Ak-Koyunlu?"

"Well enough, though nothing comes easy," Omin Hotal answered: a one-sentence summary of life everywhere on Haven. Then he gave more detail. "We used tar and pitch to control an outbreak of mange among the camels; the flocks bear well, thanks to your courtesy in allowing the females to drop their young in Shangri-La Valley; we have lost not a single pregnant woman, again thanks to your courtesy."

"I am pleased for you," Sharku said, more or less sincerely: it was convenient to let docile cattle thrive. "And your dealings with your neighbors on the steppe?" He grew alert as he awaited Omin Hotal's reply — though no *Waffenfarbe* showed his branch of service, he was an intelligence officer by training. Collecting tribute maidens also gave the Citadel a chance to collect information about foes not yet subdued.

The chief spat in the pan that held the burning muskylope dung. Saliva hissed on the hot iron; steam rose with the smoke. "That to Arik Burka, pimp and son of ten pimps, and to all his clan. The spawn of an addled land gator egg had the gall to try moving his flocks to a stretch of plain which has belonged to the White Sheep for generations. I told him I would call on the Citadel for aid if he did not desist, and he yielded. Happy the man who boasts the Soldiers for his friends!"

"May you long be happy, great chief." Inside, Sharku smiled. Omin Hotal might reckon even unleavened wheatcakes a treat, but he knew on which side his bread was buttered. The Chief Assault Leader slurped kvass, then asked, "Of what other doings have you heard?"

Omin Hotal looked owlishly down into his cup. "There is the matter of the Seven — " His wife Organa, who had drunk much less than he, suffered a timely coughing fit. He glanced over at her in surprise, then shut up.

He got away with it for a time, for yet another tribute maiden brought in a tureen full of one of the most prized steppe delicacies: a stew of mutton and oats, served in the boiled stomach of a sheep. The nature of the wrapper did not discommode Sharku in the slightest; to a Soldier, protein was protein.

"An excellent *khaagis*, great chief," Sharku said, belching appreciatively. He drank more kvass to make Omin Hotal do the same, then, voice casual, went on, "You were speaking of the Seven . . . ?"

"Was I?" Omin Hotal's narrow eyes widened for a split second; even sodden with drink, his body grew taut. *Something here*, Sharku thought, keeping his own responses under tight control. The chief might have deceived his fellow cattle; he could not hope to befool a Soldier. Well, perhaps he could hope: "I don't recall what I said."

"Liar." Snaga's voice came flat and harsh as the crack of an assault rifle. The Senior Assault Leader stood, his fur cap almost brushing the felt ceiling of the yurt. He glared down at Omin Hotal. "You boast you are the Soldiers' friend, then seek to lie to us? I ought to break your back and leave you out for the stobor, like a baby that doesn't deserve to live."

Sharku made a tiny gesture with one finger: *enough*. He didn't want Omin Hotal reviled past the point at which rage ousted fear. As Snaga folded back down to a crosslegged pose, Sharku said, "Do you fear we will take out our anger on you, great chief, for passing on what others do? That is not the Citadel's way: if we shoot the messenger, who then will bring us messages? Speak, and no harm will come to you. By Allah and the spirits I swear it."

"Swear also by the ship that brought your kind here, the *Dol Guldur*," Organa said harshly. "You are an infidel; you would take Allah's sacred name in vain for your own profit."

Since she was right, the Soldier could only sit still and endure the accusation. "If you would have it so, *khatun*, I will swear by the *Dol Guldur*," he said slowly. From his belt pouch he pulled a silver coin with the image of the ship stamped on it. "Keep this, if you would, in memory of the oath." To his mind, it was as conditional as any other, but Organa did not have to know that.

Omin Hotal looked toward his principal wife once more. Now she nodded. The chief said, "It is a bad business, Soldier of the Citadel, a feud whose roots run back many T-years."

"What feud doesn't have roots like that?" Snaga sounded openly scornful.

Again Sharku twitched a finger in warning. "Go on," he urged Omin Hotal.

"I shall." Something — maybe fear — had come close to sobering the nomad chief. Picking his words with obvious care, he said, "The matter of the Seven, Soldier of the Citadel, springs from that of Juchi the Accursed."

Sharku needed all his discipline not to come to full, visible alertness at hearing the name. So much trouble for the Citadel, for all the Soldiers, had sprung from one stupid Breedmaster's mistake in a little outlying Base. Was there now to be more? It had already bitten him in the ass in a small way, when he went looking for Juchi's sister/daughter. If he had not been a Soldier, he'd have started believing that Juchi and all his seed carried a curse directed at the Race in general.

He kept his voice deliberately neutral: "The bandit Juchi, called the Accursed, is dead, Omin Hotal. I saw his quartered corpse outside Nûrnen not long before I fared forth to meet you here."

"Aye, Juchi is dead. I too have heard the tale of that corpse, and of the dishonor the lords of the Citadel inflicted upon it in hopes of terrifying those who — how shall I say? — love the Soldiers not. But dishonor, Soldier Sharku, has a way of turning to cut the hands of those who seek to wield it as weapon. For, you see, Juchi's daughter — his sister as well — Aisha still lives."

"Oh, fuck," Mumak mumbled. Sharku was inclined to agree with that assessment. He'd always had trouble believing a worthless peasant like Yegor could have killed Glorund the Battlemaster. Glorund, after all, had slain Juchi, who bore Soldier's blood in his veins.

But if Juchi was of Soldier stock, then so was Aisha, born — if legend spoke true — of him by his own mother, herself a woman with some Soldier genes. If Glorund decided legend was a lie . . . when a Cyborg eliminated data, they no longer existed for him. All at once the probable manner of the Battlemaster's passing seemed clear. His own arrogant overconfidence had killed him — not the first Soldier to die thus.

"You see the difficulty, Soldiers of the Citadel," Omin Hotal said. "In Aisha, both Soldier blood and that of the steppe cry out for vengeance against those who slew her father/brother and dishonored his corpse. Were such not a contradiction in terms, I would call her a woman *ghazi*. You know this word, Sharku of the Citadel?"

"I know this word, Omin Hotal," Sharku answered gravely. Literally, *ghazi* meant *warrior of the faith*, one who spread Islam by the sword. In practice it meant raider, one who spread Islam by plundering the lands and goods of his non-Muslim neighbors. The combination of fanaticism and greed was about as explosive—and as unstable—as ammonium iodide.

"There is more; there is worse." Organa's voice tolled like a funeral bell of one of the Christian churches that were common in the Shangri-La.

As he had promised, Sharku met bad news like a Soldier. "Tell me the rest."

When Omin Hotal hesitated, his wife spoke again: "Aisha preaches *jihad*, holy war, against the Citadel. Great is the booty she promises the people of the felt tents: all that you Soldiers have, and possession of the valley as birthing-ground for women and livestock both. Such is enough and more than enough to tempt any plainsman. She leads a band of seven *mujahidin*, if so I may term them when more are infidel than not."

"Infidel?" Sharku echoed, puzzled. Most of the plainsfolk on the Great Northern Steppe professed Islam of one sort or another, although minorities around the fringes were Buddhist and Christian and whatnot. The main non-Muslim group was —

"The Bandari have their hand in this *jihad*, Soldier of the Citadel," Organa said, fitting a new tile into the mosaic. "Aisha somehow is kin to the folk of the Pale as well as to the steppe and the Citadel."

"Oh, fuck." This time, Mumak didn't bother to whisper. Again, Sharku shared the sentiment. The Bandari were the worst foes the Citadel had. The Frystaat blood many of them carried gave them a strong genetic heritage. They'd kept or redeveloped more technology than any other group on Haven save only the Soldiers. Maybe worst of all, they were *literate*. Like the Soldiers, they drew their schemes from a vastly larger database than mere clan memory. Add in that, as the nomads said, any two Bandari could cheat Shaitan at dice, and they became very unpleasant customers indeed.

Sharku thought hard and fast. "Do you" — his gaze swept severely from Omin Hotal to Organa and back again — "swear by Allah and the spirits you have told me the truth here?"

The chief shook his head. "No, Soldier of the Citadel, I cannot, for how much truth lies in the stories that have come out of the west I cannot say. But by Allah and the spirits, Soldier Sharku, and by the memory of fair dealing between the Citadel and the White Sheep Turks, I have reported truly what I heard."

That would have to do, Sharku realized. He inclined his head to Omin Hotal. "We Soldiers forget neither foes nor friends. Your service shall be remembered and rewarded, chief of the White Sheep Turks." He had to work to keep his voice steady. *What am I supposed to do now?* yammered in him.

A fourth tribute maiden carried in a tray of sliced apples, pears and clownfruit candied in honey. Her smile came unforced as she offered it to Sharku. Here, he thought, was one determined to make the best of things when she went to the Citadel. Here also, he decided, was the one he would bed after the feast was done. He was not one of the Soldiers who was turned on by fear.

When the fruit was gone, Omin Hotal rose, a little unsteadily, from the mat. "Come, Soldiers of the Citadel. You have seen the girls who will accompany you back to the Shangri-La Valley. See now the other gifts the White Sheep Turks grant you from our abundance."

In the flowery language of politeness, *gifts* meant *tribute*; *abundance* was *whatever we happen to have*. Sharku also spoke that language: "Your generosity always astounds, Omin Hotal. Let me be amazed once more."

"Come, then." The nomad chief left the yurt first, to show again that he trusted the Soldiers with his woman. When they followed, he led them to the place where the tribute lay piled, a couple of hundred meters off. "Behold," he said expansively. "Fleeces, beeswax, tallow, cowhides and horsehides. Herbs from which you brew your medicines — tansy, foxglove, fireweed."

Sharku checked the fleeces and hides to make sure Omin

Hotal had not concealed poor ones under those that first met the eye. He opened pots of wax and tallow at random to see if they were full, and stuck his knife into a couple to search for false bottoms. He inspected the baled herbs closely, to learn whether the chief was trying to sneak weeds past him. Omin Hotal grinned like a tamerlane all the while. He gained repute among his clansfolk by being thought so sneaky.

When the examination was done, the chief said, "Tell me if you would, Soldier Sharku, what simple you brew from fireweed. No shaman with whom I have spoken knows any use for the vile, burning stuff."

"You may not believe it, Omin Hotal, but an extract of the leaves goes into a syrup that soothes sore throats," Sharku answered easily. Omin Hotal shook his head in wonder. As a matter of fact, Sharku lied. What the Citadel extracted from fireweed was nitric acid, essential to manufacturing smokeless powder.

Ufthak nodded at the string of ponies tethered beside the tribute. "I have seen worse animals than these, chief of the White Sheep."

"They are yours," Omin Hotal said with an extravagant gesture. "Let the maidens ride some, and let the others bear our gifts."

"Behold — Omin Hotal is generous," Sharku said loudly, as if for all Haven to hear.

The nomad chief swelled up with pride. He pointed to a yurt next largest after his own. "The maidens who go to join the Citadel await you there. More food and drink also await, for your further refreshment. When you come forth, everything will be in readiness for your return to the Shangri-La Valley."

"Again I thank you, Omin Hotal," Sharku said. He had to glance at Mumak to keep the Senior Assault Leader from making toward that yurt too soon. As a matter of fact, Sharku did not want to go that way at all. Could he have done so without mortally offending his host, he would have headed out into the steppe at once, to see what more he could learn of the disquieting news the chief and his woman had passed on.

*But no,* he decided reluctantly. A tribute party could easily attract raiders, and could not easily spare the loss of a quarter of its strength. Moreover, he wanted to sit down with the Threat Analysis Computer and feed in the new data. And Sharku wondered what the TAC already knew. Among them, those considerations outweighed his desire to fly like an ice-eagle across the plains.

On to other desires, then. After more polite talk, he let Omin Hotal lead him to the second yurt. As he went in, he saw the tribute maidens sitting crosslegged on the floor matting, just on the women's side of the shelter. Behind them, embroidered blankets partitioned off four nominally private spaces.

Sharku remained alert. He eyed each blanket closely, checking with his infrared-sensitive eyes to make sure no one — brother, outraged friend or lover — crouched in ambush behind it. He also studied the tribute maidens with care. Once, some T-years before, a beardless youth had donned his sister's clothes and knifed a Soldier to death. A lot of tricks worked once. None had any business working twice.

These were, however, the maids who had served the food in Omin Hotal's yurt; he recognized their distinctive female scents. Sharku nodded to the one who had brought in the candied fruit. Beneath swarthiness, her full cheeks colored. He heard her heart speed up. "What shall I call you, fair young one?" he asked her.

"I am Toragina, Sau — Soldier of the Citadel." She flushed deeper, and bit her lip at the slip she'd made.

The Chief Assault Leader let it pass. "My name is Sharku, as you may have heard." He reached out, closed his hand on hers, drew her to her feet with effortless strength. Though she cast down her eyes with becoming modesty, she was the one who led him to a nook.

Within were mats and furs and pillows stuffed with horsehair. She sat beside Sharku, so close that their thighs touched. He did not smile, not where it showed, but he was pleased. He'd hoped she'd be bold. Even so, he waited a little before he put a hand on her. If that boldness was just a facade, he didn't want to knock it down by leaping on her like a cliff lion. First impressions lasted, and she'd stay inside the Citadel the rest of her life.

She was a Turk, so her long tunic fastened on the left; plainsfolk of Mongol stock closed theirs on the right. She didn't flinch when he undid the topmost brooch, or the next, or the next. In fact, she turned toward him to make his work easier. Now he did smile. She shrugged out of the tunic herself, before he could take it off for her. The dim, flickering light of a butter-filled lamp showed breasts small but shapely. She lay back against the piled furs.

Taking her was duty and pleasure at the same time. Given a choice, Sharku would have spent all his seed with Chichek. Being a Soldier, he was not given a choice. Since he had to do this, he took pride in doing it as well as he could, both for its own sake and to help the Soldier to whom Toragina was eventually assigned. He soon discovered she was no maiden. He didn't care, so long as she wasn't pregnant by some nomad — and his nose would have told him if she were. That she knew something of what she was doing only added to both their pleasure. He was sure of hers — no cattle woman could pretend well enough to fool one of his kind.

Between rounds — not long, given who and what he was — he listened to the noises floating from behind the other blankets. Mumak and Ufthak seemed to be pleasing their women well enough. That was all to the good. Snaga . . . He frowned. The next time Snaga thought of anyone but himself, in bed or out of it, would be the first. One of the tribute maidens was getting an introduction to the Citadel she might better have done without. Nothing to be done about that now; if it turned out Snaga had seriously abused the girl, Sharku would do his best to get him taken off this duty henceforward.

"You have a lance of steel," Toragina exclaimed as he enfleshed himself once more. She bit his shoulder, hard enough to hurt. Trained reflex almost made him smash her into unconsciousness with the side of his head. He held himself still, just in time, then abandoned himself to what he was doing. Untrained reflexes had their place, too.

After two more joinings, he could tell she was getting sore. She tried to deny it, which flattered him. He could have gone another couple of rounds, but was happy enough. Smiling, Toragina fell asleep almost as soon as his weight left her. He covered her with furs; being unaugmented, she'd feel the chill.

He listened again. Mumak had not only gone to sleep, he was snoring. Sharku chuckled. That would be something to rag him about all the way back to the Citadel. By the squeals from another nest in the yurt, both Ufthak and his girl were still going strong. And so was Snaga, though his tribute maiden, far from sounding passionate, had started to whimper.

"Enough, all," Sharku called in Americ. "Remember, we'll be riding horses, not girls, in a few hours. Rest while you can." The last four words belonged in any warrior's maxim book.

Snaga at least knew how to obey. He quickly came one last time, then turned himself off as if he were an electrical appliance. Ufthak muttered something that sounded suspiciously like, "Yes, sir, grandfather, sir," but not loud enough to compel Sharku to notice it. He brought his tribute maiden to a final peak, gasped himself in the same instant, and also began the deep, even breathing which quickly spiraled down to sleep.

Having given the order, Sharku refused to obey it. He sat crosslegged beside Toragina, again weighing the data he'd had from Omin Hotal and Organa, wishing he could do two things at once: a startlingly un-Soldierlike feeling. *One step at a time* belonged in the maxim book, too. He'd already figured out the proper course. He would follow it. Why, then, was he unhappy with his choice?

# ● CHAPTER THIRTEEN

Battlemaster Carcharoth collected arcane lore. He knew the beast from which his own name came — the wolf — though it was in an ancient, imagined language no man had ever spoken. It suited him, in the muscular ranginess of his body, in his iron-gray hair, in the tenacity with which he hunted down and destroyed threats to the Citadel.

His senses were enhanced far beyond those of any wolf, though. And to let them leap further still, he had at his fingertips technology unmatchable elsewhere on Haven (unmatchable even in the Citadel, should any of it chance to fail). As he did every couple of cycles, he let himself into the citadel within the Citadel that housed the Threat Analysis Computer. This was the only terminal that could access and control the AI, although there were others, many others, where the machine's insatiable appetite for even the most inconsequential information was fed. Dedicated pickups were scattered all over the Citadel, and over the older parts of Nûrnen as well, although they could not be replaced or manufactured these days.

*Glorund should have done this more often,* he thought. But Glorund, full of Cyborg certainty, had decided he was his own best TAC. And now Glorund was dead, and Carcharoth was wearing his boots. The new Battlemaster did not intend to repeat his predecessor's mistakes; he knew he would make enough of his own.

His fingers moved over the keys polished smooth by three hundred T-years of worried Soldiers; it was faster than the voice-recognition system, with Soldier reflexes. The query was a familiar one: *THREATS TO THE CITADEL — RANK ORDER.*

A light blinked on the screen while the computer processed data. Carcharoth had no idea how it worked, but had no doubt that it did work. The TAC had saved the Citadel untold trouble over the generations since the *Dol Guldur* had brought it from Old Sauron.

The computer whirred, a sound all but inaudible even to the Battlemaster's ears. Letters marched across the screen, orange-yellow on velvety black:

THREATS TO THE CITADEL:

1. AISHA CALLED THE DAUGHTER OF JUCHI
2. Cyborg SIGRID
3. THE BANDARI
4. STEPPE CLANS

OTHERS TOO LOW A PROBABILITY TO BE EVALUATED.

Carcharoth thought something extremely rude. Had the augmentations that made him Cyborg not obviated the need for overt emotional release, he would have sworn out loud. He almost did anyhow, augmentations or no augmentations. Fat lot of good augmentation had done Glorund, by the gods the Battlemaster did not believe in.

He typed in a new query: THREAT ANALYSIS OF AISHA IF PROVEN NOT TO BE DAUGHTER OF JUCHI. If she wasn't, and if the Soldiers could show she wasn't, maybe that would make her less of a nuisance.

But the TAC scotched his optimism almost at once: THREAT LEVEL OF SUBJECT WOMAN UNCHANGED. PROBABILITY OF SUCCESSFUL PROPAGANDA CAMPAIGN TOO LOW TO EVALUATE.

*Worth a try*, Carcharoth thought. He considered the Threat Analysis Computer's first response, found it strange. He went to the keyboard again: WHICH STEPPE CLANS INCLUDED IN THREAT ANALYSIS LISTING? The machine usually supplied a chieftain-by-chieftain listing — why not now?

He found out why in seconds: ALL STEPPE CLANS KNOWN TO SOLDIERS AND WITHIN ONE T-YEAR TRAVEL TIME OF THE CITADEL EXPECTED TO BE HOSTILE. EXCEPTIONS: WHITE SHEEP TURKS, CLANS OF OMIN HOTAL (PROBABILITY 86% +/− 3); CLAN OF TOGHRUL (PROBABILITY 59% +/− 6); ROLLING PLAINS TURKS, CLAN OF GASIM (PROBABILITY 53% +/− 8); COSSACK STANITSA OF

CHERNINSKY (PROBABILITY 51% +/- 3). PROBABILITY OF OTHER EXCEPTIONS TOO LOW TO BE EVALUATED.

The Battlemaster stared at the screen. If he understood what the TAC was trying to tell him, the whole bloody steppe was going to throw itself at the Shangri-La Valley. He wondered if the Gatlings had enough ammo to mow down every nomad on Haven. Automatic calculation told him the answer was no, but it also told him he was being foolish. The Gatlings had plenty of bullets to make survivors who wanted to keep on surviving give up their assault.

Carcharoth noticed something else: the steppe was going to blow up, but it ranked only fourth on the computer's list of worries. That meant the three threats ahead of it had to be real doozies. The Bandari always showed up on the TAC's list, particularly since Angband fell and uncorked the giant cul-de-sac of steppe at whose southern end the Pale lay. The whole mess with Aisha was Glorund's fault, though the previous Battlemaster was too dead to take all the blame he deserved. But Sigrid —

Seeing Sigrid's name on the threat list was like a stiletto in the heart. *The TAC must figure she's gone rogue*, Carcharoth thought. He had trouble believing it; no Cyborg had ever betrayed the Citadel. Revolted against its leaders, yes, in the early years. Betrayed it — and the Race — no. But the database for female Cyborg Soldiers was too small to be statistically significant. Sigrid had been gone a long time now. Maybe she wasn't coming back.

Or maybe she was. With an army behind her.

"Rivendell," said Sigrid.

The Maasai could not have understood her irony. "Katlinsvale," the woman said. "And a rift valley, yes."

They stood on the brink of it. Two cycles of travel had brought them here, afoot and unaccompanied but for the dogs that had made Sigrid their herd. Sigrid had set the pace, Cyborg pace. She was not surprised to discover the Maasai could match her, except when she pressed.

She looked down. The valley opened without warning,

as if the earth had parted at her feet, steep walls plunging down a kilometer and more from where she stood. To Cyborg eyes the whole long narrow cleft glowed with heat — hot springs concentrated at the valley's head and dotted along its length. They supported a profusion of vegetation, a jungle after the barrenness of the steppe, as rich as Shangri-La. And no word of it had come to the Citadel.

The Maasai went over the side. Sigrid followed her onto a track that descended through a dizzying pattern of switchbacks and sudden plunges. There was another, there had to be, for horses and carts, for sheep and goats. This was a challenge. She would take the hard way, the one that paid in death if one misstepped.

It was a long way down. Sigrid thought of the ropes in her pack, and of rappelling down the slope; but there was a certain pleasure in taking the slow way. In feeling by degrees the increase in the air's pressure, and tasting the richness of it: sulfur and minerals from the springs, sharp tang and sudden sweetness of growing things, the underlay of dung and smoke and sweat that marked humanity.

They farmed here. They had to, to support a population of pregnant women and animals. The fields followed the curves and hollows of the land, laid out in patterns as sophisticated as any she had seen outside of Nûrnen. The houses that watched over them were surprising: not houses at all but yurts like those on the steppe. They looked as if they could be moved at the dwellers' whim, or shifted when the pattern of tilled and fallow changed, to be closest to the fields that needed most attention. Even the barns looked temporary, and the granaries, like the yurts, sat on wheels. Nomad thrift, farmer's foresight.

Women worked in the fields. Not all were big with child. Mother Clan, those would be. Midwife-warriors, farmers, keepers of the valley.

They looked no softer than their sisters on the steppe. Good stock, strong stock. Stock that would breed well on Soldier lines.

The Mother Clan had its fire far up the valley, above a chain of springs and steaming pools. Its central yurt was marked like Margit's by a skull on a spear — Katlin's own, broad and sturdy — surmounted by an odd carving in —

Plastic. Not carved, then, but molded, and barely weathered by what must have been generations. If the thing was life-size, the creature it represented was about as large as a Terran cat, and vaguely felinoid in shape. Small for a predator in Haven's arcticlike ecology.

"Valecat," said the Maasai, "and a sister, of sorts. She breeds without the male, you see."

"Ah," said Sigrid. "A form of humphrodite."

The Maasai shook her head. "No. She has no male, absorbed into her body or otherwise. She conceives of her own essence. If she has a mind or an instinct to vary her line, she exchanges essences with a sister. She lives only here in this valley. She chooses on occasion to share a yurt or a barn. She hunts vermin as an earthcat will, but we never could keep an earthcat here. Valecat won't allow it."

"Appropriate," Sigrid said.

*Probably a relict species*, she decided. Haven had a number, since it had been undergoing a mass extinction when humans first arrived. Oddities like asexual reproduction might well flourish in a confined micro-environment like this valley. The springs were probably mildly radioactive, as well. Inevitable that it would become a symbol to the tribe.

"Surely. And a sign. While valecat favors us, we know that our way is the right way."

Sigrid raised a brow, but forbore to comment.

Katlin was unexpected. She could not have been as old as Sigrid. She was, it was clear, both chieftain and shaman. And she was vastly pregnant.

"Twins," Sigrid said, looking at her.

She smiled at Sigrid. Two young women, but older than she, had assisted her from her yurt and helped her to sit by the fire. It was so placed that one could look down the length of the valley, over the steaming pools to the fields and the orchards and the wild spaces where Haven flora grew unmolested, and up the steep walls to the distant sky. Her eyes lifted to the last, but her voice was clear and direct. "Yes, twins. Their father was a Soldier. I have high hopes of them."

"If they are viable."

She lowered her eyes to Sigrid. They were blue; she was fair, Soldier-fair, with a Soldier's strong bones, but not a Soldier's coldness. "They will be," she said. "I chose their father carefully. I disposed of him with my own hand. I was sorry to do it. He was a good lover."

Strange to hear her speak so, warm and light and child-simple. "He thought to go back," she explained. "He meant to take me with him. I was a great prize; I would make a good Soldier, he said, and a worthy mother of Soldiers."

"So you would," said Sigrid.

"No," Katlin said. "I might have gone, for curiosity, but he killed Katlin-before, thinking to steal me; and I was Katlin-next. He was sorry after. Soldiers hate to make mistakes."

"Mistakes can kill you."

"He didn't die for that. His mistake was to come here at all, where a Soldier can live and love, but never leave."

Sigrid looked down at the chain of pools. A herd of horses had come down to the lowest, not to drink — the water was foul for that — but to roll and splash, and to lie, ears slack, drowsing in the warmth. They were all mares, heavy with foal, attended by dogs like those that lay, one at her feet, one at a cautious distance. The he-dog sighed and laid his head on her knee. She forbore to push it away.

"Our dogs like you," Katlin said. "Margit's clan speaks well of you. Would you stay with them, or would you choose another?"

"I am content," said Sigrid.

Katlin nodded. "So I'm told. That's rare in a Soldier, contentment. And you are more than Soldier. You'll not always be satisfied to live under another's command."

"I am no threat to your place. Or," said Sigrid, "to Margit's."

"Did I say you were? We grow, you know," said Katlin, resting her hand on her belly. "Our herds are larger than they've ever been; our children thrive. Time's coming for a clan-founding. We've always resisted it; we've kept our numbers low, or turned the men away at the gathers. But Katlin-before died, and Katlin-now carries twofold, and we have a sign. We have you."

"One could grow weary of being a symbol."

Katlin laughed. "But, Cyborg woman, we are all symbols. The world is a symbol, a sign to any who can read it. And now that tells me, 'Take what is given. Grow. Wield the weapon set in your hand.' Would you be Sigrid over Sigridsfolk?"

Sigrid spoke carefully, quietly. "You offer me much, who am a stranger, who could be the most bitter of your enemies."

"So you could," said Katlin. "If you are, you will die, as Hama died, because it's necessary. And we'll mourn you at the gather, when we remember the dead."

"I may not be so easy to kill."

"Of course not. We'd not want you else. You'll rule well, and you'll be free. You can forge a new race."

Subtle, supple words. Words as meticulously calculated as a First Rank's speech to his troops. Breedmaster Titus could have done no better, manipulating Sigrid's mind and her instincts to serve his will. Offering her power, freedom, a race to mold as she would. But not as Titus had done, creating the beautiful monster that was Sieglinde and the simple failure that was Sigrid — dividing the race into Soldier and breeder, warrior male and helpless female. She would create a race more perfectly balanced, using the knowledge of the Breedmasters from before the fall of the *Dol Guldur*, blending it with the knowledge preserved here. They would remember her as they remembered the masters of Old Sauron, with reverence and awe.

Delusion. She snapped herself out of it. It was, if possible at all, only remotely so. No credit to her that she had succumbed so easily. She was far less in control of herself than she had imagined. The anger that had sent her from the Citadel festered deep, and the desire that had brought her here, while laudable in its concern for the Race, did not bear close scrutiny. It was not the desire of a Soldier to do his duty. It was little more than vanity.

She spoke in the Clanmother's patient silence. "If I am given the rule of a clan, what prevents me from summoning my kinsmen from the Citadel and taking your valley and your people?"

"Nothing," said Katlin.

"And yet you trust me."

"The nomads have a proverb," Katlin said. "A man will gamble on anything. A woman gambles only on a surety."

"Insane," said Sigrid. She stood. Katlin watched her calmly, head bent back on a neck that seemed as fragile as a wheatstem.

It was not in fact much less breakable than Sigrid's own. Necessary deceptions. Women among the nomads lived by them. Women in the Citadel used them — Soldier women too, relegated to the status of portable wombs and bowing to the cant that was fed them: how few, how precious they were; far too valuable to risk.

If these tribeswomen were mad, they were no more so than Sigrid. She supposed she was sane, if she could know she was not.

That was the trap's heart. She stood by the lowest pool, knowing that Katlin watched her, and the Maasai beside the Clanmother. Deliberately she took off her lion cloak. The scent and sight of it sent the basking mares wallowing and floundering out of the water, fleeing to the safety of an upper field. She folded and laid the thing on the edge of the pool, then the rest of her garments one by one. The air was cold on her skin, the water warm as she slid into it, warming toward the vent, cooling toward the edges. Its chemical reek clogged her nostrils. Its steam blurred her eyes. When she dived beneath the surface, her hearing changed, dulling to the upper world, sharpening below.

It was as close to sensory deprivation as she would come, short of the tank in the Citadel. She surfaced, sucked oxygen again and again, hyperventilating. Then she went down.

Quiet. Blood-warm. And, once the surge of her dive had settled, still.

Her timesense ticked unregarded. Her brain spun for a while that subjectively was endless; objectively, less than half a minute. Then, as the water had done, it quieted.

*Datum.* She was angry. She had been angry since she knew what she was, and what it meant.

*Datum.* She had defied the Breedmaster's command. She had left the Citadel — had, in effect, stolen herself.

*Datum.* She had found what she reckoned, with judgment admittedly impaired by anger and resentment, knowledge worth the price of disobedience. The mare, the Maasai, the tribe that had bred them both.

*Datum.* The tribe welcomed her. It saw her full potential. It proposed to use that potential to the full, and not simply to breed sons.

*Datum.* She could live this life. It offered possibilities that were, if not infinite, then more extensive than those in the Citadel. There she was a failure and a flawed seed. There Sieglinde was the culmination of the Breedmaster's program.

*Datum.* She had been manipulated into this condition, first by the Breedmaster, latest by the Clanmother. The latter was quite as insidious as the former. She knew precisely what would trap and hold Sigrid. What promises to make, what to leave unsaid. She saw considerable advantage in a clan dominated by a Cyborg — even knowing a Cyborg's dangers.

*Datum.* First of those dangers was the key to the rest. The ability to make choices.

*Datum.* Emotionally based but, for the purposes of computation, valid. Given to choose, she would choose this: freedom from the constraints of the Breedmaster's error, and a race to make in her own image.

Just at the edge of anoxia, just when her body could not draw a molecule more of hoarded oxygen, Sigrid surged into the air. It was cold and reeking and blessedly rich in her starved lungs.

The two dogs watched her from the pool's edge. The

he-dog quivered; his tail slapped the crusted rock. The she-dog, having ascertained that her herd was safe, went to work on the fleas that beset the base of her tail.

No one human kept them company. The ledge on which the clanfire burned was empty.

Sigrid sluiced water from her skin and dressed as she had undressed, deliberately, without haste. Her pack was as she had left it, her pistol in its holster, her ammunition unmolested. She buckled on the gunbelt, sliding the knife in its sheath to fit nearest her right hand.

She was ready to face her decision. She put on the lion cloak, fitting its head over her damp hair. The bonecarver in Margit's clan had made a brooch to fasten the cloak at the shoulder, a graceful stylized creature that she had taken then for a maneless cliff lion, but knew now for a valecat. Her finger traced the smooth curve of back and tail. Everything, as Katlin said, was a symbol.

No one was startled that Sigrid would accept what Katlin offered. Had not the omens foretold it? There was a feast to celebrate, and beer with the kvass, and even wine from vines in the most sheltered region of the valley. "And even at that," the vintner said, "we lose more than we grow." What there was, was good, and surprisingly strong.

It would take time to endow the new clan. For the beginning of that time, Sigrid was sent back to Margit to be trained in the ways of Katlin's folk. With that done, she would begin her travels among the rest of the clans, gathering the women who would be her clansisters.

She was of them now. There had been a rite in the middle of the feast, after the wine had had time to warm everyone but before it made them drunk. She shared blood and wine with Katlin and with the Maasai, and then with the rest who were there: blood from each, a drop into the cup, and wine mixed with it. Sigrid wondered if they knew how nourishing it was, apart from the meaning they laid on it. She doubted they knew what she could do with blood and augmented taste and smell. With this many, mixed so promiscuously, it was a wild confusion of data: fertile, infertile, pregnant, not, someone with a developing disease of the blood, someone else who had been at the wine since before the feast, someone else still who carried the iron tang of the Cyborg.

That was herself. Even her blood overrode the rest, battling the wine to dominate her senses. It made her dizzy, but gloriously so. She was of the tribe. The tribe was part of her, blood and bone. When she was dead her skull would keep vigil from a spear, watching over the doings of her daughters and her daughters' daughters.

Eyelight was cold, glaring down on Margit's herds. Sigrid watched them no less balefully. When Byers' Star rose again, she would leave this clan. Lais' clan waited. There were young women already in the camp behind, eager to follow her. There had been tears enough at the Starset feast, and a regret or ten. But no refusals.

Sigrid drew the lionskin closer about her. It had seemed a useful passport into the clan. It had become a symbol in itself. Young fools talked of getting themselves a lion, to prove that they could fight. To talk of getting themselves a man would have been more practical, in Sigrid's mind.

She was fertile again. Gathering was most of a T-year off. Here among women, paradoxically, she wanted — needed — a child more than she ever had in the Citadel. She had not even told her daughter she was going away. Signy would by now, and properly, have been taught to despise her as a deserter and a breaker of orders.

What stirred in her, she realized with some surprise, was pain. She was doing what she could not help but do.

Her hands were fists in the tanned, supple hide. She had chosen her path. She would not, could not, veer from it. Old guilt, old pain — programming only. Reflex. Conditioning that she, who was Cyborg, had broken. Nothing bound her to the Soldiers or to the Citadel. She had given them years of her service. They had paid her by holding her captive, and refusing her any rights but those of a broodmare. She owed them nothing.

Nothing.

Whatsoever.

Her body moved. It took her back through the camp, which slept in the waning hours of Haven's day, as Cat's Eye sank toward truenight. She walked neither quickly nor slowly, concealing nothing, retrieving what was necessary. The dogs followed as they always did. They too were programmed by their genes and their training.

She found herself smiling. She smiled too much of late. The tribe encouraged it. Humor, even humor as black as a Soldier's heart, had no place in a Cyborg's world, but on Katlin's ground it was welcomed. Life, Katlinsfolk insisted, was unbearable without it.

The smile died before she returned to the herd. The horses were accustomed by now to her terrifying garment. They snorted at it but did not run.

The horses she looked for were, by chance or design, near the edge of the herd, and together for once: the mare and all her daughters. One or two others grazed with them. They made a small herd within the larger one, with the bay mare its chief and its guard.

She raised her head at Sigrid's coming and blew out, but gently, with a quiver of the nostrils that was a greeting.

Cat's Eye hung just above the horizon. Unaugmented sight would find the light very dim, the long shadows deceptive. Sigrid made herself part of one.

She whistled softly between her teeth. The dogs wheeled at the signal. The he-dog grinned in dog-delight. The bitch sidled toward the herd. A flick of Sigrid's hand altered her course.

Sigrid drew a slow breath. Herding with dogs was not a skill she had studied. These, bless their good genes, would do as she told them.

They cut out the mare and her daughters. The bitch, spinning and wheeling, flashing wicked teeth, meeting stubborn eyes with eyes as implacable as any Cyborg's, drove the rest back to the larger herd. Sigrid thought briefly of counter-manding the order. But the mares who trotted away, ears flattened with resentment, were not the best or the swiftest. And they did not carry the mutation.

The bitch returned to the small new herd, white legs flashing, black body merging with shadows. When she turned to glance at Sigrid, white muzzle and white blaze gleamed. Sigrid flicked her hand again.

Onward.

Away from the camp.

"Why?"

Sigrid spun.

The Maasai stood out of reach or leap. She held a crossbow, cocked.

"An assault rifle would have been wiser," Sigrid said.

"None was ready to hand," said the Maasai. Her eyes fixed Sigrid, as steady as the bolt aimed at her heart. "Why?" she asked again.

Sigrid relaxed her stance, subsiding from the balls of her feet. The Maasai did not lower the bow.

"The worst of all sins," the woman said, "is the betrayal of one's kin."

"Yes," said Sigrid.

The Maasai's eyes widened. She understood. "We are your kin!"

"So you said."

"But never you." The Maasai's finger tightened on the trigger. "You lied to us."

"No," Sigrid said.

"You let us say it all. But," said the Maasai, "you let us."

"I believed I could do it." The Maasai did not have night-sight. Sigrid knew that her shape was, at best, a blur in gloom. Perhaps that let her show more pain than she would otherwise have allowed. Perhaps it no longer mattered that this woman see how close she was to unaugmented, undisciplined humanity. "I believed this was the only choice, the proper choice. I failed in my judgment."

"And so you will go home and confess your sin, and fall on your sword."

"No," Sigrid said. "I am the Breedmaster's heir. I know now what errors he committed. I know what errors I might have committed. I shall commit none of them."

The Maasai's breath hissed as she drew it in. "You are appalling."

"I am a Cyborg," Sigrid said.

"A monster. A killing machine. A demon in woman's shape."

"I am what I was bred to be."

"No," said the Maasai with desperate quiet. "We are more than the sum of our ancestors. They determine our beginnings. We determine our destinies."

"What," said Sigrid, "no gods? No fates?"

"The gods dream us. We shape the dream."

"There are no gods. There are only the genes." Sigrid shifted slightly. The bow twitched.

Dropped.

The Maasai sprang on Sigrid.

She was strong: strong enough, almost, to sway Sigrid on her feet. She did not, even now, fight in hate, but in bone-deep horror — not of Sigrid but of what she had been raised to be. It poured out of her in a flood of soft rhythmic words. A battle song, a death-song. A song of grief for the clan that now would never be, and the Clanmother who had betrayed her word and her kin and her own heart's desire.

Sigrid's word was given long ago, and not to this tribe. Her kin were in the Citadel. Her desire . . .

Her hands closed on the slender neck. The Maasai went still. The last of the Eyelight gleamed on her face.

The mares were well on their way southward, with the dogs herding them as Sigrid had commanded. Here was treasure as great as they. Treasure for which, alive and unharmed, the Citadel might even absolve her of desertion.

The Citadel would deduce what Sigrid had deduced. That there might be more of this kind, hidden among the clans. That those clans existed unsubdued, and within the Citadel's reach. That such an order of things was not to be tolerated in any world in which the Soldiers ruled.

The Maasai's eyes were clear. She was not afraid. She would be reading her death in Sigrid's face. Death that would save her tribe. Horses could come from anywhere.

She could come from only one place, a place of which the Citadel knew nothing. Of which the Citadel should know, must know, if Sigrid would most truly serve it.

Sigrid's fingers flexed. The fine bones snapped. The body arched in spasm.

Sigrid held her until she was dead, then laid her down, carefully. She was seemly, for a corpse. The fold of the land would hide her for as long as Sigrid needed to make her escape. She had not arranged for reinforcements, or warned the guards. She had trusted too much: in herself, in Sigrid.

"Never," said Sigrid to the still form in its reek of death. "Never trust a Cyborg. Even if she is your kin."

She turned her back on the dead woman and the living clan. Her eyes blurred. She blinked fiercely. A Cyborg did not weep. A Cyborg knew no pain, and no grief, and never regret.

The horses were out of sight, the dogs driving them on. Sigrid took a step forward. Another. Stretched her stride, as fast a horse could gallop, down the long road southward. Down to the Citadel.

*Maybe she wasn't coming back*, Carcharoth thought. Or maybe she was. If Carcharoth had been an ordinary man, ice would have walked up his spine. He looked at the screen again.

THREATS TO THE CITADEL:

1. AISHA CALLED THE DAUGHTER OF JUCHI
2. CYBORG SIGRID
3. THE BANDARI
4. STEPPE CLANS

OTHERS TOO LOW A PROBABILITY TO BE EVALUATED.

He found a new question to ask the computer: PROBABILITY OF THREATS 1, 2, 3, 4 BEING INTEGRATED.

Even the TAC needed a little while to think that one over. At last the answer appeared: PROBABILITY 61% +/− 12. Carcharoth stared at the screen a long time. *Titus has to see this*, he decided. Not only was the other Cyborg Breedmaster of the Citadel, he was also Sigrid's father. He would not be happy.

Carcharoth was not happy, either. He outclassed ordinary Soldiers to the same degree that they outclassed the ordinary cattle in Nûrnen. He was used to dealing with them from a position of superiority, able to outthink and outfight everyone around him. The *Totenkopf* he wore on his collar tabs warned those around him of what he was, and let him begin every battle with it half won through intimidation.

Titus, though, was of his own kind, one of the ruling elite of the Citadel. Cyborgs did not hold the top positions on the First Council, which were largely ceremonial these days. They ruled nonetheless, and the Breedmaster was his match, near enough, with weapons or controlled fury of body. And to Cyborg data processing Titus added his own byzantine deviousness. He would be worse than a bad enemy to make. Carcharoth cast about for ways to avoid involving him in his daughter's disgrace. He found none, not with *61% +– 12* glowing on the TAC screen.

*Duty.* The word rang through Carcharoth's mind, steadied him. This was not personal, this was for the safety of the Soldiers and the security of the Citadel. Carcharoth looked at *61% +/– 12* one last time, allowed himself a nod. He really needed Titus' help here. That was how he would put it to the Battlemaster.

He picked up the phone, punched a code reserved for wearers of the death's head. The response came while the first ping was still sounding. "Titus."

"Carcharoth here, in the TAC room. I've developed something that might interest you." No matter how secure the phone system was supposed to be, the Battlemaster said no more. Titus was not one to miss nuances.

"On my way."

Before the Battlemaster arrived, the ceiling speaker came to life: "Battlemaster Carcharoth to Interrogation. Urgent. Battlemaster Carcharoth to Interrogation. Urgent."

Unlike mere Soldiers, Cyborgs had the privilege of defining *urgent* for themselves. Instead of hurrying to the interrogation chamber (*the Red Room*, they called it in

Nûrnen, and shuddered when they spoke), he called to find out what was believed to require his presence.

"Interrogation — Regiment Leader Khim."

"Carcharoth." Whatever this was, the Battlemaster thought, the chief interrogator was handling it personally, which meant *he* thought it urgent. "I'm engaged in something important where I am. What do you have there?"

"Battlemaster, two Soldiers — Section Leader Ulfast and Senior Trooper Mim — were boozing in a Nûrnen dive when they heard a drunken nomad asking about the Cyborg Sigrid in terms that suggested he was acquainted with her. They apprehended him and have just brought him to me for questioning."

As Titus had with Carcharoth, so the Battlemaster spoke now: "On my way." He paused only to scribble down the questions he had put to the Threat Analysis Computer: let Titus see them, and their answers, for himself.

But when Carcharoth closed the last secure door to the computer room, he turned to find the Breedmaster approaching. "I thought you had something for me here," Titus remarked. His voice was so perfectly neutral, he might have been saying, *Why are you sneaking away after you called me?* Assassination — of characters and of rivals — had its place in the Citadel's power games.

But Carcharoth said, "My destination is relevant to the matter about which I called you. Accompany me to Interrogation; I will brief you on the way."

Without another word, Titus fell into step beside his fellow Cyborg. The Battlemaster spoke rapidly, intently. The briefing was over by the time the two officers reached the Red Room: talking to one of his own kind, Carcharoth needed neither repetition nor flowery elaboration. Once Titus had the data, he could analyze them for himself.

The Breedmaster's long, thin face did not change expression; Carcharoth would have been shocked if it had. But Titus was slower in answering than a simple pause to process new information would have required. At length, he asked, "How did the possibility of threat linkage occur

to you? Many would not have found that question; I admit
it might not have occurred to me."

"When I discovered the magnitude of the threat from
the steppes and compared it to the low rating the TAC gave
that threat, I wondered if it might be connected with those
ahead of it. Intuitive leap." Not even Cyborgs could make
apparently disparate chunks of data fit together on command; it was like traveling by the legendary Alderson
Drive instead of through normal space. At the far end of
the leap, you were somewhere new.

"We have never had to face one of our own kind as
opponent," Titus said, as steadily as if he and Sigrid shared
no genes. "If the TAC proves correct, her elimination may
well aid us."

Carcharoth wondered whether to admire or suspect
him. Was he putting the Citadel's interests above his own,
or just trying to create that impression so that no one would
question any other schemes he was hatching? *Not enough
data*, the Battlemaster answered himself. Aloud, he said,
"In any case, we need to find out what Sigrid is doing. Not
to mention the steppe tribes, and how the Bandari are
integrated into the threat assessment."

"Indeed." Titus pushed open the door to Interrogation.
"Let us hope this nomad can shed some light on the Sigrid
question."

*I should not drink so much. Drinking so often breaks the Yasa*,
Temujin thought. Temujin's ancient namesake had laid
down the Yasa, the code of the Mongols: it held that a man
should drink to drunkenness no more than once a month
— though the great conqueror had added: "It would be
even better if men were drunk only once a year; better still
if they were never drunk at all — but what man could keep
such a law?"

*Not only that, when I get drunk I talk too much and end up in
trouble.*

The last time he'd been drunk in Nûrnen, he'd spilled a
secret to Sigrid, though she'd had to hurt him to extract it
all. Now, seeking Sigrid, he was in the Saurons' hands

again — and by every sign, they were ready to hurt him a lot worse than Sigrid had. *I should not drink so much*. Useless, useless thought. Enough to make a man take the Muslims and their stupid Allah seriously — but then, they didn't obey their own code about drink either, which showed that the Ancestor was closer to the truth.

But it had been such a good bar. He'd been looking for a good bar, a place where he could get drunk and slide under the table and not worry — too much — that he'd have his throat slit while he was passed out.

The sign above the door had drawn his eyes, as it was meant to do: a cat's white needle teeth in the grinning mouth of a bleary-eyed, ratlike face. "The Sozzled Stobor," legends in several languages proclaimed; and the beast was on its back, with a mug in one paw. He'd already tried several places, and found them wanting. He went inside. It took moment before he realized that this was the *same* bar he'd met Sigrid in — he'd been drunk then, too. That chilled him for a moment. A malicious wind-spirit might be guiding his steps along a path of disaster, always circling back to the same place like a man lost in a winter blizzard.

*Nonsense*. Besides, he wasn't allowed to be afraid of anything but thunder, as a Mongol. It was a good bar.

Even before he was served, he had a pretty good notion this was what he was looking for. The geese roasting above the roaring fire on the far wall sent out a fragrance that made his mouth water.

He sat down at a small empty table. The barmaid who came over was pretty in a mostly Caucasoid way, and wore much less than was the habit on the steppe. He recognized her only dimly; the first time here he'd had no eyes for anyone but Sigrid, even though at first he hadn't known she was a woman.

"What'll you have?" she asked in accented Turkic, smiling as she spoke. Before Temujin could answer, she added, "Don't say me." Her eyes flicked to the big man a few tables away. "Strong Sven wouldn't like that."

One look at Strong Sven convinced Temujin to keep

away from his woman. He looked like a Sauron, tall and fair and with features so sharp and angular that they might have been hewn from stone rather than flesh. Instead of a field-gray uniform, though, he wore a miner's dirty coveralls. *Some Soldier's bastard,* Temujin guessed, not that anyone with two thoughts to rub together inside his head would have used that word to Strong Sven's face.

"Tennis-fruit brandy, miss," he answered in his own bad Americ, "and a chunk of one of those birds when they're done."

He had several shots of brandy by the time he got his goose. The room was beginning to spin. Maybe, he thought, the fat-rich dark meat and bread would coat his stomach so he wouldn't get drunk so fast.

It hadn't worked that way.

Now he lay naked and spreadeagled on a hard table, shackled at wrists and ankles. He'd tried to twist free a couple of times, and only managed to add to his aches and bruises. Now he just stared up at the glowing panels in the ceiling. He'd never seen electric lights before. He hoped never to see them again.

But staring at the ceiling was better than letting his head slip sideways so he looked at the walls. Every tool hung in neat rows on them was sharp or barbed or otherwise horrific. The uses of some were obvious. He could not imagine how others might be employed, and did not want them demonstrated on his person.

The moment of his own downfall came back to him with awful clarity. It had been just a few minutes after Strong Sven beat the whey out of a townsman who'd patted the barmaid's backside. He'd fought like a Sauron, all right — viciously. Temujin had applauded his own wisdom in leaving the girl alone except for business.

He'd raised a rather shaky hand to call her over again and order another shot when, instead, he'd listened to himself asking about Sigrid. When he got liquor into him, his tongue ran its own life.

The worst of it was, she hadn't known anything. So he'd explained about the Sauron bitch in more detail — *in loving detail*, he thought now, bitterly. And the barmaid had still looked blank.

Then a hand had fallen on his left shoulder, and another on his right. When he looked up, he discovered each hand belonged to a different Sauron. Next to the two who had hold of him, Strong Sven, sculpted as he was, might have been carved out of tallow and left too near a fire, so he started to run.

Temujin had seen them come in, but they'd taken a table at the far end of the Sozzled Stobor. They couldn't possibly have heard him asking questions of the barmaid . . . if they hadn't been Saurons. But they were Saurons, and they did have those augmented ears. Temujin had forgotten about that. With a few less shots of brandy in him, he might not have. He'd never know, now.

The one on his left had said, "Who are you to be asking questions about Sigrid, plainsman?" He'd have said *bedbug* with more warmth.

Before Temujin could answer, the one on the right said, "Sigrid's gone missing. What do you know about that, plainsman?" He'd have said *sheep two cycles dead of anthrax* with more warmth — a lot more warmth.

"Missing?" Temujin croaked, appalled — he'd come searching for the cold-faced wench and she wasn't even here? She was in Katlinsvale after all? He stammered, "I — I don't know anything of that, Sau — Soldiers. I — I met her maybe a T-year ago, and —"

"You *met* her?" both Saurons said together. They looked at each other. They nodded. The one on Temujin's left picked him up. He started to struggle, then thought better of it — fool that he was, he wanted to live.

The one on his right disarmed him quickly and expertly, down to the holdout knife in his boot, and said, "Let's take him to the Red Room so they can squeeze truth out of him."

A sigh ran through the Sozzled Stobor. Temujin hadn't fully understood it then. Now he did. He wished he'd tried to die fighting.

Behind his head, a door opened. Men — two, by their footfalls — came in. The fellow who'd been in charge of Temujin spoke to them in Americ, which the nomad could follow after a fashion: "Here he is, Breedmaster, Battlemaster."

*Wan Tngri is over all.* Having professed his faith in the Eternal Blue Sky, Temujin tried to face death bravely. What had he done to draw a pair of Cyborgs down on him? *I must not show fear. A Mongol may fear nothing but demons and thunder.* Of course, some held that Cyborgs *were* demons.

They stood looking down at him, one on either side of the table. At first he saw only the death's heads on their collar tabs. Then, when death did not descend at once (and it wouldn't, not at once, oh no), he let his eyes travel to their faces. Rather to his disappointment, they looked like any other Saurons: they were Caucasoid, light-eyed, big-nosed; the one to his left had a moustache with the beginnings of snow in it. The one on his right —

He jerked in surprise against the unyielding shackles. The one on his right wore Sigrid's face, or an older, masculine version of it. The shape of the eyes was the same, the ash-blond hair, the narrow chin and proud cheekbones beneath a broad forehead. So was the thin mouth that looked as if it might be about to smile but never did.

"Do you recognize me, plainsman?" that Cyborg asked in Turkic. His voice was just a voice. Temujin didn't know what he'd expected: thunder and brass, perhaps. But no, just a voice. The Sauron added, "I *know* I have never seen you before."

Temujin wondered how he *knew*. He himself would not *know* most of the people he'd walked past in Nûrnen bare hours before. But he never thought to doubt the Cyborg. When that one said he *knew* something, he compelled belief.

"You would be well advised to answer Breedmaster Titus," the other Cyborg, the Battlemaster, said. He took one of the small, sharp tools off the wall. Temujin's testicles tried to crawl up into his belly. The Sauron, however, merely began paring his nails.

"I — I — " Temujin's mouth was so dry, it hurt to talk. The electric light glittering off the little blade in the

Battlemaster's hand loosened his tongue quickly enough. "Breedmaster, I, ah, met in Nûrnen, a Sauron, uh, a Soldier woman who looks like you."

"Did you?" Only mild interest showed in Titus' voice. "When was this?"

"Maybe a T-year past, maybe a little less," Temujin answered. He was vague about exactly how long it had been. Out on the steppe, one cycle of light and dark was much like another. Less than a Haven year, definitely.

Titus turned to the other Cyborg. "That would fit, Carcharoth."

"So it would." Still trimming his nails, the Battlemaster — Carcharoth — gazed down at Temujin. "How did you — meet — the Breedmaster's daughter? Tell us that in great detail — what is your name?"

"T-Temujin." The Breedmaster's daughter? Temujin hadn't imagined he could be in any deeper than he'd already thought he was. Now he saw he'd been wrong. Or maybe not. Being what they were, knowing what she was, they could hardly imagine he'd tried to force her. He was still alive, after all — for the moment.

Carcharoth dropped the sharp little blade. It clattered down on the table between Temujin's legs. The point just touched — not even enough to cut — the very tip of his glans. "My apologies, Temujin," the Battlemaster said, picking up the tool. "Now, you were about to say — ?" His face was the picture of courteous attention.

Temujin talked. Temujin, not to mince words, babbled. He told the Saurons everything from the meeting in the alley to the secret clan of women, to the breed of horses that could foal in the thin air of the highlands. Sometimes a mechanical voice — an even *more* mechanical voice — chimed in from the grille in the ceiling, making him repeat things over and over. Temujin didn't mind; while he was talking, the Cyborgs weren't cutting and crushing.

The Cyborgs talked, too, across Temujin as if he did not exist. "Did she bring any record of this back here?" Carcharoth asked.

"No," Titus answered. "She was — is — headstrong, as

you know. She has always been determined to show that she can be woman and Cyborg both. Investigating this clan of cattle women who might also be warriors . . . being headstrong, she might well have wanted to personally evaluate the situation, use it in her favor against my judgment if she could, before she apprised us of it."

"But what if, having evaluated this clan, she found its values more closely suited her personality than those of the Citadel?" the Battlemaster inquired. "The probability of that, I think, is not too low to be evaluated."

"True," Titus said. "Not to our advantage, but true. If that is indeed correct, then the situation will be as the TAC views it, or possibly worse."

Temujin got confused a couple of times, trying to keep up with the quick-spoken Sauron dialect of Americ. He also got even more frightened, something he hadn't imagined possible. If he'd heard what he thought . . . Sigrid was — a Cyborg? He shivered in his shackles. The spirit that made the two of them meet had had only malice in its heart.

His shiver drew the attention of Breedmaster and Battlemaster. Carcharoth started playing with the little cutting tool again. "Tell me, Temujin," he said, "having encountered Sigrid once, why you came back to Nûrnen to seek her out a second time."

The nomad could not take his eyes off the blade. But even its threat did not make him answer quickly. After some time spent sorting through the muddle of his own thoughts, he said, "Revenge, maybe. And — " His tongue clove to the roof of his mouth. Not even the knife could make him say what else he'd thought, not to the Saurons, most especially not when one of them was her father. If he said what else, Carcharoth might carve him with even more fiendish ingenuity than if he kept his mouth shut.

Titus sniffed, turned to the Battlemaster. "Note the pheromones?"

The word meant nothing to Temujin, but Carcharoth nodded. "He wants her. What game was she playing, the night she found him?"

"I do not know." Titus' words came out machine-flat, but

Temujin heard — or imagined he heard — pain lurking under them. The Breedmaster went on, "I know her genes, I know her training, I know the biomechanicals that made her one with you and me, but herself — ? In the end, not all things are calculable."

"Yes," Carcharoth said. "Under the circumstances, however, do you agree we would be expedient to try to track her down and, if she has indeed gone rogue, to take appropriate measures?"

"Under the circumstances, the expedience of this course is undeniable," Titus said. "Its practicality, however, is open to question. Can mere Soldiers be relied upon to take appropriate measures against a Cyborg?"

"I admit the probability is low," the Battlemaster answered. "But we will have the advantage of surprise, for surely Sigrid would not dream that this nomad here might return to Nûrnen for her, and thus give us some clue as to her whereabouts."

"No doubt you are right," Titus said. "Who can calculate the foolishness of cattle?" He paused a moment in thought. "If we send out, hmmm, two sections under an Assault Leader, they may possibly generate a threat of sufficient magnitude to persuade her to return with them to the Citadel."

"Rather than leave her bones on the steppe, you mean? Were you not the one who just questioned whether Soldiers could deal with her at all?" Now it was Carcharoth's turn to ponder. "I certainly would not risk more than two sections on the task, not in view of our other difficulties at this time. But her genes are undeniably valuable — and you are her father."

"I tried not to let that influence my suggestion," Titus said coldly. "Perhaps I failed."

"In any case, if they fail to make contact, the search team will still be available to gather intelligence on the tribal movements the TAC predicted," Carcharoth mused. He seemed at last to remember Temujin was present. "As you said, Battlemaster, Sigrid will not have anticipated this nomad's reappearance — nor that he might guide the search team toward the clan of females she was investigating."

Carcharoth looked at Temujin, too. The plainsman tried to hide on the flat, matte-black surface of the table. The Battlemaster said, "If he can be relied upon to guide them in the right direction."

"That should not be a problem," Titus said. "For one thing, his self-interest is involved, as, if he leads us astray, he will be moving further from the object of his desire. And for another, the Soldiers of the search team will have access to overtly coercive measures to ensure his cooperation." The Breedmaster ran a gentle forefinger down the midline of Temujin's belly. "You would not care to be overtly coerced, would you?"

Temujin shook his head. He wasn't altogether sure what Titus was talking about, but, as with the more arcane tools on the wall of the Red Room, he didn't want to learn in detail.

Carcharoth went from one corner of the table to the next, unsnapping Temujin's shackles. "Sit up, sit up," he said almost jovially, and helped Temujin do just that. The power of his arm under Temujin's back showed the nomad that he was in truth of Sigrid's breed. "Besides which, Breedmaster, why should he not be willing to come to our aid, when he has passed into our hands and out again without being tortured. Eh, Temujin?"

Now Temujin nodded, as eagerly as he could. Nor was he lying, or not entirely. After all, he remained intact. But if Carcharoth thought he believed that a Sauron Cyborg dropped knives by accident, then the Battlemaster, for all his augments, was a fool.

## CHAPTER FOURTEEN

Erika bat Miriam fan Gimbutas scrunched down behind the rock and peered sideways around it, shivering slightly despite the thick layers of clothing. Iron-shod hooves clanked on the rough stone of the pathway, up in the Shield Range that separated the Eden Valley from the high-steppe areas of the Pale. The air was frigid here even in summer, though mild compared to the Afritsberg range to the east, where carbon dioxide fell with the snow on the highest peaks. It was near to truedark, the arch of Cat's Eye only a thin sliver, the sun down, only two of the other moons visible. Wind blew grit into her face, soughing down from the steppe toward the valley. The young girl looked over her shoulder; a thousand-meter cleft behind her dropped its way through canyon and badland to the valley floor, with only the occasional patch of reddish screwgrass and litchen.

Voices. Her half-sister Shulamit, and Shulamit's young man Karl bar Yigal fan Reenan. They were leading their horses, with an extra mount and a pack-muskylope each. Dressed for travelling on the steppe, sheepskin jackets and bag-hats, scarves. Not armed, beyond the usual saber and knife and bow in its case on their saddles, but the leather sacks slung over their pack-animals gave off an occasional betraying clink. Armor-bags. You didn't wear armor in the Pale except on duty.

" . . . three weeks," Shulamit was saying. "Maybe four."

"That's *if* they're at Cliff Lion Springs, the way those *hot-not* traders said."

"*Everyone* says they are. Three weeks."

"With only two horses each? You want to *kill* them?"

"We can buy barley at Ashkabad."

"*Oive*. Stop right next to my father's house?" Yigal bar

Rhodevik was in the Eden Valley right now, but the rest of the household was still north in the Tadjik trading-city. The People had a settlement there, a town for traders under Bandari law.

"We don't have to go into the Pale enclave —"

The voices faded around the corner. Erika licked dry lips. *Piet and Ruth, but they're going to get into* trouble *now!* she thought. They *were* sneaking off to join the Judge, *Tanta* Chaya — and the Seven. Attacking the Saurons.

Shulamit's father had been killed by Saurons in the raid after the fall of Angband Base; Miriam bat Lizbet had remarried Erika's father Shmuel afterward. Erika remembered Shulamit standing up at her bat mitzvah, even though it was four years ago now and she had been only ten herself. Standing up at the end of the ceremony and cutting her thumb, putting blood and salt in the brandy cup and swearing to kill a Sauron Soldier for every year her father had missed of his threescore-and-ten. Yohann bar Rimza had been forty T-years when he died; Shulamit would have to kill a whole *platoon* to fulfill the oath.

*I've got to stop her*, Erika thought. *She'll get killed.* It was impossible to imagine her big beautiful brave sister *dead.* All bloody, like the farmhand who'd fallen under the haycutter last year; she swallowed bile. *And if they have to come back, Karl will be here too.* Even if he did still treat her like a child. *I've had my bat mitzvah*, she thought resentfully. *I'm on the clan rolls.* She was fourteen T-years now!

Glowering, she worked her way backward and stood, picking up her bow and turning to the blind cutoff where her pony waited. The basalt walls closed around her, rising up fifty meters to the near-vertical cliffs; it was even colder in here, and her nose-hairs crinkled. Dark, too. Her horse was tethered to the wall, a dim bulk in the gloom, on the last flat spot before the end of the ravine angled sharply upward. There was slick ice underfoot, that might have lain here a century or more without melting. The animal was rolling its eyes and snorting, whickering greeting but trying to look over its shoulder in the too-narrow space.

"All right, Fancy," she called to the pony. "Oats for you

when we get home. What's *wrong*, Fancy?" she continued sharply, as it almost pushed her over in its eagerness to leave the cleft.

Then she could see past it. At first only a pair of yellow eyes ten meters up the slope; they blinked at her, horizontal slit pupils . . .

*Oh, please, not a cliff lion*, she thought, with a sudden coppery taste in her mouth. They were very rare in the Shield-of-God range — too near the dense population of the Eden Valley — but there were still a few . . .

She backed, step by step despite the pony's increasingly frantic tugging on the reins. Any second now, he was going to go crazy — and when he did, he'd trample her flat, lay her out like a fish on a platter for the cliff lion's supper. Not that it would make much difference. Her bow might succeed in annoying a cliff lion, possibly.

Moving as fast and yet as steadily as she could, she snubbed the left rein tight around the saddlehorn, where it would hold him if he tried to run, and kept hold of the right rein. She was *not* going to lose Fancy, even if he was a stupid lackwit of a pony. Still clutching the rein, thanking the Three that Fancy was still attached to the other end — shivering, running with sweat, but still blessedly mindful of his training — she reached for the quiver at her waist and slid an arrow into the centerline cutout of her bow. It was a light weapon, no wheel pulleys at the ends like the massive *bare* built to punch through armor, just a hornbacked hunting bow for a young girl, but it did have a ten-kilo draw. *I'm a good shot. Daddy said so.*

The eyes followed her, and then she could see the body as she backed out onto the open ground. Not a cliff lion. Stobor. About the size of a small dog, but with claw-tipped paws nearly monkey-agile, long whip tail, narrow pointed muzzle with splayed ripping teeth showing past the lips. The hide was pebbly and the gray of rock, the long thin fur-feathers that speckled it reddish brown. They splayed out abruptly, doubling the apparent size of the beast. It gaped its mouth at her, black and yellow.

"*Hoo-eee-eee-hu-hu-hu-heeeeee*," it screamed, high and

shrill. The sound bounced off the walls of the great canyon, echoing hugely back and forth. It was gaunt, even for its rat-thin breed. Gaunt with the long winter and sparse spring.

Fancy tried to go wild at the sound, plunging and snorting, half-rearing against the shortened reins. The bow jerked in her hand. She jerked back as hard as she could without losing the arrow, and for a miracle (*thank Mother Ruth and Father Piet and Yeweh and Christus, and Allah and the Spirits too, just to be sure*) the pony stopped cold, trembling violently, but not enough to spoil her aim again.

Stobor were pack animals. Fifty or more might be within calling range, and they could run right up cliffs. She drew slowly — *pray Yeweh it doesn't know about bows* — and laid the shaft to her ear, the aiming-pin on the animal's belly as it stood to scream maniac laughter at her again. *Whup*. That turned to a scream of pain as it fell to its side, scrabbling with paws and teeth at the black-fletched quilling that bloomed against its skin.

Erika scrabbled into the saddle, then hauled back on the reins as Fancy, his patience finally exhausted, tried to bolt. He bucked and sunfished, but she held on. *Death*. Death to try to gallop back down the trail. Held to a crabbing canter, the pony moved sideways down the faint trail. Rocks kicked away from the shod hooves, falling swiftly in Haven's heavy gravity, to bounce and crack and splinter gunshot-loud on their way to the valley floor a thousand meters down.

Behind her the screams were joined by more laughter as the stobor's pack-mates held their brief and bloody feast. They'd be finished soon.

*"Erika!"*

"Pa!"

Erika drew a shuddering breath; Fancy hung his head and slobbered more of the foam that flecked his neck and flanks. Her father was not alone; one of the apprentices was with him, and they both had their bows out at the sight of her winded horse, pale face and empty quiver. Tom

Jerrison was there too. Erika winced slightly at the sight of the big graying man, sitting his horse awkwardly with his sledgehammer over his shoulder. Jerrison was Karl's father's man. An Edenite, not a Bandari, one of the old Americ-descended folk who had held the valley back before the Founder's time. Tom Jerrison had been cast out of his church congregation, shunned; Yigal bar Rhodevik had taken him in. Now he was Yigal's shadow, his right hand, and that meant Yigal was near here somewhere.

*Karl and Shulamit are in even more trouble than I thought*, she realized unhappily. From the thundercloud look on her father's face once his first relief was past, so was she.

"Stobor," she said helpfully, waving her bow back at the rocks. Here in the foothills the trail was a little more definite; farmers took sheep and muskylope to the higher ground in summertime.

"I'm going to have the skin off the *totchkis* of those two young *sklems*," he said grimly. "Sending you back alone."

"But, *Pa*!" Erika wailed. "It wasn't like that at all! They didn't know I was following them, I did it so I could find out where they're going. They could get *killed*, you've got to make them come back!"

"*Nu?*" he murmured after a moment, tugging at his dark-brown beard. "Is that the way of it?" Then aloud: "Well, your mother should hear it; also Yigal."

Erika fell gratefully silent as they turned their mounts westward into the valley proper. *I know it's right to tell on them.* Somehow she doubted very much that Karl and Shulamit would agree, and she blanched slightly at the thought of facing her half-sister after the *Sayerets*, the Scouts, brought them back. Fancy was mostly steppe pony, and as tough as ponies came; he recovered quickly, eager for his stall, but she found herself willing the journey to take longer.

The great lowland opened around them as they left the last of the Shield-of-God range behind. It was day now, sun and half-full Cat's Eye to the west behind the Afritsberg, the white-topped peaks that closed the other side of Eden. Quite a warm summer's day, too, well above freezing, and they had all opened their sheepskin jackets. The reddish-green of native screwgrass and the sparse truegreen of earth alfa-grass was dotted with sheep and horses and muskylope. Then the land dropped further, down to the alluvial trough of the valley proper.

The chill air tasted of dust and greenery, as the irrigation channels tinkled with meltwater; the farms that lined them were broad streaks of grainland against the drabber colors of land too high to water. The fields were planted with rye, barley, oats and *ryticale*, or bushy with potatoes, shaggy with amaranth. The sprouts of the last planting were just showing, the gray-brown earth damp with irrigation water. Earth walls separated them, with an occasional grove of carefully tended birch or ash, more common orchards of clowntree fruit or Finnegan's fig, sometimes an apple tree in a sheltered, south-facing spot. Traffic thickened, carts and wagons drawn by muskylope, travellers on horseback, an occasional string of Bactrians. A few brows went up at the party's curt answers to nods and waves. Farmers and their families were hard at work, reaping grain with cradle-scythes in some fields; in others hoeing and raking, driving ox-drawn harrows in plumes of dust, spading in potatoes. Whitewashed cottages and rammed-earth sheds stood here and there.

Erika scrunched her head down into the collar of her jacket as they turned off the main road from Strang to the rutted lane that led to home. It was all her family's land from here; three small farms rented out to Edenites on shares, with the water rights. Then the mudbrick wall that enclosed the houseyard, the *werf*, with its creaking windmill and water tank. Then the house itself, big and low-slung, of adobe brick like most but painted in gay geometric patterns, roofed in good red tile and with diamond-patterned glazing for the windows; her family was a long way from the wealth Karl's father had, but they were solidly prosperous. Coalsmoke from the chimney, from the hearths of the two forges . . .

Usually there was a good deal of bustle; her parents were both smiths — that was the fan Gimbutas clan trade — and they had half a dozen apprentices, plus Moishe and Esther,

her younger siblings, and a maid and a cook and the stablehand. There would be visitors more often than not, kinfolk, one of the tenants in for business or with some metalwork to do or just for a gossip, clan-cousins with a load of iron barstock from the smelters in the northern valley, buyers looking for swordblades and gunlocks, a pedlar. Today was something else entirely. *Soldiers* stood in the cobbled courtyard, horses picketed, their riders shining in their armor of lacquered leather and brass and steel. Lancers and riflemen, with the *Sayeret* lightning blazon, hard-looking young men and women. A banner-staff stuck in the ground with the fan Reenan leaping antelope and the Pale's national flag—

*Oh, Yeweh and the Spirits of the Founders, it's the* kapetein, she thought. The newly elected *kapetein*, Barak bar Sandor fan Reenan. Ruler of all the Pale and the People. *I wish the stobor had ——* She stopped herself; the memory of those fanged mouths darting at the heels of her horse was too recent. *I almost wish the stobor had caught me.*

Miriam bat Lizbet came out of the kitchen door, with the maid behind her; they each held a handle of a big platter-shaped wicker basket. It usually carried laundry, but now was heaped with loaves of round flat bread, wedges of cheese, and links of sausage. Old *Tanta* Bethel followed with a tray bearing mugs of eggbush tea. The soldiers came forward, their politeness turning to grins.

"Hmmph," Miriam said, looking her daughter over. "*You* tend to that horse, my young *meid*. And then you've got some talking to do!"

"It's not *fair*." Erika kicked the post of the kitchen door as she sulked out.

"No it isn't," her father said with a wry smile, sinking back to his chair by the kitchen table. Miriam took his hand, as callused and work-roughened as her own, and they turned to look at the other two at the table.

*Kapetein* Barak sprinkled a little beet-sugar on a cut Finnegan's fig and ate it. "Good lunch," he said.

*Tanta* Bethel sniffed and left, wiping her hands on her apron.

"Think we'll catch them?" Yigal bar Rhodevik said. He was a square-faced man, his teak-dark skin and light eyes showing the blood of Frystaat. So did the gaunt muscularity of his face, and its premature aging; few of that breed lived much past fifty T-years.

"Those two?" Barak said moodily, pulling at his gray-white beard. "With a day's start? My *Sayerets* are good, but they're not angels, *kerel*. No better than a one in two chance. Less as they get north — too many of the border guards are caught up in this Seven nonsense themselves, in their hearts. Already dozens have slipped over the border. Hundreds."

"I'm concerned about my daughter, *oom*," Miriam said bluntly. "My sister and nephew are trying their best to get themselves killed, but I want Shulamit back."

"And I my son," Yigal countered. "I could almost wish he'd get that *wildechaver* Shulamit pregnant — then we could marry them off."

"They're too young," Shmuel said. "Also they make each other *worse*, not better."

"*Gevalt.*"

Everyone nodded, sighed, drank more of the hot sweet tea. "I have to be concerned with *everyone's* sons and daughters," Barak said. "One reason I didn't want this job. Curse Chaya for a fool! She was a good Judge, but I *still* say she's a fool. And now she's got the whole northern steppe boiling, her and Aisha. Every *hotnot* sheep-stealer thinks he's going to be a hero and slay the Saurons." He worked one thick shoulder, feeling the click of bone that had never been quite the same after a Soldier's rifle-bullet nicked it. "They should live so long."

"Karl and Shulamit should live longer," Yigal said. Then he sighed. "Well, if we can't help them by stopping them, maybe we can help them by helping them?"

Barak ate another biscuit and brushed the crumbs out of his beard; his wrinkled eyes flicked sideways to the householders. Shmuel smiled and spread his hands. "I know, I know — secrets."

When the door closed behind them the *kapetein*

leaned forward. The kitchen was warm and comfortable, thick walls cheerful with tile, a low fire glowing in the ceramic *chagal* stove. Tables lined the walls, racks for knives and spices; a thick-walled icebox was built into one wall. Barak sighed. He was sworn to protect places like this, but sixty T-years had taught him that protection didn't mean being defensive.

"I can't send the *h'gana* to war against the Citadel," he said bluntly to the younger man. *Younger. I remember when forty seemed older than Haven. Oive.* "Too far, and we'd lose too much — those poor *gayam* are going to get their rocks kicked up around their ears, *kerel.* But."

"But, there are ways of killing a cat that don't involve choking it to death with cream," Yigal said; a little of the worry melted from his face, and he laid a finger beside his nose.

Barak spread a hand. "And the tribes will hurt the Saurons." They both nodded; the feud between the Citadel and the Bandari was as old as the People. "More if we give them a helping hand."

"Weapons," Yigal mused.

"I was thinking of sending Ari bar Kosti with a brigade up to harass Quilland Base's outposts . . . but weapons and skills too, yes. And with the skills, people who can look after those young hotheads and the others like them. Let the *hotnots* go charging into the Sauron Gatling guns. If they kill Soldiers, good — if they die, also good."

Yigal winced a little at the blunt pragmatism of it, but nodded again. The tribes did not hate the Bandari the way everyone hated the Saurons — most of them did not — but the Pale was not popular. All of the Three Faiths were infidel to the mostly Muslim plains nomads, and the Pale was full of good grazing, rich herds and loot, by tribal standards. Nor did the People suffer attack meekly; blood feuds from old raids and wars sizzled across half of Haven.

"I can afford something," Yigal said. "I can raise more from our kin."

"The *kapetein*'s special funds are full," Barak said.

The Pale's granaries were stuffed with food, the treasury

with hard cash, and more out on loan; the armories were full. *Mordekai's husbandry*, Barak thought.

"The fan Gimbutas will make contributions, others . . . even the Edenites." The Church elders who ruled among the Pale's non-Bandari inhabitants thought of the Saurons as literal Spawn of Satan.

"Weapons, that we'll need permission for. Rifles?" At Barak's nod, he said, "And?"

"No." The ruler of the Pale shook his head decisively. "What the Saurons haven't met in combat, they can't evaluate. Not the 'little Ariksas,' not yet. We'll see how this *jihad* goes before we commit the fan Gimbutas' little pets. We *will* send more help to you-know-who."

Yigal grinned. Aiding the rising in the Shangri-La had been partly his idea.

"And finally, I'll send something to Cliff Lion Springs that'll hit the Saurons harder and heavier than any weapon Clan Gimbutas has ever forged," Barak continued happily.

Yigal's eyes narrowed. "I *know* you, Barak bar Sandor," he said. "You've got your drillbit-eating expression."

"Chaya deserves it," Barak said. "There I was, all ready to peacefully retire — commanding the *h'gana* was all I ever wanted to do — and she goes and lands me with *this* job. Who was my worst problem when I was commanding? Who did I have to spend half my time restraining, otherwise he'd cut every throat from *Burg Kidmi* to the North Sea and call it a mitzvah? Who did Judge Chaya, so reasonable she was and so kind to the *hotnots*, think was a mad golem from the back hills? What help can I give her that will really be help but she'll hate like poison?

"They," he concluded, rubbing his hands together, "*deserve* each other."

"How are you going to get him out of retirement?" Yigal asked, curious. "Pretty stubborn man." *Almost as stubborn as you*, he added silently.

"*Get* him? Watch — he'll jump at it like a stobor in a box. I'll send one of his old friends . . . Tameetha, say."

"Bat Irene fan Reenan?" Yigal asked. "I don't think he likes her much." *I certainly don't*, he added to himself.

"He'll listen; they were together back in their raid-and-foray days. Isn't she some sort of relative of yours, anyway?"

"We're clan-kin," he said; both fan Reenans.

"Thought it was closer."

"Second cousins," Yigal said shortly.

"*Everything's* a family affair," the *kapetein* said with a sigh. "Whole damn Pale's a *mishpocha*."

"Uncle Hammer? Are you decent?"

Hammer-of-God Jackson pulled his toe back out of the steaming water and wrapped a long towel about himself. The bathroom was shrouded in heavy-smelling mists from the natural hotspring that bubbled up in one corner; it mixed with cold water from the tank beyond the wall to fill the deep ceramic tub in the floor.

*Smells like wet muskylope farts,* he thought. "Yes, Brenda," he sighed aloud to his niece.

Brenda Jackson bustled through the door with a tray in her hands, averting her eyes. She was decently dressed in long dress, hood and apron, as befitted a Church of the Renewed Harmonic Testament (Jesus Christ) spinster-matron of thirty-odd years; she also had the Jackson family looks, tall and light-colored and strong-boned. Hammer-of-God privately thought that both his dead brother Fight-the-Good-Fight-of-Faith Jackson's daughters looked like melancholy blond mules, with dispositions to match. His own daughters were married off and occupied with children of their own, thank the Lord.

Brenda's lips narrowed. "*That* is not decent, Uncle. You've spent too many years around those shameless Bandari harlots who swagger around in unnatural dress, instead of leaving such matters to men as God intended, blessedbethenameoftheLord, amen."

"*Amen.*" *Try fighting the Turks in a bloody skirt, then,* Hammer-of-God thought, and followed it with a prayer: *Give me patience, O Lord God. But not too much.*

"It'll bring a judgment on them, by God and His Son, upsetting the natural order where men command and women obey. Now take your medicine and get in there and soak, Uncle."

Hammer-of-God shrugged. "Get in the tub?" he said, his fingers covertly loosening the towel.

"Well, that's what I *said*, Uncle, and it's what the *mediko* said so — eeeeek!"

Hammer-of-God stood naked and grinned as she fled, apron over her face. Then the smile died; he gulped down the vile-tasting medicine and slipped into the steaming water.

*I'll never hear the end of* that, he thought glumly, looking down at his body. From one end to the other it was a record of his career in the army of the Pale. The puckered shape of arrow-wounds, a little ragged where the surgeon's spoon had gone in to get the barbs out. Long scars, jagged or smooth, from knives and sabers. Knotted lumps of keloid from scraping and dragging, the inside ache of the places where bone had knitted over breaks, worse every year now. The angry red on his thigh from the last one, the pain that never went away. *So I don't heal like I used to*, he muttered to himself. *I'm not ready to lie down and die yet either*.

"Or maybe I am." Lie down and let Brenda and Ruth cosset and boss him into an old man; when he was very daring, he might ride into Strang and have a brandy or two and visit a *real* harlot. *Give me chastity, O Lord*, he prayed. Then, because he was an honest man in his fashion: *But not quite yet*.

"Thirty mortal T-years, and what has it gotten me?"

*Quite a bit*, he admitted as he slid down further in the water, leaving only his beaky nose and gray-streaked sandy moustache showing. A good farm owned free and clear, and general respect, if not liking. Silver in the bank and sheep out on shares; not riches, but enough to be comfortable. *And it cost me my only son*.

Enough. He would not think of that. Nor give Barak bar Sandor the satisfaction of seeing him come sniffing around for another command, the way he'd prophesied Hammer-of-God would. "Liar," he said to the ceiling. "I don't love fighting. I love *winning*. You should understand that, you chess-playing crafty haBandari son of a bitch. Sorry, God," he added automatically. "Old soldier's habits." The Elders were at him to be a better example to the young.

*Good example my ass.* It should be example enough that you could get ahead even if you were an Edenite. The Elders were far too fond of keeping young men — and still more, young women — down on the farm, for his taste. Blaming the Bandari for it, as well. Not that they weren't arrogant enough, but you *could* do it. Edenites mostly did their military service as infantry, garrison troops, and few went into the professionals. *He* had, grimly practicing with horse and bow to make up for the training haBandari clansfolk got in childhood, learning to read Bandarit because that was what the military manuals were written in . . . *facing down all those snotnoses who thought I couldn't be anything but an ignorant peasant.*

Good years, good years. Perhaps it would be best to rest — serve the Lord with his heart and prayers, rather than deeds, for a change.

A sound alerted him. He came up, blowing and shaking the water out of his ears, shivering a little as the air caught his wet body. "Brenda?" he said, reaching for the towel. The woman *would* not leave him alone for a moment. Thirty years of killing ragheads for Christ, and he was being pecked to death by professional virgins.

He raised the towel toward his face, rolling his neck to relax the muscles. That saved his life as it brought the glitter of the knife into his peripheral vision. Reflex made him try to lunge aside, but he was still standing in the tub, knee-deep in water. His feet shot out from under him, and he felt a thin line of white-glowing cold along his belly as the curved knife rammed by.

*Fool*, he thought, grappling with the figure in dark leathers. A lunging stab. Foolishness; you had to cut to kill quickly with a knife.

The man was faceless behind a knitted wool mask. They went over into the water, and the stranger's arm came down hard on the edge of the tub. There was a crackle of bone, and the knife spun free onto a floor awash as their struggle dumped half the contents of the bath. Hammer-of-God whipped his forehead into the masked figure's nose, felt it squash flat. The assassin snarled and tried to grapple again, but his right arm wasn't working, hanging limp at an odd angle. The Edenite rolled on top, hammered two knuckles into the smaller man's throat; his groping hand found the hilt of the knife and he thrust it up under the other's ribs, wrenching the hilt back and forth. The would-be killer arched, gurgled, fell back limp into water turned red. Hammer-of-God rolled out onto the floor and lay wheezing, shuddering with aftershock.

The door opened. Brenda screamed. Her uncle forced himself to his feet, feeling at the oozing line across his lower stomach. That had been a *sharp* knife, and if it had been a few centimeters lower . . . he shuddered. He might be pushing late middle age, but there were certain parts he wasn't ready to give up just yet. The screams trickled off to gasps, and his niece stood with her hands over her mouth.

"*Hotnot*," Hammer-of-God said, stripping the mask off the floating body. High-cheeked and slant-eyed, Turki or maybe Uighur by the looks. Nondescript clothes, the sort a wandering laborer might wear; the knife was short enough to be legal for aliens in the Pale. He must have crept in through the window and stayed motionless for hours behind the clothes chest. Underneath, the limbs were bound tightly in windings of linen; now *that* was interesting.

"*Hashashin*," he said, nodding to himself. Shi'a fanatic, pledged to don his own winding-sheet before he set out to kill. The face was pathetically young in death, younger than Hammer-of-God's own son had been.

He straightened and put a snap into his voice, the tiredness gone from it. "Get hold of yourself, woman!"

Another figure pushed past her. A woman too, but in the wool and leather of the Bandari clans, drawn saber in her hand. A decade or so younger than Hammer-of-God, but equally weathered. He recognized her; one of his staff officers in the old days.

"You can't even stop killing them in your *bath*?" Tameetha bat Irene said with a stobor grin. "Give it up,

Hammer — the *p'rknz* didn't intend you to rest and rot until you're dead."

"Un-un-uncle," Brenda whispered. "There, uh, there's a Bandari named Yigal bar Rhodevik — a fan Reenan — he's, he says he's got a message for you."

Tameetha nodded, lifting the body with a grunt and carrying it out. "So it's the *kapetein* got a message," she called over her shoulder.

"Yigal," Hammer-of-God mused. *And the* kapetein. It was still strange to think of anyone but old Mordekai with that title attached to him. *God grant him mercy.*

He shook his head. "No, *God* has a message for me, Brenda. Fetch my clothes. And my sword."

"My name isn't Issachar," Hammer-of-God Jackson said.

Barak looked puzzled. All he could remember was that Issachar was one of the Ten Tribes, back on Earth. Yigal bar Rhodevik leaned over and whispered the quotation in his ear: "*Issachar was a large-limbed ass, bent down under heavy burdens.*"

"Besides," the Edenite ex-soldier went on, "I'm a man of peace, these days."

Barak nodded at the sword by his side, and Hammer-of-God flushed slightly. That grew deeper as two of the *Sayeret* troopers went by outside, carrying the canvas-wrapped body of the assassin.

"Put that in the barn!" Hammer shouted out the window. "And Tameetha — you're going to wear that away."

The Bandari woman was stropping her fighting-knife on a leather strap wound round her left fist. The sound was hypnotic; nostalgic, as well. In the old days with the *Sayerets* he had fallen asleep by a hundred campfires to that rhythmic *wheep . . . wheep . . . wheep.*

"Some people chew their nails," she pointed out genially, and pulled out a hair from her braid. "Gray, Yewehdammit," she muttered, and dropped it. The strand fell apart as it touched the edge. "Hammer, you're going to say yes — why make them court you with baklava and flowers before you get into bed?"

"You shut up," hissed Yigal, a merchant's anger at someone queering a negotiation mixing with old irritation.

"Why, cousin — here I am, going off to look for your prodigal son."

"The *kapetein* asked you for help, I didn't," Yigal bit off.

"What sort of relative would I be if you had to ask?" she said — irrefutable logic, to one of the People — and started stropping the knife again.

*Kapetein* Barak picked up another wedge of clownfruit-and-apple pie and used it to chase some of the cream around his plate; Brenda and her sister had wasted no time in laying out an impromptu feast, with the honor of the house involved. "Going to get fat in this job," he said. "Every kitchen I visit, they bring out the dainties. Never could resist a good piece of pie."

Hammer-of-God looked at him and snorted; the blocky frame held not an ounce of spare flesh.

"So why should I go back to gnawing rotten muskylope in a snowstorm, when I could stay here?" he demanded. *Court me, Barak*, he thought. *For thirty years I jumped when you said "kermitoid." Now plead a little.* The living room of the farm was warm and comfortable, a coal fire in the stove, good rugs on the floor, a shelf of books — not only the inevitable massive Bible and Renewed Christian Harmonic Testament, but Bandarit volumes from the printshops of Strang and Ilona'sstaadt.

Yigal took a pull of his beer. "Because you're bored to distraction," he said. "Same reason Tameetha here wants to get back in harness."

Tameetha had never married, very unusual for one of the People although not unknown; instead she had lived by arms, in the Pale's service and as a free-lance. The teak-dark color of her skin and the gaunt muscularity that showed tightly defined under it suggested more than a little of the Frystaat heritage so common among the fan Reenans, the heavy-gravity adaptation. Rumor was divided on why she had never settled; some held she had been disappointed in love as a girl, others that she was secretly carrying a torch for Hammer — *hard to believe,*

Yigal thought — others that she was bent for women or just liked fighting too much to settle down. He had his own suspicions, but her skill was not in dispute.

Hammer grimaced. "Tameetha, in case you hadn't noticed, likes to kill people — which is sinful. She also enjoys fighting, which is not only a sin but stupid, too." The woman blew a kiss.

" 'I bring not peace, but a sword,' " Yigal quoted.

*Well, that's tit for tat*, Hammer thought.

"Besides," Barak said, "we need you. Lot of young *sklems* heading north to join the Judge, dreams of glory in their eyes."

Hammer-of-God spat into the fire. "No room for glory in the grave," he said.

"You know that. They don't."

"My son doesn't, nor that *wildechaver* girlfriend of his," Yigal put in. "They showed the *Sayerets* a clean pair of heels."

"Says something for their fieldcraft," Hammer-of-God observed. Outrunning the Scouts was no easy task.

"But nothing for their brains."

Hammer-of-God raised his own stein. "Send someone else," he said, wiping foam off his moustache with the back of his hand. "Someone the Judge gets along with better. Send Ari, he's good."

"He's needed here," Barak said. "I'm going to be giving him a brigade to keep Quilland Base's mind off the rest of Haven. He can handle that; he's a good solid field commander. This, this *thing* with the Seven, needs another order of skills entirely."

"Yohann bar Non —"

" — is in the . . . you-know-where."

Hammer-of-God nodded. Nobody should talk aloud about the Shangri-La Valley project. He *hoped* nobody was talking about it aloud; an uncomfortable number of people knew about it these days. Yohan was as tricky a covert-operations manager as the Pale had, among his other talents; the tribes called him the Ice-Eagle. Barak used him as a troubleshooter, the way Mordekai had used Hammer-of-God in the old days.

"Things are moving, we have to seize the time. I can't order you, old friend," Barak said, his thick shoulders slumping a little. "I am asking."

Yigal murmured: " '*Play the maid's part: say no, and take it.*' "

"How much can you give me?" Hammer-of-God said at last, not looking at either of them. To himself he muttered: "After all, Saurons *are* the spawn of Satan. Maybe God has been getting me ready for this."

"Of supplies and money, as much as you need," Barak said; Yigal nodded. "Specialists, any who want to go — Sapper, for one, we can spare him now. And plenary authority, from *kapetein* and Council. A thousand or so of the People are heading up to join the Seven already, so you'll need some impressive parchment to wave at them."

"Oh," Hammer-of-God said, smiling slightly — showing his teeth, at least, "I don't think establishing my authority will be much of a problem."

The home-field of Hammer-of-God's farm was crowded, the pastures packed almost solid with gray felt dome-tents and picketed animals.

*Next crop will be good*, he thought automatically: a lot of free fertilizer.

The news had spread quickly, and a great many old friends had shown up over the past couple of cycles. Most were from the survivors of the special retaliation unit he'd led once, the bunch known in the old days as God's Brass Knucks. Every one of them a proved fighter — well, they were alive, weren't they? — nearly as scarred as he was. And far too many fresh-faced youngsters who listened to those lying songs about it all. His cousins Be-Courteous and Smite-Sin, as well. *For my sins. I'm going to be shorter on old comrades after this is over. Mercy, please, God; and if you have to take anyone, take those two.*

"Saurons' bane," he said, leaning into a supply wagon and checking under the tarpaulin.

Flintlock breechloaders, neatly packed muzzle to butt and shining with protective oil. The Pale's answer to the Sauron assault rifle, and far better than the alternatives.

Crisp linen packets of fifty paper cartridges, each with the pointed head of a bullet peeking out like the head of a cock from its foreskin. Pottery eggs just the size to fill a palm, with wooden loops at the top; pull and throw, five-second friction fuse. Small kegs; *gunpowder, storage of.* Three-kilo ingots of lead. Coiled slowmatch cord. Baskets of arrowheads. Spearheads. Best of all, little steelbranch caskets of silver slugs, the most necessary thing of all for war. He replaced the covering and dropped to the ground, feeling only a slight twinge in his bad leg, and looked back at the rest of the wagon train.

"Fighting Saurons," he said, "one of life's rarer pleasures."

Angband Base had fallen at the beginning of his career. For a moment he looked into space and past the years: the spiked head of the Sauron rolling at Chaya's feet, the look in her eyes, the look of one who walked with God. *I thought we were kindred souls. But she saw another facet of Him, mostly.* After Angband the People and the Saurons had been like two cliff lions with overlapping territories, snarling and pissing along the boundaries but not risking a head-on clash. Waiting for a chance to spring.

The party was forming up. All well-found, good remount strings, full equipment. Quivers stuffed with arrows, lances and rifles in their scabbards, bedrolls tightly laced, everyone had heard about *his* standards. And Sapper sitting on the buckboard of the next wagon, smiling his dreamy little smile, with his mapcase beside him. If it existed on Haven, Sapper could draw you a map of it and tell you how to undermine it or blow it up or burn it down. He'd been the one to survey the road down to the Shangri-La, originally: nobody had called him anything but Sapper for so long they'd forgotten his birth-name.

"Well, you know the tribes," Yigal said. "You've killed enough of them. Now you can apply your knowledge differently. And keep these reckless *wildechaverim* under control."

Hammer-of-God laughed, a sound that started as a rippling chuckle and turned into a full-throated guffaw. The severed head of the *hashashin* on its pole above seemed to share the joke, leering with dried-out lips pulled back from yellow teeth.

"Barak is sending *me* to restrain the *reckless*?" he gasped.

Yigal snorted. "*Sekkle tvaz*," he said: "It's only reasonable. He said you were a ripe throat-cutting bastard, but you hadn't lived this long by being hasty about it."

"Save me the *tzionut*, I'm not in a mood for flattery and hot air," Hammer-of-God grunted, swinging into the saddle with one hand on the pommel. *Not too old for that yet*, he thought with satisfaction.

"Yeweh be with you, my friend — and kick my son's behind when you see him," Yigal finished.

Hammer-of-God leaned down to fist the other man on the shoulder. "His for starters, Yigal — his for starters." He rose, stood in the stirrups.

"*Ons trek, hulle pelmakim*," he shouted with grand irony: let's get going, you stainless heroes.

Whips cracked, and the draught-muskies bent to the yokes; the drovers shouted the immemorial cries — "Trek! Trek! Bosman, Witje, Samson, *trek*! Veeery nice!"

Hooves scattered dust as the horsemen cantered ahead. Behind him, the last sound was the weeping of the farm's women.

# ● CHAPTER FIFTEEN

The sky was wide as all creation. The steppe stretched end-lessly under it, rolling to the horizon. The jagged teeth of mountains lifted it up and thrust it into the leer of the Cat's Eye.

Shapes moved on it, ant-small. A hawk, hanging in the thin air, would have known the gait of steppe ponies, some jogging at tether's end and two carrying the weight of riders, with burdened pack-muskylopes trotting behind. They were much too few for a caravan, much too many for an accident, and they were squabbling at a volume that took no notice of the emptiness around them.

"And I say you should have turned east at that wash, and stopped heading north!"

She was stocky, sturdy, and swathed to the eyes, but there was no mistaking the female musk in that voice, or the righteousness of its tone.

He was probably the same age as she, but he sounded younger, with a squeak in his outrage. "And I say you're the one who made us overshoot the track, out past that cliff lion's lair!"

She hauled her pony to a halt. "There hasn't been a cliff lion anywhere near here for a T-year at least, or we'd have seen the signs."

"Hasn't been a tribesman near here, either, or we'd have the whole Horde down on us by now, the way you're yelling."

"*I'm* yelling! And who's been yattering at me like a firewalker in heat since —"

Her teeth clicked together. His hand was up in a gesture no sane steppe-rover, ignored. His face was set, listening. She strained to hear.

Wind. Grass. A hawk's cry.

He was a throwback: Frystaat genes, Frystaat senses, almost as keen as a Sauron's. She was plain ordinary Bandari, with maybe a trace of the blood of the Founder's people, and a cull-baby or two from five or six generations back. She opened her mouth to call him on his blatant ruse to shut her up.

He slipped off his pony and dropped the reins. The pony, ground-tied, did not lower its head to graze. Its ears were pricked into the wind. Its nostrils flared. It was nomad-trained — it would not whicker.

"Karl —" she said.

And shut up. She left her own pony beside its brother and pulled out her bow. No need to waste time stringing it, though she checked it over quickly. It was a Bandari *bare*, carried strung, since it relied on the pulley action of the wheels at the tip of either stave. Karl had the pistol they'd liberated from clan stores: they took turns with it, day on and day off. He eased back the hammers, checked the priming in the pans, and counted the half-dozen paper cartridges in the pouch at his belt.

Without speaking they ripped open the lacings on their war bags and hauled out their armor, helping each other on with it: cuirasses made from overlapping plates of three-ply muskylope hide boiled in wax and backed with drillbit gut, snaps and buckles and edging of brass and steel. Small round bucklers edged and rimmed with iron. Helmets like rounded buckets with cutouts for their faces. Armguards . . . The ritual was familiar from the training that began in childhood — and alien. This time it was real.

Shulamit was fast, but Karl was ahead of her, armed and out by the time she got the helmet properly on. She scowled at his broad back with its line of brass-gold braid. "You're just going to run into whatever it is? Just like that? *Gevalt!*"

She had more to say, none of it complimentary and some of it creative, but she said it at the trot. The ponies would stay where they were. No time to hobble them, none to run a line, and Karl getting farther away with every stride he took, blast his retrograde hide. Just like him to leave her with the whole thing, packs, ponies, and all, and hare off after wild drillbits.

She cursed more luridly yet and slanted back to the ponies. She found a hollow that would more or less conceal them, and offer them enough grass to distract them. She got them hobbled. She hobbled the muskylopes from left foreleg to right rear, which was the only way to hold them. She left packs and saddles on, and wouldn't old Barak tan her hide for *that* if he knew. Then she took the trail over the stony ridge that Karl had chosen, and she had not even begun to exhaust her inventory of his faults, failures, foolishnesses and shortcomings.

Steppe only looked like a solid surface. Like the ocean Shulamit had never seen but often heard of, it was full of strange deeps and hollows; in places it dropped away altogether, falling sheer into the cleft of a valley — especially here in the foothills of the Atlas Mountains, northern wall of the Shangri-La lowlands.

This valley was shallower than some she'd seen. It was long and thin and curved like a Mongol's scimitar, much deeper in the middle than at either end, with a steep wall on one side and a gentler slope on the other. Fortunately or unfortunately, she and Karl were on the gentle side. They were up above the valley, but the cliff was higher than they were, and the Three alone knew what was up there, looking down.

Karl lay flat in the grass behind a cluster of rocks. She dropped down as soon as she saw him, and crawled rapidly to his side.

"Shulamit!" he hissed. "Idiot! What about the horses?"

"Safe," she shot back, much more quietly than he, and conspicuous about it. She squirmed closer, peering between the two biggest boulders.

It looked like a caravan at first glance. A scout ran well in the lead, on foot, but with a handful of ponies and — dogs? Black-and-white animals circling the horses and running ahead. The body of the caravan was about a klick behind, concealed from the scout by the curve of the valley, and moving a touch more slowly.

Except that if this was a caravan, it had no pack animals, a bare handful of remounts, and was armed to the teeth.

One of the riders faltered. His horse went down.

Another reached out a hand and pulled him up behind. No one stopped to deal with the horse.

"Pursuit," said Karl. "And desperate, if they're killing horses."

It seemed leisurely from up here. The pursuers were barely trotting — probably had no strength left for more. The pursued seemed to be in better case. He was moving at a trot with his horses, and not as if it bothered him, or as if he had any intention of occupying the saddle one of them wore. He did not look back. Shulamit wondered for a wild moment if he even knew that he was being hunted by nomads on spent ponies.

Shulamit glanced at Karl. She knew that look of his. Tilting at windmills, Judge Chaya called it.

"That's a woman," he said. "They're chasing a woman."

There was no telling from the looks. Shulamit supposed he did it by smell. She looked harder at the running figure. What would drive a nomad woman away from her yurt, chase her out on the open steppe, get her running the way — hell, the way Karl could when he had a good tailwind?

"She's wounded," he said. "But she's left a mark or two on the hunters, too. Look! There goes another horse. They must want her bad. I wonder why — "

He would talk till the sky fell. Shulamit pulled an arrow from the clip in the quiver attached to the side of her bow. The arrow-rest in the centerline had a horn spring to hold it in place. With fingers steadier than her heart or her lungs, which were pumping fit to burst, she nocked the arrow.

She'd practiced with the bow all her life. She'd hunted for years. She had never shot at another human being.

The bottom of the valley was rough with pebbles and boulders and outwash-scree from the rare flash floods of spring, side-gullies weaving back in the rock and volcanic shale beneath their feet. If the woman made a stand, the hunters would outflank her: elementary tactics. Shulamit and Karl could force them back into the open with an ambush in the rough ground at the side of the valley.

Shulamit tapped two fingers forward. Karl nodded, made a circling motion. He would go farther downvalley.

He thrust his own bow over his shoulder into the carrying loop of the quiver, tucked the pistol into its holster but kept the strings untied, and turned and squirmed backward, hanging by his fingertips from the edge of the draw. He dropped, falling with heart-stopping swiftness, landed in a crouch five meters below, and trotted off. Shulamit turned and made her own more cautious way down to the flats.

Karl thought he was a hero. *Hero, myn totchkis,* she thought. *He wants to rescue a* woman. Her mother had warned her about that. Men stopped thinking at their bar mitzvah, or when their testicles descended, whichever came first. Some woke up again at thirty or so, but others never got their brains back at all.

From the boulder she chose as her hiding place, she could not see the nomads, though she could see the woman they hunted, halted almost in front of her, as if waiting. She heard them, or thought she did: hoofs echoing in the cleft.

First one, then more of them appeared round the curve of the valley. Their quarry made no effort to raise weapon, although she had a saber at her side and a rifle slung behind her. She simply waited as the exhausted horses brought the hunters to within a few hundred meters.

The nomads all had plainsmen's bows, reinforced with horn and sinew. A few had muskets. An arrow or two flew at long range, one so close that Shulamit thought it had hit. But the woman was still standing, and no arrow in her.

Yet another horse went down. Then another, and another. The riders behind piled up against the ones ahead, just before they too went down. The horses shrieked as they writhed on the ground. The riders made no sound.

*Caltrops,* Shulamit thought with a slight wince. The riders behind were not stopping even for that. They spread into a line and kicked their horses forward, weapons glinting in the dull light of the Cat's Eye.

Now, at last, the quarry moved. She unslung her rifle with speed that made Shulamit blink, brought it to her shoulder. Shots rang out. No space between them. No tell-tale puff of whitish smoke.

Sauron assault rifle. Nothing else in the world made those whipshot cracks, or fired so fast. Every shot found its target, felling attackers or cutting the horses' feet from under them. Screams rose now, human screams to join the more terrible sound of horses in agony.

The rearguard of the pursuers swerved aside, trying for the tumbled rock and gully where Shulamit and Karl waited — trying to work around the terrible rifle, find cover, take the woman in the flank and rear.

Shulamit stepped out from behind the boulder and drew. The cord stretched to her ear, scritching over the bone thumb-ring. Estimate range: 120 meters. Raise the sighting-ring. Lay the pin on the target. Loose.

The string snapped the sleeve of her coat. The arrow soared out. It flew straight and keen — took a rider in the shoulder. He dropped. Another hauled him back.

Then Karl appeared on top of a hill. He hefted a boulder as big as *Oom* Yigal's armchair, hurled it a jaw-dropping distance to bounce and splinter among the riders. One of them knelt and fired back with a musket — waste of time with a smoothbore, but Shulamit's stomach seemed to leap into her mouth. Karl snatched the pistol out of its holster and aimed. The *bam-bam* of the two barrels was far and faint. The bullets missed their target by a klick and ricocheted off a rock. One of the ponies shied from the shrapnel, but the others barely noticed. He thrust the use-less thing into his belt and scrambled for his bow.

Shulamit came to herself with a start. Half a dozen of the, well, enemy, she supposed, were working their way toward her. She nocked, aimed, loosed. The arrowhead gouged into the soft volcanic rock of a boulder, just as a nomad dove behind it.

Again. Again. Snap of bowstring, whistle of shafts. A few return shots, arching high, no danger — these weren't *bare*, they didn't have the range. *Bless you, Kosti Gimbutas, for inventing the* bare, she thought in some small corner of her mind.

The nomads turned back for one last, desperate, straight-on charge at their quarry. Shulamit nocked and shot, nocked and shot, till her quiver was empty. She couldn't stop herself. Under the heat of battle she was cold and sick. She hated them, these nameless riders, these strangers who for no sane reason had become her enemies.

Something tugged at her sleeve. She whipped her head around to snap at Karl for distracting her. He was far out of reach, bow at his feet, sighting with an empty pistol. His lips moved; she couldn't hear him through the rifle's roar. She looked down with numb surprise at the tear in her coat. Bullet. Arrows were falling, but thinly now. The riders were nearly all down. Three only were still mounted and shooting. As Shulamit stared, one of them thrust rifle into saddle-holster and flung up empty hands. The other two lowered their bows. Their ponies stumbled to a halt.

The Sauron rifle held steady, but it did not fire. For an endless, terrible moment the impasse held. Deliberately, defiantly, the bowmen slung their bows behind them. The rifle was silent. The riders pulled their ponies about and kicked them into a lurching trot.

Very slowly the woman lowered the rifle. There was no sound in the valley but the ponies' retreat and a thin, high keening — whether animal or human, Shulamit did not know, or want to. With blurring swiftness the rifle whipped about. It spat.

The keening stopped. The silence was appalling.

Shulamit's throat was raw. The world kept going in and out of focus. She would be sick, maybe. Eventually.

Karl was gone. She still had the box of shells for the pistol. She had never thought to give it to him.

He loomed in front of her, doubled. The new half of him was taller than he was by half a head, and half as wide. Shulamit looked into a face as white as shock and eyes the color of glacier ice. "Where in the world," Shulamit asked, "did you get a Sauron rifle?"

"Won it." Low voice, almost sexless, but indefinably female. Like the face. No beauty, with those long bones and that cruel arc of a nose, but it did not matter in the least. The accent was vaguely Edenite, and Edenite was what Shulamit thought, reckoning up height, pallor and mad cold gaze. What else she might have thought, she was not admitting to.

"I suppose you think you saved my life," the woman said.

Karl grinned like an idiot. "Of course not," he said. "But we did provide enough of a diversion to slow them down. They're done for, now."

"Three of them live," the woman said. "They'll go back to the tribe and raise the whole of it. There was blood debt. Now there is full feud."

Cold fish, Shulamit thought. It bothered her, that was clear, but not enough to crack the ice in her eyes.

"I'll take care of them," Karl said. "They won't make it back. You'll be safe."

"And what would you do," the woman inquired, "if you caught them? Invite them to tea?"

"Kill them!" he cried.

Shulamit's glance crossed the woman's. There was a gleam under the frost. "Surely," the woman said. She shrugged painfully: wounded, Shulamit remembered, but not anywhere that was obvious. "Let them go. I'll be long gone by the time they come back." She turned. She was half a dozen strides away before either of the others realized what she was doing. Karl scrambled after her. Shulamit, muttering, jogged in his wake.

The universe was not logical. Sigrid had come to that conclusion Haven-years since. Humans were not logical, either, unless they were Cyborg; and then that cold logic, imposed on the irrational, betrayed them as often as not.

She was Cyborg. She was, by definition, logical: an organic tactical computer, and a perfect fighting machine. She was also, unfortunately, human.

The few of Katlinsfolk who had followed her so far were dead or fled. The blood-debt that had sent them after her would swell now into feud. Which was nothing at all new for a Soldier of the Citadel against the nomads of Haven's steppe.

Her trap would have taken them in any case. Her fault for delaying it so long out of nothing more or less than weakness — hoping that they would give up, accept the loss of their shaman and their horses, and go back to their hidden valley. Illogical, and inefficient. And plain bloody stupid. They would know what she was doing and where she went. Betraying them to the Soldiers whose notice they had escaped so long. Carrying their death, less swift but far more sure than the rifle she carried at her back.

Katlinsfolk had made her one of them. She would have been chieftain of a new and powerful clan, with all their knowledge at her disposal. In return she had given them theft, murder, betrayal. She was Soldier first and always. She could defy the Breedmaster, but not the Race. It was bred in the bone.

Her pursuers' deaths she had expected. She had planned them. These children who fancied that they had assisted her were the universe's contribution. The girl was sturdy enough for tribute stock, but nothing to marvel at. The boy was another matter altogether.

She knew the type. No Breedmaster's pupil could have missed it: Frystaat, and nearly pure. The computer in her brain clicked over the liabilities. Heavy-G-adapted, cardiac problems inevitable, death by fifty T-years probability verging on certainty. High metabolism, with tendency toward inefficiency — he would need to eat often and in quantity, and he needed every scrap of linen, wool, leather and metal he was wrapped in, to prevent hypothermia. But the assets . . .

With frequent need for fuel and susceptibility to cold came exceptional resistance to heat and thirst. Muscular strength well within Soldier norms. Stamina likewise. Night-sight excellent by cattle standards though insufficient for a Soldier. Other senses on the high end of unaugmented norm. He might not know why he followed her so closely, but his nose was wiser than he.

He was also, and incidentally, highly decorative to look at. Dark skin set off brass-bright hair and green eyes. By Soldier standards he was excessively thick-boned and muscle-heavy, although for a Frystaater he was a slender adolescent. He was as agile as a boy of a third his bulk, even dragging reluctantly behind as she dealt with the dead. She found herself making an effort to conceal her strength as she dug the grave with knife and hands and pitched the bodies in. Wise, logic told her. Neither of her self-appointed rescuers had named her Soldier. Let them reckon her less.

The girl stood apart and glowered. The boy hovered while Sigrid searched the bodies for anything of use. Clearly he was above such things. But when she began to dig, he labored beside her with set face and swallowed bile. None of the dead was his kill. The girl had, maybe, wounded one, and that one had escaped. Still, he acted as if he had seen his first honest bloodshed. When he leaned over the pit's edge and gagged up his breakfast, Sigrid said nothing, merely handed him a packet. He took it in a hand that tried not to shake. "What . . . ?"

His Americ, she had noticed already, was heavily accented. As the last fallen Katlinsdaughter dropped gracelessly into the grave, data, clicking together, yielded a name.

Eden Valley.

And what were Edenites doing on the high steppe?

And what was an Edenite doing showing nearly pure Frystaat traits?

Her glance flicked to the lumpish figure of the girl. Sul-len eyes — blue, and that was surprising, but at this distance they seemed almost black. Rat's nest of rough black hair under the bucket helmet. Leather armor faced and studded with metal. Two knives, saber, unusual and highly efficient bow still strung and clenched in her fist. She was a picture from a Soldier's manual, marked and labeled. *Bandari.*

Sigrid nearly, perilously, laughed aloud. Good genes and Soldier instincts be thanked that she had feigned less strength than she had. Even at that, the boy was eyeing her in admiration and the girl in distaste, because she was so evidently capable of doing her own digging and hauling.

The boy's cheeks were ruddy mahogany. He looked away from her, into the open grave. And, bless his innocence, discovered only now what should have been obvious from the first. "These fighters — they're all women!"

"So they are," Sigrid said. *Ah well,* she thought. Her pheromones would overpower anything the Katlinsfolk could emit, and those who were whole enough for their sex to be discerned were well wrapped in leather and furs. She had not tried to lay them tidily — they were dead, they could not care — but some impulse had made her cast them in so their faces were turned to the sky. Tough weathered faces most of them, even the young ones, but none had ever known a beard.

He scrubbed his free hand against his trousers, again and again. The other clutched Sigrid's packet of field rations in a deathgrip. His throat worked. "Women. We killed women."

"I killed them," Sigrid said, flat and cold. "They hunted me. They would have taken my life had I not taken theirs."

"But," he said. "How — "

"That is a tale for a camp and a fire and a place safe from marauding enemies. Not for an open grave in a valley vulnerable to ambush."

He had discipline. He pulled himself together. They closed the grave in silence, and piled it with stones against predators. Sigrid topped it with a bow that had escaped intact. Ribbons fluttered from it, painfully bright in that bleak place.

For the ponies she could do little except slit the throats of the wounded and strip them of usable gear. The Bandari boy had no qualms about robbing animals. He went about it with a bandit's thoroughness and a honey dragon's glee, turning up treasures she would not have thought worth noticing.

Some of them he laid in front of her, with a look in his eyes that made her think of the he-dog that had attached itself to her. This cattle-child was all but wagging his tail, exclaiming over this trinket and that rarity. He kept more than a little for himself, she noticed, with an air that reckoned it only proper.

"This isn't a tribe I ever saw before," he said.

Sigrid shrugged. No one had, who would admit to it — until a drunken Mongol boasted to a Soldier in a tavern in Nûrnen town. Memory files yielded his name. Temujin. He had thought her a man. She had taken too much pleasure in enlightening him. Good stock there, for cattle,

but never as good as this boy who bent over a pony's carcass, rifling its saddlebags.

"You should know," Sigrid said after some consideration, "that these were not my only pursuit."

He straightened with quickness that was startling, as if
his bulk were an illusion.

"We were a procession," she said. "These warriors
tracked me far, and crossed out of any lands they had
kin-right or clan-right to. They had to dispose of a band
that rode against them. That band's kin . . ."

Behind Sigrid, breath hissed. The girl spat something in
what must have been Bandarit: not a tongue Sigrid had
seen any profit in learning. The boy answered in Americ.
"So we move. Here, Shulamit. Bundle this up. We'll lend
her one of our remounts, and make for — "

The girl — Shulamit — snapped back in Americ that
had no air of courtesy to a stranger. "*Shai lo kablos addad* —
She had horses. What happened to them?"

"Safe," Sigrid said, "and by now, hidden." *Best you go*, she
was going to say, *and sever yourself from me. This is my war.*

But the boy was as quick of tongue as of body. "Good!
We'll round them all up and ride. What tribe is it that's
after you? We have connections with some up this way. If
we can find one of their encampments, we'll be safe for a
while at least. And if they have feud with the ones who are
following you . . ."

His genes, his beautiful genes, cast Sigrid's logic down
and trampled on it. He would eat like a starving cliff lion,
and freeze if the temperature dropped. And his companion was cattle. It did not matter. The imperative was as
strong as that which forced her back to the Citadel.

One sleeptime, two, three — no more than it took to
take what she wanted, and then she would let him go. The
tribesmen were a quarter cycle behind, maybe more. She
had set a trap for them already, one that failed through
Katlinsfolk's interference, but it had lamed horses and
wounded men. Then Katlinsfolk had had to fight them,
and had lost none of their own, but taken one life that
Sigrid was sure of. She had left them fighting and fled with

all the speed her herd could manage. Katlinsfolk were hardy and their hate was hot. They had driven themselves to the utmost to catch her, and so they died.

She took a moment to savor the irony — Soldier allied with Bandari against the Soldier's enemies. She would not be quick to share it with these children.

They went in search of their herds. Hers was five horses strong, fine stock and valuable enough to look at, but it took more than eyes to see how truly precious that mare and her daughters were. The mare could foal on the high steppe outside the safety of a valley — and she had passed that trait to her offspring. It was the rarest of mutations: one that not only benefited its possessor but bred true. Sigrid had paid in blood for that prize. She would bring it to the Citadel, or die trying.

The Bandari mounts were larger than most steppe ponies, to accommodate Karl's mass, but otherwise unexceptional. They were all together, hers and theirs, with the dogs standing guard, looking highly pleased with themselves. The she-dog, as always, kept her distance. The he-dog eyed the strangers with narrow mistrust but grinned at Sigrid, circling from her to the horses and back again. The muskylopes stood in their usual resentful clump, blowing complaint through hairy nostrils and occasionally taking a half-hearted lurch against their hobbles.

"Yes," she said, "you did well." She had stopped caring that it was inefficient to talk to a dog. The beast understood tone if not words. And, like a young Soldier, he needed praise on occasion, to keep up his morale.

He leaped a clear meter in the air and somersaulted, which was his whoop of exuberance, and came down lashing at the nose of a pony that ventured to stray.

"Wonderful," said the boy, who still lacked a name.

She would remedy that. "Sigrid," she said.

He blinked, caught off guard.

"My name," she said, "is Sigrid."

"Oh," he said. Then: "Karl. Karl bar Yigal" — and in a rush of pride: "fan Reenan."

Her head bent a fraction. Her eyes, controlled, forbore

to widen. No wonder, then, his quality. He had it direct from the source: Piet van Reenan himself. Soldiers hated the man who had killed so many of them and defied them to the end, but they accorded him full respect. He had been a worthy enemy.

"And this," said Karl, "is Shulamit bat Miriam fan Gimbutas."

Shulamit did not look at all pleased to be introduced. Sigrid favored her with a flat stare and a flatter, "Honored."

The girl muttered something. "*Gayamske shiks nefkeh.*" It was in Bandarit; it did not sound friendly. Sigrid ignored it.

"I don't care what it looks like!" gritted Shulamit. "I don't like that bitch and I don't want to travel with her."

They were speaking Bandarit while the stranger — Sigrid — did something with her horses. They were out of armor, which was chillier but more comfortable. Camp was made in a spot a few klicks east of the scimitar-shaped valley, and the trail to it concealed as best they knew how. Sigrid was good at trailcraft. Karl had not expected her to be anything else, but watching her work was a pleasure. She never wasted a move or a word, and she made no mistakes.

Behind them, toward the site of the one-sided battle, a chorus of whooping cries rose. Too low-pitched for stobor: a pride of tamerlanes had found the bodies of the horses. Perhaps the other bodies as well. Like their smaller cousins, tamerlanes had almost prehensile paws, adapted for climbing. They worked well on shifting medium-sized objects such as the rocks in a cairn.

Karl flinched a bit at the sound, then looked at Shulamit and sighed. "You don't have to like her to admit that there's safety in numbers. We've seen how she can fight."

"Yes," snapped Shulamit, "and we've seen what kind of trouble she'll draw down on us, too. She's got half the tribes raised against her — and I'll bet a rifle to a grass-stem that she's not telling us everything she's done to stir them up."

"Then she needs us all the more, to help her get away from them."

Shulamit spat just to windward of his foot. "Where do you keep your brains, fan Reenan? In your pants?"

He was not going to get angry, no matter how much his fists ached with clenching. "Look," he said with all the patience he could muster. "Did you know where we were before we found her?"

"Yes!" she shot back. "We were north of Eden Valley, and heading eastward along the Atlas foothills."

"But where were we?" he pressed. She set her jaw and said nothing. "We were lost, Shulamit. We took a wrong turning somewhere — all right, maybe it was at that wash — and we were going exactly nowhere. We need her to help us get back on the track."

"And do we tell her why?" Shulamit demanded. Trust her not to thank him for admitting a mistake.

As for telling Sigrid . . . "I think we ought to," Karl said. "If she doesn't already know that the whole steppe is rising, she'd better learn it soon. She might want to join us. She's good in a fight. And," he said, clinching it, "she's got a Sauron assault rifle."

Shulamit was born stubborn. "So she has. How did she get it? Maybe she's one of them herself."

Karl struggled for patience. "Saurons don't breed females. You know that. That's why they need tribute maidens. She's tribe-bred, I'll bet money on it. There were a couple just like her in the tribe that was chasing her."

Shulamit set her jaw and looked more mulish than ever.

"I'm travelling with her," Karl said. "And I'm telling her where I'm going. You can do what you like."

That hit the mark. For a moment, he thought she might cry. That was so shocking, he almost gave way.

Then she said nastily, "All right. Let's be a caravan. We'll live together and die together, with a mob of happy nomads dancing on our bones."

He should have felt more triumphant than he did. Fighting with Shulamit was normal — a day wasn't a day without a good squabble. But this made him uneasy. It had new edges, edges that cut.

Fights always ended with one of them grabbing for the

other, and then a good long tumble in the grass or
whatever was handy. This time neither made the move.
Shulamit turned on her heel and stalked off to poke at the
campfire. Karl watched for a while. Then he angled
toward the horses.

Sigrid was checking feet. Steppe ponies seldom went
shod, and their feet were tough enough to handle anything. But Karl could see that these had come far over
tough country.

"I have some blanks," he said, "if you want to put on shoes."

Sigrid did not start or turn. She reminded him somehow
of Chaya. She had the same unflappability, the same air of
containment that could seem, in most lights, like coldness.
"I may do that," she said, "in a day or two. They're good for
a while longer."

He ran his hand along the back of the oldest mare.
"Good stock," he said.

Sigrid clearly did not do small talk. Having finished with
feet she turned to stomachs, measuring out a handful of
grain for each. Her dogs watched with interest. She rummaged in a saddlebag for strips of dried meat. The male
snapped his out of the air. The female let hers fall to the
ground precisely between her forepaws, and sniffed it carefully before gnawing on it.

Karl's own stomach growled. He'd eaten the ration packet
when he remembered he had it, but that barely whetted his
appetite. Sigrid's glance was, he thought, sardonic. His
cheeks burned. Chaya would have said something about
growing boys. Sigrid, if she thought it, kept her mouth shut.

She had a predator's stride, long and smooth. It was easy to
mistake her for a man, with her body flattened to anonymity
in nomad leather and furs, and that long blade-boned face.
But there was nothing male about her. When she squatted by
her packs and took her hat off and ran fingers through hack-
ed-short, flax-fair hair, his innards wound up in a knot.

Food helped a little: bread baked in the ashes of their
fire, dried fruit, cured meat. Sigrid had a healthy appetite.
Karl found himself outclassed, for once. Shulamit, whose
stocky frame needed next to nothing to keep it going,

watched them with bemusement verging on scorn. When she had eaten she spread her blanket conspicuously on the other side of the fire, and turned her back on it and them.

Karl felt obligated to apologize for her. "She's not usually like this," he said. "We got lost, you see, and that put her out of temper. And she never killed anybody before."

"Nor did she this time," said Sigrid.

Karl didn't know whether to be relieved or disappointed. "I didn't either, did I? We weren't much help."

"No," Sigrid said.

"You never pretty things up, do you?"

"Should I?"

Karl looked at her. She added a cake of dung to the fire. No frills to her. Nothing but the clean cold self.

"We did what we could," he said. He wanted it to sound dignified. It came out with another whining *didn't we?* on the end.

"Why?"

Her question rocked him back on his tailbone. "Why? But why not? You were all alone, and there were a whole tribe of them."

"Two dozen," she said, "on half-dead horses."

"Twenty-four against one. We couldn't ride away and leave you to it."

"I could be your worst enemy," she said.

Something in her tone made him shiver. He shook his head hard. "You're not our enemy. Our enemy is in the Citadel."

Did she go stiff?

No. A spark had escaped from the fire and landed in a clump of dry grass. She beat it out with her hat.

She settled back on her heels. Her hat was in her hands; she did not put it back on. Without it she looked younger. With a small, not at all unpleasant shock, Karl thought that she might not be much older than he was.

She had given him his opening. "We're going there," he said. "To the Citadel."

One brow went up. "Have the Bandari consented to pay tribute at last?"

Karl was on his feet. It was nothing he thought to do; his muscles did it for him. "Don't — by the Three, don't — "

She was not in the least intimidated by his bulk. She looked up calmly, ice-eyes, stone-face, with a hint, the barest hint, of a smile. "Why else would any of your race want to go to the Citadel?"

"To conquer it!"

She laughed. It sounded like water under ice. "A mighty army of two?"

"Hundreds," he said. "Thousands strong."

She looked around. Cat's Eye, setting, cast long shadows. Wind chittered through the dried grass. "Do I see them?" she asked.

"Oh, stop it!" he said if she had been Shulamit; then blushed. But he was too angry to stay embarrassed. "Of course you can't see them! They're mustering klicks away from here. Shulamit and I were heading up around the beaten tracks, in case anybody came after us — figuring to cut back west and catch the army before it marches."

"Tell me about this army," said Sigrid.

He did not like the way she said that.

She must have sensed it. "I, too," she said, "have enemies."

Heat ran through him. "Who on Haven doesn't, while the Saurons keep us under the yoke?" He was tired of hulking over her. He squatted back down and leaned forward. "That's what the army is about. You, up with your tribe — did you ever hear of Juchi?"

Sigrid's breath hissed. "Juchi? Juchi the Accursed?"

"The very one — the nomad *khan* who took Angband. He's dead. Saurons killed him. Cut him to pieces and hung his head on a spike."

"He killed a Cyborg," said Sigrid as if to herself. "Him and his daughter between them. Oh, that Breedmaster was a fool, who set him out for the stobor."

"That's what everyone says," Karl said with a shiver. "Me, I'm glad the old bastard did it. Juchi the Sauron would have been a monster to end all monsters. Juchi the nomad was the best chance we've had for freedom since *Dol*

*Guldur* landed. He couldn't finish what he started, he had too much *tsouris* on him for that. But when the Saurons killed him, they finished themselves off."

"How?" Sigrid asked. Her voice was so cold it burned. "He's dead. What can he do?"

"Be a symbol," Karl shot back. "Cry for vengeance from his spike in Nûrnen. His daughter by his mother — she's still alive. She's found allies. They're the Seven. The Seven against Nûrnen."

"Who?"

"Aisha," said Karl, "bat Badri" — giving her the Bandari matronymic. "Chaya who was Judge in the Pale. Her son Barak, the one they call Young Lightning. Sannie his lover. Karl bar Edgar fan Haller — I'm his namesake. And two Turks from the tribes: Kemal and Ihsan, princes of Tarik's clan and grand-nephews of Dede Korkut. They all owe the Citadel a blood-debt a thousand times over. They're raising Haven against the Saurons."

His heart was beating hard. He wanted to reach out, grab hold, as if his hands could transmit to her what he felt. But that, he knew in his gut, would not be wise. "It's war," he said. "War for the world. They tried to stop us at home. Told us we were too young, shut us up like children when we argued. Juchi wasn't any older than we are when he killed his father. Aisha when she followed her father/brother into the wilderness — she wasn't even that old. We're grown, we're weapons-trained, we've ridden caravans. We decided to go in spite of everybody. We took what we needed and got out. If anybody's after us, he'll have to find us with the army."

"And where is that?"

"Coming at the Citadel," Karl said, "from the west."

Informative, Sigrid thought. Half of the continent was west of the Citadel.

"But that's not all we've got. There's supposed to be a diversion in the Shangri-La Valley, too. A big one — as big as the whole valley. Riot, insurrection, civil war. They'll have to drain the Citadel to take care of that. And we'll take the Citadel."

Sigrid sat on her heels in the dying Eyelight. Her face was blank.

All at once she got up. Karl snatched, but she was too quick. He half-rose to follow, sank down again. Shulamit's eyes were on him across the fading fire.

"You told her," she said. "Nobody knows about the second half. We wouldn't either, if we hadn't listened in the right places. If she goes running to the Citadel—"

"She'll have to ride through the army to get there," Karl said with more confidence than he felt. "And her horses can't take much more of this pace. It's a lot of news, that's all. She needs to chew it over."

Sigrid heard them. They spoke Americ, whether automatically out of the rest of the conversation or so that Sigrid could hear, she did not know. She would put little past Shulamit. Cattle, that one, and a bitch, but clever. Clever cattle were dangerous.

She dismissed Shulamit abruptly and completely. The story Karl had told, the names he had named — had the TAC foreseen? Did the Citadel know what was coming against it? Everything Intelligence learned went into the TAC, but even its power to extrapolate was not unlimited.

Juchi was a Breedmaster's mistake. So — and this was not common knowledge east of the Pale — was his twin, Chaya. If Juchi had ever known of his sister, Sigrid had not heard. But the Citadel knew. Breedmaster Titus had run the data once when Sigrid was there to see it, data culled from intelligence reports and collated by the TAC. Presumably the Bandari knew their precious Judge was a Sauron — but then, they were curiously flexible for a people who made so much of their Law. Perhaps they considered acculturation more important than genetics.

Seven against Nûrnen. Sigrid had read in the archives. Citadel-bound, denied many of the liberties granted her male counterparts, she had had time to assimilate odd quantities of data. So these cattle reckoned themselves great heroes, and gathered to pull down the Citadel.

It was possible — remote, but possible — that they might succeed. If the Citadel fell for the diversion and sent the bulk of its troops south and west, it would be vulnerable to attack from the steppe; in theory, even a scratch garrison should be able to hold the walls, but life did not always run as it should in theory.

Sigrid was in no great awe of Battlemaster Carcharoth. He was capable, but he was Cyborg, and she who was of his breed knew its chief shortcoming: data not reckoned germane were immediately forgotten.

Cattle uprisings had grown common since the fall of Angband. None had been of significant size. If this one was as large as the boy believed, the Battlemaster would conclude it was a Priority One emergency, resolution required immediately and with all due force. He would not expect it to be a diversion. And he would not expect an attack on the Citadel. Angband had fallen, but Angband was a mere Base. The Citadel was the heart of Sauron on Haven. Its primacy made it invulnerable.

Weak logic, worse strategy. Sigrid called it arrogance. She had enough of it herself, but Katlinsfolk had taught her to recognize the danger in it. Even before she came to them she had been an anomaly. She did not erase data when she excluded it. She subfiled it, cross-referenced for retrieval. She suspected that that might always have been a trait of female Cyborgs, those few who had ever been permitted to survive to adulthood. Full bicamerality was a characteristic of the female mind.

She knew her duty. That was to reach the Citadel with all speed, and alert the Battlemaster to the doubled danger. But her horses, with their priceless genetic inheritance, could not keep the pace she would have to set. She could divert them to a Base, if any was manned in the crisis, and if anyone there had sufficient expertise in either genetics or horsemanship.

Or . . .

She was Cyborg. Cyborgs made decisions independently, without reference to Command. She looked enough like certain cattle — Edenites, Katlinsfolk, smaller enclaves of Norameric and other Caucasoid types — to pass. And when cattle thought *Soldier*, they did not think *woman*. Soldiers were male, so desperate for females that they took tribute in women's flesh and bred their sons on cattle. Soldier women rarely went outside Base walls to correct the impression.

What she had done in Katlinsvale, she could do among the Seven. Join them. Fight for them. Betray them to the Citadel.

Luck had provided her with a contact: these Bandari children, the one so trustful, the other so wisely suspicious. Messages could be sent to the Citadel. Sigrid would infiltrate the army. They would trust a woman, especially a woman vouched for by one of their own.

She glanced back toward the fire. Karl was on the other side of it, stooping over the hump of blankets that was Shulamit. After a moment the blankets flurried; he vanished underneath.

Her ears were quite keen enough to hear what they did there. She felt her lips stretch in a thin, humorless smile. Young flesh, hot blood. Karl was not thinking entirely, maybe, of his squat little Bandari. Shulamit was binding him in the best way she knew how. She should know a young male's fidelity was only as strong as his female's pheromones. And Sigrid could control hers.

She would take one more gift back to the Citadel when she had saved it. It would be a son, she thought, and he would live to be a Soldier. Barring lethal recessives — but the Citadel held technology for that.

She went to her blanket in as much content as a near-renegade Cyborg could know. Sleep would heal the hurts of the long pursuit. And when she woke, she had her duty, clearer than it had been since she left Nûrnen. If she dreamed — if the dreams were nightmares — then so be it. One paid a price for what one was. That, like illogic, was universal law.

# • CHAPTER SIXTEEN

" . . . on *all* the tribes, *all* the people of the black tents!" Aisha was shouting. "Disgrace, shame, shame and eternal shame that we submit to the Lidless Eye!"

*She's certainly overcome her shyness*, Chaya thought ironically.

Seeing the tall figure of the woman who strode back and forth on the rock ledge like a hungry cliff lioness, the former Judge was caught up in it despite herself. Byers' Sun was down, but two great fires burned on either hand, and behind her the vast red arch of Cat's Eye rose from the horizon. The stars above were many and harshly bright, three of the sister moons floating among them like silver ghosts. Breath steamed up from the multitude.

The Seven were grouped around the foot of the rock; beyond them shaggy ranks of the warriors carpeted the steppe, like a lumpy garment of felt and sheepskin and leather and wool caps. Narrow black eyes gleamed, and the men of the nomad clans leaped up to scream their approval and hammer dagger-pommels on shields or swordblades. Beyond them the women sent up their high ululating trill. Aisha raised her hands for silence, and it fell.

*Power*, Chaya thought, looking up at her sister/niece's flushed face. *So alone for so long, and now they hang on your words. But you'll discover power is a fickle lover, always asking for more.*

"What do you give the Saurons, the sons of Iblis, the servants of Shaitan?" Aisha said. She made a broad gesture of mockery. "Nothing — nothing but the pick of your herds, your bowed heads and humble words, your *women*."

A long, low growl at that. "How many men die without sons, their yurts empty, as the girls who should have been theirs go to the beds of your enemies? How many of us have they slain — how many lie unavenged? How many hungry ghosts wail on the steppes of Haven?"

She paused. "And what do they *keep* from you, the pork-eating infidel? Why, they keep nothing — nothing but the rich lands of the world, the lowlands of the Shangri-La where your wives and your flocks could bear in safety and your herds eat their fill of fat grass. Yes, the Saurons do *nothing* — nothing but imprison you in these lands of hunger, where your children beg for a scrap of jerked muskylope from their fathers' empty hands. Their feet are on the bones of your dead, their treasuries bulge with your wealth — and your fairest daughters' bellies swell with their spawn. They sit in their power and they *laugh* at you!"

"What can we do?" growled a chief whose gray moustaches fell past his chin. "Juchi was a great warrior, however *kismet* cursed him — and Juchi is dead."

"Yes, my father is dead," Aisha hurled back the words. "But before he died, he cast down Angband Base. Before he died, Glorund the Cyborg — Glorund the very Battlemaster of the Citadel — was dead. Dead by this hand" — her arm flew up, a knife flashing in it — "as they admit themselves."

A low murmur swept through the crowd at that, below the trilling of the women. *Cyborg* was another word for *demon* on the steppe. Chaya could feel their anger, their shame — that a woman, even one out of legend, did what they could not — and the stirrings of hope. Hope, the most dangerous and deadly of all emotions.

"To ride against the Citadel is death, you say," she went on, pointing out this man and that. "You — Ilderim *Khan* of the Dongala Khel — Raman Qul *Khan* of the Ak Djelga — Yakub Bey whom they call the Gray Tamerlane — do you not face death every season, saber in hand, fighting your own kinsmen, men as poor as yourselves, for half a dozen mangy sheep, for a waterhole of stinking black slime, for enough land to graze one camel?

"The Saurons," she went on, "call you *cattle*. Are you cattle? Are the people of the black tents cattle to the accursed of Allah, the servants of the Lidless Eye?"

Shouts of "No!" erupted. Aisha overrode them. "Or are you of the blood of the great *khans*, of Temujin, of Kubilai, of the Iron Limper? Are you the sons of the Kalmuk, the Kipchak, the Tatar, and the Krim? Or are you *cattle*?"

A young chief leapt to his feet, shaking off the hands that would have held him back. His sword flashed out, the crescent of his faith against the ruddy glow of Cat's Eye.

"North, south, east, west — where shall you find the Kirghiz?" he shouted exultantly. "By the Silver Hand of Iskander —we are *here*!" And he cast the blade down at Aisha's feet. She caught it up, touched it to her lips and returned it to him.

"Eternal glory and the opened gates of Paradise to him who falls in the Holy War," she cried, her voice the chilling screech of a stooping ice-eagle. "Fame and wealth beyond the dreams of men to the conquerors of the Citadel!"

The warriors erupted in riotous acclaim. The chiefs were sober of spirit, stroking their beards and the hilts of their sabers; they glanced at the Seven out of the corners of their narrow eyes, appraising.

*Seeing the Pale behind this thing, because I am here,* Chaya knew. The Bandari were not loved among the steppe peoples, but they were respected. *Seeing Barak my son as a promise that the armies of the People will follow. Seeing Kemal, a prince of his tribe. And seeing that their young men will ride over whoever tries to stop them.*

What had they *done*?

Aisha's hand caught her wrist. She swallowed against a tight throat, looking out over the eager lion eyes. Imagining . . . how many? Sprawled sightless, with the stobor ripping at their flesh, and the weeping of the women and children.

Now she must speak. "Aisha's blood is my blood," she said. "Juchi was my brother. That the Saurons slew him is the way of things, for he was a warrior and struck many a blow against them. For them to dishonor his corpse — to set it out to terrify us into submission — is a thing not to be borne."

She fell silent for a long moment, a wave of unaccustomed dizziness coming over her.

"Fire," she said. Then louder: "Fire! *The Citadel will burn!*"

*      *      *

"What was the bit about fire in aid of?" Barak murmured to her, as they rode out of the nomad camp. "You setting up as a prophet in your old age, *ama*?"

The trilling and the shouts and the occasional musket fired into the air followed them, until all sound faded into distant dun-colored rolling horizon. All sound save the clump of hooves, and the silver bells on the harness of their camels. The Seven were more than seven now, as they headed down the final stretch to the oasis of Cliff Lion Springs. A solid little *kammando* of Bandari followed them, and nearly five hundred warriors of Tarik's tribe, wild young men, but showing the effects of a generation under the Pale's tutelage in their order and fine weapons.

"If I were a prophet, I'd prophesy peace," Chaya said, shaking her head. "I . . . just thought I smelled fire, that's all."

*If there is ever peace, anywhere on Haven*, she thought. *Haven. Refuge. Yeweh's little joke.*

These days more than ever, Chaya was hardly on good terms with fate. The long trueday rocked on; they stopped, ate, watered their stock, rode again. Dozed in the saddle, took turns riding scout. The cluster of humans and animals was lost in the vastness, like ants crawling across a sheet of crumpled linen. No wonder, she thought, that so many prophets came out of the steppe, the desert, the wilderness. In the solitude, it was easy to dream dreams and see visions.

Her head came up. Once again, she smelled smoke. Smoke on the steppe. She could imagine the acrid stinks of burning grass, of fear, of trampled beasts or those left behind to burn as flames swept across the grasslands, driving before it tamerlanes and cliff lions and all creatures with a hope of survival, while the great ice-eagles soared high overhead, trusting instincts to escape the downdrafts that would snatch them into the fire's jaws. Fire, devouring all, as the God-bloody Saurons had engulfed Haven during the Wasting . . .

Someone slapped her horse's flanks. She jolted back to attention.

"You were drifting," Kemal warned her. He too could blame fate. Prince no longer; exile instead.

"I was thinking," she replied. They wound slowly up a saddleback between two eroded volcanoes, then down to the plateau once more. Faint in the distance was a patch of darker green, with a mist of fog above it.

"You were drifting."

How had Kemal managed to come up behind her like that? After all these years, were her senses finally dulling? Had some recessive finally emerged that was known only to fate and Grima, the unmourned Breedmaster everyone assumed was a fool? Sixty T-years. Saurons did not live long lives, most of them.

She would run her own risks. But six rode with her from the Pale in the wake of the most disastrous Ruth's Day in Bandari history...*Kemal. Ihsan. Karl, here for love of Aisha. Aisha, exile once more. Sannie, following Barak—and Barak, my son, my son...*

"Do you smell smoke?" she asked Kemal and Ihsan. Their heads came up and they sniffed. Under the impassivity their schooling required of warriors in the presence of women — even an aged, disgraced Judge — she sensed their alarm. It was high summer; the shin-high reddish bunchgrass of the steppe was nutritious, but dry.

Not they. She glanced at Barak riding up ahead, Sannie by his side. *Girl, you were not my choice as a daughter-in-law. But you'd have lied or killed for my son. Welcome to the family.*

Aisha, then, riding somewhat to the side under Karl's watchful eye. Too proud to shake after a speech to warriors who might have offered bride price to her in the days she had been a princess in her tribe, or stoned her and Juchi out of an encampment.

*The poor girl,* Chaya thought. *Girl. I am getting old, you must be nearly thirty-five T-years now. I wanted to promise you a home, rest...I owe you. I owe you all.*

The two tribesmen, satisfied she would not fall from her horse, galloped off. They cast long double shadows in the bunchgrass under the angry glare of the Cat's Eye and the pinpoint of Byers' Sun. The followers spread out instinctively in the way of those used to the steppe, not wanting to eat each other's dust or miss a chance at forage for their beasts. There were others travelling along: the first spray of those attracted by Aisha's preaching and the rumor that ran like grassfire over the plains. *Galandat* and *fuqara* and *malamati* among them — the Sufi dervishes and holy fools and travelling preachers, a few saffron-robed Buddhist lamas and a wild bone-clanking shaman as well. They came for a few cycles, listening, black intent eyes drinking in the words, then drifted away. Some in repudiation: this was not an orthodox movement. More to scatter and spread the word to their fellows and the tribes, in a chain-reaction like sparks dropped in trails of gunpowder.

Chaya settled herself more comfortably in the saddle, but there was no comfort for her. *Old bones*, she thought. Instinct brought her mount's head up, nostrils flaring. *Water*. Chaya's nose wrinkled as she too scented water and sulfur, too. At the same moment, Lightning's hand flickered at Sannie and they rode point to the other five. They were approaching one of the rare hot springs oases that made the high steppes survivable, even in the winter. Aisha might be able to speak with the warriors and merchants who found haven in such a place along their road. There was no appeal from the beasts whom the warmth, the water and the easy prey might attract.

Rumbling began deep in the ground and built up. The pack-muskylopes tossed their heads, frightened. How did you explain geysers to the beasts, anyhow? Geysers meant warmth, if the oasis's guardians admitted the Seven to its safety.

Which of the tribes controlled this oasis? No one could *own* such a treasure; a hundred blood feuds in the past had proved the truth of that. Still, one did not willingly stop at an oasis controlled by a tribe actively hostile to one's own. Which one? Time had been when Chaya remembered all the tribes, their rulers, their heirs, and the principal *khatuns* and warriors in each. Time had been when she was Judge and not an exile, call it what nobler terms some might. And never mind this nonsense about a deputy. Yeweh, but she was weary! She was too old for this.

Karl turned his horse and rode toward her and the two Turkic warriors.

"Cliff Lion Springs!" he cried. "I came to this oasis once when I was a boy."

Chaya raised an eyebrow.

"Three tribes have farmers here. They're peaceful. They're too busy working their fields and the caravans that pass through to feud."

*Until now*, Chaya thought. Rumor travelled even faster than fire on the steppe.

"How long, *khatun*?" Kemal asked her. They had to stay for a while, since they'd been telling people to rally here.

"In!" Karl said. "For at least five cycles."

"What! So long?"

"Are you mad?"

"Who put *you* in charge?" All three shouts burst out just as the rumbling in the earth exploded. At Cliff Lion Springs, a geyser burst from a brilliant, bubbling spring, lavishing warmth on the chill, thin air. Kemal's horse reared, and all seven riders laughed, somewhat shamefacedly.

"We've been on the trail and pushing hard for ten cycles," Karl repeated. He could be stubborn even by the People's legendary standards. "We're bone-tired."

*Aisha and I are bone-tired*, Chaya translated. *True enough for me*.

There would be caravans in that oasis. Men to whom Aisha might preach her *jihad*, assuming they had not heard of it already. Merchants might pass the word still further. And Lion's Rock was well known on the trade routes. Every nomad camp they had stopped at would spread the word. Here they might rest while an army gathered about them. Assuming the *pr'knz* found them worthy of assembling such an army.

Once again Chaya smelled smoke. The unwelcome vision of earlier that day flashed through her mind: this time wave upon wave of armed warriors, until the waves crested and washed them up by Nûrnen and, please God, into victory.

The men's voices went on, bickering with Bandari persistence.

"What makes you think you're in charge, fan Haller?"

"If it's a matter of people's health, bar Heber, I *am* in charge. Some of us don't have Sauron blood and need the rest. And even those of you who do could use it."

*Not too tactful, are you, Karl, my friend? Better, I suppose, than saying Chaya's too old to ride hard. For that, I'd probably have to whip your butt.*

"And if you don't like it," Haller added, "you can just shove it."

Chaya barely managed not to snort. Barak, bless his heart, didn't want to be *kapetein* . . . but he had a ruler's reflexes.

Kemal snapped a salute far more appropriate to a *kha-khan*. Barak grinned and copied him, extravagantly humble.

"We can decide who's in charge once we're settled," Karl bar Edgar said. Reasonable behavior, for once: Chaya decided she had heard a wonder.

Tribes had emblems: the White Sheep; the Ice-Eagle; the Black Horse. *Razziah*, or raiding parties, had banners. The Seven had nothing but their own reputation and a few hundred followers to herald them as they rode into Cliff Lion Springs. The ground trembled slightly from the hot springs that bubbled up from some volcanic fastness. Overhead loomed the distinctive, lion-shaped rock formation from which the oasis took its name. It mostly looked like jaws from which depended huge fangs, the result of boiling, mineral-laden water dripping down the cliff for untold years.

Channels took the purer water out to fields of ryticale and amaranth and fodder; there were thickets of clownfruit and tennis-fruit and Finnegan's fig. Veiled women and men in long ragged coats and turbans looked up from the fields. They were still gathering in the last of the grain, squatting to reap it with sickles and glean every kernel, every stalk. Other women carried food packed in

clay jugs on their heads, walking up to the hot springs —
living here, they never had to burn precious fuel for cooking. Square flat-roofed mudbrick and fieldstone huts stood
in clumps, tethered muskylopes and donkeys — no horses
— with chickens and children running between them, and
rounds of yak and muskylope dung drying on the roofs.

The light of the Cat's Eye picked out eerie shadows from
the rock face and made it seem as if the Cliff Lion's fangs
dripped blood. Not the best of omens, by any means.
Chaya saw Kemal and Ihsan make signs against ill fortune
and reach for the blue glass eye each wore about his neck.

Silently, the Seven rode into the oasis at the head of their
party. With long practice, Chaya refused to look to left or
right. A few yurts, pulled to one side, marked a family party
of nomads, a minor sept, perhaps, of a smaller clan. More
tents and staked-out Bactrians marked a merchants'
caravan. Even the fearless boychildren who usually ran
wild under the light of the Cat's Eye shrank back — or were
snatched up by their mothers.

One lad, close to manhood by his size and by the
weapons he carried, herded the others, swatting one on the
backside. "Stand proud!" he ordered. A little girl laughed.

"Farmers," muttered Ihsan to Kemal.

"And not the best of the breed," said his lord.

Whispers rose. Chaya could hear them, and she knew
that Barak and Aisha must also hear buzzing about "the old
blind man." At the whisper of "some say she's his daughter,
or his sister, or both . . ." Aisha stiffened, then whirled to
face the men who were talking. Her black eyes made nothing of the growing darkness as she studied their features.

*Ghazi*, she could hear them murmur. Warriors of the
Faith.

They fumbled for their amulets. *Baraka*, one whispered.

*Ruach*, Chaya translated into Bandarit. The gift of spirit.
Of prophecy. Sometimes, when she was very tired, the veil
between past and future seemed to part for her too, and
she saw strange sights and knew stranger things to be true.
Such a mood had been on her the night she had conceived
Lightning. At such times, she knew, the person as she was

and the person she was in spirit moved apart; and madness was very near.

It would be hard if, after all Aisha had suffered, she must run the risk of madness as well. Prophecy, charisma, madness, magic — Aisha's words were painfully close to all of them. She moved men out of themselves. And one who moved men, moved the whole world.

A young man, one of the peasants the nomad tribes had settled at the oasis, approached Kemal. Though the evening was cold, he wore no jacket. His eyes slid soon enough from the warriors to the women who accompanied them: he saluted respectfully and with more formal courtesy than Chaya would have expected of a farmer.

Kemal accepted his respects like the prince he was, but waved him — with a sardonic grin at Karl bar Edgar — to Chaya.

He was too young, perhaps, to be the headman in this place. Probably the headman was holding aloof, lest the seven newcomers prove to be seven bandits, not seven *ghazi*. Still, he had courage to come out. With a minimum of words and a few gestures of surprising courtesy, he pointed out where the Seven and their entourage might picket their beasts, where to get fresh fodder (for a very reasonable fee), and what springs to use. The man's eyes flickered at Sannie and Aisha.

*I must warn them to be circumspect.* She had no fears for Aisha and Karl; Aisha, for all her age, was still virgin, and Karl wooed her with the care a wise man would have accorded a maid scarcely out of her mother's tent. But she knew perfectly well that once they had set up camp, Sannie and Barak would soak out their aches and their sorrows in one of the heated pools.

Chaya dismounted more rapidly than she intended. When no one was looking, she sniffed. Sulfur. Smoke, from the cooking fires of everyone in the oasis.

For a moment, the Seven stood indecisive. Aisha was used to setting up her own spare camp; just as clearly, Kemal and Ihsan were accustomed to their women and servants doing so, unless they were sleeping hunter-fashion against their saddles beneath a hobbled horse. The two tribal nobles solved the problem by deciding that organizing their new-found followers was their work. Barak did the same with the Bandari present. Aisha looked a little lost as a tent sprang up and fires lit themselves as if by magic. Village women came to show the newcomers how to boil water and cook food in the baking-hot volcanic sand around the fumaroles.

"You come with me," said Karl. "The comedian."

"Where?" Barak asked with very little enthusiasm.

"I'm for checking the sanitary arrangements. If the trenches aren't long enough . . ." He limped over to the pack animals and pulled out a shovel, which he handed to Barak.

"Karl, Yewehdammit, these people know how to run an oasis. Get that boy who greeted us to dig. Or these odds-and-sods we've picked up."

"My guess is his people want as little to do as possible with us. Besides, more people are going to be coming in," Haller said. "We've got to get things organized."

Once again, the smoke Chaya had smelled all day wreathed about her. Visions formed in it: tribes chanting under banners, a *h'gana* of Bandari screaming HA-BAN-DAR! and herself, always herself looking into the sweaty face of a fearful man and raising a pistol . . . no!

*Please God, we can keep the losses to the Seven of us.* Even as she thought, she knew the hope was worse than futile. *Let Karl be wrong.*

"*Khatun*, you let your physicians rule you?" Kemal asked.

"Right now, sir, he is the only one who has made any constructive suggestions."

Settling, digging, cooking, and collapsing into sodden sleep stole what energy they had left.

*. . . blood exploding from what had been a face . . . the gun, hot in her hand . . . she hurled it from her . . . people recoiling from the stink of the powder and the blood, though they bathed in it . . . and the smoke, choking her. . . .*

"God, *no*!" She sat up, the sweat of her worst fears drying. Sannie was gone; Aisha slept. The Sauron genes, the God-bloody Sauron genes. She couldn't even wake screaming and have people comfort her. She laughed as soundlessly as she had prayed. Old as she was, hadn't she outlived the need for comfort? Lost it on the steppe? Comfort was for other people. Even now, she must comfort them by denying her worst fears: that as she grew old, the madness that was the worst of Sauron tampering with genes and body would claim her and destroy what she loved best.

She could sense the sky lightening. Byers' Star was rising, sharing the sky with Cat's Eye. She sniffed, reached for awareness. Many of the caravans had left, muffling the bells on their beasts' harness to slink away in the long darkness. Even in her sleep, she perceived them as cowards and no threat, so she had not waked herself.

Moving deftly, softly, she rose. In a far part of the space allotted to them, Kemal and Ihsan washed hands and feet, then prostrated themselves to pray. They had become particularly observant since leaving the Pale.

Karl strode toward her.

"What makes you think people will come?" Chaya asked, without even a greeting.

"You know as well as I do," he said. He nodded out toward the clusters of tents, the ones who had joined them on the journey here. "These are just the fastest. Haven't you watched their eyes as Aisha speaks — as *you* speak? They'll come; for hatred, for glory, for loot, some because they must. Because the army will pass, and it will ride over them unless they ride with it. And many will come to follow the Bandari Judge who pledges to unite Pale and tribes against the Citadel."

"I do not want to lead."

"Who else is there?"

*It is Aisha's fight.* The words, contemptible as they were, quivered on her tongue. She forced them back. Aisha was her sister and her niece; and Aisha, for all her years, was a girl in some ways. She lacked experience to lead, not to mention having no talent for treachery.

Chaya ran her eyes over the physician, who seemed to be gagging on words of his own. Like *I won't have it* about Aisha and leadership. At any other time, she might have rejoiced. Now the fan Haller's love for Juchi's daughter — which had healed him even as it led him into danger — was just another reason to fear pain.

*You will lead.* After prayers, Kemal and Ihsan joined her and Haller over their small cookfire. This smoke was familiar, the smells wholesome. Chaya busied herself heating water for tea. "I thought Bandari women did not serve men." Kemal accepted a cup of tea, some flatbread, and some dates, lovingly grown under glass in the Pale; another gift from well-wishers as they left.

"It is written," Chaya replied, "that long ago, before the Bandari came to Haven, the Judge Golda would serve breakfast to her generals before they went off to war. And the only shame accorded her was that she was not a better cook."

Karl all but choked on his egg tea. Covering his discomfort, Chaya greeted her son and Sannie and waved away an offer of help from Aisha. "So, tomorrow, it will be someone else's turn."

The others nodded, reassured by the pattern she had established: matriarch nourishing her tribe. She sighed. Trying to resign her Judgeship did not mean she could lay down her power. She didn't envy the "deputy" old *Oom* Barak had appointed, back home — the job was tough enough with all the symbolic authority behind you. She glanced up into the sky. Even though it was overcast, the glare hurt her eyes.

Ihsan looked around the oasis. The earth rumbled; a plume of water and scalding steam shot aloft. "This is a rich place," he said. "Usually, though, the farmers come to sell fruit, handcrafts, jewelry to the caravans."

"We are *haram*," Aisha said. Outcast; unclean. Then her hand shot before her mouth.

"Are you abashed at speaking truth or speaking before a man?" Chaya snapped. This bashfulness must cease — and now, before these armies that Karl prophesied came to pass. "You are certainly quick enough to speak to Karl or Barak. Or to a crowd of a thousand warriors more drunk on glory than they could get on arrack or hemp."

Aisha glared at her. "Well, we *are*."

"*He* doesn't think so." Barak pointed at the young man who had met them the night before.

"He looks different," Sannie observed.

"Dressed differently," Kemal agreed. "Like a warrior, not a farmer." A world of contempt rode in his voice. On the steppes of Haven, pockets of farmers existed on the sufferance of the wandering tribes. What little wealth there was dwelt in the yurts of the nomad *khans* and *noyons*, not among the tillers of the soil.

The young man wore the leathers and silks not just of a warrior, but of a prince. Or princeling, rather; his wrists stuck out of the jacket, and boots and breeches barely met. The silks were shabby, faded, and frayed in places, but they were very clean.

"Why would he dress up to sell us clownfruit?" Chaya asked. She saw the others' hands and eyes locate weapons.

"He doesn't look like he's peddling anything," Karl said. Instead, the young man bore what looked like a roll of carpeting.

"If he knows what we are, he ought to know we can't buy housegoods," Ihsan said. "Shall I send him away?"

Outside the circle of their fire, the young man paused.

"*Khatun*." The young man met Chaya's eyes. No cringing, no elaborate, self-abasing honorifics, and no fear.

Ihsan swung to his feet, hand out to wave him off.

"Wait," Chaya said. Again, the smoke wreathed her about. *Send him away*, she told herself, but she knew she would not. "Let him approach."

The young farmer walked past Kemal and Ihsan. The tribesmen glowered, but he met their eyes as if used to staring down warriors. His glance went to Aisha and seemed to soften. She gasped and set down the bread she was eating. Karl Haller's hand reached out to touch her shoulder, then dropped away.

He bowed with more polish than Chaya had ever seen in a farmer, and dropped down at a respectful distance.

"Your pardon, *khatun*, for not greeting you properly last night. The people were afraid."

Interesting: not "*my* people."

"But you are not."

"No," said the man. "I am not." Like a merchant about to display prize wares, he set down the carpet he bore and unrolled it. On it rested a *shamshir*, hilt and scabbard so richly tooled and inlaid with silver wire that they could belong only to a tribal chief. He drew blade from sheath just far enough to show that the weapon had been lovingly tended. Calligraphy gleamed on the blade. Chaya did not need to pick it up to see the maker's mark. How strange after more than a lifetime to see a fine blade and know it to be the work of her husband Heber, fallen in the taking of Angband from the Saurons. Her hands itched to touch it, as if to touch her husband's hand.

Aisha's eyes widened. Her lips formed a name. The farmer smiled.

"Our father always said you had his sharp eyes, my sister. Yes, *khatun*. I am Dagor. Son of Juchi. And I welcome my kinswomen to — such as it is — my home."

"My hawk, my brother, my little prince . . ." The words tumbled from Aisha's lips as her hands went out to her brother. At the moment she would have touched him, he pushed their father's sword into her hands. Wonderingly, her fingers traced the fine calligraphy. Tears spilled over her cheeks, then dried.

"Where have you been all these years?" she asked.

"Going to and fro upon Haven and walking up and down on it," he replied. "Actually, that has been *your* lot, hasn't it?"

"But what . . . ?"

"What did *I* do?"

"You were so close to manhood; I thought, surely he will be a warrior, his place is safe in the tribe. . . ."

"Safe? My father's son, and you thought I would be safe in the tribe he led?" Dagor glared at Ihsan and Kemal. "Oh, I was *safe* enough. I was fed. I was cared for, as long as I might stay among the women. But I felt myself a man, and they — your father, Kemal — feared my father's son. So he sent me to the encampments of Aydin . . . that set of traitors. 'Treat him with honor. Remember he is the son of a *khan*,' they were told. Honor? When they came into control of this oasis and needed to add to the numbers of men who farmed it, they left me here. They all but *sold* me, me, who had been heir to my father's tribe."

Kemal rose, hand on his dagger. Ihsan whispered urgently in his ear. "How do you expect us to believe you?" Ihsan asked.

Dagor reached out and took his father's blade from his sister. "Only blood and oil should touch the blade once it has been quenched, my sister. Not tears." His voice was curiously gentle; Chaya's trained ears could hear hints of the accent of the tribes around Tallinn.

"You think I want your place as heir?" Dagor laughed bitterly. "Nothing would persuade me to go back, not if every man in that tribe begged on his knees. Would Tarik Shukkur *Khan* welcome me? Yes, I heard you. I can hear anything you whisper. I have Sauron blood, remember? Lots and lots of it. I say your father threw me away to a tribe he could trust to make sure I would be no trouble to him, then lost his power and the tribe's birthright because he could not see that his ally was a stobor among the flock. And those two-legged stobor *sold* me so the tribe would not be dishonored by the presence of an accursed man's son.

"They have treated me well enough here. They even forget my father's sins, they are so grateful — proud in a way — that I can speak to warriors and merchants not as a slave but as a man of honor."

He spat. "Little did they know how little honor is mine. They know now. They may not wish me to stay, and I have no place to go. Walking up and down on Haven," he repeated. "I saw my mother defamed and dead, my father disgraced, my sister torn from her tents to wander Haven with no protection but a blind man, no home, no other kin. . . ."

"If it comes to your sister's care . . ." Karl bat Edgar cut in. He rested a hand on Aisha's shoulder. Chaya smiled as her niece leaned her cheek gratefully against it.

"You seem a decent man," said Dagor. "Ask me, and I will consent. But I ask as my sister's brideprice, man of the Pale, that you return my honor to me. You have come here and snatched the life I made from me. The people I live among could endure me as long as Juchi, my father, was a distant horror, a matter of stories around the fire. But now that curses walk among them, my place here will be gone. Give me another life — and permission to ride with you."

Chaya poured another cup of tea and set it in Dagor's hand. He nodded thanks, one of the graces of his early life, drank, and belched politely.

"You take much upon yourself, nephew," she said. "And you ask much — and of the wrong person. I decide who rides with us and who bides at home. And I say: you shall stay here."

Aisha's instinctive protest, coupled with Kemal's and Ihsan's instant agreement, hurt Chaya's ears.

"Please," she said, prying the sword from Aisha and wrapping it in the tiny carpet. "Take this back. Keep it in honor, in memory of your father — and of my husband, who forged this blade for him. But, in the name of Allah, put this thought out of your mind. Give away the old garments that no longer fit — in any sense. You have been granted chances most men pray for: a chance to live clean of blood and blood feud. An escape from the curse of your father's and mother's blood. It is a gift, a grace. *Take it!*"

"I remember when we were boys. You were a good fighter and a brave one. But you are a farmer now," Kemal said. "You would hold us back."

As if signifying that Dagor disrupted important business, Kemal bent to his task of repairing a bridle.

"Let me," said Dagor. The leather was old, tangled and rigid and cracked; the metal buckles were twisted, as if a horse had pulled against restraint in a fit, or stepped on the piece of tack while it lay on the ground. The young man's fingers moved on the dirt-fused straps, careful and delicate. The iron buckles straightened into usefulness, shedding rust.

Kemal took it back with a grunt of thanks. Then he

swore under his breath as he tried to bend one of the buckles himself; he could not, and the torsion heat in the metal was enough to scorch fingers callused hard by rein and bow and sword.

Dagor bowed himself before Chaya. "Chaya *Khatun*, I beg you."

She shook her head to clear it of the sounds of bells, the reeks of burning flesh and grasslands that she knew were only in her mind. She bent to stir the campfire, then drew from it a stick the flames had only charred, not devoured. She showed the wood to him.

"I beg you, Dagor. Listen to me. *We are death-sworn.* I have dreamed . . . I have seen . . . We carry destruction with us; for the Saurons, but few who ride with us will see their homes again. There is no room for glory in the grave. Let me save one brand, at least, from the burning. Your duty is to keep the blood alive, not spend yourself on vengeance — shall Juchi and Badri perish as if they had never been, shall the Breedmaster's malice triumph in the end? So, *no*. Marry. Have children. Prosper here, and become a *khan* among those who serve the caravans."

Dagor's face set in pure rejection. "Am I to have less honor than the women among you? You, my sister, do you say this as well?"

Aisha reached out to embrace him. He shook her off with a vehemence that would have hurt a woman who lacked Sauron blood. She went pale and still.

"It's no great blessing for any of us, Dagor," Chaya said. "For God's sake, man, it is a *gift* I am offering you. Not to have to be a warrior. Not to pour your blood out on the ground. *Hear* me, Dagor. I am offering you peace."

"No! If I am unworthy to ride with you, I will ride alone. Or walk alone. And when I can no longer walk, I will crawl. . . ."

Was the ground shuddering from a worse tremor than she had felt here, or was she shaking that hard? Steam bubbled from the nearer fumaroles like low-lying clouds. Her head came up. At the very edge of her awareness came the sound of harness bells.

Aisha, Dagor, and Lightning had also cocked their heads. None of the others had heard yet.

Dagor rose. "They are coming here, and I must prepare for them. 'Fresh fruit, hotsprings oyster pearls for the great lords.'" He hunched over, a terrible parody of the way a farmer might cringe before warriors as likely to take as to buy.

Aisha cried out in wordless protest.

"Why, what else has been left me, sister? It is not you whom I blame. May Allah light your way."

He bowed, prince again, not lout, and left their fireside.

"So be it." Chaya sighed and let the branch drop into the flames.

"Aisha?" Karl Haller asked.

Aisha had been listening to the approach of the caravan. At the sound of the physician's voice, she turned toward him, her face lightening. Karl had called her back to life before, Chaya knew, and found renewed life for himself. A pity he could not have won over Dagor, too.

"We have no time to grieve," Aisha said. But she brought her hand up to touch the physician's face in front of all of them; and the hurt in the air lightened a little.

"I will speak to your brother later," he promised.

"You will not find him."

Karl rose to his feet. "Will he walk out alone onto the steppe?" Except for Saurons, that was suicide.

Aisha shook her head mournfully. "Not as long as there is someone he can kill." She let him pull her up to stand beside him. "I am sorry, Karl. For everything but this."

Men arrived as the Seven rested. A few scarred dusty warriors one day; a noble's following the next, with a hall of embossed leather for their liege and knock-down dome tents for themselves. A whole clan, with their women and children in yurts on wheeled carts. *Khans* sent the eager youngsters who turned a ruler's hair white with worry over feuds and *razziah* and sword-backed intrigues over successions; Tarik was not the only one to think of that trick.

Merchants of Ashkabad and Tsharburdjak sent horses, draught-muskies, bundles of arrows, sacks of dried meat, gunpowder and muskylope lard and leather and cracked grain. Their contributions to the Holy War.

Aisha preached to gatherings whose screams of exultation shook the stony face of the Cliff Lion, then wept and shivered in the privacy of her tent, in the comfort of her aunt's arms. Chaya judged and soothed, keeping peace among violent young men with old hatreds. Barak and Kemal assigned campgrounds and set the riders to exercise and competition; Karl swore and pleaded and bullied the growing horde into Bandari notions of sanitation, and almost wept with relief when half a dozen men and women with the twined-snake-and-staff emblem on the backs of their leather jackets rode in, their pack-train carrying camel-loads of medicines and tools.

Barak pressed an ear to the ground. "It's a *big* one," he said. "I don't think it's traders, either. They're moving fast, and they're moving light. They wouldn't if they had yurts." He rose. "*Ama*, it is an army they bring you. Are you ready to be a general once more?"

If he had put his hand into her chest and squeezed her heart, it could not have hurt more. "I am ready to receive them."

She pulled her clothes straight and let the younger men and women put their camp in order. Kemal brought her the bags from his horse and camels.

"Sit against these, *khatun*. To be a prince, you must also look like one."

Her back straight, her eyes dry, Chaya watched the riders approach, meet the scouts, deploy. Lightning's hearing had been right, of course. Dust billowed across the darkling hills, a mist of blood under Cat's Eye. Steel sparked within it, and the hooves were an endless thunder. Not a caravan, not even a raiding party, but a veritable army approached. Old Barak had trained her; she selected a section, counted, multiplied. And swallowed hard.

*I expected hundreds. Not this.*

"Ihsan, tell me. Who bears a tamerlane's skull as a standard?"

Kemal's blood-brother raised his eyebrows. "Does it glitter?"

Chaya nodded.

"So? The Gold Tamerlanes come from the east. They are a rich tribe, very fine fighters. The Citadel's hand lies heavy on them. Do any ride with them?"

"I see an ice-eagle, mounted on a spear as if in flight," Barak told him.

"Those are Kurds! I would not have thought they would hear this much or come this far to fight," Kemal said.

"They are mighty haters, my prince," Ihsan said. "And the tribes who dwell in the cliffs by Dyer Base have reason to hate. We can expect more of them to join us as we near Nûrnen."

"They are, I have heard, a blade that cuts both ways," Chaya said. "They have no friends but the mountains."

Aisha shook her head. "All blades do. I wonder what my brother will do with my father's sword."

With a snap of fabric as the wind caught them, the tribes' banners flared out. Tamerlanes, eagles, swords and stars danced on the wind, wreathed by lettering. *God is great. In the name of Allah the merciful, the lovingkind.* The warriors rode toward the oasis. They swept past Dagor's upright, lonely figure: he was a farmer, not worthy of notice when battle was at hand. Seeing seven people awaiting them, they screamed war cries. On either side, young men on the stocky, blood-red horses that were the steppes' pride broke from the army and rode in circles, pulling up sharply to make their horses rear in greeting.

Steam from the hot springs wreathed up before the approaching riders. They looked like a mirage now: an endless army.

*What have I wrought?* Chaya asked, and knew it for the wrong question. She had not wrought it, any more than she had wrought her brother's sword or her own. But here it was, hers to command — if she could.

Her son had turned to face the south. With the Gold Tamerlanes in sight, he dared not lose his dignity by casting himself upon the ground to listen for hoofbeats. "We will have other company soon."

Since the Cat's Eye rose, the oasis had bubbled and seethed like the fumaroles that surrounded it. From campsites ringing the central area, cookfires reeked of meat and dung. The complaints of camels and the whinnies of high-bred uncut horses, too closely picketed together because of their numbers, rose above the shouts of men escaped from the constraints of their lives into the release, as they thought, of war.

The farmers never stopped scuttling from fire to fire, backs bent, voices perpetually raised in pathetic whines. Without Dagor to lead them, they seemed no more than serfs of the tribes. Over Kemal's protests, Chaya sent him to see they were not robbed blind. An old man, his skullcap leathery with the sweat of T-years, flung himself before her. "Food they demand, great *khatun*, but they will eat us bare! And then what will they do? What shall we do when they leave?"

She flung him silver. It was not money the farmers needed, but a chance to recover from this curse in the form of too much trade. Money could not buy more than the land would yield; it would vanish like spring ice in bringing grain from elsewhere. The food that would have lasted until secondharvest and on through winter was gone already. This growing army would have to keep moving, lest, like a fire, it burn itself to the ground and scorch forever any place where it remained too long.

"Like a plague of locusts in the old stories," Sannie muttered.

"Just so, Sannie-girl," Barak said, throwing an arm about her shoulders. "But they're *our* locusts."

Chaya's back ached as if claws of fire had raked it. She had spent the day greeting *khans* and heirs and notable warriors, in getting tribes and patronymics right, in joining men's hands and forcing them to at least temporary truce.

That much was statecraft. That much she could do. The management of an army? She had plotted the downfall of Angband Base. She had ridden with one tribe, perhaps two. But men and weapons kept pouring in, more than even she had ever seen. She shut her eyes, hoping, for once, for the visions that plagued her. But they came when they would, not at her need. Perhaps, if she could rest . . .

*Aisha can lash them into frenzy. I can keep them from cutting each other's throats. The rest . . .*

The tumult around the waterholes had subsided. Truenight settled, freezing even in summer, and very dark. Nothing but starlight, one of the sister moons, and, to Sauron eyes, the diffuse heat-glow of the hot springs. Chaya sat in the opened flap of her domed tent nursing a mug of tea when Barak raised his head. "Company coming," he announced.

"At truenight?"

"They must be very good. Or crazy," he replied.

"One of us had better watch for them, or the tribes will be sure it's bandits."

"Make it two," said Barak.

Chaya rose, groaning inwardly at the effort it took to make her movements look unforced.

"Let me come," said Karl bar Edgar. He had changed into leathers bearing the twined-snakes insignia that anyone who had ever known Bandari would revere and spare. He let her set the pace.

"Stop watching me," she snapped.

Behind her, he chuckled.

Chaya and Barak saw the warmth of bodies moving against hoarfrosted steppe long before Karl's binoculars caught the glint of starlight on metal. Fine horses, sturdy muskylopes, heavy wagons —

"They're *ours!*" Karl exclaimed.

"Barak, you bastard." Chaya blinked furiously. The old *kapetein* had been so angry at his election that he had refused even to see the Seven off. And now . . .

"I don't believe it," Karl fan Haller said. "I don't believe it."

The Bandari rode into the oasis. Theirs was not a caravan or a raiding party, but a combination of both. Heavy-armed riders guarded wagons that bore the mark of the fan Reenan and fan Gimbutas clans, or the Pale's symbol from the armories.

"Some of that's from Ashkabad," Karl muttered. "Why is Yigal fan Reenan sending it to us?"

Some wagons rode especially low on their axles. Chaya would have bet they contained weapons and tools. When she saw the man who drove the lead wagon, she was certain.

"He's sent us engineers, too. That's Sapper, remember? The one who built that dam?"

"I don't like it, I don't like it at all," Karl muttered. "There's enough here for a good-sized war."

"Then it may even be enough," Chaya said. "Let's greet our friends."

"Ho, *chaverim*!" came a shout hailing them. A couple of riders trotted forward, then dismounted before any of the tribesmen watching — fully armed despite the restraining oaths that seemed now to have all the power of lullabies — could decide they were raiders.

"I don't believe it," Chaya said flatly.

"Neither do I," said the *mediko*. "My least-favorite patient. Hammer-of-God, why the hell did they let you out of your cage?"

Ignoring Karl, the newcomer came forward. Tall, with the sandy coloring and light hair of the Edenites, he wore leathers and felts like a tribesman and more weapons than any other man she had ever seen. He had a limp so slight that it could have been no more than cramps from riding all day. *Stubbornness*. She had seen that wound when he was brought in on a litter raving with fever, after the journey up the southern escarpment. Fungus-infested wound deep enough to push a fist into. *Madness*. That was still there in the pale cold eyes.

The eyes. She always remembered the eyes, as she had seen them so long ago, the night Heber died and Barak was begotten.

Still mad — though the years had tempered the madness with experience and sharpened it with caution. Still doing the Lord's work with hammer blows. It was an irony, that she had tried to follow the path of forgiveness, and the Christian soldier worshiped the God of Joshua. *Jesus forgives; Hammer doesn't*, went the joke in the *h'gana*, the army of the Pale.

He came to stand before her. No, before the Judge.

"Your Honor," he greeted her. Bandari did not go in much for what old Piet's books called "spit and polish." Just as well, or Chaya would have had to learn how to respond to it.

"Hammer-of-God, I am no longer 'Your Honor.'"

"Let anyone say that in front of me," he said. "*Kapetein* Barak doesn't think so either."

Chaya paused. "I always thought," she said frankly — it was a relief to be able to do that, as an exile — "you didn't like me."

Hammer's lined face split in a grin. "I didn't. You drove me to sinful rage many a time. But I always *respected* you, which is more important . . . Your Honor."

"What are you doing here?" Karl's demand broke the moment, much to Chaya's relief.

"*Oom* Yigal and Barak damned well drafted me!" The Edenite braced hands on hips and shook his head. "After you *medikos* took all the cash I had in payment for telling me I was old and tired, I was minding my own business and my own fields, when the old man rode out and made me an offer I couldn't refuse."

"Stubborn," she said. "How long did it take your arm to heal after fan Reenan twisted it?"

He laughed. "Where do you want us, *ama*?"

"You really want to know? I wish to hell you had never come out."

"So do I," Hammer-of-God said. "So does *Oom* Yigal. And so will those two no-goods, his son Karl and that Shulamit of his. I hope you've got them tied up good. Bring them back if you can, Yigal said. He didn't say anything about tanning their butts."

"Karl, Shulamit — here?" Chaya asked. "We haven't seen them." *Not* another *cousin!* she thought. This was turning into quite the family outing. A real *mishpocha. I'm sorry, Miriam, Dvora.*

"*Shaysse!*" Karl and Hammer-of-God swore simultaneously.

"You're telling me they ran off to join us, is that it?" she demanded.

"Them and half the young fools in the Pale."

"We don't have them. Karl and Shulamit, that is. Plenty of the young fools, and more every cycle."

She spoke to the Edenite's back, as he gestured his people in. "Sapper, you're going to take over. They say they haven't seen our two runaways. I'm going to pick out a few horses and a couple riders and go . . ." He started forward, his limp noticeably worse.

"Your leg!" Chaya exclaimed.

"Stop worrying, *ama*. I figure I have one more campaign left in me."

"You're going nowhere!" the *mediko* said. "Except, maybe the hot springs over there. Just what the doctor ordered. How's Yigal doing?"

"Best thing about being a civilian was getting away from you bloodsuckers," Hammer-of-God retorted. "He's holding up, so far. The fan Reenans don't live the longest lives on Haven, lucky bastards."

She motioned him toward their fire, letting him set the pace. "You don't have to tell them what to do or even watch them. They know how to make camp all by themselves." It got a laugh from him.

"Was getting rid of the *medikos* the best thing about civilian life?" Chaya asked.

"Second best. First best was not having to fight. Working my own land. Watching my sisters' boys grow up — not like me, thank God, Whose judgments are just and righteous altogether. Chaya, we've seen eye to eye, haven't we? On occasion?"

She looked up at the Edenite. "Flattery — Yigal didn't pay you enough, so you want to borrow money from me?"

He snorted. "I'm asking for the truth. *Kapetein's* been calling this a crusade. He was of half a mind to send out the artillery. Damned near broke Sapper's heart when he decided against it." He lowered his voice. "Ties in very well indeed with the plan for you-know-what. More than a distraction, he says. Is it?"

"That bad? It's worse. We've never lied to each other. Not in the years you were our best general when it came to the tribes, not when we disagreed, either. You know how they feel about feuds, or working out a curse. Well, we've got both."

Hammer sighed and sank down on his saddlebags, rubbing at his leg.

"Hammer-of-God." Kemal's shadow covered the newcomer. Ihsan stood nearby, his hand on his swordhilt. "Tell me, to what do we owe this pleasure — a pleasure I have long awaited?"

There were a number of ways of interpreting that; one was that this was outside the bounds of the peace treaty between Kemal's tribe and the Pale. The nomad's face was full of fierce gladness.

"The blessings of Allah upon you and your house," Hammer said courteously. "Come, sit, we will talk." He could speak half a dozen tribal dialects perfectly, and Kemal's native tongue was the first he had learned.

"Shall I sit and break bread with the slayer of my father?" Kemal said in the same level tone. His voice was calm, but a hand's-breadth of bright metal showed between his hand and the chape of his sword-scabbard.

"Shall we make war on each other, Kemal Mustafoglu?" Hammer-of-God said. "Did those valiant warriors" — he signed to where the men of Tarik's tribe were picketed — "come this far to fight mine? Or are we at war with the Saurons, each of us?"

Sweat broke out on Kemal's face. "My father's blood — "

" — will wait for vengeance. If you break your oath to the others of the Seven, will the *jihad* against the accursed of God be ready to pick up once more when we are done with each other? I see many warriors here, many banners, many tribes.

Which of them does not see the faces of the slayers of their fathers, their brothers, among the others here?"

"Oh, you are a serpent, and your tongue is sharper than your sword," Kemal whispered. Ihsan waited behind him, tensed like a cliff lion waiting for its prey.

"The *kapetein* sent me to see the Saurons suffer as much as possible. Yigal fan Reenan sent me, because his son Karl has run off to join you."

"They made a bad choice of errand boy," Kemal said, with ominous slowness. "And I think there are many *ghazis* here, many warriors of the Faith, who will agree with me."

Hammer-of-God chuckled into a silence that stretched. "You have a lot of tribes here. A lot of tribes mean a lot of feuds. There's one thing all of you agree on. You all hate Saurons. But we're a long way from any Saurons. So you need something else to agree on to hate. And here I am. So focus on that, and keep your knives off each other."

"I will kill any man who touches you," said Kemal, soft and fervent. "Oh, such a man I would slay as one who snatched my beloved bride from the bed of our wedding night."

The Edenite nodded in complete understanding. "I give you my word. I'd rather kill Saurons than any of you."

The pause lasted past the time when knives might have been drawn. Kemal laughed harshly. "Allies. Your word is good, as all men know. But when we are not, when the Saurons are cast down and my oath fulfilled . . ."

"I'll let you have a head start," said Hammer-of-God. He waited. "Well?"

Kemal snapped his fingers at Ihsan, who went to the fire and returned with bread and salt. The older man shared it out, and the nomads ate as if every bite were gall.

"In the name of Allah the merciful, the lovingkind, be welcome," Kemal muttered. Ihsan echoed him. Both men walked off.

*Please God, to explain things to the other leaders,* Chaya thought. Now that Hammer-of-God was their guest, anyone who harmed him must answer to their swords. And vice versa, of course.

Hammer-of-God nodded to the others of the Seven, politely averting his eyes from Aisha, who actually dared a smile for him. As they stood there, his own people came up. "*Sayeret*," he said: Scouts. Several quiet, weathered-looking fighters with armor the color of the steppe rose and left.

"You think you'll be all right?" Chaya asked.

Hammer-of-God shrugged, munching away on the ritual hospitality. It looked very dry. "No point wasting it."

"We can feed you better than that."

"We brought our own supplies."

"Tonight, save them. We can't manage a wedding feast, but there'll be enough."

The last whisper died from around the cookfires. The tribes, like the Bandari, were great gossips; and to the usual fare about Juchi's curse and the Seven they added scandal about the Bandari caravan, the Bandari women warriors and the unwelcome presence of the one among the Bandari whom they hated above all others, but must greet as an ally. All in all, a very pleasant night at the beginning of what looked like a very promising war.

Chaya had to restrain herself from blurting that out in front of Kemal and Ihsan. Long after the other fires had been banked, the Seven sat around theirs, talking with the newcomers until shoulders sagged and voices turned drowsy. Barak and Sannie slipped away, hand in hand. Kemal bowed formally, on his most oppressively good behavior before the general he distrusted most. Hammer-of-God waved off Karl bar Edgar's offer of help and limped toward the hot springs.

Aisha and Chaya sat gazing into the fire. "There's no sleep for me tonight, child," the older woman said. "I'm going to walk about the camp."

"Will you be safe?" Tribes-bred Aisha still found the idea of a woman unaccompanied somewhat shocking — except for herself, of course, and she had always walked with her father.

"At my age? What about you?" *Girl, I could wish you and Karl would simply sneak off like my son and Sannie. Be a little happy for as long as you can.*

Aisha laughed. "I am who I am. Who would touch me?"

"You could find a place among the other Bandari."

To Chaya's astonishment, Aisha leaned over and kissed her cheek. "Our mother would have loved you," she said. "Loved you as a daughter, if she had known."

Chaya almost jerked away. "I . . . knew Badri. From the destruction of Angband. Before she . . ." *Before she married my brother and her son.* "We were friends."

Aisha looked down humbly. "I'm sorry."

"For what? Treating me like the family we are? I knew our mother. I liked and respected her. Remember this, girl. She was the property of a Sauron, yet she destroyed him and all his kind. Think of *that* instead of . . . of the other things. And be proud of her for once."

Chaya made her voice harsh, forcing the words out past a lump in her throat. "You sure you won't bed down with the others? They'd welcome you."

Aisha sighed. Then she gathered up her packs. "If you'll be all right, I guess I will." She moved off into the darkness between fires, her steps unerring. Chaya heard her voice explaining, heard another woman's voice rise in welcome, and turned her attention back to her own thoughts.

Needing silence, she wandered away from the camps, away from the fields (soon to be stripped bare) and the huts where the farmers no doubt cowered. A map pyrographed on leather — Dagor's work, perhaps — nailed up at the beginning of the trail warned her which springs and pools to avoid. A glance locked it in her memory. Then she entered a place so blasted it made the rest of Haven seem like a garden.

The Cat's Eye shone on a landscape straight out of some nightmare of Gehenna. On one side of her, bubbles plopped and broke stinking in mud pools. Beyond them, the land was sere. Stubs of trees thrust upward, coated by minerals from centuries upon centuries of geysers. Their cones jutted upward; one spouted a thin plume of steam and white water.

Sprays burst from a grotto of squat, rounded rocks. Chaya's skin tightened, sensing the violent heat of that water and the power locked far underfoot. Would it explode one day, peeling this entire place off the face of Haven? Would peace come only with death?

She shuddered. The water falling back into the pools sounded like bells. The sulfur smell grew strong.

Some of the pools came in tiers, a pleasant place to relax at the end of the day or to soak out aches. She was sure her son and Sannie had found one such place. Perhaps Hammer-of-God, looking for a pool to soak his leg, had quite literally stumbled in on them. She grinned. Well, if she hadn't heard any shouting . . . She went on, past a pool in which luminous blue and red bubbles flickered, as if fire had been contained in glass and sunk beneath the water.

How quiet it was here, except for the steam and the water. The ground was warm, even through her boots. When she rested a hand on a rock, it was warm and slick with salty water. This pool before her looked inviting. Her thoughts flashed back to the leather map.

Warm water. Safe water. Heavy with salts, it would buoy her. Soon, she promised herself. First, she needed to think. Sighing, she sank down. What was the line? *By the waters of Babylon we sat, and wept as we remembered Zion* . . . Time was when she remembered all of the psalms. Time was . . . time was . . .

She let her head sag back against the rock. *Go to the rock for comfort?* No, that came from somewhere else. That was right. *How shall we sing the Lord's song in a strange land?*

Her mind raced backward in time, counting over her mother and her mother's mother to Ruth, the first Judge on Haven, to all the other Judges there were. Only that dawn, she had spoken of Judge Golda who had cooked for her warriors, then sent them off. Judge Golda, it was, who had faced a need to bring the Wasting down upon her enemies, who longed to kill herself to avoid it — and then found another way.

*Ama, sister, help me!* she pleaded.

There was no help for the likes of her. It was in her blood, in her blood, in her blood. Overhead the Cat's Eye glared redly on the pool. A moment ago, it had looked so tempting. Now, if she entered the water, she would be bathing in blood.

The ground and the rock supporting her back and head

trembled. Somewhere, a geyser erupted. Her nose protested the stink of minerals. Her head whirled and her ears rang. Warm fluid bathed her face. She clawed at it, and shut her eyes lest she see her fingers come away red. The reek made her gag.

She remembered the psalm again, the terrible lines: *Happy are they who dash the heads of their enemies' children against the stones*.

She remembered too well. Shocked, she heard herself whimper. Then her mind was seized, thrust to look upon a vision of a child, casually thrown from a wall, falling, falling, falling. Children crying, children bleeding, children falling and dying — and all of them somehow her own, as banners thrust like lances about her and the flash of blades blinded her. Riders charged behind her, their teeth and the teeth of their horses grinning like the jaws of skulls, forcing her forward.

A huge roaring came — the guns that could hurl death over Sauron walls — but they were aimed at her.

She screamed hoarsely and fell, spasming, then going rigid. Smoke engulfed her, and the clamor of the bells and the child's scream thrust her down.

For a long moment, Chaya stared into the Cat's Eye, and it stared back. So had it been her whole life. She watched the Cat's Eye, and the Cat's Eye watched her. She yawned, like a great cat herself. It would be good to rest here, where the mists of hot water rose up to comfort her. So good.

She drowsed. But the Cat's Eye stared at her as a hungry animal stares at its mistress. Shaking her head a little, she tried to rise. It was hard work. She gave it up.

No one was around whom she could ask, "What happened?" Just as well. She could draw her own conclusions. At least, she had no need to ask, "Where am I?" She knew that perfectly. She was in Cliff Lion Springs, by a hot pool; and she had clearly suffered a seizure. She remembered smoke and crying out and falling, but nothing more. She remembered hearing that sometimes, after a fit, you lost memory.

She had lost more. Not just a belief so deeply buried that she had only now begun to realize how strong it was: that, with her Sauron blood, she was invulnerable to anything but violence. She was vulnerable now to the worst of the Sauron bloodlines: recessives coming out to betray her, body and soul. Would she collapse first, or would she plummet into the chasm between madness and true vision?

She moaned and spat out the wadded cloth she found, in surprise and a stab of shame, between her jaws. She lay straightened out on her side, as if someone had come along while she was unconscious, kept her from rolling into the pool or crashing into the rocks as she convulsed, then laid her out in the most comfort that could be afforded.

"Laid her out." *Not yet, Chaya*, she told herself. *Not yet*.

She smelled, not smoke, but the acrid reek of her own urine. The humiliation brought her back to full awareness. Now she found herself able to move. She must cleanse herself, soak away the sickness and the fear. She stripped off the fouled clothes and lowered herself into the pool. The water, heavy with minerals, was soft to her skin. She floated easily. She could have lain like that forever, but when her head began to loll to one side, she knew she must sleep.

Reluctantly she climbed from the pool. Even more reluctantly, she picked up the clothes her body's weakness had soiled. She hated the idea of seeing them, let alone touching or wearing them. Fabrics caught her eye, neatly draped over a nearby rock. She snatched them up; the suppleness of clean leather, wool and linen caught on her roughened hands. She found herself shivering, and dressed fast. Even for one of tainted Sauron blood, the night was cold.

She wadded up her other clothes, buried them under a flat rock, and headed back to the camp of the Seven. She wanted to sleep, but she did not want to be alone. Perhaps someone was there, someone who could tell her who had nursed her through her fit, then vanished so she would not have to feel shame when she awoke.

Someone knew she had betrayed herself. She hoped that knowledge would not cost her more than she could pay.

# ● CHAPTER SEVENTEEN

Almost home. Sharku was not a man given to flights of poetic fancy, but he thought that one of the loveliest phrases he'd ever heard. When he got back to the Citadel, he'd stand on tiptoe so he could kiss the shower head in his apartment's refresher cubicle. Only those who spent a lot of their time away from plumbing could fully appreciate it when they had it.

He'd kiss Chichek, too, most thoroughly. Toragina had entertained him well enough on the journey back from the yurts of the Ak-Koyunlu. He doubted she would end up unassigned, to do menial labor and bear children to whatever Soldiers the Breedmaster decided. She would make some Soldier a companion better than the usual run of tribute maiden. But Chichek was something special.

An uxorious Soldier! How the nomads would have laughed, had they known.

He wondered what Gimilzor had learned while he was gone. Children changed so fast. Wasn't it yesterday — day before at the earliest — when the boy had been only a wailing lump swaddled in a blanket of soft muskylope wool? Now he was reading, field-stripping a toy assault rifle, learning the tricks of unarmed combat and of controlling his own enhanced body. Whereas Sharku just went on, cycle by cycle. So far as he could tell, *he* hadn't changed since Gimilzor was born. But his son's growth made a lie of that.

Ahead in the distance reared the glittering peaks of the Atlas Mountains, the northern rampart of the Shangri-La Valley. The snow that topped those mountains never melted; some of it was $CO_2$. The peaks reminded Sharku of the spine that might top a dragon's back; like a dragon's armor, they shielded the softer valley from danger all around. Already the land was falling toward the pass; invisible to the eye, but the air was a trifle thicker, the grass taller and more lush than on the high northern steppe.

His party had taken a wide detour around the northern foothills of the Atlas range to approach the Citadel. Here near the great fortress of the Soldiers, traffic on the steppe was heavy: merchants coming to trade with and cater to the richest folk on Haven, a couple of tribute parties like his own, nomads bringing their animals or their wives to give birth in the thick lowland air of the Shangri-La Valley. Soon they would meet the customs stations and the paved road.

He twisted to look behind him. Scattered here and there out on the steppe, he saw examples of all the groups that had crossed his mind. And there, less than a klick away and closing fast, he also saw a lone runner eating up the ground with the unmistakable untiring lope of a Soldier.

His vision leaped the distance to give him a better look: a young fellow, beard still patchy, dressed in the furs and leathers of the plains. Not a man he knew by sight, which puzzled him a little; he thought he at least recognized most of the Soldiers of the Citadel likely to pull steppe duty. Turning to his companions, he pointed out the approaching runner. "Any of you seen him before?"

Mumak, Ufthak and Snaga all looked back at the fellow. "No," they said in the same breath. Mumak added: "He's one of ours, though. Couldn't be anything else, not moving like that."

"Raggedy-ass excuse for a Soldier," Snaga said. "If he's what our distant Bases turn out these days, no wonder the cattle overran Angband."

Sometimes Sharku wondered if Snaga had any brains at all. As patiently as he could, he said, "It wasn't just cattle, if you'll remember. One of ours run wild led them. It's Juchi's fault. Curse him, he's got the whole steppe boiling against us even after he's dead."

"Raggedy-ass," Snaga repeated. Not for the first time, Sharku decided some selection board had been asleep at the switch when it made him an officer.

Ufthak said, "Maybe he's been doing intelligence work among the cattle. That would account for the way he looks. You travel among the barbarians on that kind of mission, you don't want to be conspicuous." Ufthak, now, knew how to use his wits, Sharku thought. He wasn't just a fighter, he was a Soldier.

Maybe the fellow trotting along through the calf-high grass heard the men of the tribute party speaking Americ. Maybe he recognized the field-gray they wore. Whatever the reason, he swerved toward them. His clothes looked ragged, but his boots were new — from the gaunt look of his face, he'd run far and fast and without time or opportunity to eat enough, wearing out footwear as he came. When he spoke, he blew all of Ufthak's fine theorizing into a cloud of muskylope flatulence. Not only did he use the Turkic dialect of the plains, he addressed the men of the Citadel as if they were others, not comrades: "You fellows, you're — Saurons?"

"We're Soldiers," Sharku answered stonily; Sauron was an other-people label for the descendants of those who had reached Haven in the *Dol Guldur*. The Chief Assault Leader studied the newcomer, who effortlessly kept pace with the tribute party's horses. "So are you, by your genes. Who are you, anyhow?" *What are you?* was the unspoken echo to the question.

The stranger's mouth twisted. Sharku noted that for a couple of reasons: first, the stranger didn't like the question, the answer to it, or both, and second, he'd never had proper Soldier schooling in controlling his musculature. Maybe Snaga had a point after all, Sharku thought reluctantly.

The stranger's breath hissed out in a sigh — not weariness, not with the way he moved, but resignation. He dipped his head in what might have been either salute or challenge. "Saurons — Soldiers, if you'd rather — know I am Dagor son of Juchi. Having heard that, do with me as you will." His head came up again. His eyes locked with Sharku's. It was challenge, then; whatever else was in this young man, he held no resignation.

Sharku needed all his discipline to keep from staring. In Turkic, so Dagor could hear and fear, Snaga said, "Kill him. If he lies, he deserves death for his presumption. And if he's telling the truth, he deserves death for who he is."

Much as Sharku disliked agreeing with Snaga about anything, he thought the other Soldier was right this once; at least, he found nothing missing from Snaga's analysis. Then Dagor threw back his head and roared laughter. Yes, he had spirit, whoever he was. Sharku said, "Have a care with your mirth, stranger. Your life is in peril."

"By Allah and the spirits, why should I not laugh?" Dagor retorted. "I went to the oasis where the Seven gather their hosts against the Citadel, seeking to set my sword among theirs, and they cast me out, may they roast in Hell forever. So I decided I would have my revenge upon them — after all, Saurons, I share your blood as well as theirs. And now you'd sooner kill me than hear me out! The bards on the steppe would set song round the several sides of such stupidity."

"Hold, there," Sharku said. "You know of the Seven?"

"Know *of* them?" Dagor said. "Do you just hear with those augmented ears of yours, or do you listen? I know them well. With two, indeed, I could scarcely be more closely connected. Aisha, whose name even you will know, is my full sister, and Chaya, till lately Judge of the Bandari, is my father's sister — and my three-quarter sister as well."

He fairly spat out the last of that; Sharku guessed he'd had it spat in his face scores of times. The Chief Assault Leader kept his mouth shut tight. Incest was only a word, not a curse, in the Citadel, where bloodlines counted so much. And even if that hadn't been true, Sharku wasn't about to offend the most precious intelligence source he'd ever set eyes on.

Maybe he heard something behind him, maybe he just sensed it. Without turning, he snapped, "Hold, Snaga. We'll bring him with us."

"Waste of —" Snaga began.

"Waste of what?" Sharku interrupted. "Waste of a mount? He's come this far afoot. He can go on to the

Citadel that way at need. Waste of food? The same applies. Waste of time? I don't think so — and in such matters my will is the controlling one."

Dagor's eyes had flicked from one of them to the other. He might not have been able to follow the Americ — that was Sharku's guess, though he wasn't sure of it — but he could read tones and maybe expressions; even Soldiers got careless sometimes. Now he said to Sharku, "If that other Sauron doesn't care for me, tell him I'll fight him. We'll see how he likes me afterwards."

When Snaga heard that, he laughed loud and long. He was not a man who often laughed; the noise burst from his throat like water forcing its way out through a clogged pipe. He actually beamed at Dagor. Speaking Turkic himself, he said, "Of course I'll fight you. Few offer me their lives as gifts, but I make a habit of taking them when offered."

"Have a care, Snaga," Mumak said. Snaga glowered, but his comrade went on, "Remember that, between them, his father and sister put paid to a Cyborg Battlemaster. He's no bad-genes cattle lad with more testosterone than he knows what to do with, for you to play with like a cliff lion and a calf."

The reminder sobered Snaga, but having gone so far he could not back down if he intended to show his face in the Citadel again. He started to dismount. "Hold!" Sharku commanded. He shifted to Turkic. "No fighting now. If Dagor wins, the Citadel will have lost a Soldier. If Snaga wins, we'll have lost an intelligence resource we can in no way make up. Let there be truce." He was confident Snaga would obey; of wild Dagor he was less certain. Now he locked eyes with the young stranger. "Or do you think you can take the four of us at once?"

By the way he shifted his weight, Dagor was ready to try: a case of testosterone poisoning after all, Sharku thought. But he mastered himself. He might be wild, but he was no fool. "Let there be truce . . . Soldier. As you say, I am coming to join you and yours. Let there be no more blood between us than that which was borne in the past."

"Aye, that is a sufficiency," Sharku said, in one of the choicer understatements of his career.

The tribute maidens chattered among themselves as the journey south resumed. Enough of the talk had been in Turkic for them to have figured out what was going on. Juchi, curse him, was a legend on the steppes, and to have his son appear out of nowhere was a marvel greater than any they'd encountered among the yurts of their clan. They'd have plenty of juicy gossip for the women in the Citadel, too.

Snaga rode close to Sharku. "Permission to speak to the Chief Assault Leader," he said in the most robotically formal voice he owned.

"Go ahead." Sharku had a pretty good idea of what was coming.

It came: "I must protest the Chief Assault Leader's equalizing the probabilities of victory for myself and that — that savage. I resent the imputation of weakness with which you have burdened me."

"Go ahead," Sharku said in a different tone. "If you really don't like it, Snaga, wait till we're back home and then try and kick *my* ass."

"Let it be as the Chief Assault Leader wishes," Snaga said, by which he meant he knew too bloody well he had no hope of kicking Sharku's ass.

Had Sharku not been trained from infancy to control his reactions, his grin would have been as wide and toothy as a land gator's. But he decided to let Snaga down easy, lest he find himself sipping distillate of oxbane in his tea one fine morning: little men avenged themselves over little things. "Think, Snaga," he urged. "After we bring the wild one here into the Citadel, where is he likely to go for questioning?"

Snaga thought. Like Sharku, he'd learned to mask what went on behind his eyes. Even so, his voice had lost that robotic quality as he answered, "The Red Room."

"Exactly," Sharku said. Neither of them had named or looked at Dagor. If he truly didn't understand Americ, he'd have no idea that they were talking about him. *Well, that's his hard luck,* Sharku thought. *Nobody asked him to cast his lot with us in the first place.*

# ● CHAPTER EIGHTEEN

The *mediko* in Karl bar Edgar was horrified, over-worked, desperately worried. Cliff Lion Oasis was past the saturation point. No matter how fast they dug, the latrine trenches kept filling. Dry and hot — for the steppes — weather meant windborne disease in the dust. Typhus, for starters, lice which could spread further. Of lice they had enough to conquer Old Sauron, if only they could train them up to war. Cholera morbus. Dysentery, which had killed more armies over the centuries than any weapon.

The man in him (*no, the boy*, he admitted) was happy as he had rarely been. With his wife Miriam there had been a steady warm glow; companionship, pleasure, children, shared work. With Aisha, there was the sort of giddy intoxication adolescents were supposed to experience, and that he never had. He distrusted happiness so extreme. It was too fragile.

"Dammit, we've got to get *moving*," he burst out, as Hammer-of-God joined him on a low rise of tumbled boulders. Absently, he noted that exercise and a course of hot baths were helping the warrior's injured leg muscles.

"Of course we will," Hammer-of-God said. His complacency irritated Karl beyond bearing.

"You're loving this, aren't you?" he said.

A shrill cry went up. *"Prayer is better than sleep —"* it began. Instantly, rugs were unrolled, men washed, then bent in prayer — in the direction of the star around which Earth circled, hence of Mecca. Mecca, like most of Earth, was tumbled ruin with nothing human left but the bones.

"Of course I am," Hammer-of-God said. "God made me for a purpose. Happiness is the service of God; and this is the purpose for which He made me."

"You're very certain of that."

"Of course. I asked, and He told me."

Karl shivered slightly. The other man's voice held utter sincerity. Hammer-of-God Jackson talked with God, a deity Who, in those conversations, tended to resemble nothing so much as an omnipotent Hammer-of-God Jackson. Now *there* was a thought to make a man shudder. So was the force of raw belief unrolled before the Hammer and him.

"They're not really that pious, most of them," Hammer-of-God said, as if reading his mind. That was disconcerting as well, the alternation of exaltation and detached analysis. *Is he sane?* Karl thought. Then: *is any of us?*

"They just don't want to be outdone; the steppe mullahs won't be shown up before the Tadjiks, and the Kherkessians" — he nodded to a group of men with Astrakan wool hats and silver-sheathed daggers worn in echelon on chest-straps; wild-looking men, handsome as hawks, their black hair long and carefully tended — "are self-conscious away from their *aouls*." The very word had a predatory sound, for all that it meant simply *fortified village*.

The prayer ended and the camp dissolved back into its usual milling chaos. Sapper was crouched before a smoking field of fumaroles, with a clipboard in one hand and a clock the size and shape of a turnip in the other. A crowd of women, children and carefully nonchalant warriors watched him. He stood, nodded — and the geyser thundered free, breaking high into a wash of bitter mineral-tasting droplets.

"Djinni," the crowd moaned, surging backward.

"Poor superstitious fools who know not Christ," Hammer-of-God said.

Karl snorted; he was a believing man in his way, but no fanatic. "Something I've always wanted to ask you," he said. *But never dared before*. "How is it that you get along so well with the Bandari clansfolk, since they're not of your faith?"

Hammer-of-God looked at him. "Some of you are Christian," he said. "Possibly heretics, but I'm called to be a soldier of Christ, not a theologian. Those who sacrifice to the Founders? Piet was a saint; there's no error in praying for the intervention of saints — just going through the chain of command, as I see it. I'm privileged to talk to the Commander-in-Chief, but I'm special-forces."

"And the *Ivrit*?"

"Oh," the other man said, waving a negligent hand skyward, "you have to make allowances for the Boss' relatives."

Karl gaped — humor was not something he had ever associated with Hammer-of-God, and the man's long bony face was perfectly serious. Then Hammer's eyes changed, looking out over the *mediko*'s shoulder to the plains.

"Let me have your spyglasses," he snapped.

Mystified, Karl obeyed. He shaded his eyes with his hand and squinted; it was early trueday, Byers' Sun and Cat's Eye both behind him. There was traffic all over the steppe to the west, groups coming and going; the pickets checked them over lightly and sent them through. Eventually, he saw the group Hammer-of-God sought. Three mounted figures, about a dozen horses, some pack-muskies.

"Ah! Stay where you are, you little *mamzrim*, bastards . . . you spoiled-bastard runaways . . ."

Hammer-of-God plunged into the crowd with a certainty of purpose that sent tribesfolk scattering out of his way even before they recognized his face or distinctive gait. Now Karl too could see his target: a knot of three people. The tallest was half hidden by some horses and two dogs. Karl caught a glimpse of a pale face before the — what? trader? horsebreaker? — turned away. The other two . . .

"Front and center, *boy*," Hammer-of-God growled. "Don't even *think* about getting away. So help me, if I'd had the training of you . . ."

The stocky figure turned; he was dressed in a long sheepskin jacket with the fleece turned in, winter wear in high summer. Blood darkened a face that had been tanned in the womb against the sun of Frystaat it would never see, and green eyes flashed with anger and apprehension. His namesake, then. Young Karl bar Yigal fan Reenan, now standing in an awkward brace.

" . . .training of *both* of you," the Edenite continued, his glance taking in the blue-eyed girl who tossed a shock of dark hair, but held her ground. "You wouldn't have sneaked away from your duties to follow the war."

"Uh . . . sir," Karl's namesake began with what was really admirable pluck, not backing down, and actually getting a word in edgewise.

Hammer-of-God would have none of it.

"My *men* call me 'sir'! You may when you've earned the right; and right now, what I see is a badly trained, badly disciplined *boy*." Surrounded as they were by tribesmen, the older man kept his voice down, but the words stung all the worse for that.

Young fan Reenan stiffened further, Shulamit poised to spring beside him.

"You think you can? Go ahead. I'll paddle your spoiled butts," Hammer-of-God said. "Your father, young fan Reenan, rode up to my farm to chase me out of retirement. He's not in shape for a ride like that any more, and you know it. You really think you're worth that kind of pain?"

"Just because I'm his heir . . ."

"Dammit, he'd do the same for a dog he loved!" That came out as a growl.

The stranger's dog responded with one of his own. Hammer-of-God snapped his fingers, and the dog, if not the youth, subsided. Young Karl's Frystaat blood might make him more than a match for the older man in brute strength, but never in craft. He glared green rage, but knew better than to challenge.

"If I wanted to lie, I'd say he sent us after you to make sure you didn't get your stupid asses captured by Turks. Or Saurons. That would be a fine thing, wouldn't it? The first Bandari on Haven captured by Saurons — a fan Reenan. *Oom* Piet wouldn't just turn over in his grave; he'd circumnavigate this God-rotted planet. We'd have to abandon you, you know that?"

"My father has other sons."

Hammer-of-God shrugged, a Bandari gesture he'd made his own over the years. "*Any* man's child is precious

to him." Pain ached in his voice. "And Yigal's not the only
man you're a son to, lad," he said. "You're all the son Tom
Jerrison's got. He's put his whole life into you. You going to
let some Sauron steal his harvest?"

Young Karl flinched. He looked down, a boy now, not a
soldier subjected to a dressing-down, deserved or not.

The harsh voice turned gentler. "You going to behave
now? Do I have to put guards on you and send you back to
the Pale?"

"No, sir."

"Now I'll take that word from you. If you could get this
far, I guess my *Sayerets* can use you." Hammer-of-God held
up a hand. "You're under their orders, mind. Disobey
them even once and back home you go, like a spoiled brat
with a sore tail."

Young Karl's head was up, his eyes fairly blazing with
pride. "I won't fail you, sir."

"No? I guess you won't. First, I need your report on what
you've seen. I think the Judge will want to hear it too. She'll
be glad — relieved!" — he shot over his shoulder as he
turned toward the center of the camp, confident that
people would get out of his way — "you've been found."

"What about *me*?" Shulamit bat Miriam burst out.

"Shulamit, shut up!" Karl hissed at her.

"Don't you think a girl can ride and fight just as well as
he, is that it? We fought *hotnots* on the way up. And I
killed . . ."

"Bragging about it, young *meid*? I wouldn't. Not here.
Not anywhere. I'll take young Karl in charge because what
he needs to learn, I can teach him. But now, let's consider
you, Shulamit bat Miriam fan Gimbutas. You already know
how to fight. You're damned good, in fact. Had better
training than I got at your age. But I can't teach you a Bandari woman's responsibilities so you grow up like Judge
Ruth or Ilona. That's for Judge Chaya, or maybe Aisha,
who knows enough now to be thankful. And to *listen*."

Hammer-of-God set a long, limping stride toward the
camp's center, and thrust one arm out, as if expecting to
knock the third, half-hidden newcomer off-balance. They

both swerved, both of a height. For a moment, the newcomer glared at him, in arrogance and some mild surprise.

Bringing up the rear, Karl bar Edgar snatched a look at the stranger. Tall. Very pale. Lean in a way that would have been lanky if it weren't controlled. Probably very strong. Altogether unusual on the steppes. A wild surmise seized him. The stranger melted into the crowd with incredible ease, but not before Karl the *mediko* saw two more things: what looked like a cliff lion's skin draped about the stranger's shoulders, and below it the subtle rise of small breasts.

*Ah*, he thought, with a mental sigh of relief. For a moment, he'd been afraid the stranger was a Sauron. But it was a woman instead.

About the time Aisha was deemed old enough to cover her hair like a grown woman, Badri had taken her to watch her father at his judgments. Women did not sit in the *majlis*, though it was whispered that Bandari women not only attended, but spoke up. Juchi might well have allowed Badri to do so, Aisha-the-girl thought with pride. After all, as much as anything else, it had been by her courage and her wits that Angband fell.

But Badri, subtle in the assurance of her power, preferred to listen from outside, to counsel Juchi later, when no voice would be raised in dissent and when her man was most likely to listen and be swayed. This was wisdom, she taught her daughter. A woman destined to rule a *khan*'s tent watched and listened and learned the law in case she might need to advise her husband or counsel a son, Allah forbid, come too early to rule.

There sat her father, and there, dressed like a prince, deferred to and indulged by all the men present, her brother Dagor, commendably trying not to yawn and to listen in case, Allah forbid that too, his father asked him to speak.

It had been longer than she cared to remember, and a flash of a mirror. Everything was the same, and everything was different — reversed, as in the strange book Judge

Ruth had treasured, *Through the Looking Glass*. (Karl fan Haller had told her stories from that — had given her a mirror of her own.) Carpets and cushions stitched from *kilims* too battered to use, but still bright-hued; the gleams of embroidery and jewelry, harness and arms amid clothes mostly brown or gray; riding boots tracking dust and dung into the tent; smells that assaulted the nose as the voices assaulted the ears.

But it was a mirror image of the *majlis* Aisha remembered. Here, women ruled with the men — except for the few women from each tribe who passed through the crowd, some veiled, all holding trays full of food.

Aisha took a skewer of lamb, contemplated a second, then waved the woman on. She had begun, however much it shocked her, to become used to food that was abundant, adequate even for her. (Karl had told her she didn't eat enough for her supercharged body.) The tribeswoman went on, though not without a glare of *Who do* you *think you are? You should be here helping me*.

Here Aisha sat, dressed as a prince, with a saber in her lap and watching her kinswoman render judgment. The Judge had even sent her own son out of the tent, so it was Aisha who sat listening as her brother had listened. She hoped she would not be asked to say anything. Speaking was still hard, let alone giving orders to so many men, even if they called her *khatun* and *ghazi* rather than other words they knew. When she preached to the crowds, she did not have to watch the faces of individuals or listen to them answer.

Now, two *medikos* stood before the Judge, shaking their heads. A Bandari Scout ran in to report that still more tribes had been spotted, heading for the hot springs — and one of the farmers, deprived of her brother's voice on their behalf, let out what Aisha could only describe as a howl. There was little food as it was and less of it *hallal*, ritually pure; soon there would be none.

Chaya spoke to comfort him. "Soon, we shall be leaving and you can purify your land."

"If you depart, who will protect us from the Saurons?"

Most of the tribes who owned this oasis were nominally subject to Quilland Base. The nomads left behind by the horde could scatter and flee, but farmers could not.

Aisha winced at the peasant's whine. She had heard it near the Citadel. All that was missing was the crisscross, the farmers here being Muslims of a sort. That struck her as odd; Islam was a faith for the wandering tribes, for herdsmen and merchants and warriors. The crisscross Bog was a good god for peasants like luckless Yegor. He was dead, too. Like her father.

"Trust in Allah," Aisha heard from one of the Gimbutas clan, and forbore to search further.

"Your mangy sheep are eating my sheep's grass, and your men do not respect my wells!" a *khan* from nearby shouted at a newcomer.

"Shall my sheep starve while yours get fat? Is that the charity Muslim owes to Muslim on *jihad*?"

Not that it mattered: the sere grass was clipped so close to the ground by grazing beasts that it was a wonder they had not already begun to starve.

"We will be moving soon," Chaya repeated. She waved her hand as if to brush smoke away from her face. "Then it will not matter which fields you use. Honor? Your honor is your honor — and it lies in your courage for marching against the cursed Citadel."

The tall woman, part Bandari and part Sauron, raised her head. Her eyes looked strange, as they had for many days now. "I tell you, *khans*, the day will come that this campaign will be sung of and praised as if it were a *hajj*, with blood shed as freely as you offer prayers during Ramadan."

Aisha suppressed a shiver. What in her childhood she would have called power quivered in the thick air. In the past days, she had seen Chaya become more and more the prophet, less and less the friend and kinswoman she loved. It was another thing they shared, and she was still not easy with it.

Another mutter, this time from a warrior who rode with Gasim, one of the most powerful of the *khans*. Barely moving her head, Aisha listened as Chaya had taught her, using her augmented hearing to spy on what might be danger.

"Talk of honor is fine," the man Kumar said. "But from those with Sauron blood? Juchi's seed is doubly accursed. And it is said that his own son . . ."

"You think . . ."

"Had I been the *khan* who ruled after Juchi, I should not have allowed the young serpent to grow."

*Flick*. Aisha's mind registered faces and voices. She shot a brief warning glance in their direction. *Flick*. She would know these men if they spoke again. She would be watching. And Chaya would know.

Where *did* her brother wander? She would have given him her life's blood, accursed gift that it was, had he only accepted what was offered him.

"And who would have killed a man of that line and lived? Even the women are warriors," Gasim muttered, gesturing with his chin at Chaya and Aisha herself.

The Judge was speaking earnestly about boundaries. A foolishness between clans that rode as they would, as Chaya, who had ridden with them, should know. Well and oasis rights, now, that was a different story.

"Dagor should have been killed at once!" the tribesman went on, *sotto voce*.

"There is only shame in killing a boy who is kin to you," Gasim muttered. "Even if that kinman's very life sticks in your throat. No more of this, if you wish to live. You know who would avenge him. And she is watching you."

Kumar spat on the precious rugs of the Judge's tent. "I should fear a woman?"

"Not just a woman. A *ghazi*. And a Sauron of the Accursed One's line. She killed the Battlemaster of the Citadel, wine-bibbing fool; will she hesitate with *you*? This is no ordinary woman; this is She Who Must Be Obeyed!"

At least the blood that made her outcast made her feared. And there were even others who did not fear her. At his *khan*'s word, Kumar's bluster subsided. Aisha caught a mutter about whores before he was sent outside. A moment later, the tent erupted into shouts of outrage as a

Kurd claimed that one of the *mujahidin* had hamstrung his horse in a practice round of *buzkashi*. Aisha saw how Chaya shook her head imperceptibly. The close air in the tent and the shouting must be affecting her. She was old — she was Juchi's age, but a life within the Pale had kept her younger. Aisha rose to open a tent flap. The air would be chilly, but it would be fresh and clean.

A rush of cold air and the people it heralded made her stop where she stood. Pushing forward into the tent came the big Edenite, Hammer-of-God. The warriors glared at him, but he had always treated Aisha with respect. The enemy of all tribes — but who except an enemy knew them as well as kin? After him walked a youth with the dark and blond coloring that made him stand out and brought him the respect of much older Bandari. Shulamit was beside him, the runaways, cousins to her and Chaya. It would have meant a whipping in the yurts, perhaps. For the sake of that clever girlchild who had offered Aisha an amulet, Aisha hoped not.

And following them came Karl the *mediko*. Aisha felt the blood rush to her face, warming her all over. His blue eyes sought her dark ones, and he smiled. He had dragged her back to life when she was dying on the steppe, had cursed her when she sought release, had followed her into this *jihad* which was likely to be the death of all of them.

He had brought her back to life in another way. Had held her hand as she wept. Had laid her arm over her shoulders in front of all the assembled Bandari. "An acceptable future," Chaya had called him, healed now of his wife's death, back in the Pale. Even Dagor, before he vanished, had respected him, or why would he have said he would give her to an outlander? *The Bandari are my people now*, Aisha told herself.

At the great oath-taking, she would be wed to Karl bar Edgar. It seemed like joy beyond all hope; she hated to admit that the planned ceremonies terrified her worse than fighting a Cyborg Battlemaster. That was ingratitude.

Seeing Karl bar Edgar's lined, clever face, she wanted to fling her arms about him the way she had seen Bandari women do. Meeting his eyes with a tent full of people watching her was hard enough.

*Courage*, she told herself and held out a hand. He was at her side, holding it, bending over her in a way that made her feel protected and delicate, though she knew that when they stood, they were of a height.

"You found them," she said. It was not what she wanted to say. Her fingers tightened on Karl's. "It is good to see you, *khan*."

"Karl," he corrected her. She lowered her eyes, flushed again, then tossed her head, angry at her own shyness.

"That's better." With his free hand, he tilted up her chin. She had seen Bandari, and seen that wild Shulamit, now enduring a scolding from the Judge, kiss their men. Karl had rarely kissed her. Would he claim her like this, before her other kin? Her lips trembled.

"I'd like to get you by yourself," he muttered. "Our wedding can't come too soon to suit me."

Behind her, she could hear Chaya's voice, reprimanding the two scapegraces, then trailing off.

"Are you well, *ama*?" the Edenite asked her.

"Just these damned background noises," said Chaya. "As soon as I filter out all the harness bells . . ."

"Shulamit," Hammer-of-God said sternly, "I hope you see the Judge needs help."

"I didn't think you were just turning me over to the women and kiddies," the girl retorted. "Waste of a good fighter."

"I'd look after her," the younger Karl offered. "Let her come scout with me."

"She can be attached to the headquarters unit. Tameetha bat Irene commands it."

"The old battle-axe . . . oops," Shulamit said.

Hammer nodded, grinning. "*Not* the way to talk about your *aluf*, unless you want to be sorry and sore," he observed.

"Why can't I serve with Karl?"

"Because I want the two of you separated," Hammer-of-God said. "At least in waking cycles. What one of you doesn't think of, the other will."

Shulamit's eyes flashed to her friend and went smoky in a way that Aisha finally understood.

She waved over one of the serving women. She had a responsibility to see that her promised husband was fed, even if she could not be a proper wife in other ways.

Karl bar Edgar waited for her to choose first, which startled her *and* the woman holding the battered tray. "You don't eat enough," he said, and held out a skewer. This one held meat patties, ground fine and heavily spiced.

Judge Chaya turned. Seeing Aisha with Karl, she rummaged through a stack of what looked like maps and beckoned. Still clasping Karl bar Edgar's hand, Aisha rose.

"Better watch that hand, Karl old man," one of the Edenites muttered. "You may never get it back in the same shape."

He stood among several big-shouldered men who'd ridden out with the guards to look for Karl and Shulamit. She put name to him: Be-courteous Jackson. Some sort of kin to Hammer-of-God and vilely misnamed. Well, there were bad ones in every bloodline.

"What if he sticks something else out? 'You will be gentle, won't you?'" His voice went up in an offensive falsetto. "Question is, which one of them is going to say it first?"

Chaya's head went up and her eyes glittered. Hammer-of-God started toward his kinsman as if he had Sauron hearing.

"Let me," Karl said courteously. With astonishing speed, he cut the man out of his knot of friends, twisted one arm up behind his back, and marched him to the back of the tent.

"Out!" he said shortly and shoved him, emphasizing the order with a kick to the man's buttocks.

"Nice job," Hammer-of-God approved. "Want me to help throw him in the midden? He ought to be right at home in the manure, cousin or no cousin. God, families."

"Any throwing gets done, I do it," Karl said. "Aisha's going to be my wife."

He yanked the tent flaps shut and tied them.

"Don't let him in till you're told otherwise," he shouted at the Bandari standing guard.

Then he came back to Aisha and put his arm around her as if she were much younger and smaller and weaker than she was. "I don't want you to be upset," he said. "I know you could tie him in knots. But I'm glad you let me do it. If he does get back in, I'll do it again."

That would be all they'd need. Edenites raising Cain until some tribesman seized upon the insult to Aisha — as if she could be insulted like a veiled maiden — followed by drawn steel and brother-killing all around. One death would involve every tribe — and the Pale — in a blood feud that would distract them from their hatred of Saurons.

If *she* were Sauron, she would try to start one. The thought struck her as something Chaya should hear, and she made a mental note. It was hard, this thinking like a Judge. Chaya had enough to worry about without Aisha running to her like a maiden afraid of her wedding night.

Sapper appeared by Chaya's side, holding out a sheaf of papers. He pointed at them and smiled in answer to the Judge's calculating grin.

"Something for the oath-taking," Aisha told Karl.

More than ever, she dreaded the display, the songs, the jokes. Tribute maidens? Calling them "maiden" even before they left their yurts was often a case of wishful thinking. In the tribes, virginity was a thing everyone claimed to prize — but sought to do away with as soon as possible.

Aisha knew girls got lessons — she regulated her pulse to calm — on where to put all the arms and legs, not to mention everything else, on their wedding nights. There had been no time for Badri to explain. And since then, life had been not a matter of protecting a virginity no one prized, least of all in her, but of keeping herself from getting raped. The way the Cyborg would have used her, then killed her. She tightened her lips, though she knew Karl would worry. He had reason to worry. He needed to know she was giving him counterfeit instead of a dowry. She had tried to tell him that before. He hadn't listened.

Had she married at a proper age, it would not have mattered. A man like Kemal, say, who had actually begun to bargain for her before she joined her father in his exile, would simply insist upon submission. And she would know no better. At least, *her* tribe was civilized. In some tribes, women were cut before they were married, to make them faithful.

Her Karl was a woman's *mediko*, strange as that idea was. He would know women's bodies as well as a midwife. She told herself his knowledge would have to serve them both, more shame to her. And if it were not, she had Sauron blood. She could endure a little pain if it bound her to the man who had chosen her.

But she was abruptly certain that if people came to inspect her sheets for a smear of blood in token of her lost virginity, she might breach the truce herself. Living as she had, she doubted the barrier had survived, assuming a woman of Sauron blood ever possessed such a thing.

Chaya didn't need to hear that, didn't need to have to face it. Aisha didn't think she looked well. From the way Hammer-of-God gestured, sending a sullen Shulamit over to take a tray and place it before the Judge, he didn't think so, either.

Best slip away and deal with her fears in a decent privacy. She began to move toward the tent flap. Byers' Sun was setting. It would be dimday soon; truenight would come later. And after that, dawn and the oathtaking Chaya was planning with such care.

Karl's hand slid up to her wrist and tightened. She knew—and so did he — that she could have snapped his arm, but the gentle touch held her where she was.

"It isn't the idea of marrying me, is it?" he whispered.

She shook her head, brazenly meeting his eyes for longer than she had ever done.

"It's all this? I don't like it either, but it's the custom. In the Pale, weddings can last for weeks." He too looked tense now. He had lost his last wife to a miscarriage. "As long as it's just the fact that this is public, Aisha, I don't want you worrying. We'll both have to be gentle with each other. Lord, I'm glad you're part Sauron. I heard they can control their fertility without drugs, and the idea of dragging a pregnant woman along on this crusade . . ." He snorted and shook his head.

Aisha narrowed her eyes. "Don't you *want* a son?" If Byers' Sun had suddenly cast bright warmth over all Haven, she could not have been more surprised. She would be Karl's wife. A measure of her worth was the sons she could bear him. Even at her age.

"I don't want to risk you. Maybe we should wait till this campaign is over."

Was he repudiating her? She would kill him: no, she would kill herself, and the *afrit* take this fantasy of the Seven against the Citadel. Panic threatened; then she looked again at her promised husband. She did not see disgust in his face, which he could not control like the Sauron-born, but remembered fear and sorrow, renewed as he faced the prospects of his Aisha pregnant on the steppe, away from the safe haven of a birthing valley.

"Ah, my life has been risked so many times. At least, this risk would give you a son. I would dare anything for that."

"I *have* a son," Karl bar Edgar said. "I have nephews. I would prize a daughter with your loyalty."

Aisha started to shake her head.

"Aisha . . . so long as the child thrives. Were you not more to Juchi than many sons?"

She shook her head. "Poor Dagor."

When Karl's arm went about her, she let herself rest her head on his shoulder.

Even for one of the Seven, steering through the crowd in the Judge's tent without causing irreparable injury by bumping into some rank-proud *khan* or irritable Bandari took some time. Judge Chaya, Hammer-of-God and Kemal were deep in a screaming match about the order of march.

"You can't *all* ride in front!" Hammer shouted, exasperated. "Take turns and satisfy everyone's honor — unless you're less interested in your own face than grinding mud into your enemy's."

The tamerlane's grin on Kemal's face indicated a direct hit. The prospect of putting his boot on Sauron necks was enough to soothe any man here.

"I knew I would regret placing you under my personal protection," Kemal said.

"Right. Later. You can try to kill me later. After we take out the God-bloody Saurons."

"I don't even want to hear that kind of talk," Chaya snapped. "Not before the oath-taking, and certainly not after it. What would you think if everyone who was able took the oath in as many languages as he could?"

"Wouldn't take long for some of these fools. They can barely speak Turkic, much less Americ or Russki."

"Impressive." Hammer-of-God grinned. "It's more real if you hear it in your own language."

He saw Aisha approach and moved aside to bring her and Karl into the circle around the Judge. "Is that what you're going to do with their wedding? Vows in . . . Turkic, Bandarit, Russki, Arabic . . ."

"Nothing of the kind." Chaya pulled out a document from the pile beside her. "Aisha, I ask your pardon." All her remoteness was gone for the moment. "I drew this up last night for you to look at, you and Karl."

"Aisha, it's our marriage contract." Karl put out a hand to touch it. His was admirably steady. Aisha suspected hers would not be. "They call it a *ketubah* in Ivriot."

In the yurts, she would not have seen her marriage contract until after the wedding, and it would have been signed for her. She puzzled out the words. "No dowry?"

"It's not customary, no more than a bride price," Chaya assured her. "This look all right to both of you?"

Karl nodded.

"But . . ." Aisha said.

"Aisha, I haven't had much time for you, but I have noticed one thing," Chaya said. "You hate the idea of the wedding we planned to cement the oath-taking."

"But if it's necessary . . ."

"Let's say it would be useful. But I've got a little leeway. Thanks to Sapper, I just got a little more. So, since this is likely the only wedding you'll ever have, I can give you the wedding gift you want. Privacy. I can do what we call a civil ceremony right here. Or, if you like, we can send for an imam. I warn you, though, that'll probably create family problems about who's entitled to hand you over to your husband."

Aisha turned to Karl bar Edgar. "*I* give myself," she announced. "That is . . ."

"With all my heart." Karl reached for a pen and handed it to her.

"I wouldn't even have been asked to look at the contract," she murmured. Her eyes blurred, and she let the tears come.

No elaborate robes or feasting or men riding horses about the camp, firing into the air. No gifts. Just a man who looked at her and saw a woman he said he loved — Aisha, not a Sauron cull or the daughter of a coupling that all Haven called abomination, or even the Allah-touched *ghazi.*

Given that, what need did she have of anything else? She remembered how to sign her name, even to the calligraphic flourish Badri had had her taught. Karl signed after her.

"Now," said Chaya. "Do you, Aisha bat Badri . . ."

The crowd in the tent pressed round, witnesses to the sudden wedding. Aisha found Shulamit and Sannie standing by her side, which was as much a surprise as anything else.

"Give them room to breathe, people," someone ordered on one side, even as Kemal, Aisha's distant kinsman, pushed back eager onlookers. The serving women clustered together, forcing out a few dutiful tears.

"Here, Karl. I didn't think you had a ring anywhere about you. We've been passing this one back and forth for years." Chaya pulled the ruby from her ring finger. "It's yours again, Aisha. Wear it in the best of health."

Karl placed the ring on Aisha's left hand and squeezed it. She clung to his hand, feeling about fifteen T-years old. "But I have nothing to give you."

"Let me be the judge of that," Karl said.

"Meanwhile, I *am* the Judge. So if you two will let me finish . . . that ought to do for the glass."

She pointed to a tiny flask lying haphazardly on a stack of books. Dutifully, Karl set it down.

"All *right!*" he said, and brought down his boot, grinding

the glass into the crimson rug. The Bandari cheered, Shulamit clapped her hands, and even the dour Edenites applauded.

"We smash a glass at the end of each wedding," Chaya said. "It used to symbolize the destruction of the Temple back on Earth. Now it stands for the Wasting of Haven by the Saurons. Remember that sorrow, even as you build a life together."

Chaya stretched out her long-fingered hand and clasped both of theirs. "By the authority vested in me by the Pale of Settlement as leader of this campaign, I now pronounce you husband and wife."

The ring blazed like red fire on Aisha's hand.

"Come on, fan Haller, kiss your bride," Hammer-of-God ordered, grinning. "Before someone else does."

Lips brushed Aisha's mouth, and clung before she knew what was happening. Rocked off balance, she clung to her husband's shoulders, then steadied and kissed him back, while the Bandari cheered and the serving women tightened their fingers around their throats to produce the keening shriek that passed for rejoicing on the steppe.

As a Sauron, she knew she was physically stronger than he. But he was strong enough to hold her so tightly her blood raced. When he ended the kiss, she was breathless, though not from lack of air.

"Now," Chaya said, "where *did* I put that *vadaka*?" She produced a bottle and, for a miracle, clean glasses. Sannie slipped outside and returned laden with skins of kvass.

Some she tossed to the serving women. Others she passed with ceremony — hospitality from one of the Seven — to the leading *khans*. Chaya passed tiny glasses to Aisha and Karl. "*L'chaym!*" she proclaimed. "To life!"

Aisha, who never thought to have much of one, drank and smiled. To life.

"Now," Chaya said, "that's that. You've got till dawn after truedark. Not as much time as I'd like to give you, but if you start *now* . . . I had Sannie look you out a nice place. Yeweh knows, she and Barak have had plenty of practice. She'll take you there, make sure you're not disturbed."

Chaya bent to kiss Aisha's forehead. There was a time when Badri had kissed her in just that way. Imagine it: Badri, seeing her daughter married. She clung to her kinswoman, trying not to weep. "What are you waiting for?" Chaya asked. "Get out of here before I decide I have twenty more things only you or Karl can do. Besides the one."

"Come on." Sannie tugged at Aisha's sleeve. "I found a real nice place."

Still, Aisha hung back, watching the Judge.

Chaya's eyes went strange, and the voice that fell from her lips was stranger yet. "I promise you, sister and niece. You and your husband will never be parted in all the days of your lives."

Hand in hand, Aisha and Karl followed Sannie into the weird rock gardens of the hot springs. Aisha tried to hang back as a proper wife should, but Karl pulled her forward. "You want to be a good wife to me?" he said in her ear. "Then stay at my side."

Sannie turned a bend in the trail and promptly disappeared.

"Come on!" her voice urged. "This is the best place Barak and I ever found." They followed her and saw her pause in front of a compact, obviously new tent hidden in the shadows of two smooth boulders. To one side a hot spring bubbled, making the air warm and moist. The smell of sulfur was barely perceptible, and the lights that bloomed in the depths of the water cast a glow like lanterns over the tiny camp.

"Be happy, you two." She flung her arms enthusiastically around Karl. *Will I ever feel comfortable enough to do that?* Aisha wondered. Then, with more reserve, Sannie turned to Aisha. "I just want you to know," Sannie said. "We're going to be sisters. I'll do my best to be a good sister to you."

"So will I," Aisha said. "Oh, so will I." She hugged the Bandari woman carefully.

"Now, I'm going to get out of here," Sannie said. "You two . . . be happy. You deserve it."

She disappeared around the bend in the trail, leaving Aisha alone with her new husband.

Karl bent and peered within the tent. "There's food in there, *vadaka*. They obviously don't want to see us for a while." He rummaged through parcels. "Quite a wedding feast they gave us when they haven't got enough food for themselves."

Not just abundant food, but foods she had learned were favorites of her new husband's — even the few favorites she had let herself enjoy.

"Should we . . .what if they need us?"

"Then they'll have to wait," Karl said. "When you're a *mediko*, you learn that. So we'll accept their gifts, I think, and thank them later. Right now, *we* need us." He touched her face.

Her glance went past him to the sheepskins and furs heaped within the tent. A bridal bed for a tribal princess, indeed. *Allah, now what?*

She shook her head. "I'm . . . sorry. I'm acting like a child."

He smiled. "No, you're not. You're acting like the inexperienced woman you are. It's all right, Aisha." He brushed the hair that had escaped from her braids back off her face. "You're Aisha. One of the Seven. Too strong — you would say too old, too — to be as nervous as a bride on her wedding night. But that's what you are. But think it through. If you were Aisha before all this happened . . ."

"I'd expect my husband to teach me," Aisha answered.

"Well enough. And I will. Everything I've wanted to do with you."

He undid the fastenings of her jacket and slipped it off. "Look at that hot spring. Think how good the water would feel."

It wouldn't be truly cold for awhile yet, Aisha thought. She nodded and backed away a step.

"You'd feel better getting undressed by yourself, wouldn't you?" Karl asked. "All right. Let me know when I can turn around."

She eased out of boots, breeches, shirt, and undergarments, then slipped into the water. Its warmth seemed to seep into her bones, and she sighed with pleasure.

Taking that for a signal, Karl turned around. To her shock, he pulled off his own clothes and joined her in the water. She had seen him naked before, when they all took dustbaths on their way to the Pale. It was different this time.

"It's getting cold. We'll be warm in here, though. And when we're finished . . ." He gestured at the tent.

He looked down. The lights in the water illuminated her body — and his. "You're lovely," he said, and ran a hand from her face to her shoulder. Then he drew her into his arms. Aisha relaxed as water and desire warmed her and his hands slid over her back and breasts and sides.

It seemed the most simple, necessary thing in the world to fold her arms about him and cling as his hands and lips touched her.

"If we stay in the water much longer, we may both be too relaxed." He laughed against her skin. "Let's go into the tent. I'll dry you off."

The wind stung them as they climbed from the pool.

"That's *cold*!" he yelped. Aisha managed not to laugh, but she was glad to burrow into the sheepskins that Sannie had left temptingly open. He followed her and drew the soft fleeces about both of them. Then he shivered, so she put her arms about him.

"I'll warm you," she offered.

He had had his hands on her a long time before, when she was ill. And he had touched her just a moment ago. Now his hands felt different, more assured and more insistent. She felt heat rising from her skin, felt her muscles relaxing even more than they had in the hot water; and she drew him close against her.

Stories she had overheard as a young girl came back to her. They were lies. If her husband left no place on her body untouched, he also left her no room for fear. She felt no tearing or any of the pain the old stories had led her to expect — a little awkwardness because she was nervous; but she was used to depending on her body, and the strain of newness was quickly gone.

"Aisha . . ." His husky voice made her name come out

like a sigh. "It's been so long! Move with me, girl. Rock with me. Hold me."

She wrapped arms and legs about him. Above and within her, she felt him tremble and clasped him even closer. It was a dance, she thought. Her body caught the rhythm from his own, and she opened under his touch.

She gasped, dazzled by pulses inside that snatched control of her body even as he gasped and spasmed upon her. She found herself crying as she had when she first came to the Pale. That time, he had stroked her hair and shoulders. That time, he had told her, "Get it out of your system. Let it go."

Now, he ran his hands over her entire body, reassuring her, setting her on fire. "You can let go, Aisha. I've got you safe." His fingers probed like no *mediko* she had ever imagined, and she gasped, heating up again.

"I should have done that the first time I wanted to," he murmured. "Professional ethics be damned."

She laughed. Astonishing that he knew her mind so well.

"Even the way I was?"

"You needed me. Not just my skills, but *me*. Do you know how good being needed is?"

She nodded against his chest. "I thought I needed you. And now . . ." She ran her hand over his chest.

"You tie me to life — risking it to know I've got it back. God help me, I joined the Seven to be with you."

"I don't want to risk . . ."

"My dearest, I made the choice a long time ago. To be secure, or to live. When . . . Miriam died, I was secure for a long, bitter time. And dead inside. Now, I'm alive again, because you're with me."

He rolled off her, then drew her to lie with her head on his shoulder as if she had been an inexperienced young girl. So gentle he was with her. He didn't, couldn't know she would do anything to thank him — if thanks were possible. (*They're not necessary*, her Karl would say. Like a good wife, she would not gainsay him. But she would not be swerved from her purposes, either.) She was outcast, fated to wander lifelong, and she was Sauron, guarded all her life against feeling what she felt.

It was not submission. Islam, she knew, meant exactly that; but even now she could not bow to the will of Allah. She had been on her own too long.

A child, she thought. A wife and child to replace what he had lost in heart and life. A child to share this man's compassion and decency as well as the gifts she carried deep within her genes. A child who would be special as her line was special. A child to survive — she knew that as surely as she believed Judge Chaya's prophecies — the holy war that waited outside this tent and these magic hours. Revelation struck her: she was ready as women of Sauron blood always knew themselves to be.

Deep inside her came a melting, a certainty. . . . She had never felt either, but instinct woke and reassured her. "A child," she murmured, as she drifted toward sleep. A private miracle, like this time snatched from war. Hers, and Karl's.

And for the first time in years, prayer came to her simple and unforced. *Allah grant it.*

The air stank of sulfur, dung and tension. The Cat's Eye's baleful glare cast red shadows over the plain beyond Cliff Lion Oasis. Steam rose from the hot springs. It was tinged the color of old blood; the same ruddy light stained Chaya's leathers, which had been bleached as close to white as the finest leatherworkers among the Bandari could make. A Judge's robes would have been better, but she had abandoned them.

As she saw it now, she was no Judge. Yet here she was, playing Judge in front of the massed tribes of Haven. Years of practice had taught her when an audience wanted to believe. The need in this one reached out to snare her. Briefly, she shook her head, dizzy with revulsion. They wanted to believe. She wanted to use their belief. And so she would. A man back on Terra had preached what he called the Mother of All Battles. It had turned out to be the Mother of All Massacres. None of the tribes had ever forgotten or forgiven.

Chaya thought she knew why he had done it. And how.

Behind her stood the other Six. Kemal and Ihsan wore their finest felts and furs, flung open to show the splendor of embroidered silks. Their weapons — they must have spent every moment they weren't scheming or sleeping in polishing them — fairly glittered as they reflected the Cat's Eye's bloody light.

All the men who thronged this open place were armed. Anything else would have disgraced them and the ceremony she would seduce them into joining. Behind them, banners whipped in the wind.

At Chaya's back stood Barak, her son, and the greatest lie of her life. She knew, and the records knew — and now Barak knew too — that he was not the son of Heber, not a descendant of Piet van Reenan, but the son of a chance-met and quite deliberately slain Sauron from whom Chaya took the life of a son as bloodprice for the death of her husband. Sannie stood at his shoulder, watchful, stubborn, loving in her way.

Next to them stood the one decent thing to come out of this entire charade. Aisha and Karl had emerged with Byers' Sun from the blasted land by the hot springs, not quite wanting to touch each other in the sight of the tribes, not quite wanting to look at each other in public, but with such a sense of gratified passion and accord wreathing them that it soothed even Chaya. She could be cynical about everything else, but not about the way those two lives had flowed together — for as long as it lasted.

There was a truth. Perhaps corruption ran in their blood, but she could always hope.

Around the Seven massed the tribes and the Bandari. Her general seemed to have constituted himself her personal guard. That too was truth. *Try it.*

Light flickered in her eyes. She didn't flinch, not quite. *Heliograph*, she knew. Sapper, stationed in the waste between grassland and hot springs, signaled to one of his men, whose mirror flashed the message to her. *Time*. It was all a matter of timing.

Underfoot, the ground trembled. A pillar of steam hissed up from one of the smaller pools, and the air grew momentarily warmer.

What was that line about asking for bread and being offered a stone? These men and women asked for belief, and they'd get theatricals. Still, if her kin were to be avenged and a great evil stopped — she remembered the devastation around Angband Base, and her lips thinned.

The crowd's shouts and mutterings died into awed murmurs. She gauged that she stood fully in the light of the Cat's Eye. Her cue.

She raised her arms. The knife she had palmed in her sleeve slid gleaming out and shone redly, as if it had already drawn blood.

"We are here to march on the Citadel, we, the finest fighters on Haven. We are here — we who have shed each other's blood — to shed the blood of our common enemy. The blood that the cursed Saurons have shed cries out to Heaven for revenge. The very ground itself and all of us who walk or ride upon it cry out to drive these people from the earth. And toward that end, I call upon all of you to swear the oath of blood-kin."

Deliberately, watching the crowd — her audience! — Chaya drew the blade down one arm. Blood stained the white leather. She let it drip upon the ground with an effort of will as much as body: left alone, the wound was slight enough to clot almost instantly.

"Let the ground receive this sacrifice," she cried. "Let the ground remember faith kept and oaths broken. Let the ground remember how the Saurons tormented it.

"Let the ground be the judge. Let it receive this blood. Let it swallow all oath-breakers.

"I call on all who would ride with me to shed their blood in token of their faith."

She let the flow of blood slow to a very tiny trickle. Then she repeated her call to oath-taking in Arabic, then *Ivrit*, then Russki, working through all the languages she knew and a few she had memorized for the event.

Following her lead, her son cut his arm and swore. Aisha swore after him, her blood as quick to cease its flow as that of her kin. Kemal, Ihsan, Sannie. Karl spoke last of the Seven, his face grave. Chaya suspected that he itched to get his hands on the cuts made by the oath-taking. Well, he was going to have a lot more work than he could handle.

"Let this symbol of my art testify to my willingness to take this oath," he declared and slashed his arm, not with a knife, but with a scalpel.

*Keep it moving*, came a signal from one of Sapper's people — Timothy. He nodded, and Mark went trotting off toward the engineers.

"Now," Chaya said in a voice pitched to carry to the farthest reaches of the crowd, "the rest of you."

The air began to stink of blood as well as holiness. One of the minor geysers spewed sulfurous water: drops fell on the blood as it soaked the hard ground.

One by one, the *khans* came up, slashing their arms and repeating the oath, some in one language, some in many, some — like Gasim — obviously mouthing words they had learned to gain face among the other leaders. The man of Bod — from the far, high snows — swore in a tonal language Chaya knew to be Tibetan, though she could not understand it. *Wonder if he's lying*, she thought, then shrugged off the thought. Not in a reincarnate culture. Lies were for people who thought you lived only once.

And not even for all of them, as Kemal turned with elaborate, ironic courtesy to Hammer-of-God. "You've seen enough of our blood," he remarked. "Let's see yours."

The Edenite flicked hand to breast, lips and brow, then slashed his arm, taking the oath, repeating the oath, swearing in almost as many languages as Chaya laid claim to. *We're not all dumb* peasants, she heard his voice rasp in memory. *Besides, I had to do something while the damned medikos had me tied down, and I like learning things.*

"My oath stands for my men. I will answer for their conduct with my life," he added. "Unless there is any objection . . ." He flicked blood off his blade into the fire, cleaned it, then bound up his arm neatly.

"The strangers," Gasim muttered. "Let them take the oath now." His eyes fell first on Karl fan Reenan, who shrugged and swore, even in the Farsi common around Ashkabad. Shulamit pressed forward and was humored:

Chaya sensed her rage, as she sensed the hates and fears and hopes of every man and woman in the crowd of warriors and worshippers.

*Keep it moving*, Timothy gestured. *You're doing fine, but don't let it get away from you.*

A glance up at the Cat's Eye confirmed his signals.

"That one!"

Karl fan Reenan leaned forward. So did half the people nearby. The stranger Gasim had singled out was very tall for a woman, about of a height with Chaya. What made her stand out most, though, was her coloring — frost-fair, with features like the blade of a knife before it is quenched in blood. She strode forward almost contemptuously. Disdaining Chaya's knife, disdaining even Karl's scalpel, for a blade of her own, severely plain of hilt, surpassingly fine steel. She spoke the words of the oath and repeated it in Russki. That wasn't all that surprising, given that the folk of Belarus were often fair. But some awareness twinged at the base of Chaya's consciousness, and she thought that Russki might not be the stranger's birth tongue.

Her eyes met Chaya's, who saw an irony almost equal to her own. She refused to acknowledge it and waited until the newcomer nodded respect. She was owed that much at least.

The pale woman's blood flowed; she bound up her arm with a clean cloth.

"Don't see why she bothers," Shulamit said *sotto voce.* "It'll stop in a minute."

Young Karl shoved her. "Will you *stop* that? Would you rather have her bleed herself white?"

"No chance . . ."

A hiss, and the two adolescents were separated before they could quarrel and break the mood Chaya had worked so hard to create. The dung fires smoked, stinking to high heaven against the reek of the blood. The Tibetans swung mallets against bronze gongs and blew those sinister bone horns of theirs; she had never liked to speculate on where they got the bones. The curved *radongs* bellowed like beasts in pain.

She sensed the belief in the crowd, the wildness held in

restraint — barely. Like icemelt off a glacier, waiting only for a rock to shift before it plunged down a hillside, it could sweep away all that lay in its path.

Or it could turn a mill and feed the children of entire towns. But there was always that moment of peril before you knew whether the power you had released would obey your will or destroy you.

Barak gave her a thumbs-up. *You're doing fine*.

But she wasn't. She had smelled that smoke, heard those bells before — before she had collapsed in the blasted land by the hot springs and been tended by some anonymity who had yet to claim a price of her. Her head spun, and she felt surrounded by an aura of light and sensations surrounded her.

If she hurried, she could race through the remainder of this spectacle and take herself to her tent — maybe even have in decent privacy whatever seizure might be coming. It was too much to hope that Karl bar Edgar might tend her; he had her medical records. *A treat for you, Karl. See senile deterioration in a Sauron 'breed.* Juchi had not lived long enough for it to start in him.

Urgency came upon her, and a frantic, shamed desire not to let her son and Aisha see how her genes betrayed her — how their own might turn on them to their destruction.

But the faith was there; the oath; and the spilled blood. It remained only for her to take those threads of belief, of fanaticism, and of controlled violence into her hands, and of them weave a noose strong enough to hang every Sauron in the Citadel, hang him higher than the Haman of Bandari festival tales.

The familiar rumble was building under the earth. She knew what that meant, knew she had limited time either to consummate this ritual or to flee. God, she hated the idea of twitching and spasming in front of half the tribes on Haven, like some filthy shaman in pelts and bone beads. But if she fled — what would become of them all?

They were watching her. Clearly the oath to one another was not enough. Kemal drew his sword and strode forward as the other *khans* muttered approval. He laid the sword at Chaya's feet.

"I have sworn to my brothers," he said. "But I will swear again to one of us who has been warrior and scholar and who leads the Seven."

Only her will kept her on her feet. She could not flee now, even if she wanted, without collapsing the entire structure she had spent blood to build. Damn these tribes! What barbarians they were, demanding an oath made flesh — and now she knew: that flesh must be hers.

*Kapetein Piet was right. We have moved from history to legend, and none of us is civilized. Especially not me.*

*Real* Saurons had training, she knew, that let them rifle their memories as fast they might snap a neck. She tried to imitate it. Saurons. Myths. There was an oath once, taken when a tribe, no, a king set out to oppose Saurons. What was it?

She was not Cyborg to have an eidetic memory, but even now, hers would serve, unless her genes ripped the wits from her. She drove her will back into the reaches of her memory. Ahhh . . . she had it now.

"Come forward, Kemal," she told him. She let her voice wrap about him, almost seductive. "Kneel before me." He stiffened, then dropped to his knees, caught up despite himself.

Over to one side, Sapper's engineers waved frantically. The rumbling beneath their feet grew louder. Chaya felt the earth shake, and knew that it was not part of the seizure that must come soon.

"Repeat after me: I swear loyalty and service to my brothers and to the Judge of this host, to speak and to be silent, to do and to let be, to come and to go, in need or plenty, in peace or war, in living or dying, from this hour henceforth, until my Lord release me, or death take me, or the world end. So say I. . . ."

Kemal's eyes met hers. He looked stupefied yet exhilarated, as if he had been smoking hemp or eating hashish. But he added his name and patronymic with a flourish.

The tall, pale woman looked startled. Interesting.

Chaya bent to take up his blade and hand it to him in

token his oath had been received. *Don't you just wish you could see yourself?* She knew she was shaking. The gongs grew louder. Judging from the others' expressions, no one else could hear. Best finish while she could.

"And this do I hear, Chaya bat Dvora, Judge of the Pale, Leader of the Seven, and I will not forget it, nor fail to reward that which is given: fealty with love, valor with honor, oath-breaking with vengeance."

Barak glared at Mark, Sapper's man. *Well, where* is *the damned thing?*

For a moment, the entire camp was still.

And then the great geyser erupted in steam and spume, a column of scalding water ejected into the chill air.

It stank of sulfur and blood, like the pits of hell. She knew a moment of wild exultation. She had unleashed the torrent, and now it would flow into the channels she had devised.

Then the clamor of the gongs rose and struck her down. Even as she collapsed, she heard the warriors cheer and clash their weapons.

Foam ran down her chin. Her back arched, and she cried out. For an eternity, she thought that no one noticed. Hoped, maybe, was a better word.

"Quick, the Judge! She's fallen!"

"Your Honor . . ."

"*Tanta* Chaya!"

"Sister!" Pure panic in Aisha's voice, in Barak's eyes.

*I will not be cattle!* She forced some remote corner of her awareness to hold aloof from the convulsions that racked her. To remain aware. She rose above the pathetic, spasming, aging body she knew to be hers. The Edenite general thought to restrain her? It would not work; she was still too strong . . . no . . . her son had joined Hammer-of-God.

Both men's lips were bleeding: she had struck at them. Her own lip bled too; she could taste the iron tang. She could not feel it. She wondered if she would wake up paralyzed — or at all. It hardly seemed to matter. Now the wave had been set free. For all she cared, it might roll over her, provided it reached the desired shore.

"She's had one of these seizures before. I was there. Don't worry, Barak — help me get this cloth between her teeth. For Christ's sake, man, it's not a death sentence."

*Oh, but it was, it was, the instability coming out in the genes.*

Karl bar Edgar knelt by her side, helping to turn her, ordering around men half a head taller than he and infinitely more wealthy. At this moment, though, he was *khan* and they were—all of them—warriors yet to win the name.

To his surprise, he was not alone. Aisha had not fled; Barak was at her side; and even the tall, pale woman had edged forward, fascination writ large on her features.

*You.* Her eyes met the stranger's, then glazed over. She felt her feet drumming against the bloody ground. Voices spoke in wonder: "The falling sickness! Ai-yai! Like Kubilai's son or . . ."

*Khan*, king, tsar . . . Caesar. She had the falling sickness. That alone removed this from the realm of arms and into the realm of holiness, as *jihad* was holy.

Then the lightning struck her down. She screamed — a strangled noise of horror and obedience mingled — and as the black cloud of unconsciousness offered itself to her, she embraced it, clasping it to her breast like the lover she had awaited all her life.

# ● CHAPTER NINETEEN

Cliff Lion Springs. It was Orodruin on some maps in the Citadel, early ones made in the flush of mythmaking that followed the descent of the *Dol Guldur*. Most placenames had since gone back to native usage, unless there were Soldiers close by to keep up the custom.

Sigrid was inclined to call it Cesspool Springs, herself. She could smell it for a good hour before she got to it. The horses did not appear to mind the reek of sulfur and manshit. It was water and warmth and a place to rest. The yearling had a stone bruise on her hoof that needed a good soaking and a few cycles' layup.

The Bandari were bickering, as usual. In the last couple of cycles it had been essentially one-sided: Shulamit pricking and nagging, Karl answering in monosyllables or not at all. He was nicely sunk in a pheromone fog. Sigrid would have done something about it at the last rest stop, but Shulamit had got to him while Sigrid saw to the yearling's hoof. Just as well, Sigrid thought. In the crowd at the oasis there would be greater opportunity, and paradoxically more privacy.

Now they were squabbling over whether to creep in like bandits or ride in like decent Bandari, and never mind the parental army that might be waiting. Karl had waked up a bit and sprung for the open route. Shulamit was for circumspection. "You never know," she said darkly, "what our parents could have got up to. If they caught Erika . . ."

"They'd never catch Erika," Karl said. "She's too clever. She wouldn't have told on us, either."

"Wouldn't she?" said Shulamit. "*Tattletale* is her middle name. Bet you she went straight back to papa and told him everything she knew."

"Bet you she didn't."

Sigrid intervened before Karl lost something he valued. It was likely to be his hide, the way Shulamit was glowering at him. "We go in quietly, like honest traders," Sigrid said. "If we're seen, we're seen. If we're not, well enough."

Karl gave in promptly, or his gonads did, which was essentially the same thing. Shulamit would have argued, but she knew by now that Sigrid did not play that game. Bandari, by reputation and in Sigrid's recent experience, had to debate everything up, down, inside out and backwards, and then fight over it for a cycle or so before they settled on the conclusion they had started with. Sigrid had also seen how efficient they could be at their hours of weapons practice, otherwise she would have been convinced that the whole martial reputation of the breed was based on their own bombast.

As it turned out, both Karl and Shulamit were proved right. They rode in as if they had every right to, mixing in with a largish merchant caravan, and no one stopped them. As they came to the outer ring of yurts, they were briefly swept round by a troop of wild black-haired horsemen on black horses. Sigrid eyed those with some interest. Breeding for color, or for any one trait, was a mistake, but there were a few halfway decent beasts in that lot. Somebody would be outcrossing, then, or doing enough culling to keep the stock hardy.

While the upper layer of her mind pondered bloodlines and desirable recessives, the rest cataloged the camp. The whole oasis was overrun, and it was a big oasis. At current rate of influx it had, she calculated, about half a cycle before its population hit critical mass. Then the carefully dug latrine system — nice bit of work, that; Battlemaster Carcharoth would have approved — would overload. Meanwhile she noted that the nomads were being kept in something like order, that no feuds were being pursued right at the moment, and that the rough series of concentric circles looked in on a much smaller agglomeration. The Seven?

One long scan had it all in memory for access later. The raw numbers were impressive. It was like an exercise for

Soldier-trainees, a purely hypothetical worst-case scenario. Suppose the whole steppe rose, got rid of its inextricable snarl of feud and counterfeud, found a leader charismatic enough to hold the whole improbable alliance together, and massed against the Citadel. There was still no basis for supposing the army had high-tech weapons, except gut feeling that in a Cyborg meant near certainty. Bows and swords and antique muskets did not mass against assault rifles. They had something else here, or access to something else.

Karl and Shulamit were looking cocky now that they were in the camp, or on the edge of it at least, and so far undetected. "We'll camp over there," said Karl, "inside the perimeter but far enough out that there's grass for the horses. I suppose there's a rota or something for water. Should we go straight to Judge Chaya now and confess our sins, or do we wait till we've scouted things out a bit?"

That was the signal for another round of squabbling. Sigrid cut it off before it could start. "We camp. Then we reconnoiter."

A shrill wailing stopped her cold. It also stopped the camp. In less time than it took to break down and reassemble a Kalashnikov, every nomad in sight was down on his prayer rug and bowing toward invisible Sol.

They could not move the horses sidewise or back without trampling the faithful. The merchants closed them in behind. There were people up front, heading the newcomers away from the center of the camp. None of those was praying, which marked them Bandari or Edenite even without the differences in clothing and coloring. The Edenites ran to lanky fairness — some common ancestry with Soldiers there, old Noreuropa and Norameric stock.

One big, fair man was visible on what must have been a scout post, standing next to a shorter, darker man and scanning the arrivals with a Soldier's eye. He stood like a soldier too, if not a Soldier, with a cant to the body that meant a bad leg. Edenite, that cast to the features and that set to the mouth. Bandari overlay — training, but not from youth as the two with her had it. His youth, in fact, was a good while gone. He was as gray as an old wolf out of a Terran vidtape, and he carried himself as men did who had held command for so long it had become a habit.

The prayer ended. The camp went back to its milling and shouting. The Edenite's eye passed lazily over the caravan, paused at Sigrid's horses — appreciative glint there, before it went on — and froze.

Karl was fussing with the girth on his pony's saddle. Shulamit had her hands full with her remounts. The chestnut had decided that it had had enough of the camel pressing up behind it and was expressing its displeasure with squealing, kicking emphasis. Neither youth noticed the man who bore down on them. Sigrid reckoned that it would be less trouble to let him take them by surprise. There was nowhere to run, in any case, and they would only fall into one of their endless squabbles.

No point in inviting scrutiny. She moved unobtrusively between the mare and her oldest daughter. The dogs, even the independent-minded bitch, pressed against her shins.

The Edenite was in a fine fury, and unleashing it well before the objects of it could have heard him. *Spoiled brats* was the least of it. *Runaways* went without saying. She rather liked *brass-brained, brass-balled son of a rabid tamerlane bitch*. He did not see Shulamit yet, then. She was not that easy to see. Unlike Karl, who looked like nothing else on this part of Haven.

He got his reaming-out, and Shulamit too, since she could never be left out of anything. Sigrid could easily have slipped away in the midst of it. She chose not to.

She was glad of her Soldier training. It kept her face straight through all of it, even the part about the first Bandari on Haven captured by Saurons. An unaugmented human would have laughed aloud.

The Edenite was a soldier, no doubt about it, but he had never learned much about control. He finished with a blast that made even Shulamit flinch, and wheeled about on his game leg.

Sigrid had seen the flash of his glance. She was ready for the arm that swung as if to flatten her for the crime of simply being there. Clever, she thought: play at blind temper, get a good look at the stranger's face. He got his look, but not as long or as clear as maybe he hoped. So did the man with him, who looked both amused and fascinated. The one was wearing a *mediko*'s insignia — and that did not mean a shaman or an herb-healer, not in a Bandari army. He would be as good as they got outside the Citadel. She gave him enough expression to lull suspicion. Complete control was dangerous here. She had to remember that.

Neither reared up and howled, *Sauron!* The Edenite dragged Karl with him toward the center of the camp. Shulamit pushed sullenly in their wake. Sigrid took the animals in hand — her horses and the Bandari ponies both — and made herself scarce.

It wasn't the pain of getting his just deserts, and being busted clear down to a pup in the process, that made Karl want to kick something. It was that he'd got it in front of *her.*

She hadn't laughed, but he knew she'd wanted to. He was getting good at reading her. She wore that cold arrogant face to protect herself. No wonder, too. A woman alone on the steppe needed every defense she could muster. She had a tragedy in her past, he was sure. Something grim and heroic, that made her what she was.

He booted himself back into the present, unpleasant as that was. She'd disappeared, horses and dogs and all. His heart stabbed. What if he couldn't find her again?

Well, then he'd comb the camp till he did. Meanwhile he had some music to face. Hammer-of-God stopped dragging him once it was clear that he wasn't going to bolt — probably none too soon for the old bastard, too, with that leg.

Another man moved up beside Karl. Karl braced himself for another blast. He got a smile and an arm around the shoulders — stretching a bit, that, and the smile broadened to a grin. "I swear," said Karl bar Edgar, "you've grown another foot across since I saw you last."

"Not that much," said Karl, but his lips were twitching. It

was impossible to keep a good sulk going around *Oom* Karl.

The *mediko* snorted. "You're as big as Yigal already, don't say you aren't."

They veered round a knot of yelling Mongols. One of them made a grab for Shulamit. He got a fist in the gut. "Damn," she said. "Hit too high."

Karl spared her a grin, but his mind was still on *Oom* Karl's words. "Yigal's all right?"

"He'll be righter when he's tanned your hide," said the *mediko*, "but yes, he'll do."

That was comforting, coming from *Oom* Karl. Karl didn't think, most times, about how old Yigal had been getting lately. It came too close to thinking about how old he would get, thanks to his Frystaat genes.

*Live while you can,* he thought. It came wrapped around another thought, with an ash-fair face in it, and a long elegant body in leathers and furs.

Judge Chaya was looking old. That came as a part of what else Karl had been thinking, but it was true. She had the kind of face that stopped showing age as soon as it hit maturity, long and lean, with strong prominent bones, but now the bones were sharp, the flesh fallen away. Her eyes focused as keenly as ever, looked right through him, but they didn't, somehow, look as far. Or else they looked farther than ever, and blurred with the distance.

Her speech was a variation on Hammer's, with more resort to Duty and less to Family. He'd have thought it would be the other way around, considering Bandari and Edenite priorities. It wound down a lot sooner than he'd expected. Hammer sounded worried when he asked was she all right. She said she was. Karl knew she was lying, but he was too relieved to have got off so lightly to want to call her on it.

Chaya kept Shulamit with her, not surprising since they were family. Karl minded less than he might have. Shulamit was getting a little hard to take, he admitted to himself. Yatter, yatter, yatter, and she was rude to Sigrid. She was rude to everybody, come to think of it, except Chaya, and that was good solid fear.

He got out as soon he could, under cover of a flap between Karl bar Edgar and General Hammer and one of the General's Edenite cousins. Aisha was in it. Poor Aisha. She looked like Chaya, of course — Chaya was her three-quarter sister, and her aunt too — but much younger. She carried herself like a tribeswoman, but when she forgot she moved like, well, Sigrid. She didn't act like a woman about to get married, except when Karl bar Edgar's eye fell on her; then she lit up like a lamp.

It was colder outside the yurt than in, with Byers' Sun getting low enough to cast long shadows across the camp, but the breathing was easier. Hammer had told him to go in with the Scouts. That was worth the rest of it, because it meant he was trusted — he wasn't going back to his father like a brat too young to fight. He'd do it, and do it as well as he could, for pride. But he had something else to do first.

"Karl! Karl bar Yigal!"

Karl stiffened and spun. Barak bar Heber looked him up and down. He was thriving on all this, grinning like a stobor alpha male in a flock of fat sheep. "Well, you rascal. You took your time getting here."

"We took the long way around," Karl said. "I've had two sets of talking-to. Do I get another lecture, or can I just assume it's included in the others?"

Barak cuffed him. He ducked, but he still got enough of a buffet to make his ears ring. "That's for running off like a pup. The rest goes without saying."

"Hammer said it," said Karl. "And Judge Chaya."

"I'll bet they did," Barak said. "Where's Shulamit?"

"Helping the Judge," said Karl. "I'm to be in the *Sayerets*, the Scouts." He said that with pride.

"Splitting you up, then. Sensible of them. The two of you were always six times as much trouble together as you were separately." Barak paused. "I hear you had company coming in."

Rumor travelled fast. Karl kept his tone casual. "Oh. Yes, we did. Has there been any trouble?"

"None at all," said Barak. "Horsebreaker, is he?"

"She." Careful, Karl told himself. Not too quick. But

Barak caught it anyway. His eyes started to sharpen.

"She's bringing horses to sell for remounts?" the Judge's son asked.

"I don't think they're for sale."

"No?" Barak looked ready to say something else, but somebody yelled his name. Something was up. There was a lot of flurry and shouting, and what looked — and sounded — like a dogfight. "I'll talk to you later," Barak said. Then he was off.

Karl took a deep breath. Saved again. At this rate he might even get away with it. All of the Seven who could care about him were accounted for, and Hammer was tied up in the tent, literally since he'd thrown out his cousin. Karl was as free as a man could be. He set off with a spring in his step.

By starset he was walking more like a man with a mission, and not finding what he was looking for, either. No one had seen the tall blonde woman or the black-and-white dogs or, more to the point in this camp, the horses. Since the last he had seen of his and Shulamit's ponies and baggage had been in Sigrid's charge, he had more to think about than simply losing her, but she was what he was thinking of. Mounts and weapons were easy enough to come by. There was only one of her.

Amazing how many nooks and crannies the oasis held. It was mostly flat, with dips and rises, but the springs bubbled out wherever they had a mind. Streams wandered every which way, some so hot they boiled, others so cold mist hung above them, and smokes and steams, geysers and fumaroles, made the going interesting to say the least. The tribes kept a wary distance from the most active places, and with good reason. The earth quaked and trembled even more there than it did elsewhere, and sometimes belched out boiling water or steam. A body could cook in here.

Karl was never warm enough. It was his greatest grievance with the world he had been born to: that he was designed for a hotter climate. From what the old stories said, warmth was the only virtue Frystaat had — it sounded like a version of the Muslim hell, and had been given to

Piet van Reenan's ancestors in the fond hope the planet would kill them all. It almost had, come to that — like Haven, but backwards. Karl, born to Haven, bred to Frystaat, was always cold. But here, for once, he felt almost comfortable. He picked his way carefully, avoiding the pits and the crusted pools, keeping to where there was grass or what looked like a track. Horses had been up this way. The ground was too stony to tell if they were horses he knew, but they'd come by recently, and he was in a mood to gamble.

He moved quietly by force of habit. It was good practice for scouting, and he liked to surprise people who expected him to be clumsy, with his heavy-world bones and his big feet. Not a stone shifted where he walked. He made less sound than the wind in the grass. He ghosted round an outcropping of stone crusted over with pallid crystals, and stopped cold.

The ground dropped away at his feet into what must have begun as a sinkhole. It was a shallow valley now, with a chain of pools running down it from the rise on the other side. The highest one bubbled like a cauldron on the boil. Successively lower ones looked cooler, till the one at the bottom, the one that seeped away into the ground again, barely steamed. There were horses in that one, standing hipshot or lying down. He recognized Shulamit's chestnut war horse and Sigrid's narrow-headed bays. The dogs were on the bank, one lying with head on paws and eyes on the horses, the other sitting up with one ear pricked and one flopped over, staring straight at Karl.

He saw them in a glance and promptly forgot them. She was standing in one of the higher pools, one that looked just short of boiling. Her clothes were spread on a rock, dark with washing, and she was as naked as she was born. Her skin was so white it shone.

She wasn't the way he'd thought she'd be, not in the least. Tall thin women ran to ropy muscle and a lot of sharp angles, and breasts like an afterthought or barely there at all. She had muscle, true enough, but it was long and smooth and molded to the elegant bones. She looked as hard as a boy, but there was nothing boylike about her. Her breasts looked as if they belonged exactly where they were, curving just enough above the high arc of the ribs. The nipples were an impossibly tender shade of pink, like the flush in her cheeks as she met his eyes through the curling steam.

He was one big burning blush from toes to braid-end. Then she smiled.

It wasn't much of a smile, but for her it was as broad as a grin. It stopped him on the verge of turning and bolting. It looped a noose around his neck and pulled him down off the track, past the drowsy horses and the dogs — one sparing him a glance, the other a grin and a tail wag as he went by — and up again along the chain of pools. She never moved, not one muscle, except her eyes that held his. They were the color of silver, or of rain.

He halted on the pool's rim, just before he fell in. "Hello," he said. It sounded unbearably inane.

"You need a bath," she said.

Her voice was the same as always, cool and husky, but it was different too. Friendlier? He was aware suddenly of himself, how leather could smell if you lived in it too long, and how long it had been since he washed properly, all over. As a matter of fact, he stank.

But — here? With her?

She was on him before he knew it, moving with that blinding speed of hers — like — like —

Never mind. She stripped him as neatly as a farmer could shear a sheep, and with about as much resistance: his muscles did the fighting for him, he had nothing to do with it. It had no effect, either. Through the thunder of blood in his ears, he was amazed. Skill, that was it. Speed. She couldn't be stronger than he was. Nobody was. Except Yigal, and he was growing old. And young Barak. And . . .

Cold cut him to the bone. She wasn't even shivering. She half-led, half-dragged him into water so hot he yelped and lurched back toward the shore again, but she held him till the heat melted and flowed through the whole of him. Hands like steel. Not a shift, not a sway as he struggled, as if she were made of immovable metal, or stone. But so narrow, so elegantly slender. Hips that just barely curved. Skin as fine as silk, or the buttery leather the Dinneh had, cured, they said, in the brains of the beasts it came from. She smelled of salt and sulfur and subtle musk, so subtle it barely touched his senses, but he knew it was there.

She was taller than he was. He wasn't used to that. Shulamit — guilt stabbed at the thought of her, but it faded fast — Shulamit came just to his chin. He came just to Sigrid's. He didn't feel small, not at all. He was as wide as three of her, as heavy as — two? One and a half? She packed an amazing amount of mass in those narrow bones.

She had soapweed mixed with something sharp and pleasantly scented. She washed him with it, not too slow, not too light, the way he liked it. Just the way he liked it. How did she know? She took her time. Something kept him from lunging at her, maybe the way she held him with her eyes, or maybe just the steel-strength in her hands. She explored every inch of him.

He still hadn't touched her, not with his hands. After she ducked him under to rinse him, while the water was still streaming from him, he reached for her. He half-expected her not to be there, but she was. She let him pull her to him, neither helping nor resisting. Her skin was fever hot and even softer than it looked, like silk stretched over steel. Her face was rapt and a little mad. She looked like Chaya. But stronger. And beautiful as Chaya never had been, a terrible, death's head beauty, white as a bone and cold enough to burn.

No one, not Shulamit, not any of the women in the Pale, had ever been as strong as he was. He always held back, no matter how hot he was, till it was a habit, and he stopped having to think about it. It shocked him to the bone to find himself out of control, taking Sigrid in one great lunging rush that carried them clean out of the water and onto a fortunate patch of grass. He pulled back, appalled — or tried. Her arms and legs were locked around him. So was another part of her. Sanity ran gibbering for cover. No one — no one —

She did something indescribable with muscles he'd never known a woman had. His own muscles responded out of sheer self-preservation. The thrust should have split her from crotch to sternum.

"Is that all you've got?" she asked.

She wasn't even breathing hard. He snarled something, no matter what, and let red rage carry the rest of it.

"*Yeweh*," he sighed, some considerable time later. He was wrung to a rag. She looked a bit ruffled, and she was smiling. He supposed that was a good thing, except for where her hand was going. He caught it and held it against his hip. "What in the name of the Three are you?"

"Djinni," she said, or he thought she said. She was nibbling his ear, which was one sure way to drive him wild. "You're almost strong enough for me."

He'd spent his rage a long time ago. Three times? Six? He'd lost count. His hair was out of its plait and falling all over them both. She left off torturing his ear and played with a hank of it. He mustered the energy to pull her in closer. She let him do it. Everything was letting and not-letting, with her.

She looked as relaxed as he'd ever seen her. Her white hand on his brown flank seemed to fascinate her. So did the yellow bush in his groin. That was not growing anything worth looking at, not immediately and maybe not for the rest of his life. She closed that long hand around it.

"Is it dead, do you think?" she asked.

That was a joke; he could tell by the way she slanted her eyes at him. "Deader than Diettinger," he said.

She stiffened, just for an instant, just enough to detect. Then she laughed. He'd never heard her laugh like that before, low and almost warm. "Ah, but will he rise again?"

"I hope not," he said. Then when she laughed harder: "You know what I mean!"

"Do I want to?" She raised herself on her hands. Her breasts swayed, distracting him.

But not completely. "What do you mean, I'm almost strong enough for you?"

"So," she said. "You do listen."

Shulamit — guilt again, but as weak as the rest of him — would have added something about the penetration of sound through six meters of skull. Sigrid lowered herself onto his body, trapping him from head to foot, but not with all her weight — just enough to keep him still. "I always mean what I say," she said.

"I'm as strong as you'll ever find." He sounded lame to himself, as if he had anything left to prove.

"You are proud of that," she said. She'd gone remote again, and cold. Weird, with her body so warm on top of him.

"I should think I have a right to be," he said stiffly.

"So you do." She smiled her faint cool smile. "You're young, after all. You've a lot of growing in you yet."

"And you're as old as Judge Chaya, I suppose?"

"Not quite." She was laughing, damn her, inside that narrow skull of hers. "Nor quite as dead as One-Eyed Diettinger. Nor, I wager, are you."

No. Temper had done it again, brought back the dead. He rolled her over onto her back and gave her what she wanted.

Sannie and Barak between them got Chaya to rest a little after starset. It took doing. Shulamit helped as much as she could, but she got in the way more often than not. Finally Sannie snapped at her, "Go to bed yourself. You're dead on your feet."

They'd given her a place to sleep in one of the smaller yurts, but she tossed and turned. Finally she got up, pulled on the clothes she'd taken off, and picked her way over other, less restless bodies. The trouble, she told herself, was that she'd got out of the habit of sleeping alone. And piled in a palm-sized yurt with a dozen other women was alone. Company meant one big yellow-headed lug with more balls than brains.

General Hammer had him off with the *Sayeret*. She'd envy him more if she didn't suspect she'd see more action where she was.

He wasn't where the Scouts slept. He wasn't out on duty, that anyone knew. He hadn't reported at all.

She dragged up her heart from where it had dived to her boots. No way he'd gone running again, not when they'd finally got where they wanted to go. So where else would he be?

Most people were asleep in the bloody light of the Cat's Eye, getting settled in for the dark of truenight. But luck hadn't left Shulamit. She found a Mongol woman nursing a baby by a yurt, who remembered very well a brass braid and green eyes and muscle from ear to ear. Not that she put it that way. She had the muscle a few feet lower and rising fast.

He'd been alone, the woman said. A Mongol would not have missed a tall blonde woman with two dogs and a herd of horses. Shulamit was less relieved to hear that than she might have been, especially when the path she was set on left yurts and people behind and went deeper into the springs. Karl wasn't the type to brood in solitude. Public sulks were more his style.

She was puffing when she came to the bend. What made her want to run those last furlongs, she couldn't have said. Maybe just needing to move, because if she didn't, she'd kill something. It wasn't so easy to say that any more, since she'd seen that Sauron rifle roaring in the cleft, and the havoc of blood and brains it left behind.

Saurons, now. Saurons she'd kill, and count every *Yewehferdamt* one of them toward her father's blood price. It was other people she'd be sparing of. Thinking like that made her feel virtuous.

She needed to feel virtuous about now. Guarding Chaya was noble duty and honorable and would pay off in time, the sooner the better — but she was the baby of the group, and they made sure she knew it. Barak, blast him; he'd called her *kitten* and laughed when she scowled. And she got all the scutwork, to the great relief and obvious pleasure of the woman who'd been doing it before she got there.

Her breath was back, or most of it. She walked the rest of the way around the rock.

And there he was. His mahogany butt pumping away, and long white legs wrapped around it, and his braid-crinkled yellow hair hanging down, hiding both their faces.

Karl had a kink about his hair. He wore it long because he was vain of it, but then he never took it out of its braid except to wash it and comb it and braid it up again. He never let Shulamit touch it, and squawked when she wanted to play with it. He was less tender about his cock, and less shy of it, too.

Now it was all loose in the bloody light. So was he. If that was rape, Shulamit was a Sauron.

The tears in her eyes burned like acid. Her mouth was full of bile. Her knife was in her hand. Stab him, stab him and stab him and stab him and —

He never knew that she stood there. The other one, the white-faced bitch — she did. He rocked to a climax and dropped on his face, heaving for breath. Sigrid lay where he had left her. She looked cool, relaxed, sated. Her head turned slowly. She smiled. Right into Shulamit's eyes.

"Bitch," Shulamit said without sound.

Sigrid laughed, also silently. She didn't even care enough to be smug. She saluted Shulamit with the lift of a brow and the flip of a hand, then pulled Karl back onto her. She did it as easily as if he'd been a bundle of rags. And Shulamit knew what he weighed. He'd come near to crushing her more than once, when he got excited and forgot to be careful. Sigrid was a Sauron — and nobody would believe her. Sauron women were hens' teeth, not even a myth.

She turned and ran. She imagined that Sigrid's laughter followed her all the way down the long twisting path into the truenight.

The boy slept long and hard, the way boys did. Or so Sigrid assumed. She spent some hours in prowling the camp, which was tucked up tight in the darkness, and came back to find him still asleep. She considered waking him up and tossing him out, but he was no trouble as he was.

She sat on her haunches in the age-old posture of the

nomad and watched him sleep, while her mind processed
the data it had acquired. She was able, as she did that, to
reserve a portion for herself. Her body was well and
profitably exercised, and the deep need, the prime imperative, was satisfied. Even while she sat there compiling and
collating databases, the cells went about their essential
business, dividing and multiplying.

The he-dog thrust a cold nose into her hand. She rubbed
his ears absently. Inefficient, like talking to him, but
pleasurable in its way. Like watching Karl fan Reenan
sleep.

What she felt, she realized not entirely with displeasure,
was similar to what she felt when she looked at Harad, her
sister's eldest son, or Signy, her own daughter. She had not
seen either of them in more than a T-year. Harad would
have begun his Soldier training. Signy had been in training
since birth. She, like her mother, was Cyborg.

The boy shivered in his sleep. Sigrid threw another
blanket over him. He had given her what she wanted. He
would be appalled if he knew what he had given it to. She
doubted that he would kill himself over it, or castrate himself, though his blocky little bint might be pleased to do the
honors. Bandari were cattle, with cattle absurdities about
breeding. It had not kept this one from doing his best to
cooperate. With help, she admitted, and a solid dose of
pheromones. But he was a willing victim.

She happened to be smiling, practicing a new kind of
facial control, when he woke. He could not see as well in
the dark as she, but he saw well enough. He smiled back
completely by instinct. She watched him remember, and
blaze up like a beacon in her night sight: a glorious blush,
and on top of it a wide white grin. He said something in
Bandarit, then in Americ: "Good morning, madam."

"Not for a good while yet," Sigrid said.

His face fell a bit, but not enough to matter. "It's an old
line. A custom of sorts. The lady usually says, 'You're
welcome, sir.'"

"Interesting," said Sigrid.

"Well? Am I?"

Presumptuous. She picked him up bodily and kissed him till he wheezed, and went to cook breakfast.

He sat where she had dropped him, looking poleaxed. She tossed a waterskin at him. "Fill it," she said.

He obeyed less promptly than a Soldier should. For a Bandari in his condition it was quick.

He ate almost as much as she did. That muscle mass took a great deal of fuel. She was taking nourishment now for two. She stoked herself rapidly and thoroughly. Later she would see what she could obtain in the camp. There was a huge concentration of disposable income here, as such things were measured on the steppe. Several markets had established themselves around the army's fringes, to take advantage of it. None of them had been open when she reconnoitered, but by now people should be awake to man the stalls.

As fast as she ate, she was done before he was. Well enough. He did not need to be reminded that, by cattle standards, she ate enough for a platoon. She could of course go without for considerably longer than an unaugmented human, and operate at reasonable efficiency until she dropped, by deliberately reducing her metabolism to a lower level — even hibernating.

As he finished eating, he began to sigh and fidget and patently work himself up to something. She spared him the effort. "You have duty."

He blushed again. "Actually, I never reported."

Her facial control was slipping admirably. He flinched at her expression. "You — never — reported?"

"I wanted to see you first."

Clearly he thought that excused him. If he had been a Soldier she would have knocked him flat for his stupidity, and whipped him for his lack of discipline. She fixed him with her coldest eye. "You had better go."

He wilted dramatically. She was to soften, no doubt, and forgive him his sins. She turned her back on him, busying herself with the cookfire.

He wavered for a long while, sighing and shuffling his feet. She did not turn. "I'll come back," he said.

She did not respond to that, either.

"Maybe I won't!" he cried behind her. "Maybe I'll go out on scout for days on end. Maybe when I come back I'll be too proud to come crawling into your blankets. Maybe I don't care if you ever look at me again!"

Good, she thought. She straightened, still without turning. There was the filly's hoof to see to. And then, again, the larger camp.

When she looked again, Karl was gone. Her ears, tuned to his footfalls, heard him far away, running with that long light stride, not a Soldier's lope but akin to it in speed and ground-covering efficiency.

She allowed herself a slow drawing of breath. Better he leave angry. She was done with him. There was no graceful way to explain that, and none that would not betray the truth. This way he would go back to his Shulamit. She would make him pay, Sigrid knew, but she would also make sure he stayed.

There was, of course, no surety in the human equation. But Sigrid chose to give the variable a definite value, for the moment. She filed it all under *data, incalculable,* and left it there until she needed it, where in a male Cyborg it would have been erased. She kept one memory for herself, to examine when she had leisure: a moment just after nightfall, a turn of brass-blond head, a sudden flash of smile.

The camp was awake as she had expected, torchlit and humming. She haggled for a basket of flat steppe bread and a wheel of cheese, and exchanged a bone-handled knife from Katlinsvale for a clubfooted kid. She had the Mongol dispatch, gut and skin the kid on the spot, and got a sack of Bandari sweets for the hide. Prices were high, she supposed. So was the energy in the baklava. She shouldered her pack full of bread and cheese and meat, and worked her way through the honey-nut-dripping pastries as she walked.

The effect was of course calculated. People were less wary of a lone rangy woman with sticky fingers and a mouthful of sweetness than of a lone rangy woman with her hand on her swordhilt. She did not carry her rifle here.

It was buried in a cache near the chain of springs, where the she-dog stood guard over the horses.

The he-dog trotted at her heel. He seemed to have decided she was his charge, not the mares. Since she had not ordered him to stay behind, she could hardly shoot him for disobedience. He conducted himself sensibly, ignored the dogs that challenged him, and growled at men who approached too close. Some of them had larceny in mind. The dog's warning saved them some considerable inconvenience, such as the loss of a hand.

She squatted by a yurt to consume the last of her baklava. It stood on a rise not far from the center of the camp, part of it and yet subtly separate. The design branded on it was a repeated pattern of leaping antelope and crossed thunderbolts. From beside it she could see a fair spread of camp and oasis, including the largest market and the densest concentration of farmers' huts.

The dog kept her company by gnawing on a bone, raising his head occasionally to warn off intruders. He was just far enough out of the way to keep from being kicked or stepped on.

"Nice dog."

Sigrid licked her fingers as carefully as her sister Sieglinde's cat, and with much the same air of self-absorption. It gave her time to study the man without giving away too much of her intention. She needed the time, and the feint.

This was a Sauron. Not a Soldier, no. He did not have the training. He stood too loose, his face too easy, too transparently readable. But that face was more nearly pure Sauron than most in the Citadel, short of the Cyborg bloodlines. Most Soldiers these days were only half of the Race. The other half was native, constantly reinforced with full- and three-quarter-bred Soldiers, constantly diluted with fresh tribute maidens.

There was native blood in him, a little. Russki and Mongol, she judged. Given time enough, she could name the tribes. The rest . . .

Three-quarters at least. Judging from his clothing and

the badge on his hat, he called himself Bandari of the Springbok clan. Fan Reenan, like Karl. If he was fan Reenan, then his mother had not been telling the truth about his father. And if his mother was Bandari by blood, then Sigrid had lost any claim to Breedmaster's training.

He was down on one knee, introducing himself to the dog. The dog was amenable. It smelled the Soldier in him as keenly as Sigrid did. "Does he have a name?" the man asked.

"No," said Sigrid.

He shrugged and smiled easily as all these people did. It was disconcerting to see those muscles in such free use, and to know from precisely which bloodlines they came. The conclusion was inescapable.

"Barak," said Sigrid, "bar Heber fan Reenan." And every part of it a lie but the first.

"At your service," he said.

He expected a return of the courtesy. "Sigrid," she said, and added on impulse that she would analyze later, "Erda's daughter."

"Sigrid bat Erda, we would say." Barak dipped his head in greeting and salute. "You came in with our runaways, I hear."

So he would have, with the ears he had. Sigrid nodded, taking care not to do it too tightly. Loose, loose; easy; slack. Like cattle. These of all eyes would see how she differed, this of all minds, however untrained, would record the data and come eventually to the right conclusion. He was already aware of her as a Soldier would be: twitch of the nostrils, shift of the body toward her and then away. Scenting that she was female, and ripe. Perceiving that someone else had been there before him.

She damped her signals, but gradually, or he would sense that too, and be suspicious.

A pity, rather, that she was carrying the Frystaater's son. She would have been glad to preserve something of this line. It was dangerous, but primarily because it was wild Sauron, untrained and uncontrolled. Brought into the Citadel and bred back to the parent stock, it would be a useful contribution to the Race.

Who knew? She might have the chance. He massed this army, he and his mother and their band of lunatics and visionaries, to storm the Citadel. When the Citadel failed to fall, he would have to be disposed of. She would be pleased to attend to that.

As far as he could know, she simply nodded and half-smiled. "They're well, those two?" she asked. "Hides still intact?"

"Mostly." Barak scratched the dog's ribs. The dog rolled over and wriggled, grinning like the idiot Sigrid had never taken him for. "You have horses to trade, I'm told."

"No."

She had surprised him. No Soldier would betray it so openly, with widened eyes and stiffened back. "You do have horses," he said, half a question, half not.

"Not to sell."

"We need remounts. The more the better."

"Not mine." She paused. "Unless you think you might try a little appropriating of stock for the army's use? If so," she said, "mine aren't suitable."

"Mares," he said, "I'm told. All in foal?"

"The elder two."

"You'd be wanting to get to a valley, then."

She smiled internally at that. Her mares needed no valley to foal safely. "I was going," she said, "toward Shangri-La. Until I met your runaways."

"And they convinced you to join the war?"

"They made me curious to see what this war was."

"If you aren't going to join us, you'd better hurry with your horses. It won't be easy to get into the valley once we surround the Citadel."

"You're going to prevent the women from going through? Keep the mares from foaling?"

"Of course not," he said, as if she had proposed something abominable.

"That's foolish," she said. "An army could get in disguised as pregnant women, and neatly outflank you."

He shouted with laughter, so sudden that she nearly lost control and went for her weapons. "*Yeweh!* What a sight that would be! Wouldn't work, though," he said. "We'd start to suspect something after we saw a couple of hundred big bony ladies with rock-solid bellies. Unless they sent out their women," he mused, "but those are tribeswomen. Tribute stock. Captives."

"Few of them are adequately trained to fight," Sigrid said.

"You seem to know about it," he said. "From up around Lermontovgrad, are you?"

"It's obvious to you?"

He shrugged. "You've got a bit of the accent. Not much, true. What's a valley woman doing bringing in steppe ponies? Toughening up the local breed?"

She would not be trapped into making more of the accent he fancied she had. She had, it was true, undertaken to smooth out her flat Soldier vowels. That the result struck him as Valley Russki was interesting, and could be useful. "I have an interest in horsebreeding," she said, "and a . . . connection with a tribe who breed unusually fine stock."

He could not fail to catch the hesitation. "I hear you had a little trouble getting here."

"My mares are a tempting prize."

"So is a lone rider on the steppe."

"Your runaways were helpful," said Sigrid.

"You wouldn't sell your mares for anything, then."

Tenacious. That was Bandari. Soldier, too, but Soldiers were not merchants. "My mares are meant for a gift," she said.

"To your man?"

She felt her lips stretch in what was not a smile. "To my father."

"You're a runaway, too."

He seemed much amused. She was glad he could be, and that he wasted so much of his augmented senses on easy assumptions. "No, he didn't want me to go. He ordered me to stay. I disobeyed."

In the Citadel it would have been a bitter confession, and prelude to discipline. Here it gained her a grin and a salute. "Something you had to do, yes? Well then, we won't try to buy your gift horses. I can't speak for the nomads, mind. Some of them might decide to try a little appropriation of good breeding stock, to keep their hand in."

"They may try," said Sigrid.

"No bloodshed here," he said, suddenly stern.

"May I knock heads together? If necessary?"

The corner of his mouth twitched. "Only if absolutely necessary."

"I'll bear that in mind," said Sigrid.

They were making myths here. The spectacle was impressive, the effect calculated to a minute degree, with the geyser timed to erupt at the crucial moment. Sigrid suspected that it had been like this on *Fomoria* — with all due apology to the noble dead, that she compared them with cattle — when Galen Diettinger renamed the ship *Dol Guldur* and took the device of the Lidless Eye, and wielded Old Terran archetypes against the populations of Haven. Humans, and that included humans who carried the modified genes of Old Sauron, needed their myths.

Sigrid was not immune to it. The blood-red light. The stink and the smoke, like an image of the Christers' Hell. The massed tribes. The Seven on a rise above them, and their chief in front of them all in pure and shining white. Sigrid tuned out the words the woman cried in her strong age-thinned voice. She watched the face instead. Barak stood beside and behind his mother, but even without his presence Sigrid would have known who the old woman was. Chaya daughter of Badri and the Soldier Dagor, sister of Juchi the Accursed, sister and aunt both of the woman who stood among the Seven, that one Soldier bred as Barak was: Aisha, daughter and sister of Juchi.

Such complications. So typical of Soldier bloodlines, so absurdly abhorred by the cattle. If cattle had had any sense at all when it came to breeding solid stock, Juchi's curse would have been no curse, and this army would not have gathered.

No, Sigrid thought. The fault ultimately lay with the Breedmaster who exposed Juchi and his sister. Juchi was dead, and well disposed of. Chaya lived to carry on the feud. There was a paradox to confuse one's database. Soldier blood raised by the Soldiers' implacable enemies, the untamable and intractable Bandari.

Sigrid, chance and good genes willing, would balance that with a paradox of her own. She found Karl fan Reenan in the crowd, unmistakable even to cattle senses with his bright hair and dark face, and noted that Shulamit was there, but not beside him. He was not aware of her, not consciously. He was fixed on the Judge's spectacle, concentrating on her speech. She ended it with a grand flourish and a flash of blade in flesh, and the sudden scarlet stream of blood.

Sigrid's whole self focused on that single point. Chaya was using control, however weak, however incomplete. The blood did not clot as soon as it flowed. It kept on, dripping in long slow gleaming drops to the earth beneath her feet.

Just so it had been in a vale leagues away, across a wall of dead: just so, when Katlin's folk took Sigrid into their tribe and sisterhood. Just so; and just so Sigrid had responded to it — but then she had been a part of it. Now she was alien, and outsider, and enemy. She looked at this shedding of blood in a cause that these people reckoned great, and saw only waste.

Priceless, priceless waste. In that blood was encoded more genetic data than any Breedmaster on Haven had ever had access to. Sigrid was trembling, she discovered, as she never did, even with lust. This went beyond mere physical passion. It was data. Knowledge. Intelligence.

She moved through the press of bodies toward the front and the intoxication of blood. The rest of the Seven took oath one by one. She took little specific notice. She knew which of them was Soldier bred, and which not. It was written in their faces.

The *khans* and the minor leaders began to swear. There was surprisingly little jockeying for position. She recorded every face, with the name its owner attached to it and the languages in which he swore. Leaders took oath for their people, she noted. Hammer-of-God, the big Edenite, was explicit about it, and no more reverent than he had to be.

Then one of the Mongol *khans*, the one with the most evident power and position, Gasim, demanded that the "strangers" swear. It was Karl fan Reenan he meant, or the boy chose to think he did, coming forward with the air of a man who does another man a favor. It played well. He could have declared loudly that he was not a stranger, he was Bandari of the Pale. Sigrid doubted he refrained out of prudence. He was glad to take the oath, proud to spill his blood on earth that by now was muddy and iron-reeking. He was not shy, either, to show off his command of languages, of which he had a fair sampling.

Boy-strut, every bit of it. Sigrid would have smacked him if he had been a Soldier under her command.

Shulamit came up after him, sulking enough for a dozen, and all but spat her oath. "I'll keep faith with you. I'll kill Saurons in the name of that faith, and go on killing them till every last one of them is dead. Or," she said, "I'll die trying."

The Mongol *khan* could not be seen to approve. She was a woman, after all. But his narrow eyes gleamed before they left her to rove the crowd. Sigrid knew before they fastened on her, what he would say.

"That one!"

Stupid, she upbraided herself. Standing in front where she could not possibly be missed. Towering over surrounding people, most of whom were squat, black-haired, sallow-faced Mongols. All but begging the *khan* to single her out.

Bloodlust was a weakness in any soldier. Lust for the data encoded in blood was damned near fatal.

Instinct would have damped every reaction, smoothed every emotion from her face. But not here. She took her cues from the eyes that stared at her. Arrogant — not too much. Not enough to telegraph *Soldier*. Contemptuous? Yes. She could afford that. But again, not too much. Keen

as a Soldier in battle, for this was battle, of the most subtle
and deadly kind, she strode to face the rebels' leader.

Barak, allegedly bar Heber, was more truly Sauron by
blood. This woman was more truly a Soldier. Age, discipline, the experience of a Judge in the Pale — they honed
a mind and a body.

They also honed it, ultimately, to nothing. Sigrid spoke
words that seemed suitable, in the softened Americ she had
been using and then in the Russki of Lermontovgrad, for
Barak whose eyes were alert and whose ears were listening
for just that. She offered no other languages. It was otiose
to speak various dialects of steppe Turkic, and the related
Mongol tongue, or to betray that she was picking up Bandarit and their holy *Ivrit*. She certainly was not going to
offer them her command of Old Terran Anglish, Old
Latin, or any of several computer languages.

And as she spoke, she studied the woman in front of her.
Chaya's bleeding was long since stopped, the blood clotted
as Soldier blood should. Sigrid did not need the fresh blood
to gauge the woman, inside or out. One close, concentrated
look was enough.

The Judge was dying. It would not be a quick death, but
as deaths went it was reasonably easy. Chaya was — what?
Sixty T-years? Seventy? That was old for a Soldier, between
accumulating poisons and late-emerging recessives. A Soldier who lived that long was prey to certain particular
forms of decay, most of them mental and none curable.

The dementia was well begun, from the look of it. And
once it had begun, its progress could be rapid. The army
could lose its primary leader before it even reached the
Citadel, or find itself under the command of a madwoman.
This oath might even be part of it, exquisite calculation or
no. Delusions were a common effect of the syndrome:
delusions, visionary episodes, hallucinations.

All of it clouded her eyes as she looked into Sigrid's.
Her senses were blunted, her analytic faculties dulled or
nonexistent, or she would have known at once, without
hesitation, what faced her on that bloody height.

She only knew that Sigrid had taken oath, and that there

BLOOD FEUDS: *A Novel of War World*　　465

had been no kneeling or bowing or homage in it. In the manner of despots or of dignitaries with delusions, she wanted something of that, and waited for it. Sigrid gave it to her. A nod was small enough price to pay. She shed blood with her own knife, bound the wound up rapidly to conceal the speed with which, even under control, it clotted. Then at last she was free to withdraw, taking her analysis and her conclusions with her.

Shulamit hadn't intended to get stuck beside Karl after her oathtaking, but when she worked her way back into the crowd, there he was, broad as a brick wall and twice as ugly. At least he didn't try to say anything. He was too busy goggling at the next victim.

*Her.*

Shulamit stiffened in every muscle. She felt the hackles go up, knew the tickle of the growl in her throat. "Bitch. Fucking bitch."

*"Shhhh!"* someone hushed her.

She hunched her shoulders and balled her fists. She was not, in spite of appearances, blind mad. She never quite got that far. Her eyes were perfectly clear, and her mind was clicking rapidly along, taking note of every twitch of Karl bloody ballbrain fan Reenan's face, and every move it reflected, as the white-eyed bitch separated herself from the crowd and stood in front of Chaya.

They were almost exactly the same size. And, as gray as the old woman was and as blonde as the young one happened to be, they had damned near the same coloring, too. And the same kind of face, long and narrow, with a nose like an axeblade. And the same kind of figure, no curves to speak of, and the same way of carrying it, and the same bloody bedroom voice. They could have been kin. They could have been sisters.

Truth had a taste, Shulamit discovered: the slow-breaking kind, like valley brandy. First the shock, sharp and fiery. Then the spreading, paradoxical sweetness. Then the heat flowing from the stomach outward, and the fumes rising to the brain, making it reel with certainty.

The bitch was a Sauron.

Once Shulamit said it, even to herself, it felt real. It felt right. It was all there. The way she looked. The way she moved. The way she walked instead of rode, and covered ground without ever seeming to tire. The way she talked — she was talking nice Valley Americ now, with a slight Russki accent, but that wasn't the accent Shulamit had heard the first time she spoke. That accent had been much flatter and harder, especially in the vowels. Sauron accent. And if that wasn't enough, Shulamit went back to the one that clinched the rest, that and the resemblance to Juchi's sister. The way she had picked up Karl as if he weighed no more than a baby, and wrapped him around her finger, and around most of the rest of her as well. That was Sauron strength. It could be nothing else.

No wonder she had a Sauron rifle. She was a Sauron.

Shulamit watched her take the oath in the blood-red light. Something, the angle of the light, the way she bent her head, turned her face for a moment into a skull, a death's head over the blood of the swearing. Shulamit shuddered so hard she almost fell. Why not? Why shouldn't it be a Cyborg, too?

Absurd, of course. There were no death's head females. But if the Universe was going to hit them with a traitor in their midst, it would be just like the luck to give them the worst kind of all, the ultimate traitor, a super-Sauron.

Shulamit wasn't thinking straight, or she would have watched her mouth. She said what she thought when the bitch wrapped up her cut — not to keep it from bleeding, of course, but to keep people from seeing how fast it stopped bleeding. And of course Shulamit had to blurt it out so Karl could hear. He wouldn't see what the bitch was if she told him herself, with diagrams. Which he promptly demonstrated. It damned near caused a scene. Got them dragged apart, and got Shulamit thumped for using her fists where she damned well ought to.

Just as well. Karl wasn't the one who had to know. Everybody else was busy. Including the Sauron, who wouldn't be leaving in any hurry, Shulamit didn't think. If Shulamit were a spy, she wouldn't go till she had all the information she could get hold of, from anyone likely to have any. That would take a while, even for a Sauron.

Shulamit watched her as she faded back into the crowd. Even when the geyser went up with a roar and a hiss like a million angry snakes — that would be a prime chance to slip away, but the Sauron stayed. She was watching Chaya. She stood absolutely still through the Judge's collapse, screams and uproar and all. Her face was wiped of expression, all its lines gone clean as a skull's. Her eyes were pale and deadly cold.

"I'll get you," Shulamit vowed, pressing her lips to the still-seeping cut in her arm. The blood was hot and iron-sweet. "I'll get you if it's the last thing I do."

# ● CHAPTER TWENTY

Carcharoth felt harassed. Harassment was the price a Battlemaster paid for his job, or so the saying went, but at the moment Carcharoth's account was overdrawn. It wasn't enough that all the dirty, greasy nomads on Haven were bearing down on the Citadel, armed with whatever they could lay their hands on.

No, that wasn't enough.

It wasn't enough that the Bandari were behind the *Volkerwanderung*, which meant the steppe cattle would be able to get their hands on more and better weapons than they could have otherwise.

No, that wasn't enough.

It wasn't even enough that Breedmaster Titus' Cyborg daughter might have gone feral and joined the stinking nomads. Sigrid — Carcharoth was alone, so he granted himself the luxury of a scowl. Her genes were too good to cull, too near the edge of stability to be safe. After this mess was over, Carcharoth would have to think long and hard on what to do about her.

But no, even the problem of Sigrid wasn't enough to fill his plate of troubles.

Sitting on that plate, gently steaming like a proper entree — or a pile of shit — was fresh news of rebellion in the west end of the Shangri-La Valley. Swarming nomads on the plains were one thing. Revolt *inside* the valley was something else again. Literally and figuratively, that hit the Soldiers where they lived. The TAC had predicted scattered rebellion there — in two to five T-years, no sooner.

The Threat Analysis Computer hadn't given a single solitary hint of anything wrong till the heliograph brought word to the Citadel that the garrison at Hell's A'-Comin' was under attack. Since then it had been soaking up the —

very scarce — data and saying very little. It wasn't any scattered rebellion, either; big chunks of the New Soviet Men and the Sons of Liberty, the two largest vassal nations in the western valley, had risen, with more joining them all the time. A hundred and fifty thousand fighting men — cattle, but trained and armed. Garrisons had been overrun, river traffic on the Xanadu cut back to nothing.

So Carcharoth felt harassed. When the ceiling speaker said, "Battlemaster Carcharoth to tribute reception area, Battlemaster Carcharoth to tribute reception area. Urgent," he had to suppress a most un-Cyborglike reaction to tell *it* where to go.

He hurried to the tribute reception area, taking a few seconds along the way to imagine the new asshole he'd ream for the Soldier who'd unnecessarily called him away from serious business. When he found Sharku there, he had to let the fantasy die: the Chief Assault Leader was as capable a field-grade officer as the Citadel had. With him were his comrades in the tribute party, the usual tribute maidens doing their usual gaping at being inside a structure more solid than a yurt, and a man he did not know but tentatively identified as a Soldier out of uniform.

The Soldiers did not usually go in for spit and polish among themselves. Sharku nodded to Carcharoth and said, "I know you have problems of your own, Battlemaster, but — "

"Son, you don't begin to," Carcharoth interrupted. "This had better be interesting, because I'm busy enough to wish I were triplets."

"I'll keep it short for now, then," Sharku said. "You can have me amplify later, at your leisure."

"Leisure?" Carcharoth said. "Leisure is for when you're dead, if the worms give you any. What's up?"

"Big nomad movement — "

"I already know about that," the Battlemaster said. "It showed up on the TAC. Details will be helpful, but not vital. Anything else?" Fully prepared for the answer to be no, he began to turn away. So much to do, so little time to do it in. . . .

But Sharku answered, "Yes, Battlemaster." Carcharoth had to turn back. Nodding to the male stranger, Sharku said, "Battlemaster, this is Dagor, Juchi's son. He seeks to join forces with the Citadel, and offers intelligence data as his price of entry."

It was a truism that Cyborgs could not be taken by surprise. Like any truism, it had its holes: Carcharoth's immediate predecessor as Battlemaster, for instance, had no doubt been surprised by the knife that cut his throat. But Cyborgs made a point of never showing surprise. "Is he?" Carcharoth said mildly. He addressed Dagor: "Are you?" Seeing incomprehension in the other's eyes and body language, he switched to Turkic and asked, "What languages have you?"

"This one we speak now, Russki, Bandarit, a little of the Mongols' speech, a few words of Eden Valley Americ," Dagor answered promptly and apparently willingly. "I cannot follow your dialect of Americ. I am sorry."

"No matter." Carcharoth studied the stranger with lively curiosity. Though no Breedmaster, he carried in his head enough data to make what he thought of as a battlefield evaluation of a man's genetic potential: rough, but serviceable until somebody flanged up something better.

Without warning, he dropped a hand to his knife. The speed with which Dagor reached for his own weapon put him somewhere near the middle of the first quartile for Soldier's reflexes. The speed with which he disengaged when he saw Carcharoth hadn't drawn said he wasn't stupid.

"Well!" Carcharoth said. His own Turkic was better than fluent; whatever he did, he did well. "I'm sure we'll have a great many questions to ask of you, Dagor son of Juchi." *The Breedmaster who exposed your father was not a fool. He was an imbecile.*

"Shall I take him to the Interrogation Room?" asked one of the officers with Sharku: Snaga. Carcharoth had the name after a millisecond's flip through the database between his ears. The fellow quivered with barely concealed eagerness; the Battlemaster wondered how Dagor had managed to yank his chain so hard.

"No, not unless we have to. Let's try to keep him in one piece a little longer, shall we?" Carcharoth replied in Americ. Snaga wilted, both at the answer and at his tone. *Too bad for you, Snaga*, the Battlemaster thought. He dropped back into Turkic: "Why do you wish to join the Soldiers, Dagor? This is — shall we say? — an uncommon desire among the folk of the steppes."

"Few on the steppes have my breeding," Dagor returned, to which Carcharoth had to nod. The young Sauron (Carcharoth thought of him so, for, whatever his breeding, he was no trained Soldier and might never be one) went on, "Besides, I would avenge myself against those on the steppes who would not accept me as one of theirs. I have spoken of this somewhat to Sharku here." He fixed Carcharoth with a measuring stare. "My hope was that those who dwelt here might be less inclined to shy at shadows."

Untrained or not, Carcharoth thought, the fellow *acted* like a Soldier. He turned to Sharku, staying in Turkic so that Dagor could understand: "Assign him a billet among the unpartnered Soldiers during the debriefing process. Let them know there is to be no hazing of any sort. If he is damaged, those responsible will suffer tenfold. If no individual can be proved responsible, all in the barracks will suffer tenfold. Make that clear, Chief Assault Leader — *very* clear."

"Aye, Battlemaster," Sharku said. He hesitated, then added, "Forgive me, Battlemaster, but interrogating him strikes me as urgent."

"Under normal circumstances, I would agree with you," Carcharoth said. "Circumstances, however, are anything but normal." In a few clipped words, he explained about the rising in the west end of the valley, and about the TAC's blindness to it. A very rare occurrence, although not completely unknown.

Sharku's brows came together as he thought hard. "Battlemaster, the timing of these two events strikes me as something other than coincidental. Some other factor has intervened to increase the severity of the unrest and escalate it to open revolt earlier than predicted."

"A certain amount of paranoia is an asset to an intelligence officer, but only a certain amount," Carcharoth said, shaking his head. "Were there a route from the plains — or would it be the Pale? — into the valley, I might take your hypothesis more seriously. Were there such a route, however, we would have seen painful evidence of it long before this — and it would have become known to the Threat Analysis Computer. The TAC has been exhaustively briefed concerning the uprising, and finds no such connection."

"Where the Pale is concerned, I take nothing on trust," Sharku said stubbornly.

"I take the facts of this world on trust," Carcharoth said in a voice that should have brooked no argument. "Among those facts, let me note a couple: first, that the Citadel is unquestionably proof against any assault the nomads of the steppe can muster, and second, that control of the Shangri-La Valley is not only what gives us control over the bulk of Haven but also what allows us to survive as a technological civilization. Without the foodstuffs we realize from the valley, we would have to do our own farming, and low-tech farming is so labor intensive that it would leave us no time for anything else."

Sharku glared. Carcharoth could not blame him; being lectured as if he were in an officer training seminar had to sting. But the Chief Assault Leader had spirit. He shot back, "Maybe the TAC didn't foresee this rising because it knows less about how Haven is made than the Bandari do."

"No." Carcharoth dismissed that idea out of hand, and when a Cyborg dismissed an idea, it was gone for good. "If we start distrusting the Threat Analysis Computer, what shall we trust? Without it, we might well have failed to survive here."

The Chief Assault Leader snapped to attention. Among the Soldiers, that was almost a slap in the face. The Battlemaster adjusted his blood chemistry and the circulation in his brain away from anger. Like a military machine, Sharku droned, "Request permission to instruct the TAC to hypothesize overland connection between the Pale and the valley, and to analyze the rebellion taking this hypothesis into account."

"Permission denied." Carcharoth went icily formal himself, exchanging insult for polite insult. "It is the Battlemaster's judgment that the uprising of the agricultural populace within the Shangri-La Valley is of higher priority than any movement of steppe peoples, and that the resources of the Citadel must be committed to suppressing this uprising and preventing its spread. The Battlemaster shall present this recommendation for action by the First Council. The Chief Assault Leader of course retains the privilege of offering to the Council his alternative strategic plan."

Sharku held his brace as if carved from stone. Snaga smirked; even an ordinary Soldier might have missed it, but Carcharoth didn't. Dagor just stood wide-eyed and watched the argument, understanding that it was one but not what it was about. The tribute maidens also stared, but Carcharoth hardly bothered to notice them.

He did notice the other two Soldiers — Mumak and Ufthak, their names were, he recalled from his data store — exchanging glances. He didn't care for that; if they doubted his judgment, he had to wonder whether he'd been hasty. He reviewed the argument in his own mind. No, it was incontrovertible. Let Sharku imagine all the mountain routes he wanted — if they really existed, the TAC would have known about them long ago. Impossible to hide the subtle evidence that such communication existed, and the TAC could deduce a whole map from a single irrelevant fact. Since the TAC didn't know about it, the valley revolt and the plains uprising were unconnected. Between them, as he'd said, the valley came first.

"Well, of course I'm not sure," Hammer-of-God said mildly, ignoring the *khan's* glare.

They were sitting in the commander's tent, with a big map pinned to the wall behind him — an object of awe even to the illiterate majority — and eating *kefir*, honey-colored sweetened milk-curd, out of bowls.

"But," he added, "I don't *think* Quilland Base will set out to attack us."

He turned and tapped a finger on the map. The Great Northern Steppe wrapped around the Atlas mountains, west and north and east, like a vast elongated C on its side, five thousand kilometers around. Cliff Lion Springs was at the top of the western arm, where the mountains turned south to the Pale. Nearby — fairly nearby, five hundred kilometers — was Quilland Base: westernmost Sauron outpost since the fall of Angband, and commanding a valley of some size in the outer Atlas foothills.

"Quilland Base has its own worries," he said.

"How do you know?"

"How do I know, O Ilderim *Khan* of the Dongala Khel?" Hammer-of-God laid a finger along his nose. "A little lizard whispered in my ear that a brigade of haBandari rode north out of the Pale not five cycles ago, and harries the western outworks of Quilland Base's lands," he said. "They have their own problems."

"By Shaitan!"

"Istagfarullah!"

Faces high-cheeked and flat, or lean and hairy under pugaree turbans, broke into grins; men whose fathers and grandfathers had been knifing and ambushing each other since time out of mind slapped backs and slurped strong green eggbush tea from the same samovar. All as if never a sheep had gone astray, a horse been lifted, or a girl been snatched from a waterhole.

Ilderim *Khan* was of the bearded variety, with a strong hook nose; there was gray in the beard, and a deep furrowed scar plowed across the empty eye socket above his left cheekbone. He tugged at his beard now, and blinked the single eye at the map. Then he drew the long *chora* tucked through the sash that held his grimy green coat closed, and used it to point.

"Those Saurons are infidel pigs with hair on their livers," he said, "but they are no fools, by Allah and the spirits! If the Bandari riders harry them *here*" — the point of the elongated butcher knife moved west — "what of the smaller outposts here, here, here, east along the foothills?" He flicked the weapon east. A chain of outstations reached back toward Dyer Base and then the Citadel.

"None of them is of any size," Hammer-of-God said. "Let the little dogs yap."

There was a stir of uncertainty. "Not so little that we can have their teeth in our arses as we ride east," Ilderim said stubbornly.

Silence fell, until Aisha leaned forward. Her hands were clenched white-knuckled on her knees — it was still an ordeal for her to speak in public like this — as she said: "Ilderim *Khan* is wise." The man stroked his beard and nodded. "As is Hammer-of-God. Though these small forts have few Sauron warriors — "

"Couple of squads each," Hammer said helpfully. Aisha nodded thanks.

" — still, they control . . . not the steppe, they are too few . . . but they control the hearts of many. Who has dared to attack them? Now and then a lone Sauron is killed, but when has one of their posts been overrun — save by Juchi? If we pass by and let them harry us, many will say we are an army that flees, not one that attacks."

This time the Seven as well as the chiefs nodded slowly. Aisha went on: "This one here, this is Shamrabad, isn't it?"

Hammer nodded. Juchi's daughter continued: "My father and I passed through there, many years ago, but I remember it well. A village of farmers brought there long ago from the Saratov Valley near the Base, with an outpost they use to collect their tribute — occupied much of the summer." Haven summers were nearly one and a half T-years long. "The first harvest is in, and the first shearing from the sheep, and the lambs, and the wild muskylope herds" — there was a vast seasonal migration from the Atlas foothills to the uninhabited swamps of the far north — "so they will be there once more."

Everyone was looking at Aisha now. She flushed darkly, but plowed on: "How many are we?"

Tameetha bat Irene leaned forward. She had been stropping a knife on a leather strap wound round the knuckles of her left hand; now she murmured in the Edenite general's ear. Hammer nodded.

"In fighting men? Five thousand sabers," he said. "Influx's been dropping off the last few days."

"But those are the best, the wildest, the strongest," said Ilderim *Khan*.

Aisha nodded. "And they must have a victory — so that all others will be inspired to join us. Hammer-of-God, let us plan together."

Chichek ran her warm, smooth hand down Sharku's chest and belly toward his groin. "What troubles you, my love?" she murmured in Turkic. They'd made love twice when at last he returned to his quarters, but he was having trouble rising for a third round. For a Soldier, that was close enough to impotence for government work.

Soldiers were disciplined. Soldiers did not question orders; they obeyed. Soldiers most assuredly did not complain. In the privacy of his own cubicle, in the privacy of his own bed, in the arms of the woman he'd longed for and loved, discipline dissolved. Sharku slammed a fist into the mattress, hard enough to make him and Chichek bounce on the springs.

"The Battlemaster is blinder than the accursed Juchi who set this catastrophe in train!" His voice was a shouted whisper, as if he wanted to scream his frustration to the sky but at the same time dared not speak it aloud.

"He is a Cyborg," Chichek said doubtfully. To the women of the Citadel, even more than to the ordinary Soldiers, Cyborgs were creatures of marvelous, maybe even supernatural, powers. Tribute maidens from the nomad peoples learned that awe even out on the steppes: in some Turkic dialects, the word for Cyborg was *afrit* — demon.

"He is an idiot," Sharku retorted. "Out on the plains, the tribes are moving, and the Bandari have a hand in it. Can it be coincidence that rebellion breaks out at the same time in the valley — and in the part of the valley nearest the Pale? But the Threat Analysis Computer says there is no connection over the mountains, so the events cannot be connected. The TAC is an idiot, too!"

"It is a computer. How can it be wrong, sun of my life?" To Chichek, the TAC was definitely supernatural, as much an oracle as the ones at which shamans or priestesses prophesied in exchange for livestock or grain or silver.

Sharku knew better. "The stinking thing is only a machine. It did not predict the rising in the valley, so there *must* be something it doesn't know. Maybe it is wearing out." Even saying those words sent dread running through him. The TAC had come from Old Sauron aboard the *Dol Guldur*. Repairing it was as far beyond the abilities of the Soldiers on Haven as rebuilding the ship that had brought them here three centuries ago. Sharku continued, "Or maybe it just has bad data. If I told you dirt made good soup and you didn't know any better, you might cook up a batch, but could you eat it afterwards?"

His woman smiled. "No. That would be something our son was more likely to try."

"So it would." Sharku smiled, too; he couldn't help himself. Gimilzor had shot up like a fireweed plant while he was gone. The boy lay asleep in the cubicle's other bedroom, having exhausted himself in hand-to-hand combat with his father. With the reaction time and strength he was already showing, he would be a Soldier to watch. Already Sharku would have bet on him in unarmed fighting against most men of the cattle tribes.

"He missed you," Chichek said. "I know it is the Soldiers' way to train the boys to be hard. It is the way of the folk I came from as well, and rightly; Haven is a hard world." She hesitated. "Promise you will say nothing to him if I tell you this."

"Wait." Just under her left breast, a little ways out from the nipple, Chichek had a spot that was exquisitely ticklish. Sharku found that spot. Chichek writhed and squealed and pulled away from him. He laughed. "There. Now you can say I tortured it out of you."

"Monstrous man," she said. In other contexts, he might have killed to avenge himself for those words. She spoke them with love. After another moment, she remembered what they'd been talking about. "He cried in his bed a few times after you set out. Never when I was there to see it, never so I heard it, but I found the pillow wet more than once when I came in to look at him after he fell asleep."

"He's a little boy," Sharku said. Let Gimilzor cry now, if he would. Soon enough, he would do what he had to, and do it dry-eyed. *I do what I must,* Sharku thought, *no matter how moronically the Battlemaster is acting.* His rage ripped free again. In the strangled shout he'd used before, he cried out, "They will not *listen* to me!"

"Did you not say that Carcharoth offered you the privilege of presenting your report to the Council along with his?" Chichek asked.

"He could hardly deny it to me, our usages being what they are," Sharku said. "But will the Council listen to the Cyborg Battlemaster or to a Chief Assault Leader who they think is seeing stobor under the bed? Carcharoth doesn't need the TAC to compute the answer to that one."

"What will you do, then?"

"Submit my bloody report, of course. What else can I do?" Sharku said bitterly. "And after it's rejected, I'll take my assault rifle and tramp across the Shangri-La Valley to deal with this rebellion, whoever turns out to be in back of it. Then I'll tramp back here and get to see you again for a while." He enfolded her in his arms. "That's the time that's worthwhile, flower of mine."

For all that he held her close, he still remained limp. She poked him in the ribs. "You wore yourself out on those girls fresh from the yurt," she complained, but her eyes were laughing at him.

"It's part of my duty," he answered seriously. "Except at the time, I don't particularly enjoy it."

"Ah, but what about at the time?" Chichek said. "And what about now?" Her hand closed around him, grew insistent. Under such ministration, he thought dizzily, a man of the cattle who had died the cycle before of old age would have risen. As for a Soldier — Chichek laughed again. "What about now?"

He rolled over onto her; she opened herself for him. His reply was quite without words, but satisfied them both. It also considerably relieved Sharku: a Soldier who had reason to doubt himself was hardly a Soldier. Chichek murmured something happy he didn't quite catch; she was already most of the way toward sleep.

Sharku started willing himself in that direction, too. Soldiers had a knack for it, and a corresponding knack for waking on the instant. Before he quite let go of his conscious mind, though, Sharku remembered how few on Haven, either cattle or Soldiers, died of old age.

*I am bored*, Trooper Shagrat admitted to himself. The wind keened about his ears, gritty with loess dust and very little moisture picked up from the snowfields on the Atlas Mountains that reared behind him. The Lidless Eye snapped and fluttered on the flagpole, a little tattered. Early summer, such as it was up here. Shamrabad had to be about the worst hole in the entire area administered from Quilland Base, and collecting the tribute brought here the safest, most routine duty on the roster. *Ugly little arsehole of a place*, he thought. The fact that it was second-cycle day — Byers' Sun up, Cat's Eye full, and three of the sister moons in the sky — only made it more bleak.

Nothing behind him but the crumbling mudbrick walls of the little fort — less a military post than a seasonal tribute-collection station, with a few windowless huts, some stables, and a packed-earth courtyard. Nothing ahead of him but the town itself, if it deserved the name. The hovels looked like heaps of the dry earth itself, with stone sheep-pens and straggling kitchen-gardens behind them. A goat cropped the sparse herbs on a flat roof. A tiny onion-domed church and an equally seedy mosque dominated the hamlet; it was too small even to support a teahouse or a tavern. Women and children were busy with their chores. Most of the men were out hunting, as the wild muskylope herds came down from the heights; the outskirts of the town were thick with bone-and-twig frames where strips of the meat hung to air-cure. He could see the cloud of dust and hear the drumming hooves where one herd moved out of a long dry valley and onto the rolling steppe, kilometers away. Fields were hard to tell apart from steppe, since the first crop was cut and carted. The *qanats* were easier to spot, lines of dirt mounds like giant drillbit holes marking the maintenance shafts, snaking south into the mountains.

More women lay or squatted on mats in a compound near the fort: tribute maidens, waiting to be sent back to Quilland along with the sacks of threshed *ryticale*, sacks of cheeses, herbs and hides and bales of wool. The grain and goods were stacked near them, with the milling herds of pack animals and the empty wagons. *I'm even bored with fucking*, Shagrat thought, which he wouldn't have believed possible for a young Soldier in his prime. He pulled up the collar of his greatcoat and settled the assault rifle cradled in his arms. He longed to be back at Quilland Base; to have someone to *talk* to. Drill and field maneuvers, competitions, some hunting, going into town to a tavern or a cockfight occasionally, or a stallion duel, or even watching a *buzkashi* game. *Anything*.

How the cattle here endured whole *lives* spent like this was beyond him; but then, who understood cattle?

Footsteps sounded behind him. "Gorthaur," he said without turning.

"Shagrat," his relief answered. The other Soldier stopped beside him, on the top of the fort's earthwork mound. The gate was below them, poles lashed together with rawhide that years of dry cold had turned as iron-hard as the native wood.

"Hear the report?" Gorthaur said, offering a vacuum flask.

It held almost-coffee, slightly spiked, more for taste than anything else; getting a Soldier drunk required truly heroic imbibing, which was something he regretted intensely right now.

"What, Senior Trooper Azog is letting us lowly Troopers know what's in dispatches?" he said.

They both glanced back; Azog was in the largest hut with a woman, and they spoke in almost subvocal whispers. With the background of the wind, it was safe enough. Azog was old, for a Soldier — fifty T-years — and would never be promoted past the lowest noncommissioned rank. Many of the green young Troopers under him would, which made him even more of a martinet.

"Raids on the western outposts," Gorthaur said.

Shagrat perked up. "Serious?" *Fighting*, he thought. If he had believed in any god, he might have given a prayer of thanks.

"HaBandari," Gorthaur said. "Lots of them."

"We'll be reassigned, if they've had casualties," Shagrat said; that *was* half a prayer.

"We've been told to redouble alertness," Gorthaur said ironically.

Shagrat gave a snarled almost-laugh. "*Here?*" They were so far east that the next Soldier outpost — a month's travel farther on — reported to Isengard Base, which was under direct Citadel authority.

"Look — there's the Bandari horde now," Gorthaur said; he was what passed for a humorist, among Soldiers.

Shagrat had seen the wagons long before; he had heard the squealing of their ungreased axles for the better part of an hour. Coming in from the outlying hamlets, of course. Farms lay scattered along the foothills for kilometers here, what with the fertile wind-borne soil and the — usually — reliable water the *qanats* gathered from glacier-fed springs. That and the Soldier presence made settlement possible. The Soldiers usually didn't interfere much in the internal disputes of cattle, since constant culling by warfare improved the genetic quality of tribute maidens. They did forbid raiding of the occasional useful area like this. That and the odd punitive expedition against nomad bandits who couldn't resist the temptation allowed peasants to exist here.

"Wonder what they're bringing," Shagrat said idly. His eyes went into telescopic mode. Four wagons, each loaded high with — barrels.

"Liquor, by the Lidless Eye." Gorthaur echoed his thought, licking his lips.

"Might be," Shagrat said. Barrels were seldom used for

anything but liquids, since wood was so rare and expensive on the steppe; they had to be painstakingly fitted together from small twisted brushwood. There were full skins among the loads too, bulging whole sheepskins of *something*.

The wagons were pulled by stocky draft-muskylope, the type bred for plowing, lower and thicker-bodied than the rangy wild animals. The drivers were women. He focused on the first, a middle-aged one with a square face. There were two more of the same type; the last one in line was younger and pretty enough, he thought indifferently. There were twoscore girls from the farms and herding tribes hereabouts in the pen below, though. Right now those barrels and skins were what held his attention.

"We'll have to inspect it," he said hopefully.

"Those are the standing orders," Gorthaur agreed.

"Finnegan's fig brandy," the wagoner said, bowing low.

Shagrat grunted; he could smell that. Some of it must have leaked, because the reek covered everything, almost hiding the scents of humans and animals. Even the stink from the gallows alongside. Human figures hung there, a few lucky ones by their necks, others by their ankles or their arms. One was still moving. The Soldier grunted again, as the wagoner leapt down and knocked the bung out of a barrel, filled a horn with the straw-colored liquid that ran out, and took a preliminary swallow herself.

"Hand it over," he said, now that he knew it hadn't been poisoned — his nose could detect most toxins anyway — and took the horn she gave him and drained it. His pale brows rose. "Not bad, for a change," he said, holding it out for a refill.

Gorthaur snatched it out of his hand and drank. "Some comrade you are," he gasped, wiping his mouth.

"Plunder and pussy, there's no friendship where they're concerned," Shagrat said.

They took other samples at random, making the woman drink first. It was *good* Finnegan's fig liquor, double-distilled, over a hundred and twenty proof, and sweet with hydromel and spices.

"Take it through," Shagrat said. His Adam's apple worked as he emptied the curled muskylope horn again a final time.

The woman bowed low again in the Russki fashion, the cap in her hand brushing the packed dirt. "*Pajalsta*, excellence," she said humbly. "In the fort?"

"Of course in the fort, you brainless cattle bitch," he said in his whistling nasal accent, and kicked at her. She went sprawling in the roadway and hauled herself up to her knees, bowing again and again: "*Izvenete*, excellence; *pajalsta*, *veno vat.*"

*Pardon, excellence; mercy, for I am guilty.* He nodded in satisfaction.

Aisha swallowed and kept the fur cap pulled down over her eyes as Tameetha picked herself up and jammed her own cap back on, looking away from the gallows. *Juchi's body hangs like that.* She stayed dismounted, leading the train of six draught-muskylopes that pulled the first farm wagon. All the drivers in the four-wagon train were women, to excite less suspicion — and they had to be women who could move quickly. The Bandari warrior-woman Tameetha, herself, Chaya, and Shulamit to guard the Judge. Hammer-of-God and her husband — she glowed slightly at the thought, even now — had nearly had an apoplexy at the thought, but Chaya and she had overridden them. Who had a better chance?

They walked the animals forward; one blew out its nostrils in a blubbery sigh, sweet with the scent of hay. Some of the tribute maidens in the holding pen next to the fort looked up at them curiously; others lay apathetic, and she could hear some of them weeping. *Be glad*, she thought fiercely. *Vengeance comes.*

The gate creaked open, and they pulled up in the big empty courtyard. Her ears caught a faint rhythmic creaking that ended in a grunt, and then a door opened and a Sauron came out. He was grizzled and half-bald, the lean muscularity of his breed turned ropy in middle age; he wore only loose trousers.

"What's this?" he said, sniffing. Aisha could smell him, the mingled stink of Sauron and rut.

"Liquor, Senior Trooper," the young Sauron who had kicked Tameetha said. "From — " He snapped his fingers at her.

"The farm of the *boyar* Petrenchsky, lord," she said, doing another sweeping one-handed bow.

"In ahead of time with his quota," the noncom said in Americ. "Wonders never cease."

"Shall we get some locals to unload?" Shagrat said.

"Why bother? This is the last. We'll just put the teams back in the traces tomorrow and leave." He switched to Russki: "Get going, cattle."

"Excellence?"

*What are you doing?* Aisha thought frantically. None of them had arms beyond beltknives.

"Get going!"

"Excellence, our carts . . . the boyar will beat us if we return without our teams and carts!"

The older Sauron slapped her, an open-handed blow that sent her rolling half a dozen meters. "Not worse than I will if you don't get going, cattle," he said flatly.

Tameetha was grinning savagely as they trudged out of Shamrabad. She wiped at the blood running from nose and mouth with the edge of a shawl.

" . . . because if I hadn't complained, it would look suspicious," she said to Aisha. "Besides, I was enjoying myself. I used to like doing the theatricals at the *Parim* festival."

"How long have we got?" Chaya asked tightly.

"A few minutes. Can't say any closer," Tameetha said.

Shulamit spat aside; her mouth had filled with the spit of nausea, waiting there under the gallows. Aisha patted her on the shoulder; the young Bandari *meid* jerked, then threw her a glance of thanks.

"Shulamit," Tameetha added, "try to walk as if you wore skirts all the time."

Shulamit began a snarl, then looked up. "Uh-oh," she said.

They were at the edge of the little hamlet, with harvested fields to either side; children were gleaning the last grains of fallen *ryticale* and barley among the stubble. Ahead was the great cloud of dust from the muskylope herd . . . and now it headed straight for the little town. The children pointed in wonder, until an older boy caught the gleam of steel behind the hairy, plunging backs. Then they scattered for their houses.

"Barak's not behindhand. *Come* on," Shulamit said; she hiked her skirt up in both hands — showing very un-peasant-like leather trousers — and began to run for the clownfruit orchard where they had left their gear. "Unless you all want to get run down!"


"That's not brandy," Gorthaur said, hefting one of the whole-sheepskin bags; they were made by sewing the hide closed again along the slit used to skin the animal. "It's muskylope lard."

Which was liquid at all temperatures above freezing, and highly prized for lamp-oil, lubricant, cooking and a dozen other uses.

"Petrenchsky is overfilling his quota," one of the squad said.

"Petrenchsky?" Azog said. "When Haven melts, Petrenchsky will pay more than he has to — he tried to short us once while we had a son of his as hostage, and we staked the brat out for stobor."

He stopped, turning. "*Listen.*"

They did; the drumming of muskylope hooves was much louder. Shagrat threw himself down and pressed an ear to the hard ground.

"Horses!" he shouted.

None of the Soldiers needed to be told what to do next. They were all at least halfway up the steep earth ramp to the firing parapet when the casks of gunpowder in the wagon beds went off. There was not all that much explosive, but it vaporized the oil and almost pure alcohol . . . and then *that* exploded. Shagrat never lost consciousness; he even kept a grip on his assault rifle as he cartwheeled down the outside slope of the fort's earthen mound. He lay stunned for an instant, watching Gorthaur sail past above, spreadeagled and screaming, with his hair and uniform on fire.

*Crack*. Shagrat fired and ran down the earth mound. The fort was a pillar of flame behind him. Ahead, Shamrabad had vanished in a cloud of dust and a sea of mop-haired, wild-eyed muskylopes, a thunder of hooves and bawling blubbering cries; but behind them came riders on horseback and the glint of steel. *Have to find cover*, he thought, and darted into a checkerwork pile of baled wool. *Crack*, he fired again, and a rider in a boiled-leather breastplate pitched backward over the cantle of his saddle.

That brought more of them, leaping their horses over the bales and the pyramids of sacks.

"Gur! Gur!"

Their yelping war cries were like stobor, or the fabled wolves of Terra. Wide-nostriled horses and shouting nomad faces beneath fur caps or turbans or spiked helmets. *Crack-crack-crack-crack*, a man down with each shot, a mound of kicking screaming horses, but there were more and more of them. Forcing him back lest he be crushed under dead animals and men.

*Whack*. An arrow hammered into his thigh, into the bone. He wheeled and fired, and the next shaft went wild over his head. The rider fell, spilling arrows from the quiver at his belt, and bounced away with one foot through the stirrup as his horse bolted, shrilling its terror.

More shafts sprouted in the bales of wool as Shagrat ducked and popped back up; but there were formed ranks of the enemy coming at him now, and the powerful hornbacked bows shot almost as fast as a rifle. Out in front of him Senior Trooper Azog plunged into the enemy ranks, his skin blackened and smouldering; tore a nomad from the saddle, threw him under the hooves of a charging horse. Grabbed a *shamshir* in either hand, beheaded a horse, cut a man in half despite his steel-splint armor. He went down under a mound of enemy dead, and more clambering over him in a circle of rising and falling blades.

*Whack*. Another hit, in Shagrat's shoulder. Flights of arrows rising and then falling at him like edged rain. Hits, shoulder, chest, leg, pelvis. The last magazine fell from fingers slippery with blood, and they were on him. He clubbed the rifle — the hot barrel burned his fingers — broke a man's neck, caved in another's chest. Whirled, dodged, slowed down by his wounds but still faster than any cattle, who hampered each other as they reined in around him and leaned over to slash with yataghans and stab with javelin and lance.

Another man loomed in front of him and he checked for a second, for sight and scent said *Soldier* while the armor and weapons said *enemy*. Soldier-quick reflexes tore the rifle from his hands, grabbed, lifted with Soldier strength, threw him ten meters to bounce off a wall.

After that he saw little. Consciousness faded, and the last sound was a voice speaking plains Turkic:

"*Shabash, Barak Bahadur!*" Then: "*This whore's son is alive still — with a dozen shafts in him, by Shaitan!*"

"*Bhisti-sawad!*"

The little party of nomad warriors reined in at the entranceway to the mud-walled compound. The tribute maidens within surged back from the wall, the bolder ones who had been craning to see what went on as Shamrabad fell to the sudden, overwhelming attack. The flames in the fort had died for want of fuel.

"*Bhisti-sawad!* — heavenly!" the nomad subchief said again, slapping his thigh; the leather-leaf armor rattled. "We have fought, we have conquered — and here, is this not the best plunder of all, brothers? *Aiee*, but the Sauron dogs pick well, pimps of a line of pimps that they are. Look at that moon-faced beauty there!"

Some of the women — girls — screamed as he leered at them. He started to dismount, then checked himself and turned with a scowl. The pony turned under him, responsive to the shift in his balance.

Shulamit halted behind Tameetha, reins knotted on her horse's neck and her bow in her hands; the thumb-ring was locked around the shaft, but she kept the head pointed downward for now. The *hotnots* looked ugly, a full dozen of them, which made her acutely conscious that only five of the People were here with her. The chief had nail-studded hide armor and an iron helmet with leather cheek-guards, the others only sheepskin jackets and astrakhan caps. But they all carried *shamshirs* at their sides; most had bows, one poised a javelin ready with the thongs around his fingers. Their leader had two pistols thrust into his boot-tops as well, and a short musket across his back.

"What do you *yahudi* do here?" the chief growled. "We got here first. Go find your own women."

"I *am* a woman, or had no you notice, fool begotten of fool?" Tameetha said in her roughly accented Turkic; she and the plains chief were stirrup to stirrup. By the sudden widening of his eyes, he hadn't, even with her lack of a beard. "And these maidens are under protection of another woman — Aisha daughter of Juchi. They also women of the tribes, in case you no see good, O *khan* of the closed eyes."

Aisha's name daunted them a little, but the chief snapped back: "Maidens? These are Saurons' sluts — their own fathers would spit upon them now; they are fair plunder. Why should we not enjoy them?"

"Because Aisha and the Judge order it. You swore to obey them. Go."

She stabbed a finger at his face for emphasis. He slapped at it, and Tameetha grabbed his wrist. They strained together for a moment, until she jerked him out of the saddle. He went tumbling into the dirt.

"Shulamit, Uri, Mordekai!" the Bandari officer barked.

When the nomad chieftain came to his feet spitting blood and dust, he found himself looking at three bows drawn to the angle of the jaw, the pile-shaped arrowheads winking ruddy under Cat's Eye. There was a long moment of tension, and then he threw up a hand; his men let their hands fall from hilts.

"I, Ai Bash of Aqcha, will remember this," he grated after he had remounted.

Tameetha smiled. "Don't try ravishing women until you can out-wrestle them, Ai Bash of Aqcha," she said sweetly. There was a muffled chortle from behind the chief; he turned sharply in the saddle to glare his followers into silence, then spurred off.

"Shulamit," Tameetha said. "Ride to headquarters — quickly — and tell Hammer we need some reliable troops here. Of the People, not *hotnots*. About a squadron, if we're going to keep the flies from the honeypot."

She turned to the gateway, taking off her helmet, and called in Turkic: "Peace, oh daughters of misfortune! You nothing more to fear have."

Shagrat woke to see a face he recognized. It was the driver of the wagonload of Finnegan's fig brandy, but now she wore armor. Armor he recognized from familiarization lectures, Pale-made gear. *Bandari*, he thought dazedly; his lips drew back in a snarl. *Sneaky Jew bastards!*

The snarl of anger turned to one of pain as he suddenly became aware of how much he hurt. Control clamped down, but raggedly. Then the rest of his surroundings began to clear; he was staked out naked and spread-eagled on the slope of the mound beside the fort. The bodies of his comrades dangled from their own gallows, in place of the cattle hanged as examples. They were all there and all dead, he realized . . . that took a moment, because many of the bodies had been hacked to pieces, and he had to count appendages to make sure. He tested the bonds that held him; no luck there, heavy hide lashings secured to thick stakes driven deep.

The Bandari woman was speaking. "*Veno vat*, excellence," she said mockingly, making the low bow. Then she switched to Americ, a thick guttural dialect of it that he could barely follow: "I am *very* guilty. But I am discourteous; the boyar Petrenchsky sends his greetings, and says his carts were well spent."

She was standing by another woman he recognized.

One of the tribute maidens. A very pretty one, except for the bruises. More of them crowded on either side.

"And my new friends here wish to speak with you as well."

The girls he had helped collect as tribute stood silently, a little circle of them, watching him with shining eyes. The one beside the Bandari held a small curved knife, and two of the others had brought a brazier, its wrought iron glowing cherry-red.

"Don't you remember me, Shagrat, of the great strong *baz-baz*?" the tribute maiden said kittenishly as she stepped forward. Tameetha thrust her hands through her belt, watching and moistening her lips.

"It is your darling Zulfiya!" the maiden said. She smiled. "Shall I be gentle with you, my heart?"

Shagrat began to twist frantically at the rawhide ropes that held him.

"And," the Acting First Citizen prompted—

# ● CHAPTER TWENTY-ONE

Sharku had little respect for the men who sat on the Council now. Most of them were overage, Soldiers risen as high as they could and then elected because they had the time — many of them lived down in Saurontown in Nûrnen, not on active duty at all. The First Council's functions were largely ceremonial anyway, these days. The Battlemaster and his staff ran most operations.

That had not been what Galen Diettinger intended when he landed the survivors of the *Dol Guldur* on Haven. A hologram of the man who had been Captain of that ship and founder of the Citadel was fixed to the wall behind the Council's table, flawless and perfect after three centuries. It showed a tall man in the plain coverall worn by the forces of the Sauron Unified State — even plainer than the Citadel's gray uniform, for it lacked the insignia of the Lid-'ess Eye. Diettinger and Lady Althene had invented that—trieved it from the same mythos the original discoverers of Sauron had drawn on to name the planet — that and much else. The great banner on the wall above the picture rippled slightly in the breeze from the ventilators.

Sharku stood braced to attention. The Acting First Citizen spoke: the office had been formally vacant for centuries. Sharku himself was a scion of Diettinger's blood, in the female line, through a daughter born to a Havener tribute maiden. Having read Lady Althene's works as few did in these days, he had always mildly regretted not bearing her genes as well.

"Have you anything further to add, Chief Assault Leader?"

Sharku resisted the temptation to steal a glance at the Cyborg beside him. "In summation, Second Rank," he said, "I believe we are the victims of a subtle and long-prepared deception and disinformation plan, and our current movements are conforming to that plan. This is an invitation to strategic disaster."

Silence, absolute and complete, from the six men before him and the vast audience in the tiers behind. Soldiers did not fidget.

"And?" the Acting First Citizen prompted.

Bitterness overflowed in Sharku. *I knew they would not listen.* Had he believed in Fate, he might have comforted himself with the thought that it was a curse — always to speak truth and never to be believed. The rationalist doctrine of the Soldiers gave no reassurance, even one so bitter.

"And," he added, "this is of a pattern with our recent history." He might as well speak his mind, having already ruined hopes of further promotion by defying the Battlemaster. He would be lucky not to be sent to the Tierra del Muerte to fight the Dinneh.

"We Soldiers," he went on, "are unmatched at tactics, in actual fighting. We are masters of the operational art of war. At strategy, and at the long-term political, social and economic management which underlies strategy, we are . . . less adept. That was why we lost the Secession Wars, lost Old Sauron. First Citizen Diettinger was a brilliant long-term strategist; he saved the Race from extinction. He never intended Haven to be our final resting place" — Sharku used the phrase with malice aforethought — "but instead a base to recoup our numbers and strength for another attempt at interstellar mastery.

"Instead," he said, "what have we done? We have not even definitively pacified this planet. Our technological base has declined steadily; from sheer lack of resources, yes, but also from unwillingness to display energies that might attract attention. We do not even know if the Empire of Man still exists; it has been three hundred T-years, yet we still hide from its ghost. The first generation built the Wall — when it fell, we never attempted to rebuild it, partly because it would be visible from space if this planet were ever surveyed. Instead, we sit on our ancestors' achievements, contenting ourselves with meaningless victories over cattle armed with bows and swords."

The Council was showing slight signs of impatience; only a Soldier could have recognized them. *I'm going to get this on the record anyway*, Sharku decided.

"Lady Althene called Haven the largest and most ruthless experiment in human eugenics ever conducted. This is an accurate appraisal. This planet has been selecting and culling its inhabitants since its first settlement. For the last three T-centuries we have been increasing the selective pressure toward martial achievement — and making the inhabitants a free gift of our genes as well, in a steady diffusion. Is it any surprise, then, that their level of achievement is increasing exponentially? A simple extrapolation of curves will indicate the logical conclusion of *that* — while this environment lacks sufficient stress to promote such an adaptive increase in *us*."

That *did* bring a stir. The thought that cattle might someday outdo Soldiers in fighting ability was . . . what was the cattle phrase? Ah, yes. *Heresy*.

"In conclusion," he said, "the uprising in the Shangri-La is a strategic deception engineered by the cattle of the Pale. Commitment of our main reserve force is an unwarranted risk at this stage in what is, in my opinion, a major war. That is all."

"Thank you for your historical analysis," the Acting First Citizen said.

*Meaningless, meaningless*, Sharku raged within himself. The Soldiers had a deliberately now-oriented culture. On Old Sauron, that had not been an impossible handicap; there were other castes, other subcultures. Here . . .

"Battlemaster Carcharoth has submitted a plan—" Sharku listened impassively as the Second Rank outlined the Cyborg's mobilization of the whole reserve strength of the Race.

" — Chief Assault Leader Sharku has submitted a counterproposal that one regiment only be so detached, with another from Firebases Two through Six" — the valley garrison towns along the Jordan-Xanadu River system — "while awaiting developments. Vote, please."

Sharku was surprised; one member of the Council, Gimli the Archivist, voted in his favor.

"Majority of five to one for Battlemaster Carcharoth's proposal. Proposal is affirmed. Execute. Dismissed."

The Grand Muster, the Soldiers were calling it. Carcharoth didn't know whether he approved, but had not suggested forbidding the name. Surely this was the greatest force the Citadel had sent into battle in the memory of living man; the Soldiers' aura of might had made the large-scale employment of might unnecessary for generations. All along the Xanadu River, the garrisons would be moving in readiness to join them as they moved west. But the Battlemaster thought the Soldiers should have learned enough about soldiering to know how seldom it was grand.

The women and children of the Citadel knew better, that was certain. Carcharoth looked down from the outwalls of the great fortress into the inner ward. Mates and brats swarmed round the gathering men, getting in their way, slowing them down, and generally being nuisances. How much more convenient it would have been were the Soldiers a monastic order dedicated only to war. But then, of course, it would have died out in a generation.

The Battlemaster, as befit his rank, was a student of the histories the Soldiers had brought with them from Old Sauron aboard the *Dol Guldur*, as well as those seized after the landing on Haven. He knew such that monastic orders had existed back on legendary Terra, and knew also that they'd been imperfect both in monasticism and in discipline. Of course, the Soldiers had the advantage of better genetic material with which to work.

Any Soldier worthy of the name could use his eyes to simulate binoculars. Cyborgs could play the same trick with their ears, filtering out extraneous conversations and background noise to focus on what they wanted to hear.

Much of what he focused on, he didn't like. Here a pregnant woman squeezed herself against a Senior Trooper in an heirloom soft-armor jacket, hard enough to hurt herself or him or both of them. "You keep yourself safe, do you hear me?" she said. "Who will protect your baby and me if you fall?"

A Soldier's answer should have been something like, *My duty comes first.* The Senior Trooper hugged his woman and replied, "Don't worry, darling. I'll watch myself." Carcharoth opened a new mental file and gave it *fainthearts* as an access code. If the Soldiers whose names he put there performed well in the upcoming action, he'd take those names out of the file when they got home. If they didn't, he'd deal with them personally. He promised himself that.

It was some consolation that the Soldier-born women weren't undermining morale; but they were only about a third of the total. Every second conversation he monitored between Soldiers and tribute-maiden females seemed to give him a name for the *fainthearts* file. "I'll be home again as soon as I can," a veteran Section Leader told his sons, one of whom looked almost old enough for enrollment among the Soldiers himself. "You needn't fret about me. I won't do anything stupid."

Another Trooper held a kiss with his woman so long that she, who used oxygen less efficiently, came close to passing out. When at last he let her go, he murmured, "I'd sooner spend my time in bed with you than out there where I'm liable to get my ass shot off." The Soldiers to either side of the fellow might not have heard him, but Carcharoth did. The Trooper's name went into the file.

And there — there stood Sharku in front of his assault group. Soldiers so often fought in small units that it was hard to remember their ranks really did correspond to places in the chain of command. The lives of a couple of hundred men would depend on the Chief Assault Leader's judgment and skill.

Like most of the other Soldiers, Sharku was fondling his woman (the Battlemaster admitted she was worth fondling) and hugging his little boy. Gimilzor, that was his name, Carcharoth remembered. Yes, he was one of the better boys of the coming generation.

For that matter, Carcharoth had thought his father a

promising officer until he developed this foolish fixation that the revolt in the Valley was somehow linked to the movements on the steppe. The TAC didn't see that, and if the TAC didn't see it, it wasn't there. That had been proved too many times to doubt.

Carcharoth hurled his hearing down onto Sharku like a spear. The Chief Assault Leader was saying, " — hope we can wrap this idiotic campaign up in a hurry, that's all. I've told everyone in the Citadel it's a feint, a diversion, but no one listens. No one, curse it!"

"*I* listen," Chichek said loyally.

"I'm glad you do, my flower, but you don't wear the death's head on your collar tabs, worse luck," Sharku answered. "I think the fools who do are looking through the skull's eyes and not their own."

"I believe you, Father," Gimilzor declared. "When you come back from smashing the rebels, maybe you should do the same to the people who will not hear you." The boy thought like a Soldier already, Carcharoth noted — move forward, attack, smash the position in front of you. In a lad, it was charming, a harbinger of good things ahead. If Sharku agreed with the lad, it was treason.

But Sharku said, "They are our leaders, son. I will obey them. If we don't obey the officers set over us, how are we better than cattle? Even if they are wrong here, odds are it won't hurt us. The Citadel is a mighty fortress, and should hold against whatever the steppe nomads can throw at it, though I do worry that the Bandari are part of this — they know too much."

Gimilzor straightened to his full height. "I will help to hold the Citadel."

"I'm sure you will, son." Sharku laughed and ran a hand through the boy's hair. "Still, though our garrison here be mostly the young and the old, I hope with all my heart that they will not need you at a gun."

"At need, I would take one," Chichek said. "Many women here would."

"Again, may there be no need," Sharku said. Carcharoth, however, stored that idea away, too. Cyborgs were more accurate than polygraphs at determining where loyalty truly lay. He and his fellow masters should have no trouble telling which tribute maidens were safe to arm if an emergency arose. Soldier women first, of course — they had some training already, as backup. But the others as well, at need. Like Sharku, though, he could not believe an emergency so great would occur.

The Chief Assault Leader squeezed his woman hard enough to leave her gasping, tossed his son high into the air. He did not catch the boy as a fond father among the cattle would have done. Instead, he let him land on his own. Gimilzor lit rolling, and bounced to his feet with speed some adult Soldiers would have been hard pressed to match. Yes, the boy had spirit, Carcharoth thought.

Display was not part of the Soldiers' military style. The gates opened; the men assigned to the expeditionary force filtered out to form ranks in the pass that led down into the Shangri-La Valley. Wives and children milled about in the inner ward, which seemed strangely empty despite their presence. Carcharoth did not need to augment his hearing to take in their wails.

As the Battlemaster watched the Soldiers assembled outside the Citadel, he compared what he was seeing to the countless stories he knew of men going off to war. One that passed through his mind was the mustering of the men of Gondor in *The Lord of the Rings*, the myth-cycle from which his own folk had derived so many of their outward trappings here on Haven.

He wondered if the whole history of his race would have been different if the explorers who found the home world called it, say, Gandalf rather than Sauron. By all surviving records, Sauron had been a world that deserved to be named after an evil power, but might the name itself in some way have impelled later settlers to try to live up — or down — to it? He erased that train of thought: too few data from which to form any conclusion. Whether or not it was true, though, enemy propaganda had surely made the most of it, all the way from the titanic struggle with the Empire of Man through the exile of the surviving fragment here on Haven. So much, to flow from a random choice by an explorer whose name was long vanished from every record.

Now even the Soldiers had come to identify with their place on the dark side of the mythos. Carcharoth would have bet an assault rifle against a broken bow that the mythical Sauron's forces had been better organized than the random levies Denethor called up to defend his city against them. They needed organization; they didn't have the author on their side. In real life, as far as the Battlemaster could tell, good and evil were not only hard to tell apart but were often of more or less equal strength. Of course the cattle, those who could think so deeply, were bereft of moral sense and no fit judge.

He wished he were trotting at the head of the two regiments moving west. Only reluctantly had he agreed with the Council that the Battlemaster saw to all the military concerns of the Soldiers in every part of Haven, and so needed to stay in the Citadel, the greatest communications center on the world. Ghâsh was a fiery Brigade Leader, more than capable, but still . . . *"Delegate,"* Carcharoth thought, *is a fancy military term for "sit around on your ass."*

Well, if he had to sit around on his ass, he decided he might as well accomplish something useful. He descended from the wall and went off to ask more questions of Dagor. Until dispatches arrived from the western end of the steppe, it was all he could do.

*"Horrosho."*

Yohann bar Non's mother had spoken Tallinn Valley Russki as her native tongue; she had been a tribute maiden in Angband Base, bearing her first child to a Soldier not long before it fell. She had married in the Pale afterwards, but her son still used that language occasionally, in dreams or when deeply moved.

*"Horrosho,"* he repeated softly. Then, in Bandarit: "Most excellent." He took a deep breath of the resin-scented air, rich as kvass, full of the life-giving moisture that soaked the cropped ash-blond beard and long braid.

The forward command post of the southern expeditionary force was set up in a stand of tall redwoods, on a mountain slope overlooking the seacoast plain, and heavily camouflaged. Yohann had never seen anything like the giant trees, but these foothills were a unique environment — well-watered, and low enough that Terran life had an advantage. The air was already thick enough to be slightly intoxicating, and the endurance of his troops was increasing substantially; a necessary factor, after the grueling march down the escarpment. Careful, painstaking logistical preparation had made it possible. Now for the reward.

His Sauron-bred eyes could see a dozen kilometers from here under Byers' Sun and Cat's Eye. Rolling forested slopes; then an open cultivated plain dotted with villages and towns, and many small streams running from the mountains to the sea. The sea . . . the great stretch of ruddy-silver water was also like nothing in his experience; imagination and maps could not prepare you for it. Left, eastward, were more mountains and the huge salt-marsh wilderness of the Xanadu delta, where it met the spectacular tides of Haven's seas. Cat's Eye and the sister moons between them could raise walls of water a dozen meters high and send them ripping inland.

Khanut Base and town were spread out along a narrow fiord with ancient Imperial tide-locks at its entrance. He sincerely hoped those were not damaged in the coming fighting. The docks and sea-going craft whose masts showed above the rooftops of the towns were a major prize.

Again he studied Khanut Base itself. Fairly recent construction; the Imperial-era city here had been taken out in the *Dol Guldur*'s strike and only rebuilt two hundred T-years ago. Most of the defenses pointed seaward — corsairs and the navies of the southern-hemisphere island nations were the major challenge here. Landward was mainly a curtain wall and ditch, more than enough for containing rebellious peasants or barbarian raiders from the forests. Not enough for the ten thousand Bandari who were coming down from the Pale in stages, with the two thousand allied nomad cavalry and three thousand Tallinn

Valley infantry. Plus the rifled cast-steel cannon, the spigot mortars, the iron-carts with their steam-powered battering rams, all the painfully accumulated surprises old Mordekai had commanded.

Not now that the bulk of the Sauron force, fifteen hundred Soldiers, had entrained for the Shangri-La. He could see the last of the electric locomotives hauling its load of carts northeastward, toward the tunnels. Too risky to attack them there, but as soon as they passed, the massive charges of gunpowder would be brought forward and dropped down the access and ventilation shafts. Experiments on fragments of Imperial structural materials had shown they would not be able to withstand it, not in confined spaces.

The Saurons had thought the area impassable — even the forest tribes did not go there. *Always fight against nature rather than men when you can,* Piet van Reenan had said.

"How very true," Yohann murmured, turning to his staff and repeating it aloud.

Several were Orphans like himself. All of them looked eager. He was not at all disturbed by the prospect of fighting Saurons, his remote blood-kin. A culture was a matrix, a framework for the survival of bloodlines. His matrix — knowing the compulsions were subconscious did not affect their power — was the one initiated by Piet van Reenan and his helpers; now it was coming into conflict with the one Galen Diettinger had founded, and he was thoroughly committed. He had risen high in the Pale; his wife was of the van Reenan line, and Yohann's very promising sons, someday . . .

"Shimon," he said, "your *Sayerets* will activate their infiltrators in Khanut Town as per plan *Shin-Tov-Shin.* Hendryk, I want the artillery ready to move down to the lateral road" — he traced a line on the map — "by truenight, and I don't care if it's possible. Uri, you — "

And so it went, down the line, setting in motion the fall of Sauron in this part of Haven.

# • CHAPTER TWENTY-TWO

Without warning, Temujin's muskylope foundered. He flew over its head and fell hard on the cold, grassy steppe. Something hit him in the pit of his stomach. He rolled to a stop, retching and trying to force air into his lungs.

The Saurons with him were not mounted. Nonetheless, this was the third muskylope their burning pace had killed. They called to one another, and held up. One of them walked over to the muskylope. He looked down at the poor gasping beast for a moment, then stooped, took its neck in his hands, twisted sharply. Temujin winced at the sharp pop of snapping vertebrae.

"Fresh protein," the Sauron announced. He glanced over to Temujin. "You all right?"

"I'll live," the nomad wheezed.

"Good." The Sauron detached the bayonet from his rifle, started butchering the still-twitching muskylope. His comrades gathered round for their shares, stuffed themselves with raw, dripping chunks of meat. The Sauron tossed one in Temujin's direction. It landed in the dirt. "Feed your face," the butcher said. The words carried the flat snap of an order.

Temujin ate. His own people, no less than the Saurons, were used to making do with very little and to making that very little stretch very far. The muskylope meat was hot and gamy and tough. He hardly noticed. As the fellow who'd cut it off the carcass said, it was meat. When meat came along, you got outside of it.

Besides, refusing would have annoyed the Saurons. He didn't want to annoy them. Out here on the steppe, they lacked the sophisticated tools of torment on display in the Red Room. Still, what they could do with blades, fire and their own ingenuity was plenty to keep him on his best behavior.

He'd tried to escape one freezing truenight. He was, after all, a man born to the plains, a nomad, not someone whose true home lay in the unmoving Citadel. And, he thought, these Saurons were just Soldiers, not Cyborgs like — Sigrid. He knew he was an idiot, he'd proved he was an idiot, but he could not drive her from his thoughts, from his dreams.

He'd been positive he was away clean. The Saurons' hadn't bothered setting any special guard on him, so he'd just walked off from their camp in the darkness. Once he'd gained a couple of hundred meters, he'd been sure his hunting and battle knowledge would let him disguise his trail so no one — maybe not even . . . Sigrid (that pause again) — could follow him.

He'd gone more than a klick and done some serious but silent exulting when an Americ voice not five meters from him abruptly pricked his bubble of optimism: "Cut the shit, fool. Don't you know I can see you by the heat your body gives off? I'm bored with tracking you, so now you get your lesson."

The set of lumps he'd taken had been painful but not permanently damaging; the Saurons needed him in shape to ride. The fellow who beat him even carried him back to camp afterward, as casual about his whimpering weight as if he'd been a pony. He hadn't tried to run, or to bother the Saurons in any other way, since.

Between mouthfuls of muskylope, he asked, "What will you — Soldiers — do when you get to Katlinsvale?"

The commander of the Sauron force was a scar-faced Assault Leader named Atanamir. He answered, "Scout, take what we need, destroy the rest."

"Just like that?" Temujin said.

"Just like that," Atanamir agreed. "Who'll stop us? Cattle? *Female* cattle?" He laughed loudly. So did a good many other Saurons.

"Sigrid might be there," Temujin said. "Sigrid the Cyborg."

Atanamir had the full measure of Sauron arrogance, but didn't seem crazy with it, not by Sauron standards, anyhow. He sobered abruptly. "We worry about that as we find evidence of it, and modify plans accordingly. We bring her back if we can, kill her if we can't. Not even Cyborgs outrun assault-rifle slugs."

Sigrid's lean, hard body bleeding, pierced by copper-jacketed lead . . . Temujin made a horrible face, not sure whether he wanted that more than anything else on Haven or dreaded it enough to throw away his own life to prevent it.

His Americ had improved a great deal since he'd involuntarily started associating with the Saurons. It was, he thought, a clipped, compact tongue, utterly without the rhetorical flourishes that made Turkic, for instance, a language in which to rouse warriors to fighting frenzy. Even so, it had terms to describe states and conditions that Turkic could not encompass. One of those descriptions fit Temujin like a good pair of wool socks. He was *fucked up*.

One of the Saurons finished fixing bridle, saddle and reins to the next muskylope from the string the Soldiers had brought with them. His eyes pinned Temujin down as if he were a cockroach under a boot. "Climb on, nomad."

Temujin mounted the muskylope, flattening along its broad back. The beast tossed its head, snuffled out a long, burbling complaint through hair-filled nostrils and wide, blubbery lips. The plainsman felt it quiver under his weight. Keeping up with the Saurons, even without a rider, had left it worn to the point of exhaustion. Carrying him at that same pace would soon kill it. The Saurons didn't care. To them, it was an expendable resource, and a renewable one at that.

Atanamir rose from his crouch. He wiped blood off his chin as he walked over to Temujin. "How much farther to this Katlinsvale, cattle?"

Temujin knew he dared not lie. The first time he was caught in a falsehood, he'd lose a thumb. The second time, he'd lose some other projection he valued even more. But telling the truth here was not easy, either. "Assault Leader, I beg you to remember I know of this place by rumor only. We should be fairly near, but since I know neither exactly where it lies nor just how far we've travelled, I can give no exact answer."

Atanamir glanced down at something strapped to his leg. "We've come just over 1,300 klicks. Trouble is, that only fills one of your variables. I give you another — hmmm — fifteen hours. If we don't see evidence by then, you'll have to take off your boots whenever you want to count higher than nine."

The plainsman would have found Atanamir less frightening — and easier to hate — if he'd been full of gloating, sadistic anticipation. But he wasn't. He just seemed an ordinary man going about his ordinary business. If that ordinary business involved mutilating Temujin, he'd take care of it without undue fuss or bother, and then go on to the next item on his list.

The Saurons loped ahead, a few a klick or so in front of the rest to serve as scouts, another handful the same distance behind as a rear guard. In the middle were the rest of the Soldiers, Temujin and the muskylopes not yet killed. The arrangement was compact and logical. Even if he'd had Sigrid's abilities, Temujin didn't think he'd have been able to escape.

These other, ordinary Saurons seemed about as far above him in physical prowess as Sigrid had. Of course, they were men, so being dominated by them wasn't so hard for Temujin to take. And they spoke about the object of his affection — or obsession — with great respect and caution. Whatever else one could say, he'd picked a remarkable woman with whom to entangle his fate.

One of the Sauron point men came sprinting back to Atanamir, who ran with the main body of Soldiers. The Saurons' steady, ground-eating lope had already both awed and appalled Temujin. Now he saw a Sauron really in a hurry, and was awed all over again. It was as if the fellow had shot himself out of a bow.

Atanamir listened to whatever the messenger had to say, then let out a call that Temujin hardly heard but which sufficed to bring the spread-out central band of Soldiers to a dead stop. The Saurons' commander waved for Temujin to halt his muskylope. He obeyed. The animal shuddered under him in weariness or relief or the two of them commingled.

"Tell everyone, Gaurhoth," Atanamir said.

"I don't need to tell, Assault Leader," the Sauron scout answered. "They can see it for themselves — there." He pointed to the northwest.

Temujin looked — there, following Gaurhoth's finger. He saw nothing out of the ordinary: just more steppe, klicks and klicks of klicks and klicks. He was, however, not a Sauron, for which he fervently thanked the spirits. Whatever Gaurhoth was pointing out, the Soldiers saw it. They grunted as they looked across the plain, then at one another and toward Atanamir.

Some of the grunts had words in them: "Dust." "Bloody fucking lot of dust, for us to see it that far." "Lot of bloody fucking nomads then, too." "Maybe a trick — animals out in front, to make 'em look like more than they are." "Dragging brush on ropes, maybe." Several more sets of eyes turned toward Atanamir.

The Assault Leader shook his long, fair head. "They're really plainsmen, I think. I was briefed on this before we set out — some sort of expeditionary force moving on the Citadel, if you can believe that shit." The Saurons laughed at the audacity of that, cliff lion-like, with tongues lolling out. Atanamir went on, "I hoped we'd be through before we ran into 'em, but their van is moving faster than I figured."

"So what do we do, Assault Leader?" Gaurhoth asked. "Go around 'em? Forgive my saying so, but it would waste a lot of time."

"So it would," Atanamir agreed. He grinned, as if encountering something new and interesting in the course of daily routine. "What do you say we go through 'em instead? I don't care how many cattle there are up there. There'll be a lot fewer of 'em after we're done. Let's go."

It was as simple as that. The two sections of Saurons spread out into a long, thin skirmish line and swept forward toward the foes who were still invisible to Temujin. Atanamir and everybody else seemed to have forgotten all about him.

He thought about wheeling his muskylope and getting the hell out of there, but he didn't have the nerve. He was too grimly certain the Saurons would be able to hunt him down and punish him once they were done with the plainsmen ahead. If he rode slowly after them, they could find nothing for which to blame him. He slapped the muskylope's fuzzy side. It snorted resentfully but plodded forward.

Temujin wondered whether Atanamir was crazy with Sauron arrogance after all. At any rate, if *he'd* had only this relative handful of men under his command, he'd have tried to get some notion of just how big a force he faced before he went and attacked it.

"Damn," Atanamir said mildly, turning the captured weapon over in his hands.

It was a flintlock rifle, about breastbone-high on a man of medium height. The trigger guard was a lever that curled around the grip section of the stock and ended in a loop. Atanamir put his thumb through the loop and pressed down.

"The iron block behind the hammer is the breech?" one of the younger Soldiers asked, like a tyro on a training field, which, Temujin thought, this mostly was.

"Yes." A wedge cammed down and the block slid back along a track that tilted its forward edge up at the same time. "A brass cylinder is sunk into the breechblock, with a rim protruding; the rim fits inside the edge of the barrel, and expands for gas sealage when the weapon is fired."

The Sauron reached down into the dead enemy warrior's bandolier and came up with a paper cartridge. He sniffed at it. "Black powder, meal-ground. The paper is soaked in saltpeter and highly flammable."

After a moment's study the Sauron bit off the end of the cartridge and pinched the torn paper shut. He pushed the L-shaped frizzen forward and let a pinch of gunpowder fall into the pan. The spring-loaded frizzen clicked back over the powder as he moved his hand to push the paper cylinder and long pointed bullet into the brass tube. The action went snick-*click* as he pulled the lever back to its rest position under the stock. Another *snick* as he thumbed back the hammer.

"Coming in from the left," another Sauron called.

Atanamir turned without exposing himself over the barricade of dead men, horses and muskylopes ahead of them. Some of them were not quite dead, but no matter.

The Sauron advance had swept into the nomad host like iron shot into a vat of treacle, swiftly at first, then slowing from sheer friction. They were on a slight rise in the steppe now, with a gully on their right flank. Several hundred meters to their front were a line of low hummocks, probably frost-heave from a bed of permafrost such as was common on the steppe; from behind that a hundred or so riflemen were pinning the Saurons down. Further back and all around swarmed mounted nomad warriors. *Swarmed* was exactly the right word, because the steppe seethed with them even in the dimday twilight — perhaps more so than they would have under bright light, dun masses twinkling with the steel of lance-heads and swords.

Temujin had seen a fair amount of steppe warfare, for a man his age — one civil war, numerous raids, and the endless skirmishing with their Muslim neighbors that the clans subject to his father Yesugai always suffered. At a pinch, his tribal confederation could muster a full *touman*, ten thousand fighting men. He was pretty sure he could see at least three times that from here —

— and the Saurons didn't seem worried at all. Annoyed, yes. Worried, no. Oddly enough, their calm was contagious. If he'd been in command of this force, Temujin thought, he'd be gibbering with terror behind a stone-faced mask put on to hearten the troops. As it was, Atanamir just looked like someone who'd found a light chore turning into real work and wanted to get it finished.

The rifle fire from the front intensified, big soft-lead slugs going *crack* overhead or hammering into the barricade of flesh left over from the first assault on the Sauron position. Hooves drummed through the earth; Temujin could feel it through his belly, pressed to the dirt. He looked to the left. A thousand horsemen were charging in on the flank of the Sauron position.

Atanamir adjusted the rear leaf-sight of the captured

rifle and fired. Still doll-tiny, a horse crumpled and its rider
tumbled free. The standard of yak-tails on a long pole he
carried fell into the dirt until another rider bent low and
snatched it up.

"Nine hundred meters," Atanamir said, sounding a little
impressed. "But it throws very high."

Several others of the Sauron party were firing, with their
assault rifles on semi-automatic. The sharp whipcrack
reports were a continuous stutter, brass flying out in
streams as if the weapons were on full automatic. Men and
horses dropped all along the front of the charge, but one
Sauron who rose too high to get a better angle fell back
with the top of his head clipped off. At three hundred
meters the casualties were gruesome; then the horsemen
loosed a volley of arrows on high arching trajectories and
wheeled around to flee.

Temujin knew a familiar fear, almost homelike, as he
heard the arrows whistle. He curled himself into a ball and
tried to burrow under the high-peaked saddle of the dead
horse in front of him. *Thwack.* One quivered in the wood
and leather not two centimeters from his nose. The springy
horn and sinew of the plainsmens' composite bows could
send a shaft a *long* way. More fell all around him, into
coarse gritty dirt with a *shink* sound, or into flesh with a
duller, wetter noise. Some of the flesh was living; when he
raised his head, he could see Saurons tending to their
wounds. One man pushed a shaft through the fleshy part
of his leg, then snapped off the head and pulled the wood
free. Another dug a point from a comrade's shoulderblade
with his bayonet. Both wounded men were expressionless
and silent, and their blood stopped flowing with unnatural
speed.

"Ammo," Atanamir called. The Soldiers reported; none
had more than two hundred rounds left, a total shrinking
steadily as they replied to the harassing fire from the
entrenched riflemen ahead.

"Noise in the gully," a Soldier called from their right.

Seconds later a pottery globe about the size of a tennis-
ball fruit arched up out of the deep wash. The Soldier

who'd called out caught it and half-rose to throw it back with a blurring snap. It exploded below the rim of the *wadi*, a crash of sound followed by screams of pain. The Soldiers chuckled at that, but something else came out of the depths. Arrows, fired blind to arch up and drop, but quite a few of them, and more all the time. The archers were in good cover, and to rise and fire at them the Saurons would have to expose themselves to rifle fire from the west.

"Damn," Atanamir said again. "Mewlip." The young trooper who'd asked about the rifle looked up. "Take this." The Sauron commander tossed him the captured weapon. "Familiarize yourself. Your absolute — absolute — mission priority, should we be overrun at any time on this patrol, is to report back to the Citadel with the intelligence. Bandari rifles, several hundred of them at least."

"Bandari?" Mewlip said.

"Unmistakable — and most Bandari, even, are armed with bows. It costs to make these by hand. I repeat: mission priority.

"Everyone," he said a little louder. "We're pulling back."

*Saurons retreating!* Temujin exulted. It was a heady thought, enough to make him envy the men out there fighting the patrol. Men who dared to march on the Citadel itself!

Of course, the barricade around him contained the bodies of at least a hundred of those men.

"How?" someone asked, jerking his head behind him. Dust there marked bands of horsemen closing in behind him.

Atanamir grinned. "We'll roll over the lip of that gully and move east along it, right through those fucking bow-men," he said. "They think they've got us pinned. Ought to surprise 'em."

The Soldiers laughed.

Over the next couple of cycles, Temujin seriously began to wonder whether Atanamir was the crazy one, or he himself.

The Mongols had a tradition of herding that went back

to Earth, the wonderful world from which their sins or
crimes (depending on which shaman you happened to listen to) had caused them to be banished. They guided and
used flocks and herds of sheep, goats, camels, horses, yaks,
musk oxen, muskylopes . . . if it had hooves (or even the
broad horn-soled padded feet of muskylopes), they could
master it.

The Saurons were herders of men.

"You wish us to join you in war, men of the Citadel?"
Omin Hotal said cautiously.

The Sauron patrol were squatting and eating hugely on
the rugs the chief of the White Sheep Turks had set out.
Temujin just lay and groaned for the first half-hour or so,
before he could gather enough energy to think of food; for
the last half-cycle the Saurons had been carrying him,
occasionally debating whether it was worth the trouble.

Atanamir looked around. Temujin followed his gaze; the
encampment was huge, much larger than the sept of even
a great chief like Omin Hotal. The other septs and clans of
the Ak-Koyunlu were gathered close, clusters of yurts and
herds spreading to all the horizons under the trueday
brightness, pounding the steppe to dust and overburden-
ing the wells where warriors quarreled shrilly as they
labored to haul up the skin sacks of water. The air was thick
with that dust, with the smoke of dung fires and the smell of
dung, with the sweat of men and horses soaked into leather
and felt. The tribe was mustering for war . . . and not only
the tribe. There were big, fair Caucasoid-looking men in
camp, dressed as plainsmen but with differences — baggy
red breeches, brimless conical caps, many bare to the waist
and all sporting crosses and icons about their necks. Their
standard of a double-headed crowned eagle stood next to
the white sheepskin of the Ak-Koyunlu, their bear-shaped
scalp-locked chief sat next to Omin Hotal.

Atanamir stared, until the Turk and the Cossack bowed
their heads. "We require your warriors, Omin Hotal, Oleg
Cherninsky," he said. "Unfortunately, we do not have
enough ammunition with us at the moment to kill all the
advancing horde by ourselves, and it is inconvenient to

send for reinforcements at the moment. Therefore you will cooperate under our orders."

Both chieftains bowed with hands on hearts. For the first time, Temujin began to understand why the warriors of the Citadel called the other folk of Haven cattle. White Sheep women scurried about with trays of dried meat and flatbread, and skins of kvass. Temujin grabbed a sack and drank thirstily; it wasn't the ultra-strong *kara kumiss* his own folk brewed, but even Turkish kvass was better than nothing.

"The horde is advancing at about twenty klicks per day," Atanamir calculated. That was good speed, for a force burdened with yurts and herds. "We estimate their numbers at about thirty thousand fighting men, less the several hundred we killed."

*Hetman* Oleg Cherninsky swallowed. "My *stanitsa* can muster two thousand sabers," he said, "counting graybeards and lads whose balls have barely dropped. We could send to our kin in other settlements of the Sir Brothers, but that would take too long — ten days." Haven days, say a tenth of a T-year.

"Three thousand," Omin Hotal said. "Four, perhaps five, if our cousins of the Kara-Koyunlu join us."

"They will," Atanamir said, as calmly as a man stating that Cat's Eye would be full in another twenty hours. "With fifty-seven Soldiers" — three had been lost in the clash with the horde — "and seven thousand of your men, the odds are in our favor. We'll sleep, then see to tactical dispositions."

The chiefs left, like schoolboys dismissed by the master. Temujin felt the kvass reviving him; he reached for a bowl of soft cheese and wild onions, scooping up a mouthful with some flatbread and munching on a skewer of grilled goat meat. It was an improvement on raw muskylope, and the serving-wench smiled at him as she ladled out more. *Better, much better,* the Mongol thought. The Saurons would demand women for their stay — they always did — and with a little luck, he'd get some too.

"They obeyed quickly," he said to Atanamir.

"Of course," the Sauron said, belching and reaching for
a bowl of sweet cakes. His angular face looked more gaunt
than usual; the past cycle had been strenuous even by
Sauron standards. "A guilty man seeks to please."

"Guilty?"

Wordlessly, Atanamir turned the bowl the cakes rested
in. It was cast glass, fine work, with an embossed rim of
running tamerlanes about the edge.

*Bandari-made,* Temujin realized — his father had some
like it, bought at vast expense from the Pale's traders. The
sort of gift an embassy brought, to sweeten negotiations. If
the Saurons had turned up a little later, the White Sheep
might well have been riding under the banner of the
Seven.

Perhaps not. The horde was sweeping across the Great
Northern Steppe like land gators, leaving wreckage in
their path; the White Sheep would be fighting for their
lives and their land, if they did not join it. The Kossacki
even more so, for they had a fortified town and farms as
well as wandering herdsmen. The followers of the Seven
were vacuuming up everything, including the seed corn.

*Not exactly a smooth force,* Temujin thought a cycle later,
watching the last of the Kossacki ride in. He felt much better, well rested and dressed and mounted on a good horse
the Saurons had ordered up for him — Atanamir seemed
to regard him as something of a pet, these days.

There were several hundred of the shaven-headed warriors in this party, clustered around a two-wheeled cart
drawn by a pair of muskylope and crowded with big barrels.
The tops of the barrels had been smashed in, and the Kossacki were singing loudly in their harsh dialect of Russki,
laden with Turkic loan-words and seemingly divided between the obscene and the scatological. Every once in a while
one would spur over to the barrels and sink his head in the
potent amaranth vodka without dismounting, coming up
red-faced and blowing, long moustaches dripping over gap-
toothed grins. Many were swaying in their saddles, and not a
few were lashed over them, limp as sacks of grain.

Their *hetman* laughed, showing a few spikes of teeth. He slapped his keglike belly, bound around with a studded belt that held saber, silver-hilted flintlock pistols and many knives. The gray-blond scalp lock hanging down his back bobbed with his mirth.

"We drink *na umor*, to the death!" he boasted. "Then we fight — *na umor* — to the death!"

Atanamir looked at him silently. The chieftain flushed, growled and heeled his horse away.

"Buffoon," one of the Soldiers muttered. Temujin agreed; he shuddered to think what his father or his father's *noyons* would say to warriors sousing themselves on the eve of battle.

"They'll fight pretty well, for cattle," Atanamir said.

*That migrating horde isn't likely to have much in the way of discipline either,* Temujin reflected.

Watching the army grow as if from nothing, watching the clansmen follow the Saurons' orders as if they'd never imagined they might do otherwise, made Temujin's eyes widen — he was a chief's son, but Yesugei never dreamt of obedience like this.

At last, curiosity (maybe even a more dangerous fault than a fondness for strong drink or a loose tongue) made him approach Atanamir. "May I ask a question?"

"Ask," the Sauron said; he'd developed a half-scornful affection for Temujin as they'd journeyed together, and tolerated more from him now than he had when they first set out from the Citadel.

"How do you make these men follow your commands? I've had no choice but to do as you say, but there were many of you and only the one of me. Now there are many nomads and only a few of you. Soldiers you may be, but if they turned on you, they could kill you all. Yet they do not turn. Why?"

"The term is military fear," Atanamir answered. On matters military, he spoke seriously, even to one as lowly in his eyes as Temujin. He had the attitude of a shaman spinning tales of the *tngri* to one who, though never worthy of becoming an apprentice, nevertheless might learn something from them.

The only thing Temujin learned was that his Americ still had gaps in it. "What do you mean, fear?" he asked. "These are warriors you have gathered here. What good would they be to you if they shivered instead of going into battle?"

"Not what I meant," Atanamir said, serious still. "You're right, plainsman — they could wipe us out. But how many of them do you think we'd take with us before we went?"

Temujin considered that. Fifty-seven Saurons, fifty-seven assault rifles in their hands, against plainsmen with muzzle-loaders and bows? "It would be a slaughter to make the women wail," he admitted.

"Bet your ass it would," Atanamir said. "So that's half of what military fear is all about — they know we could hurt them. But it's only half. Suppose we all went to sleep and not one of us woke up while they were cutting our throats?"

Temujin supposed just that, with a bloodthirsty eagerness he did his best to hide from the Sauron hunkered down beside him. It was one of the few pleasant thoughts he'd had since he went, sozzled, from the Sozzled Stobor to the Red Room.

But Atanamir continued, "Even if the cattle knew they could get away with that, they still wouldn't. And that's the other half of military fear."

"I do not understand," Temujin confessed.

"Think," Atanamir urged. "You're not a Soldier, but you're not stupid, either." Now he sounded like a man guiding a boy at his first swordstrokes. When Temujin still looked blank, he asked, "What happens to these cattle if they wipe out two sections of Soldiers?"

*Every woman in every clan from here to the Valley of the Dinneh spreads her legs for them*, Temujin thought. That *was* a pleasant thought — it had been a long time. But since that probably wasn't the answer Atanamir was looking for, he kept quiet.

The Sauron said, "What will the Citadel do to them and their clans afterwards?"

A light went on in Temujin's head, cold and bright and piercing as the fluorescents that had glared down at him from the ceiling of the Sauron torture chamber. "Something dreadful," he whispered.

"You have it," Atanamir said. "They *know* that, down below where they don't think it, they feel it in their bones. So they don't even think about trying to bushwhack us. And that's what military fear is all about: not doing something they might be able to pull off because they know something a whole lot worse would come down on them afterwards. You got it?"

"Yes," Temujin said, and he did. Just when he didn't need any more reasons to be terrified of the Saurons, they'd given him a new one. They were surely *chidkur*, spirits of the dead that battened on the living. But the wind blew the thought out of his head, and the Saurons remained.

"Cossaki, *stanitsa* of Cherninsky," the Scout said. "They will fight to bar our path. The Ay-Koyunlu Turks have joined them. Two thousand Cossack sabers, five thousand riders of the White Sheep and the Black; the Saurons are thirty, perhaps twice that — they come close behind."

Hammer-of-God Jackson grunted, making a mark on the glossy enamel of the folding map with his chalkstick. His table was set up at one end of the big tent; crowded within were sixty of the generals, mullahs, chieftains, kings, sultans, tribal presidents . . . whatever . . . that the *jihad*-crusade-*Volkerwanderung* had inherited or thrown up. When he turned to the assembled leaders of the horde, most of them were watching him as if he had performed some magical rite. The chilly air was heavy with the scent of sweat, horse and human, and felt, leather, grease, smoke from dung fires soaked into hair and clothing.

*Some of them probably* do *think maps are magic*, he reflected with a groan.

"*Khans* — " that was the safest address for the leaders; he had Turks, Mongols, Dinneh, Arabs, Kurds, Tadjiks, Russki of various sorts, Spanjols, Bo, Ghorkalis, of every faith from the Islamic majority through Buddhism to followers of Christ of ten dozen heretical varieties . . . Hellmouth take it, there were even a dozen Polaki from some island out in the southern seas.

"Here is our situation." His finger traced along the line of the Atlas Mountains from west to east, in the direction the horde was moving; toward the Citadel and the entrance to the Shangri-La.

"We already have the largest host ever gathered on Haven. We are moving across the Northern Steppes like a wind of fire. Behind us even the grass is gone."

No surprise with thirty thousand mounted men, plus their dependents and families and the livestock to feed them, all crammed into the corridor between the foothills and the northern tundra-swamps, just turning treacherous and liquid now that ground level did not freeze hard every dimday. Hammer sent a silent prayer of thanks to his strait God that this was happening in summertime, when the carrying capacity of the pastures was at its height. Even so they were eating the land bare, sweeping up all the remaining grainstocks of the farming valleys, every head of livestock within reach, all the wild muskylope heading north with the season.

"We cannot stop, or we starve. We cannot go back, or we starve. Every people on our path must either join us, or fight to stop us, or starve. The greater our numbers grow, the faster we must travel — or we starve."

Which meant that anyone who could not keep up was left behind; stobor and cliff lions, tamerlanes and land gators were flocking in from half the continent to feast on the leavings, man and beast. Military patrols every stop period kept them from snapping up the rearguards as they slept; nobody had ever seen predators in such numbers, or so bold.

"These Cossaki, and the White Sheep Turks, they have decided to fight rather than join. With their accursed masters, the Saurons — the first real force of the enemies of God we have encountered."

"What shall we do with them?" a man asked. Running Wolf, Hammer noted. Dinneh, one of a small band who had force-marched down from the Tierra del Muerte to join the Seven. "The tribesfolk, not the Saurons."

"God is with us; God is great; God is our strength," Hammer said. He smiled, then, an expression so feral that even the hard men before him blinked at it. "Those who oppose us, fight against Him. *And they went in unto that city and slew all therein, both the young and the old, the male and the female, the ox and the ass and the sheep, with the edge of the sword, leaving not one alive to breathe; and Joshua burned the city with fire.* So says the Lord!"

A long snarl of approval swept over the armed figures crouched on the rugs of the tent, a rattle of steel and a gleam of teeth in dark faces. The fierce eyes dropped a little when Chaya rose, resplendent in her stainless robes.

"I see . . . I see a pillar of smoke by day, and of fire by night," she said. Her voice was a penetrating whisper, the pale eyes locked on some horizon beyond the red-hued steppe outside. She walked forward, and the crowd parted for her like tall grass before a wind. "They who put their faith in fire, in flame their faith shall be repaid."

They watched her, Hammer-of-God thought, with more reverence than they watched their own imams and bonzes. It would have been a beautifully executed strategy, if he could be sure it was a strategy and not nerve-wracking reality. He had found her in the Waste the night of her first convulsions; the entire army had seen her scream and topple in the the throes of prophecy at the oath-taking's height.

*Lord God of Hosts, God help us if it's real.*

Not the sort of prayers the Elders of his church would have approved of, regardless of all the time they spent braying on about prophecies. Show them the real thing, though, and watch them turn white as fresh dough and begin to shake. He wished he had time to enjoy the spectacle.

He flicked a glance at Karl bar Edgar, standing at Judge Chaya's side. His new wife was with him. Between Karl's medical skills and Aisha's fighting skills, the Judge was as safe as Hammer-of-God could make her.

*Don't let her see through me. I have enough trouble with this mob.* Another prayer that wouldn't have passed muster in his father's church. Too damned bad. *In thy hand only is victory, O Lord God of Hosts.* He'd just have to do his best.

Karl nodded — which Hammer assumed to mean "no fits imminent" — and thinned his lips, which wasn't a good sign at all. Even a worn-out old professional soldier could see that the Judge was worn out too. Old, he thought of her, for the first time. He had spent most of his life following the Judge's orders, or conspiring with the *kapetein* to find a way around them. She had stood like a monument in his life. And now, as he thought he saw it start to fall, he was more afraid than he'd been since the death of the *kommandant h'gana* who had first whipped him into shape.

"What of the bloody Saurons?" Kemal asked; as one of the Seven he had a rank among the first line of commanders, although only a few hundred of his own people had followed him eastward. Many more from other tribes were sworn to him now.

"We defeated this force once — we can do it again."

"At heavy cost," Kemal said. Four hundred dead, and twice that number wounded. The horde was balanced between exaltation — they had forced Saurons to retreat in open battle — and shock.

Hammer nodded, glad to be back to practicalities. "There are a maximum of sixty left," he said, his voice coldly analytical once more. "Each carries no more than two hundred rounds of ammunition after what they expended in the first encounter. If every third round kills one of ours — an optimistic estimate from their point of view — then each Sauron will kill sixty or so. Thirty-six hundred dead; we can spare them."

There was an intake of breath. "With seven thousand plainsmen fighting beside them, how many shall we lose?" someone asked.

"You swore to the Holy War," Hammer-of-God said. "Nobody promised you an easy task."

Silence fell; everyone knew their only hope was to swamp the Saurons with numbers — a strategy of holocaust, trading a hundred lives for one.

"If three score of them can kill a tenth of the greatest

host Haven has ever seen, how may we prevail against the Citadel?" Ilderim *Khan* said. "There are *thousands* of the sons of Iblis there, behind great walls."

Aisha leaned forward. "We have shown that the Saurons are not invincible."

Ilderim and several of the older leaders snorted. "*Khatun*, we took a small outpost of boys, commanded by a tired old man. By a trick. A clever trick, by Allah and the spirits, a trick I shall tell my grandchildren — but a trick. We drove back a force which did not know our numbers or determination. We shall not trick three score of warriors in their prime, ready for a fight."

The others nodded. Warfare on the steppe was a matter of raid and ambush and subterfuge more often than not, but when armies collided . . .

"True enough, by Malak Ta'us," a chief said, a slim dark man with chiseled features and a long embroidered coat.

"Stuff your blasphemous Peacock up your devil-worshiping backside," growled another leader, a thick-bodied man in a shirt of scale mail, with a strong hook nose and a bushy beard that flowed down over the steel scales. "If you're a woman, why didn't you tell us earlier? We might have gotten some use out of you."

"Gazakardian *Khan!*" Chaya said sternly, and the two men came half-erect, clapping their hands to their swords. "Remember your oath!"

Aisha put a hand to Gazakardian's wrist; the thick limb trembled slightly, and the sword sank back in its scabbard with a *snick* of steel and brass against oiled wood and leather.

"I remember," he growled, looking aside.

"Then make your apology," Chaya said, and turned to the first man: "Which you, Shaikh Hoshyar, will accept with the graciousness of your noble lineage, I am sure."

Sweat broke out on Gazakardian's face. Silence stretched. At last, he said: "I spoke in anger, but my anger should be with the Accursed of God, not you . . . Shaikh Hoshyar."

Hoshyar waved. "The words are gone, swallowed up in

the ocean of your goodwill and courtesy, O Gazakardian *Khan*," the Yezda said. "What is evil, but a word?"

Some of the others smiled at that; Gazakardian's tribe, the Hayq, lived fairly near Hoshyar's Yezadi folk in the foothills of the Tierra del Muerte country, on the northwest edge of the Great Northern Steppe. Being neighbors, they hated each other like poison, of course.

"Be still!" Aisha said sharply to the Muslim chiefs. "These are the words of brave men — it takes more courage to acknowledge wrong and grant forgiveness than to quarrel like fools in the face of a greater enemy. If some of us are *nasrani* and others follow the Peacock Angel . . . by Allah, we can all agree that the Saurons are under the curse of whatever spirits wish men well."

She turned to Hammer-of-God. "Still, for the good of our cause we must win a convincing victory. The more victories, the more the warriors' spirits will rise — and the more we will conquer."

Hammer nodded sardonically. "Thirty-six hundred dead is the worst possible case," he said. *One which might wreck us.* The tribes would take any losses necessary to break the Citadel, but they had to *believe* it. Aisha's rhetoric could whip them into a frenzy, but the *khans* here were mostly older men, survivor-graduates of a lifetime of warfare in a very hard school. Pessimists to a man. Let them become convinced the thing was impossible and they'd turn on each other in a minute. The biggest horde Haven had ever seen would become the biggest and bloodiest *battle* Haven had ever seen. All by itself.

"I presume none of you are *afraid* to fight the Kossacki or the White Sheep?" he said dryly. That brought the expected bristle. *Chaya is the impartial Judge, Aisha inspires them — and they can resent me, like a good tough sergeant who makes his officer look good.* "Our first task will be to peel as many of them away from the Saurons as we can. Then we make the Saurons come to us."

He flipped over the map and drew on the reverse. "We've fought Saurons before, and beaten them off, although it always costs. Their Dark Lord gives them great warrior skills — but they tend to arrogance and overconfidence. Note how they're driving the fighters of the tribes before them. Their most effective strategy would be to use their Sauron abilities and firepower to break our line in close coordination with their allies — but to them, all who aren't Saurons are cattle to be driven. Here's how we'll proceed. . . ."

*This ought to do*, Shulamit thought. Nice and high, up here on the hill, so nobody could steal up on her, but with plenty of large rocks for concealment. She unwrapped her belt; it was new, bought from one of the recent volunteers from the Pale. Quite nice, triple-ply sheepskin with the fleece left on the inside, adjustable lacings, a chiseled-steel buckle and plenty of pouches and fastenings. Saber and dagger went within reach, and she looked out over the plain as she unfastened the armor.

Byers' Sun was slipping below the horizon, but Cat's Eye was up and full, plenty of light — enough to tell a dark thread from a light, according to the traditional test. The rolling plain below the rocky hillside was reddish-brown, mottled with clumps of moving humans and animals, out to the limit of sight in every direction. Metal winked at her from weapons and gear; wagons lumbered behind their long strings of muskylope or oxen; trains of pack-beasts drew straggling lines across the plain. Pillars of dust rose from herds of slaughter-beasts and mounted warriors each leading his remounts; the geometric regularity of the Pale's fighters stood out against the vast sprawl of the host, ant-small at two kilometers' distance.

That was where she should be, with the others. The old battle-axe who led the squad she was in, and the others, all sniggering at her for carrying on about Karl. *Nobody* would take what she said about Sigrid seriously!

Ten minutes later she rose from behind the boulder, readjusting her loincloth and pulling up her trousers with weary discomfort. *Just* what she needed — constipation in the middle of a war. Then she froze and dropped the trousers again to check.

*Oh,* no, *not* now. It was ten Haven days since the last time, sure enough, although she'd never been very regular. Then a wave of relief: no bleeding *quite* yet. Although she felt bloated and edgy enough. She wouldn't need the packets of moss in linen in her warbag for a T-day or two.

Then she froze again. She'd been very careful about taking her herbs — not that she'd had much *reason* to be careful the past month or so. Had the Sauron bitch?

*Did she* want *to be careful?* The hateful scene at Cliff Lion Springs played itself out again in her mind. Many people — Bandari among them — haunted Sauron culling grounds for abandoned babies; there were even stories of women lying with lone Saurons to get pregnant, to bear children who would have the enemy's strong blood yet be raised human. What if it had been the other way 'round, this time? No Bandari woman had ever gone as tribute maiden to the Saurons — but the ice-bitch might have stolen the seed of the fan Reenans none the less. Blood of the Founder raised in the Citadel!

"Karl bar Yigal fan Reenan, you are *stuuuuppiiid!*" Shulamit screamed in mingled jealousy and rage, shaking her fist at the sky. The lurch of the trousers round her ankles, and the cold wind on her thighs, brought her back to herself. She had come here for privacy — the last thing she needed right now was constipation jokes from her squadmates — but it was not safe to attract attention alone.

*Yeweh and the* anima *of the Founders.* A glint of steel, heading toward the base of the hill. *Hotnot* riders.

She pulled up the trousers and began the complicated squirm-swing-grab of putting on armor without someone to help. With the skill of long practice she caught the tie at her left shoulder and slipped it into the bronze buckles set into the curved leather plates, then fastened the latches down along her side and bent to touch her toes to make sure everything was working. Shulamit kicked viciously at a rock. It bounded away down the slope and shattered with a crack against a harder boulder. The Bandari *meid* followed in its wake with cautious speed, but the four strangers still managed to get between her and her string of ponies. Turks, she saw at a glance — Mongols fastened their coats the other way, and these were too sharp-featured for that breed as well. Of the Red Stobor tribal federation, from the markings on their horses; she couldn't place the clan, but the whole kit-and-caboodle had come in to join the trek about two weeks ago, just before they left the oasis. One of them had a flintlock pistol through his belt. They had dismounted, and her own hobbled ponies were on the other side of them.

*Spirits damn it*, she thought. *Hotnots*. They were trouble wherever you met them.

"Hello!" one of them called as she walked into hailing distance. The others spread across her path.

"Go bugger a goat," she snarled back, coming reluctantly to a halt. It looked as if she would have to talk to them, after all.

"Have you ever heard of lo-mid-hi?" Shulamit said with vicious sweetness, smiling and knocking the tribesman's hand aside again. That was the third time he'd tried to fondle her butt. *Third time is enough.* She *had* told him to go away, the first time. Nobody could say she was stretching things.

"I do not know this word, beautiful one," he said eagerly. Behind him his comrades nudged each other, chuckling and winking.

"It means, handsome warrior — "

Shulamit's right hand rested on her hip; the left was behind her back, pulling out a short rod of iron barstock she kept tucked into a fold of her broad sheepskin belt.

"*Lo.*" A sharp huffing exhalation of breath.

Her right hand shot out, knuckles down and fingers crooked, as her body pivoted away. The heel of the palm thudded into his pubic bone and the strong fingers clenched around his testicles, twisting. The leather trousers saved the nomad a little, but not much. He screamed, high and shrill.

"*Mid.*" A shout.

She turned back toward him on her heel, driving the

weight of her body from heel through gut to shoulder behind her left fist as it punched into his sternum. He was not wearing armor, and his lambskin jacket was open to the waist; the hard muscle of his belly shocked at her fist, jarring her wrist. The striking knuckles had been accurately placed in the soft spot all humans have just under the breastbone, though, and the nomad's scream cut off in an agonized *hooof* as he doubled over. Wonderful what a sap in your hand did when you punched somebody.

"*Hi!*"

The last word was a shriek of rage as she drove her knee into his face, not as hard as she could have; that would have killed him. Enough to drop him stunned, spitting teeth and bleeding from a broken nose.

"Low, middle, and high," Shulamit said, wheeling on his companions. "That's what you get if you touch Bandari women uninvited."

The flurry of blows had taken less than twenty seconds. Enough time for the nomad's three friends to gape with shock and then drop their hands to their weapons. Shulamit bared her teeth and half-drew her saber; she was in her harness, except for the helmet and shield she'd left on her horse. None of the plainsmen had more than a leather coat . . . and all of them knew the reputation of the People.

"You . . . you . . . that is the *gur-khan*'s son!" one of them sputtered. "You laid hands on the *gur-khan*'s son, you harlot!"

Shulamit's Turki was heavily accented but fluent: "I *punched out* the *gur-khan*'s son," she corrected him. *Yes, he does have turquoise on his swordbelt, and those are good weapons.* A pity he wasn't alone; then she could take them. Fair recompense for the trouble he'd caused her. His horse was worth having, too.

The young Turk was crawling and moaning, one hand to his nose and the other leaving off clutching at his crotch to go for a knife. Shulamit kicked him in the ribs with judicious force and he collapsed again.

*Men*, she thought. None of them was worth the fletching on the arrow it would take to shoot them.

"And what's he going to do, go whining to his father — *maybe* his father — that a woman beat him? What's the matter with you *hotnots*, you don't have enough of the ewes and muskylope mares you usually screw? *Gur-khan's* son? He's the Prince of Perversion, bothering a human female instead of bending over for his boar-pig brothers as would be natural for him. Go on, go complain to your pork-eating fathers — all forty of them."

The olive faces of the nomads darkened further: *son of ten fathers* was about as insulting as you could get, in their tongue. They were young men, only a few T-years older than her seventeen, but there was a wealth of experience in the way they drew their curved *shamshirs* and spread out without wasting words. Shulamit skipped back a step as her own saber came out; the look on their faces was like cold water on the hot coals of her anger. It made her remember she was not really angry at *them*. She reached across and drew her knife left-handed for want of a shield, crouching slightly and letting the tip of her saber weave in a tight, controlled circle.

*P'rknz hammer me for a fool, they really mean it,* she thought uneasily. *They could* kill *me*. She was far too young to die; there was so much left to do! Dying in a useless brawl was *not* what she had planned. *I'm almost as stupid as Karl.*

She would have to lunge; the *hotnots* wouldn't be expecting it, their own swordplay was all with the edge, body flat-on to an opponent. Shulamit crooked her right knee slightly, keeping her left back and bent ready to spring. Thrusting, the blade should be parallel to the ground so it didn't catch on ribs. Nasty thought, the steel grating on bone. She had tried it on butchered muskylope strung up at the practice ground: part of the drill was to get you accustomed to the feeling. You had to be something special to take on more than one opponent hand to hand, the clan armsmasters said. Shulamit knew she was better than average for her age, but she had fought only once in earnest. Fighting for the Sauron bitch, if only she had known it then.

*I wish I'd shot her in the back. I wish I had her assault rifle right now.* The thought reawoke her anger; that and danger narrowed her vision down to a tunnel. She barely heard the hooves clattering on rock behind her. Only the startled retreat of the Turks made her begin to turn.

*Whack.* The steel-shod butt of the lance caught her between the shoulderblades, banging on the hard lamellae of her armor and throwing her forward. She came up rolling and turning, to meet the same metal driving into her belly. Another gunshot crack, and she went on her back winded and gasping for breath; reflex started to bring her sword up, and common sense stopped it. The stocky figure on the big horse was also in Pale armor, and she recognized the face and markings. Tameetha bat Irene fan Reenan. *Not* a good idea to draw on her appointed *aluf*. Shulamit sheathed her blade and tried to rise, wheezing; the older Bandari heeled her mount forward, and its shoulder knocked the girl flying again. This time she landed on rocks, with a howl of protest.

"*Shut* up," Tameetha barked.

Shulamit rubbed her stomach; the older woman was *strong*. The twelve-foot lance swung back as she wheeled her horse between Shulamit and the nomads. Legs clamped to barrel and the big horse reared, the pawing menace of the ironshod hooves sending them scrambling away. The honed edges of the arm-long lancehead caught the light of Byers' Sun as she flipped it up to an overarm grip, prodding the air. One Turk reached slowly toward the bowcase slung at his back. The steel rammed forward to rest a hand's-width from his throat.

"Don' even tink abut it, boy," Tameetha barked; her Turkic was understandable, but worse than Shulamit's. "Go hum. Tek yur frien', en go hum."

Silent, they gathered up the gasping, bleeding young man and walked in stiff-backed anger toward the horse. Shulamit rose rubbing her bruised buttocks and decided on a preemptive attack. Preemptive self-defense, the old legends called it.

"They started it!" she said, and pointed up to the slopes of the rocky volcanic hill that rose out of the steppe. "I went up there to take a leak and they started bothering me when

I came down — I *told* them a couple of times to go away, but the stupid *hotnot* kept trying to grab my ass, so I gave him lo-mid-hi, then they drew on me first!"

Tameetha rested the lance-butt on the toe of her boot and leaned forward: "Save the slather for Barak, bat Miriam — and sniffing around him means you're picking a fight with Sannie, too. Yeweh, Christ, and the *anima* of the Founders, because your Karl is a brainless boy who thinks with his testicles and is ready to fuck mud — that's normal for a male his age — is that any reason *you* have to act stupid? He screws some *shiks*, you carry on like the world's ending, in the middle of a war, already. For your information, it doesn't wear out with use! Wake up and smell the tea brewing, you bliddyful of a *meid*! There's a battle coming on, and I don't *need* this shit."

"Battle, *tanta aluf*?" Shulamit gulped.

Tameetha gave her a stobor grin. "Auntie officer am I, now? You hadn't noticed, eh, wrapped up in your more important affairs? Yes, a battle."

Shulamit whistled for her horse. It took three tries; her mouth was dry.

# ● CHAPTER TWENTY-THREE

"Will we win?" Chaya said quietly.

"Oh, we'll win, all right," Hammer-of-God said.

The Seven stood on a low hill, surrounded by messengers. Hammer-of-God had a few more complex items of equipment: a tripod-mounted pair of binoculars the length of a man's leg, a heliograph and a map table. He was uneasily aware that those meant less than they might have. With a Bandari force he would have had a fully articulated chain of command from regiments down to squads, trained officers, and the whole force would be well-disciplined and literate. With only about fifteen hundred of the People here, nine-tenths of the force were *hotnots*. Of those, only some of the Mongols and a few others had any idea of discipline; the rest were brave, hardy, mobile and about as cohesive as a bar brawl. Fighting by clans and tribes . . .

*So are most of the enemy*, he reminded himself. The sixty Saurons were a different matter, but he had a plan for them. *A plan that depends on their doing what I want them to.*

Out on the plain, a dust cloud was moving. High-plumed dust, pink against the ruddy sky. Horsemen, beyond the furthest limits of the Seven's forces.

"Kemal," he said. "The White Sheep are moving to our flank. Get around them. Barak, you—"

"Get ready for it," Barak called from the ridge ahead, to the west. "Mount up."

"Get ready for *what*?" Shulamit whispered, as they swung into the saddle with a long rattling clatter of gear.

Some of the Bandari troopers on either side of her laughed at that; Tameetha turned and glared at her. A hundred and fifty of them were strung out in a line three deep, well back from the ridge. From here what they saw was what they had seen all day: columns of dust across the rocky landscape, too far away to make out the men and horses beneath as anything but bug figures. Blocks of them moving back and forth, sometimes meeting, sometimes disappearing behind a hill. A glint of weapons, faint shouts far-off mixed with the discordant harp music of bowstrings and the occasional scrap-metal sound of combat.

Once they heard the *phutphutphutphut* sound an older fighter said was Sauron assault rifles, different from the close-range banging she had heard in the valley where Sigrid fought. They had all gone tense at that, but nothing happened. Sometimes a message came for them to move, and they trotted off across the rocky steppe to a place not visibly different from the one before. Passing others moving, or dead men and horses, or wounded ones, which was worse. Karl bar Edgar had gone by once with wagonloads of bloody figures who shrieked at the bumping of the wheels, his face fixed and pale.

It was trueday, too bright for stars and well above freezing; Byers' Sun overhead, and Cat's Eye's lidless orb squatting in the west in banded dull-red majesty. Four of the sister moons were in the sky as well, as if the heavens crowded to look at what humans did. Shulamit remembered her fears and hopes; if this was a battle, it seemed like neither, only a vast chaotic bewilderment where nobody seemed to know what was going on. She twisted slightly in the saddle to look behind her; Sapper and his crew had their dozens of modified wagons there, fronted with planks and covered in greasy-green drillbit gut, fresh and stinking vilely of decay and metallic salts. There were loopholes in the planks, and riflemen crouched behind with the long-barreled weapons of the Pale. Behind them came a wooden frame on wheels, assembled from local timber and metal parts brought from Eisenstaadt, the Gimbutas town in Eden Valley. A long wooden lever with a cup on one end, the other thrust through a huge knot of cured muskylope sinews, and windlasses to bend it back. Sapper was whistling cheerfully as he worked about it; he had a small barrel inside a larger one, and was pouring sacks of lead balls into the gap between.

Karl bar Yigal grinned ingratiatingly as he trotted back from over the ridge and took a place in the ranks a little down from her; the horses jostled a bit as the line readjusted, stirrup irons clanking together. This was no clan regiment, with its ancient traditions and blood ties, but they all had the training and they'd been together for weeks now, long enough for drill to shake them down into a unit.

"Lot of *hotnots* over there, but I didn't see any Saurons," Karl said.

"Apart from your girlfriend?" Shulamit snapped back.

"She's not my — she's not a Sauron!" Karl half-yelled, standing in the saddle to gesture over the shoulder of the man next to him.

"She had a Sauron rifle," Shulamit said, stabbing a finger at him. "She *looks* like a bloody Sauron, she *talked* like one when we met her — who else but a Sauron wanders around the steppes alone and lives to tell about it?"

"Does she waddle and quack like a Sauron, too?" someone asked, with amusement in his voice.

"Hell, does she fuck like a Sauron, eh, man, Karl, hey?" another laughed.

"*Shut up or it's the gauntlet*," Tameetha rasped.

That brought real silence; running between a line of your comrades while they lashed you with their belts was no joke. Ahead of them Barak raised his hand to shade his eyes; augmented eyes, Shulamit remembered with a chill. His hearing would be sorting out whatever-it-was across there as well. Then he turned and cantered down toward them.

"All right," he said, drawing up near the center of the formation; he gave her a slight distracted smile when she waved. "Over there" — he pointed behind him — "our *hotnots* are fighting theirs, and falling back toward us by Hammer's plan. When they retreat, the enemy will push forward. We come over the hill and get them moving back sharp. *Don't* shove in among them or scatter them; keep them grouped and moving back. The Saurons are behind them. We want a big screen of enemy between us and them. When the Saurons pitch in, which they will, you'll hear the retreat sounded. Retreat *quick*; in good order, but quick. I've seen what their weapons can do. The range is about a thousand meters; that's where you'll rally, while Sapper and his merry band play their tricks."

After that was only waiting; once Shulamit put on her helmet and buckled the chinstrap, even the sounds were muffled. She shifted in the saddle, conscious of thirst and a humiliating need to piss, and the ache of Karl's presence only five meters away. It made her angry, and she was *tired* of being angry, but she couldn't stop. He *should* say he was sorry, or at least *believe* her . . . and she was frightened, too. Sigrid was a Sauron, but sixty more of the real article were only a kilometer away, and coming closer. She wiped her hand down the cold nappy surface of her wool pants, below the armor. Judge Chaya and Hammer-of-God knew what they were doing; but the Judge had been acting very strange lately, and Hammer was *always* strange. Even for an Edenite.

*Saurons killed Da.* She had been eight when they brought back his body. So strong and alive, and then lying there in the box, and the hands that used to lift her up toward the ceiling still and wastedlooking. *I promised, Da.* Thirty lives to pay for the years he missed. Treason to be afraid because she had yet to see her third Haven year.

It was almost a relief when a pair of *hotnots* came over the ridge; Mongols, Yek clansmen in embroidered jackets. They galloped down and past the waiting Bandari, waving to Barak as they slowed their mounts and cantered off. Barak shouted: "Bows ready!" More noise sounded from beyond the ridge, an angry insistent buzzing.

Beside her a man she hardly knew murmured, but not to her: "Lord God of Hosts, Who stayed the sun in its course, You know I must be busy now. I will have no time to think of You; but may You think well of me."

Shulamit slapped on the gloves tucked through her belt and pulled the *bare* out of the case at her left knee, as sweat turned dank under her harness. Her hands tingled as she unfastened the cap on the quiver, to the right of the saddlehorn. Forty arrows in there, five in the clip attached to her bow. She pulled out a red-feather broadhead and slotted it through the cutout of the handgrip. There was a gentle click as the horn spring caught the shaft and held it there, a crisp sound as the bone nock rested on the horse-hair of the string. She pulled the shaft to half-draw, testing the tension and the smoothness of the pulley wheels. Then she looped her reins around the pommel of the saddle. It took both hands to handle a bow from horseback, and hence a well-trained mount. The chestnut was her best, and first-rate apart from a neurotic hatred of camels. Shulamit sympathized with the mare: camels stank.

"Left wheel." The formation turned, changing from a line to a column. "Advance, at the walk."

They rode north, then the formation bent like an L as the head of it turned west and over the ridge. Ahead of her riders rose like a living wave, manes and helmet crests and the points of slung lances. The iron *ting* of horseshoes on rock echoed, and the thudding sound of four hundred hooves on dirt. Then the chestnut's muscles were bunching between her knees as they rose, and the view ahead hit at her like an invisible blow to the face. The Mongols were racing off to north and south, except for the dead who stayed, and a few caught among the Cossack host in circles of thrashing sabers. There were half again a thousand of the *gayam*, a vast dun mass shaped like a C with the blunt end toward her. They recoiled at the sight of the Bandari, then edged forward again when it became clear how few the People were; and at the menacing stutter of an assault rifle at their heels.

They had no order, but they rocked forward almost as one creature, a vast shaggy mass flowing across the plain to meet her, bright with bristling banners and teeth that were metal swordblades and spearheads. And they screamed as they charged: *"Na Umor! Umor!"* To the death! Death!

The Bandari stretched out, racing at a pounding gallop across the front of the enemy line; their three-deep formation was staggered, and she could see through the two to her left. Enemy closing fast, three hundred meters, two. Broad-cheeked shouting faces, red coats daubed with tar, shaven heads with scalp locks and long moustaches, here and there a helmet or a leather breastplate. A ram's horn snarled and dunted from somewhere along the Bandari line: *Draw.*

She threw arms and shoulders and gut muscle against the draw of her bow, holding it as the base of her thumb rested in the angle of her jaw. The string creased her nose; she raised the lowest sighting pin until it rested in air above the nearest Cossack rank. Another blatting call.

*Loose*. The string rasped over the thumb-ring of her gauntlet and whacked against the leather of her arm-guard. For a second the whistling of a hundred and fifty arrows drowned shouts and hoofbeats. The shafts rose in a blurred cloud, seemed to pause an instant at the height of their trajectory with a wink of sunlight on steel, then swooped downward. The Kossacki checked briefly — that was long range for their unaided bows, middling for the People, but they had no experience of the Bandari *bare*. Then their formation shattered like crockery under a sledgehammer as the long arrows sleeted down. Men fell, dead or screaming and plucking at the iron in their flesh; horses reared, tumbled; others too close and fast to stop plowed into them and fell in turn, multi-ton pileups of kicking, shrieking meat taller than a man. Shulamit felt a complex shudder at the thought of being caught like that, unavoidable for a lifelong rider.

Her hands stripped another arrow from the ready clip with automatic skill. By the time the clip was empty the Bandari had ridden the full length of the Cossack formation, and the *gayam* were advancing much more slowly, in clots and dribbles rather than a solid mass. The next horn-call was more complex; it was called the *Parthian retreat*, for some reason. Shulamit recognized it easily enough: the trumpet codes were learned as early as writing in the Pale. Most of the horses knew it too; slowed of their own accord before the riders drew them up and wheeled right, spurring back into a gallop in extended order toward the western ridge. They turned in the saddle to shoot behind them as they rode; the Kossacki seemed to recover some of their spirit to see their foes retreat, and came on again against the slower rain of arrows.

They stopped when the other two companies of ha-Bandari surged up over the ridge on either side, and

the original one halted and turned about. They stopped
and wavered and turned back; then the Sauron rifles
sounded behind them in earnest. Shulamit set her teeth at
the sound; the *soldati* were giving their "allies" no choice
but to attack the People or be slaughtered.

*That's the friendship of Saurons,* she thought. Fury ground
her teeth together, memory of long arms and legs wrapped
around Karl. *Friendship of stobor. Thickheaded yellow-thatched
Litvak* fool. Pack-muskylopes lumbered up to the Bandari,
and their handlers tossed bundles of spare arrows to the
waiting fighters. Shulamit grabbed two, filled her quiver
and clip, took a moment to rinse out her mouth and spit.
One long swallow of tepid leathery water from her canteen
was like a taste of heaven.

"Ready," Tameetha said, a few paces ahead. "Remember, listen for the calls; don't get caught up." More softly,
looking down to where the Kossacki milled and began to
advance again: "*Gayams naktness,*" she whispered. *Barbarian
madness.*

Everyone cased bows. The front rank unslung their lances
and brought them down; Shulamit drew her saber and
smoothed a hand down the chestnut's neck before she took
up her shield by its central handgrip. The horn blatted.

"*HA-BANDAR!*"

The deep guttural shout launched the fighters of the
Pale into the charge. Shulamit shouted too, as much to
clear the tightness from her throat as anything else. The
Kossacki howled like files on rock and spurred their
horses, not enthusiastic but too experienced at steppe warfare to receive a charge at the stand. Their formation
stretched and scattered as it advanced, trying to lap around
the tighter Bandari lines. Few arrows came from it; the
enemy had shot their quivers empty earlier in the day, and
had no organization to refill them.

They struck.

Shulamit could never remember exactly what happened next; it was as if a flash of white light seared her
memories. Flickering images remained. Tameetha spear-
ing a Cossack out of the saddle and pivoting her lance at

the grip to let it drag free. The chestnut shouldered into an enemy mount, and the lighter *gayam* horse going down, her own legs gripping convulsively as the Pale warhorse staggered then half-jumped, half-walked across the fallen beast and its rider. Well-trained, the chestnut stepped on the human. Hard.

The wind of a blade's passage across her face; full awareness snapped back. She brought the shield around and up and cut to her left, then the man was past her. Another coming up on her right; the momentum of the charge was stalling, and the chestnut slowed automatically. This one was a bareheaded man, young, with a cut on his cheek. Wild blue eyes above a button nose, a chain around his neck strung with crosses and odd-looking little portraits. He rode hunched over like a jockey, his stirrups short, a curved sword rising for a cut as their mounts brought them into range.

*"Umor!"* he screeched at her; the voice broke in comical surprise as he saw that the face below the crested helmet belonged to a girl younger than he. There was nothing chivalrous about the cut he tried, a simple overarm swing aimed at her shoulder. That would bisect her to the navel, or break bone through the armor.

Reaction was automatic, from ten thousand hours of training starting the month she learned to walk. Lean forward, twist the wrist to set the sword horizontal to the ground. Muscles in line from point to arm to braced feet. Buckler around and up, over her head.

The young Cossack ran right on to the point. It wasn't like skewering a muskylope carcass; there was a soft, heavy feeling as the saber punched in beside his navel. His slash weakened and banged feebly off her shield, scarcely even driving her hand down on the stiff horsehair of her helmet crest. Something seemed to travel up the blade to her hand and into her arm; their eyes met, blue to blue. His went round, and his mouth did too, like a cartoon drawing of a surprised face done in charcoal on the side of a barn. The follow-through was as automatic as the thrust: twist sharply (crisp poppings resounded through the blade), *wrench* the hilt back as the horses passed. The eyes, the eyes stayed

locked on hers, rolling up into the fair brows, Shulamit
turning in the saddle and watching as the body toppled
over the high cantle and the front of it was *all* blood, a sheet
more crimson than Cat's Eye —

"*Look alive!*" Tameetha's voice screamed at her.

She snapped around to the front, fear tightening the
loose feeling in stomach and throat and drying her mouth
of the rush of gummy saliva. A Cossack was staring at her,
eyelids drooping as if he was sleepy; then the *aluf* freed her
lancepoint from his back with a wrenching effort. Nobody
seemed to be near them. Beyond her Shulamit could see
Karl fighting, his forged-steel war-hammer blurring in a
circle as if it were a spoke on a spinning wheel. It snapped a
sword and struck a skull that spattered away from it, and
Karl's face was locked in a grimace that seemed half terror
and half disbelief.

Tameetha whacked the dead Cossack's horse across the
rump with the shaft of her lance. There was a rough sympathy to her voice as she jerked her head to Shulamit,
motioning her back. "You only have to lose that cherry once,
too," she said. Then shouted: "Pull back, pull back! Rally!"

Shulamit wheezed out a shuddering breath as the Bandari fighters dressed their ranks; the enemy were milling a
hundred meters away, caught between two fires and
unwilling to face either. The flexible armor seemed to be
squeezing at her ribs as she panted.

*Where did all the bodies come from?* she wondered, dazed.
The open ground between the forces was littered with
them, almost all enemy. *Where was the fight? All I saw was* —

Assault rifles snarled again, much closer this time; the
Cossack screams turned hysterical, and she thought she
could see figures on foot through their thinning ranks,
figures in gray. The ram's horn sounded, quick and hard:
*retreat, retreat.* The Bandari turned once more and spurred
their horses, the weary beasts taking a little longer to reach a
gallop, their masters more urgent. More firing from behind
her; she risked a look. The enemy was scattering every which
way, crying their panic, more of them going down with each
instant as invisible death combed them from behind. *Four*

*hundred meters*. Lightning had said that the danger zone was a thousand. Then there *were* figures in field-gray dodging among the last Kossacki, running fast as horses themselves, jinking and turning with unhuman agility.

Fear jerked at her, but the moan turned into a snarl as hatred overpowered it. Hate was strong, like the salt taste of blood on her lips.

*Seven hundred yards*. Just beside her a trooper grunted as something smacked between his shoulder blades. He crumpled off his mount, down even as she grabbed at him. Beyond him a horse reared and screamed and collapsed, throwing his rider; the Bandari on either side swooped down and came up with an armpit grip, carrying the unconscious woman with both her feet off the ground. A sound like a giant insect buzzing, and the chestnut pig-jumped under her, squealing. Her heart lurched again as she turned. A red line across his haunch, not too deep but bleeding freely; she had to slug back on the reins to keep him from bolting. More of the People down, but they were nearly out of range.

Ahead, Sapper's wagons rumbled over the ridge and down toward them, running along propelled by gravity and enthusiastic hands. Wagons and riders passed in a flash of combined speed and the riders pulled up at the ridge. Shulamit reined in once they were safely downslope, invisible from the enemy side. Then she slid from the saddle and dropped the reins on the ground; that meant *halt in place* to the chestnut. It shuddered and twisted to sniff at its injury; she got out some ointment and treated the wound, soothed the animal with soft words and careful stroking. Then she cleaned the bloody saber and walked back to the ridge and crouched to look over it, drawing the sword through a balled-up rag without glancing down until she was sure it was clean. Nobody objected, although only officers were supposed to dismount.

There was a grim fascination in what happened below. The Saurons had halted for an instant when the wagons appeared, puzzled by the unfamiliar sight. Then the long flintlocks began to crackle from behind the timber shields, firing bullets the size of a small woman's thumb. One tall figure in field-gray dropped, then two more. The others went to ground and fired from behind what scanty cover the open plain offered. Single shots, but so close together that they might have been automatic, and the shields of the wagons rippled with the impacts. Triple layers of drillbit gut — drillbits ate rock — and inch-thick steelwood planks turned them; the rifles behind spoke with metronomic regularity at six rounds a minute. The folk using them might not have enhanced genes, but the weapons were as accurate as the Citadel-made copies of the ancient AK, and the marksmen keen-eyed and well trained. Ammunition was ferociously expensive and the People thrifty, but they didn't begrudge practice rounds.

It looked to be a curiously bloodless and remote way of war, compared to what she had just experienced. Shulamit winced at the memory of those blue eyes, so surprised. *He was trying to kill* me, *it's only fair*, she thought. Barak laughed beside her; she started. He was even quieter than Karl, when he wanted to be.

"Look," he said. "Behind them."

A line of dark figures; she squinted. Men on foot, loping along with bundles of javelins and short, massive recurved chopping knives.

"Gurkhas," she said. They were the only infantry in the Seven's host, and came from the Atlas Mountains not far from here. Very friendly to the People; haBandari merchants had helped their villages in a famine a generation ago, and often hired their young men as caravan guards.

"Bloody clever of Hammer," Barak said respectfully. "Even if the Saurons did go at it like a bull muskylope charging a gate in springtime."

"Won't . . . won't they just turn and finish off the Gurkhas?"

"No," Barak said, shaking his head. His eyes looked a little odd, shining redly with Cat's Eye light, as a cat's might. "They want *us*, Shuli."

Even the diminutive gave her a little pleasure; he was the Judge's son . . . well, sort of. And handsome. And *smarter* than Karl, even if he wouldn't believe her about Sigrid either. At nineteen T-years, Karl was such a *boy* sometimes.

"Because of Judge Chaya," Shulamit said, nodding wisely. The Seven would fall apart without her; Aisha's preaching had rallied the tribes, but it was the Judge they trusted.

"And because we're us," Barak said grimly. "That feud's as old as the Citadel. Right about now they're going to decide that it's worth the casualties to storm those wagons, and — "

Perhaps the Saurons had some ancient technology of communication still, or perhaps their senses let them call to each other without humans hearing it. Just then the whole line of Soldiers rose and charged, faster than galloping horses. Behind the wagons Sapper's hand whipped down, and the catapult cut loose with a whit*bang* of sound. The rear wheels jumped into the air — that had earned the device its name of *jackass* — and a barrel flew up into the sky, trailing a line of blue smoke from its fuse. The slowmatch ended just as the tumbling wood was halfway down from its apogee, about twenty meters up. The Saurons had seen it, had even thrown themselves flat again with supernal speed. It did them no good. The explosion was a massive *crack* in midair, black smoke with a winking eye of red in its center. The malignant wasp-whine of a thousand lead musket balls was louder. Dirt and dust spurted up from a broad circle as the metal shrapnel flayed the ground and everything on it.

Half the Saurons rose again, some staggering with wounds that would have killed ordinary men; they met a crashing volley from the concealed riflemen, and another keg-bomb went lofting skyward, then a flurry of pottery hand grenades when the range closed. Barak was grinning like a cliff lion with its paws on a kill.

"*Now* we attack," he said. "A feint, a feint, a diversion — and *then* the real thing." They turned and slid down towards the waiting horses and their comrades. "*Up and at 'em!*"

The first part of the battle had not been too bad, Temujin thought. The Saurons had stayed well back — the role of the Turks and Kossacki was to fix the enemy in place, after all. Dust clouds maneuvered across the western horizon, and Atanamir sent messengers to direct his tributary allies. After a while *Hetman* Oleg Cherninsky came riding up with a thousand or so of his men, horses blowing, many clutching wounds or reeling in the saddle. The Cossack chief might have a fat belly — covered right now with a chain-mail shirt — but he was a good rider. There was blood on the guardless saber in his right hand, and the small nail-studded shield in his left was hacked and battered.

"*Slava bogdu!*" he said, crossing himself as he halted in front of the Saurons. "They press us back; they are too many, and they fight like men possessed by wind demons. We just took a charge from those Jew devils — "

"HaBandari?" Anatamir said. "How many rifles?"

"No long guns, a few pistols, but their bows are fearsome. And they are all in full harness, while most of my men have only their *tulups*, their coats."

Atanamir nodded, then looked past the Kossacki. "Deploy there," he said. "We will support you."

Temujin had thought he knew battle. He'd fought before; he was used to the bang of muzzle-loading muskets, the arrows' whistle and hiss, groans from wounded men and shrieks from wounded beasts. But this —

He shuddered. The chaos that ravened around him might have been spawned by the thirteen terrible *ayungghui-yin tngri*, the *tngri* of the thunder. Mongols were trained to fear neither man nor beast (the training, in Temujin's case, had proved incomplete), but even the almost mythical Chingiz *Khan* of Terra, nearly a *tngri* himself, was said to have dreaded thunder. And why not? What man could contend against the heavens?

The steady, deadly chatter of the Saurons' assault rifles had been bad enough — one of them spat as much lead as a dozen of the longarms he was used to, maybe more.

But the Bandari had rifles, too, lots of them. Their blackpowder blasts were deeper, more prolonged, less harsh than those of the Saurons' weapons. That in itself might have been comfortingly familiar — had he not been both unarmed himself and on the wrong end of the Bandari rifles, and had they not put out a volume of fire far greater than that of any black-powder weapons he'd known.

Amazing clouds of smoke rose from the Bandari wagon-barricade. The sulfur stink of it drifted down the wind toward him, and the long reddish blades of the muzzle-flashes stabbed through it.

They also threw bullets worse than the round balls he was familiar with. A Sauron only a few meters from him went down with a groan, clutching his shin. Another bent to check him. "Shattered that bone to shit," he reported.

"Tell me something I don't know," the wounded Soldier answered, his face paler than Caucasoid genes alone could account for. "I'm not going anywhere any more. Have to do what I can from here."

What Temujin would have done from there was go into shock. But the Sauron rolled onto his belly and began banging away at the nomads and Bandari ahead. However much he had reason to hate them, Temujin had to admit the men of the Citadel died hard. They were stalled now, though; gone to ground to fire back, with one very unwilling Mongol to their rear. The Kossacki had scattered off to either side, wavering as the Bandari lancers struck and retreated, covered by their horse-archers. Beyond them, the White Sheep Turks were in a death grapple with the main body of the nomad horde. . . . Temujin rose to his knees, to see better, and to see if there was a way out of this hell.

A swag-bellied cylinder spun through the air from behind the Bandari riflemen. *Blam!* The blast from the powder-filled barrel knocked Temujin sprawling. Another one flew, and another. *Blam! Blam!* More reports sounded from farther away, where the White Sheep fought. Not only were the blasts deadly in themselves, they also spread panic through the ranks of the Saurons' hastily patched-together army. Men who would have stood against the most galling gunfire wheeled their horses and muskylopes and galloped for the rear. Some animals, maddened with fear, spun and bolted that way regardless of their masters' wishes in the matter. He writhed backward on his belly.

"Mewlip!" Anatamir called. "Gaurhoth! *Now.*"

The two Saurons whom the leader had designated to bring word of possible defeat worked their way backward,

out of the killing zone where their comrades were trapped
between Bandari firepower and their own pride. He saw
their faces as they passed, set and blank, concealing the
pain it took to leave the field of battle — leave in defeat, to
flee. Sauron discipline held them to it, and at a little distance they rose to run. Mewlip sped directly east, his
comrade south by east, making for the Cossack village and
the documents and samples cached there. They ran faster
than horses, their field-gray uniforms almost invisible
against the dark steppe. Byers' Sun was sinking, and Cat's
Eye balanced the horizon like a giant red ball; wisps of high
cloud surrounded it, like rays.

Before they were out of sight, a band of horsemen came
charging in from the south, the left; Kossacki, and in full flight,
boiling up heedlessly out of a long declivity in the steppe. Behind them and among them rode warriors unlike any
Temujin had seen. Their horses were taller than most: they
wore armor of overlapping mottled brown leather plates,
rimmed with metal, and steel helmets. Their swords were less
curved than was usual on the plains, their lances longer, and
their odd chunky-looking bows seemed to have tiny wheels on
the tips. They shot and hacked and stabbed among the fleeing
enemy with a disciplined, methodical ferocity.

A Cossack wheeled his horse. "*Na Umor!*"

"*HABANDAAAR!*" A rider speared him out of the saddle
with a lance. The lighter steppe pony went down at the
impact of the big horse.

Then the whole mass dissolved as the Saurons opened
up indiscriminately; the Kossacki crumpled, and the
enemy — the Bandari, he realized — those who lived,
turned and fled at the blatting call of a trumpet.

And some beasts were riderless. A shaggy pony paused
near Temujin for a momentary blow. Two arrows stood up
from the high-cantled saddle, which was wet with blood —
rider's blood, by the looks of it. He looked at the pony. He
looked at the Saurons. They were busy getting killed. Oh,
they were doing a fine job of slaughter on their own, too,
but the only way any of them would get out alive was to run
away. The Bandari rifles came too close to matching their

own, and there were too many of them. But running away wasn't how Saurons did things.

So . . . Very smooth, as if he weren't anybody in particular at all, surely no one a Sauron would be the least bit interested in, Temujin crawled over to the steppe pony. It rolled an eye at him and started to move away, but stepped on its own reins instead. A moment later, he was in the saddle. The pony didn't like him, but Temujin was used to that — steppe ponies didn't like anybody. Maybe they got it from being around camels too much. He hauled down on the reins. After a moment of snorting and trying to turn in circles, it obeyed him. Its likes didn't matter now. In another moment he was trotting east, away from flying pieces of metal that were trying to kill him.

"Thank you, *Atagha Tngri*, supreme over all, protector of horses, my *tngri* who gives me a mount to ride with my thighs," Temujin intoned. In just a few seconds now, he'd be away from the Saurons forever.

Off to one side, one of the men of the Citadel saw him, recognized him, swung toward him. A keg of gunpowder landed right beside him before he could squeeze the trigger of his assault rifle. When the smoke cleared, nothing was left, not even a corpse. The rest of the Saurons were leaping up for their death-charge; he saw a small figure he thought was Atanamir take three paces and fall, jerking time and again as he was struck by the flying lead.

"Thank you, *ayungghui tngri*," Temujin choked out. Maybe the thirteen thunder gods weren't so terrible after all. He kicked his heels into the horse's sides. Tired as it was, it was ready to gallop as long as he wanted to get away from the terrifying noises and smells of the battle.

Then he was in the middle of the rout, and no one cared about him any more: just one more fugitive among thousands. He couldn't have been a Cossack; they wore wool, not leather, and their fur caps were shaped like the top fifteen centimeters of a drum, whereas his looked more like a cowflop. But he could have passed for a White Sheep Turk unless someone noticed on which side his tunic closed. He was also wearing Sauron boots, a pair he'd been given at the Citadel in case he needed to guide the Soldiers on foot, something his high-heeled native footwear was very unsuitable for. He didn't think people would be taking note of such details right this minute.

"Now I need a weapon," he said. A gun, a sword, a toothpick — anything would have been an improvement on his present declawed state. The pony's saddle had a quiver and bowcase, but both were empty. Many of the fleeing men around him were weaponless, too.

The retreat washed back through the Cossack village and the thicket of encampments around it. Women ran shrieking among the huts and tents, some looking for their men, others cursing them for joining the Saurons and bringing this disaster down on the clan. Canvas and felt and thatch fell onto cooking fires, and the first tongues of flame licked up. A few men paused to swing women up behind them; most did not. The first bands of pursuers were thrusting recklessly among the fugitives, slashing men out of the saddle and dismounting to rummage among the yurts and buildings — less foolhardy than it seemed, when your foemen thought only of flight. Horses trampled wicker chicken coops. Squawking, screeching, fluttering birds and flying feathers only added to the insanity.

Out the other side of the village, blowing fluff off his nose. He wished he could have grabbed a hen. Even raw, he would have eaten it.

A hundred meters ahead of him, a Turk with a bloody wound in his back slid off his horse and crashed to the ground. He had a short musket slung over one shoulder and a saber on his belt. Temujin grinned. He brought his own mount to a halt, got down, and hurried over to appropriate the weapons. He thrust the scabbard through his own belt, checked the priming of the musket — it was loaded — and thoughtfully transferred a full pouch of Citadel-minted silver coins to his own coat pockets.

When he looked up fifteen seconds later, the steppe pony was trotting off with the rest of the rout, at a better clip than it had shown with him aboard it.

"Fuck you, *Atagha Tngri!*" he shouted to the uncaring sky.

Maybe the horse god would blast him for such blasphemy? . . . No, no such luck. Wearily, he started east on foot.

"Halt, dog!" the voice commanded in rough Turkic.

The Sauron boots *were* much more comfortable for running in; unfortunately, they conferred nothing of a Sauron's speed. Temujin dodged right, then left, arms and legs pumping. The lariat that settled over his shoulders jerked him off his feet and dragged him a dozen meters before the owner dropped it. Temujin spat dirt and struggled to a sitting position.

There were twenty or so in the party that overtook him; all hard-looking warriors, all on horses — itself a mark of status. Lean hawk-faced men with loose pugaree turbans around their heads and long beards, except for their leader with his iron helmet and nail-studded coat. Several of them rode off a little to one side to cover him with their bows. The chief pulled a pistol out of his sash and gestured with it.

"Lay down the weapons, pork-eating whey-faced son of a Turk," he said. His men were talking among themselves in another language. *Farsi*, Temujin thought. He hoped they wouldn't realize he was Mongol. The only Farsi speakers he knew well were the Tadjik tribes around Ashkabad, near his home . . . and they did *not* love their Mongol neighbors.

Moving slowly and carefully, Temujin put the musket down at his feet, then dropped his captured saber by it.

"The knife too," the chief said, a snag-toothed grin splitting his hairy face. "And the little knife in your boot; and if you have any others, when we find them we will use them on *you*, Sauron-lover."

"Why couldn't you be a pretty girl?" one of the others asked, leering, as he frisked Temujin. "*Bhisti-sawad!* Silver — look, brothers, good silver of the accursed spawn of Shaitan from the Citadel. They paid a high price for this whore's son's worthless sword arm." He backhanded Temujin across the face. "I'd still rather he was a girl."

The other Tadjiks hooted and laughed as the chief appropriated the purse and shared it out. One looked over at Temujin. "He'll do as well," he said. "Woman for duty, boy for pleasure, melon for ecstasy — and this one has a bottom like a peach." He made a grab for the area in question.

Temujin's hand snapped down to the wrist, twisted, wrenched. The Tadjik screamed in pain and staggered backwards; Temujin jumped clear and dropped into a fighting crouch, eyeing a leap toward his weapons — the Tadjiks had sheathed theirs. Most of them were laughing at their friend's discomfiture; one popped the dislocated limb back into its socket with a nerve-grating *snap*. The injured man reached for his saber.

Then the chief's words drove even that worry from Temujin's mind.

"Look at the son-of-ten-father's feet!" he snapped. "Those are Sauron boots." He spurred close, looking down at Temujin closely. "This swine's get is no Turk," he said. "Look at his tunic — he's a Mongol, or my name isn't Bakhtiar."

The Tadjiks' faces changed. "By Allah and the spirits," one said softly. "Didn't the spy say a Mongol rode with the Sauron dogs? At their heel, speaking often with their leader. A young man . . ."

Sweat broke out on Temujin's face. Another noose settled over his shoulders, and the Tadjiks remounted.

"The *khan* must know of this," one said.

"The Seven?"

"If the *khan* orders."

Their leader smiled unpleasantly as he snubbed the braided-leather cord to his saddle. "You can wrestle, Sauron-lover," he said. "Can you run?"

The chestnut started, flicked her ears, snorted and danced a half-step sideways, bringing her head around with more energy than Shulamit thought was in her after the long day's pursuit. They were near the gateway of Cherninsky, the Cossack town. Not much of a town, earth wall and rammed-earth huts, in a little hollow that hardly deserved the name of valley, less than a thousand meters below the steppe. Flame belched skyward from within the shattered gates, along with screams and howls; men were staggering out of the gates, the wounded from the last fighting or looters with a good bit. Shulamit turned her head away from them, toward the heap of dead the chestnut shied from; poor pony, she'd had a hard day. The dead were Gurkhas, mostly, and a few Kossacki. They must have been good ones, to take that many with them; the little men with the knives were *tough*, even by haBandari standards.

Then the dead moved.

Fear brought her hackles up; it also raised her bow. The figure that struggled erect was nearly naked, except for a head-to-foot coating of blood. Gut slid free through his torn belly and broken bone showed in half a dozen places, but the face held a sculptured calm. He drove toward her at a quick hobbling run, pale eyes intent. Shulamit drew and loosed without aiming, snap-shot. It cracked his breastbone, sinking to the feathers on the right side; she could hear the wet popping sound of bone parting. He turned half away at the impact and a spray of blood came out of his mouth and nose, then stopped. He turned toward her again and came on, the same brisk lurch. Fumbling, she stripped another shaft from the clip and drew, loosed, again and again, the horse backing and rolling its eyes in panic. It squealed and reared in protest, then quieted in obedience to her legs and voice.

At the fifth arrow, he fell. His outstretched hand was almost to her stirrup. It opened and closed, clawing at the packed earth. The body twitched for minutes, for longer than it took to soothe her trembling horse into control. She dismounted and leaned against the chestnut, hugging the saddle and her warm horse smell, shaking a little until the velvety nose came around and prodded against her ear, and the thick lips nibbled at her hair.

"*Ja*, I'm all right," she husked, unslinging her water bottle and taking a drink.

It came right back up, with what little was left of her breakfast. She turned aside and bent over with hands on her knees, coughing and retching until the last of the bile was gone, then washed her mouth out again and took a swallow, cold on her raw throat. Then she set her mouth and walked back to the man. *No, a Sauron. A soldati.* No doubt of that, not when it took five arrows to kill him after he should have been dead for hours. No doubt from the face, either, all slabs and angles. Like Sigrid's. Eyes the same silver color. She hesitated for a moment, then used her foot to turn the head away so she didn't have to look in his eyes while she did it. The saber came out heavy in her hand, painful where the calluses were worn with harder work than she'd ever done in training. She knew what she had to do.

Shulamit took the hilt in both hands for the first cut at the neckbone.

It was truedark before the celebration really got under way. They needed time to care for the wounded and sort the loot and clear up the worst of the damage here near Cherninsky, and to rest a little. The Cossack women and children were inside, allowed to surrender — there had been a screaming fight between Hammer and Judge Chaya about that — and were guarded by the Bandari presence. Not many outsiders were in this part of the camp, most of them feasting with their kin; a few at a time came to watch from the shadows outside the circle of bonfires, or to stare at the fifty-six Sauron heads that looked down blindly from poles. There had been many more spectators, *khans* and princes and warriors, a few hours ago. When Hammer-of-God Jackson stood beneath the heads on a wagon draped in the banner that carried the Lidless Eye. Others of the Seven beside him; everyone had made speeches, and got endless cheers. Shulamit had liked Hammer-of-God's best.

He'd pointed up at the heads fairly often as he loomed like an iron idol over the crowd. Shulamit had caught snatches of words: *bear them before us . . . messengers to the tribes . . . lie of Sauron invincibility . . . headless in Hell . . .* — and they had cheered him, crying hail to him and Judge Chaya and Aisha, and death to the *soldati*. Shulamit had been more interested in the kvass and clownfruit brandy going the rounds, easing her head and taking away the taste in her mouth. Now her head was spinning as she broke away from the dance circle, a little away from the great fires. She looked up into the sky, into the bright stars and three of the sister moons, watching sparks drifting across them like the spaceships of legend.

The assault rifle across her back hardly seemed real, but it was hers by right, now. Back at the fires they were singing as they stamped in concentric rings, not the happy songs but something older. Something from before the Empire of Man and even the CoDominium, from Earth the lost and lovely. A song of wars and terrors and hates a thousand years dead, and still living; perhaps that was why few of the *gayam* were here, they remembered too:

> *"Turn around and go back down*
> *Back the way you came —*
> *Can't you see that flash of fire*
> *Ten times brighter than the day?*
> *and —*
> *Oh, Lord, the pride of man, broken in the dust again!"*

A hand tugged at her sleeve. It was a girl, a Kurd — they wore no veils and were friendlier to the People than most — with a tray of muskylope ribs grilled in honey.

"You killed a *Sauron*, young *ghazi*?" she said in an awe-filled voice, looking at the rifle. Such a thing was worth a hundred fine horses. And it was fame more precious than that, to take a Sauron's weapon in battle.

"I finished him," Shulamit replied, taking the meat in both hands and ripping off a mouthful. This time it stayed down. "I brought Barak his head." It was beginning to seem real. One down, twenty-nine to go.

The Kurd peered closer, her jaw going slack. "You're a girl, too!"

"He's just as dead for all that," Shulamit said, grinning at the slight note of disappointment in the other's voice. "Run along and you'll find another *ghazi* to give you the kind of kiss you're looking for."

The Kurd grinned back at her. "A *ghazi* girl — good for us!" she said, and swayed off.

Off by the fires the circles had melted into two, one of women and a larger one of men; they moved clockwise and counterclockwise. Someone beat out the rhythm on a captured kettledrum. The women's high sweet voices soared like descant hawks about the harsh male chorus:

*"Turn around and go back down,*
*Back the way you came —*
*Terror is on every side,*
*And your leaders are dismayed.*
*The mighty men we've beaten down,*
*Your kings we scatter in the waste:*
*and —*
*Oh, Lord, the pride of man, broken in the dust again!"*

Shulamit listened, tearing at the flavorful meat with strong white teeth. An old song, but not often heard; *Ivrit* originally, and it woke memories some thought better forgotten. The Sauron heads looked down on it, desiccation already peeling their lips back from their teeth, making them grin at some private joke. She unhooked a flask from her belt and drank, eyes watering at the bite. The savage music suited her heart tonight.

*"Turn around and go back down,*
*Back the way you came —*
*Take a warning to your peoples*
*That the Sword of God is raised!*
*and —*
*Oh, Lord, the pride of man, broken in the dust again!"*

Another figure watched the celebration from the shadow of an overturned wagon, wrapped in a dark blanket. No mistaking the ash-pale hair as she stared up at the poles and the captured banner. Two hounds sat at her feet, their eyes glinting red in the firelight, like their mistress'.

*"Turn around and go back down,*
*Back the way you came —*
*See Babylon, that mighty city*
*Rich in treasure, wide in fame*
*We have brought her towers down,*
*Made of her a pyre of flame.*
*and —*
*Oh, Lord, the pride of man, broken in the dust again!"*

Red in the firelight, Sigrid's eyes turned toward

Shulamit. Moving away from the light and falling into shadow. The Bandari girl tossed the bone in her hand toward the dogs; they ignored it, growling, as she wiped her mouth with the back of her hand and rested it on the butt of the Citadel-made assault rifle.

"One down, twenty-nine to go," Shulamit said again, baring her teeth. It was as unconscious as the dogs' gesture, and as sincere. Silence answered her, and she jerked her head toward the fires and the singers, as their voices united for the last verse. "You should listen: *Babylon is fallen*. And so is Old Sauron, and there's a curse on her seed. Where are our enemies, Pharaoh, Romans, Germans, Philistine, time out of mind? Ashes on the wind — as the Citadel will be."

For answer she had only silence, still, and the gleam of Sauron eyes.

*Living* Sauron eyes.

Living — for now.

She turned on her heel and walked off; Barak stood apart from the fires as well, brooding with his own rifle in his hands. Brooding on his heritage, perhaps. . . . He looked up and smiled as she approached. Behind her the sound swelled as the rings halted and raised their linked hands:

> *Thy holy mountain be restored —*
> *Thy favor on Thy People, Lord!"*

# VOLUME ONE

## THE END